John Corbet Anderson

Shropshire, its Early History and Antiquities

John Corbet Anderson

Shropshire, its Early History and Antiquities

1st Edition | ISBN: 978-3-75258-473-8

Place of Publication: Frankfurt am Main, Germany

Year of Publication: 2022

Salzwasser Verlag GmbH, Germany.

Reprint of the original, first published in 1864.

Shropshire:

ITS EARLY HISTORY AND ANTIQUITIES.

COMPRISING A DESCRIPTION OF THE IMPORTANT

British and Roman Remains in that County:

ITS SAXON AND DANISH REMINISCENCES:

The Domesday Survey of Shropshire

ILLUSTRATED BY NUMEROUS DRAWINGS ON WOOD.

London

MDCCCLXIV.

TONG CHURCH.

SUBSCRIBERS' NAMES.

Copy for Her Majesty's Library.
The ROYAL INSTITUTION, Albemarle Street.
The CITY LIBRARY, Guildhall.
The LONDON INSTITUTION, Finsbury Circus.
The LONDON LIBRARY, 12, St. James' Square.

Acton, Major J. P., Gatacre Park, Bridgnorth.
Allen, Rev. Wm., St. George's, Donnington, Salop.
Allen, Mr. Harry, Victoria Hotel, Newport.
Bradford, Right Hon. the Earl of.
Boyne, Right Hon. Viscount.
Berwick, Right Hon. Lord.
Boughton, Sir C. Rouse, Bart.
Baddeley, William E., Esq., M.D., Newport.
Badger, Mr. T., House Agent, Savings' Bank, Shrewsbury.
Barnes, James R., Esq., The Quinta, near Chirk.
Baugh, Mr. E., Bookseller, Ellesmere.
Bayley, J., Esq., Bicton Heath, Shrewsbury.
Bennett, Edward, Esq., Bedstone.
Bickley, Mr. T. W., Second Hand Bookseller, Shrewsbury.
Borough, J. C. Burton, Esq., J.P., Chetwynd Park.
Boucher, Mr. J. B., Professor of Music, Shrewsbury.
Burd, Edward, Esq., M.D., Shrewsbury.
Burd, Henry, Esq., The Laurels, Shrewsbury.
Burd, Laurence, Esq., The Laurels, Shrewsbury.
Burr, George, Esq., Woodfield, Shrewsbury.
Burton, Rev. H., A.M., Vicar of Atcham, and Rural Dean of Shrewsbury.
Canterbury, His Grace the Archbishop of,
Cleveland, His Grace the Duke of.
Chancellor, Mr. A., Bookseller, Shrewsbury.
Charlton, St. John C., Esq., J.P.
Clay, Chas., Esq., Whitchurch.
Clive, Lady Mary Windsor.
Copy for Library of Shrewsbury Institute.
Corbet, Sir Vincent R., Bart., Acton Reynald.
Corbet, J. Dryden, Esq., J.P., Sundorne Castle.
Corbet, Miller, Esq., Solicitor, Kidderminster.
Corbett, Mr. T., Agricultural Engineer, Shrewsbury.
Corser, George Sandford, Esq., Shrewsbury.
Cotes, Miss, Bicton.
Cotes, John, Esq., J.P., Woodcote.
Cranage, Dr., Old Hall School, Wellington.
Cresswell, Mr. S. G., Shrewsbury.
Cresswell, Mr. J., Wine Merchant, Market Square, Shrewsbury.
Crump, Mr. Vincent, Confectioner, Shrewsbury.
Cunliffe, Rev. Canon, Wrexham.
Curtler, J. Ashmore, Esq., Solicitor, Ellesmere.
Dartmouth, Right Hon. the Earl of.
Davenport, W. S., Esq., J.P., Davenport, Bridgnorth.
Daniel, Mr. T., Mason, Abbey Foregate.
Davies, Corbet, Esq., Solicitor, Shrewsbury.
Davies, Mr. Thomas, Ellesmere.
Davies, Mr. Richard, Printer, Shrewsbury.
Davies, Mr. David, Coach Builder, Shrewsbury.
Dodson, Mr. R., Statuary and Mason, Shrewsbury.
Dodwell, Mr. W., Hot-water Engineer, Wyle Cop, Shrewsbury.
Drayton, Mr. George, Bookseller, Shrewsbury.
Ebrall, Mr. S., Gunmaker, Shrewsbury.
Ebrall, Mr. S. Browning, Shrewsbury.
Edgerley, J. Faulkner, Esq., Shrewsbury.
Edwardes, T. H. Hope, Esq., J.P., Netley.
Evans, Mr. W., Glass Stainer, etc., Shrewsbury.
Evans, Mr. R. E., Accountant, Shrewsbury.
Everall, Mr. Robert, Builder, Shrewsbury.
Farror, Miss, The Stone House, Shrewsbury.
Fenton, Henry, Esq., Shrewsbury.
Ferrington, Francis F., Shrewsbury.
Fielden, Rev. O. M., Whittington.
Fleet, Mr., Tailor, High Street, Shrewsbury.
Forester, Rev. R. T., Elmley Lodge, Leamington.
Forth, Mr. John, 8, Pride Hill, Shrewsbury.
Fox, Mr. G., George Hotel, Shrewsbury.
Frail, John, Esq., Clerk of the Races, Shrewsbury.
Frail, S., Esq., Solicitor, and Coroner of the Borough of Shrewsbury.
France, Richard S., Esq, Monkland Hall, Shrewsbury.
Furmston, Rev. Edward, Cocksbutt.
Gaskell, J. Milnes, Esq., M.P.
Gatacre, E. L., Esq., of Gatacre.
George, A. B., Esq., M.D., Whitchurch.
Godby, Augustus H., Esq., M.D., Newport.
Gore, J. R. Ormsby, Esq., M.P.
Gosnell, Mr. T., Mudie's Library Branch, Newport.
Goucher, Mr. J., Chemist, High Street, Shrewsbury.
Griffith, Thos. Taylor, Esq., Wrexham.
Groom, Thos., Esq., Edgely House, Whitchurch.
Hill, Right Hon. Viscount, Lord-Lieutenant of Shropshire, etc.
Hancocks, William, Esq., J.P., Blakeshall House, Kidderminster.
Harnage, Sir George, Bart., Belleurdine.
Harries, John D., Esq., Surgeon, Shrewsbury.
Harries, Mr. Geo., Tobacco Manufacturer, Shrewsbury.
Harries, Mr. G. E., Saddler, High Street, Shrewsbury.
Heighway, Mr. John, Shrewsbury.
Higgins, Robert G., Esq., Newport.
Hill, Rev. John, The Citadel, Hawkstone.
Hickman, Mr. Henry, Dentist, Shrewsbury.
Hobson, Mr. Robert, Bookseller, Wellington.
Horton, T. E., Esq., Priors Lee Hall, Shropshire.
Horton, S. L., Esq., The Grove, St. George's, near Donnington.
Howard, Hon. and Very Rev. Henry, D.D., Lichfield.
Hughes, Mrs., High Street, Newport.

Hughes, Mr. Edw., Wine Merchant, Shrewsbury.
Humphreys, Mr. Jos., Land Agent, Dogpole Court, Shrewsbury.
Jebb, R. G., Esq., J.P., The Lyth, Ellesmere.
Jones, R. Parry, Esq., Whitchurch.
Jones, A. C., Esq., Prior's Lee.
Jones, Horatio M., Esq., Shrewsbury.
Jones, Mr. J., Cheese Mart, Shrewsbury.
Jones, Mr. Thomas Y., Law Stationer and Lithographer, Shrewsbury.
Kennedy, Rev. Benjamin H., D.D., Head Master, Grammar School, Shrewsbury.
Kenyon, J. R., Esq., J.P., Pradoe.
Knights, Mr. Hammond, Croydon, Surrey.
Laing, Mr. J., Photographer, Shrewsbury.
Lawrence, Richard, Esq., Cantlop.
Lee, John, Esq., Whitchurch.
Legge, Col. the Hon. Arthur C., Caynton, Shiffnal.
Lloyd, Rev. T. B., Whitehall, Shrewsbury.
LLoyd, C. S., Esq., J. P., Leaton Knolls.
Lockett, Mr. John, Bookseller, Market Drayton. Six Copies.
Loxdale, James, Esq., J.P., Albrighton, Wolverhampton.
Maddock, Mr. J., Swan Hill, Shrewsbury.
Mainwaring, S. K., Esq., Oteley Park, Ellesmere.
Mansell, Mr. J., Baths, Coton Hill, Shrewsbury.
Masefield, J., Esq., Newport.
Maude, Rev. J., Vicarage, Chirk.
Minshull and Hughes, Messrs., Booksellers, Chester. Two Copies.
Minshall, Chas., Esq., Oswestry.
Mitton, Mr. George, News Agent, Shrewsbury.
Morgan, Mr. T., Printer, Shrewsbury.
Morris, Charles J., Esq., Oxon, Shrewsbury.
Mousley, H. K., Esq., Whitchurch.
Nightingale, Mr. Chas. G., Dental Surgeon, Shrewsbury.
Owen, G., Esq., Mayor of Oswestry.
Owen, Mr. C. W., Wine Merchant, Oswestry.
Payne, Fredk. A., Esq., Pentre Urcha, Oswestry.
Pardoe, George, Esq., J.P., Nash Court, Tenbury.
Patchett, W., Esq., Greenfields, Shrewsbury.
Parry, Edw., Esq., The Factory, Shrewsbury.
Peake, Rev. John, Ellesmere.
Peake, Rev. J. R., Head Master Grammar School, Whitchurch.
Pelham, Rev. A. Thursby, Connd, Shrewsbury.
Phillips, Jas., Esq., Severn Villa, Shrewsbury.
Phillips, Mr. Edw., Tailor, Shrewsbury.
Piercy, Robt., Esq., Worthenbury, near Wrexham.
Plowden, Wm., Esq., Plowden Hall.
Powell, Mr. J., Printer and Stationer, Mardol, Shrewsbury.
Provis, W. A., Esq., The Grange, Ellesmere.
Rigg, Rev. John, B.D., Sec. Master Grammar School Shrewsbury.

Roberts, Thos. Lloyd, Esq., J.P., Corfton Hall
Robertson, Henry, Esq., M.P.
Robinson, C. B., Esq., Frankton Grange.
Rocke, John, Esq., J.P., Clungunford House.
St. Asaph, Right Rev. the Bishop of.
Salt, Wm., Esq., Shrewsbury.
Salter, Mr. Jackson, Bookseller, Oswestry.
Sandford, Humphrey, Esq., J.P., Isle House, Shrewsbury.
Saxton, Rev. C. Waring, D.D., Head Master Gram. School, Newport.
Scarth, Jonathan, Esq., Shrewsbury.
Shaw, Mr. John, Birdstuffer, &c., Shrewsbury.
Short, Rev. Ambrose, Head Master Gram. School, Oswestry.
Silvester, Messrs. H. P. and C., Booksellers, Newport.
Slaney, Mr. R., Wine Merchant, Shrewsbury.
Smith, S. Pountney, Esq., Architect, Shrewsbury.
Smith, C., Esq., Shrewsbury.
Smith, Mr. Russell, Bookseller, 36, Soho-square, London. Two Copies.
Southam, Mr. Thos., Wine Merchant, Shrewsbury.
Spence, Mr. James G., Coal and Iron Merchant, Shrewsbury.
Stanton, George, Esq., Shrewsbury.
Trevor, Right Hon. Lord A. P. Hill.
Taylor, Richard, Esq., Abbey Foregate, Shrewsbury
Taylor, John, Esq., Shrewsbury.
Tibnam, Mr. William, Bookseller, Shrewsbury.
Tipton, Edward, Esq., Shrewsbury.
Tomline, George, Esq., M.P.
Tudman, Edw., Esq., Whitchurch.
Tudor, Mr. Abraham, Shrewsbury.
Tulett, Mr. Anthony, Croydon, Surrey.
Windsor, Right Hon. the Baroness.
Walker, John, Esq., Southgate.
Warner, Mrs., Newport.
Warter, H. de Grey, Esq., J.P., Cruck Meole.
Watton, John, Esq., Murivance, Shrewsbury.
Wem, T, Esq., Donnington.
Wem, Mr. Wm, Snedshill.
Westmacott, George, Esq., Mill House, Wem.
Whitmore, Rev. George, Stockton Rectory.
Whitwell, Francis, Esq., Surgeon, Shrewsbury.
Wicksted, Charles, Esq., J.P., Shakenhurst.
Wightman, Rev. C. E. L., St. Alkmond's, Shrewsbury.
Wilde, Mr. Peter, Bookseller, and Publisher of "Shrewsbury Observer."
Williams, Henry, Esq., Hinstock Hall.
Williams, Edw., Esq., Lloran House, Oswestry.
Wingfield, Capt., Onslow.
Wood, Edw., Esq., Culmington, Bromfield.
Worthington, Archbd., Esq., Whitchurch.
Wynn, Sir Watkin W., Bart., Wynnstay.
Yate, J., Esq., Madeley Hall.

INTRODUCTION.

SHROPSHIRE, beautiful in scenery, and rich withal in mineral wealth, has a history which, in its earlier phases at least, is inferior in interest to that of no other county in England. Upon its soil, the last great battle for British independence is said to have been fought; and the extensive remains of British earthworks and fortifications which, in a connected chain, extending over the whole southern and western portions of the county, concentrate in the vast military works, Caer Caradoc and Oswestry, indicate the fierce nature of that struggle which Caractacus made, to stay the declining fate of his country. The ruins of the city of Uriconium or Wroxeter, and of their highway, Watling Street, as well as numerous vestiges of other Roman settlements and roads scattered throughout Shropshire, attest how futile, after all, had been the efforts of the heroic Briton to resist the victorious progress of the Latin invader; whilst, at the same time, the study of these interesting memorials tends to enlarge our acquaintance with the history of our country during that period of nearly 400 years in which it remained subject to the Romans.

After the departure of the Romans came the Saxons, when the history of Shropshire, including Pengwern or Shrewsbury, the capital of the old British Kings of Powis, whose wattled halls the fair-haired heathen fired; the early history of the county of Shropshire, we say, will be found to contribute towards the elucidation of the question as to how the German invaders eventually made themselves masters of England. It was " Offa the Terrible," of Mercia, who finally annexed Shropshire to the land of the Angles or England; and he it was who, to secure his acquisition, cast up that remarkable entrenchment known as Offa's Dyke. This great earthwork traverses the border for upwards of a hundred miles over mountain and plain, in its course northwards, forming the boundary between Shropshire and Montgomeryshire.

Next came the descent upon the shores of our country of the dread sea-king rovers of the North—the Danes; to stay whose destructive ravages, King Alfred's high-spirited daughter Ethelfleda, Lady of the Mercians, reared fortresses both at Chirbury and Brugge or Bridgnorth: Danesford by Severn, in its name, implying that the grisly worshippers of Odin were no strangers to Shropshire.

Finally occurred the advent of the Normans; and if a perusal of the history of Shropshire is in any degree calculated to enlarge the reader's acquaintance with the knowledge of his country's history during the British, Roman, Saxon, and Danish epochs, surely this work may claim to contribute something to the general fund of information relating to the Norman Conquest of England, and that Anglo-Norman era, concerning which our general histories, it may truly be said, are miserably scanty in the amount of accurate information they convey. Among the movers in that great social revolution which eventually laid our country prostrate at the feet of William the Conqueror—a revolution the influences of which to this day are powerfully felt, not only in our political constitution, but in our laws, language, and manners; among the leading actors in that great drama, the Saxon Earl Godwin was a Shropshire landowner. Sweyn, his out-lawed eldest son; Earl Harold, who afterwards disputed the succession to the English throne with "the Bastard" count of the Normans; Edith, the Lady, the Confessor's lovely yet unhonoured Saxon Queen, as well as her husband King Edward, the last legitimate Anglo-Saxon Monarch; Edwin and Morcar, the brother Mercian earls, whose sad fate affords a lively comment on the Norman rule; and Edric, the Forester, who, long after William's victory at Hastings, and his coronation in Westminster Abbey had become accomplished facts, continued, in his western haunts, to baffle every effort of the Conqueror to reduce him;—Domesday Book reveals the fact, that these Saxons were all more or less connected with Shropshire.

On the Norman side again, we have William the Conqueror himself, and Roger de Montgomery the palatine Earl of Shrewsbury, ranking as chiefs among the Shropshire proprietors. Beneath one or other of these held Warin the Bald, and his successor Rainald the Sheriff, the Corbets, William Pantulf, Ralph de Mortemer, Roger de Laci, Picot de Say, Gerard de Tornai, William de Warrene, Norman Venator, Richard Fitz Osbern, Helgot, and a host of other vassals and retainers of more or less note, who, having drawn their long-swords at Hastings, or else contributed to extend and consolidate the Norman Duke's victory over the north-western border, received as the meed of their service some portion of Shropshire ; when, transferring themselves and their families thither, innumerable Saxon holders were dispossessed of their respective patrimonies, and their lands apportioned out among the iron-clad strangers. To the unhappy conquered was left life only; and this upon the hard condition of being mere hewers of wood and drawers of water, as it were, to their oppressors. No one could conceive what spoliations and sufferings our vanquished Saxon countrymen endured at the hands of their Norman conquerors, unless he had access to such sources of information as Domesday Book. Yet that venerable and authentic record is a sealed document to the majority of those who desire to learn more concerning the history of their country. To supply a felt deficiency in this respect, the reader is herewith furnished with the entire *Domesday* survey of the county of Shropshire, resolved from the obscure Latin contractions of the original into our own language. There is no controverting facts ; and he who will look carefully over the Tables of the *Domesday* Hundreds of Shropshire, inserted in this book, comparing, as his eye scans their contents, the third columns, in which are entered the names of the Saxon owners of each respective estate in Shropshire in the time of the Saxon King Edward, with the fourth, fifth, and sixth columns, which give the names of the chief-tenant, the mesne or next tenant, and that of the sub- or under-tenant of the same estate in 1086, just twenty years after the battle of Hastings had been fought ;—he who will do this may learn how wholesale that eviction was which attended the conquest of England by the Normans.

The principle upon which these Tables of the respective *Domesday* Hundreds to which they refer have been constructed is this:— In the first column will be found the modern name of the place alluded to ; by way of contrast, the second column furnishes the reader with the name by which that place was known eight hundred years ago, or, in other words, when William the Conqueror's Commissioners surveyed Shropshire. The third column gives, as we observed, the name or names of the Saxon owner or owners of the place described in the time of King Edward. The fourth column gives the name of the *Domesday* tenant *in capite* ; the fifth column exhibits that of the *Domesday mesne* or next tenant ; the sixth column gives the name of the *Domesday* sub-tenant ; whilst the seventh and last column gives, in opposition to the title of the Table, the name of the modern Hundred in which the place is now included.

With respect to the order in which the various places are entered on these Tables, as a general rule, the estates which the Norman Earl himself retained are entered first; then follow those which belonged to the largest holder in the particular Hundred in question under the Earl, given as the places are entered in the original record; and so, gradually down the scale until we arrive at the lesser holders.

Glancing at the pre-Norman history of Shropshire then, yet making Domesday Book the great basis of local investigation, it has been our study, as nearly as possible, to furnish the reader with a literal translation of that majestic record. Each place spoken of in the following work is treated separately under a distinct heading, and throughout the book described in the same order as it is entered on the Tables. By adhering to this simple arrangement, we avoid giving offence to our local subscribers; whilst, at the same time, the general reader has presented to him a fac-simile almost of the Shropshire *Domesday*, and otherwise becomes possessed of much valuable matter very closely connected with the history of his country.

Besides the complete *Domesday* survey of Shropshire, it may be mentioned that this work embraces the three great Ecclesiastical surveys of the county: namely, Pope Nicholas' Taxation, taken about A.D. 1291; the *Inquisitiones Nonarum*, or Inquests of the Ninths, taken about A D. 1341; and King Henry the Eighth's *Valor Ecclesiasticus*, of the year 1534.

A border county, with the early history of Shropshire, is interwoven that protracted struggle, made by the brave Welsh against the asserted supremacy of the Anglo-Saxon and Anglo-Norman kings; a struggle which terminated only when the Principality was conquered by Edward the First.

To treat of the great primeval forests of Shropshire, and its highly interesting British and Roman remains: of the Saxon, Danish, Anglo-Norman and Welsh reminiscences mingling with, and involved in a description of Oswestry, Wroxeter, Shrewsbury, Bridgenorth, Ludlow, and its other towns;—to show how these towns originally acquired their charters of freedom, some from kings, others from the fostering hand of the church, or from their feudal lord; and, emerging from the darkness and tyranny of the middle ages, gradually became the important municipalities they now are ;—to give the histories of its rich abbeys and other ecclesiastical foundations ; to trace the line of their succession from the conquest of England by the Norman of the Mortemers, and those other Shropshire potentates, whose time appears to have been divided between rebelling against their sovereign, in bloody fray with the Welsh, or else in hunting around those gloomy border fortresses through whose grated donjons scarce penetrated the light of day ; in short, to produce a work, which, within the compass of an ordinary volume, shall present the reader with the essential outline of the early history of Shropshire—such has been the endeavour of the author.

How much of history is comprehended in the knowledge of topography ! How much of history is involved in the mere names of places ! Works of this nature supply the reader with the necessary facts from which he arrives at his conclusion respecting the past. It is only through the medium of such minute details, dry and fatiguing as their examination may appear to some, that the economy of the middle ages can be clearly understood ; and we venture to assert, that one perusal of a book of this kind will give the reader a more accurate notion of the Norman Conquest of England and the feudal period, than he could possibly derive from any general history, however ably written.

A word now, in reference to those works relating to Shropshire and its antiquities, which have preceded this one, and to the labours of whose authors I must acknowledge myself very deeply indebted. First, there is Hartshorne's " *Salopia Antiqua,* or an enquiry, from personal survey, into the Druidical, military, and other early remains in Shropshire and the North-western Borders," a work of distinguished merit. Next follows Owen and Blakeway's " History of Shrewsbury," of the very highest order of excellence. Then Blakeway's " Sheriffs of Shropshire ;" Dukes' " Antiquities of Shropshire ;" Wright's admirable " History of Ludlow ;" and last, yet greatest of all, Eyton's " Antiquities of Shropshire," which, commencing at *Domesday,* strictly speaking, is a manorial history of the county. Concerning this work, the erudite Thomas Wright has pronounced that it is, " in its limits, the best local history that this country possesses." To this laborious and valuable undertaking, the author is specially indebted. In fact, the present book owes its existence to the circumstance of its publisher having become possessed of the wood-engravings which adorned Eyton's pages. As only 300 copies were printed of Eyton's "Antiquities of Shropshire," it seemed a pity that cuts of such merit should lie idle,—hence the present publication, which, although largely indebted to Eyton's work, nevertheless, both in its system of arrangement, its rendering of *Domesday*, and in its subject-matter, assumes the form of an original production, as any one who will be at the trouble to compare the two works may convince himself of. Being foreign to the purpose of his undertaking, the learned Eyton omits in his volumes all mention either of the Roman Wroxeter or the town of Shrewsbury. Recent investigations made on the site of the former, however, having concentrated public attention on this great Roman settlement on the Welsh border, it seemed essential that a page or two should be devoted to Uriconium or Wroxeter; whilst the early history of the capital of Shropshire is so interesting and instructive, that a description of Shrewsbury forms an important feature in the present work.

With respect to the notices of early Incumbents of the Churches of Shropshire, the rule is to notice one only, and that one the earliest mentioned.

Finally, to advert to the system of spelling names adopted in these pages. The names used are those of the original documents quoted, a variation of spelling is thus introduced, but the gradual changes which have occurred in our nomenclature are laid before the reader.

SHROPSHIRE.

Its Early History and Antiquities.

Domesday Hundred of Alnodestreu.

Modern Name.	Domesday Name.	Saxon Owner or Owners, T. R. E.	Domesday Tenant in capite.	Domesday Mesne, or next Tenant.	Domesday Sub-Tenant.	Modern Hundred.
Morville	Membrefeld	Rex Edwardns	Rogerius Comes	Ecclesia, Sancti, Petri, etc. iu part.		Stottesden.
Oldbury	Aldeberie	Eluuard	Idem	Rainaldus Vicecomes	Radulfus	..Ibidem.
Fulwardine	Fuloordie	Elmund	Idem	Rainaldus Viecomes	Radulfus	..Ibidem.
Upton Cresset	Ultone	Elmund	Idem	Rainaldus Vicecomes		..Ibidem.
Eudon Burnell	Eldone	Æluuard	Idem	Rainaldus Vicecomes		..Ibidem.
Middleton Scriven	Middeltone	Edric	Idem	Rainaldus Vicecomes	Alcher Albert	Ibidem.
Aston Eyre	Estone	Sessi	Idem	Rainaldus Vicecomes	Alcber	..Ibidem.
Glazeley	Gleslei	Elunard	Idem	Rainaldus Viecomes	Azo	..Ibidem.
Aston Botterel	Estone	Elric	Idem	Rainaldus Vicecomes	Tochil	..Ibidem.
Badger	Beghesovre	Brunthi	Idem	Osbernus	Robertus	Brimstree.
Ryton	Rultone	Wiuar / Bricstual	Idem	Osbernus		..Ibidem.
Brockton	Broctone	Bruniht	Idem	Osbernus		..Ibidem.
Meadowley	Madolea	Austin	Idem	Helgotus	Ricardus	Stottesden.
Broseley	Bosle	Gethne	Idem	Helgotus		Wenlock.
Sutton Maddock	Sudtone	Comes Morcar	Idem	Gerardus		Brimstree.
Stockton	Stochetone	Eduin / Ordui	Idem	Gerardus	Hugo	..Ibidem.
Hatton	Etone	Turgod / Turgot	Idem	Gerardus / Rainaldus	Willielmus	..Ibidem.
Albrighton	Albriestone	Algar / Godhit	Idem	Normannus		..Ibidem.
Bishton	Bispetone	Turgod	Idem	Normannus		..Ibidem.
Faintree	Faventrei	Ulchetel / Archetel / Uluiet / Æluui / Ordui / Ordrie	Idem	Walchelinus		Stottesden.
Willey	Wilit	Hunnit	Idem	Turold	Hunnit	Wenlock.
Deuxhill	Dehocsele	Eccles'a Sanetæ / Milburgæ	Idem	Ecclesia Sanctæ Milburgæ		Brimstree.

Manors probably in Alnodestreu, but whose Hundred is not stated in Domesday.

Eardington and Quatford	Arditone & Quatford	EcclesiaSanctæ Milburgæ	Rogerius Comes			Stottesden.
——?——	Bolebec	Stenulf	Idem			—?—
Chetton	Catinton	Godeva Comitissa	Idem			Stottesden.
Donington	Donitone	Eduinus Comes	Idem			Brimstree.
Tong	Tuange	Morcar Comes	Idem			..Ibidem.

Manor probably in Alnodestreu, but whose Hundred is mis-stated in Domesday.

Charlcott	Cerelecote	Elsi	Rogerius Comes	Helgotus		Stottesden.

THE old Alnodestreu Hundred of William the Conqueror's time has ceased to exist. Scattered and broken up by isolated portions of the Hundreds of Bascherch and of Patinton, the limits of old Alnodestreu present us with an example of those eccentric territorial divisions which abounded in our country at the time of the Conquest. It is supposed that we owe to the administrative abilities of Henry I. that reform, which, re-arranging the divisional system of Shropshire, swept away Alnodestreu Hundred, with all its confusions, and assigned its various manors to the then newly created Hundreds of Stottesden, Brimstree, and Munslow. In Richard I.'s time, however, the Liberty of Wenlock sprang into existence, when that portion of Alnodestreu Hundred, which had been given to Munslow Hundred, and one manor out of Brimstree Hundred, viz., Badger, were retransferred to Wenlock.

Membrefelde or Morville used to be *caput* or centre of the Hundred of Alnodestreu; and here, consequently, was exercised that local jurisdiction which, together with the manor, realised £10 annually. Two-thirds of the *curial* income went, in Saxon times, to the Crown, and the remaining third to the Earl of Mercia. After the Conquest, the Norman earl took the whole profits of the Hundred Court.

Morville. According to Domesday Book,[1] the Norman Earl Roger de Montgomery held of the Crown the Manor of Membrefelde, with its eighteen berewicks, or hamlets. King Edward had held it in Saxon times. Here were twelve hides. Of these hides, we are informed, that the Norman earl held four in demesne. A supplementary note indicates, however, that two out of the said four hides were held by Richard Pincerna, under the earl. The remaining eight hides had, in Edward the Confessor's time, constituted the endowment of the collegiate church of St. Gregory of Membrefelde, in which ministered eight canons. But this church with five hides of its territory, had been given by the Norman earl to his newly founded monastery of St Peter, at Shrewsbury. The other three hides, Earl Roger had given to his own chaplains.

---

[1] " Ipse Comes tenet Membrefelde cum xviii berewichis. Rex Edwardus tenuit. Ibi xii hidæ. Una ex his berewichis, Calvestone, de i hidâ est in Wirecestrescire. De *hac terrâ* iiii hidæ sunt in dominio, et ibi ii carrucæ, et vi aliæ carrucæ possent esse. Ibi ix villani et vi bordarii cum iii carrucis, et adhuc duæ aliæ possent esse. Ibi iiii bovarii.

" Huic Manerio pertinet totum Alnodestreu Hundredum. Duo denarii erant Regis Edwardi, et tercius Comitis. Inter

Summarily, then, when the Domesday commissioners surveyed Shropshire,[1] in 1085-6, the Norman earl held this Manor and Hundred *in capite*. Of the manor, he retained two hides in demesne; two hides were held under him by Richard Pincerna; five by the monks of Shrewsbury; and three by his own chaplains.

Domesday supplies us with certain facts as to the relative value, cultivation, and occupation, of these respective portions. In demesne (two hides) there were two ox-teams, and work for six more. Here were nine villains and six boors, with three teams; and there was room for two more teams. Here were four neat-herds. The annual value of this portion, including the revenue of the Hundred Court, was £3.

St. Peter's five hides employed in demesne two ox-teams, and totum reddebat x libros. Modo, quod Comes habet valet iii libros.

"Ecclesia hujus Manerii est in honore Sancti Gregorii, quæ tempore Regis Edwardi habebat de hâc terrâ viii hidas, et ibi serviebant viii canonici. Hanc ecclesiam cum v hidis terræ tenet ecclesia Sancti Petri de Comite. In dominio sunt ibi ii carrucæ et iiii aliæ possunt esse. Ibi ix villani et unus hordarius et iii presbyteri cum ix carrucis, et iiii bovarii; et unus miles tenet i hidam, reddens iiii solidos monachis. Totum hoc valet lxvii solidos.

"Reliquas iii hidas tenent capellani Comitis et v homines de eis. Terra est vi carrucis. Ibi sunt ii carrucæ. Totum valet lx solidos et xviii denarios.

"De ipsâ terrâ hujus Manerii tenet Ricardus Pincerna ii hidas et ibi habet i carrucam et ii servos et vii villanos cum i carrucâ, et molendinum reddens x summa annonæ. Ibi ix carrucæ plus possent esse. Valet xx solidos.—*Domesd.* fo. 253, a 2.

[1] The Domesday Commissioners for Worcestershire and other (probably adjoining) counties were four Normans: namely Remigius, Bishop of Lincoln, Earl Walter Giffard, Henry de Ferrers, and Adam, brother of Eudo, the king's sewer. (*Cotton*, MSS., Tib. A. xiij.) As the Commissioners travelled through the country, taking the survey, they examined sheriffs, barons, reeves of hundreds, priests, bailiffs, and even villains—in short, whoever they liked; but the detailed information seems generally to have been derived from the answers of jurors empanneled from each Hundred. The result is the famous *Domesday Book*, which, as Hume has justly observed, is "the most valuable piece of antiquity possessed by any nation." The cotemporary writer of the Anglo-Saxon Chronicle has left on record what were the national feelings of his Saxon countrymen respecting William the Conqueror's great territorial survey. He says, "After this, the king had a great consultation, and spoke very deeply with his *witan* concerning this land, how it was held, and what were its tenantry. He then sent his men over all England, into every shire, and caused them to ascertain how many hundred hides of land it contained, and what lands the king possessed therein; what cattle there were in the several counties, and how much revenue he ought to receive yearly from each. He also caused them to write down how much land belonged to his archbishops, to his bishops, his abbots, and his earls; and, that I may be brief, what property every inhabitant of all England possessed, in land or in cattle, and how much money this was worth. So very narrowly did he cause the survey to be made, that there was not a single hide nor a rood of land, nor—it is shameful to relate, that which he thought no shame to do—was there an ox, or a cow, or a pig passed by, and that was not set down in the accounts; and then all these writings were brought to him."—*Anglo-Saxon Chron.* p. 458, Bohn's Ed.

This work on the early history of Shropshire embraces the entire *Domesday* survey of the county. The reader, therefore, has an opportunity of judging, so far as Shropshire is concerned, whether or not the Saxon writer of the foregoing was justified in his severe stricture on the Conqueror's great undertaking.

might employ four more; here were nine villains, one boor, and three priests, with nine teams among them; here were also four neat-herds, and a knight who held a whole hide under the monks, at a rent of four shillings (*per annum*). This portion was worth £3 17s. (*per annum*).

The three hides held by the earl's chaplains were sublet to five freemen. The arable land was sufficient for six ox-teams; but here were only two. The total annual value was £3 1s. 6d.

Upon the two hides of land of this manor held by Richard Pincerna were one ox-team; and two serfs, and seven villains had another team; but the land was capable of employing nine more teams. A mill here rendered ten horse-loads of grain. The whole was worth 20s. *annually.*

ST. GREGORY'S, MORVILLE.

The church spoken of in *Domesday*, in connection with this Manor had been originally a Saxon Collegiate Church, attached to which was a parish of vast extent; but before the survey was taken, the Norman earl had given it to Shrewsbury Abbey. In 1118, the monks of Shrewsbury built a new church at Morville, and Geoffrey (de Clive), Bishop of Hereford consecrated it. As the day was remarkably fine, numbers flocked to the ceremonial. But, after the company had broken up, a tremendous thunderstorm suddenly arose. A party of five, two of whom were females, were overtaken by it on their way homewards, when a flash of lightning struck the two women and the five horses belonging to the party, and killed them.[1]

About 1138, Bishop Robert de Betun granted an appropriation of *Momerfeulde* (Morville) Church to Shrewsbury Abbey, enjoining, at the same time, that it should be colonized with monks from Shrewsbury, changeable at the abbot's discretion. Thus Morville became a priory subject to Salop Abbey, and not only it, but its chapels also; for within eighty years after *Domesday*, no less than seven chapels had been built and endowed by the barons and knights of Shropshire, in the great parish of St. Gregory, These the bishop consecrated, as a "protection for the poor, and having respect to the warlike troubles of the time"—for it was the stormy and disastrous reign of the usurper Stephen.

Shorn of its original influence; Morville remained a cell or priory of Shrewsbury Abbey until the Reformation.

---

[1] *Contin. of Florence of Worc. Chron.*, p. 230 Bohn's Ed.

CHANCEL DOOR, MORVILLE.

FONT, MORVILLE.

In 1291, the Church of Morville, with three of its chapels, viz., Astley, Aston Aer, and Billingsley, was valued at £17 6s. 8d. *per annum*. In 1341, the parish of Morville was assessed only £10 3s. 4d., as the *ninth* of its wheat, wool, and lamb, because there had been a murrain that year; many tenants had thrown up their holdings through poverty, etc. Morville Church is not specially mentioned in King Henry VIII.'s *Valor*.

PILLAR AND CAPITAL, MORVILLE.

On December 4th, 1545, the site of the Cell or Grange of Morville, with its houses, kitchen, pasture, barns, stables, buildings, etc., in a state of utter ruin, was granted by the Crown to John Dudley, Viscount Lisle, and Lord Admiral of England.

The oldest parts of the present Church of St. Gregory's, Morville belong to that interesting transitional period when the pure Norman style of architecture began to change into the early English. The massy walls of its tower are strengthened at the angles by flat Norman buttresses. The upper portion of this tower, however, consists of much later work. On the north side of the chancel is a door, which, notwithstanding the date, 1683, inserted over it, evidently belongs to the twelfth century.

CHANCEL ARCH, MORVILLE.

Within, the nave is separated from the aisles by semicircular arches, resting on square piers, in the sides of which are semi-shafts. The form of the abacus is octagonal. A handsome Norman semicircular arch divides the nave from the chancel. The font is a curious and interesting relic.

Early Incumbent.—Roger, Chaplain of Morville, Thirteenth Century.

Much difficulty has been experienced in identifying those eighteen *berewicks* or members, which, according to the Conqueror's survey, belonged to the Manor of Morville. The one mentioned in Domesday (supposed to be erroneously), described as Calvestone in Worcestershire, is believed to be Cold Weston, far to the south of Morville. We learn, from Salop Abbey Chartulary, the names of eight more of these berewicks. They were as follows:—Astley Abbots, a township which, at a very early period, engrossed to itself the manorial dignity of Morville, and the church of which, about 1138, styled the "chapel of Estleya," yielded a pension of 8s. to Salop Abbey: Astley Parva; Norley; Croft; Haughton; Kingslow, held, under the abbey, by a family of wealth and importance, in the thirteenth century; Harpswood, and Billingsley; all of which were granted by the Norman earl Roger to Shrewsbury Abbey. The latter then spelt *Biligesleaye*, according to some authorities is the place where, in 1055, Earl Harold, Edward the Confessor's vicegerent, held the Peace Conference with Griffin, Prince of Wales, and Algar, the rebel Earl of Mercia.

Billingsley Church, originally subject to Morville, was founded and endowed by Herbert de Castello, Lord of Castle Holgate, very early in the reign of Stephen.

Early Incumbent of Billingsley.—Ralph Sagon, 1322, presented by the Abbot and Convent of Salop.

Road, Colemore, Stanley, Severn Hall, Dunvall, Rucroft, Cantreyn, the Haye, and Bunewall now Binnall, may have been the remaining nine berewicks of Morville. At any rate, all these formerly were held by tenants of Salop Abbey, who did suit to the Abbot's Court at Astley.

Aldenham, Underton, and that tract of land which was afterwards occupied by the castle and borough of Bridgenorth, and Tasley, the lords of which were the Corbets of Tasley; also, in all probability, were members of the Domesday Manor of Morville.

Tasley Chapel was existent in 1138, as, when, at that date, Robert de Betun, Bishop of Hereford, granted to Salop Abbey an appropriation of the Church of Morville, a pension of half-a-merk

BILLINGSLEY CHURCH.

p. 6.

UPTON CRESSETT CHURCH (*see* p. 51).

was included from the subject "Chapel of Tasseley."[1] In 1291, the Church of Tasselye, in Stottesden Deanery, was under £4 annual value. In 1341, Tasley Parish was rated only 20s. to the *ninth*, because storms had destroyed the crops. There were no sheep in it, etc.

Early Incumbent of Tasley.—Sir Robert de Stamford, 1277. Patron, Sir Thomas Corbet, of Tasley.

Eardington and Quatford are thus noticed in *Domesday*:— "The Earl himself holds Ardintone. Saint Milburg held it in King Edward's time. Here are v hides. In demesne, is 1 ox-team, and 4 serfs, and ix villains, and ii boors with iii teams; and there might be viii teams more (employed). Here a mill worth 5s. (*per annum*), and a borough, called Quatford, rendering nothing. In time of King Edward (the manor) was worth 40s.; now (it is worth) 30s."[2]

From the above, then, we learn, that in 1085, the borough or town of Quatford was subordinate to Eardington: it soon, however surpassed Eardington in importance.

Quatford derives its name from the Saxon, cpatpopb, Cwatford, in allusion to the neighbouring ford over the Severn. Under date 896, the Saxon Chronicle informs us, that, when King Alfred and the Londoners compelled the Danes to evacuate their stronghold by the River Lea, abandoning their ships, the bold Northmen traversed England until they came to Cwatbricge, by Severn, where they went into winter quarters. Florence of Worcester corroborates this account, when he describes the pagans as placing their wives for security in East Anglia, leaving those ships behind which the Anglo-Saxon King had contrived to obstruct the passage of into the Thames; and making a forced march, on foot, as far as a place called Quattbrycge; where, having built themselves a fortress, they passed the winter.

"In the summer season," continues this authority, "part of the pagan army, which had wintered at Quattbrycge, went into East Anglia, and the other parts as far as Northumbria;"[3] committing dreadful ravages, doubtless, as they marched.

---

[1] *Salop Chartulary*, No. 334.   [2] *Domesday*, fo. 254, a 1.
[3] FLORENCE OF WORCESTER. *Chron.*, p. 84. Bohn's Ed.

Quattbrycge here spoken of was Quatford, and an adjacent ford of the Severn, in its name of Danesford, bears witness to the fact of the heathen Northmen's visit to this neighbourhood.

About a quarter of a mile below the village, upon a rock precipitously overhanging the Severn, there are indications of a keep having formerly stood. Upon the side next the river, the rock rises nearly 100 feet perpendicularly above the Severn : where the rock slopes on the other sides, the fortress was surrounded by a curvilinear ditch, cut for nearly two hundred yards through the solid rock. This huge fosse, according to Hartshorne's measurement, is three yards wide at the bottom, and at least four in depth below the average level of the meadow above it, whilst the summit of the keep upon the top of the rock is about twenty-five feet above the same level. There are indications of an inferior keep a little nearer the ford. Judging from existing remains, if this was the site of the Danish fortress alluded to by the chronicler, it is certain that the Normans afterwards occupied the same spot. The appearance is essentially Norman, and when, some years ago, by the directions of Mr. Smallman, of Quatford Castle, the semicircular fosse was cleared out, there were found embedded in the rubbish great quantities of red-deer bones and boar tusks, (trophies of its former Norman proprietors' hunting prowess), two small horse-shoes, and an iron spur of Norman character.

Who, then, was the Norman proprietor of Quatford Castle? undoubtedly, Roger de Montgomery, the Earl of Shrewsbury, who built it probably as a hunting residence; for around Quatford then stretched the remains of the great primæval forest. The Conqueror's survey speaks of a *new house* at Quatford,[1] which expression clearly referred to Earl Roger's Castle, then, perhaps, in the course of erection.

Ordericus Vitalis informs us,[2] that, after Earl Roger's death, his son Robert de Belèsme built a very strong castle at Bridgenorth, on the River Severn, and transferred the town and people of Quatford to the new fortress.

QUATFORD CHURCH.

After the murder of his first Countess, Roger de Montgomery married Adelais, daughter of Ebrard de Pusey, one of the chief nobles of France. In contrast to his former wife, this lady, we are told, "excelled in understanding and in piety, and oft per-

---

[1] "Nova Domus."   [2] *Eccl. Hist. of England and Normandy*, Bk. X. ch. vii.

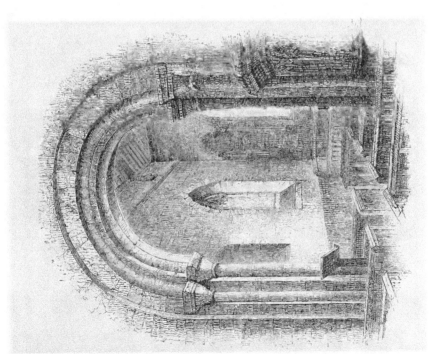

CHANCEL, QUATFORD.

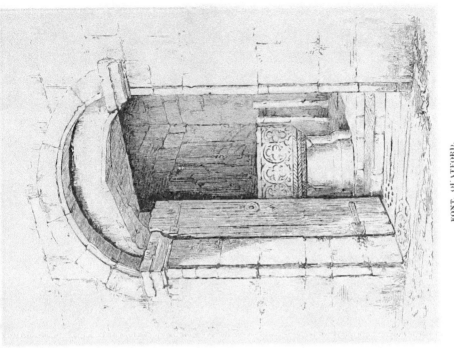

FONT, QUATFORD.

suaded her Lord to befriend monks, and to relieve the poor." Where Quatford Church now stands, at the time the earl's second marriage took place, grew the forest.

The Countess Adelais arrived in England in 1083-4. On her voyage to England, according to the legend, a storm shook the vessel in which she sailed to such a degree, that the mariners despaired of reaching land. It happened that a certain priest who was in her retinue, wearied by over-watching, fell into a slumber; and as he slept, he dreamt that he saw a matron standing before him, and thus addressing him;

"If your mistress and her suite desire to be liberated from the instant danger of horrible shipwreck, let her make a vow to God, and promise faithfully to build a church in honour of the blessed Mary Magdalene, on the spot where it happens that she first meets the earl, her husband, and exactly where a hollow oak tree grows by a pigstye."

The priest awoke, and told the particulars of his vision to the Lady Adelais, who, when she had heard them, vowed to perform everything fully. The storm ceased, and the lady reached the shore. Travelling inland to rejoin her lord, after many days she first met Earl Roger at Quatford, at the very spot where the oak tree, indicated in the vision, grew. She at once entreated her husband to aid her in carrying into execution the vow she had made when in danger of shipwreck. Earl Roger concurred; and thus, according to the legend, Quatford Church was built and amply endowed.

It is interesting to learn, that this romantic story [1], credible in itself, has been found to be minutely consistent with other ascertained facts.

Originally collegiate, Quatford Church ceased to be such after Robert de Belèsme transferred the castle and borough of Quatford to Bridgenorth. There remained for Quatford Church a parish identical with the *Domesday* Manor of Eardington. In 1291, the church here was worth under £4 *per annum*, and, consequently, not taxable. It is uncertain whether or not the village of Quatford was assessed to the *ninth*. Quatford Church is not mentioned in the *Valor*, of 1535.

The architectural features of Quatford Church are interesting. It is supposed that the present church preserves the ground plan

---

[1] Narrated in the *Chronicle* of JOHN BROMTON, pp. 988-9.

of the Norman earl's original foundation; although, with the exception of a small window on the north side of the chancel, and the chancel arch, which belong to the late Norman or transitional period; there are no details earlier than the fourteenth century.

The chancel arch, as well as parts of the walls of both nave and chancel are built of *calcareous tufa*, which, according to Hartshorne, "must have been brought hither up the Severn, out of Gloucestershire, as the nearest deposit of this formation lies at Stroud, in that county."[1] The font, which is low and circular, rests on four clustered massive shafts: its sides are enriched by quatrefoils, inscribed within circles. Near the door are some curiously incised sepulchral slabs.

INCISED SLAB, QUATFORD.

Early Incumbent.—Sir William de Chetinton was Chaplain of Quatford early in the 13th century.

Between Quatford and the larger portion of the old Manor of Eardington flowed the Severn. We learn, from the cotemporary foundation-charter, that Eardington was included among those lands which the Norman earl gave to his collegiate church of Quatford.

"In time of King William," says this charter, "Roger the earl and Adelaysa the countess built a church in Quatford, in honour of Our Lord Jesus Christ, and St. Mary Magdalene, and all the saints of God. They gave Ardintone, except the land of Walter the Smith and that land which lies between the water and the mount nigh to the bridge, and except that land where the borough [of Quatford] is built, and all its *hays* and *proper chaces*, quit of all service and thing." Upon this, Eardington became divided into two portions, allotted to two stalls of the earl's prebendal church viz., the prebend of Eardington and the prebend of Alveley.

Only a small tenement in Eardington remained in lay hands; it was the Moor[2] (the More Ridding), which was held *in capite* of the crown by the following curious kind of *petit* serjeantry :—

---

[1] *Salopia Antiqua*, p. 232.
[2] It is supposed that the following entry in *Domesday* relates to this tenement :—"The Earl himself holds Bolebec. Stenulf held it in King Edward's time. Here is half a hide, geldable. The arable land is for one ox team. It was and is waste" (*Domesday*, fo. 254, a 1) and accordingly acquired in time its name of *the Moor*.

"The king's tenant at the More held his land (a virgate) by service of appearing yearly in the exchequer, on the morrow of Michaelmas Day, with a hazel rod of a year's growth and a cubit's length, and two knives. The treasurer and barons being present the tenant was to attempt to sever the rod with one of the knives which was to bend or break; the other knife was to do the same work at one stroke, and then to be given up to the king's chamberlain for royal use."

The object of this service apparently was to secure for the king a good knife: yet what originally induced the monarch to look to his tenant in this out of the way spot for such an implement is involved in obscurity.

Bridgenorth.

It was during that dreadful period, when England, from one end to the other, groaned under the attacks of the heathen Northmen, that Ethelfleda, Lady of the Mercians, cast up, to stay the destructive ravages of the Danes, on the "western bank of the River Severn, at the place which is called Brige,[1]" a fortress.

Ethelfleda, the Mercian heroine, possessed a large share of her father King Alfred's spirit, ruling over the province of Mercia with much vigour after the decease of Ethelred her husband. She died A.D. 918.

The Danish and the Saxon rule had both passed away, when, after the conquest of England by the Normans, Roger de Montgomery obtained the Earldom of Shrewsbury. To him succeeded Earl Hugh, and then Robert de Belèsme became third and last Norman Earl of Shrewsbury. In him we have presented to us the very worst type of the ferocious Anglo-Norman noble; and if contemporary accounts can be relied on, Robert de Belèsme was little better than a monster. Able, active, and singularly cruel, "having usurped the vast estates of his ancestors in Normandie and Maine, to the disherison of his brothers," by payment of £3000, Robert obtained from Rufus the Earldom of Shrewsbury, when he exercised great severities. In fact, the more he acquired, the prouder and more cruel he became, so that "the English and Welsh, who had long treated as idle tales the accounts they had heard of his making his cruelties a jest, now tortured in his iron grasp, felt, to their sorrow, that the reports were true."[2]

[1] ROGER DE HOVENDEN. *Saxon Chron.* FLORENCE OF WORCESTER.
[2] ORDERICUS VITALIS. *Eccles. Hist. of Norm. and Eng.* Bk. X. ch. vii.

It was this man who reared upon the site of the Saxon burg, or fortress, which the Lady of Mercia had erected, a Norman castle. One of the most able engineers of his day, Robert de Belèsme, says the contemporary writer, "built a very strong castle at Brigge, on the River Severn." Bridgenorth Castle was a fortress of the first class. It was between the tenth and fourteenth centuries, the period in which De Belèsme built this stronghold, that feudalism erected its most important fortresses. Unlike those castles and defences of an earlier period, which were simply adjusted to the situation of an already existing town, oftimes but ill adapted by nature for defensive arrangements, the Norman De Belèsme's fortress was a true feudal structure. Reared upon the most favourable site that could be chosen, its military architect took advantage of every configuration of the country: and there, high overhanging the banks of the Severn, the Castle of Bruge, with outworks, and a moat of correspondingly vast proportion, in days of yore bade defiance to the surrounding neighbourhood.

Its ruins, could they speak, might tell of pageantries and banquets, as of many a secret tragedy enacted in the damp, dark dungeon; or these stones, had they a tongue, might boastfully recall the stirring time when the iron storm of war rattled ineffectually upon the surface of the grey and massive walls of Bridgenorth. Its revels are over; the miserable captive too has had his release; and a hoary fragment is all that remains of the once famous stronghold.

Robert de Belèsme, with other Anglo-Norman nobles, conspired to dethrone King Henry I., and place the English sceptre in the hands of his elder brother, Robert Curthose. But the astute Henry accommodated matters between himself and his brave but indolent brother; when, having broken up the Confederacy, he summoned De Belèsme before his court, to answer many accusations against him. The rebellious peer sought refuge in flight, when the king, proclaiming him an outlaw, assembled his forces and leading them northwards, attacked Bridgenorth. It was towards the autumn of 1102 that King Henry I. laid siege to De Belèsme's castle, the defence of which had been entrusted to Roger, son of Corbet, Robert de Neuville, Ulger the Hunter, and a garrison of eighty mercenaries. Earl Robert himself retired to Shrewsbury, from whence he sallied to annoy the king. Yet all to no purpose. Owing to William Pantulf, that vassal whom the Norman earl had formerly so unrighteously oppressed, the king refused to listen to the specious arguments adduced in De Belèsme's favour by his brother peers. The siege of Bridgenorth was vigorously pressed, and, at the end of three months, its governors surrendered the fortress to the king. This they did according to a preconcerted arrangement with Pantulf, shutting up the mercenary men-at-arms in one part of the fortress, whilst, at another, they " let in the king's troops with a royal ensign, amidst the cheers of the townsmen."[1] The stipendaries, however, obtained leave to depart with horses and arms, when, marching out of the fallen stronghold, they bitterly complained that they had been outwitted by their chiefs, whom they charged with treachery.

When Robert de Belèsme heard that Bridgenorth had fallen, he became almost frantic. After the capture of the castle, the king issued orders for his army to march by "Hunel-hege," the dangerous pass of Wenlock Edge, and besiege Shrewsbury. "This road," says Ordericus, who probably remembered it when a child, "was for a thousand paces full of holes, and the surface rough with large stones, and so narrow that two men on horseback could scarcely pass each other. It was overshadowed on both sides by a thick wood, in which bowmen were placed in ambush, ready to inflict sudden wounds with hissing bolts and arrows, on the troops on their march. There were more than 60,000 infantry in the expedition; and the king gave orders that they should clear a broad track, by cutting down the wood with axes, so that a road might be formed for his own passage, and a public highway for ever afterwards. The royal command was promptly performed, and vast numbers of men being employed, the wood was felled, and a very broad road levelled through it."[2]

At length, driven to despair, Robert de Belèsme surrendered at discretion. After consulting with his friends, he went to meet the king as he approached Shrewsbury, when, confessing his treason, he humbly laid the keys of the town at the king's feet, and sued for mercy. Thus Beauclerk reduced the turbulent noble, who was permitted to retire unmolested to Normandy. A shout of tumultuous joy rang throughout England when it became known that the monster was banished. Boiling with rage, de Belèsme crossed over to Normandy, when, like the dragon in the Apocalypse, says the chronicler, cast out of heaven, cruelly vented his wrath on the dwellers of the earth, so the last Norman Earl of Shrewsbury,

---

[1] ORDERICUS VITALIS, Bk. XI. ch. iii. [2] Ibidem.

driven from England, spent his fury upon Normandy. Sweeping their farms of all that could be carried off, he devoted them to the flames, and inflicted the torments of death or mutilation on all who fell into his hands. There is something appalling in the spectacle presented to us in the conduct of this implacable villain.

To return. Upon the fall of De Belèsme, the palatine Earldom of Shropshire escheated to Henry I., who, now combining in his own person both the Palatine and Royal dignities, governed the province by a viceroy, indifferently called Dapifer, Seneschall, and sometimes Sheriff, an office which posterity has assimilated to the wardenry of the Western Marches. His jurisdiction was not confined to Shropshire, or even to the Marches of Wales; but it extended into Staffordshire, and probably into Herefordshire. Presiding over all causes, both ecclesiastical and temporal, his decisions were afterwards recognised by the crown as irreversible. In short, he was to the district he presided over, what, in the absence of the sovereign, the justiciar, or chief justice of a later period was to England. Such was the power accorded to his representative by the king in the lately escheated palatine Earldom of Shropshire; the ordinary Sheriff or Sheriffs of the counties included in his province, however, still remained.

The first to represent King Henry I. in this new capacity, was Richard de Belmeis. As to Bridgenorth, maintained as a royal castle, it became a seat of provincial government.

On his Welsh expedition in 1121, Henry I. halted here, several of his charters about that period being dated at Brug. Tenacious of office and power, at length De Belmeis' increasing maladies totally incapacitated him from discharging his vice-regal duties, and, retiring to the Priory of St. Osyth, in Essex, which he had founded, he died there.

Pagan, or Pain Fitz John then held court at Bridgenorth, as the king's representative, in the earlier years of whose provincial power Bridgenorth became the temporary prison of Walleran, Earl of Mellent, whom Henry had brought over from Normandy. In 1128 this stronghold became the prison of Meredyth ap Lhywarch, who had been given up by Lhewelyn ap Owen.

From the Pipe Roll of 1130, we learn, that Milo de Gloucester, Sheriff of that county, had sent a quantity of wine by the king's order to Brug. Sending of wine was a usual item of sheriff's accounts, and this was undoubtedly for the king's use.

The close of Stephen's reign found Hugh de Mortimer, of Wigmore, of the Usurper's party, seised of the Castle of Bridgenorth. Upon the accession of Henry II., this proud baron refused to do homage, and, fortifying Bridgenorth, bad defiance to the king. But Henry quickly led his forces westward against the recusant noble, and, detaching from him his confederate, Roger, Earl of Hereford, who held the "Tower of Gloucester," forthwith the active king laid siege to Mortimer's three Castles of Wigmore, Cleobury, and Brug. Cleobury, after a short siege, the king took and destroyed, when the crest-fallen Mortimer surrendered up Bridgenorth and Wigmore to his sovereign. Bridgenorth having been recovered, from this period it served both as a fortress, a prison, and a royal residence.

We may infer what the castle originally was, from the following items, culled from the Shropshire Pipe Rolls, relative to its repairs in the respective years mentioned. At Michaelmas, 1166, the sheriff accounts 6s. 8d. for repairs of the "Well of Brug;—a good well was an indispensable requisite in every castle. In 1167, in obedience to the king's writs, £30 13s. 4d. was expended on the works of the "Tower of Brug;" in 1168, £14 5s. 6d.; and a further sum of £26 6s. 4d. accounted for in the following year. In 1169, £15 8s. 6d. for the same object, and so on, until during the thirty-four years Henry II. was in seisin of Bridgenorth, the recorded expenditure for repairs and additions amounted to £213, a sum equivalent to about £10,000 of the present time.

During the reign of Richard I., the expenditure was in proportion. Among the expences connected with Bridgenorth Castle in the time of John, the work charged for in 1212, is specified to have been at the "barbican and draw-bridge."

Yet, as when, through the Anglo-Norman period, Bridgenorth frowned in its might, we have no direct evidence. The earliest description of this castle is supplied by John Leland, the antiquary, who visited it about the middle of the 16th century. "The castle," he says, "standeth on the south part of the towne, and is fortified by east with the profound valley (of the Severn) instead of a ditch. The walles of it be of a great height. There were two or three stronge wardes in the castle, that nowe goe totally to ruine. I count the castle to be more in compasse than the third part of the towne," then about a mile round. "There is," he continues, "one mighty gate by north in it, now stopped up, and a litle posterne made of force thereby through the wall, to enter into the castle.

The castle ground, and especially the base court, hath now many dwelling-houses of tymbre in it, newly erected."[1]

The sheriff of Shropshire was usually *ex-officio* keeper of the two castles of Bridgenorth and Shrewsbury, the constable or chief resident officer in each in ordinary times being appointed by him. Occasionally, however, the Crown immediately nominated the constable. Besides this officer, there was a porter or warder at Bridgenorth, whose office likewise was permanent, and, in time of peace, perhaps half-a-dozen castellans as a regular garrison. There was no necessity for a greater number, as, in war-time, *castle-guard* service was due from neighbouring tenants of the Crown.

Bridgenorth Castle served also the purposes of a prison, and a palace. In June, 1163, Henry II. invaded South Wales, and, having ravaged Caermarthenshire, Rees, prince of South Wales, came to him at "Pencadayr beside Brecknock, and did him homage and gave him pledges." Accordingly, both at Michaelmas, 1163, and also in the two following years, the sheriff of Shropshire charges for the maintenance of hostages at Brug, in the latter year £4 12s., being charged for the keep of twenty-five hostages. In 1173-4, England, being greatly disturbed by the unnatural rebellion of Prince Henry, Guy le Strange, sheriff of Shropshire, charged for victualling the castle of Brug, for 92 horse-loads of corn £9 0s. 6d.; for 120 hogs £10 4s.; for 120 cheeses £2 6s. 8d.; and for 20 horse-loads of salt 10s. Total outlay, £22 5s. 2d.

Having frustrated the machinations of his enemies, Henry II. made a progress throughout his kingdom, the ostensible object of which was the punishment of all those who, during the late troubles, had trespassed on the royal forests. It is presumed, that during the course of this progress, the king visited Bridgenorth. King John was at Bridgenorth Castle upon the 11th and 13th of November, 1200, with a noble retinue, such as none but a fortress of the first-class could have accommodated. John also stayed here on the 13th, 14th, and 15th of March, 1204. In the king's train were the Bishops of Lincoln and Hereford, the Earls of Essex, Pembroke, Chester, Salisbury, Warren, Leicester, Warwick, and Hereford; also William de Braose, the provost of Beverley, Hugh de Nevill, and William de Briwere, with their respective suites.

---

[1] LELAND's *Itinerary*, Vol. IV. part ii. fo. 182, a

King John's writ is extant in which he orders his treasurer and chamberlains to deliver to Geoffrey Fitz-Piers (sheriff of Shropshire) £40, which said Geoffrey had paid in the King's Chamber, to discharge the king's expenses at Brug."

Again, in 1212, King John visited Bridgenorth, and under the following circumstances. The disunited Welsh princes, soldering up their petty feuds for the moment, had laid siege to the castle of Mathraval in North Wales, defended by Robert de Vipont, one of John's most active lieutenants. Retribution for crimes of deepest dye at length had overtaken King John. He had been expelled from his French provinces; his unhappy kingdom lay under an interdict; his nobles openly defied his authority. Altogether the affairs of John were in a most desperate condition. Yet, surrounded as he was with appalling difficulties, the following well-attested facts will serve to dispel the too generally received notion that John was at all times a coward and incapable.

On Thursday, July 26th, 1212, John passed from Bristol to Melkesham, Wilts, from whence he sent £300 to the sheriff of Herefordshire "to succour Robert de Vipont, who was besieged in Wales." Next day the king was at Devizes and Ludgarshall, both in Wilts. On the 29th, he was at Winchester. It was Sunday. That same day he passed back to Marlborough, Wilts; reached Tewkesbury on the 30th, and was at Worcester on the 31st. On the 1st of August, he travelled from Worcester to Bridgenorth, upon which journey the sumpter-horse that carried the king's bed broke down and was left at Bridgenorth. We learn, also, that two of the king's valets, with their jaded horses and attendants, the king's falconer with his hawks, the two carters and four sumpterers who carried the king's wardrobe, with their nine horses, accompanied the king's march no further. Certain coffers, which contained relics, were also left by the king at Bridgenorth, over which, during the three nights they remained there, wax candles were burnt at the superstitious king's expense. On the following morning, Thursday, the 2nd of August, the king, in urgent need of both horse and knight, ordered 60s. to be given to Buchard de Gratelon, whose horse in pawn at Brug was forthwith redeemed; when, that same day, spurring his slender troop more than fifty miles over bad roads, and in the dead heat of summer, right into Wales, John Plantagenet raised the siege of Mathraval, and levelled its castle to the ground. On the following day he returned to Bridgenorth. It was Friday; but the king ate meat twice, for which he atoned by feeding a hundred paupers with bread, fish, and beer.[1]

Notwithstanding tremendous exertions, the prospects of the king grew darker daily. Yet Shropshire and the western counties held fast their loyalty to the last; the storm, meanwhile, closing over the devoted head of John. On the 14th and 15th of August, 1216, the king made his final sojourn with his faithful castellans of Bridgenorth. Bereft of the larger portion of his kingdom, deserted even by Longespée who, like the other barons, had at length done homage to the French Prince Louis; a prey to anxiety; an ill-timed and fatiguing march across the Wash of Lincolnshire, in which, by the sudden rising of the tide, he lost both baggage and regalia, as well as many valuable records, threw the unhappy king into a fever, of which he died at Newark, October 18th, 1216. His heart was deposited in a golden urn at Font Evraud; but his body, by King John's dying request, was carried to Worcester, where a noble monument commemorates his unchanging attachment to the faithful city.

Bridgenorth Castle was visited by Henry III. both in 1221 and in 1223.

Among many notices connected with Bridgenorth, it may be observed, that, the Inquiries of the King's Commissioners in 1255 led to several statements relative to the castle. The Borough Jury reported, that when the king was at Brug, the lord of Albrighton was bound to find fuel for the castle, that being the service due on his fee of Little Brug, and the lord of Bobbington and Quat owed ward to the castle in time of war,—that, as long as the king held in hand the Manor of Worfield, the produce of hay and of the mills there used to come to the castle, and the tenants of that Manor used to do *Hirson* in time of war, and take up their quarters in the castle for ward thereof if required.

During the civil convulsions that characterised the close of the third Henry's reign, " by Council of the Magnates," that is, by coercion of the Committee of Reform appointed by the " Mad Parliament" of Oxford, the imbecile Henry III. granted custody of the castle of Brug to Peter, son of the arch-rebel Simon de Montfort. The confederate barons, however, do not appear to have long retained possession of Bridgenorth, as we learn that James D'Audley, the royalist sheriff of Shropshire, on July, 1261,

---

[1] *Itinerary of King John*, see preface to the patent Rolls of that King's reign, by T. DUFFUS HARDY, Esq.

laid out 100 merks in corn, and victualled the castle. Every exercise of the kingly prerogative being keenly contested by the confederates for some years about this time, it is difficult to decide who were the *bonâ fide* constables of Bridgenorth, or even the real sheriffs of Shropshire. Appointments and re-appointments succeeding each other in rapid succession, accordingly as either party obtained the ascendancy. Yet, from the records which have come down to us, it appears certain, that " the good men and true " of Shropshire were hearty royalists, assuming the offensive against Montfort's nominees. Hamo le Strange, a royalist, seems to have been in possession of Bridgenorth throughout this stormy period.

After the battle of Evesham, which blasted the hopes of the confederates, and restored the king to his prerogative, the gratified Henry favoured Shropshire with a visit; and great were the rejoicings at Bridgenorth, the sheriff accounting no less a sum than £30 8s. 4d. which he had paid for corn, oats, oxen, and sheep supplied on the occasion of the king's late visit to the castle.

With respect to Bridgenorth Castle as a prison, a couple of notices will suffice; and these will show what *good* old times they were in which our Anglo-Norman ancestors lived. To an enquiry made in 1274, as to the excesses of public officers, the Jurors of the Borough replied, that Robert Trillee, under-sheriff of Shropshire, maintained " certain satellites, who wrongfully extorted money " from messengers and other travellers on the king's highway." " The same Robert had caused these satellites to seize Richard de Dodemonston at midnight and carry him about from one wood to another, threatening his life; which Richard offered a fine of three merks payable to Trillee, if he might be taken to the castle prison of Brug, with his head on his shoulders." Hugh de Donvile, constable of Bridgenorth, and also bailiff of Stottesden in 1274, was accused of many excesses of power. Donvile, backed by his brother and others, kept an approver[1] in the castle prison, " who impeached many faithful subjects and harmless men for the sake of lucre."

Nor did the scoundrel oppress the innocent only; he allowed the guilty to escape. By his connivance, Henry le Pleidour, an outlaw, whom Donvile had arrested in Shropshire, got off by

---

[1] The approver was a most formidable instrument of feudal oppression. He was a self-confessed felon, an informer, and a bravo. A person accused by an approver might, if he chose, be tried by a jury; but the practical alternative was that he had either to fight a duel with his accuser, or else bribe his employer.

giving a false name, when arraigned before the justices. Calling himself John de Womburne, the criminal appealed to a Staffordshire jury, who, knowing nothing about him, of course acquitted him. As to what money Donvile got for his connivance in the job none of the jurors could tell.

So much for Bridgenorth Castle.

THE BOROUGH OF BRIDGENORTH.

This is presumed to have been a foundation immediately consequent on the transfer of the castle from Quatford, in 1101. Speaking of De Belèsme's succession to his brother's earldom, the Norman chronicler says, "Having thus secured it, he exercised great cruelties on the Welsh, during four years. He built a very strong castle at Bridgenorth, on the River Severn, transferring the *town* and *people* of Quatford to the new fortress." [1]

From the confirmation of its privileges by King Henry II. it appears that the new borough was recognised by Henry I. The following is the purport of a document which merits attention, from the circumstance, that it is the earliest written charter implying royal recognition of any Shropshire borough:—

"Henry, King of England, and Duke of Normandy and Aquitaine, and Earl of Anjou, to his Justiciars, and Sheriffs, and Barons, and Ministers, and all his faithful of England, greeting. Know ye, that I have conceded to my Burgesses of Brugia, all their franchises, and customs, and rights, which they or their ancestors had in the time of King Henry, my grandfather. Wherefore, I will and strictly command that they have them, well and in peace, and honourably and fully; within the Borough and without, in wood and in field, in meadows and pastures, and in all things, with such comparative fulness and honour as they held them in the time of King Henry, my grandfather. And I forbid any one to do them injury or insult, in regard to their tenements.—Witnesses: T. Chancellor and Henry de Essex, Constable, and Wm. Fitz Alan : at Raddemore."

Eyton assigns the year 1157 as the probable date of the foregoing. The reader must not forget, however, that Shrewsbury was a much older borough than Bridgenorth, yet it has no charter earlier than that of Richard I. It may be added, that, according to a great authority, there are no examples of civil incorporations in England, except London, till the reign of Henry II. [2]

---

[1] ORDERICUS VITALIS, B. X. ch. vii. [2] HALLAM, *Middle Ages*, vol. i. 211.

When the barons, knights, abbots, and burgesses of the kingdom, in 1159, contributed a royal aid in form of a *donum*, Shrewsbury and Brug were the only boroughs in Shropshire that were assessed; the former raising fifty merks and the latter ten, and paying the same through the sheriff at the Exchequer.

According to Madox, "The yearly *Ferme* of towns arose out of certain *locata* or demised things that yielded issues or profit. Insomuch that when a town was committed to a sheriff, fermer, or *custos*, such fermer or *custos* well knew how to raise the *ferme* out of the ordinary issues of the town, with an overplus of profit to himself."

But Bridgenorth soon escaped out of the clutches of the sheriff, and obtained the privilege of paying its own *ferme* or chief rent directly to the crown, without being subject to the extortion of an intermediate officer; as we learn, that at Michaelmas, 1170, the burgesses of Brug and Salop had fined with the Crown, in sums of twenty and eighteen merks respectively, "for having the *ferme* of their *vills*"—each had paid the said fine and was *quit*. The terms on which the burgesses of Brug obtained this privilege were, that they should pay $2\frac{1}{2}$ merks per annum in addition to the quota of £5, which for ten years previously they had contributed to the general ferme of the county.[1] Yet not until the burgesses of Bridgenorth had again fined in a sum of thirty merks, and two coursers, "to have their town at *ferm*," did they realize, to its full extent, their privilege. According to the Pipe Roll of the year ending Michaelmas, 1176, in that year the burgesses rendered their first annual account of the full *ferme* of their *vill*. It was 10 merks, namely, $7\frac{1}{2}$ (£5) which they used to pay through the sheriff, and $2\frac{1}{2}$ merks the "*increment* of their *vill*," which they had already paid for five years themselves.

At this juncture, King Henry began to issue writs to the burgesses, which are in the nature of *drafts* on their annual debt; the first of which in that very year directing them to make a payment "in corrody (entertainment) of his sister, the wife of David ap Owen," which draft the burgesses duly respected and took credit for it in their own account with the Exchequer.

Yet, besides the annual contribution to the royal revenue, this borough, as a demesne of the Crown, was subject to other imposts, and every now and then, under the title of a *donum*, Bridgenorth

---

[1] *Rot. Pip.* 16 Hen. II., Salop.

was mulcted of a heavy sum. For instance, in 1187 it was assessed at 15 merks; in 1214, 50 merks; in 1227, another 50 merks, and so forth.

That Bridgenorth was a corporate town in 1180 may be inferred from the circumstance that Ranulph de Glanvill, the Justiciar visiting Shropshire in that year, left the burgesses of Brug subject to the heavy amercement of 20 merks. They had made a false averment, reporting a suit as compounded which was not compounded: the burgesses were amerced corporately for a return which could only have been made in their own Borough Court.

It appears that this court took primary cognizance of certain legal matters beyond the usual routine of self-government, therefore the burgesses of Brug had special privileges. At the county assizes of 1203, the earliest of which we have detailed records, the Borough of Brug as being among those hundreds or boroughs claiming an exclusive jurisdiction was summoned to send its jury. From the report of it, we glean that the "assize of cloth" was not held in the borough.[1]

A second royal charter was obtained for this borough in 1215. About this time, the burgesses of Brug began to encircle their town with a stockade or barrier of woodwork, a precaution necessitated by the disturbed character of the period, allowances of timber for the purpose being made out of the royal forest of Morf.

Again, in May, and also in June, 1220, Henry III. granted timber to the loyal burgesses, out of the "royal forest near Bruges," to assist them in the enclosure of their town. To enable them to complete their defences, the king also empowered the burgesses to charge $\frac{1}{2}$d. on every cart bringing things into the town for sale, and if such cart came from another county 1d. Other tolls were specified on pack-horses, cattle, and barges; the right of enforcing all which was granted them from June 24th, 1220, until the end of four years following, the license constituting, says Eyton, an early instance of a royal grant to take "customs" or "murage."

In November, 1222, the Borough of Brug was among those whose bailiffs were addressed on the subject of the *aid* granted by the King in Council for the King of Jerusalem.[2] It is the first

---

[1] The Assize of Cloth was an ancient statute regulating the measure and price of such manufactures. Its non-observance, in any borough, subjected the same to a fine.

[2] It was the period of the 6th crusade.

positive recognition which occurs of the bailiffs or provosts of the town.

We read, that on September 1st, 1226, King Henry III. having just left Bridgenorth, granted, until he came of age, to the men of Bruges, an annual fair of three days' duration, namely, "the *vigil*, the day and the morrow of St. Luke the Evangelist, unless some neighbouring fair be thus interfered with."

It will be recollected, that Henry III. declared himself of age at the Council of Oxford, in February, 1227, and announced to all privileged bodies the necessity of having their charters renewed, by which he netted over a £100,000. Accordingly, the burgesses of Bridgenorth applied to the king to have theirs renewed, which Henry, for a consideration, graciously granted.

Stephen de Segrave and his fellow justiciars, sitting at Gloucester in 1227, amerced the *vill* of Brug in one merk "for the flight of Osbert le Puleter," a felon, whose escape had not been prevented. This was demurred to, however, by the burgesses as an encroachment on their liberties. They claimed exemption from making *trace* (pursuit, hue or cry), through their town after felons, and there is no notice taken of the liquidation of the *item*.

On August 16th, 1256, this borough obtained its fourth and fifth charters from the Crown. At loggerheads with his barons, the king confirmed and extended the liberties of his faithful burgesses of Bridgenorth, doubtless in anticipation of the aid he required and afterwards received from them. On the other hand, Simon de Montfort, the opponent of the lawless Henry III., out-bade the king for popularity by summoning two knights from each shire, and deputies from boroughs, to attend the National Council—the origin of the British House of Commons. This, the great leader of the barons in rebellion against Henry III., did in the year 1265; and thus, in the hands of Providence, a squabble between a worthless king and a band of selfish feudal lords, was the means of vastly extending the freedom of the down-trodden people. Upon the termination of the civil war, in recognition of their devotion to his cause, and "for the losses which they had sustained in the time when the kingdom was disturbed, and because they faithfully adhered to the king and to Edward his son," Henry III. renewed to the burgesses their long-expired licence to take *customs* or *murage*, and excused them various sums of money which they owed to the Crown. Enough, however, has been said respecting the Borough of Bridgenorth.

Among the first recorded Members of Parliament for this borough were Andrew Bolding (provost of Bridgenorth in 1294), and Fremund de Erdinton, who were summoned to the Parliament which met in November, 1295. Their manucaptors were Robert Tinctor, Robert Crowk, John Glydde, and Roger Bonamy. Roger Bonamy and Thomas de Isenham appear as burgesses of the Parliament which was summoned for May 25th, 1298, to York. Their manucaptors were John Glydde, Simon Dod, Roger de la More, and Andrew Bolding. Roger Bonamy, provost or chief bailiff of Bridgenorth, with Richard Robert, provost of Bridgenorth in 1299, were returned as burgesses for the Parliament which was summoned to meet at Lincoln on January 20th, 1301. These ex-provosts were both returned as members for the Parliament which was summoned to London for September 29th, 1303.[1]

Church of St. Mary Magdalene.

Associated with the religious history of Bridgenorth and its suburbs, first in importance and antiquity stood this church. When Robert de Belèsme transferred the castle and people of Quatford to the stronger fortress he had reared on the banks of the Severn, he removed also the collegiate church his father had so richly endowed; henceforth, therefore, the dean and prebendaries of St. Mary Magdalene performed their sacred offices in the chapel built within the precincts of Bridgenorth Castle. From the Sheriff's account, we learn that on the accession of Henry II., the canons of Brug were entitled to a recognised composition or payment of 10s. per annum in lieu of the tithes of the king's demesne, which sum continued to be paid and charged in each annual account of the sheriff, until the year 1176, when, the king ordered the burgesses of Brug to pay the 10s. to the canons of St. Mary. Henceforth, therefore, they made the payment annually, and took credit for it in their account with the Exchequer.

The church of St. Mary Magdalene enjoyed all those privileges and immunities which attached to royal free-chapels. From a petition of the burgesses of Brug to the Parliament of Winchester in 1330, praying that they might have the use of the King's Chapel as a parish church, it would seem that originally no parochial cure had been attached to it.

The collegiate body consisted of six prebendaries, generally non-

---

[1] *Parliamentary Writs*, vol. 1.

resident; the superiority of the dean appearing nominal only. The immunities claimed by the church of St. Mary Magdalene extended to all the churches and chapels which belonged to its prebendaries. At the Salop Assizes, November, 1221, the jurors of the borough and hundred of Bruges returned the church of St. Mary of Brug as of the king's gift, and that there were six prebends therein, which six clerks held by gift of the king and his ancestors. In 1228, a precept issued to the sheriff of Shropshire, commanding him to allow to this chapel all tithes of the king's demesnes of Brug in fairs and mills. By a patent of 1246, King Henry ordered the canons of Bruges to render obedience to their dean Peter de Rivallis, in the matter of remedying deficiencies in the decorations of their chapel:—the collegiate body sadly at variance, neglect of the sacred edifice appears to have been the consequence.

In 1254, the dean of the King's Chapel of Brug was commissioned by letters patent to assist Bernard de Nympha to collect certain moneys from those who had vowed the crusade for the use of the Earl of Cornwall. This prince, brother of Henry III., was undoubtedly the hero of the seventh crusade, which took place in 1240-1. Dugdale[1] says, that the earl went a second time to the Holy Land, accompanying William Longespée, and that he again returned thence in 1242. The statement, however, does not appear founded on fact. Yet, even if it were, it is admitted on all hands, that the Earl of Cornwall never afterwards went to Palestine. How comes it then, that, in 1254, the dean of Brug was commissioned to collect moneys from those who had vowed the crusade for his use? The *cruce signati*, or those who vowed the crusade, were permitted to compound the obligation by money payments, which, collected under papal authority, were supposed to be allotted to those who personally fulfilled their vows.

It was a common occurrence at this period for the Pope, by means of his emissaries, to proclaim a crusade; in furtherance of which he was accustomed to furnish to the King of England a mandate, the purport of which was, that the Holy Father "by virtue of the authority given him from God," granted to the king enormous tithes of the whole English church, to provide, as was said, necessaries for the king's pilgrimage. King Henry worked in concert with the Pope, and when our country had been well

---

[1] *Baronage.*

drained of its gold, the Holy Father and the equally unscrupulous king, neither of whom had the most remote intention of applying the money to the purpose for which it had been collected, shared it between them. Or England was fleeced thus:—the Pope so arranged matters with the money-loving Earl of Cornwall, that, "with averted eyes and closed ears," he stood by whilst the Holy Father—"kisses to his blessed feet"—riddled his country. It was a profitable speculation this for Earl Richard, who, although not intending to go on pilgrimage, from one archdeaconry alone is said to have carried off £600. Nor was the earl over particular as to the way in which his agents went to work to cash the Pope's order, for, under date of 1250, M. Paris observes, that Bernard de Nympha (the man alluded to), a clerk armed with the papal documents, collected a large sum of money from the crusaders for the use of Earl Richard, in such a dishonourable way, that it appeared robbery rather than justice.

To return to the king's free chapel in the castle of Brug. Secure in its independence, it does not appear that the Bishops of Lichfield ever held ordinations there. The visit of Master Rigaud de Asserio, Clerk of the Papal Chamber, to England in 1317, however, threatened the rights of several royal free chapels, including Bruges and St. Mary's, Salop. This agent of Pope John XXII. was authoritatively commanded, in spite of all customs, privileges, and indulgences, to enforce the neglected collection of Peter's Pence in England; but King Edward II. interfered in defence of his free chapels, and forbade the nuncio to enforce his exactions against those establishments.

The taxation of 1291 values the spiritualities of the church of Bruges and its members at £54 13s. 4d. From the "Inquisition of the Ninth," taken in 1341, the dean and canons of Brug were specially exempted.

Among the DEANS OF ST. MARY MAGDALENE, Alexander, dean of Brug, 1161-1171, appears the earliest. On the 13th April, 1214, a Poictevin of the name of Hugo or Hugh de Tanney, was appointed to this deanery by John—the king's object being, as he avows in his grant, that the friends of the presentee "who are very necessary to the king in the parts of Poictou, may be placed under obligation." Of the dean who succeeded this one a more lengthened notice is required.

Appointed to the deanery of the chapel of Brug in 1223, Peter de Rivallis, a Poictevin by descent, was ostensibly the nephew, but in reality the son of, that Peter de Rupibus, Bishop of Winchester, the corrupt but powerful minister, first of King John, and afterwards of Henry III. Upon the downfall of the great Hubert de Burgh, in 1232, de Rivallis, through the influence of his relative, was appointed "Treasurer of the Chamber," an office which gave, says Eyton, "custody of all the Crown escheats and wardships, and his success in replenishing the royal coffers was most unequivocal." By an extraordinary patent, dated July 2nd, 1232, this Poictevin dean of Brug was granted the custody (shrievalty) of Shropshire and Staffordshire for life, and also that of the counties of York, Berks, Gloucester, Somerset, Dorset, Devon, Lancaster, Northumberland, Essex, Herts, Lincoln, Norfolk, Suffolk, and Kent.[1] In fact, Henry the Third was infatuated, and having dismissed all his former counsellors, according to the cotemporary chronicler,[2] the weak monarch "put confidence in no one except the aforesaid Bishop of Winchester and his son Peter de Rivallis; after which he ejected all the castellans throughout all England, and placed the castles under the charge of the said Peter."

It was the misfortune both of Henry the Third and his misguided father John, that they preferred to be surrounded with foreigners rather than be led by the counsels of their own subjects, who, born within the realm, had a great interest in its government. King Henry's Poictevin and Gascon favourites were for the most part needy adventurers, who flourished by advising him to measures obnoxious to the great body of his barons. Those high-mettled potentates could ill-brook the indignity of seeing aliens whom they despised preferred before them to the highest offices, and still less were they inclined to submit to be arbitrarily taxed at the caprice of a tyrannical monarch to support the extravagance of a set of dissipated foreign courtiers. True, these very murmurers themselves were of foreign extraction, and scarce 200 years had yet passed since their ancestors had landed with Duke William on the English shore; and the great separating line between the conquering Norman and the subject Saxon and Danish people was still distinctly visible. But time had begun to soften down those feelings of bitter animosity with which the opposing races had for so long a period regarded each other, and of late,

---

[1] Pat. 16 Hen. III.   [2] ROGER DE WENDOVER.

both bent on curbing the abuse of irresponsible power, and mutually needing assistance, had drawn nearer together. The Great Charter, won by their united exertions, and framed for their common benefit, was the first pledge of their reconciliation.

Foremost among the haters of the system represented by the elevation of the alien Dean of Brug, was the chivalric Richard Marshal. He had suffered in person by the ascendancy of this man and his minions. His lands had been confiscated to them, and other indignities heaped on him through their advice, and accordingly the baron bore them a mortal antipathy. Confederating, then, with Llewellyn, Prince of North Wales, Marshal attacked the king's troops, and defeating John de Monmouth, who ineffectually endeavoured to oppose his progress, at length he laid waste Shropshire, the county in which De Rivallis was chiefly interested, and sacked and fired Shrewsbury. It was a dreadful sight, says the chronicler, to see in the lanes and meadows of England the corpses of the slain, whose naked and unburied bodies afforded carrion for the kites. At length, Peter de Rivallis and his alien uncle had recourse to guile, to do that which, by fair means, they could not accomplish. "They wrote letters," says Roger de Wendover, "and forced the king, although ignorant of their purport, to set his seal to them." These letters, addressed to Fitz-Gerald and other magnates in Ireland, announced the forfeiture and proscription of the earl, and promised them that if they could bring Marshal, dead or alive, to the king, the earl's inheritance in Ireland should be shared amongst them. The plot succeeded. To entice the earl over to Ireland, his lands were invaded by the treacherous lords of Ireland, of which no sooner had Marshal intelligence than he crossed the channel with only fifteen knights in his train.

Notwithstanding the inferiority of Marshal's force, at first success attended his efforts, but at length he was entrapped into an engagement against fearful odds. Choosing, however, rather to die on the field with honour, than quit it in disgrace, the brave earl deliberately arranged his little band, and, exhorting them to quit themselves like men, he inspired them with the noble reflection, that if they fell, they died for justice and the sake of English laws; then, lowering his lance into its rest, he heroically dashed into the thickest of his enemies. Determined to sell life dearly, desperate were his efforts; but at length, hard driven, his horse being killed under him, and overwhelmed, Marshal was stabbed in the back, and carried prisoner to his own castle. There, as he lay wounded, his cruel enemies required of him his castles and lands; and, whilst he hesitated, they produced the forged charter. At seeing it, Marshal became much excited, and neglecting his wounds, a physician whom his enemies had summoned, "with a long heated instrument, laid his wounds open and probed them so often and deeply with it" says the cotemporary historian, that his acute sufferings flung him into a fever, and clasping the cross deliriously to his bosom, Marshal died. Thus, through the cunning of the Dean of Bridgenorth and other aliens, fell, on April 16th, 1234, in the prime of his life, " the flower of chivalry in that age."

Meanwhile, the high hand with which his Poictevin favourites were carrying affairs, had awakened a tempest that threatened to involve both Henry the Third and his ministers in a common destruction. At a council held at Westminster, in February previously, the Bishops, with Edmund elect of Canterbury at their head, had informed the King, that the counsel which "Peter, Bishop of Winchester, and Peter de Rivallis" gave him was neither wise or safe, but "dangerous to the whole kingdom;" and that Marshal's insurrection would not have occurred if his people had been governed by law and justice. Continuing to address the weak monarch, they warmly added: "There is scarcely any business of importance in the kingdom transacted under your seal, or by your warrant, without being also under the seal and by the warrant of Peter de Rivallis, from which it is clear they (your subjects) do not consider you in the light of a king."

Henry III. preferred to sacrifice his favourites rather than himself; so, promising the prelates that he would yield to their counsels, he ordered the Bishop of Winchester to his Bishopric, and dismissed the Poictevins. As to Peter de Rivallis, the facile Henry at once stripped him of his trusts, declaring, with an oath, "that, if he were not a beneficed person, and admitted to the rights of the clergy, he would order his two eyes to be torn out." The king's indignation reached its climax on receipt of the news of "the murder of the marshal," when, by the direction of his new council, Henry demanded of the late ministers not only an account of all moneys they had received, but also of their misuse of his seal. Upon this, overwhelmed with affright, Peter de Rivallis and his former colleague fled to the sanctuary at Winchester for refuge.

At length, under a safe conduct, they appeared before the king at Westminster. Peter de Rivallis was brought up for trial first. He came before the court "in a clerical dress, with his head shaved, and wearing a broad chaplet, and reverently greeted the king, who was sitting on the bench with the justiciaries. The king, eyeing him with a scowling look, thus addressed him: 'Traitor,' said he, 'by your evil advice, I unknowingly affixed my seal to letters containing treacherous designs against the marshal. It was also by your evil counsel that I banished him and others of my natural subjects from my kingdom, and thus estranged their affections and regard from me; and by your ill-advice was it, that I made war against them, and have wasted my own money, as well as that of my subjects.' He also demanded of him an account of his treasury, and of the wardship of youths of noble families entrusted to his care, as also of escheats, and several other revenues incident to the crown. When the king had thus accused him of these and many other offences, and charged him with treachery, he did not deny any of the charges brought against him, but, prostrating himself on the ground before the king, implored his mercy. 'My lord king,' he said, 'I was brought up and enriched in worldly property by you; therefore, do not destroy the man you have made, rather give me time for deliberation, that I may be able to give you a due account respecting the things demanded of me.'

"To this, the king replied: 'I will send you to the Tower of London, there to consider on the matter, in order to give me a proper account.'

"Peter replied: 'My lord, I am a priest, and ought not to be imprisoned or consigned to the custody of laymen.'

"The king then said: 'The archbishop is here, and if he will become security for you, I will give you into his charge, in order that you may give me a proper answer to my demands.'" "To speak briefly," adds Roger de Wendover, "the king sent him to the Tower, and took charge of all his lay possessions; for, under his clerical habit, he was armed with a coat of mail, which was not befitting a clerk." Having been kept in the Tower two days, the archbishop then restored Peter to sanctuary at Winchester.

King Henry's wrath, simulated probably to clear himself of the odium attaching itself to the foul murder of Marshal, lasted only a short time. In June, 1236, Peter, Dean of Bridgenorth, with his alien relative, were restored to the royal favor, de Rivallis in 1249 appearing as joint custos of the Great Seal, during the temporary absence of the chancellor from Court; and from November, 1256, to April, 1258, occupying his old office of Treasurer to the King's Wardrobe. Thus much for the alien Dean of Brug.

Among other presentees to the Deanery of Brug, occurs William de Montfort, March 2nd, 1265, whose name, coupled with the date at which he obtained the grant, indicate his relationship to Simon de Montfort. Under the diocese of Coventry and Lichfield, and the archdeaconry of Stafford, the following was returned in the Valor of 1535: "Thomas Magnus, Dean of the Collegiate Church of St. Mary Magdalene, holds the prebend of Ludston, which is worth, in glebe land, clear of deductions, £4 per annum. He also holds the Rectory of Claverley, which is worth in tithes, offerings, etc., £36 per annum." £40 *per annum*, therefore, was the value of his Deanery.

Among the *Prebendaries* of this once great Collegiate establishment, occurs John Mansel, who, Chancellor of England from November, 1246, to October, 1249, through a period of twenty-five years was employed in various offices by King Henry III. This man was reputed to be the richest clerk in the world! The enormities of the principles of plurality and non-residence, which prevailed in the days of Henry III., may be inferred from the circumstance, that, no less than 700[1] ecclesiastical livings are computed to have been held by Mansel, the king's chaplain, at one and the same time. When such intolerable abuses prevailed, is it any wonder that our Anglo-Norman forefathers kicked at the mis-rule of the Third Henry?

A CHANTRY in the Church of St. Mary Magdalene, was founded by Richard Dammas about 1294, which remained till the Dissolution.

CHURCH OF ST. LEONARD.—When, in the time of Henry VIII., Leland, the antiquary, visited Bridgenorth, he wrote: "There is but one Paroch Church in the towne, a very fayre one, and dedicated to St. Leonard."[2] Eyton supposes its foundation to be coeval with that of the borough, although described as the "Cemetery of St. Leonard" the first notice relating to it is not older than the middle of the 13th century. It was in the king's gift.

Unnoticed, either in the Taxation of 1291, or the Inquest of the Ninths, the *Valor* of 1535, however, recognised two Chantries

---

[1] HUME, *Hist. of Eng.* Ch. 12. [2] *Itinerary*, Vol. IV. part ii, fo. 182 a.

in St. Leonard's Church, namely, those of "St. Thomas," and "St. Mary the Virgin." The founders of these Chantries were Burgesses of the Town; their revenues were derived from borough property. These Chantries remained till the Dissolution.

THE HOSPITAL OF THE HOLY TRINITY, dedicated also to the Virgin Mary and St. John the Baptist, is reputed to have been founded by Ralph le Strange, Lord of Alveley, in the time of Richard I. Usually called St. John's, this foundation was doubtless originally designed for the relief of poor impotent people, and for the entertainment of travellers on the road; and, like others of its class, was placed by the road-side. The hospital alluded to, stood in the Low Town of Bridgenorth, within the angle formed by Mill Street and St. John Street, and, thus placed, it commanded every highway by which travellers could approach the town from the eastern end of the bridge over the Severn. It had a Master, or Prior, a Chaplain probably, and a certain number of regular brethren. According to the *Valor* of 1535, this House was a dependency of Lilleshall Abbey, which long before had obtained custody of it.

THE LEPER HOUSE OF ST. JAMES, intended as a refuge for persons afflicted with formidable, and perhaps contagious, diseases, stood without the town, not far off from the Hospital of the Holy Trinity, and probably owed its foundation to the sanitary precaution of the community of the borough of Brug. Founded previously to 1224.

Connected with Bridgenorth, appears to have been a "maladrerie," of still older date than the Leper House of St. James. It lay on the Oldbury side of the town. "The language used in certain early charters of these Leper-Houses, would seem to indicate that the term 'leprosy,' was applicable only to contagious disease, or what was believed to be so. On the other hand, it is well known that paralytic affections were classified under the same term 'leprosy,' in the middle ages; and, whereas, paralysis can scarcely have been accounted infectious even then, it would appear that the term was used to denote severe disease, in a much more general sense than modern notions can at once apprehend."[1]

Among the ancient religious foundations of Bridgenorth, was THE MONASTERY OF ST. FRANCIS, belonging to the Franciscan, or Grey Friars, known also as the order of Friars

---

[1] EYTON'S *Antiquities of Shropshire*, note Vol. I. p. 347.

Minors, a monastic fraternity, introduced into England early in the 13th century.[1] Founded during the reign of Henry III., this House at Bridgenorth was one of nine subject to the custody of Worcester, the English province of the order of Franciscans being subdivided into seven custodies, or districts, over the convents in each of which presided a separate custos, or keeper. The House in question lay to the west of the Severn, under the Church of St. Leonard's, adjoining which are some vaults known as the "Friars' Caves." Their great hall, or refectory, is still, or was but lately, in tolerable condition. It is not known who founded this establishment, although the brethren claimed Ralph le Strange for founder; yet this could not have been, as Ralph died twenty-four years before the order was introduced into England. Unaccounted for in the *Valor* of 1535, the revenues of this House fell into lay hands at the Dissolution.

Hewn out of the red sandstone hilly formation that faces Bridgenorth on the east, the road which led through Morf Forest towards Worfield, passed under a cave, "THE HERMITAGE," where, says tradition, a brother of King Athelstane

> Far in a wild, unknown to public view,
> From youth to age, a reverend hermit grew.

Yet, whether it existed in the Anglo-Saxon era, or not, certain it is, that anciently there was a hermitage in this suburb of Bridgenorth; for we read, that in 1328 John Oxindon was presented by King Edward III. to the "Hermitage of Athelwildston, near Bridgnorth."[2]

Among early tenures in Bridgenorth, "THE FEE OF LITTLE BRUG," held of the Crown by *petit sergeantry*, deserves mention. Sometimes called Southbridge, this suburb of Little Brug consisted of two short continuations of Hungary Street or St. Mary's Street, and of Whitburn or Raven Street. These lying outside of St. Mary's and Whitburn gates, unite in a road, which, leading north-west at first, afterwards branches off towards Shrewsbury. The angle formed by these streets (one of which is still called Little Bridge Street), and subtended by the town wall, will represent the Fee of Little Brug. There is a legend, that during the siege of Brug by Henry I. in 1102, "Sir Ralph de Pitchford, one of the

---

[1] St. Francis, founder of the order of Minorites, died 1226; and within ten years afterwards, his followers obtained a footing in England.
[2] *Pat.* 2 Ed. III. p. 1, m. 33.

king's commanders, behaved himself so gallantly, that Henry granted him an estate in the neighbourhood, called the Little Brugge, to hold by the service of finding dry wood for the king's great chamber in the castle, as often as he should come there."[1] From a fragmentary Roll in the *Testa de Nevill*, drawn up about 1212, we learn, that Ralph, son of Hugh de Pichford, held Little Brug by gift of King Henry, grandfather of King John, by service of finding dry wood for the chamber in the castle of Brug, at the King's coming there. This family of Pitchford is presumed to have descended from the Domesday "Norman Venator." Now Ulger the Hunter (Ulger Venator), according to the contemporary chronicler,[2] whose connection with the family of the Earl of Shrewsbury would give him access to precise information on the subject, was one of the three knights concerned in the surrender to Henry I. of de Belèsme's stronghold of Bridgenorth; yet, in what way the Sir Ralph de Pitchford of the legend, and Ulger the Hunter, were connected, is the question. Singularly enough, however, the representatives of each, under a writ of "mort d' ancestre," contested certain property in Lee Brockhirst. The De Pitchfords held Little Brug *in capite*, having tenants under them.

HAUGHMOND ABBEY also, from ancient time, held in Little Brug, having acquired, previously to 1172, the mill of Pichefort and half a virgate of land from Richard de Pichforte, who, "for the health of his soul," gave them to the monks.

Among other religious communities which had property in Bridgenorth, LILLESHALL ABBEY, by grant of Sibil de Linley about 1195, acquired all her lands in Brocton and in Brug. Sibil further bestowed her body for burial in that house. In 1255, 30s. rent in Bridgenorth accrued to Lilleshall, whose possessions in this borough were largely increased in the reign of Edward IV. by the acquisition of the hospital of St. John.

Besides Haughmond and Lilleshall, BUILDWAS ABBEY and the WHITE NUNS OF BREWOOD had estates here.

Finally, the famous KNIGHTS TEMPLARS derived an income from Bridgenorth.

Undoubtedly, the family of greatest wealth and importance in ancient Brug, was that of Le Palmer, whose interest in messuages,

---

[1] GROSE, *Antiquities of England and Wales*, Vol. V. p. 3.
[2] ORDERICUS VITALIS, Bk. XI. ch. iii.

streets, "shops," and the "fields," about old Brug are attested by numbers of ancient deeds. Robert and Walter le Palmer, the latter of whom was founder of two great families in the borough, occur between 1176 and 1205. The family of Le Palmer furnished a provost to Bridgenorth no less than eighteen times between 1220 and 1331 : the names of members of it also frequently appear on the earliest list of burgesses of Parliament returned by Bridgenorth. About 1250, a silver drinking cup value 12s. is specified as being in the possession of Walter le Palmer of Brug. The house in High Street, of Edmund le Palmer, who died about 1331, was dignified with the appellation "a hall," *Aula Edmundi le Palmer.*

Another family, which probably derived its surname of De Castello or De Castro, from residing in or near the castle ; and also the Fitz-Roberts, early acquired prominence in Bridgenorth.

Chetton. "The Earl himself," says *Domesday,* "holds Catinton. Godeva, the countess, held it in time of King Edward. Here is i hide geldable. In demesne are iii ox-teams ; and vi serfs, ii female serfs,[1] iv villains, and i boor, with a priest, and a provost have iii teams, and yet there might be ii more teams. Here is a new mill, and i league[2] of wood. In time of King Edward, the manor was worth 100s. ; now it is worth 45s."[3]

Conjointly with her husband, Leofric, Earl of Mercia, the Countess Godeva built and magnificently endowed the monastery of Coventry. Godeva's name still lives in ballad and in song. The manor of Chetton, which in Saxon times had belonged to this lady, after the Conquest came into the hands of the Norman Earl of Shrewsbury, when, upon the forfeiture of Robert de Belèsme, Henry I. granted Chetton to a subject, whose interest here soon lapsed to Damietta, an heiress. She married a royal favourite, Ranulf de Broc, who acquired notoriety by the part he took in Henry the Second's contest with the famous Thomas à Becket.

After the king had confiscated the see of Canterbury, and pronounced sentence of banishment on the numerous relatives of the Archbishop, it was to Ranulf de Broc, that Henry entrusted the execution of his orders, who discharged the office committed to him

---

[1] *Ancillæ*, is the expression of the original record.

[2] *Leuua.* or *Leuga* as Domesday has it.
[3] *Domesday,* fo. 254, a. 1.

with such severity, that he called down upon his head a special excommunication from à Becket. "Ranulph de Broc," wrote the exiled Archbishop, "has taken possession of the property of the church of Canterbury, which by right is a provision for the poor, and withholds the same, and has arrested our men as though they were laymen, and detains them in his custody."[1]

For nearly a hundred years after his decease, Ranulf's descendants retained an interest in Chetton; but by 1284 Roger Corbet had acquired the manor, which he held directly of the Crown by the following extraordinary service. His "man was to take 1 bow, 3 arrows, and a caltrop, and also a cured hog, and when he reached the king's army, he was to deliver to the king's marshal half thereof, and the marshal was to give him daily of the said *half-bacon* for his dinner, as long as he stayed in the army, and he was to stay with the army as long as the hog lasted."[2]

The Church.

The mention of a priest in the *Domesday* survey of Chetton, implies the existence of a church here in 1086. It was probably founded by the Countess Godeva. The church of Chetynton with the chapel of Lustone, in 1291, were returned as worth £16 *per annum*; the rector of Cound had a portion therein of 4s., and the abbot of Wigmore one of 10s. In 1341, the parish was taxed only £7 4s. 4d. to the *ninth*, because much land lay uncultivated on account of the poverty of tenants, etc. The *Valor* of 1534 represents the rectory of Chetton as worth £10 19s. 7d. *net* value.

Early Incumbent.—Richard Folyott is the first recorded Rector of Chetton, 1255.

Donington is thus alluded to in Domesday Book:—"The Earl himself holds Donitone. Earl Edwin held it. Here iii hides. In demesne are iv ox-teams and [there are] viii neat-herds, and ii female serfs and xii villains and ii boors with iii teams; and still there might be vii more teams [employed] here. There is a mill rendering [annually] v horse-loads of corn, and a wood one league long and half-a-league wide. In Wich there are v salt-pits [belonging to the manor] which render 20s. [per annum]. In King

---

[1] Archbishop Thomas à Becket's *Letter to his Suffragans*. Rog. de Hoveden, sub. ann. 1165.
[2] Kirby's *Quest*.

Edward's time the manor was worth £20 [per annum]; now [it pays] £9."[1]

After the forfeiture of the Norman Earl de Belèsme, the seigneury of this fine manor, and also that of Tong, were granted by Henry I. to his viceroy Richard de Belmeis, Bishop of London, who accordingly became Lord of Donington and Tong. In the time of Henry II., Richard de Belmeis, representing that collateral branch whose ancestor had been enfeoffed in Donington, held this manor under the Lords of Tong, the elder house.

Of this man or his son we read, that in 1189, Aaron, the rich Jew of Lincoln, having died, his chattels and securities escheated to the Crown, when, among others, it was found that Richard de Belmeis had owed the deceased Israelite £4 8s. 6d., to which accordingly the Crown laid claim; and Richard paid the amount into the Exchequer, through the sheriff of Shropshire, by successive instalments, the last of which is entered on the Pipe Roll of 1200. The reader hardly requires to be reminded, that throughout the Anglo-Norman period, the once renowned chosen people of God were subject to the most iniquitous oppressions and indignities at the hands of all classes. Abandoned to the rapacity of the king and his unscrupulous ministers, the revenue arising from Jewish exactions was so considerable, that a particular Court of Exchequer was set apart for managing it.[2]

Walter de Belmeis next became Lord of Donington, who, in 1221, having been challenged by Geoffrey de Eswell for breach of the king's peace and for robbery, his accuser, although bound over to prosecute, did not appear before the justices in Eyre, and so was to be arrested—the jury meanwhile acquitted Walter. To Walter succeeded Roger his son. In 1284, John de Beaumes, occurs as holding the manor of Donington, under Roger la Zouch, by one knight's fee. John left two sons, Hugh and John, the latter of whom, resigning his interest in this place to his elder brother, Hugh de Beaumeys, in 1316, was accordingly returned as lord of the manor of Donington. Hugh was returned as a "man-at-arms," liable to attend the Great Council summoned to meet at Westminster on May 30th, 1324.

Neachley, Shakerley, Kilsall, and Humphreston, the last of which is presumed to derive its name from some early tenant, were all in Donington manor, and each had its under-tenants.

A word now as to those salt-pits which, *Domesday* says, were

---

[1] *Domesday*, fo. 253, b. 2.   [2] MADOX, *History of the Exchequer*.

attached to this manor. Wherever, in the Conqueror's record, *salinae*, salt-works, or salt-pans, are mentioned in connection with any manor, some local advantage, a salt spring, or the sea near at hand is indicated. We read in *Domesday* that "In Wich there are v salt-pits, which render xx shillings." Wich appears to have been a generic term, applicable to any place where salt was produced. We are not to suppose that in Donington there was a district called Wich wherein were five salt-pits, any more than that Donington lay on the sea-coast where marine salt was manufactured. Eyton's explanation seems the correct one, namely, that five *salinae* in Wich, that is, in one of the large salt districts of Cheshire or Worcestershire, were adjuncts of this manor, and had been so in Saxon times.

DONINGTON CHURCH.

The Norman earl, Roger, who founded this church, bestowed it on Shrewsbury Abbey. Bishop Roger de Belmeis wrung the advowson from the monks; but on his death-bed he was careful to restore it. This was in 1127. In 1291 the annual value of the church of Doniton, in the deanery of Newport, was £2 13s. 4d. The Commissioners for the Ninth of corn, wool, and lamb, in 1341, taxed the parish of Dunynton only £1 3s. 4d. In 1534 Donyngton Rectory was valued at £14 *per annum*, less 13s. 4d. for Synodals and Procurations, and a pension of 6s. 8d. to the Abbot of Shrewsbury.

Early Incumbent.—Simon, Parson of Dunyton, concerning whom the jurors of Brimstree Hundred reported in 1256 that "he had been slain by unknown malefactors, who had also burnt his house, and the vills of Dunyton and Tonge had made no pursuit after the assassins."

In Donington Church windows are two coats of arms; they are—
    I. Gules, ten Bezants, four, three, two, and one.
    II. The same with a chief ermine.

The first was the arms of Alan la Zouche, Lord of Tong; a very ancient charge, the Byzantium gold coin, the Bezant indicating the eastern or crusading origin of the fantastic science of heraldry. The second, the coat of a member of the same family, presents us with an interesting example of early differencing.

𝕿𝖔𝖓𝖌, like fertile Donington, was also retained by the Norman Earl himself. *Domesday* thus records the fact:—" The same Earl holds Tuange. Earl Morcar held it. Here iii hides geldable. In demesne are iiii ox-teams; and viii serfs, and iii villains, and ii boors with iii teams. Here is one league of wood. In King Edward's time [the manor] was worth £11 [per annum]; now it is worth £6."[1]

Doubtless the earl honoured both Donington and this manor occasionally by his presence. Near were woods in which the Norman seigneur might hunt, and trout-abounding streams, such as a devout catholic would prize; so Earl Roger built him a church here in token of his special regard.

Upon the forfeiture of De Belèsme, Tong became a royal demesne, when Henry I. granted it with Donington to Richard de Belmeis, who, from being a confidential clerk in the service of Earl Roger de Montgomery, rose to be Sheriff or Viceroy of Shropshire, and ultimately Bishop of London. De Belmeis stood high in favour with the Norman Earl—attesting his charters frequently. He also figures as a witness to the charters of Earl Hugh. His non-participation in the rebellion of Robert de Belèsme probably recommended this able scholar to the notice of King Henry I. "The said Richard," says Eadmer, "was a most able man in secular affairs."

The post, however, to which he was assigned, that of "warden of the marches," owing to the unsettled state of the border, required all De Belmeis' tact to manage; the Welsh, ever ready to assert their freedom, were constantly making irruptions on the lands of their neighbouring Anglo-Norman oppressors; assassinations and disorders were rife. Surrounded by such circumstances, there is but too much reason to fear, that "Richard, Bishop of London, whom the king had appointed warden of the marches," lent himself to schemes of the grossest treachery, and that more than one Welsh chieftain lost his life at the hands of assassins in the pay of this prelatic viceroy of the Anglo-Norman king.

The great Christian Church of St. Paul's, which Sebert, the tributary king of the East Saxons, had reared upon the site of the Roman temple of Diana in London, was destroyed by fire in the year 1087, when the Norman bishop, Maurice, began the foundation of a new church, to be erected on a much larger and

---

[1] *Domesday*, fo. 253, b. 2.

more splendid scale. To this great work, both he and his successor De Belmeis, each of whom presided twenty years over the diocese, devoted the principal portion of their episcopal revenues; yet St. Paul's Cathedral was not finished until long afterwards. Besides his princely donations to St. Paul's, Richard de Belmeis was a great benefactor to the Priory of St. Osyth, and also to the Nunnery of Clerkenwell. Struck with paralysis, it is supposed that this Anglo-Norman prelate retired to St. Osyth's, and died there. At any rate, there he was buried, and a marble tomb within the Priory Church long bore the following inscription:—

"Hic jacet Richardus Beauveis, cognomine Rufus, London: Episcopus, vir probus et grandævus, per totam vitam laboriosus, fundator noster religiosus, et qui multa bona nobis et ministris ecclesiæ suæ Sancti Pauli contulit. Obiit xvi Januarii, mcxxvii. Cujus animæ propitietur altissimus."[1]

Upon the decease of the prelate, his nephew, Philip de Belmeis, became Lord of Tong and Donington; and he, upon the breaking out of the civil war, took part with the usurper, Stephen, with whom he was at the siege of Shrewsbury. Like other great men of his day, the Lord of Tong was liberal in gifts to the Church. He gave lands to Buildwas Abbey, and, some years afterwards, founded, near Tong, that Augustine institution, the germ of the afterwards magnificent abbey of Lilleshall. The piece of land which Philip de Belmeis granted, "for the foundation of a church in honour of the Holy Mary, Mother of God," bounded by the ancient Roman Watling Street on the north, and eastwards by the rivulet, which, flowing from north to south, supplies Tong Mere, is still called "the Grange." Seised of lands in Shropshire, Sussex, Leicestershire, Staffordshire, Cheshire, and probably other counties, Philip did not long survive this grant, when to him succeeded another Philip, and afterwards Ranulph, his brother, who was employed by Henry II. in Wales. Ranulph, dying without issue, about 1167, with him terminated the elder male line of De Belmeis.

The manor of Tong, with Ranulph's other possessions, now devolved to Alice, his sister, who, having married Alan la Zouche son of Geoffrey, Vicomte of Rohan, in Brittany, upon his death, Tong passed to the La Zouche's descendants of this heiress.

---

[1] Weever's *Sepulchral Monuments*, p. 607.

The accession of King John to the Anglo-Norman throne, in accordance, it is true, with King Richard's last will, nevertheless was contrary to the law of primogeniture, and manifestly an injustice to his nephew Arthur, son of his elder brother Geoffrey, Count of Brittany, in favour of whose superior claims to the succession, a large body of trans-marine nobles had declared themselves. It is not improbable, that, descended as he was from the reigning earls or dukes of Brittany, Roger la Zouche, Lord of Tong in 1199, entertained similar sentiments. But when John added to his other crimes that of the murder of young Prince Arthur, the Bretons, determining to avenge it, arose against the parricidal tyrant, and Roger la Zouche joined them. Hence, when summoned to the Salop assizes of October, 1203, Roger *essoigned* his attendance, his excuse being that he had gone beyond sea.

It was never to a certainty known that John did murder his nephew; yet, as Horace says, "All the footmarks led to the lion's cave, but none led back again." The Bretons, joining themselves to Philip Augustus of France, the English monarch's barbarous act led, as is well known, to his expulsion from his French provinces. On the other side, La Zouche's chivalric sympathies involved the forfeiture of his English possessions.

Tong now was given to William de Braose, the same whose wife and heir the fickle tyrant John afterwards starved to death in Windsor Castle.

De Braose had held the Manor but a short while, however, when Roger la Zouche, returning to his allegiance, paid a hundred merks for seisin of his lands, and recovered possession of Tong. Roger accompanied the English king in his expedition into Ireland, in 1210, and in 1214 he attended him into Poictou. Adhering to King John, that sovereign gave La Zouche many valuable manors which had become forfeit to the Crown. Upon the death of John, La Zouche assisted the Earl of Pembroke and other loyal nobles to retain the throne of England for his son, young Henry III.

La Zouche's loyal services were rewarded by fresh grants. He had license to hold a fair at his Devonshire Manor of Northmolton, and, in the same year, namely 1218, the Sheriff of Norfolk and Suffolk received orders to give him lands which had belonged to the "Vicomte of Roain," who, a collateral descendant of the house from whence La Zouche himself sprang, appears to have inherited considerable estates in England.

When the English king lost his continental possessions, every man who held land by feudal tenure, that is military service, on both sides of the channel, was constrained to elect between two allegiances. He could not personally fight for opposite suzerains. He was compelled to elect on which side he would remain, when, the decision arrived at, the suzerain of his choice doubtless rewarded him, whilst the other deprived him of his estates.

Such would appear to have been the circumstances under which Roger la Zouche obtained possession of the English lordship of the Vicomte de Rohan. This vicomte, representing, as we said, an elder branch of that house from which La Zouche sprang, adhered to the French suzerain, and forfeited his English fief; on the contrary, La Zouche, from motives best known to himself, elected for the English allegiance, and parted with his foreign possessions: as we learn that, on January 22, 1219, the sheriff of Devonshire was ordered to give Roger the lands which had once been Joel de Maine's, the grant being, as is expressed, in recompense of lands which Roger "had lost in Brittany in the king's service."

At the Salop assizes of Nov. 1221, Roger la Zouche sued the Abbot of Shrewsbury for the advowson of Tong, without success. Roger also had a quarrel with the Abbot of Buildwas.

On April 2, 1230, Roger la Zouche has the king's letters-patent of protection, dated at Portsmouth, "so long as he should be with the king in foreign parts"; from which it appears that he was one of those nobles who accompanied Henry III. in his expedition into Brittany, being with the king all the while that he "was lying with his army at the City of Nantes, doing nothing except spending his money."

Enfeoffing Henry de Hugford in lands at Tong, in a curious deed noticed by Dugdale in his Baronage, the only acknowledgment Roger la Zouche reserved was "a chaplet of roses, payable to the grantor and his heirs upon the feast day of the Nativity of St. John the Baptist (June 24), in case he or they should be at Tong; if not, then to be put upon the image of the Blessed Virgin in the Church of Tonge."

Roger died at an advanced age, about 1238, when Alan la Zouche, the eminent justiciar, became Lord of Tong. The finale of this eminent baron is briefly indicated by M. Paris, under date 1269, when, "about the same time," says the chronicler, "John de Warenne, Earl of Surrey, slew with his own hand, in Westminster Hall, Alan de la Zouch, the king's justiciary, in consequence of some words which passed between them." Long previously, however, Alan had given the Manor of Tong with his sister Alice, in *frank marriage* to William de Harcourt. Alice la Zouche, wife of William de Harcourt died, after having borne him two daughters, whereupon the Lord of Tong espoused Hillaria, the sister of Henry de Hastings. This was in 1256. A few years later, and his barons rebelled against the mis-rule of Henry III., when William de Harcourt, joining de Hastings and the confederates, ranged himself against Alan la Zouche, his brother-in-law, and the royalists. It was Harcourt's error to miscalculate the signs of his time. He had chosen the losing side, and, in 1265, his estates became forfeit. Yet, notwithstanding this, Alan La Zouch's powerful interest secured for his nieces, Orabel and Margery de Harcourt, Tong, and other lands which were theirs in right of their mother. Orabel, the elder of these ladies, married Henry, son of Henry de Pembruge; Margery, marrying John de Cantilupe, both she and her husband died without issue. Henry de Pembruge, therefore, in right of his wife, became Lord of Tong.

He, the grandson of Henry de Pembruge, of Pembruge, Herefordshire, represented a house with which many Shropshire families claim affinity. It was alleged, that Henry, his father, an adherent of Simon Montfort, even after the battle of Evesham, had insulted Prince Edmund, second son of Henry III., and set fire to Warwick, where, however, being taken prisoner, he was handed over to the keeping of Roger de Mortimer, under whom he held his Manor of Pembruge, who clapped him into the dungeon at Wigmore. Instead of striving to reclaim the unsteady faith of his vassal, Mortimer was intent rather on extorting from his prisoner his lands, in which nefarious scheme he succeeded to a considerable extent. Upon his accession, however, the Lord of Tong strenuously set himself to recover the fallen fortunes of his house, and apprising the justices of his readiness to redeem his father's lands, according to the *Dictum de Kenilworth*, upon the refusal of Mortimer to surrender them, Henry de Pembruge sued him before the Justices Itinerant, and also before the king, at Westminster. Owing to the gigantic influences opposed to him, the Lord of Tong, however, experienced but partial redress.

Inquisitions, taken after the decease of Henry de Pembruge, in 1279, report him to have held land in Worcestershire, Wiltshire, Herefordshire, Leicestershire, and Tong in Shropshire; and Fulk, his son, then a minor, the juries found to be his heir. Soon after attaining his majority, Fulk died, when, on June 20, 1296, th king's writ of *diem clausit extremum*, issued to the escheator *citr* Trent, and the inquests which followed found, among other par ticulars, that the deceased held the Manor of Tong under Sir Ala La Zouche, and that he owed no service thereon. The Tong juror valued the capital messuage at 5s., the fishery of the *vivary* a 2s. 8d., the dovecote at 1s. 8d., the water-mill at 2s. *per annum* They enumerated various rents due from the free tenants of the manor, among which was one of a *chaplet of roses*. The whole manor and income they estimated as worth £20 19s. 8½d. yearly. They found Fulk, infant son of the deceased, to be his heir.

The lands of this heir were entrusted by King Edward II. to Oliver de Bordeaux, until he should attain his majority, which happened in 1312.

Fulk de Pembruge was included among those adherents of Thomas Earl of Lancaster, who, having participated in the death of Piers Gaveston, had the king's pardon. This Lord of Tong served as a knight of the shire of Salop, at the parliament of York, in 1322. Indeed, to judge from his various employments, as a commissioner of array, inspector of levies, etc., and his frequent summonses to councils at home, and military service abroad, the Lord of Tong was not only a very active, but a useful and im- portant personage in his time.

About 1334, Fulk Pembruge III. died, when it is supposed Robert, his brother became his heir, who was father of Fulk Pembruge IV. This Fulk was twice married, first to Margaret, daughter and eventual sole heir of William Trussel, of Cublesdon. She died without issue. Fulk then married Isabel (or Elizabeth) Lingen, and, dying without issue, about 1308, thus ended the male line of his succession at Tong. Isabel, widow of Fulk Pembruge, remarried twice afterwards, namely, to Sir Thomas Peytevine and Sir John Ludlow. The heir of Sir Fulk Pembruge of Tong was his grand-nephew, Sir Richard de Vernon, who died in 1451, seised of various Vernon and Pembruge estates in Buckingham- shire, Derbyshire, Staffordshire, and Shropshire. A succession of knights and nobles continued to possess the Lordship of Tong, con- spicuous among whom was Stanley.

A younger branch of the De Belmeis family, distinct from that which furnished lords to Donington, appears among the under tenants in Tong. Thus, Robert de Beaumes occurs, in 1255, as a vassal of the Lords of Tong, whose son, again, Hugh de Belmeis, loyally adhering to Henry III. throughout the civil war, as one of that monarch's valets, attended him at the siege of Kenilworth Castle, where he lost two horses. Being with the king, at Cambridge, on March 15, 1267, Hugh obtained the royal licence to hunt the fox, the badger, and the wild cat, anywhere in the royal forests of Shropshire or Staffordshire. Towards the latter end of the same year, being at Salop with King Henry, that monarch, "in recompense of the long and laudable service which his beloved valet, Hugh de Beaumeys, had rendered him, granted to said Hugh the marriage of Isabella, widow of Robert de Beysyn, lately deceased, or, at least, the fine which belonged to the king for the said marriage"; and again, on July 5, 1270, the king, by letters patent, granted him "the marriage of Hillaria, widow of William de Harecut, deceased, or else such fine as said Hillaria might be about to make with the king for her own marriage; or, in the last place, such forfeit as would be coming to the king if Hillaria married to any other, without licence of the king or of said Hugh."[1] Unhonoured, however, with the hand of either lady, although probably enriched with the fines of both, the king's favourite valet found a rich wife elsewhere. And thus it was, that, in the feudal times, the suzerain concocted the marriages of our Anglo-Norman ancestors.

In Albrighton Parish, is a messuage still known as Beamish Hall. Perhaps it was once the seat of this branch of the Belmeis family. In a note, Eyton remarks, "The name Beamish is yet to be found among the poorer classes of Tong or its neighbourhood." Does it rest, then, with the poor alone to represent the lordly De Belmeis or Beaumes, in the place where once they held such high state? Alas! how are the mighty fallen!

RUCKLEY, an ancient member of Tong, was, excepting its wood, given by Philip de Belmeis, in 1138-9, to Buildwas Abbey.

TONG CHURCH.

Like that of Donington, Tong Church was founded, endowed, and bestowed on Shrewsbury Abbey by Earl Roger de Montgomery, previously to 1094. When he induced the monks to consign to him the advowson of Donington, Richard de Belmeis, Bishop of London, also compelled them to part with Tong Church; yet, as he lay dying at St. Osyth's, the remorseful prelate, by a formal

---

[1] *Patent* 54, Hen. III.

act of restitution, took care to restore both churches to Shrewsbury Abbey.

Pope Nicholas's taxation in 1291, valued the Church of Tonge in the Deanery of Newport, the Archdeaconry of Salop, and Diocese of Coventry, at £4, besides the Abbot of Shrewsbury's pension of 6s. 8d. therein. In 1341, Tong parish was assessed only £3 6s. 8d. to the *ninth*, because the Abbots of Buildwas and Lilleshall held lands here, etc. Preparatory to founding the Collegiate Church of Tong, Isabel, widow of Sir Fulk de Pembruge, purchased in 1410 the advowson from Salop Abbey; reserving to the abbot, however, that pension which his predecessors had been wont to receive from the church of St. Bartholomew the Apostle. Accordingly, in 1534, the Abbot of Salop returned 6s. 8d., as paid by the College of Tong. In 1535, the value of the parochial church annexed to the said college was stated by the Master of Tong College to be £6 13s. 4d., less 14s. to the bishop and archdeacon.

Early Incumbent—Ernulf, Canon of Lichfield, instituted to this church about 1190.

Although parts of its south aisle may be referred to the 13th century, by far the larger portion of Tong Church was erected at the commencement of the 15th century. Consisting of a nave with aisles, a chancel, and central octagonal tower with a low spire, it is a fine example of the early perpendicular. All the roofs are of timber, excepting the fan vaulting of the

CORBEL, SOUTH AISLE, TONG.

chapel on the south side, which chapel, by the way, belongs to the latest period of Gothic.

Within the walls of this sacred edifice are several splendid monuments, the oldest of which is thus noticed by Sir William Dugdale, who visited Tong Church in Sept., 1663:—"Towards

(SUPPOSED)
MONUMENT OF SIR RICHARD VERNON AND WIFE IN TONG CHURCH.

the north side of the church stands a faire tombe of alabaster, whereon do lye the figures of a man in armour (partly mail and partly plate armour), and of his wife on his right hand, and on her chin a wimpler. Upon the helm whereon the man resteth his head is this crest (upon a wreath), viz., a Turkish woman's head with a wreath about her temples, her haire platted and hanging below her shoulders, with a tassel at the end of the platting. This is sayde to be the monument of Sir Fowke Pembrugge, knight, sometime Lord of Tong Castle."[1] Sir Fulk Pembruge, the last of his line, died 1408-9. It was his widow, Isabella, who founded the collegiate church of Tong. As in Dugdale's time, the popular notion still is that this monument commemorates Sir Fulk Pembruge; yet, from the half-effaced heraldic insignia it displays, the learned Eyton concludes that this is the tomb of Sir Richard Vernon, treasurer of Calais, who, the first to inherit the estates and arms of Pembruge, died in 1451.

The reader will remember Roger la Zouche enfeoffing Henry de Hugford in lands at Tong, and reserving to himself only "a chaplet of roses, payable to the grantor and his heirs upon the feast-day of the nativity of St. John the Baptist (June 24), in case he or they should be at Tong; if not, then to be put upon the image of the Blessed Virgin in the Church of Tong." And it will also be remembered that, on the death of Fulk de Pembruge, Lord of Tong, in 1296, a quit-rent of a *chaplet of roses* was enumerated among his dues. Towards the close of the eighteenth century, a writer in the *Gentleman's Magazine*, when visiting Tong Church, among the other monuments, observed "one of alabaster, to the memory of a *Vernon*," the tomb in question. "The effigies," he continues, "lie on an altar-tomb, and had the remains of a garland of flowers (then nearly reduced to dust) round the neck and breast. The sexton told me that on every Midsummer-day (June 24), a new garland was put on, and remained so until the following, when it was annually renewed. As this is a singular custom, I could not forbear noticing it, and wish to be informed what was the origin of it."[2] The custom alluded to, without doubt, had its origin in the earlier part of the thirteenth century, when Roger La Zouche enfeoffed Henry de Hugford in lands at Tong. The old lords of Tong, with their knightly successors, have long since been numbered with the things that were, and "the image of the

---

[1] DUGDALE'S *Visitation of Shropshire*, at the Herald's College, Church Notes, p.18.
[2] *Gentleman's Magazine*, Vol. LXX. p. 934.

Blessed Virgin" has disappeared before a purer faith; yet still, for hundreds of years afterwards, the quit-rent of the "chaplet of roses" continued to be paid—aye, even until the nineteenth century; with this difference only, that the garland, no longer attached to an image that had ceased to exist, was hung around the "neck and breast" of the effigy of an old lord of the manor.

An epitaph upon another monument in Tong Church is, by an eminent authority,[1] asserted to have been written by Shakspeare. The verse in question runs as follows:—

> Not monumental stone preserves our fame,
> Nor sky-aspiring pyramids our name;
> The memory of him for whom this stands
> Shall outlive marble and defacer's hands.
> When all to Time's consumption shall be given,
> Stanley, for whom this stands, shall stand in heaven.

It is to be observed, that Shakspeare was not yet thirteen years old when Sir Thomas Stanley, whom these lines commemorate, died; yet monuments were not always erected immediately upon the decease of the parties they are intended to commemorate. Formerly, the windows of Tong Church were enriched with many brilliant coats of arms illustrative of the history and alliances of the Pembruge's and Vernons.

Although no mention is made of it in King William's record, yet at the time of the Conqueror, and for generations afterwards, an extensive forest, formerly known as the Royal FOREST OF BREWOOD, existed in the part of Shropshire we are describing. Weston and Bishop's Wood bounded it on the north, Brewood and Chillington to the east, whilst Albrighton, Donington, and Tong formed its southern and western limits. By one grant after another, King John surrendered the more imperative rights of the Crown in this district.

In the Anglo-Norman period, the forest laws, as my readers are aware, were very stringent and oppressive. According to Spelman, sixty-eight forests, thirteen chases, and seven hundred and eighty-one parks, in different parts of England, were retained by the king, the slightest trespass on any one of which sometimes occasioned the ruin of the offender. Considering the passion evinced by both Norman and Saxon for the pleasures of the chase, these royal forests were little better than so many traps set to allure

---

[1] SIR WILLIAM DUGDALE.

WHITE-LADIES.

people into heavy and oppressive fines, which went to swell the King's Exchequer.

Within the boundaries of Brewood Forest, at the beginning of the thirteenth century, existed two rival religious establishments, —St. Leonard's, known as White Ladies, a convent of Cistercian nuns, which was in Shropshire, and St. Mary's, a convent of Black or Benedictine nuns, in Staffordshire.

It is a singular circumstance, that no chartulary, or even legend, exists to throw a light upon the origin of the former of these convents. Supposed to have been founded in the time of King Richard, or John, the charter of the latter monarch calls the sisterhood "Nuns of St. Leonard of Brewud." The property of this sisterhood, acquired by gradual instalments, each representing the consignment of some female member of a wealthy or powerful family to the service of religion, in time came to be represented by a large aggregate. Their House was parochially and manorially independent. The sisterhood elected their own superior.

In 1535-6, the Prioress of St. Leonard returned £31 1s. 4d. as the gross annual income of this House, derivable from demesne lands at White Ladies, and from various rents in Nottinghamshire, Staffordshire, and Shropshire.

White Ladies was a Norman structure. A wood-cut representation of this interesting ruin is appended.

Oldbury. Situated in the Manor of Oldbury, and fronting the castle-hill of Bridgenorth to the south, is a large artificial conical mound of earth. This earthwork, which still goes by the name of "The Old Castle," is supposed by an authority,[1] to be the site of that fortress which, according to the Saxon Chronicle and Florence of Worcester, Ethelfleda, Lady of the Mercians, built on the western side of the Severn, in the year 913. If such be the case, then Oldbury, literally *Old Borough*, once possessed a castle which had an existence antecedent to that at Bridgenorth.

When William the Conqueror's commissioners surveyed Shropshire, they found that Rainald, the sheriff of the county, held eight manors under the Norman Earl of Shrewsbury, in the Hundred of Alnodestreu; and a part of Hatton. Oldbury, one of the sheriff's manors, is thus described in Domesday Book:—" The same Rainald [Vicecomes] holds Aldeberie, and Radulf [holds it]

---

[1] Eyton, *Antiq. of Shrop.* vol. i. p. 131.

of him. Eluuard held it and was free. There is i hide and iii virgates geldable. In demesne is i ox-team, and vii serfs, iii Frenchmen, ii cottars, and i boor, with ii teams; and still there might be two more [teams]. Here is a mill of 2s. [annual value], and a wood which will fatten 100 swine. In the time of King Edward it was worth 30s., now it is worth 13s. He [Rainald] found it waste."[1]

OLDBURY CHURCH.

Helyas de Constantine founded and endowed a chapel with cemetery, at Oldbury, about the year 1138. This chapel, subject to Morville, passed with that mother church to Shrewsbury Abbey. The Church of Holdebury, in the Deanery of Stottesden, in 1291, was valued at £4 18s. 4d. In 1341, the parish was assessed at £1 5s. to the *ninth*. In 1534, the annual value of this rectory was £5, less 6d. for Archdeacon's synodals.

Early Incumbent.—Robert de Hastings was Rector of Oldbury about 1200.

Fulwardine, now "Fowswardine Farm," a small tenement in Sidbury, was not overlooked by the Conqueror's commissioners, for we read in *Domesday*, that "the same Rainald holds Fuloordie, and Radulf [holds] of him. Edmund held it [in Saxon times], and was a free man. Here half a hide geldable. In demesne there is i ox-team and iv serfs, i villain, and i boor, with i team; and yet there might be i more team besides. In time of King Edward it was worth 16s., and afterwards 6s.; now [it is worth] 10s."[2]

Upton Cressett. The following, from *Domesday*, is supposed to refer to Upton Cressett: "The same Rainald [the Sheriff] holds Ultone. Edmund held it, and was a free man. Here are iii hides geldable. In demesne are ii ox-teams, and iii serfs, i free neat-herd, vi villains, iv boors and i radman,[3] with iv teams, and there might be iv more [teams] besides. The wood here will fatten xxx swine. In King Edward's time it was worth 40s., and afterwards 10s.; now it is worth 25s."[4]

---

[1] *Domesday*, fo. 255 a, 2. [2] Ibidem.
[3] A Radman was a grade higher than either the serf, villain, or boor. The tenure of some, however, obliged them to pay a rent in the shape of agricultural labour to their lords; others, again, were inseparable from the land; whilst some were free men.— See *Introduction to Domesday*.
[4] *Domesday*, fo. 255, a 2.

FONT, UPTON CRESSETT.

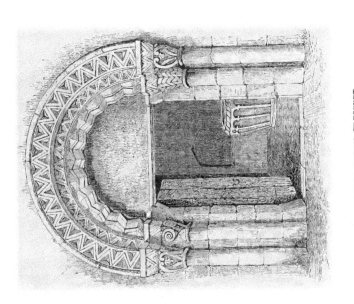

DOORWAY, UPTON CRESSETT.

The early Lords of Upton derived their surname of Hupton, or Upton, from this place; on the contrary, the manor derived its distinctive title of Cressett from that family of Cressett, who, after the failure of the male line of Upton, succeeded to this, their inheritance.

The Church.

The precise date of the foundation of Upton Cressett Church is unknown. To judge from its architecture, it belongs to the 12th century. Pope Nicholas' taxation in 1291, valued the Church of Upton, in the Deanery of Stottesden, at £3 6s. 8d. In 1341, the assessors of the ninth of wheat, wool, and lamb, taxed the parish only 17s., because there were only two fleezes of wool in it, and no lambs; 4 virgates lay untilled, on account of the poverty of tenants, etc. In 1534, the rector of Hopton Cressett's preferment was worth £4 15s. 8d. *per annum*, less 6d. for synodals.

Early Incumbent.—Richard Nowe, 1354.

Eudon, now Eudon Burnell, a township in the Parish of Chetton, at the period of the Conqueror's Survey, was also held under the Norman Earl of Shrewsbury, by Rainald the Sheriff, for *Domesday* informs us that: "The same Rainald holds Eldone. Æluuard held it, and was a free man. Here are ii hides geldable. In demesne are iii ox-teams, and vi serfs, i villain, v boors, and i Frenchman with ii teams. Here is wood for lx swine. It was worth 30s. Now it is worth 40s."[1]

Criddon, like Eudon Burnell, also in the Parish of Chetton, apparently was overlooked by the Domesday Commissioners; for, although no mention is made of it in King William's Record, it is certain that it figured as an independent manor from a very ancient period.

The Saxon termination *bun*, here, as in Eudon, signifies a *hill*, or *down*. The first syllable of the name Criddon, may derive from Criba. Crida was the name of the Saxon Chief who founded the kingdom of Mercia, A.D. 586.

Middleton Scriven is the subject of the following entry in Domesday Book: "Rainald [the sheriff] holds Middeltone [of

---

[1] *Domesday*, fo. 252, a 2.

the Earl], and Alcher and Albert hold of him. Edric, a free man, held it for two manors. Here ii hides geldable. In demesne are ii ox-teams, and v serfs, vi villains, and v boors, with iii teams, and there might be iii [teams] more [employed]. In the time of King Edward [these two manors] were worth 13s. [per annum]. Now 28s. They were waste [literally worth nothing, when they came into the hands of Rainald].[1]

The Saxon word tun, signifies a town, and the original village here probably derived its distinctive appellation from its occupying a position between certain other Mercian villages.

The Church.

The Church of Middleton was returned in 1291 as under £4 annual value. In 1341, the parish was taxed only £1 3s. 4d. to the *ninth*, because the wheat had been destroyed by storms, there had been a murrain among the sheep, 3 carrucates of land lay untilled in consequence of the poverty of the tenants, etc. In 1534, the preferment of the rector of Mydulton, in Stottesden Deanery, was valued at £4, less 6d. for synodals.

Early Incumbent.—Sir Wm. de la Lowe, Priest, 1303.

Aston Eyre, Aston,[2] Eston Eyre, or Wheaten Aston. According to *Domesday*: "The same Rainald holds Estone, and Alcher [holds it] of him. Sessi held it in King Edward's time, and was a free man. Here are ii hides geldable. In demesne are iii ox-teams, and vi serfs, i villain, v boors, and i Frenchman with ii teams. There is a wood that will fatten lx swine. .[In the time of King Edward the manor] was worth 30s., now 40s."[3]

The Alcher alluded to above, had an interest also in other Shropshire manors; in three of these he held, as at Aston, of the fief of the Sheriff; whilst in Harcott he held directly under the Earl. Hence it came, that upon the forfeiture of Earl Robert de Belèsme, Alcher's descendants became tenants *in capite* of the Crown. Alcher gave his lordship of Albrighton to the then just founded Abbey of Shrewsbury, and was succeeded by his son, Robert Fitz Aer, who founded and endowed Aston Church about 1138.

Hugh, son of Hugh Fitz Aer, was returned in 1316, as Lord of Aston Aer.

---

[1] *Domesday*, fo. 255, a 2.
[2] Aston, or Eston, implies a town situated to the east of something else.
[3] *Domesday*, fo. 255, a 2.

Church or Chapel of Aston Eyre.

This was built about 1138. The Fitz Aer's feudatories of the lords Fitz Alan, doubtless espoused with their chief the cause of the Empress Maude and legitimacy, against Stephen the Usurper. Such was the period when the Church of Aston Eyre was consecrated. "Know all men," says the ancient deed, "both now and hereafter, that, on the day of the dedication of the Cemetery[1] of Eston, I, Robert, Son of Aher, gave to God and to the chapel of the same *vill* of Eston, one virgate of land, containing sixty acres, and all tithes of my demesne of the same *vill*, and one mansion, for the health of my soul, and of all my predecessors and successors. And that my gift may be free and quit of all reclaim by me, or by my heirs, and may ever remain firm and stable, I have fortified it with this present writing, and with the impression of my seal. These being witnesses: Robert, by divine grace, Bishop of Hereford; Reinald, Prior of Wenlock; Peter, the Archdeacon; Richard and Eluric, Deans; Alan de Opton, Fulcaius de Aldreham, and many others."[2]

Shortly afterwards, Robert de Betun, Bishop of Hereford, deemed it necessary to specify the cemeteries or chapels, which the warlike troubles of the time had induced him to consecrate. Eston was among the number, the bishop expressly mentioning, that the "defence of the poor" was one of the objects he had in view in consecrating these chapels. It was thus that the church in the middle ages often became a stronghold for the people, it being nothing uncommon for both church and church-yard to be crowded with the effects of those in the neighbourhood, who placed them there for protection. During the horrors of those 15 years which succeeded the pious act of Fitz Aer, even the churches afforded, however, but an uncertain protection; Malmesbury, who witnessed the scenes he has described under date of 1140, adding, that "the legate repeatedly excommunicated all violators of church-yards, and plunderers of churches," but that little attention was paid to his ecclesiastical thunderings.

The doorway and tympanum of the original structure of Aston Eyre chapel (of which a wood-cut is given) still remain a monument of the benevolence and devotion of Robert Fitz Aer.

---

[1] As the early Christians were driven to worship in vaults and burial-places, the words *Cemetery* and *Church* became synonymous.

[2] The original deed is in the possession of Mr. G. Morris, of Shrewsbury.

Erected in a district where Shrewsbury Abbey claimed a prescriptive parochial jurisdiction, the church of Aston Eyre appears to have been most unjustly dealt with by the abbey, which not only appropriated part of its endowment, but claimed to present

DOORWAY AND TYMPANUM OF ASTON EYRE.

to the residue. The remonstrances of the founder's heir proved unavailing; the diocesan bishop awarded the right of advowson to the abbey, when, about 1230, the "Lord of Eston" formally quitted to Salop Abbey all claim in the chapel his ancestor had erected and endowed.

In the *Taxation* of 1291, the chapel of Astone Aer, described as an adjunct of the church of Morville, no separate valuation is given; but the annual value of the Vicarage is stated to be under £4.

In the *Valor* of 1534-5, this chapel is not mentioned; the curate of Wheaten Aston, however, had a salary of £5 16s. 0½d. chargeable on the cell or grange of Morville.

Scarcely anything is known relating to the Early Incumbents of Aston Aer.

Glazeley. In old British phraseology, Glass-LLe signified "green-place," when Anglo-Saxon usage having changed the terminating *lle*—a place, into *leaʒ*—a district; accordingly, we have the etymology of the modern Glazeley.

It is recorded in Domesday Book, that: "The same Rainald holds Gleslei, and Azo [holds it] of him. Eluuard held it [in Saxon times], and was free with his land. Here ii hides geldable. In demesne, is i ox-team; and [there are] vii serfs, iiii villains, v boors, one radman, and a priest with iii teams, and still there might be ii more teams. Here is a mill of 5s. [annual value]. [In King Edward's time the manor] was worth 25s. [annually]. Now, 20s."[1] Thus, Eluuard the Saxon's free manor of Gleslei, wrenched, like Oldbury and Eudon from him, was given to the Norman, when all three devolved to the fief of Rainald the Sheriff.

Respecting Azo, who held Glazeley under Rainald at the time of the survey, his interest in this, as in other manors, in time came to be represented by the elder house of Le Strange. Accordingly, in 1165, we find John le Strange holding Glazeley of the Barony of Fitz Alan. About 1175, Simon and William de Perepunt,[2] of Norman extraction, their grandfather probably having fought at Hastings, as the name spelt Perepond appears on the Roll of Battle Abbey, figure as witnesses to a curious deed, in which John le Strange I. notifies his remembrance of Fitz Alan's grant of Wroxeter Church to Haughmond Abbey. Alan succeeded Simon at Glazeley, after whom came Guy de Pierrepoint, otherwise called Wydo de Gleseleg. Guy had three sons, the eldest of whom, Alan, in 1255, was reported by the Stottesden Jurors, Lord of Glascle, holding its hide of land of John le Strange for half a knight's fee. Alan did no suit, excepting twice a year at the sheriff's *tourn*, nor did he pay *stretward*, or *motfee*. Sir Alan was succeeded by another Wydo; and so, until far into the reign of Edward III., the descendants of the Norman de Pierpont from time to time figure in old charters, the Escheat Rolls,[3] or other national records, as lords of the manor of Glazeley.

GLAZELEY CHURCH.

Indicated by the mention of a priest in the *Domesday* entry

---

[1] *Domesday*, fo. 255, a 2.

[2] Pont St. Pierre is a *vill* in the diocese of Rouen, situate at the confluence of the rivers Andelle and Seine.

[3] The *Escheat Rolls*, otherwise called *Inquisitiones post mortem*, commence in the reign of Henry III., and are records of the writs addressed by the Crown to the proper officer to summon a jury, when the death of any tenant *in capite* involved a right of wardship, or marriage, or a fine by such tenant's successor for livery. The returns of these Juries also form part of the Record, and usually contain statements as to the extent and value of the deceased's property, its tenure, and the name and age of his heir.

relating to this manor, about thirty years after the survey, this church had acquired such a standing, that Ingelbert, its priest, claimed parochial jurisdiction over the neighbouring manor of Deuxhill, belonging to Wenlock Priory. The monks had founded a chapel there; hence the dispute. But De Belmeis, Bishop of London, then Viceroy of Shropshire, presiding judicially in the Chapter in which the claim was preferred, rejected it on the ground that *all St. Milburg's lands constituted but one parish.*

According to Pope Nicholas' *taxation* in 1291, the church of Glasleye was worth £4, the Prior of Wenlock having a portion of 6s. 8d. therein. The church of Glaseley, in Stottesden Deanery, in 1341, is entered at £4 6s. 8d., yet the assessors of the *ninth* taxed the parish only 19s. in consequence of a want of sheep and lambs, non-cultivation of one virgate through poverty of its tenants, etc. In 1535, the joint value of Deuxhill and Glazeley was £4 13s. 4d., out of which a pension of 8s. went to Wenlock Priory.

Doubtless, very early in the 12th century, there were Incumbents of Glazeley; the Hereford registers, which commence 1275, however, take no notice of the circumstance; nor is it known when the combination with Deuxhill, which existed in 1534, commenced.

Aston Botterell, is thus noticed in *Domesday*:—"The same Rainald holds Estone, and Tochil [holds it] under him. Elric held it [in Saxon times], and was free, together with this land. Here i hide geldable. In demesne is i ox-team; and [there are] vi serfs and ii villains, iii boors and iii radmans, with two teams amongst them all; and still there might be a third team here. [In King Edward's time] the manor was worth 14s.; now it is worth 15s."[1] This manor probably derived its early name of Estone from its lying to the east of the Great Clee Hill.

Although more than one person is represented by the Saxon name Aluric, Alric, Ælric, or Elric, which so often occurs in *Domesday* as connected with Shropshire, it is probable that the Aluric who held Udecote [Woodcote] in Recordin Hundred, and the Elric who similarly held Estone in Edward the Confessor's time, were one and the same person; and for this reason: in 1085 the successor to both these manors was Tochil—the name is Saxon—who, it is not unreasonable to suppose, was one of those favoured

---

[1] *Domesday,* fo 255, a 2.

but unpatriotic few, that, by a sufferance rarely exercised, was permitted to hold, under Norman Lords two manors which, widely apart, were his by descent. In a record of law proceedings a century afterwards, we find that the Lord of Woodcote sued the Lord of Aston for the latter manor, a circumstance likewise strikingly indicative of their early association.

Tochil, degenerate scion of the conquered race, early in the twelfth century gave land to the Norman Abbey of Shrewsbury.

It is not very clear how the family of Botterell, from whom this place acquired its distinctive title, succeeded to Aston; yet it is certain that among the fines offered to the Crown at Michaelmas, 1202, was one by Robert de Wudecot of 10 merks, that he might have trial concerning one knight's fee in Eston against William Boterell. About 1240, Philip Boterel is returned as holding one fee in Aston of the Barony of John Fitz-Alan.

In 1316-17, John Boterel was lord of Aston Botterel.

ASTON BOTTERELL CHURCH.

This is first mentioned in the *Taxation* of 1291, when, as the church of "Asheston Botel," in the deanery of Stottesden, its annual value is stated to be £10. In 1341, the parish was assessed only £2 5s. to the *ninth*, because there were no sheep or lambs in it, two virgates lay untilled, etc. The *Valor* of 1534 represents this preferment as worth £7 1s. 1d., out of which 7s. 8d. went for procurations and synodals, a pension of 6s. 8d. was payable to the Lady of Brewood, and a portion of 4s. to the Rector of Castle-Holgate.

Early Incumbent.—Thomas Boterel, September 27, 1278, has the episcopal license to study for a year.

Badger. The pretty dingle here, with its purling brook, is celebrated throughout the county of Shropshire. Variously written in ancient times, the etymology of Beghesovre or Badger is uncertain. It may derive from a combination of the Anglo-Saxon Ƿen a *bank, brink,* or *shore,* and Beccer *of the brook,*—the bank of the brook; while Bécer, the possessive case of the Anglo-Saxon word Béce, a beech-tree, has an equal applicability to local circumstances.

Domesday says:—"Osbern holds of Earl Roger Beghesovre and Robert [holds] of him. Bruniht held it and was a free man. Here is half a hide geldable. The land is [enough for] ii ox-teams. In demesne is i team, and iii boors with i team. The wood here will fatten thirty swine. [In King Edward's time] its value was 7s; now 10s."[1]

---

[1] *Domesday,* fo. 257, b 2.

The Osbern who held this and two other manors in Alnodestreu Hundred, under the Earl of Shrewsbury, in the Conqueror's day, was none other than the powerful noble, Osbern Fitz-Richard, Baron of Burford and Richard's Castle, whose heirs continued for centuries afterwards lords of the manor.

Of Robert, sub-tenant here in 1085, nothing further is known than *Domesday* relates. Thomas de Beggesoure became sub-tenant here about 1224, to whom his younger brother Philip, having taken the cross, surrendered up his tenancy in the following terms:— " Know all men that I, Philip de Beggesoure, have rendered and quit-claimed to Thomas de Beggesoure, my brother, his heirs and assigns, all my land in Bechebiri, which I held of him (that namely, which Reginald and William le Sage held under me), for five merks of silver, which the said Thomas hath given me for my journey to Jerusalem. Witnesses, Sir Walter de Huggeford," etc.

Philip de Beggesoure, it would seem, was one of that countless multitude who left kindred and land to join the crusade against the infidel. He fought in the sixth crusade, which, first proclaimed in 1215 by Innocent the Third, and afterwards by succeeding Popes, may be compared to a drama having three acts, namely, the expedition of the King of Hungary, the war in Egypt, and the campaign of Frederick the Second in the Holy Land. The Christian army, under Andrew of Hungary, most gallantly commenced its conflict with the Moslems; but, by discord, its forces were disunited and eventually fell before the Saracens. The war in Egypt was signalised by the capture and re-capture from the Christian forces, after a bloody contest, of the city of Damietta. The expedition under Frederick the Second of Germany, whose conduct at first was vacillating, notwithstanding that monarch was exposed to the anathemas of the tyrannical Gregory IX., left Palestine in a more favourable condition than it had known since the days of Saladin; a treaty which was entered into between the German monarch and the Saracens, securing to the Christians the possession of their kingdom for ten years. Roger de Wendover[1] avers, upon the authority of Hubert, one of the preachers of the crusade in England who quoted the number from his roll, that 40,000 picked men, with the bishops of Winchester and Exeter, left England in 1227 to join this crusade.

Upon the decease of Thomas de Beggesoure, Philip, his son,

---

[1] ROGER DE WENDOVER, vol. ii. p. 489, Bohn's Ed.

became Lord of Badger, who, marrying without license of the Crown, paid a heavy penalty for so doing. He was one of those northern nobles whom Geoffrey de Langley and his fellow Justices of the Forest in 1250 so unscrupulously fleeced to fill the king's exchequer. Alluding to this memorable *Iter*, the monk of St. Albans [1] observes, that the Commissioners of Henry III. " cunningly, wantonly, and forcibly extorted such an immense sum of money, especially from the nobles of the northern parts of England, that the amount collected exceeded the belief of all who heard it. Geoffrey de Langley," he continues, " was attended by a large and well-armed retinue, and if any one of the said nobles made excuses, or dared to give vent to murmurs, as the judges were their enemies, he ordered him to be at once taken and consigned to the king's prison ; nor could any one reply to the demand by any reasonable arguments for fear of giving offence. For a single small beast, a fawn, or hare, although straying in an out-of-the-way place, he impoverished some men of noble birth, even to ruin, sparing neither blood nor fortune."

The Pipe Roll gives the enormous sum of £526 0s. 6d. as the amount of the penalties inflicted by this visitation on Shropshire.

Wenlock Priory had manorial rights in Badger from time immemorial. Like Broseley and Willey, Badger, in the time of Richard I., was transferred to the franchise of Wenlock.

BADGER CHURCH.

This church was founded in the earlier part of the twelfth century, and it remained in the gift of the lords of the fee. They were bound, however, to present their nominee to the Prior of Wenlock, who again presented him to the bishop. In the taxation of 1291, this chapel, entered as of less than £4 annual value, was therefore not assessable. Neither Badger nor Beckbury appear in the assessment of parishes in 1341. According to the *Valor* of 1534, the Rectory of Bagesore was worth £4 11s. 2d., of which 3s. 4d. was due at the translation of St. Milburg to Wenlock Priory, and 4s. *per annum* for synodals.

Early Incumbent—Roger, clerk of Baggesour in 1211.

Throughout the long war with France, in the fourteenth century, the king exercised the mediate right of patronage, "seeing," as Edward III. expressed it, "that the Priory of Wenlock is in our hands by reason of the war." [2]

---

[1] MATT. PARIS, vol. ii. p. 358. Bohn's Ed.   [2] PAT. 23 Edw. III. p. 1, m 23.

Ryton. When speaking of places thus named in Warwickshire, Dugdale assigns to them an etymology "obvious enough, forasmuch as the soyle there is of a light sandy disposition, and beareth rye best of any grain."[1] The Shropshire Ryton is thus alluded to in Domesday Book:—"The same Osbern [Fitz Richard] holds Ruitone [under Earl Roger]. Wiuar and Brictstual held it [in Saxon times] for two manors. Here v hides geldable. The land is for viii ox teams. In demesne are ii teams and iii serfs, with iii boors. Here a mill rendering viii horse-loads of fine wheat. In King Edward's time the manor was worth 30s. [per annum], now it is worth 20s. He [Osbern] found it waste."[2]

Osbern's interest in Ryton does not appear to have passed to his descendants; yet we have no means of judging how this happened, as there are no hints of any forfeiture having befallen the early barons of Richard's castle. It might have been that a baron, the bulk of whose fief lay in distant parts of this or in other counties, finding an outlying manor a mere incumbrance, and that the services with which it was charged were more than it was worth to him, neglected to comply with the terms of his tenure, and the manor reverted to the suzerain. However, it came to pass, Ryton appears to have become subject to the re-disposal of the Norman earl, or, upon the forfeiture of De Belèsme, of the Crown.

Engelard, a man of importance in his day, was tenant *in capite* of Ryton, in the time of Henry I.: being made castellan of Stretton, hence his name of De Stretton.

In 1165-6, the return of the tenants *in capite* of the kingdom, known as the *Liber Niger*,[3] was made, when Engelard de Stretton, being one of the king's vassals, returned that he "has only one knight, viz., Richard Fitz Odo, and that he has no knight of the new feoffment," which means that he held only one knight's fee *in capite*, and that the knight then holding it under Engelard was Richard Fitz Odo.

Of the knight, Richard Fitz Odo, returned in 1165 as holding

---

[1] Dugdale's *Warwickshire*.
[2] *Domesday*. fo. 257, b 2.
[3] The record called the *Liber Niger* or Black Book of the Exchequer, is mainly the result of an order made in the year 1165 or beginning of 1166, on every tenant *in capite* of the Crown, to return a list before the first Sunday of Lent (March 17, 1166) of all who held under him by knight's service; stating whether such tenure was of old or of new feoffment: that is, whether it had existed from the days of Henry I., or had arisen since. It is a valuable national record.

this manor under Engelard de Stretton, styled simply Richard de Ruiton, either this man or his son appears as witness to various deeds affecting land in the neighbourhood, between the years 1190 and 1230. In 1211, Richard de Ruiton is entered as one of the king's tenants by serjeantry, in the county of Salop, his service being to find one serving foot-soldier with a lance, for the ward of the king's castle of Shrawardine. His successor was John de Ruiton, after whom came William de Ruiton, who gave lands to Wombridge Priory. But Buildwas Abbey profited to a much greater extent by the grants and alienations of this William. He had sold Ryton Mill to Hugh, Lord of Weston, who gave it to Buildwas Abbey, the lord of the fee confirming the grant in the following terms: "I William, Lord of Ritton, have granted and confirmed to God and Saint Mary, and the monks of Bildewas, a certain mill in the *vill* of Ritton, which the monks have of the gift of Sir Hugh de Weston. I have granted it free from all earthly service, with easements, and free pasturage for their horses and beasts of burden coming to the mill in places nearest thereunto, except corn-fields, and meadows under crop; also I grant that the miller for the time being may have around the same mill, cocks, hens, capons, geese, ganders, chickens, and ducks; also, I quit the whole *bylet* at the back of the said mill, as on all sides the water bounds it; also a certain meadow in the *vill* of Ritton, which the monks have of the gift of Thomas de Marham, near the meadow called the Moremede, which they have of my gift; witnesses, Sir Hugh Weston, etc. By another deed, similarly attested, the Lord of Ryton granted to Buildwas "a certain plat of ground in the territory of Ruton, thus bounded, viz., from a certain cross which stands on the boundary between Cospeford [Cosford] and Archesleg [Atchley] along a road to Crassitismere [Crasset's mere], and thence along a made fence to a certain white thorn, and thence to the headland of a certain culture, which extends to Trendelleswallemerch, and thence to a place called Munebehatch, and thence along the highroad, as far as the first-named cross." He grants to the monks also "common pasture for all their animals in their granges of Gospesford and of Hatton, without number, taxation, or count, through his whole Fee of Ruton, except in a tract of land fenced by a footpath, which passes from his greater Stew to the highroad outside his court-house at Atchley, towards Ryton, and so along the said road to Calvercroft, and thence to Cecilie's Meadow. If the monks' cattle happen to stray within this boundary, they shall not be impounded, but restored without trouble; but if they be found there with a keeper, surety shall be taken from said keeper for reasonable damages, to be settled by two umpires, within eight days after the trespass.

The monks may also make a bridge across the water of Wergh [Worfe] over which they can drive their cattle to said pasture from Hatton."

Such, and so extensive, were the privileges conferred by the Lord of Ryton on Buildwas Abbey, which, passing subsequently to the statute of mortmain,[1] required a royal licence; and such was granted, after an inquisition held in 1285 had reported in favour of the monks. Does the reader of the present day ask what had the monks to do with agriculture; we answer, more than is generally supposed, for they were the first systematic farmers, and, to this day the broad acres of England bear the impress stamped upon them by their former monastic possessors.

Better was it for the community at large, including the great subject population, in that period of oppression which succeeded the Conquest, that the land should be intrusted to the keeping of a set of harmless and industrious monks, than that it should continue to lie comparatively neglected in the hands of the iron-clad Norman nobles. Yet Edward was right in passing the statute of mortmain. It was high time; otherwise the wily men of the cloister would have relieved the thick-headed superstitious lay lords of every acre.

RYTON CHURCH.

Ryton Church is inferred to have existed in 1186, from the circumstance that the priest of Ryton attested a charter of that date. According to Pope Nicholas' taxation, in 1291, the church of Ryton, in the diocese of Lichfield and Coventry, the archdeaconry of Salop, and deanery of Newport, was valued at £2 *per annum*. In 1341, the parish was taxed 10s. only to the *ninth*, because much land lay untilled by reason of the poverty and

---

[1] The statute of mortmain (mortmain signifies such a state of possession as makes it inalienable), passed in the year 1279, during the reign of King Edward I. It prevented the clergy from making new acquisitions of lands, which, by the ecclesiastical canons, they were for ever prohibited from alienating. King Edward's object was to maintain the number of knight's fees, and, as a consequence, the military force of the kingdom, and also to prevent the superiors from being defrauded of the profits of wardship, marriage, livery, and other emoluments arising from the feudal tenures. So great a check did this enactment give to the acquisition of lands by the monks, that they specially entitled it, "*the statute*."

quitting of the occupiers, etc. The *Valor* of 1534 returns £6 as the value of this benefice, less 6s. 8d. for procurations, and 1s. 5d. for synodals.

Early Incumbent.—Bernard, Priest of Ryton, about 1186.

Brockton, deriving its name from the brook which flows through it,[1] is thus mentioned in *Domesday:*—" The same Osbern holds Broctone. Bruniht, who occurs above [i.e., under Badger], held it. Here i virgate of land and viii acres. There is land [enough for] i ox team. Here i boor with ii oxen. [In the time of King Edward this land] was worth 8s. [per annum] ; it is now [worth] xii pence. He [Osbern] found it waste." [2] As in Ryton, and, probably from a similar cause, Osbern Fitz Richard's seigneury in Brockton reverted to the crown some fifty years after *Domesday.*

On the re-arrangement of the divisional system of Shropshire, in the time of Henry I., Brockton became involved with the neighbouring manor of Sutton.

The Broctone of the Conqueror's time, says Eyton " was possibly represented by a tenement of two virgates, held, subsequently, under the Crown by *petit sergeantry*. The immediate tenants bore the name of Russel, and their service was that of castle guard at Shrawardine." In 1211, a William Russel was the king's tenant in Brockton, holding it by service of " the finding of one serving foot-soldier, with a bow for ward of the king's castle of Srawrthin." [3]

The Feodary of 1284 gives Alexander le Cold as holding half a virgate in the *vill* of Brocton *in capite*, by service of going with the king into Wales in time of war, with one lance, for a week. In later times, the Burnels of Langley held in Brockton.

Meadowley derives its name from the Saxon Mæðeþe-leaȝ which signifies *the district of meadows.*

"Helgot," says *Domesday,* " holds Madolea [of the Norman earl]. Austin held it. Here half a hide geldable. He [Austin]

---

[1] A small stream, still known as the mad brook, gave a name both to Madeley and Brocton.

[2] *Domesday*, fo. 257, b. 2.
[3] *Testa de Neville*, fo. 254.

was a free man. Richard holds it of Helgot. The [arable] land is [enough for] vi ox teams. In demesne is i team and iii serfs, and i radman with half a team and ii boors. In time of King Edward it was worth 30s. Now it is worth 11s. When [Helgot] obtained it, it was worth 2s."[1] Beyond the above notice, there is nothing of interest attached to the early history of this small manor.

Charlcott and **Bold**, both of which are now in the parish of Aston Botterel, in William the Conqueror's time formed one manor, which is thus noticed in Domesday Book:—"The same Helgot holds Cerlecote. Elsi held it [in Saxon times] and was free. Here is half a hide, geldable. There is land for ii ox teams. It is and was waste. It used [in time of King Edward] to be worth 10s."[2]

The name Charlcott is derived from the Saxon words ceopl and cot (*ceorl-cot*) a husbandman's abode.

Bolb is the Saxon term for a house or hall.

The church of Bold, in Stottesden Deanery, in 1291, was valued at £4 6s. 8d.; but the parish was taxed only £2 6s. 8d. to the *ninth* in 1341, because two virgates lay untilled, the tenants having quitted through poverty; there were no sheep in it, etc. No mention is made of either church or chapel here in 1534.

Broseley. It is conjectured, that the following entry in *Domesday* refers to Broseley. "The same Helgot holds Bosle. Gethne held it, and was a free man. Here is i hide geldable. The land is [capable of employing] ii ox-teams. In demesne is one [team], and [there are] iiii serfs, and iiii boors, and i radman, with i team. In King Edward's time [the manor] was worth 16s. 1d., now 12s. He [Helgot] found it waste."[3] Of Helgot's successors not a trace remains.

It is presumed, that the discerning Henry I. bestowed the lordship of Broseley upon Warin de Metz, of Lorraine, from whom it is thought descended in after times many lords of Broseley; yet it is conjecture. Certain it is, however, that the Fitz Warins, de

---

[1] *Domesday*, fo. 258, b. 1.   [2] Ibidem.   [3] Ibidem.

Burwardsley's, d'Eyton's, de Covene's, and the de Pyehford's, all, at one time or another, had an interest in the Manor of Broseley, beneath whom again held undertenants.

BROSELEY CHURCH.

Subject to the mother church of St. Milburg, at Wenlock, within the bounds of whose vast Saxon parish it stood. The date of the foundation of Broseley Church is unknown. In token of its affiliation, and probably as a condition of its origin, the Incumbent was taxed with an annual pension of 2s, payable at the feast of St. Nicholas, to the mother church. No cure of souls went with the new foundation, whose Incumbent was usually beneficed elsewhere.

In 1291, the church of Burewardsleye, in the deanery of Wenlock, was valued at £6 13s. 4d. *per ann.* In 1341, the parish was assessed only 42s. to the *ninth*, for the growing corn had been destroyed by tempests; a large portion of the parish, owing to the poverty of the tenants, lay uncultivated, etc. In 1535, this preferment was valued at £8 5s. 8d. *per ann.*, less 7s. 2d. for synodals.

Early Incumbent—William, Parson of Burwardesleg, about 1230.

Sutton Maddock, although unmarked by its compound name in *Domesday*, is identified with the following entry:—" The same Gerard holds Sudtone. Earl Morcar held it. Here are iiii hides geldable. The [arable] land is [enough for] xii ox-teams. In demesne are ii teams and vi serfs, and xii villains, and iiii boors with vii teams; and a certain knight has here i team and ii serfs. In the time of King Edward it was worth 40s. [per annum], now it is worth the same." [1]

Manorially associated from earliest time with Iteshale or Shiffnal, it is supposed that Sudtone was so named from its position in the southern quarter of that great Saxon parish. With Tong and Donington, these had constituted an estate of the Earls of Mereia.

In the desperate attempt which, in 1068, the English made to liberate themselves from the yoke of their oppressors, the brothers Edwin and Morcar, joint tenants of the earldom of Mercia, as is well known, took a part. The Conqueror's vigor was too great for the patriots, however; sanguinary vengeance and devastation,

---

[1] *Domesday*, fo. 259, a 1.

accompanied by a wholesale spoliation, followed, when in 1071, among the remnant of scattered Saxons who sought that camp of refuge, the marsh-environed Isle of Ely, were Edwin and Morcar. Here, in the last refuge of Anglo-Saxon independence, the Mercian earls might have smiled at the futile efforts of William's heavy-clad Norman men-at-arms to dispossess them; but the Englishman foolishly suffered himself to be duped by the false protestations of "the Bastard," and quitting the camp of refuge for the Court, as he had been persuaded, scarce had Morcar set foot beyond the patriot entrenchments, than seized, he was loaded with irons, and cast into a dungeon. Edwin then left the Isle of Ely, to make another grand effort for the deliverance of his country and captured brother. Yet no sooner was he in a position to make the attempt, when some of his attendants betrayed him to the Normans. At the head of twenty of his knights, Edwin made a heroic defence against enormous odds, retreating backwards as he fought. At length, stopped by a swollen brook, he fell, overcome by numbers. His enemies cut off his head, and carried it to the Conqueror, who wept, it is said, over the fate of one whom he would fain have attached to his fortune.

Committed to the custody of Roger de Beaumont, who probably guarded him in one of his castles of Beaumont, Brionne, or Pontaudemer, some sixteen years afterwards, as the Conqueror lay on his death-bed, he was reminded of Morcar, the Saxon noble, who still languished in prison. Full of remorse at the remembrance of his many atrocities, the dying Conqueror released him. Immediately upon the death of his father, the hard Rufus, however, again sent back to a prison the unfortunate Earl of Mercia, out of which it does not appear that he ever returned.

Such was the end of the Saxon earls Edwin and Morcar,—such the calamities inflicted by the Norman Conquest on "two brothers," who, even according to Norman authority,[1] once "were zealous in the worship of God, and respected good men. They were remarkably handsome, their relations were of high birth and very numerous, their estates were vast and gave them immense power, and their popularity was great. The clergy and monks offered continual prayers on their behalf, and crowds of poor daily supplications."

Upon the re-distribution of the conquered province of Mercia,

---

[1] ORDERICUS VITALIS, B. IV. ch. iv.

Earl Roger de Montgomery entered Shropshire to possess and rule, when Gerard de Tornai, one of his followers, received as the meed of service, eighteen valuable Saxon manors, of which the largest was Sutton.

Gerard was one of those western magnates who, upon the accession of Rufus, rebelled against him. At any rate, de Tornai's career in Shropshire terminated, about 1088, in a total and absolute forfeiture. The disinherited baron had a daughter, Sibil, wife of Hamo Peverel, who, by special favor of the suzerain, king, or earl under whom Gerard de Tornai had held, acquired a succession to the forfeited estate, under a title from the first ambiguous. Some[1] say that the Peverels descended from a Saxon ancestress, who, first concubine of William, Duke of Normandy, afterwards married Ranulf Peverel, of Hatfield. There is much mystery about the matter, yet certain it is, that the Shropshire Peverels attended the Court and enjoyed the favor of Henry I. Of this branch, Hamo Peverel undoubtedly held Sutton during the reign of that king. Some twenty years after the death of Hamo, Jorwerth Goch, a Welsh prince, the "Red Edward" of border traditions, was associated with the Fief of Gerard de Tornai.

This Cymrian renegade was one of those tools used by the Anglo-Norman kings to disintegrate the national unity of North Wales. Whether Jorwerth acquired Sutton by marriage or as a bribe, is unknown. His elder brother, Madoc, was in the pay of Henry II. The following, from the Pipe Roll, may illustrate the policy of the Anglo-Norman kings with respect to their attempts at the acquisition of Wales. William Fitz Alan, Sheriff of Shropshire, in 1157 rendered account of a sum of £7 6s. 4d., being the current year's *Ferm* of the land of Gerard de Tornai. Of this sum he had paid £3 6s. into the King's treasury; the balance of £4 0s. 3d. he had handed over to Gerverd Coch, by orders of Becket, the Chancellor, and Leicester, Chief Justice of England. At the same time, by order of the King, he had made presents of £8 10s. to Maddoch, and £2 to Gervase.

The year 1157 was the one in which Henry II. undertook his Welsh campaign. It was a failure; and the Anglo-Norman sovereign sought by trusty agents to accomplish that which he was unable to do by more open means. Intrigue and bribery accord-

---

[1] DUGDALE, *Baronage*. Eyton questions the scandalous story. See *Antiquities of Shropshire*, vol. ii. p. 104.

ingly were the order of the day; and we may infer the lavish extent of the latter when we learn that the enormous amount of £91 *per ann.*—a salary equivalent to 60 times the pay of a common soldier of that day, or £4,500 modern currency, was appointed for the maintenance of Jorwerth Goch, who regularly received this amount, as the Pipe Rolls reveal, for the years 1169, 1170, and for forty-seven weeks of the year ending Michaelmas, 1171, at which period a pacification was effected between the King of England and Rese, Prince of South Wales. The services of Gervase were therefore no longer needed, and we hear no more of him.

In 1186-7, Madoc, son of Gervase Ghoc, granted to Wombridge Priory the advowson of his church at Sutton. To Madoc succeeded his brother Griffith de Sutton, the peculiarity of whose serjeantry is explained by a return of the year 1211. " He holds," says the record,[1] " Sutton and Brocton, of the gift of King Henry II., by service of being *Latimarius* (or King's Interpreter), between England and Wales." Griffin, the Welshman, gave land to the monks, one of his grants to Wombridge Priory being a rent of 24 cocks and hens, which he received for an *assart* in Sutton. To Griffin succeeded another Madoc as Lord of Sutton, and from him it was that the manor acquired the distinctive appellation Sutton Maddock. He held it forty years, a chief among the knights who constituted the Court of the County of Shropshire. Madoc sold Sutton to John le Strange, who thereupon became lord of this manor. The aged "Latimarius" fell, it is supposed, in one of the many conflicts that took place between the English and the Welsh towards the close of Henry III.'s reign. Madoc's end is enshrouded in uncertainty; yet the probability is, representing as he did a house that, connected with the English king, had caused an immense deal of injury to be inflicted on Wales, he fell at the hands of his enraged fellow-countrymen.

Sutton Maddock abounded in sub-infeudations and tenancies, the principal of which granted by Griffin Goch, Lord of Sutton to Ralph de Sandford, may be termed the Sandford Fee. Ralph, by purchasing, largely extended his footing in Sutton, when, worldly-wise, he sub-let his acquisitions to the utmost advantage. One of his tenants was Margaret, *daughter of Richard, the priest* of Brocton—how about priestly celibacy?

There was also the BURWARDSLEY FEE, the COCUS FEE, and the

---

[1] *Testa de Nevill,* p. 56.

tenure of *Begesour in Sutton and Brockton,* the holders of each of which doubtless were good men in their day; for they gave lands to the monks. Yet both they and the shorn occupants of Wombridge Priory likewise have long since passed away, and a few half-obliterated mouldering parchments are all that survive to remind us that they once lived.

SUTTON CHURCH.

This church, about 1186-7, was given, as we have said, by Madoc, son of Jorwerth Goch, to Wombridge Priory.

In 1206, the Bishop of Coventry sanctioned an appropriation thereof by Wombridge Priory. In 1291, the church of Sutton Madok was valued at £4 13s. 4d. In 1341, the parish was rated at only £3 to the *ninth,* because four virgates of land lay untilled, etc. The Valor of 1534-5 omits to notice this church under the deanery of Newport. From the acknowledgment of the Prior of Wombridge, however, we learn that he received £3 6s. 8d. per annum "tithes of the church of Sutton Madok."

Early Incumbent.—"Radulf the clerk," 1187. Probably the last resident rector of Sutton; he was followed by the deputies of Wombridge Priory, at first styled chaplains or priests, and afterwards vicars.

Stockton. This word derives from the Saxon Stóc, meaning the *stock* or trunk of a tree, and tun, a *town* or enclosure. The manor is thus described in Domesday book:—"The same Gerard [de Tornai] holds Stochetone, and Hugo [holds it] of him. Eduin and Ordui held it [in Saxon times] for two manors, and were freemen. Here i hide geldable. The land is [enough for] iii oxteams. In demesne is half-a-team, and i serf, and i villain, and i boor, with half-a-team. In the time of King Edward, the manor was worth 12s. [per annum]; now it is worth 4s."[1]

Forfeit, with the other possessions of the rebellious De Tornai, the manor of Stockton next appears as held *in capite* of the Crown by serjeantry of service at Shrawardine Castle.

It appearing that persons throughout the kingdom holding lands of the king by serjeantry, having wholly or in part alienated the same without license of the Crown, a commission issued in 1246

---

[1] *Domesday.* fo. 259, a 1.

to Henry de Wingeham *Escheator citra Trent,* appointing him with an associate knight in each county and a jury if he pleased, to make inquest into the state of all serjeantries. Shortly after, a similar commission, issued to Robert Passelewe, treasurer of King Henry III, in virtue of which he visited many counties to "*take fines*" and "*make arrentations*" of serjeantries, that is, to provide for the due fulfilment of the services attached to the tenures, and exact a certain annual rent in money by way of composition for every alienation without license of the Crown. One of the results of Passelewe's visit to Shropshire was to find that the "serjeantry of John le Bret, which was formerly Henry de Stockton's, in Stockton, for which he was bound to provide for the lord king one serving foot-soldier, with bow and arrows, for fifteen days, at his own cost, in garrison of Shrawardine Castle in time of war, etc.," had become in part the subject of alienation.

The vill of Ewdness, a member of the *Domesday,* Stockton probably became detached when, after the forfeiture of De Tornai, both were in the king's hands. It then constituted a distinct serjeantry, the service being that its tenant should accompany the sheriff of Shropshire when, twice every year, the latter conveyed the ferm or revenue of the county to the Exchequer, the king paying all charges.

STOCKTON CHURCH.

This is supposed to have been founded by one of the De Laci's, seigneural lords of Highford, shortly after *Domesday*. According to the taxation of 1291, the church of Stockton, with its chapel (Boningale), was worth £4 13s. 4d. ; the Prior of St. Guthlac, Hereford, also receiving a pension of 6s. 8d. therefrom. In 1341, the parish was assessed only £3 6s. 8d., because a recent murrain had destroyed the sheep, etc. In 1534 the rectory of Stoketon, with the chapel of Bonynghal, in the deanery of Newport, was valued at £14, less 6s. 8d. for procurations, and 2s. 3d. for synodals.

Hatton is twice alluded to in *Domesday*. In one part of the Conqueror's record we are told that:—"The same Gerard holds Etone, and William [holds] of him. Turgod held it and was a free man. Here half a hide geldable. There is land enough for iii ox-teams. In demesne is i [team] and i serf and iiii boors; also, there is i guest [*hospes*] paying a rent of 2s. In time of

King Edward its value was 12s.; now it is worth 11s. He [Gerard] found it waste."[1]

In another place, *Domesday* says, that:—"The same Rainald [the sheriff] holds in Etone half a hide. Turgot held it for a single manor and paid geld."[2]

The Etone of *Domesday* is identical with the modern Hatton. A small stream called Tuy Brook, of which traces remain, coursed through the original manor, dividing it into two equal parts, one of which lying to the eastward of the stream, Adam de Hetune gave to Buildwas Abbey in 1189.

The monks now had an eye to the land on the west of Tuy Brook. A footing they acquired here when John de Hemes gave to Buildwas a virgate and 12 acres of his demesne in Hettun. They obtained a further hold, when Walter, son of this John, with assent of his mother, his heirs, and his friends, added to his father's donation "all the land which is between the road of Hyvclith [Evelith] and Tinbroc," for which the monks received the grantor, his mother and his heirs, into their fraternity. About 1248, Robert Traynel, Lord of Hattone, for the health of his soul gave them the remaining portion; and thus, at length, the monks of Buildwas Abbey acquired complete possession of this manor, which continued in their hands until the Dissolution.

Albrighton derived its name apparently from having been founded or owned by some Anglo-Saxon Alberic or Albrecht.

According to *Domesday*:—"The same Normannus holds Albricstone. Algar and Godhit held it for two manors. Here one hide and a half geldable. There is land for iiii ox-teams. In demesne are iii such teams; and xiii serfs and iii villains, and iii boors with i team. The wood here will fatten 100 swine; but at present it is in the king's hand. In time of King Edward the manor was worth 21s. [per annum]; now it is worth 16s. He [Norman] found it waste."[3]

It is not unlikely that the Algar alluded to above was Algar, Earl of Mercia, whose extensive possessions included Pattingham, a manor not far distant from Albrighton. "Normannus Venator," or Norman hunter—for such was his name—held six other manors

---

[1] *Domesday*, fo. 259, a 1.   [2] *Ibidem*, fo. 255, a 2.   [3] *Ibidem*, fo. 259, a 2.

besides Albrighton under Roger de Montgomery, the Norman Earl of Shrewsbury; the service by which he held them probably being implied in his name. The locality of two of his manors cannot be determined; but in the other five he appears to have been succeeded by the Pichfords, who, for two centuries, held the fief of Norman Venator of the Crown. Albrighton was the reputed *caput* or centre of this fief, the whole being held by service of one knight's fee.

The gallant services of Ralph de Pichford, at the siege of Brug in 1102, have been alluded to.[1] Upon Ralph's decease, his son Richard de Pichford became Lord of Albrighton, who again was succeeded by Hugh. In 1194, this Hugh de Pichford paid 20s. scutage, or shield-tax, the sum assessed on every knight's fee held *in capite* for King Richard's redemption. In 1195 and in 1197 De Pichford's scutage was assessed at the same rate in support of Richard's war with France; but, in the years 1199, 1201, -2, -3, -4, -5, -6 successively, from some cause or other, King John charged him scutage enormously in excess of the current assessment on a single knight's fee. Thus, in 1199, he was charged 40s., although £1 6s. 8d. was the current rate; in 1204 he was charged six merks, the rate being only two-and-a-half. These facts indicate one of the causes that alienated from King John his impoverished feudatories.

To Hugh succeeded Ralph de Pichford II., who assessed to various *scutages* and *aids* in 1235, was charged two merks for the *aid* levied on marriage of the sister of King Henry III., and in 1245 £1 to the aid for marriage of the king's daughter.

Besides their stated service according to feudal custom, the king was entitled to *scutage* or *aid* from his tenants in these three cases; the king's captivity, the knighting of his eldest son, and the marrying of his eldest daughter. It was one of the points stipulated for in Magna Charta that the king should impose no scutage or aid upon his subjects without the consent of the barons.

The King's Exchequer, in the Anglo-Norman time, was also largely recruited by the system of fines and gifts. Thus, this very Ralph de Pichford, in 1232 fined 40s. with the Crown, for the privilege of holding a market and fair at his manor of Albrighton, for which he obtained the king's charter; and we read, that, in 1234, he gave the king the large sum of 300 merks to have

---

[1] Page 33.

marriage of the heirs, and custody of the lands in Ireland, of John Fitz-Dermot, deceased.

In 1252, Ralph himself was dead, as, that year, Fitz-Nicholas fined 100 merks with the king for custody of his land, and heir, including the marriage of the latter. De Pichford's estate, in 1254, was charged 40s. to the *aid* for knighting Prince Edward, the king's eldest son; 40s. in 1260, for the scutage of Wales; and, when the army destined by the ambitious Edward I. for the conquest of that country, stood summoned to meet at Worcester on July 1st, 1277, John de Pychford, knight, acknowledged his service due on a knight's fee at Albrighton, and was ready to discharge it in person. Ralph de Picheford, son of John, succeeded him as lord of Albrighton. He was the last of his line who had an interest here, as he sold the manor to Sir John de Tregoz, upon whose decease, Albrighton fell to his grandson, Sir John de la Warre.

There were various under-tenants in Albrighton.

ALBRIGHTON CHURCH.

This church has a western tower, the lower part of which belongs to the 12th century, which tallies with the mention of Nicholas, priest of Albrighton in 1186-7. The church of Albryton, in the deanery of Newport and archdeaconry of Salop, in 1291 stood at £5 6s. 8d. When Ralph de Pichford sold the manor of Albrighton to Sir John de Tregoz, he sold the advowson of this church to Walter de Langton, bishop of Lichfield and Coventry, upon which sale a fine was levied by special order of the king. Bishop Langton retained the advowson but a short time. In 1341, the parish was rated only £3 6s. 8d. to the *ninth*, because the abbot of Buildwas had three carucates of land in the parish, etc. The Valor of 1534 gives the vicarage of Albrighton as worth £6 *per annum*, less 8s. for procurations and 2s. for synodals; but the honest abbot of Dore returned it as worth £6 13s. 4d.

During the alterations which a few years since were made in Albrighton church, in lowering the floor of the south aisle, a very ancient stone altar tomb was discovered lying about eighteen inches below the surface. In the early English style, it is ornamented by a number of coats of arms relating to the Pichford, the Despencer, and other families. From the circumstance, that neither Sandford in his Church-notes of 1660, nor Johnson in 1699, mention this tomb, it is inferred, that it had lain under the ground for over 200 years. This relic of the past has been carefully placed outside the church.

Early Incumbent.—Nicholas, priest of Albriton, 1186-7.

We read of John de Aston being admitted to the "newly-founded" vicarage of Albrighton in 1329, on presentation of abbot and convent of Dore.

Johnson particularly noted in 1699, in the south aisle of Albrighton church a marble tomb, which is now nowhere to be found. He adds that the windows of the south aisle contained twelve coats of arms in "very old glass." These associated the names of Langton, De Burgh, Montford, Pichford, Giffard, and Davenant with this house, which, many ages ago, was set apart for the public worship of God.

Bishton, originally Bishops-ton at some period anterior to existing records, doubtless, was attached to some episcopal see.

Domesday informs us that:—"Normannus [Venator] holds Bispetone. Turgod held it and was a free man. Here i hide geldable. The land is [capable of employing] vi ox-teams. Here two Frenchmen with iiii villains and ii boors have iii teams. There is a wood which will fatten x swine. In time of King Edward the manor was worth 30s. [per annum]; now it is worth 10s."[1] Like Norman Venator's other manors, Bishton descended to De Pichford, when it gradually became a mere member of Albrighton.

Faintree, now a township in the parish of Chetton is mentioned in Domesday Book. From that record we learn, that:—"Walcheline holds Faventrei. Ulchetel, Archetel, Uluiet, Ælwi, Ordwi, and Ordric held it, and those thanes were free. Here are ii hides geldable. There is land enough for v ox-teams. In demesne is one team and a half; and i serf, ii villains, and v boors, with ii teams. In time of King Edward it was worth 27s.; now 20s. He [Walcheline] found it waste."[2]

Willey, in 1086, was a member of the fief held by Turold de Verley, under the Norman earl. *Domesday* says:—"The same

---

[1] *Domesday*, fo. 259, a 2.   [2] *Ibidem*, fo. 257, b 1.

ALBRIGHTON CHURCH, A.D. 1835.

Turold holds Wilit, and Hunnit [holds it] of him. This same [Hunnit] held it [in Saxon times] and was free. Here half a hide geldable. The arable land is for ii ox-teams. Here those teams are, together with ii villains and ii boors. Its value was and is 5s."[1]

It is a disputed point, whether Turold, the *Domesday* lord of Willey was a Saxon or Norman. Blakeway says he was a Saxon. Eyton argues that he was a Norman. The latter, however, shows that the name occurs in Normandy before the Conquest, and was borne by several who profited by the Norman invasion. Assuming that he was a Norman, this man then held thirteen manors under Earl Roger de Montgomery. Exhibiting a partizanship, although it was but slight, with the wicked De Belèsme, Turold managed to escape summary forfeiture upon the fall of his suzerain; and, granting lands to Shrewsbury Abbey, he died before 1121. Robert, his son, succeeded, of whom nothing further is known than that, like his father, he also gave lands to the monks. By the close of the 12th century, Fitz-Turold's interest in Willey had passed to Chetwynd, who held under Fitz-Alan.

As to Hunnit, who held under Turold at the time of the survey, he doubtless was one of those few who were suffered by the conquerors to retain an interest in a soil that had been their fathers'.

"This continuous Saxon interest in the manor," says Eyton, "was probably the cause of its non-diminution of value since the time of Edward the Confessor, as well of its being cultivated to its full capability when the *Domesday* Commissioners took their account of it." The Norman *gentile-hommes*, better at wielding lance or long-sword than at handling the plough, affected to despise such homely but useful avocations. Yet, when they permitted any of the subject race to hold lands, it was not the policy of their oppressors to suffer them to retain them in places where, old associations awakening, might lead to a spirit of resistance; and there is a strong presumption that Hunnit was eventually thus dealt with. At any rate, a new feoffee, in no way related to Hunnit or his heirs, Warnerius by name, it is supposed became lord of Willey, whose family inheriting other estates of the fee of Chetwynd, perhaps acquired Willey by favour of its chief lord. This Warnerius, or Warner, was ancestor of a family which took its surname from the Manor of Willey.

Third in succession from Warnerius, occurs Warner de Willeley,

---

[1] *Domesday*, fo. 258, a 1.

who, marrying the daughter of Roger Fitz Odo, with her acquired much property. Not satisfied with such increase, however, this man was convicted of an act of treacherous oppression, which, even in a period when oppression was rife, brought down on him the censure of the law. Coveting the land of one whom feudal law bound him to protect, Warner de Willeley and his wife contrived that his vassal, by a false information, should appear guilty of a capital crime. The assumed felon was arrested, and his chattels sold by a king's bailiff. Should he be finally outlawed, his lands of course became forfeit to the lord of the fee. It was a deeply planned scheme; yet, cunning although it was, there remained for the unfortunate victim a chance of obtaining, at the hands of the king's justices, that equity which a local court denied him. The case was gone into at the assizes of November, 1221, when the innocency of the accused being fully established, the oppressing lord, with his satellite, the king's bailiff, in their turn were committed to prison. It was a characteristic of that dark age that no crime was without its fiscal equivalent. The culprit who could pay, got off, and, accordingly, a fine of five merks released the scoundrel, Warner de Willeley, who shortly afterwards figured as one of the principal personages in Shropshire.

Leagued with others as desperate as himself, Andrew de Willeley, the grandson of this man, terminated a turbulent career upon the field of Evesham. He left an infant daughter to inherit his forfeited estate—forfeit, that is, until such time as, according to the *dictum de Kenilworth*, it was, by payment of a heavy sum of money, redeemed. Burga, for that was her name, years afterward marrying Richard de Harley, to her posterity by him was transmitted the splendid, and, at length disencumbered, domain of De Willeley.

WILLEY CHURCH.

Probably founded and endowed by the lords of the manor, this church appears as the subject of litigation in 1214. In 1291, the church or chapel of Wyleleye, in the deanery of Wenlock, was valued at £5 6s. 8d. *per annum*, a pension of 7s. being annually payable to the priory kitchen, under the title of, " The Chapel of Welyley." The parish was assessed only 40s. in 1341, because of tempests and murrain, etc. In 1534, the value of this benefice was £5 6s. 8d. *per annum*, less 6d. for synodals. The rectors of Willey without cure were probably non-resident.

Early Incumbent.—Adam de Wetenhale, 1276.

Willey, like Broseley, in the time of Richard I. was transferred to the then newly-created Liberty of Wenlock, in which it has ever since remained.

Deuxhill. "It is often doubtful," says Eyton, "whether places with this termination owe it to the Saxon heall, *a hall*, or hul, *a hill*." The manor is thus noticed in *Domesday*:—"The same church [St. Milburg] held, and still holds, Dehocsele. Here half a hide geldable. In demesne is i ox-team; and ii boors, and i cottar with i team and i serf is here. [In time of King Edward] it was worth 10s. [per annum]; now it is worth 20s." [1]

From Saxon times until the Reformation, the monastery of Wenlock possessed the manor of Deuxhill; yet, the chartularies of this once renowned priory being either lost or destroyed, unfortunately we know but little of its dependencies.

The Church

Alluded to under Glazeley, the chapel of Deuxhill, was founded as early as 1115. According to the taxation of 1291, the annual value of the church of Deukeshull, with the chapel of Mitletone, was under £4. Singularly enough, it is not mentioned in the Inquisition of 1341. In 1535, Deuxhill was united to Glazeley, of which the then value has been given.

Early Incumbent.—Sir Robert de Mudle, chaplain, 1278, was presented by the prior and convent of Wenlock to the chapels of Middleton Priors, and Deuxhill.

During the war with France, in the 14th century, the king presented to Deuxhill; and, for the same reason, viz., because the king held in his hands the alien priory of Wenlock, in 1388, the Crown was still presenting to this church. Yet the hero of Crecy and Poictiers had long since sunk into a premature grave; the broken-hearted Edward III. had followed: and now that great war, which for fifty long years the English kings had waged for the crown of France, lingering in the hands of the weak Richard II., drew to a close.

Pickthorn. The shrub we call *rest-harrow*, from its arresting the use of that implement, is by the Scandinavians called "Puk-

---

[1] *Domesday*, 252, b 2.

torne," i.e., devil's-thorn. It may have been then, that this name originated from a prevalence of some such plant in the locality and that in the *Domesday* Pichetorne, we have another proof of the wide-spreading hold the Vikings of the North once had over the midland counties of England. Not many miles distant from Pickthorn is Danesford. Chester and Derby, as is well known were "Danish Burghs."

We read, in Domesday Book, that, "The same church [St Milburg] held [in Saxon times], and still holds, Pichetorne Here is half a hide geldable. In demesne is i ox team; and villain, and ii boors with ii teams, and ii serfs. It was and now is worth 7s."[1]

At what subsequent period the Baskervilles became enfeoffed in Pickthorn by Wenlock Priory is unknown. Of this family, whose surname has been variously traced to Basqueville in the Pays de Caux, or to Boscherville in the forest of Roumare, near Rouen the Norman localities whence issued, probably to take part in Duke William's adventure, the founder of the Anglo-Norman Baskervilles, whose branches, early in the 13th century, spread wide over Shropshire, Herefordshire, Northamptonshire, Warwickshire, Norfolk, Bucks, and Wilts; Radulf de Baskervill, in 1165, held land in Herefordshire under Adam de Port His tenure was of *old feoffment:* that is, he held or inherited his land from a period antecedent to the death of Henry I. in 1135. There is reason to believe that this man became lord of Pickthorn. Ralph Baskerville was murdered, in Northampton shire, previously to 1194, and his son had succeeded him, as at that date the Escheator accounts 8d. for the ferm of "Piketon Tomæ," which means, for Thomas de Baskerville's land of Pickthorn.

Roger de Baskerville was returned in 1316 as lord of Pikethorn in Shropshire.[2]

Cadets of the family of Baskerville figure among the under tenants in Pickthorn.

---

[1] *Domesday*, fo. 252, b 2.   [2] *Parliamentary Writs*, IV. 398.

WE have done with the *Domesday* Hundred of Alnodestreu, and now proceed to those scattered Manors, which, forming detachments of other hundreds and counties, nevertheless, at the time of the Conqueror's survey, lay confusedly intermixed among the Manors of Alnodestreu. When the old Hundred of Alnodestreu was swept away, upon the re-arrangement of the boundaries and divisional system of Shropshire in Henry the First's time, the isolated manors we are about to describe were attached to the newly created Hundreds of Brimstree and Stottesden. A glance at the annexed Table will give the reader not only the *Domesday* status of these Manors, but also their modern Hundred and modern name. He will see how Shropshire now includes manors that formerly belonged to other counties; and, if he can but imagine the nineteen manors of this Table indiscriminately intermixed with the thirty others of the Alnodestreu Table, he will, to some extent, realize the extraordinary eccentric territorial division of the county of Shropshire in the time of William the Conqueror.

DETACHMENTS OF DOMESDAY HUNDRED OF BASCHERCH.

Modern Name.	Domesday Name.	Saxon Owner or Owners, T. R. E.	Domesday Tenant in capite.	Domesday Mesne, or next Tenant.	Domesday Sub-Tenant.	Modern Hundred.
		FIRST DETACHMENT.				
Shiffnal	Iteshale	Morcar Comes	Rogerius Comes	Rotbert Fitz Tetbald		Brimstree.
Kemberton	Chenbritone	Aluric / Elmer / Uluuin / Edmer	...... Idem	Rotbert Fitz Tetbald		..Ibidem.
Cosford	Costeford	Turgot	...... Idem	Radulf de Mortemer		..Ibidem.
Higford	Huchefor	Goduin	...... Idem	Roger de Laci	Berner..	..Ibidem.
		SECOND DETACHMENT.				
Eudon George	Eldone	Edric	...... Idem	Radulf de Mortemer		Stottesden.
Chelmarsh	Celmeres	Eduin Comes	...... Idem	Radulf de Mortemer		..Ibidem.
Sidbury	Sudberie	Wiga	...... Idem	Radulf de Mortemer		..Ibidem.
Neenton	Newentone	Azor	...... Idem	Radulf de Mortemer	Roger	..Ibidem.
Burwarton	Burertone	Azor	...... Idem	Radulf de Mortemer	Helgot	..Ibidem.
Cleobury North	Cleberie	Seunard	Rogerius de Laci	Ulnuard		..Ibidem.

PART OF DOMESDAY COUNTY OF STAFFORDSHIRE.*

Modern Name.	Domesday Name.	Saxon Owner or Owners, T. R. E.	Domesday Tenant in capite.	Domesday Mesne, or next Tenant.	Domesday Sub-Tenant.	Modern Hundred.
Claverley	Claverlege	Algar Comes	Rogerius Comes			Brimstree.
Worfield	Wrfeld	Algar Comes	Hugo de Montgumeri			..Ibidem.
Alveley	Alvidelege	Algar Comes	Rogerius Comes			Stottesden.
Norley Regis	Nordlege	Algar Comes	...... Idem			..Ibidem.
Bobbington	Bubintone	Wifure	Robertus de Statford	Helgot		{ Brimstree. Seisdon, Staff.

DETACHMENT OF DOMESDAY HUNDRED OF STANLEI, WARWICKSHIRE.

Modern Name.	Domesday Name.	Saxon Owner or Owners, T. R. E.	Domesday Tenant in capite.	Domesday Mesne, or next Tenant.	Domesday Sub-Tenant.	Modern Hundred.
Quat	Quatone	Outi	Rogerius Comes	Outi		Stottesden.
Romesley	Rameslege	Achi	...... Idem	Walter		..Ibidem.
Rudge	Rigge	Edric, de Comite Leurico	...... Idem	Radulf (de Mortemer)		..Ibidem.
Shipley	Sciplei	Alsi	...... Idem	Radulf (de Mortemer)		Brimstree.

* Only one of these Manors (Bobbington) has its Staffordshire Hundred assigned in *Domesday*. That Hundred is Saisdoue, in which also will have been situated Claverley, Worfield, Alveley, and Norley.

Idsall or Shiffnal.

The Saxon word Iðes-heal signifies the Hall of Ide, and Sceafan-heal the Hall of Sceafa; and it may be, that, originally Idsall and Shiffnal represented two districts, lying respectively west and east of the stream which divides the town.

The place is thus noticed in *Domesday* :[1]—" Rotbert, son of Tetbald, holds of Earl Roger Iteshale. Earl Morcar held it. Here are 7½ hides geldable. In demesne are ix ox-teams; and [there are] xxvi serfs and xxxvii villains, and iii boors, and iii radmans, with xxvii teams. The wood here will fatten 300 swine. In time of King Edward [the manor] was worth £15 [per annum]; afterwards it was worth 6s. Now it pays £15."

We have spoken of Edwin and Morcar, joint-tenants of the earldom of Mercia, and their sad fate. A terrible comment does the above extract furnish, upon that unrighteous regime which goaded the Saxon Morcar into rebellion against the Conqueror. Here we have the annual value of a manor, reduced in a brief space of time, from £15 to 6s.—a lively evidence of that desolation which attended the abortive efforts of the patriot Saxons to throw off the yoke of their oppressors. From Roger de Montgomery, the Norman Robert Fitz-Tetbald then received the ruined manor, and he restored it to its former worth.

This Robert Fitz-Tetbald, who, besides Idsall, held three other Shropshire Manors, appears not only a witness, but a coadjutor in Earl Roger's endowment of Shrewsbury Abbey. "Robert, son of Theobald, gave them [the monks,]" says the earl, "the Church of Iteshale, with the tithes of the same *vill*."[2] From the survey of Sussex, he appears to have been by far the greatest feoffee in Roger de Montgomery's earldom of Arundel and Chichester; and, although his shrievalty is nowhere noticed in *Domesday*, doubtless it was in relation to his great southern fief, rather than to any connection with Shropshire, that Robert Fitz-Tetbald acquired his title of *Vicecomes*.

Robert, Vicecomes, does not appear to have been involved in the fall of De Belèsme. During the reign of Henry I., both his Shropshire and Sussex fiefs, however, lapsed to the Crown; yet, whether by surrender, forfeiture, or failure of heirs, cannot be determined. Henry I. retained Robert's fief until, in 1130-5,

---

[1] *Domesday*, fo. 256, b 2.   [2] *Salop Chartu'ary*, No. 2.

another large portion of the earldom of Arundel falling into his hands, this the king granted to Alan de Dunstanvill, and along with it Henry I. gave to Alan the Shropshire manor of Idsall: at least so it is supposed. Who then was Alan de Dunstanvill? Yet let us first speak of Walter de Pinkney.

The year 1139 saw an insurrection break out, which, speedily spreading, at length the whole kingdom was enveloped in the flames of a civil war. Then was witnessed in its direst form the most horrid of all kinds of war, that in which two parties of equal strength in the same country close in deadly strife; when, amid the opposing ranks are seen brother fighting against brother, and the father against the son; and when all ties of kindred and neighbourhood being fatally severed, their former friendship tends only to embitter and lend a keenness to the swords of the ensanguined combatants.

England, peaceful and happy, has yet more than once since the Norman conquest been the theatre of civil war. We might point to the reigns of John and the weak Henry III., to the bloody wars of the roses, or, nearer our own day, to the time of Charles I. Yet it may be questioned whether the confused and bloody drama was ever enacted amid circumstances of greater barbarity than during the nineteen long years that succeeded to the usurpation of Stephen. During that dark and unhappy period, England was literally in a state of anarchy. The ferocious Anglo-Norman nobility, unrestrained by any considerations, gave a full vent to their implacable rage against each other; or, sallying from their turretted dens of infamy, trampled down, without remorse, the Saxons whom they detested. Cruelty, robbery, and lust, were the order of the day, for the punishment of which no power existed in the disjointed realm. Towns and villages were burned, the fields remained unploughed, and the rude implements of our forefather's industry were destroyed, or turned to purposes of self-defence by an oppressed and dejected peasantry. The cattle, being neglected, died; and, as the inevitable result of all this sanguinary confusion, gaunt famine combined with crimson war to decimate the miserable inhabitants.

It was amid the convulsions of this unhappy period, that Walter de Pinkney became possessed of the vast Wiltshire domains of his mother, Adeliza de Dunstanvill, widow of Reginald de Dunstanvill, alias Fitz Roy, one of the numerous illegitimate children of Henry I. De Pinkney was a staunch adherent of the usurper

The unknown, but contemporaneous author of the Acts of Stephen, tells us that as this Walter made a sortie from Malmesbury Castle, over which he kept ward for the usurper, William de Dover adroitly captured him, when the Empress Maude, " having now in her power the man whom of all others she most hated, strove, both by her blandishments, and by threats of torture or death, to induce him to surrender Malmesbury Castle ; but he, resisting with constancy all the seductions of female influence and regardless of her menaces, could not be induced to comply with her demands." Hearing that his favourite had fallen into the empress's hands, the active Stephen hastened to reinforce the beleagured garrison, when, having relieved it, he turned his attention to other affairs. Meanwhile, annoyed at losing the castle through De Pinkney's obstinacy, Maude loaded him with chains, and threw him into a loathsome dungeon, where he appears to have remained some years. At length, released from prison, through the assistance of Roger, Earl of Hereford, De Pinkney again flew to arms, and, surprising Christchurch Castle, Hants, then held for the empress, he put the garrison to the sword, and entered on the lordship of a wide district. But his sacrileges and cruelties, it is said, led to the formation of a conspiracy between the men of the lordship and the soldiers of the castle.

One day, as Walter and his suite, passed from castle to church, he was waylaid by the conspirators, who, in the guise of suppliants, affected humbly to implore him to cease his exactions. More imperious than ever, De Pinkney was in the act of replying, when one of the assassins sprang forward, and severed his head from his neck by a blow of his axe.

The following is a translation of a curious charter which this man gave to Lewes Priory :—" To the Venerable Lord Prior of Lewes, etc., Walter de Pencheni greeting. Know ye that I give ye the church of Wintreburne, which my mother, Adeliza, gave ye. I give it after the decease of the clerk, my kinsman, to whom I granted it ; and as long as that clerk shall live he shall hold it of ye, and he shall pay ye every year, whilst the war shall last, 10s., and when God shall have given peace, he shall pay one merk of silver. But, after his decease, ye shall have it wholly and freely. Hugo de Cumbrevilla and his two brothers, Roger and Reinald de Insula being witnesses. This [I do] that I may partake in all the benefits of your Church." [1]

---

[1] Lewes *Chartulary*.

The deceased Walter de Pinkney had adhered to Stephen; on the other side, his brother Robert, and that Alan de Dunstanvill to whom Henry I. gave Idsall, fought for the empress. Alan granted to Wombridge Priory half a virgate of land, which Eilric held in Leies (afterwards Prior's Lee), with all the children of the said Eilric: a grant which, by the way, proves him to have been lord of Idsall, for Lee was then a member of that manor. Alan also gave to Lewes Priory, Newtimber, Sussex. Dying about 1156, Walter de Dunstanvill, Alan's eldest son, became lord of Idsall, who, heir also of his uncle Robert, succeeded to vast estates in Wiltshire and Surrey, besides a large possession in Normandy.

Of this man we have many notices. From the first, which occurs in 1156, we learn, that, by writ of Henry II., Walter's quota of the Danegeld, assessed on the county of Sussex, was excused. The sum excused was £3. Again, in 1158, he was excused 14s. 6d. his share of the *donum* of the said county. In 1156, having been assessed £1 6s. 3d. for the Danegeld of Shropshire, being in arrear, Henry II. excused Walter; and the king further excused him 16s., his proportion of the *donum* of Shropshire.[1]

When the Danegeld was levied again in 1162, Walter de Dunstanvill was assessed at, and excused £1 7s. 6d. in Shropshire, and £2 8s. in Sussex.

About 1168, having become heir to his uncle, Walter de Dunstanvill appears accordingly entered on the Pipe Roll among the Wiltshire grantees of the crown as having the manor and hundred of Heytesbury, of £40 annual value. Yet Walter had not long held his Wiltshire domains, when a break of two years and a half, which ended March 1173, in the otherwise uniform sheriff's account, appears to indicate a temporary forfeiture. Perhaps Walter was associated with the rebellion of Prince Henry. At any rate, he does not seem to have been much of a favourite with Henry II.; for, at Michaelmas, 1177, that monarch, sitting himself in judgment on those who were accused of trespassing on the royal forests, amerced Walter in £100, a sum enormously in excess of amercements inflicted on other great holders in Shropshire. Nor did King Richard show this baron greater favour, for one of the retinue of John, Earl of Moreton, and probably implicated in

---

[1] *Rot. Pip.*, 2, 3, and 4 Henry II.

the treason of that base prince, there is reason to believe that De Dunstanvill suffered forfeiture during the reign of the lion-hearted.

He certainly experienced either the civil death implied by forfeiture, or that other decease, besides physical dissolution, which was wont to happen to men in those superstitious days, namely, the abandonment of the world and retirement into a monastery. It is most likely that, in 1194, this baron died all the three deaths, and was buried, according to his desire, in Wombridge Priory, to which, with other religious establishments, he had been a benefactor.

Within the present century, an ancient effigy of a cross-legged knight, in mail armour, with surcoat, sword in scabbard by his side, left hand holding the scabbard, the right on the hilt of, as if about to draw the sword (a martial attitude), spurs on heels, head resting on a cushion, and the feet on a lion, was removed from Wombridge, where it had lain in the churchyard ever since the demolition of the old church, to the south aisle of the abbey church of Shrewsbury. It was the monumental relic of Walter de Dunstanvill.

Walter de Dunstanvill II. then became lord of the manor of Idsall, and heir to his father's other possessions, who, long a minor, about April, 1201, William Briwerr proffered to King John a fine of 300 merks to have custody of the lands and marriage of the heir of the deceased Walter de Dunstanvill. The fine was accepted, but afterwards cancelled; for Gilbert Basset proffering 600 merks, double the amount Briwerr had offered for the same wardship, he got it. According to feudal practice, if the heir were a minor, the king retained the whole profit of the estate till his majority, giving what he chose for the maintenance and education of the young baron. By granting the wardship of a rich heir to any one, the sovereign could enrich a favourite; or, by selling it, as John did the wardship of young Walter de Dunstanvill, large sums accrued thereby to the Anglo-Norman king's exchequer.

Having attained his majority, styled the king's "faithful and beloved," Walter de Dunstanvill II., in 1215, had a grant of market and fair to be held in his Wiltshire manor of Heytesbury; but, wavering, he finally seceded from King John's allegiance, when his lands were given to another.

Among the number of those who gave in their allegiance to

TOMB IN THE ABBEY CHURCH, SHREWSBURY.
(SUPPOSED TO BE THAT OF SIR WALTER DE DUNSTANVILLE).

young Henry III., De Dunstanvill's lands were restored to him—the sheriffs of Shropshire, Cambridgeshire, Wiltshire, and Surrey receiving orders accordingly; when in 1218, and in the following year, Walter paid two merks scutage for one knight's fee in Ydeshall. Dying in 1241, King Henry III. received at Chester the homage of his son and heir, Walter de Dunstanvill III., when, having paid his relief of £100, the heir had seisin of his lands.

This baron, in 1245, was assessed 20s. in respect of one fee in Ideshal, to the *aid* for marriage of the king's daughter; and nine years later, he paid a similar amount towards making Prince Edward, the king's eldest son, a knight. He had a grant of market and fair in his manor of Hydeshale, and the subject of many cotemporary notices; as one of the lord marchers, he had military summons to meet the king at Chester on July 1st, 1258, to oppose the incursions of the Welsh. Although he fought against the king at Lewes, yet no permanent forfeiture was the result; and, dying in 1270, numerous charters which Walter left behind, prove him to have been more friendly to the monks than his father had been. Indeed, except granting to the abbey of Haughmond a right of road through his land when going to or returning from Wiche, in Cheshire, where they had some salt-pits, Walter's father does not appear to have conferred upon the monks any material benefits whatever; yet, whether this indicated a lack of piety in him, as some averred; or, whether it arose from his being of a less superstitious turn than his neighbours, we cannot determine.

The customary inquisitions having been held as to the estate of the deceased baron, and his heir having been found to be Petronilla, wife of Robert de Montfort; forthwith the king's writ issued to the escheator *citra* Trent, ordering him to give seisin of all Dunstanvill's lands to "Robert de Montfort, who had married Petronilla, daughter and heir of the deceased"; and he, accordingly, in right of his wife, became lord of Idsall and other great estates. William, this man's son, sold Idsall to Bartholomew de Badlesmere, when, the race of Dunstanvill no longer connected with it, the place henceforth appears described by its other name of Shiffnal.

The manor of Idsall involved many townships or members held by tenants of various rank and importance. Of these, HUNNINGTON or HINNINGTON was undoubtedly a member of the *Domesday*

"Iteshale," deriving its name, perhaps, from the Saxon Hunnit or Hunnine, who might have held it in the days of the Confessor.

Alan de Dunstanvill, in the reign of Stephen, granted, as we have seen, to Wombridge Priory the land which Eilric held in Lees; when the canons, having obtained a footing in Idsall, they gradually improved their position, until their estate, afterwards known as PRIOR'S LEE, yielded them at the period of the dissolution £14 9s. 2d. HEM, WYKE, and LEONARD'S LEE were also members of Idsall, the latter taking its name from Leonard, its early possessor, tenant of Dunstanvill. The tenement formerly named THE CASTLE, the situation of which is still indicated by the "castle farm," was not the residence of the lords of Idsall, being simply a minor member of their manor. WOODHOUSE, HAUGHTON, and KNOWLE, also were formerly members of Idsall. About 1185, Roger, Walter de Dunstanvill's vassal at Haughton, being dead, the baron, in a charter singularly illustrative of feudal tenures and customs, granted, according to the following terms, to "Oliver, his harper, custody of the land of the deceased, for his life, together with the widow of the said Roger, whom Oliver had already espoused, with Dunstanvill's consent. Also, Oliver was to have custody of the heir of Roger, and was to take order concerning the said heir according to his own will; and this wardship was to be free of *tac* and *tol* to Oliver and his men, and free of all services, except that Oliver was to mew one sparrow-hawk annually at his own cost, or to mew a goshawk at the cost of his lord; in which case, the lord's men were to provide a cage wherein the bird should be placed." "And, together with the aforesaid wardship, I have given and conceded to the aforesaid Oliver, for his homage and service, and as a forestalment of his release from office, that reputed virgate of land which Achi and Swein of Knoll, have held, and all the *assarts* which I have given him in Long Rudigg, up to Sumerlone, as Smelebroc divides them; and quittance of *tac* and of *tol* for him and his men; and of all services and customs; in fee and inheritance; with all the appurtenances; in wood and in field; to hold of me and my heirs, by him and his heirs; rendering therefore yearly, he or his heirs, to me or my heirs, on Easter-day, certain spurs or sixpence."[1] Thus did the lord of Idsall provide for his harper, who became not only

---

[1] A copy of this instructive Charter in the original Latin is given by EYTON. *Antiq. Shropshire*, vol. ii, p.281.

a husband and guardian, but also feoffee of the *vill* of Knowle, at the fiat of the Anglo-Norman seigneur. The situation of Knowle may be identified by a small coppice still called " The Knowle Wood."

DRAYTON, STANTON, and UPTON were also held under the lords of Idsall.

Yet, besides the tenants who held all these various members of the ancient Idsall, its seigneur had other tenants in his manor of equal standing, whose interests were associated with the town itself. Thus, John de Stevinton, hereditary "seneschal of the manor of Ideshal," attests a manorial deed in 1316; and Devereux, whose name is spelt with all those varieties to which Norman names were subject, occurs as a juror in Idsall somewhat later.

SHIFFNAL CHURCH.

This large structure has been erected at various dates. It consists of a *nave*, with aisles and a south porch, north and south transept, central tower having large stair-turret at north-west angle, and the Moreton chancel or south aisle.

Parts of the south transept, north wall of chancel, and also the chancel arch, in which latter the dog-tooth ornament appears, belong to the transitional period between the Norman and early English, say end of 12th century. The south porch is early English, latter half of 13th century; the nave, the central tower, and parts of the chancel, belong to the decorated style, commencement of 14th century; the north transept is entirely of perpendicular work, 15th century; whilst the south aisle appears to be the work of the 16th century.

Although *Domesday* does not mention the circumstance, a collegiate church doubtless existed at Itesale in Saxon times, which, re-established by Robert Fitz Tetbald, soon after the survey, was given by him to Shrewsbury Abbey. The Normans first restored the Saxon collegiate churches, and then disposed of them in such a way, as that they should eventually lose their collegiate character. Thus, whilst repeating his donations to Shrewsbury, the Norman lord of the manor directed, that, as fast as the clerks or canons of Iteshale should die off, this church should come into the demesne of St. Peter. The collegiate character of the church, therefore, became gradually extinct, and its revenues absorbed in the treasury of a distant monastery. Thus the spiritual interests of the rural districts of the extensive Saxon parish of Iteshale, as in those other cases where great Saxon churches had been assigned to monasteries of Norman foundation, were utterly neglected. But in 1219, the Abbot of Shrewsbury and Walter de Dunstanvill II. were at issue respecting this church, when the advowson of Idsall returned to the lord of the manor.

The church of Ydesale, in 1291, was valued at £20 *per annum*; besides a pension of 30s. which the Abbot of Salop received therefrom. In 1341, the parish was assessed only £12 9s. to the *ninth*, because the corn had been destroyed by storms, etc., and because Hatton Grange belonged to the Abbot of Buildwas.

The Valor of 1534 represents this vicarage as worth £16 5s. 10d., less 16s. 8d. for procurations, and 2s. 6d. for synodals. The abbot's pension of 30s. out of Idsall church is duly returned among his receipts for the same year.

Early Incumbent.—Walter de Dunstanvill, rector, 1188.

Kemberton is thus described in Domesday Book[1]:—"The same Robert [Fitz Tetbald] holds Chenbritone [of the earl.] Aluric, Elmer, Uluuin, and Edmer held it [in Saxon times] for iv manors, and were free. Here iii hides geldable. In demesne are ii ox-teams, and [there are] iv serfs and iii villains, and iii boors and i radman, with i team and a half between them all; and there might be viii more teams besides. The wood here will fatten xxx swine. In time of King Edward [the manor] was worth 28s. [per annum], now 15s."

Kenberton, Chenbritone originally perhaps had been the seat of some Saxon earldorman or thane, Cenbýŕhꞇ, or Kenbert, by name.

The Norman Robert Fitz Tetbald, the same who held Idsall, and the great Sussex fief called the Honour of Petworth, was also lord of Kemberton. The possessions of this "Rothbert Vicecomes" reverted, from some cause or other, as we said, to the crown; when the king re-granted them in such a way that his Shropshire manors, of which Kemberton was one, became associated with the earldom of Arundel and county of Sussex, rather than with the earldom of Shrewsbury and the county in which they lay.

KEMBERTON CHURCH.

The Taxation of Pope Nicholas, in 1291, valued the church of

---

[1] *Domesday*, fo. 256, b 2.

FINIAL AND DEVICE OVER THE WESTERN FACE OF
CHANCEL-ARCH, SHIFFNAL.

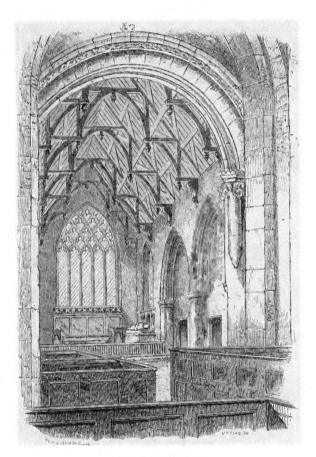

CHANCEL, SHIFFNAL.

Kemberton, in the deanery of Newport, at £2 13s. 4d. per annum. The Prior of Heringham (Sussex) also received a pension of £1 10s. therefrom. In 1341, the parish was assessed to the *ninth* of wheat, wool, and lamb £2 4s. In 1534, Kemberton Rectory was valued at £6 per annum, less 6s. 8d. for procurations, 1s. 11d. for synodals, and 5s. due to the vicar of Idsall.

Early Incumbent.—Gilbert, chaplain, 1230.

Cosford is thus spoken of in Domesday[1]:—"Radulfus [de Mortemer] holds Costeford [of the earl]. Turgot held it [in Saxon times], and was a free man. Here i hide geldable. The [arable] land is [sufficient for] iii ox-teams. In demesne is i [team]. In time of King Edward it was worth 40s. [per annum]; afterwards it was waste. Now it is worth 5s." This small outlying manor, from some cause or other, became early separated from the fief of the great Mortemer, and annexed to the neighbouring manor of Albrighton.

Higford (High-ford) evidently derives its name from the circumstance that it overhangs a fordable part of the adjacent river Worf. Spelt in *Domesday* Huchefor, this manor, described as being held by Roger de Laci under Earl Roger, is thus alluded to in King William's record[2]:—"The same Roger holds Huchefor. Goduin held it [in Saxon times] and was a free man. Here are iii hides geldable. Berner holds [the manor] of Roger [de Laci]. In demesne he has iii ox-teams and ix serfs, vii villains, vii boors, and ii radmans with v teams. Here a mill of 8s. [annual value]. The wood will fatten 100 swine. [Formerly] it was worth 40s. [per annum], now 60s."

Whatever Lacy retained of his *Domesday* tenure under the Norman earl, upon the forfeiture of the latter, became part of the greater barony which he held of the king. In 1175, however, Fitz Alan II. having married Hugh de Lacy's daughter, Lacy's seigneury over Higford, together with the lady, passed to Fitz Alan.

---

[1] *Domesday*, fo. 257, a 1.   [2] Ibidem, fo. 256, b 1.

With respect to Berner, the *Domesday* tenant of Higford, he appears to have been ancestor of that knightly race, who, deriving their name from this manor, held it under Fitz Alan.

Sir William de Hugford, one of Berner's descendants, fought for Henry III. in that civil war which beclouded the latter end of his reign. At the battle of Lewes, the king's power was shattered, himself and son being taken prisoners, when, masters of the realm, the rebellious barons compelled the king, their prisoner, to affix his seal to whatever documents they chose. Thus, on May 20, 1265, Henry III., then a captive at Hereford, was constrained by the rebels to mention Sir William de Hugford (his devoted adherent) as one of those lords marchers who were to leave the kingdom for *the peace thereof*, as it was ironically expressed. But the lords marchers of Shropshire held fast their loyal principles, until, soon afterwards, at Evesham, the king regained his prerogative.

It appears that Sir William held his manor of Hugford, including the *vills* of Norton, Apley, and Astall, under the suzerainty of Richard Fitz Alan, by the service of two knights for forty days, in war time, at his own charges. The latest notice of him is that of 1297, when he was summoned as holding lands of £20 annual value, to prepare himself with horses and arms for foreign service.[1]

Sir Walter de Hugford IV., his son and successor, sat as a knight of the shire in the Parliament which met at Westminster, on January 20, 1315; and also in the one summoned to meet at York, on May 2, 1322. He was succeeded by several generations in the male line, until, eventually, Alice de Hugford carried the estate into the family of Lucy of Charlcote.

Eudon George is the subject of the following entry in William the Conqueror's record:—" The same Radulf [de Mortemer] holds [under Earl Roger] Eldone. Edric held it [in Saxon times] and was a free man. Here ii hides geldable. In demesne are ii ox teams, and vi serfs and one villain, and ii boors with i team, and still there might be ii more teams [employed]. In time of King Edward, the manor was worth 25s. [annually], and afterwards it was waste. Now it is worth 15s."[2]

---

[1] *Parliamentary Writs*, vol. i. 291. [2] *Domesday*, fo. 257, a 1.

Edric, the forester, whom Ralph de Mortemer succeeded in this manor, was nephew of the infamous Mercian earl, Edric Streone. Florence of Worcester, under date 1006, says, "the crafty and treacherous Edric Streon, insidiously plotting against the noble Ealdorman Ælfhelm, prepared a great entertainment at Shrewsbury, to which he invited him. Ælfhelm, accepting the invitation, was welcomed by Edric Streon as his intimate friend; but, on the third or fourth day of the feast, he took him to hunt in a wood, where he had laid an ambuscade; and, when all were engaged in the chase, a ruffian of Shrewsbury, called Godwin Port-Hund, which signifies, the town's hound, who had been long before bribed by the profuse gifts and promises of Edric to commit the crime, suddenly sprung from his ambush, and basely assassinated the earldorman." A short time afterwards, his sons, Wulfheag and Ufgeat, were, by King Ethelred's orders, deprived of sight at Corfham. In the following year, continues this accurate chronicler, "the king made the before-mentioned Edric, son of Ethelric, ealdorman of Mercia. He was a man, indeed, of low origin, but his smooth tongue gained him wealth and high rank; and, gifted with a subtle genius and persuasive eloquence, he surpassed all his contemporaries in malice and perfidy, as well as in pride and cruelty": assertions amply borne out by the contemporary writer in the Anglo-Saxon Chronicle.

It would be difficult to point out a baser or more contemptible villain than this renegade Saxon, or one who has obtained a more unenviable notoriety in the chronicles of his country. To his traitorous counsel and action, it had been mainly owing that the English finally succumbed to the Dane.

Amid the horrors of that strife which raged between the Saxons and the Danes, Ethelred the Unready departed this life, A.D. 1016. "The Etheling," a resolute man of extraordinary strength, natural son of Ethelred, was then chosen king by the Anglo-Saxons. He raised the fortunes of the English, and took London from King Knut. But Edmund "Ironside's" glorious reign was but of a brief year's duration. Harassed by a sanguinary conflict with the Dane, this brave Saxon monarch had but barely terminated a hopeless struggle, by consenting to divide England with the invader, when he was murdered by emissaries of his kinsman, the execrable Duke Edric.

Satisfactory it is to know that this traitor to his country ultimately met his deserts. Knut the Great, or Canute, as he is generally but incorrectly named, had been crowned king of all England, when, one day, Edric and the Conqueror had words. King Knut despised the man, and knowing how unpopular he was, only waited for a pretext to rid his presence of him. The quarrel went on. Edric, presuming on the credit of his perfidious service to the Dane, had got the length of reproaching the king by saying, "I first deserted Edmund for your sake, and afterwards even despatched him, in consequence of my engagements to you," when, all of a sudden, King Knut's countenance changing, "thou shalt die," said he, to Edric, "and justly, since thou art guilty of treason both to God and me, by having killed thy own sovereign and my sworn brother: thy blood be upon thy head." And Knut ordered the traitor to be strangled then and there, in the chamber where he sat, and his body thrown out of the window into the Thames.[1] Such was the end of the wretch. When we read of the Anglo-Saxon army and navy being entrusted to such as this low-born scoundrel, whose mere gift of gab enabled Edric Streone to obtain the greatest influence in the councils of the nation, and even the hand of the daughter of King Ethelred, is it any wonder that England became the spoil of the Dane?

To return to the more immediate subject of our enquiry. Perhaps it was owing to his uncle Edric Streone having had the earldom of Mercia, that Edric the Forester came to possess considerable estates in that province. This powerful western Saxon thane long disdained to submit to the Conqueror. Richard Fitz Scrobi and the Norman garrison of Hereford, had orders to invade his lands, but as often as they made an inroad on his territories they lost mail-clad knights and squires. Confederating with Blethyn and Rhywallon, the princes of North Wales and Powis, Edric then retaliated on the Normans by devastating Hereford, as far as the bridge of Lugg, carrying off great booty.

At length, in 1070, even the resolute Forester made his peace with the Conqueror, whom, in 1072, he accompanied into Scotland, in that expedition in which Malcolm, king of Scots, is said to have done homage to William. It will be seen, therefore, that Edric "Sylvaticus" neither shared in the rebellion or forfeiture of Edwin and Morcar, the brother Earls of Mercia. Disunion among their chiefs then, as it had ever been, was the bane of the Anglo-Saxons. Disorganised and in confusion, Anglo-Saxon England

---

[1] WILLIAM OF MALMESBURY.

had neither the head nor the heart to cope with her subtle conquerors. Yet Edric soon forsook his allegiance to "the Bastard." Ralph de Mortimer was deputed by William to reduce him, and succeeded in doing so; when, if reliance can be placed on a monastic annalist,[1] the Forester expiated his *treason*, as the Normans called it, in a dungeon. As a reward for the services he had rendered his sovereign, King William then bestowed upon Mortimer many forfeited estates of the unfortunate Saxon, of which Eudon, the manor in question, was among the number.

In the time of King Stephen or Henry II., Eudon was held under Mortimer of Wigmore by William le Salvage, a name singularly coincident with that of the Saxon proprietor, yet it does not appear that they were in any way related. Le Savage holding also Neen and Walton under the same baron, thus these acquired the names Eudon Savage, Neen Savage, and Walton Savage.

Chelmarsh derives its name from the Saxon words Céle meɲrc, signifying chill, or chilly marsh. The Conqueror's survey thus alludes to this place:—"The same Radulf [de Mortemer] holds Celmeres. Earl Eduin held it [formerly]. Here v hides geldable. In demesne are iii ox-teams, and vi serfs, and xiii villains and viii boors, with vi teams. In time of King Edward it was worth £6 [per annum], and afterwards was waste. Now [it is worth] 40s."[2]

We learn from a monastic chronicle[3] that William de Mortimer, a younger son of the *Domesday* baron, became feoffee of Chelmarsh by gift of his elder brother Hugh. Afterwards, this powerful baron re-assumed his manor, when, having founded Wigmore Abbey, among other gifts he granted to it the advowson of Chelmarsh. Hugh, second Baron of Wigmore, dying in 1185, left four sons; Roger, the eldest of whom, succeeded him in the barony, whilst Hugh de Mortimer, one of the others, became lord of Chelmarsh and Sidbury. Hugh was killed in a tournament at Worcester, when his widow surrendered Chelmarsh to the lord of the fee, who then enfeoffed his own son Hugh in this manor. Upon his father's decease, becoming fourth Baron Mortimer of Wigmore, Hugh transferred Chelmarsh to his brother Ralph, who

---

[1] *Monasticon*, vi. p.349, No. iii.   [2] *Domesday*, fo. 257, a 1.
[3] *Monasticon*, vi. 349, No. iii.

eventually became fifth Baron Wigmore. Ralph married Gladuse, daughter of Llewellyn, Prince of Wales, and by her had several sons; Roger, the eldest of whom, succeeded him in the barony: Chelmarsh, as usual, going to a younger son. But Hugh de Mortimer, who now became lord of this manor, transmitted it to his descendants; hence these acquired the distinctive appellation of the line of Mortimer of Chelmarsh.

The male line of Mortimer of Chelmarsh expired when Hugh de Mortimer fell at the battle of Shrewsbury in 1403.

CHELMARSH CHURCH.

The advowson of Chelmarsh, granted, as we said, by Lord Hugh de Mortimer to Wigmore Abbey in 1179, was valued in the Taxation of Pope Nicholas at £10, the vicar's portion therein being less than £4. In 1341, the parish was rated to the *ninth* £5 10s., there being no sheep or lambs therein; 14 virgates lay untilled, the tenants having left, etc. Hugh de Mortimer of Chelmarsh endowed a chantry dedicated to St. James in this church in 1345, wherein service was to be performed daily for the soul of the said Hugh.

PISCINA, CHELMARSH.

The annual value of the preferment in 1534 was £6 13s. 4d., less 6s. 8d. for procurations, and 1s. for synodals.

Early Incumbents.—Nicholas, vicar of Chaumers. Sir William, perpetual vicar of Chelmarsh, 1320.

Sidbury.

"The same Ralph de Mortimer," says *Domesday*, "holds Sudberie. Wiga held it [in Saxon times] and was a freeman. Here i hide geldable. In demesne are ii ox-teams, and vi serfs, vi villains, and iii boors with ii teams: and ii other teams might be here. In time of King Edward, the manor was worth 20s. [*per annum*], and afterwards it was waste. Now it is worth 18s." [1]

Concerning the early Norman feoffee of "Sudberie," namely, South Borough, little is known. By 1240, this manor had become associated with Neenton; and, some fifteen years afterwards, Ralph d'Arraz was lord of both, holding Sidbury immediately of Roger de Mortimer, for service of one knight pertaining to Wigmore.

SIDBURY CHURCH.

The church of "Sudbury," in Stottesden deanery, in 1291 was valued at £5 6s. 8d. In 1341, the parish was assessed only 21s. to the *ninth*, because there were no sheep or lambs therein; four carucates lay untilled; 13 tenants had quitted on account of poverty, etc. The Valor of 1534 gives £4 17s. as the annual value of this rectory, less 6s. 8d. for procurations, and 1s. for synodals.

Early Incumbent.—Ralph de Elmebrug, 1291.

Neenton. In Saxon times, this place was probably called Neoþene-tun, Neowend-tun, New-Town.

We read in Domesday Book:[1]—" The same Ralph holds Newentone, and Roger [holds it] of him. Azor held it [in Saxon times] and was a free man. Here is half a hide. In demesne are ii ox-teams, and ii serfs, ii villains, and ii boors with i team, and yet there might be ii more teams here. In the time of King Edward and now, the [annual] value [of the manor] was and is 17s."

Azor, the Saxon owner of Newentone, was lord also of Burwarton. Of Roger, the Norman mesne-tenant little is known. It was him, perhaps, or his successor, who, as lord of Neuton, about 1138, granted two-thirds of his tithes to Shrewsbury Abbey. About 1240, Sir Ralph d'Arraz held two knight's fees in Sodburi and Neenton, under Mortimer of Wigmore, and he transmitted the tenure to his descendants.

---

[1] *Domesday*, fo. 257, a 1.

Neenton Church.

The church of Neuton, in Stottesden deanery, was valued in 1291 at £5 6s. 8d., exclusive of the Abbot of Shrewsbury's portion of 16s. therein. In 1341, the parish was taxed only 31s. to the *ninth*, because there were no sheep or lambs in it; a carucate lay untilled, the tenants having quitted from poverty, etc. In 1534, the rectory of Nyenton was valued at £5 10s. 8d., less 6s. 8d. for procurations, and 6d. for synodals.

Early Incumbent.—William, parson of this church, 1246.

Burwarton was a Roman fortified town or village. According to *Domesday* :—" The same Ralph holds Burertone, and Helgot [holds] of him. Azor held it [in Saxon times]. Here half a hide geldable. The land is [enough for] iii ox-teams. Here ii villains have i team. It was waste [when it came into Mortemer's hands]. Now it is worth 2s." [per annum].[1]

Over Burwarton the seigneury of Mortimer of Wigmore continued for three hundred years.

The Church.

In 1291 the church of Borewarton, in the deanery of Stottesden, was valued at £3 6s. 8d. *per annum*. In 1341, the parish was assessed 12s. to the *ninth*. The Valor of 1534-5 gives this preferment as worth £4 15s. 8d. *per annum*, less 6d. for synodals.

Early Incumbent.—Alan, rector of Burwarton, 1250.

Cleobury North is thus noticed in the Conqueror's survey :—"Roger de Laci holds of the king Cleberie. Uluuard [holds it] of him. Seuuard held it [in Saxon times] and was a free man. Here ii½ hides geldable. The [arable] land is for 4 ox-teams. In demesne is one [team], and there are i serf and iv villains, and iv boors with iii teams. Here is a mill of 4s. [annual value]. In time of King Edward the manor was worth 12s., and afterwards 7s. Now it is worth 20s."[2] A note at the foot of the page, written in paler ink than the body of the record, adds :— "The same Roger holds Dodentone, and it pertains to Claiberie.

---

[1] *Domesday*, fo. 257, a 1.   [2] Ibidem, fo. 260, b 1.

CHANCEL, BURWARTON.

FONT, CLEOBURY NORTH.

Here is i hide, and it is valued there," namely, under Cleobury. The latter entry probably refers to an adjacent portion of Dodentone or Ditton, now Prior's Ditton.

Clæia in Saxon, signifies "Clayey," hence Clee Hill; and Clæia-Buṛh, or Clayey-town, Cleobury, which is now named Cleobury North, to distinguish it from Cleobury Mortimer.

In the days of the Anglo-Saxon King Edward the Confessor, Cleobury North, then known as Ufere-Cleobyrig, namely Over or Upper Cleobury, belonged to the church of Worcester; which lost the *vill* under the following circumstances. Sweyn, the eldest son of the great Earl Godwin, ruling over Oxford, Gloucester, and Hereford, in 1046 led the English a successful expedition into Wales. "As he was on his way homewards," says the Anglo-Saxon Chronicle, "then commanded he to be brought unto him the Abbess of Leominster; and he had her as long as he listed; and after that he let her go home." The monk of Worcester, whose testimony is not to be doubted in a matter upon which he must have had the best opportunities of being correctly informed, says, that Earl Sweyn left England and went to Denmark, "because he was not permitted to marry Edgiva, Abbess of the Monastery of Leominster, whom he had debauched."[1] We learn from another authority,[2] that Sweyn was compelled to put away the abbess by the threats of Eadsige, Archbishop of Canterbury, and Lyfing, Bishop of Worcester; and that, in revenge, the son of Godwin procured that the church of Worcester should be deprived of Ufere Cleobrig and many other Shropshire lands.

To sum this story, and Sweyn's sad history up in a few words. He, the passionate representative of the noblest Anglo-Saxon house, violated Algiva, Abbess of Leominster, with whom he had fallen in love; when, enraged that the laws of holy mother church forbade him to retain her as his wife, all his mother's Danish heathen blood fired up in him, and Sweyn betook himself to the piratical ways of his viking ancestors. His cousin Bruno or Beorn, also, upon some pretence having forced on ship-board, Sweyn murdered with his axe. Thus did this earl tarnish the lustre of Godwin's house. To satisfy justice for these crimes, and appease, as he vainly thought, his conscience, the outlawed Sweyn condemned himself to make a pilgrimage to Jerusalem bare-footed.

---

[1] FLORENCE OF WORCESTER, p. 148. Bohn's Ed.
[2] HEMING's *Chartulary*, p. 275. *Monasticon* I, p. 597.

Succeeding in accomplishing this painful self-inflicted penance, on his return homewards the outcast wanderer fell a victim, either to exhaustion or the treachery of the Mahommedans.

Later in the Confessor's reign, Cleobury North was held by Seuuard or Siward, mentioned in *Domesday.*

Probably an Anglo-Dane, Seuuard no longer continued " a free man," after the Conquest, but gave place to the Norman Roger de Laci, who, in 1085, held this manor *in capite* of the king. But very shortly afterwards it passed from the fief of Lacy to that of Bernard de Newmarch, the conqueror of Brecknockshire, and from him to De Bohun, Earl of Hereford.

Respecting the Saxon tenant, Uluuard, who held Cleberie under De Laci at the time of *Domesday,* as had been the case with his fair-haired countrymen in general, he was speedily relieved of his holding. The Norman Walter de Cropus then held this manor until 1130; and he appears to have been ancestor of that family of Le Wafre who continued to hold Cleobury North, Hopton Wafre, and other lands of the Honour of Brecknock, until Lucia le Wafre carried them to her husband Roger de Mortimer of Chirk.

THE CHURCH.

As a monument of his conquest of Brecknockshire, Bernard de Newmarch, with consent of King Henry I., founded Brecknock Priory, to which this Norman scourge of the Cymrians gave " the church of Cliberia, and whatever belongeth thereto."[1]

In 1291, the church of Cleobury North, in Stottesden deanery, was worth £8 13s. 4d. *per annum.* In 1341, the parish was assessed at only £2 6s. 8d., because two virgates lay untilled, the tenants having been forced to quit from poverty; there were no sheep in it, etc. The church of Clybery North, in 1534, was valued at £5 19s. 4d. *per annum,* less 6s. 8d. for procurations, and 6d. for synodals.

Early Incumbent.—Roger de Haluton, 1294.

By referring to the Table, the reader will see that we have done with those detached manors of the *Domesday* Hundred of Bascherch, which, lying confusedly intermixed with the manors of Alnodestreu Hundred, are now included in the modern hundreds

---

[1] *Monasticon,* III, 264, No. 2.

of Brimstree and Stottesden. We now commence to describe those manors which, lying eastward of the Severn, at the time of the Conqueror's survey, were reckoned to belong to Staffordshire.

Of these, at the head of the Staffordshire lands of Earl Roger,

Claverley is thus noticed in Domesday Book:—"Earl Roger holds Claverlege. Here are xx hides. Earl Algar[1] held it. The land is [capable of employing] xxxii ox-teams. In demesne are v teams, and [there are] xxxii villains and xiii boors having xxiii teams. Here is a mill of 5s. [annual value], and 12 acres of meadow. The wood is two leagues long and a half league wide. In time of King Edward [the manor] was worth £7 10s. [annually]; now £10."[2]

The etymology of Claverley being found in the Saxon Clæꝼeꞃ, Clover; the very word implies fertility. Claverley, Worfield, Nordley, and Alveley, consisting of 23,000 modern acres, including the forest of Morf, in the days of Edward the Confessor, formed one continuous and magnificent estate, whose western boundary was the broad and navigable Severn. It belonged to the Mercian Earl Algar, from whose Saxon children it was reft by the Conqueror, and given to the first Norman Earl of Shrewsbury. And the Norman earl gave Claverley church, doubtless his own erection, with its tithes, to Quatford collegiate church; for the iron-clad seigneurs, who fleshed their long swords upon the field of Senlac, were devout.

The ungrateful son of the Norman earl, however, rebelled against the successor of that suzerain whose hand had enriched his father, when King Henry I. expelled the fierce De Belésme from his earldom, and his vast estates became forfeit to the Crown. Then it was, that Beauclerk retained Claverley in demesne, not granting it to any subject; and thus, as forming part of the king's personal estates, it came into the hands of his grandson Henry II.

The sheriff of Shropshire, as Fermor of the county, accounted at

---

[1] Earl Algar died in 1059, when his sons Edwin and Morcar succeeded to his Mercian earldom. As William the Conqueror's Commissioners for Staffordshire in their notes mainly allude to the period when Algar was Earl of Mercia, whilst the Domesday Commissioners for Shropshire refer to the time when his sons, Edwin and Morcar, had succeeded him; it is clear, that different eras of King Edward's reign are alluded to. It would seem that the Conqueror's Commissioners, when they compiled Domesday Book, consulted an anterior record or records, as well as admitted oral testimony.

[2] *Domesday*, fo. 248, a 1.

the Exchequer for the rents of those particular manors described as "ancient demesne of the Crown," of which Claverley may be regarded as a type. The fiscal or reputed ferm of the county of Salop stood, in the ninth year of Henry II., at the sum of £265 15s.; which ferm remained technically unaltered for more than a hundred years afterwards. This £265 15s. then, was summarily, the rent or income of the king's demesnes or other prerogatives in the county, which the sheriff received. He received a good deal more, but for this amount he was obliged to account to the king. Of the £265 15s. assessed on Shropshire, £15 was about the ferm of the king's manor of Claverley.

Very interesting and instructive is it to observe the effect which the commotions of those unsettled times had upon the king's returns. We learn from the Pipe Roll that William Fitz-Alan, sheriff of Shropshire, expended in 1156, the year succeeding the demise of the Usurper, no less than £145 8s. 8d.—an enormous sum in those days—in re-stocking the king's manors throughout the county. He also charges £17 6s. 4d. for waste of the county. The disorder consequent on Richard Cœur de Leon's continued absence from his dominions, also, appears to have told upon the king's demesnes in Shropshire; for, in the earlier years of his successor, not only was it found that the late king had been grossly cheated by his sheriffs, but that the royal manors were otherwise seriously affected. As an example, take the Shropshire manor of Worfield, which, like Claverley, was also a royal manor. The Pipe Roll of 1202 represents this manor as deficient in 6 oxteams, 600 sheep, 32 bee-stalls, 30 sows, and 24 cows, involving an annual loss of £6, £6, 32s., 30s., and 24s. on each item. The king's manor consequently had to be re-stocked, and the Pipe Roll which embraces the years 1208 and 1209, states that, 8 oxen necessary to make up 6 teams at Worfield had cost 4 merks, or 6s. 8d. a head; 180 sheep necessary to make up 600 in the same manor, had cost £9, or 1s. each; and similar expense was King John put to in Claverley, and throughout all his other Shropshire manors.

Again, young Henry III. experienced the consequences of the barons' coalition against his father. In 1220 (4th Hen. III.) the sheriff of Shropshire claimed an allowance of £135 17s. from the Crown, in respect of a loss of £45 5s. 8d. *per annum*, which, as fermor of the county, he had incurred during the three past years of his shrievalty: he also claimed at the same rate for three succeeding years—significant witness of the extensive waste that had befallen the royal demesnes of Shropshire during the national disturbances in the time of King John.

Like other demesnes of the Crown, Claverley enjoyed peculiar privileges. Its tenants were free from toll and other duties throughout the realm. At home they constituted a manorial court, adequate both in matters civil and criminal for almost all purposes of self-government. In short, Claverley was *extra-Hundredal*, being a hundred as it were in itself; owing no suit to, nor having any concern in other hundredal courts; yet, like the latter, it was controlled by the county court, and responsible to the king's justiciars in those criminal matters which came under the head of "Pleas of the Crown." Whenever the king's justices visited Shropshire, the manors of ancient demesne were obliged to appear before them by their representatives or juries, who reported every graver offence which had been committed within their respective liberties since the last *Iter* of the justices, and how the same had been dealt with by the county court.

Royal demesnes were assessable to tallages.

The sheriff of the county continued to be the fermor of Claverley, from the accession of Henry II. to the death of Henry III. Various other parties, however, participated in the revenues of this manor. In 1155, King Henry II. made a grant in fee to Robert de Girros, of Broughton a portion thereof, fiscally reputed to be worth 35s. annually, for which the sheriff claimed his exemption on the Pipe Roll, thus—"*In terris datis. Et Roberto de Girros xxxv/ in Claverlai.*" Again, upon the marriage of Lewellyn with the daughter of King John, lands in this manor were assigned to Madoc, son of Griffin; hence, the sheriff of Shropshire, in his account of the ferm of the county at Michaelmas, 1207, discharges himself of a sum equivalent to £5 1s. *per annum* to "Madoc, son of Griffin, in Claverlei." But, in 1229, Henry III. granted this manor in fee-farm to John Fitz Philip, to hold for life, at an annual rental of £15 payable at the Exchequer, the king reserving to himself all *Tallages* and *aids* arising from it. In 1292, the Claverley jurors reported Roger Careless and Nicholas de Warrewyk, as joint fermors of this manor, paying to the king a rent of £16. About 1311, Ingelard de Warle held it, but at his decease the king reseized Claverley.

The manor of Claverley comprehended numerous townships, namely, Broughton, Beobridge, Gatacre, Sutton, Aston, Farmcott,

Heathton, Hopstone, Woundale, Dallicot, and Ludstone, besides the hamlets of Draycott, Gravenor, Bulwardine, and Wystanesmere; all of which, as appears from various tenure rolls, were held of the Crown by tenants, ecclesiastical or secular. Lee Farm adjacent to Hopstone, was also a member of this manor.

The family of Brooke had its origin in Claverley, where its elder branch continued to be resident for many centuries.

CLAVERLEY CHURCH.

A prominent feature among the various endowments of the deanery of Bridgenorth, the succession of its rectors is involved with the list of dignitaries of that establishment.

Worfield. The particulars of this extensive manor are given in the Staffordshire *Domesday*, under the title of "Terra Hugonis de Montgumeri"; thus :—"Hugh de Montgumeri holds of the king Wrfeld. Earl Algar held it [in Saxon times]. Here xxx hides. The [arable] land is [enough] for xxx ox-teams. In demesne are iv [such teams]; and v serfs, and lxvii villains, with a priest and x boors have xxv teams. Here iii mills of 40s. [value per annum] and a fishery of 15s. [annual value], and xvi acres of meadow. The wood is 3 leagues long and 1 league wide. Here iii English have v teams with xviii villains and v boors. [In time of King Edward the manor] was worth £3 [per annum]; now £18. Of this land iii hides are waste."[1]

It appears that Hugh de Montgomery, son of the Norman earl, held this manor of the king, independently of his father. When, however, Hugh succeeded to the earldom of Shrewsbury, his seigneury over Worfield became massed with his other palatine honours, and thus descending to his brother, Earl Robert de Belésme, upon his forfeiture the whole came into the hands of Henry I.

Accounted *ancient demesne* of the Crown, King Henry II., and also Richard I., held Worfield strictly in demesne; that is, these Kings kept the manor in their own hands. Its fiscal value was £32 0s. 5½d.; or, nearly an eighth of the Sheriff's reputed ferm of Shropshire.

In the time of King John, however, Wrenock Fitz Meuric,

---

[1] *Domesday*, fo. 248, b. 1.

FONT, CLAVERLEY.

WORFIELD CHURCH.

Latimerius, or Interpreter between England and Wales, acquired an interest in Worfield by grant of that king. He lost it, when, in 1238, Henry III. assigned this manor to Ada, youngest sister and co-heir of John Scott, Earl of Huntingdon and Chester, and to her husband, Henry de Hastings, in partial satisfaction of their claims on the Honour of Chester: accordingly, this royal manor passed to subjects, who transmitted it to their descendants.

Worfield Church.

From the mention of a priest, it is clear that a church existed here at *Domesday*. It was probably founded by the great Mercian Earl Leofric. Pope Nicholas's taxation values this church at £33 6s. 8d. The advowson of Worfield remained in the Crown until, in 1318, King Edward II. gave it to Walter de Langton, Bishop of Lichfield, who appropriated it to his own cathedral. In 1341, Worfield Parish was assessed at only £13 6s. 8d.; because the growing corn was destroyed by storms; there were fewer sheep in the parish than formerly; tenants had quitted, through poverty, and their lands lay untilled; and because the small tithes, etc., were not reckoned to the *ninth*. The *Valor* of 1534-5 represents the receipts of Dean and Chapter of Lichfield, as parsons of this church, to amount to £51 *per ann*. The benefice was valued at £16 16s. 10d., less 2s. *per ann*. for synodals.

Early Incumbents.—Henry, Archdeacon of Stafford, presented to this church by King John, in 1205. Being made Archbishop of Dublin, in 1213, he vacated this preferment; when, in 1215,

Walter, son of William de Cantelupe, an adherent of John's, was presented to the rectory, by the same monarch. On August 30, 1236, Walter was elected Bishop of Worcester, yet he was not consecrated until May 3, 1237; having only been ordained deacon on April 4, 1237, and priest fourteen days afterwards.

William de Kilkenny, presented by King Henry III. Concerning this eminent personage, Matthew of Westminster, under date 1254, observes: "Master William of Kilkenny filled the office of Chancellor with great modesty and virtue;—not long afterwards the same Master William was elected Bishop of Ely."

Henry de Wengham was William de Kilkenny's successor at Worfield; and also succeeded him as Lord Chancellor of England. In 1259, says the chronicler just quoted, "the Lord Henry de Wengham, the Chancellor of the Lord the King, was by the unanimous consent of them all (namely the Canons of St. Paul's) elected Bishop of London; a thorough courtier, but what is better still, a man of morality and discretion, prudence and circumspection."

The last rector of Worfield was Sir William de Kyrkeby, 1325—1345.

Thomas Kirkby appears as the first vicar, between 1345 and 1369, the appropriation of this church having been effected in the interval.

Formerly there was a chantry, dedicated to the Virgin Mary, in Worfield Church.

Alveley, under Staffordshire in *Domesday*, is thus noticed:— "The same earl [Roger de Montgomery] holds Alvidelege. Earl Algar held it [in Saxon times]. Here i hide. The [arable] land is [enough] for ix ox-teams. In demesne are ii [such teams]; and [there are] viii villains with a priest, and iiii boors, with vi teams. Here vi acres of meadow, and a wood two leagues long and half a league wide. In time of King Edward [the manor] was worth £6 [per annum]. Now it is worth 100s."[1]

Reputed to be a manor of ancient demesne, Alveley came intact into the hands of Henry II., by precisely the same process as Claverley and Worfield, when Henry Plantagenet, soon after his accession, granted it to Guy le Strange. Who then was Le Strange, to whom, so shortly after regaining his grandfather's throne, young Henry gave this fine manor? Had this feoffee rendered some important service to royalty during its late fearful struggle against the Usurper?

The only account we have of the origin of the family of Le Strange we owe to tradition. The Fitz-Warine Chronicle relates, how William Peverel had two beautiful nieces, of whom the one, named Melette, had resolved never to marry, excepting to a knight of great prowess. To give the lady a choice, her uncle caused to be proclaimed through many lands a tournament, to be held at his castle in the Peak; at which, whoever should display the greatest dexterity, was to have his niece, with the castle of Whittington. Among the crowd of nobles and distinguished knights, who hastened to that brilliant passage of arms,

---

[1] *Domesday*, fo. 248, a. 1.

were ten sons of the Duke of Britany, the younger of whom, being named Guy, was called Guy l'Estrange, and from him the several families of the Stranges did descend.

Does the reader curiously enquire, was it he who won the lady? Guy did not win her. To that gay gathering,

> "Where throngs of knights and barons bold,
> In weeds of peace, high triumphs hold,"

speeded also Guarin de Metz, with a silver shield and peacock for crest. This knight tilted first against a son of the king of Scots, and then with a baron from Burgundy; and, as he vanquished them both, he claimed and obtained as his prize, the willing and beautiful Melette. Seated, therefore, at Whittington, between Guarin and the Prince of Wales fierce animosities reigned.

To descend from romance to sober truth. Rodland Extraneous, namely, Roland le Estrange, appears as first lay witness to a deed, which, passing in the reign of Henry I., secured to the Norfolk Priory of Castle-Acre an extensive donation. It is conjectured, that Guy, from whom, according to the legend, "came all the great lords of England, who have the surname of Estrange," was a son of this Roland; and it is probable that the Guy le Strange, to whom Henry II. granted Alveley, acquired the manor by way of recompense for services which either he or his family had rendered to the cause of legitimacy. Guy le Strange, Lord of Alveley, not only succeeded William Fitz-Alan, as sheriff of Shropshire, but had custody of his barony during the long minority of his son. In 1170, Guy a second time became sheriff of Shropshire, and in that capacity he rendered good service to Henry II., when his sons rebelled against him. One of those who attended the great court and council, which King Henry II., in January, 1177, held at Northampton, Guy appears at Michaelmas, 1179, to have rendered his last account as sheriff of Shropshire, when Alveley became in *manu Regis*, until livery should be given to the heir. That heir, Ralph le Strange, a minor at the time of his father's decease, obtained livery in 1182, when the sheriff, by special order of the king, made over to him two years' revenue of Alveley.

Mary le Strange, widow of Guy, and mother of Ralph, descended from knights and barons, appears as a widow in the King's gift, in 1186. She was forty years old, therefore, she could not have been more than sixteen years old when Ralph was born; and, as Guy le Strange was her third husband, she must have been married when very young. She had her dower in various counties.

Ralph le Strange, castellan at Carrechova, guarding the silver mines there that belonged to the Crown, died on that service, in the prime of his life. It was this man who founded the Hospital of the Holy Trinity, at Bridgnorth, endowing it with lands in Alveley. Like his father, he also was a liberal benefactor to Haughmond Abbey.

Ralph's heirs were his three sisters:—Margaret, wife of Thomas Noel; Joan, wife of Richard de Wapenburi; and Matilda, wife of Griffin de Sutton; which husbands, in the year 1196, conjointly fined 200 merks with the king, "for having all the land which was before Ralph le Strange's, together with the fortress which is called Cnukin."

PILLAR AND CAPITAL, ALVELEY.

Thomas Noel, who married le Strange's eldest sister, appears to have been a man of high influence and trust. Sheriff of Staffordshire, Thomas, with his associates, acted as Justices in Eyre for that county, in 1187. He figures also in various other capacities and public employments. In 1199, he proffered the large sum of 200 merks, that he might "freely and without hindrance marry his daughters, Johanna and Alice, to whom he would." This offer was not accepted by King John, however. Eighteen months afterwards, Thomas Noel fined at the rate of 300 merks and three palfreys with the Crown, for license to marry his youngest daughter to Thomas Fitz-Eustace Stephen;

CAPITAL, ALVELEY.

which fine being accepted, in addition, Noel promised to give the king "a better Goshawk than Geoffrey Fitz-Piers had."

Thomas Noel's daughters survived him, the former of whom, Alice, married William de Harcourt; the latter, Thomas Fitz-Eustace. De Harcourt's descendants long continued to be connected with Alveley. Fitz-Eustace's son Ralph, who adopted his mother's maiden name of Noel, in 1255, sold his quarter of a hide in Alveley to William de Hampton; the same, or one of that family, of whose former interest in this neighbourhood, Hempton, or Hampton's Load, originally a ford over the Severn, is a reminiscence.

To return to Joan, second sister and co-heir of Ralph le Strange, wife of Richard de Wapenburi. It does not appear that any portion of Alveley descended to his heir.

As for Matilda, the third sister and co-heir of Ralph le Strange, surviving Griffin, her husband, she manifested a partiality for Haughmond Abbey, by granting it lands, with mill, and a third of her fishery. Madoc de Sutton, her son, succeeding her, gave his share of Alveley, with Isabel, his daughter, in *frank* marriage to Henry de Morf. Accordingly, in 1284, Henry de Morf was said to hold one-sixth of a knight's fee in Alveley, of the heirs of Madoc de Sutton, who held the same of the King, *in capite*.

The most important under-tenant here, appears to have been Simon de Alvitheleg.

Included in the deanery of Stottesden, the parish of Alveley, in 1341, was assessed at £7 13s. to the *ninth*. The church has been alluded to before.

Nordley-Regis, so called, perhaps, with reference to Alveley, to the north of which it lies, *Domesday* mentions as follows:—
"The same earl [Roger de Montgomery] holds Nordlege. Earl Algar held it. Here ii hides. The land is for xii ox-teams. In demesne are iii teams; and vii villains and ii boors have v teams. Here is a mill of 2s. [annual value]; a wood $1\frac{1}{2}$ leagues long, by $\frac{1}{2}$ a league wide. In time of King Edward [the manor] was worth £8 [per annum], now £4." [1]

---

[1] *Domesday*, fo. 248, a. 1.

Like the three last manors we have described, Nordley was held by the Norman earls *in demesne*, and in that condition, along with them, it came into the hands of Henry I. This monarch granted a hide here in fee-farm to a tenant of the name of Fitz-Ulky or Fulky, who was to pay for the same £8 10s. annually, at the exchequer; and Fitz-Ulky's descendants, deriving a name from the vill of Astley, anciently a member of Nordley, continued for many succeeding generations to hold this land *in capite*, of the king.

Astley, although originally a member of Nordley, and held by the same tenants *in capite*, was a tenure, not in fee-farm, but by serjeantry. The serjeantry by which it was held frequently changed. Thus we read, that, in 1211, "John, son of Robert de Estleg, holds Estleg from ancient time, from the conquest; and he owes of his service, one serving horseman, with a hauberk, to accompany the lord the king, when he goes on any military expedition into Wales. The costs of the said horseman were to be paid by the king."[1] Again, in 1221, the Stottesden Jurors represented the son of the foregoing as holding this *vill* "by serjeantry of the lord king, and by service that he shall be *custos* of the king's pavilion, when the king goes into Wales."[2]

Nordley, Astley, and Alvelcy possessed a manorial court in common, which had the jurisdiction usual to manors of ancient demesne.

Bobbington is thus noticed in the Conqueror's Record:—
"The same Robert [de Stafford] holds in Bubintone v hides, and Helgot [holds] of him. Wifare held [them in Saxon times], with *sac* and *soc*. The land is [sufficient] for vi ox-teams. In demesne are ii teams, and there are iv serfs, v villains, and iii boors, with i team; there is a wood which can be depastured,[3] one league long and half a league wide. The [annual] value is 40s."[4] At the period of the survey, this manor formed part of the Staffordshire Hundred of Saisdone, where the greater part of it still remains.

Whittimere, that member of Bobbington which lies in Shropshire, had for tenants a family who, deriving their name from this

---

[1] Testa de Nevill, pp. 55, 417.
[2] Assizes, 6 Henry III., m. 9.
[3] 'SILVA PASTILIS.'
[4] *Domesday*, fo. 249, a 2.

vill, became ancestors of the families of Whitmore of Apley, and of Dudmaston, county Salop; and the Whitmores of London.

Quat, as forming part of Earl Roger's lands in Stanlci Hundred, Warwickshire, is thus described in Domesday Book:—"Outi holds of the Earl iii hides in Quatone. There is land [enough] for xii ox-teams. In demesne are iiii [such teams], and v serfs, xix villains, and xiiii boors, with x teams. Here is i acre of meadow, a wood two leagues long and one wide, and a mill of 2s. [annual value]. [In King Edward's time the manor] was worth £6; now 100s. The same Outi held it freely [in Saxon times]."[1]

It will be noticed how this redundantly-stocked manor, in the same Saxon hands both before and after the Conquest, became deteriorated in value after it was held under the Norman seigneur. Nothing further is known of Outi—the once free Saxon owner, but, after the Conquest, subservient holder of this manor, under the Norman Earl—than is related in the above extract. As neither he or any of his kin are heard of afterwards, it would seem that, like the rest of his race, he was eventually dispossessed.

Upon the forfeiture of de Belésme, Quat came into the hands of Henry I., who, dividing it into three parts, as is supposed, granted half a hide, represented by the present manor of Dudmaston, to Herbert, son of Helgot, the *Domesday* Lord of Stanton; and two other hides, one of which is represented by the township of Quat Malvern, and the other by the collective townships of Quat Jarvis, Mose, and Wooton, to his younger brothers.

Herbert Fitz Helgot, to whom Henry I. granted the manor of Dudmaston, succceding his father as lord of Castle Holgate, henceforth Dudmaston became a member of that barony. The lord of Castle Holgate, by a charter still extant, enfeoffed Herlwyn de Butailles, one of his Norman retainers in this manor; either he or his successor, transformed into Herelewin de Dudemaneston, holding it in 1165. "Thus were Norman names, and the proof of Norman origin, forgotten and buried, on acquisition of English estates."

Wydo Fitz Helgot, to whom Henry I. granted the hide of land, now identified with the township of Quat Malvern, gave this estate,

---

[1] *Domesday*, fo. 239, a 2.

together with another, to the Priory of Great Malvern, as appears from the Charter of Henry I. to Malvern, dated at Winchester, in 1127. "I give them" [the monks], says the king, "two hides of land, which Wydo Fitz Holgod surrendered into my hand, whereof one is in Worcestershire, and the other in Staffordshire, by name Quat,—quit [of all gelds and assessments], and to hold of me and my successors *in capite.*" [1] It is necessary to explain, that, when a tenant wished to make any transfer of property, the formal mode of doing so at that period was, to surrender it to his suzerain, when the suzerain re-granted it according to the tenant's wish.

In 1534-5, the income receivable by the Priory from Great Malvern was £3 0s. 9d.

The hide of the *Domesday* Quat, now represented by the collective townships of Quat Jarvis, Wooton, and Mose, Henry I. gave, as we said, to a third son of Helgot, Lord of Castle Holgate, to be held by serjeantry; namely, to provide one knight to do service for xl days at the royal castle of Shrawardine. Castle guard elsewhere, however, afterwards came to be substituted for this service. Thus, in 1255, "John Fitz Philip," a descendant of the first grantee, it was said, "holds in Quat and Mose one hide of land, by service of providing two men at his own cost [to go] with the king into Wales, in time of war, for 40 days, one with a bow and arrows, the other with a lance. And he [John] does suit to the Hundred of Brug."

Quat Church.

The first notice we have of this church is in 1255, when, valued at 10 merks *per annum*, it was in the gift of the Prior of Malvern. Pope Nicholas's taxation gives the same valuation in 1291. The Staffordshire Inquisition for the *ninth*, a mere fragment, scarcely alludes to this parish. In 1534, the preferment of the parson of Quat was valued at £15 18s. 6d., whereof a pension of 20s. was payable to the Prior of Malvern, 2s. triennially to the Bishop of Chester, and 11s. 8d., for procurations, to the Archdeacon of Stafford.

Early Incumbent.—Hugh de Duddemaneston, 1293.

---

[1] EYTON, who gives a lithograph facsimile of the original, and also a Latin rendering of this very ancient deed, says, it probably passed before 1127, but certainly before the death of Henry I., in 1135.

Romsley. As attached to the Hundred of Stanlei, Warwickshire, *Domesday* notices this manor in the following terms:—
"Walter holds of the Earl [Roger de Montgomery] i hide in Rameslege. The land is [capable of employing] vii ox-teams. In demesne there is i [team], and ii serfs, vii villains, and vii boors, with iii teams. The wood is i league long by half a league wide. [The manor formerly] was worth 30s. [per annum]; now 40s. Achi held it freely [in King Edward's time]."[1]

The Saxons, who loved agriculture and husbandry, were wont to attach to localities names savouring of farming ideas. Thus, the manor in question derives its title from the Saxon Rammeɼ-leaᵹ, the district of the Ram.

But little is known concerning Walter, the Norman earl's tenant here. Suffice it to observe, that his position was afterwards occupied by the barons of Richard's castle, when the manor of Romsley became attached to the fief which these barons held *in capite* of the Crown.

Remains of Romsley chapel, and of the encaustic tiling of its floor, are still visible. Two stones from its old doorway, carved with zodiacal signs, Leo and Sagittarius, once perhaps belonging to a set of twelve such, are also to be seen, built into the wall of an adjacent stable.

Rudge, at the time of William the Conqueror's survey, was another of Earl Roger's manors in Stanlei Hundred, Warwickshire. *Domesday* thus notices it:—"Radulphus holds of the Earl v hides in Rigge. The land is for vii ox-teams. In demesne is one team, with i serf, and iii villains and iv boors with ii teams. [Formerly] it was worth 60s. [per annum]; now 40s. Edric [once] held it freely of Earl Leuric."[2]

Domesday says Edric held this manor of Earl Leuric or Leofric, the Saxon Earl of Mercia, who died August 31st, 1057. It is clear, therefore, that in this Warwickshire portion of the Survey, the accounts given of a previous state of things, refer to the period when Leofric was living. Leofric was succeeded in his Mercian earldom by his son, Algar, who figures as earl in the Staffordshire portion of *Domesday*. Leofric was grandfather of Edwin and Morcar

---

[1] *Domesday,* fo. 239, a 2.   [2] Ibidem.

represented as earls of Mercia in the Shropshire *Domesday*. In their allusions to the bygone Saxon era, the Conqueror's Commissioners evidently, therefore, refer to various periods of the reign of Edward the Confessor.

Edric, alluded to above, was Sylvaticus, the Forester, of whom and in what way his estates, of which Rudge was one, came afterwards to be possessed by the Norman Radulphus or Ralph de Mortimer, we have spoken.

The Mortimers of Wigmore long continued to hold their seigneury over Rudge.

Shipley.

The word is another reminiscence of Saxon farming, being originally Scéper-leaȝ, the district of the sheep. It is thus described in the Warwickshire *Domesday* :—" The same Radulphus holds of the earl [Roger de Montgomery] i hide in Sciplei. The land is [enough] for iii ox-teams. Here are ii villains, and there is one quarentine[1] of oaks in length and in breadth. [The manor] is worth 5s. [annually]. Alsi held it freely in the time of King Edward."[2]

Lands in Remesleage, Sciplea, and Suthtune, identical probably with the Shropshire Romsley, Shipley, and Sutton by Claverley, were included by Wulfric Spott, the Saxon, in his magnificent endowment of Burton Abbey, at the commencement of the 11th century; yet, excepting the mention in his will, not a trace can be discovered of this remote Shropshire interest of Burton Abbey.

Concerning Alsi, the unlucky Saxon wight displaced by the Norman Radulphus de Mortimer, nothing further is heard.

Stretching away for miles eastward and westward of the valley of the Severn, in ancient times, flourished a forest. It occupied all that district where now the counties of Shropshire, Staffordshire, and Worcestershire converge—a densely wooded pathless tract, where roamed at will those four-footed denizens of the green cover which own not the dominion of man. Here, ever since vegetable life first budded, had it run riot in the excess of luxuriancy. It was a primeval forest; sublime in the grey and solemn twilight of its hoary antiquity.

---

[1] The *quarentine* was equivalent to the furlong, or 40 *perches*.
[2] *Domesday*, fo. 239, a 2.

Through this leafy region, known to our early British ancestors as Coed *the forest*, struggled against the various hindrances opposed to its onward course, the sluggish Severn. One while, some huge tree, levelled by lightning or the wind, blocked up the passage of its waters; which, then deserting their wonted channel, would transgress into neighbouring hollows, and there stagnate into reedy and mephitic pools. At another time, swollen with wintry rains, the angry torrent impetuously burst its bonds and flooded the surrounding country, carrying all before it.

The extent of the wild uncultivated tract in question may be inferred from the relative positions of Morf, Kinver, and Wyre forests, so often alluded to in the Anglo-Norman period; all of which were included in the ancient Coed. But civilization gradually obtained the ascendancy over nature; large patches of the parent forest were reclaimed, and these, ever widening, at length, smiling and cultivated distances intervened between Morf, Kinver, and Wyre. It is with the former of these Boscs or woods that we have now more particularly to deal.

MORF FOREST lay to the east of the Severn. Not only have traces of our early British ancestors, in the shape of tumuli, been found within the precincts of Morf forest, but reminiscences of each successive race that obtained the ascendancy in this island have also been discovered there. Thus Chesterton, formerly within its *regard*, implies a Roman encampment; and the Saxon Clæpep-leaʒ, or Claverley, the clover district, bespeak the fostering supervision of the agriculture-loving Saxon earls of Mercia. Again, the Danes, when out-generalled by Alfred, sought refuge in Morf forest, and, entrenching themselves there one winter, endeavoured by the aid of the timber it yielded, to construct a fleet that would float them down the Severn, that so the Viking rovers might regain their element, the main, from which the Anglo-Saxon king had cut them off. Starved out of the forest, the grisly worshippers of Odin made their dread forage westward over the Severn, when Danes-ford recalls to memory the pagan host.

Finally, Quat Castle frowning over the surrounding neighbourhood, marked the epoch of Norman supremacy.

Yes! Briton, Saxon, Dane, and Norman, each left their impress on this wood: they had their day, and passed away; and now we, the men of the 19th century, erect our schools and run our rail-roads through the valley, where haunted of yore the antlered monarch of Morf.

I

DOMESDAY HUNDRED OF RECORDIN.

Modern Name.	Domesday Name.	Saxon Owner or Owners, T. R. E.	Domesday Tenant in capite.	Domesday Mesne, or next Tenant.	Domesday Sub-Tenant.	Modern Hundred.
Wrockwardine	Recordine	Rex Edwardus	Rogerius Comes			Bradford Sor
Upton Magna	Uptune	Seunardus	Idem	Rainaldus Vicecomes		Bradford Sor and Liberties Shrewsbury.
Eaton Constantine	Etune	Wenesi	Idem	Rainaldus Vicecomes		Bradford Sou
Leighton	Lestone	Lenni	Idem	Rainaldus Vicecomes		Ibidem.
Childs Ercall	Arcalun	Seunardus	Idem	Rainaldus Vicecomes		Bradford Nor
Berwick Maviston	Berewic	Uluiet	Idem	Rainaldus Vicecomes		Bradford Sou
Wroxeter	Rochecestre	Toret	Idem	Rainaldus Vicecomes		Ibidem.
Hadley	Hatlege	Witric & Elric	Idem	Rainaldus Vicecomes	Goisfrid	Ibidem.
Little Dawley	Dalelie	Sistain	Idem	Rainaldus Vicecomes	Benedictus	Ibidem.
? ?		Wige	Idem	Rainaldus Vicecomes	Ricardus	Ibidem.
Lee-Gomery	Lega	Toret	Idem	Rainaldus Vicecomes	Toret	Ibidem.
Rodington	Rodintone	Toret	Idem	Rainaldus Vicecomes	Toret	Ibidem.
Hinstock	Stoche	Algar	Idem	Willelmus Pantulf	Sasfrid	Bradford Nor
? ?	Corselle	Goduinus	Idem	Willelmus Pantulf		? ?
Beslow	Beteslauue	Goduinus	Idem	Willelmus Pantulf		Bradford Sou
Buttery	Buterei	Turchil	Idem	Willelmus Pantulf		Ibidem.
Eyton on the Wealdmoors	Etone	Wighe & Ouiet	Idem	Willelmus Pantulf	Warin	Ibidem.
Bratton	Brocketone	Erniet	Idem	Willelmus Pantulf	Warin	Ibidem.
Horton	Hortune	Erniet	Idem	Willelmus Pantulf	Warin	Ibidem.
Lawley	Lauelei	Erniet	Idem	Willelmus Pantulf		Ibidem.
			Idem	Turoldus	Hunnit	Bradford Nor
Longford	Langeford	Eduinus Comes	Idem	Turoldus		Bradford Sou
Chetwynd	Catewinde	GodevaComitissa	Idem	Turoldus		Ibidem.
Pilson	Plivesdone	Eduinus Comes	Idem	Turoldus		Bradford Nor
Sambrook	Semebre	Ulgar	Idem	Turoldus		Ibidem.
Howle	Hugle	Batsuen	Idem	Turoldus	Walter	Ibidem.
Kinnersley	Chinardeslei	Willegrip	Idem	Gerardus		Bradford Sou
Uppington	Opetone	Seunardus	Idem	Gerardus		Ibid-m.
Shawbury	Sawesberie	Edric & Eliet	Idem	Gerardus		Bradford Nor
Cherrington	Cerlintone	Uluiet		Gerardus		Bradford Sou
Chesthill	Cestulle	Leduui	Idem	Gerardus		Bradford Nor
Longner	Languenare	Episcopus de Cestre	Episcopus de Cestre	Wigot		Liberties of Shrewsbury.
Stoke-upon-Tern	Stoche	Edmundus	Rogerius Comes	Rogerius de Laci		Bradford Nor
Waters Upton	Uptone	Gamel	Idem	Rogerius de Laci	Seunardus	Bradford Sor
Little Withiford	Wideford	Lenenod	Idem	Rogerius de Laci	Robertus	Bradford Nor
Withington	Wientone	Uluinus and Uluricus	Idem	Fulcuius		Bradford Sou
Preston on Wealdmoors	Prestune	Burrer	Idem	Radulfus de Mortemer		Ibidem.
Peplow	Papelau	Orgrim and Uluric	Idem	Radulfus de Mortemer		Bradford Nor
Isombridge	Asnebruge	Ulf	Idem	Radulfus de Mortemer		Bradford Sou
Sutton near Drayton	Sudtone	GodevaComitissa	Idem	Rogerius de Curcelle		Bradford Nor
Tibberton	Tetbristone	Ulgar	Idem	Rogerius de Curcelle		Bradford Sor
Woodcote	Udecote	Aluric	Idem	Robertus fil. Tetbaldi	Tochi	Ibidem.
Eye Farm			Idem	Robertus fil. Tetbaldi	Tochi	Ibidem.
Brockton	Brocketune	Aisil	Idem	Ricardus		Ibidem.
Haughton	Haustone	Edwi	Idem	Rogerius Venator		Ibidem.
Uffington	Ofitone	Genut and Elveva	Idem	Holgot		Ibidem.
Poynton	Peventone & Tunestau	Uluiet	Idem	Uluiet		Ibidem.
Lilleshall	Linleshelle	Ecclesia Sti. Almundi	Idem	Eccl. Sti. Almundi	Godeboldus Presbiter	Ibidem.
Longdon upon Tern	Languedune	Ecclesia Sti. Almundi	Idem	Eccl. Sti. Almundi		Ibidem.
Uckington	Uchintune	Ecclesia Sti. Almundi	Idem	Eccl. Sti. Almundi	Godeboldus	Ibidem.
Atcham	Atingeham	Ecclesia Sti. Almundi	Idem	Eccl. Sti. Almundi	Godeboldus	Ibidem.
Albright-Lee	Etbretelie	Ecclesia Sti. Almundi	Idem	Eccl. Sti. Almundi		Liberties of Shrewsbury.
Charlton near Shawbury	Cerletone	Ecclesia Sti. Almundi	Idem	Eccl. Sti. Almundi		Bradford No

Manors situated in Recordin, but whose Hundred is not stated in Domesday.

Modern Name.	Domesday Name.	Saxon Owner or Owners, T. R. E.	Domesday Tenant in capite.	Domesday Mesne, or next Tenant.	Domesday Sub-Tenant.	Modern Hundred.
High Ercall	Archelou	Eduinus Comes	Rogerius Comes			Bradford South.
Wellington	Walltone	Eduinus Comes	.... Idem			..Ibidem.
Edgmond	Edmendune	Leuinus Cilt	.... Idem			..Ibidem.
Dawley Magna	Dalelie	Grim	.... Idem	Willelmus (Pantulf)		Ibidem.

RECORDIN, the largest of the *Domesday* Hundreds of Shropshire, combined with Odenet, went, in the days of Henry I., to form the modern Hundred of ·Bradford.

𝔚𝔯𝔬𝔠𝔨𝔴𝔞𝔯𝔡𝔦𝔫𝔢, situated to the north of the Wrekin, may derive its name from *Wrekin Worthen*, "the Village of the Wrekin." After the Conquest of Mercia, when the palatine Norman Earl divided Shropshire among his vassals, he retained pleasantly situated Wrockwardine in demesne. The fact is thus recorded in Domesday Book:—" Earl Roger holds Recordine. King Edward held it. To this manor pertain vii berewicks and a half. Here v hides geldable. In demesne are iiii ox-teams; and xiii villains, iiii boors, a priest, and a radman have among them all xii teams. Here are viii neatherds, a mill of 12s. [annual value], and a wood one league long and half a league wide.

"The Church of St. Peter holds the church of this manor, with i hide, and thereon it has one ox-team, and there might be another team besides. It [namely, this hide] is worth 5s. [per annum].

"Two *denarii* [or pence] of the Hundred of Recordin, in the time of King Edward, used to belong to this manor. The Earl [of Mercia] had the third penny.

"In the time of King Edward, the manor used to yield £6 13s. 8d. [annually]; now it pays a ferm of £12 10s."[1] It was from this manor of the Saxon kings that the Hundred of Recordin derived its name.

Adhering to the cause of Curthose, Robert de Belèsme, third and last Norman Earl of Shrewsbury, forfeited Wrockwardine,

---

[1] *Domesday*, fo. 253, a 2.

and thus, as a manor of royal demesne, it came into the hands of Henry II., who granted one-half of it to Roger de Powis and his brother Jonas. Their interest here, however, was temporary, for in the year 1200, Hamo le Strange, younger brother of John le Strange II., of Ness and Cheswardine, fined 60 merks with the Crown, that he, " Hamo, might have the Manor of Wrocwrthin, late held by Meuric de Powis." Hamo le Strange accordingly became Lord of Wrockwardine, with its members—Admaston, Allscot, Leaton, Burcote, Nesse, Clotley, and Walcott; and his descendants continued to hold the manor *in capite* of the king.

The *Nomina Villarum* of 1316 duly enters *Fulco Extraneus* as Lord of Wrockwardine. The le Stranges claimed to exercise *Free-warren*; *Free-court*, with its pleas of *bloodshed, hue and cry*, and *gallows*; and the *Assize of Bread and Beer*, in their Manor of Wrockwardine.

The Church.

Wrockwardine Church was a Saxon foundation, the mother church of a district. "The Church of St. Peter," says *Domesday*, "holds the church of this manor with one hide." The Norman earl, it appears, had given the church, and Oilerius the priest, the hide to Shrewsbury Abbey. In 1291, the church of Wrocworthin, in the deanery of Salop, was valued at £10 *per ann*. In 1341, the parish was rated only £6 13s. 4d. to the *ninth*, because there were few sheep in it, etc. A patent of King Ed. III., dated July 26, 1329, gave the Abbot of Shrewsbury license to appropriate this church. The *valor* of 1534-5 gives the Abbot's rectorial tithes of Wrockwardyn as £14, and the vicarage at £8, less 7s. 6d. for procurations and 4s. for synodals.

Early Incumbent.—Oilerius, the priest who, according to Earl Roger's Charter, gave one hide of land in Cherlton, a member of Wrockwardine, to Shrewsbury Abbey, is supposed to have been Rector of Wrockwardine in 1086. This Oilerius, or "Odelirius, of Orleans, son of Constantius, a man of talent and eloquence, as well as of great learning," was one of the Norman earl's chief counsellors. He was father of Ordericus Vitalis, the celebrated Norman chronicler.

High Ercall. That the ancient British poet Llywarç Hên was acquainted with Shropshire, the names of streams and localities which he introduces into his elegies are proofs. Among other places, he mentions Ercal.

> 'The sod of Ercal is on the ashes of fierce
> Men, of the progeny of Morial.'[1]

From the circumstance that about a mile south of High Ercall, between three and four hundred paces from the eastern side of the river Roden, there is a depressed mound, thirty-six yards wide, and ninety long, with angles rounded, and encircled by a fosse six feet deep and twenty-nine wide, it has been conjectured that High Ercall is alluded to by the poet in the above quotation.

High Ercall is thus described in the Domesday Book:—" The Earl himself holds Archelou. Earl Eduin held it, with v Berewicks. Here vii hides. In demesne are vi ox-teams and xii neatherds. Here xxix villains and xii boors have xv teams. Here two mills render [or pay] xii measures of corn[2] [annually]; and here there is a fishery of [*i.e.* which yields annually] 1502 great eels. There is one league of wood. In King Edward's time the manor was worth £20 [*per ann.*]; now [it is worth] the same. According to a custom, when the countess visited the manor, eighteen sums of 20d. [each] used to be brought to her."[3]

" With the manor of High Ercall," Eyton eloquently observes, " are associated some of the greatest names in Shropshire history. Here the co-heirs of Hamo Peverel retained their last hold on the county which had nursed his fortunes. Here the Chancellor Burnell, never sated with acquisition, reconsolidated in himself a seigneury which had been severed for more than a century. In later times, Ercall was the caput of those vast estates which formed the heritage of the Newports—a heritage than which none greater has accrued to any single Shropshire family since the advent of the Normans."[4]

High Ercall came into the hands of Henry I. upon the forfeiture of Earl Robert, when the king invested Hamo Peverel in this manor, which descended to his collateral heirs.

The de Hadleys, otherwise the de Ercalls, descending from William de Hadley I., and Seburga, natural daughter of Hamo Peverel, continued, for two hundred years, to be the vassals of the mesne lords of High Ercall. To the Ercalls succeeded the Cavers-

---

[1] Llywarç Hên, p. 93.
[2] "*Summas annonæ.*"
[3] *Domesday*, fo. 253, b 2.
[4] *Antiq. of Shrop.* Vol. IX. p. 62.

wells, who became lords of High Ercall about 1345. From the Caverswells the Newports, in 1398, purchased the manor, and thus it was that this family, "pre-eminent in Shropshire for more than three centuries," became lords of High Ercall.

The various monastic establishments of Shropshire—Lilleshall, Shrewsbury, and Buildwas Abbeys, Wombridge Priory, as well as the Prioress of White-Ladies, in former times—all had a picking out of either Ercall or its members, Tern, Sleap and Crudgington, Osbaston, Moortown, or the now lost members of Shurlow and Wilsithland.

THE CHURCH.

High Ercall Church is not mentioned in *Domesday*; soon after which, however, it seems to have been founded, and to have become the mother church of a district, for Earl Roger himself gave to Shrewsbury Abbey the "*Church of Archeloua,* with all things pertaining thereto." In 1228, the monks of Shrewsbury were permitted by the Bishop to appropriate Ercall Church, which thereupon became a vicarage in the gift of the Abbot and convent.

PILLARS IN THE NORTH AISLE, HIGH ERCALL.

In 1291, the church (*i.e.* rectory) of Ercalwe, in the deanery of Salop, was valued at £20, besides a pension of £1 4s. to the Abbot of Shrewsbury. In 1341, the parish was assessed £13 6s. 8d. to the *ninth.* The *Valor* of 1534-5 gives £18 19s. 4d. as the Vicar of *Miche-Ercall's* preferment. Out of this, the vicar paid a pension of 20s. to Shrewsbury Abbey, 10s. for procurations, and 2s. 8d. for synodals.

WROCKWARDINE CHURCH.

WELLINGTON CHURCH (TAKEN DOWN IN 1789).

Early Incumbents.— { Nicholas, last rector of Ercall ; } 1228.
{ Alexander, first vicar ; }

At the east end of the north aisle of High Ercall Church, carved in freestone, reposes the mutilated effigy of a warrior-knight. Tradition says that it is one of the Ercalls.

The old Norman font, which formerly belonged to Ercall Church, is now in Shrewsbury Abbey.

Wellington. " The Earl himself," says *Domesday*, " holds Walitone. Earl Eduin held it, with v berewicks. Here are xiiii hides geldable. In demesne are vi ox-teams; and xii neat-herds, xii villains, and viii boors, with a priest, have ix ox-teams, and other ix teams might be here. There is a mill here of 12s. [annual value], and two fisheries of 8s. In the time of King Edward, the manor was worth £20 [*per ann.*]; now it is worth £18."[1]

It appears then that, when the Norman earl appropriated Wrockwardine, which erewhile had belonged to Saxon kings, he seized at the same time, and held, High Ercall and Wellington, the Saxon earl's manors. From Wrockwardine and Wellington the great Norman could view the Wrekin tower in solitary grandeur upwards into the sky. Hard by Earl Roger's manors ran the Watling Street, to remind him of a former conqueror.

Like the rest of the Norman earl's manors, Wellington became forfeit to the king by the rebellion of Robert de Belèsme, when at length it appears that King John gave Wellington to Thomas de Erdinton, in reward for the services rendered by the latter in the Court of Rome at the time of the Interdict.[2] The jurors who made this statement in 1284 added, that in King John's time there were only 14 hearths in Wellington, and 24 hearths in Arleston. Changes have since taken place in respect to Wellington, which is now a populous and thriving town.

WELLINGTON CHURCH.

As we glean from the *Domesday* report of the manor, this church was existent in 1086. From Roger de Montgomery's charter to Shrewsbury Abbey we learn, that soon afterwards, the Norman earl gave it to his newly-founded abbey. Wellington remained a rectory in the gift of the abbot until the year 1232,

---

[1] *Domesday*, fo. 253, b. 2.   [2] *Inquisitions*, 12 Edw. I., No. 88.

when the Bishop of Lichfield suffering the abbot to appropriate it, he received as the reward of his complicity, that moiety of the tithes of Wellington which enabled him to found the Prebend of Wellington, in Lichfield Cathedral.

In 1291, the Church of Welinton, in the deanery of Salop, was valued at £6 the abbot's share, £2 13s. 4d. the vicarage, and £10 the prebend.

The assessors of the *ninth* rated the parish £10 13s. 4d. in 1341. The *valor* of 1534-5 gives £11 to the abbot, £10 to the prebendary, and £10 to the vicar of Wellington. The latter had to pay out of his income, 5s. for synodals, and 10s. for procurations.

Early Incumbent.—Philip de Welinton, 1189.

Apley, now Apley Castle, Arleston, Aston under the Wrekin, Dothill, and Walcot, were all appurtenances of the manor of Wellington.

Around the Wrekin, in ancient times, stretched the Forest of the Wrekin, or Forest of Mount Gilbert, as it was afterwards called. Gradually this forest was encroached upon, until, in the year 1300, the *Haye of Welinton* was all that remained to the lord king.

That forester whose hereditary office it was to take charge of Wellington Haye, the locality of which is still indicated by *Hay-gate*, there is little doubt was ancestor of the present Lord Forrester, who now holds the very land which his ancestor held 700 years ago.

That, in days gone by, a hermit dwelt amidst the solitudes of the Wrekin, is proved by the fact, that King Henry III., by his patent of September 17, 1267, granted to "Nicolas de Denton, Heremite of Mount Gilbert, six quarters of corn; to be paid him by the sheriff of Shropshire, out of the issues of Pendleston Mill," in order, as it was expressed, "to give the Hermit greater leisure for holy exercises, and to support him during his life, so long as he shall be a Heremite on the aforesaid mountain."

Edmond is noticed in *Domesday*, thus:—"The Earl himself holds Edmendune. Leuuin Cilt held it [in Saxon times] with vi berewicks. Here are xiiii hides geldable. In demesne are vi ox-teams; and xii neat herds; and one female serf, xxxiii villains, and viii boors, with ii frenchmen have xi teams; and yet there might be xi more teams here. Here a mill with a fishery pays 10s. [annually]. In the time of King Edward the manor used to pay £14 (*per annum*), now [it pays] £15."[1]

Upon the forfeiture of Earl Roger's son, Robert de Belèsme, Edgmond, with its appurtenances, became forfeit to King Henry I., who, retaining it as a manor of royal demesne, it eventually came into the hands of his grandson, Henry II. Successive sheriffs continued to farm its revenues until the year 1227, when King Henry III., by his charter, dated at Westminster, granted the *Manor of Egmundon-cum-Novo Burgo* to Henry de Audley and his heirs, to hold of the Crown, by the service of one *sore sparrow-hawk*, payable yearly at the Exchequer.[2] And the Pipe Roll, of the same year informs us, that "Henry de Aldithele accounts one *mewed sparrow-hawk* for the ferm of *Egmendon-cum-Novo Burgo,* according as the king had given the manor to him at such a ferm. The hawk had been paid to the king himself; and Audley was quit." The barons Audley, of whom a notice is given under Ford, thus became lords of Edgmond and Newport.

The Bradford Tenure-Roll of 1285, says, that, "Nicholas de Audeley holds the manor of Egemond, with its members, viz:—Adeney, Great Aston, Little Aston, Little Halis, Pickestoke, with the vill of *Neuporte,* of the king *in capite* by charter; rendering yearly a mewed sparrow-hawk, in lieu of all services. The said manor was a demesne-manor of the king. Of the said members, William Eyssely holds Great Aston of the said Nicholas; the Abbot of Crokesden holds Adeney; John de Halis holds Little Halis; and the Burgesses of Neuport hold Neuport as a *free* borough, of the said Nicholas. And here the said Nicholas has his free court, and pleas of bloodshed, and hue-and-cry, and gallows, warren, market, and fair; and these he has used."

THE CHURCH.

Edgmond Church, founded apparently by Earl Roger de Montgomery, was, with its subject chapels, by him given to Shrewsbury Abbey. Pope Nicholas's taxation, in 1291, values the church of Egemindon, in Newport deanery, at £12 *per ann.*, besides a pension of £1 10s. to the Abbot of Shrewsbury. In 1341, the

---

[1] *Domesday*, fo. 253, b 2.   [2] *Rot. Cart.*, II. Hen. III, p. 1, m. 7.

parish was rated £11 to the *ninth*. The *Valor* of 1534-5 gives the rectory of Egmonde as worth £48, less the ancient pension to the abbot; 8s for procurations, and 4s. for synodals.

Early Incumbents :—Geoffrey Griffin is said to have been rector of Edgmond; after whom came Artald de Sancto Romano, presented in 1250.

Newport.

Founded within the royal manor of Edgmond, Novus Burgus, or Newport, belonged to that class of boroughs which had kings for their founders. Newport appears to have been founded by the Anglo-Norman king, Henry I., in whose time the burgesses of Newport enjoyed *franchises* and had *customs*. King Henry II. by his charter, dated at Brewood, between the years 1163 and 1166 confirms to the Burgesses of *Novo Burgo* all those liberties and rights which they had in the time of King Henry his grandfather. At the assizes of 1203, the new borough was represented by its own community. It was alleged against them that the *assize of Bread* was not kept in their town.

The earliest instance which occurs of the name Neuport being substituted for New Borough is in 1221, when Matilda de Stafford was named at the assizes as complainant against Nicholas de Neuport and others.

On January 23, 1287, King Edward I. at Shrewsbury, inspected and confirmed Henry the Second's charter to the burgesses of of Novus Burgus. At the assizes of 1292, the "Vill of Neuport" was represented by William Noblet, its chief bailiff, William Rondulf, Richard Alemond, Robert de Morton, Richard de la Loue, John Rondulf, and Roger Priest, jurors. Under the head, *De Libertibus*, it was presented at these assizes, that the burgesses of Novus Burgus claimed to have a court, to assize bread and beer, and to have a merchant-guild. Appearing, the burgesses explained that they had exercised these franchises from time immemorial. They adduced Henry the Second's charter, and said that both before and after that charter, they had exercised these franchises.

Involved with that of Edgmond, and subject to the same lords, the early history of Newport is meagre and unsatisfactory.

Adjoining Newport there was formerly a famous vivary, and the burgesses appear to have held their liberties by serjeantry of

EDGMOND CHURCH.

conveying the fish taken in this vivary to the court of the king, and afterwards to that of the Lord Audley, wherever it might be. About 1250, however, the burgesses, by payment of £5, obtained the following release :—" James, son of Henry de Audley, quit-claims to the burgesses of New Borough the following, viz.: that they shall not carry the fish of the vivary of New Borough anywhither except within the boundaries of Shropshire." [1]

The arms of the town of Newport (three fishes in pale), are allusive to this ancient sergeantry.

THE CHURCH.

Newport Church, coeval with the borough, was originally an affiliation of Edgmond; and, as such, belonged to Shrewsbury Abbey. In 1291, this church was valued at £2 13s. 4d. *per annum*. In 1341, the parish of Newport was assessed 40s. to the *ninth*.

On March 29, 1442, King Henry VI. empowered the Abbot of Salop to alienate Newport Church, with its tithes and oblations, and the tithes of *Littel* and *Muchel Astone*, to Thomas Draper and his heirs, so that the said Thomas might found a college in the said church, to the praise of God and the Virgin Mary, and also a chantry of two chaplains, who were to perform Divine service in a chapel of the said church daily. The *College* was to consist of a Warden, in priest's orders, and four Chaplains or Fellows, who were to pray for the king and royal family, for the soul of Humphrey, Duke of Gloucester, and for the brethren and sisters of the fraternity of St. Mary's Guild, in the said church of Newport, as the said Thomas Draper should order. The Fellows were to elect their Warden, and present him to the Abbot of Salop. The said Warden was to have the cure of souls among the parishioners of Newport, and a sufficient sum was annually to be distributed among the poor parishioners, according to the Statute, *De appropriationibus*.[2]

King Henry the Eighth's valor represents the "Church of the Guild of Newporte" as receiving an amount of £6 13s. 4d., payable by the Seneschall of the said Guild.

Early Incumbent:—John Parson of Newport: 1267.

Newport gives name to a deanery.

---

[1] *Harl. M.S.*, 1985, fo. 245, quoted by Eyton.
[2] *Patent*, 20 Hen. VI. Pars. 4, m.2.

Upton Magna. When William the Conqueror's Commissioners surveyed Shropshire, they found that the largest holder in Recordin Hundred, under the Norman Earl of Shrewsbury, was Rainald, successor to Guarin the sheriff. This Guarin, or Warin the Bald, who had been selected by Earl Roger from among his barons to fill the responsible office of vicomté, or sheriff of Shropshire, was, as Ordericus tells us, " a man of small stature but great courage, who bravely encountered the earl's enemies, and maintained tranquillity throughout the district entrusted to his government." With the shrievalty, which, in Norman times, was a hereditary office, the earl conferred upon Warin the hand of Amieria or Emeriè, his niece, and attaching no less than seventy different manors in Shropshire, besides several in other counties, to the sheriff's fief, Earl Roger's prime minister, Warin the Bald, stood the second man in the county of Shropshire. Leaving a son named Hugh, a minor, Warin died before *Domesday* was compiled, when Rainald, who held the fief of Bailleul, in Normandy, under Earl Roger de Montgomery, marrying the widow of Warin, became second Norman sheriff of Shropshire, and lord over those eleven manors in Recordin Hundred, of which Upton Magna was the most important.

This place is thus noticed in Domesday Book:—" The same Rainald holds Uptune. Seuuard held it in King Edward's time. Here v hides geldable. In demesne are iii ox-teams, and vii serfs, xxv villains, and one free man with xii ox-teams; and there might be viii more teams here besides. Here is a mill of 16s. [annual value], and a fishery rendering what it is able, and half a league of wood. In King Edward's time the manor was worth £10 [*per annum*]; now £7."[1]

Little is known concerning Rainald, the *Domesday* lord of Upton Magna. He continued sheriff of Shropshire during both Earl Hugh's and Earl Robert's times, and from the circumstance that he was confidentially employed by Henry I. in the affairs of the Border at the close of the year 1102, we judge that he escaped the ruin which befell the latter. Immediately afterwards, however, Rainald's connection with Shropshire ceased. Hugh, son of Warin, being old enough as it seems to succeed to his paternal inheritance, now stept into his fief, whilst the king, causing the shrievalty to

---

[1] *Domesday*, fo 254, b 2.

merge into the vice-royalty of Richard de Belmeis, Rainald returned to Normandy. We next hear of Rainald de Bailleul taking part in that Norman expedition which the Comte de Perche brilliantly led against the Moors of Spain. Finally, we have Rainald's loyalty suspected by Henry I. in 1119, when the baron haughtily refusing to surrender Le Château Renouard, the king destroyed his stronghold.

Meanwhile, Hugh, son of Warin, having deceased without issue, Alan Fitz-Flaald received by grant of Henry I. the honour of the sheriff of Shropshire. It is a question who the new lord of Upton Magna was; but that Alan Fitz-Flaald was progenitor not only of the great house of Fitz-Alan, but also of the royal line of Stuart, the representative of which now sits upon the throne of England, is beyond a doubt.

We do not intend to weary our reader with an intricate genealogical investigation; let it suffice to note, that, when Macbeth, King of Scotland, sought about the year 1050, to secure the succession in his own line, by putting to death, and confiscating the estates of those whom he suspected of plotting the restoration of Malcolm Canmore, the eldest son of Duncan; amongst those who fled from his reach was Fleance, son of Banquo, the murdered Thane of Lochaber. He fled to the Prince of North Wales, Gruffyth ap Lewellyn, with whose daughter, Guenta, becoming enamoured, the Welsh princess bore to Fleance a son—Alan Fitz-Flaald—the party in question. At least, such is the opinion of Eyton, who has examined the question with much learning and critical sagacity. The change from Fleanchus to Flaadus is certainly not very great, especially when we bear in mind that the nomenclature of that period was far from fixed. According to this, then, Alan Fitz-Flaald was grandson of Gruffyth ap Lewellyn, Prince of North Wales. Now, as Gruffyth married Alditha, daughter of Algar, Earl of Mercia, by whom he had Guenta, it follows that Alan Fitz-Flaald, legitimate or illegitimate, was the greatgrandson of the Saxon Earl of Mercia. Henry I., who, be it remembered, married a Scoto-Saxon princess, therefore, in giving Alan Fitz-Flaald the specific fief of the sheriff of Shropshire, may be supposed to have been actuated by a variety of motives. In the first place, he was planting in the very van of border warfare a chieftain who sprang from the native princes of North Wales. Secondly, descending as Alan Fitz-Flaald did from the Saxon Mercian Earl, Henry I., it may be presumed, acted in accordance with his well-known policy of conciliating the English. Again, he who now became lord of Upton Magna, represented a house illustrious in that land of Scots from whence Henry I. had married his queen.

ALAN FITZ-FLAALD married Avelina de Hesding, by whom he had issue three sons, William, Walter, Jordan, and a daughter named Sibil. It was Walter Fitz-Alan, Alan Fitz-Flaald's second son, who was the undoubted ancestor of the royal house of Stuart. A partizan of the daughter of that king who had enriched his family, Walter, during the stormy period of Stephen's usurpation, sought a shelter at the Court of David, King of Scots, the empress' uncle, where he became steward or seneschal to the King of Scots. The charter is yet in existence that proves how William Fitz-Alan, seneschal of the King of Scotland benefitted the monks of Melrose abbey. Its seal presents on one side the figure of an "armed knight on horseback, at full speed; a lance with pennon, couched in his right hand, and a shield on his left arm:" the legend is— *Sigillum Walteri filii Alani Dapiferi Reg.*[1] It was Alexander, the great-grandson of this Walter, who, abandoning his patronymic, in allusion to his hereditary office styled himself simply Alexander Stuart.

Alan Fitz-Flaald dying about 1114, was succeeded in his Shropshire fief by his eldest son,

WILLIAM FITZ-ALAN, who, in early manhood, founded Haughmond Abbey. This illustrious character married a niece of Robert, Earl of Gloucester, and joining heart and soul the league against the Usurper, defended Shrewsbury castle against Stephen. But the active king took Fitz-Alan's stronghold by assault, and cruelly and ignominiously hanged no less than ninety-three of his knightly captives.[2] "In no way inferior to the great earls who supported her cause, neither in fidelity, merit, valour, nor high repute," William Fitz-Alan outlived King Stephen's stormy reign, when, Henry II. having succeeded to his grandfather's throne reinstated Fitz-Alan in his estates, and conferred on him the sheriffdom of Shropshire. Now, too, it was that the king conferred upon Fitz-Alan in second marriage Isabel de Say, Baroness of Clun, the wealthiest heiress in Shropshire. Fitz-Alan enjoyed his restored estates but five years, and dying in 1160, he received sepulture in Shrewsbury abbey, as he had given land in Iseham together with his body, to that house.

---

[1] LAING's *Scottish Seals.*   [2] See page 173.

Fitz-Alan's son and heir by Isabel de Say was very young at the time of his father's decease. During his long minority, Guy le Strange, Geoffrey de Vere, and afterwards Hugh Pantulf, successively acted as sheriffs of Shropshire, the former being appointed also custos of the Fitz-Alan estates. In 1175, however,

WILLIAM FITZ-ALAN II, had livery of his Shropshire baronry; and about the same time he married the infant daughter of Hugh de Lacy, of Ludlow and Ewyas. More frequently associated with monastic charters than with political life, this Shropshire sheriff and baron-marcher died in 1210, and was buried at Haughmond Abbey, to which he had been a benefactor. A minor at the period of his father's decease, at length, on March 3rd, 1215, King John received at the Tower of London the homage of

WILLIAM FITZ-ALAN III., when the king, addressing letters patent to all the knights and tenants of the young baron, ordered them to do homage and fealty to their lord. Yet scarcely had the young noble arrived at his honours ere he was cut off.

JOHN FITZ-ALAN, William's brother, who next became lord of Oswestry and Fitz-Alan's fief, immediately upon his brother's death rebelled against King John, and confederating with the barons, the furious king burned his town, if not his castle, of Oswestry, to the ground. King John's career now closed; yet not immediately did the indignant rebel give in his adherence to young Henry III., but, in October, 1217, becoming reconciled, the king empowered him to collect the scutage of his tenants in Warwickshire, Wiltshire, Norfolk, Suffolk, Oxfordshire, and Shropshire. To this baron succeeded his son,

JOHN FITZ-ALAN II., in 1243, who fined £1,000 for livery and seizin of his father's lands and castles. In right of his mother Isabel, sister of Earl Hugh de Albini, John Fitz-Alan acquired Arundel castle and the Honour of Petworth, Sussex. Fighting on the side of the king at the disastrous battle of Lewes, this so-called Earl of Arundel was taken prisoner by the victorious barons. Towards the close of the year 1267, the greatest of the lords-marchers was laid with his ancestors in that abbey of Haughmond they had founded, when

JOHN FITZ-ALAN III, son and heir of John Fitz-Alan II. and Matilda de Verdon, became lord of Upton Magna. The enormous privileges which the lords of the marches occasionally asserted, were strikingly exemplified in the conduct of this man. In defiance of the king's oft-repeated mandate to pay £200 to his father's widow, the Shropshire noble still delayed; asserting, in contempt of the king, that, "in the *Parts of the March* where he now resided he was obliged to do nothing at the king's mandate, and that nothing would he do:" at which the king is said to have been "surprised and greatly moved." The proud noble, however, passed away in the prime of his life, leaving an infant son by Isabel de Mortimer.

RICHARD FITZ-ALAN, Earl of Arundel, the heir in question, is described in the Feodary of 1284, as holding many manors *in capite*, and amongst the number that of UPTON CUM MEMBRIS. He married an Italian lady, by whom he had

EDMUND FITZ-ALAN, who again marrying Alice Plantagenet, his descendants became entitled to the earldom of Warren and Surrey. The career of Edmund Fitz-Alan was cut short by the executioner.[1]

UPTON MAGNA CHURCH.

This, a very ancient foundation, appears to have been originally the mother church of a district, for Bishop Clinton (1129-1148) confirms to Shrewsbury abbey "the church of Uptona, together with its chapels and its pension of 20s." In 1291, Upton church, in the archdeaconry and deanery of Salop, was worth £10 *per annum*, over and above a pension of £1 to Shrewsbury abbey. In 1341, the parish was rated £8 to the *ninth*. The *Valor* of 1534-5 gives the rectory of Upton Magna as worth £12 *per annum*.

Early Incumbent.—Alard, rector of Upton in 1244.

Preston Boats, Rea, Hunkington, Downton, Sundorn, and part of Haughton, were formerly all members of Upton Magna, held by various tenants under Warin, the sheriff, and his successors the Fitz-Alans.

Haughmond Abbey.

Within that half league of wood noticed in *Domesday* as an adjunct of the manor of Upton, there might have dwelt in the Conqueror's time a hermit; but, it is certain that William Fitz-Alan, previously to 1138, in which year he became an exile from Shropshire, was a benefactor to the priory of St. John, on Haughmond Hill. To the canons regular of Haughmond, both the Empress Maude and her antagonist Stephen, gave donations; successive kings and barons vied with one another in granting

---

[1] DUGDALE'S *Baronage*, p. 316.

HAUGHMOND ABBEY (FROM THE NORTH-EAST).

CHAPTER HOUSE, HAUGHMOND ABBEY.

fertile lands to this ecclesiastical foundation, and thus the Augustine house of Haughmond swelled into the stately proportions of an abbey.

In 1291, the monastic possessions yielded a total of £157 4s. 1½d. From King Henry the Eighth's *Valor* we learn that the abbot of Haughmond, in 1535-6, represented the gross income of his house, temporalities and spiritualities included, as £294 12s. 9d. Its outgoings in chief-rents, standing dues, official salaries, church pensions, episcopal and archidiaconal dues, and alms, were £34 19s. 1¾d. The site and demesne lands of Haughmond were granted by Henry VIII. to Edmund Littleton.

Fulco appears as prior of Haughmond about 1135.

Ingenulf was abbot of Haghmon in 1156.

Eaton Constantine derives its distinctive appellation from that Anglo-Norman family of Constantine who long held it under the Fitz-Alans. *Domesday* says, "The same Rainald [the sheriff] holds Etune of the earl. Wenesi held it in King Edward's time. Here ii hides. In demesne are ii ox-teams; and iv serfs, ii female serfs, i villain and v boors with i team; and yet there might be ii more teams. Here is a fishery in the Severn, yielding no rent. A small wood yields 5d. In the time of King Edward [the manor] was worth 50s. [annually]; now 40s. He [Rainald] found it waste."[1]

The Church.

Originally a chapel dependent upon Leighton; in 1291, the church of Eton Constantine, in the deanery of Salop, was valued at 30s. *per annum*. In 1341, the parish was taxed only 10s. to the *ninth*, because it was small and poor; there had been a murrain among the sheep, etc. In 1534-5 the *free chapel* of Eton Constantyne was worth only £1 6s. 2d. *per annum*.

Early Incumbent.—Richard, son of William le Despenser, of Eton, 1301.

Leighton, near the Severn, is described in Domesday Book: "The same Rainald holds Lestone. Leuui held it in the time of

---

[1] *Domesday*, fo. 254. b 1.

King Edward. Here iii hides. In demesne are iii ox-teams; and vi neat-herds, iv villains, and vii boors, with a priest, and one Frenchman have v teams. There is a mill of 4s. [annual value] and half a league of wood yielding 11d. [per annum]. In King Edward's time [the manor] was worth 20s. [per annum]; now it is worth 40s. He [Rainald] found it waste."[1]

Within fifty years after the Norman scribe had penned the above, either Rainald or one of his successors enfeoffed a tenant here, of the name of Tihel or Tiel, who, taking his name of Tihel de Lahtune, from the place, became ancestor of those knightly Leightons who have been distinguished in Shropshire from that day to this. The De Leightons long held the manor under the Fitz-Alans, whilst under the Leightons again held sub-tenants.

LEIGHTON CHURCH.

We may infer that this was existent in 1086, from the mention of a priest in the *Domesday* account of the manor. In 1282, Richard de Leighton conveyed the advowson of Leighton to Robert Burnell, Bishop of Bath and Wells, who, within two years after, gave it to Buildwas abbey. Pope Nicholas' Taxation in 1291, represented the church of Lehton, in the archdeaconry and deanery of Salop, as worth £4 *per annum*. In 1341, the parish was assessed only £1 13s. 4d. to the *ninth*. King Henry the Eighth's *Valor* gives £8 as the income of the vicar of Leighton, less a pension of 5s. to the rector of Holgate. The abbot of Buildwas received £4 *per annum* for *ferm* of rectorial tithes of Leighton; out of which he paid 6s. 8d. for procurations to the archdeacon of Salop.

Early Incumbent.—Thomas, parson of Leighton early in 13th century.

In Leighton church is the recumbent monumental effigy of a mail-clad warrior, which, tradition says, was brought from Buildwas abbey at the Dissolution. From the arms displayed on the shield it is certain that it commemorates one of the Leighton family. The costume points to the latter end of the 13th century.

Childs Ercall in 1086, also belonged to the Norman sheriff of Shropshire. "The same Rainald," says *Domesday,* "holds Arcalun of the Earl. Seuuard held it [in Saxon times]. Here

---

Domesday, fo. 254, b 1.

iii hides. In demesne are ii ox-teams; and iv neat-herds, vii villains, x boors, a priest, a smith, and a Frenchman, have between them vii ox-teams and a half; and there might be i more team besides. Here half a league of wood produces 3d. [annually]. In the time of King Edward the manor was worth 45s. [*per annum*]; now it is worth 60s. He [Rainald] found it waste."[1] Rainald's successors, the Fitz-Alans, long continued to exercise the seigneury over Ercall, under whom the Le Strange's held a portion of the manor. King Henry the Eighth's Inquisition, however, revealed the fact, that the abbots of Combermere and Haughmond had both acquired slices of Childs Ercall.

The Church.

FONT, CHILDS ERCALL.

As appears from *Domesday*, Childs Ercall church was existent in the 11th century. In 1291 the church of Erkalive Parva, in Newport deanery, was valued at £3 6s. 8d. *per annum*. The parish was rated 48s. to the *ninth* in 1341.

Early Incumbent. — William de Prayers, acolyte, presented in 1308 by the abbot and convent of Combermere, who, at some unknown period, had obtained this advowson.

Berwick Maviston is described in Domesday Book as follows:—"The same Rainald holds Berewic. Uluiet held it in

---

[1] *Domesday*, fo. 254, b 2.

King Edward's time. Here half a hide. In demesne are ii ox-teams; and iv neat-herds, iv villains and iii boors with ii teams. Here is i league of wood paying 16d. [annually]: there might be one more team here."[1] This place acquired the name by which it is now known from the circumstance, that for centuries it was held under Rainald's successors, the Fitz-Alans, by a branch of that great family of Malvoisin or Mauveysin, which flourished in Shropshire and Staffordshire in the 13th century. The return upon the death of Saer Mauveysin in 1283, states, that the deceased had held one carucate in Berewyk, under Richard Fitz-Alan, for a whole knight's fee; and, by service of castle-guard at Oswestry, with one horseman, not heavily armed, for forty days in time of war.[2]

Wroxeter. A little to the west of the remarkable Shropshire mountain, the Wrekin, which, rearing from a vast plain its solitary crest upwards to an altitude of 1,370 feet is visible from various points of a radius of seventy miles round it, the Roman conquerors built the city of *Uriconium,* or W.roxeter. The Celtic *Bre* or *Wre, Wrc,* signifies a *hill, high* or *rotund.* The Romans Latinized *Wre* into *Uri*; for it is most likely that this station of theirs took its name from the very conspicuous natural land-mark near it. The terminative *conium* seems to be a Latinized edition of the Celtic *cond,* signifying an *embouchure,* which also exactly agrees with the situation of Uriconium, or Wroxeter.

The contemplation of the remains of this Roman city is fraught with interest to every student of the ancient history of his country; it is to be regretted, however, that we are in possession of so little information respecting its history. Planted on the north or northeast side of the Severn, near where the streamlet called Bell Brook empties itself into that river, from vestiges of its circumference that can be traced, the Uriconium of Roman times appears to have been a very large and fortified town, encircled by a vallum and fosse. Its walls were about three miles in circuit.[3] Hartshorne[4] estimates the vallum to have been fifteen feet in height, and the fosse the same in width. A piece of the "Old Wall" that

---

[1] *Domesday,* fo. 254, b 2.
[2] *Inquisitions,* 12 Edw. I. No. 2.
[3] The walls of Pompeii are less than two miles in circumference.
[4] *Salopia Antiqua,* p. 128.

CHILDS ERCALL CHURCH.

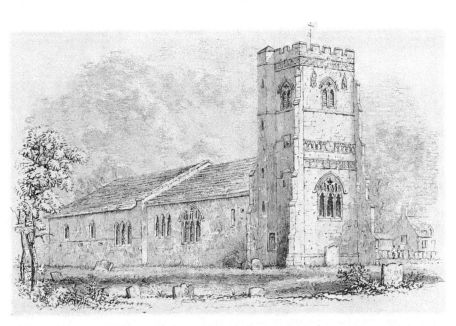

WROXETER CHURCH (NORTH-WEST VIEW).

formerly surrounded Uriconium, still attracts the attention of the traveller, as he approaches the village of Wroxeter by the high road from Buildwas to Shrewsbury. Standing in a field to his left, this huge fragment, seventy-two feet long by twenty high, presents to the eye of the lover of antiquities a genuine sample of Roman construction, being faced with small quarried stones six inches by four, with bondings of Roman tile after a certain number of courses. The interior of the wall, which is three feet two inches thick, is filled up with rubbish and pebbles.

Uriconium—Οὐιροκόνιον is mentioned by Ptolemy,[1] from whom we learn that it was situated in the country of the Cornavii whose chief city probably it was. It is alluded to also in the second and twelfth Iter of Antoninus, and by Richard of Cirencester in his first, second, and thirteenth Iter. Direct lines of roads connected the Roman city with Watling Street and those other great causeways with which the Latin conquerors networked Britain.

Various antiquities of the Roman period have been found here. In 1701, a hypocaust, or sweating bath, was uncovered, "walled about and floored, under and over," with flues and all complete. Mr. Dukes, in his manuscript,[2] gives a drawing of a tesselated floor found at Wroxeter in 1734; the form is oblong and semi-circular at one extremity; it is composed of green, red, white, and blue tesseræ, the green forming the outside border. In 1747, a paper was read before the Royal Society relative to a quantity of clay moulds for forging Roman coins which were found at Wroxeter. They had on them the head of Julia, the wife of Severus, and the inscription JVLIA AVGVSTA. In 1752, three sepulchral stones, having Latin inscriptions on them, were found in a field about two hundred yards north-east of the old wall.[3] The inscription on one of these ran as follows:—M·PETRONIVS·L·F·MEN·VIC· ANN·XXXVIII·MIL·LEG·XIIII·GEM·MILITAVIT ANN· XVIII·SIGN·FVIT·H·S·E· "Marcus Petronius, son of Lucius, of the tribe Menenia, lived thirty-eight years. He was a soldier of the fourteenth Legion Gemina. He served eighteen years, and was a standard-bearer. Here he rests." By one who has devoted his attention to the history of the fourteenth Legion, it is considered "certain that Petronius was a bearer of one of the

---

[1] PTOLOMÆI GEOG. *apud Horsley*, p. 359.
[2] Mr. DUKE's MS. *Illustrated Account of Wroxeter*, in possession of Society of Antiquaries of London. [3] Engraved in *Camden*, vol. III. p. 13.

signa of the fourteenth Legion, in the famous victory over Boadicæa, A.D. 61. . . . He may have died in consequence of his wounds."[1]

In 1788 there was a grand discovery made of Roman remains at Wroxeter. These consisted of coins, both of the Upper and Lower Empire, fragments of earthen vessels of various sizes and shapes, pieces of glass, a piece of leaden pipe, not soldered but hammered together, and the seam or juncture secured by a kind of mortar, tesselated floors of rooms, baths, and hypocausts. In one of the latter pieces of painted stucco, were found some striped crimson on a yellow ground, others intersecting chequer work of one colour, red or blue.

The following notice of a discovery made February 8th, 1798, is preserved in Mr. Parkes' manuscripts in the British Museum.[2] "Between Tern Bridge and the Severn, at Attingham, in a ploughed field, at a little more than plough depth, an enclosure of large stones was come upon, within which were ranged three large glass urns of very elegant workmanship, one large earthen urn, and two small ones of fine red earth. Each of the urns had one handle, and the handles of the glass urns were elegantly ribbed. The glass urns were 12 inches high, by 10 inches in diameter. The large earthen urn was so much broken that its size could not be ascertained. On the handle were the letters SPAH. The small urns were about 9 inches high. Within the glass urns were burnt bones and fine mould, and in each a fine glass lachrymatory; these had a most beautiful light green tint. Near one of them was part of a jaw-bone, an earthen lamp, and a few Roman coins of the Lower Empire, of little value. The whole was covered with large flat stones, covered with a quantity of coarse rock-stone." As noticed in the manuscript, this was probably the burial-place of some family of Uriconium. These remains lay probably by the side of the Roman road, which is conjectured to have communicated with *Deva* or Chester, as we have sepulchral remains marking the line of the other two well-ascertained roads which led through Uriconium.

A very curious relic was found at Wroxeter whilst ploughing near the "Old Wall" in 1808, namely, a small stamp, such as were used by Roman empirics and *ocularii*. It is formed of fine grained green schist; on it is an inscription which, rendered into English, is believed by Professor Simpson, of Edinburgh, to

---

[1] *Archæological Journal*, 1859, p. 63. [2] Add. MS., No. 21,011, p. 37.

signify "the Dialbanum or Incense Collyrium of Julius Bassus Clemens, for every eye-disease, to be used with egg."

Several urns were found here in 1810, and a quantity of silver coins in a glass vessel with two handles. Indeed, with respect to coins, so far back as the year 1829, Mr. Dukes was able to enumerate no less than 201 silver ones, one gold coin, and four counterfeit ones, which had been found at different periods at Wroxeter. The discovery is recorded of a singular altar upon which is inscribed BONO REI PVBLICÆ NATVS. It is supposed to be of the time of Constantine.[1] In 1827 a bronze statuette of Apollo holding the lyre was found. A bronze figure of Diana, and one of Mercury were discovered in 1848.

Considerable explorations have been made of late on the site of this ancient Roman city. Fragments of columns which appear to have been disposed in rows; baths, and Basilica, Temple or Hall of Justice; and a space considered to be the Forum, have been discovered. The inner sides of the walls of some of the buildings were covered with a thick layer of mortar, painted in fresco, the colours of which still preserved their freshness. Roofing tiles also were found. Various streets of the ancient Roman city have been carefully examined, and the roadway is found to be composed of small stones from the bed of the river Severn; on either side is a causeway for foot-passengers, terminated by a kerb-stone; the width of the road, including the foot-ways, being 18 feet. A water-course of wrought stone, very well made, little more than a foot deep, and a foot wide, has been opened, which runs in front of the ruins of some houses. The stones found in this water-course, and which in places block it up, are supposed to have been stepping-stones; fallen during the demolition of the adjoining buildings, or before the city was wholly deserted. The site of the ancient burial-ground was, as is invariably the case in Roman cities, without the gates; and, from discoveries of numerous urns, lachrymatories, and other sepulchral vessels, in earth and glass, it would appear that the ancient cemetery of the city of Uriconium at Wroxeter, lay without the Roman city, on its eastern side, extending along the sides of the Watling Street.

Among other things which have been turned up by the spade

---

[1] Unmentioned by Hartshorne; drawings of this altar are given both in Duke's and Blakeway's collections. Blakeway's MS. Notes on Wroxeter in Bodleian Library.

of the archæologist, it may be mentioned, are curious glass and
metal vessels. One of the vessels, in Samian ware, was a very fine
bowl, with figures in high relief, representing a hunting scene—
deer chased by a dog, a bushy tree—well executed; and there is
also the name of the potter. The remains of what is supposed to
have been a chariot-wheel, have been found, also spear-heads, the
head of a pick or adze, as well as other implements of iron, clamps,
rivets, and nails. Lead and tin also have been discovered in the
recent excavations. A painter's palette was turned up; also inta-
glios or engraved stones, bronze and bone hair-pins, combs, fibulæ,
bracelets, finger-rings, glass beads, and bone needles. These, with
other interesting discoveries, full details of which have been duly
recorded in the journals of those learned societies whose special
province it is to extend our knowledge of antiquities, have resulted
in a very considerable insight into the condition of the inhabitants
of Roman Britain.[1]

Uriconium or Wroxeter owed its foundation, it is conjectured,
to the campaigns of Ostorius, about A.D. 50. In the absence of any
certain information, it is impossible to determine whether it was
ruined by accidental fire, by the inroads of the Picts and Scots
before the arrival of the Saxons, by some irruption from the
Britons of North Wales, or, lastly, as some suppose, the Danes at
length burnt Wroxeter. From the recent explorations, it is certain that it was burnt to the ground, whoever fired it.

Among the most remarkable of the discoveries lately made at
Wroxeter, was the finding of a number of skeletons and human
bones. The position in which they were found was very peculiar.
In one of the smaller hypocausts were three skeletons, one of
which was seated or crouching in a corner, the other two were
lying extended by the side of the wall. It appeared from the
skull and jaw of the former that these were the remains of a very
old man; the others seemed to be females. At a short distance
from the old man lay, in a small heap, 132 copper coins, extending
from Claudius to Valens, or from about A.D. 52 to 379. With

---

[1] The reader will find a good deal relating to Wroxeter in Hartshorne's Salopia Antiqua, pp. 90, 91, 117—133; in
Wright's 'Guide to the Ruins of the Roman
City of Uriconium'; in the Journal of the
British Archæological Association, vols.
xv., xvi, xvii., and xix.; in the March and
September numbers 1859, and September
number 1860, of the Archæological Journal; in the Archæologia Cambrensis; and
in the Gentleman's Magazine. In the
Museum of the Shropshire Natural History and Antiquarian Society, as well as
in the Library of King Edward's Free
Grammar School at Shrewsbury, various
relics from Uriconium are deposited.

these were found small iron nails and decayed wood—the remains of the box in which the coins had been enclosed. It seemed as if, in the suddenness of their surprise, and the fierceness of the conflict in which the city was destroyed, the persons of whom these were the skeletons, had sought safety by hiding themselves in the hypocaust, and had there met their fate. Besides the skeletons in the hypocaust, numerous skulls, many of which were distorted in form, were found near the fortifications which secured the passage across the Severn, as if there had been a conflict just at this point.

Now the discovery of the coins with the old skeleton in the hypocaust has a two-fold significance. In the first place, it shows what was the current money at the time in Britain; secondly, and more important still, it presents us, it may be, with a clue to the date of the destruction of Uriconium; for it was in the year 382, just three years after the date of the latest coin discovered, that Maximus, assuming the imperial purple, withdrew the garrisons from the cities of Roman Britain, and left the enervated conquered population of this country at the mercy of their more hardy highland brethren. It is a historical fact, that in the year A.D. 396 the Britons sent ambassadors to Rome for succour against the Picts and Scots.

The Saxons called this place *Wreaken-Ceaster*. From its being mentioned, at the close of the seventh century, in the Chorography of Ravennas, as the chief city of the Cornavii, Baxter supposes that Uriconium flourished till the time of the Danes, and that perhaps even here, at one period, the Mercians fixed their capital. The kingdom of Mercia, the *March* or boundary bordering on the lands of the British tribes, founded by Cridda, A.D. 585, embraced Shropshire and the midland counties.

But when Domesday Book was written, eight hundred years ago, the famous Roman city of Uriconium had long been numbered with the dead. The varied evidences which it supplies of the progress of art and civilization in this distant province of the Roman empire—this extensive settlement of that wonderful race on the borders of Wales, had been overlooked and forgotten amid the confusion and barbarism of the succeeding middle ages. In silence profound as the grave, deep lay the charred and blackened ruins of Uriconium, beneath the accumulations of ages! As a mere manor, Wroxeter is thus described in the Norman Conqueror's record :—" The same Rainald [the sheriff] holds Rochecestre.

Toret held it [in Saxon times], and was a free man. Here i hide geldable. In demesne is an ox-team and a half, and [there are] vii teams among the serfs, mále and female. Here are vii villains, iiii boors, iiii priests, and one radman. Between them they have iiii ox-teams. Here a church and i league of wood. In the time of King Edward [the manor] was worth 40s. [per annum]; now it is worth the same."[1] Twelve and a half teams employed on a single hide of land appears so greatly in excess of ordinary requirements, that it seems to indicate "the cotemporary progress of some extensive building operations. The once collegiate church of Wroxeter was richly endowed and greatly cherished by the Norman lords of the manor; probably the fabric was of their construction. Moreover, the Fitz Alans, Rainald's successors, are known to have had a residence at Wroxeter; perhaps Rainald was its builder."[2]

Fitz Alan, Earl of Arundel, is registered in the *Nomina Villarum* of 1316, as Lord of Wrocestre.

THE CHURCH.

Wroxeter Church, mentioned in *Domesday*, was, as is indicated by the mention of four priests in the Conqueror's record, originally a Saxon collegiate foundation. As we learn from a series of ancient charters, it was given by William Fitz Alan I. on the very day that he was restored to his estates and anew received the homage of his

DOORWAY, WROXETER.

---

[1] *Domesday*, fo. 254, b 2.   [2] *Antiq. of Shrop.* vol. vii. p. 309.

vassals, to his monastery of Haughmond.¹ In 1291, the church of Wroxeter was valued at £23 6s. 8d. *per ann.* In 1341, the parish was taxed £6 13s. 4d. to the *ninth.* The *Valor* of 1534-5 gives the preferment of the vicar of *Rockcetor* as £12 *per ann.*, less 10s. for procurations and 2s. for synodals. The Abbot of Haughmond's rectorial income was £8. To the chaplain of St. Mary's chantry in Wroxeter Church, the Abbot paid £2 yearly, " by gift of the Founder."

Portioners of Wroxeter.—Roland de Viquiria was rector of the first portion; Nicholas de Troughford was rector of the second portion; Robert de Warrewyk of the third portion—in 1301.

The first vicar of Wroxeter was William de Hodenet, instituted November 11, 1347; patrons, the Abbot and Convent of Haughmon.

LITTLE BUILDWAS, parochially and manorially, was an isolated member of Wroxeter; but in 1175 this ancient status was done away with by William Fitz Alan granting it to Buildwas Abbey. In 1302, Edmund de Lenham and his wife held Little Buildwas under the Abbot. Their services were as follows:—Edmund and his wife were to place the first dish on the Abbot's table at Buildwas every Christmas-day, and were to ride with the Abbot anywhither within the four seas, at the Abbot's charges.²

Hadley is noticed in Domesday Book thus:—" The same Rainald holds Hatlege, and Goisfrid [holds it] of him. [In Saxon times] Witric and Elric held it for two manors. Here ii hides. In demesne is one ox-team, and ii serfs and viii boors with half a team, and there might be ii and a half teams here besides. There is a mill here of 2s. [annual value], and i league of wood. In the time of King Edward, [the manor] was worth 37s. [per annum]; now 15s. He [Rainald] found it waste."³ Before the end of Henry I.'s reign, Goisfrid, who held Hadley under Rainald the sheriff, had been succeeded by William de Hadley, who, with Seburga, his wife, Hamo Peverel's daughter, and Alan, their son, founded, in Hadley Wood,

WOMBRIDGE PRIORY.

Wombridge Priory, of which some slight remains still exist,

---

¹ *Haughmond Chartulary.*   ² *Inquisitions,* 31 Edw. I. No. 127.
³ *Domesday,* fo. 254, b 2.

was founded for Augustine canons. The creation of a mere vassal of Fitz Alan's, this house never attained either to the wealth or influence of its rivals—Haughmond, Buildwas, Shrewsbury, or Lilleshall.

William, last Prior of Wombridge, declared before Henry the Eighth's commissioners, in 1535-6, that the net income of his house, temporalities and spiritualities included, amounted to only £65 7s. 4d. Amongst the items, an iron forge in *Woborne* (Wombridge) produced 13s. 4d. to the monks, and a coal-mine there, £5.

Little Dawley,

in 1086, also belonged to Rainald, the Norman sheriff of Shropshire. The fact is thus recorded in the Conqueror's record:—" The same Rainald holds Dalelie [of the Earl] and Benedict [holds] of him. Sistain held it [in Saxon times]. Here i hide. In demesne is half an ox-team; and one serf, i villain, and ii boors, with half a team, and there might be ii more teams. Here is i league of wood, which the Earl holds in demesne. In the time of King Edward, [the manor] was worth 24s. [annually]; now [it is worth] 5s." [1]

" The same Rainald," continues *Domesday*, " holds of the earl ii hides and ii parts of one hide, for a manor. Wige held it in the time of King Edward. Richard holds it of Rainald, and has i ox-team in demesne; and [there are] ii serfs and iii villains with ii teams. Of this land, one free man[2] holds half a hide and two parts of a virgate; and here with his three boors he has six oxen ploughing. In the time of King Edward the manor was worth 25s. [annually]; now 20s. There might be [another] team and a half here." [1] The nameless manor here alluded to cannot now be identified. It is supposed that, depopulated, it became absorbed into the forest of the Wrekin.

Lee-Gomery,

now a township in the parish of Wellington, is thus alluded to in *Domesday*:—" The same Rainald holds Lega, and Toret [holds it] of him. [Toret] himself held it in the time of King Edward. Here iii hides. In demesne is one ox-team;

---

[1] *Domesday*, fo. 254, b 2.   [2] "*Francus homo*."

RUINED CHAPEL, MALINS LEE.

CHANCEL ARCH, STIRCHLEY (*see* p. 146).

and [there are] v [such teams] among the male and female serfs; and ii villains, and iv radmans with two ox-teams; and there might be two other teams. Here is a wood of ii leagues. In King Edward's time [the manor] was worth 20s. [annually]; now it is worth 15s."[1]

At Malins Lee are the ruins of a Norman chapel, concerning which, however, early records are silent.

Rodington, pleasantly situated on the river Roden, also once belonged to Rainald, *vicecomes*, for *Domesday* says:—" The same Rainald holds Rodintone, and Toret holds [the manor] of him. The same [Toret] held it in King Edward's time. Here iv hides and one virgate. In demesne is i ox-team and ii serfs and iii female serfs. The church, the priest, ii villains, iii boors, and iii radmans have between them all ii teams and a half; and there might be iii more teams besides. Here is a mill of 6d. [annual value]. In the time of King Edward the manor was worth 27s. [*per annum*]. Now it is worth 20s."[1]

According to the Bradford Hundred Roll of 1255, the tenants of Rodington held it for " three-parts of a knight's fee, of the fief of John Fitz-Alan; and they do ward at Oswaldistree for 30 days, in time of war, with one horse, a hauberk, a chapel de fer, and a lance; and they do suit to the hundred-court every three weeks; and the manor is geldable."

RODINGTON CHURCH.

The church and the priest described in *Domesday*, under Rodintone, appear to have belonged to the mother church of Ercall, which, with all its appurtenances, Rodington included, Earl Roger gave to Shrewsbury abbey. Rodington was assessed 18s. to the *ninth* in 1341. The *Valor* of 1534-5 gives the rectory of Rodyngton as worth £6 13s. 4d. *per annum*.

Early Incumbent.—Philip de Pontesbury, rector, resigned 1298.

Dawley Magna. When William the Conqueror's Commissioners surveyed Shropshire, it was found that the Norman,

---

[1] *Domesday*, fo. 254, b 2.

William Pantulf, held nine different manors in Recordin Hundred under the Earl of Shrewsbury, namely, Dawley, Hinstock, Corselle, Beslow, Buttery, Eyton, Bratton, Horton, and Lawley; yet, beyond the *Domesday* notices of these places, their early history is comparatively uninteresting. Respecting Dawley, whose mineral wealth and great iron-works were undreamt of in 1086, *Domesday* adds, by way of supplement to its notice of Wellington:—" Of the land of this manor William [Pantulf] holds of the earl i hide, Dalelie for a manor. Grim held it before. Here is one ox-team, and vii villains have i team. Its old value was 30s. [*per annum*]; now [it is worth] 10s."[1]

A patent, dated at York on November 17th, 1316, allows William de Morton, clerk, to surround his mansion of Dalilcye with a wall of stone and lime, and to embattle the same—whence originated Dawley Castle.

The Church.

Dawley church, founded probably in the latter half of the 12th century, was originally a chapel subject to Idsall church, and with it passed to Battle-field College. It is not noticed as an independent church in either of the great ecclesiastical surveys.

Hinstock.

In 1086, William Pantulf and his undertenants held also Hinstock, under the Norman earl; for we read in Domesday Book:—" The same William holds Stoche, and Sasfrid [holds] of him. Algar held it. Here ii hides and a half geldable. The [arable] land is enough for v ox-teams. In demesne is one ox-team; and two neat-herds and one boor. There is i league of wood here. [The manor formerly] was worth 40s. [annually]; now 8s."[2]

The Church.

"The parochial church of the vill of Hinstock" was conveyed to Alcester Abbey in 1306. This parish was taxed 20s. to the *ninth* in 1341. The *Valor* of 1535-6 represents the rector of Hynstoke's income to be £6 *per annum*, less 4s. for procurations and synodals.

Early Incumbent.—Sir William de Brugge, rector, died 1320.

Shackford.—This member of Hinstock was formerly a notorious haunt of robbers.

---

[1] *Domesday*, fo. 253, b 2.   [2] Ibidem, fo. 257, a 2.

Corselle. " The same William holds Corselle ; and Sasfrid holds it of him. Godwin held it [in Saxon times]. Here ii hides geldable. The land is sufficient for iv ox-teams. Here is one boor, having nothing. In King Edward's time the manor was worth 20s. [*per annum*]. Afterwards it was worth 40s.; now it is worth 12d. "[1]

It is conjectured that the *Domesday* Corselle is now represented by Cross Hill, about a mile south of Hinstock.

Beslow, in the parish of Wroxeter, is thus noticed in the Conqueror's record :—" The same William holds Beteslawe. Godwin held it [formerly]. Here is half a hide geldable. The land is sufficient for ii ox-teams. In demesne is half a team ; and one serf and one free man, with two boors. [In King Edward's time the manor] was worth 11s. [*per annum*] ; now it is worth 5s."[2]

Butterry, now a township in the parish of Edgmond, is thus described in Domesday Book :—" The same William holds Buterei. Turchil held it [in Saxon times]. Here i hide geldable. The land is [sufficient] for ii ox-teams. Here are only three oxen. The old value of the manor was 6s. [*per annum*] ; now 2s."[2]

Eyton-on-the-Wealdmoors. " The same William," says *Domesday*, " holds Etone, and Warin [holds it] of him. Wighe and Ouiet held it [in Saxon times] for ii manors. Here iii hides geldable. In demesne are ii ox-teams ; and [there are] iv neat-herds, ii villains, and i boor with half a team ; and there might be i team and a half besides. In King Edward's time, the manor was worth 33s. [annually]. Now 20s."[2] Warin, who held Etone under William Pantulf in 1086, was probably ancestor of that Robert de Eyton, who was lord of Eyton in the reign of Henry II. To this day Robert de Eyton's descendants continue lords of the manor.

THE CHURCH.

Eyton church appears to have been founded by the lords of the manor, and always subject to their presentation. It is " dedicated

---

[1] *Domesday.* fo. 257, a 2.   [2] Ibidem, fo. 257, b 1.

to St. Catherine, and tradition says that one Catherine de Eyton vowed its foundation in the event of the safe return of her husband, then absent on a crusade. The motto of the lords of Eyton—*Je m'y oblige*, or *I bind myself*, is further said to have reference to this vow, and its pious accomplishment." [1]

King Henry the Eighth's *Valor* represents the rectory of *Eyton-super-Wyldmor*, in the deanery of Newport, as worth £2 4s. 8d. *per annum*.

Early Incumbent.—Roger de Lye, rector, died September 3rd, 1336.

Bratton, in the parish of Wrockwardine, in 1086, was a manor distinct in itself, for we read in *Domesday*, that:—"The same William holds Brochetone. Erniet held it [in Saxon times]. Here a hide and half geldable. There is land sufficient for iv ox-teams. Here are v boors, and they have nothing [that is, no ox-team]. In time of King Edward the manor was worth 24s. [annually]; now it is almost waste. Warin holds it [under Pantulf]." [2] Like Eyton held by Warin under William Pantulf, Bratton descended with Eyton to that Robert de Eyton whose representative now owns the township.

Horton. "The same William holds Hortune, and Warin holds it of him. Erniet held it [in Saxon times]. Here iii virgates of land geldable. The [arable] land is [capable of employing] i ox-team. It is waste. Here is half a league of wood and one haye." [2]

Lawley. "The same William holds Lauelei. Erneit held it [in Saxon times]. Here half a hide geldable. The land is sufficient for i ox-team. It was and is waste." [2] Little did the compilers of *Domesday* think of the rich veins of coal and iron-stone that lay deep embowelled in the earth under what they described as a *waste* manor. But Turold de Verley shared Lawley with William Pantulf, and his portion of the manor is thus alluded to in another page of *Domesday*:—" The same Turold holds Lauelie,

---

[1] Eyton's *Shropshire*, vol. 8, p. 35. [2] *Domesday*, fo. 257, b 1.

and Hunnit holds it of him. Here is one hide geldable. The land is sufficient for ii ox-teams. In demesne is one team; and there are iv serfs and i villain here. [In time of King Edward, Turold's share of the manor] was worth 12s. [per annum]; now it is worth 10s. [per annum]."[1]

𝔏𝔬𝔫𝔤𝔣𝔬𝔯𝔡.

Besides a share of Lawley, Turold de Verley held of the Norman Earl of Shrewsbury five manors in Recordin Hundred. Of these, the most important was Longford, which is thus noticed in Domesday Book:—"Turold holds Langeford of Earl Roger. Earl Eduin held it [formerly]. Here vi hides, with iiii berewicks, geldable. In demesne are ii hides; and here viii villains have iii ox-teams. Two knights hold of him [Turold] iiii hides, and here they have iii ox-teams; and there are iiii neat-herds, vii villains, iii boors, and one radman, with 3½ ox-teams, and yet there might be iiii more teams [employed]. Here a mill. In time of King Edward, the whole manor was worth £9 [annually]. Now it is worth 44s. He [Turold] found it waste."[2]

As a general rule, Turold's manors passed to Fitz-Alan, under whom they were held by the family of the Chetwynds; but Longford, an exception to that rule, appears to have come into the hands of Henry I., who granted the larger part of it to one Hamo by name. Adam de Brimpton II., a great grandson of this man, died lord of Longford in 1274. He had held it *in capite* by service of one knight's fee. He was bound, at his own cost, to provide a guard, with a barbed horse, for forty days, whenever the king in person approached Wales. The lord of Longford held his *free court* here twice in the year, and judged pleas of bloodshed and hue and cry. He had gallows and warren, and exercised his rights in these respects. As holding Longford by military tenure of the king, Adam de Brimpton III., in the summer of 1277, was summoned for service against Llewellyn.[3] In 1297, and again in 1301, he had military summons against the Scots.

THE CHURCH.

The advowson of Longford was granted in 1155 to Shrewsbury Abbey, but surrendered back to the lady of the manor thirty

---

[1] *Domesday*, fo. 258, a 1.   [2] Ibidem, fo. 257, b 2.
[3] *Parliamentary Writs*, I. 501.

years afterwards. In 1291, the church of Longefort, in the deanery of Newport, was valued at £2 *per annum*. The assessors of the *ninth* rated the parish 30s. in 1341. In 1534-5 King Henry VIII.'s *Valor* represented the preferment of the rector of Longforde juxta Newporte, to be worth £6 13s. 4d. *per annum*, less 10s. 8d. for synodals and procurations.

Early Incumbent.—Adam Parson, of Longford attested a deed in the 13th century.

Stirchley, although eight miles distant, was one of the four Domesday berewicks of Longford, on which it continued dependant for the greater part of two centuries after. About 1247, however, Osbern Fitz-William, the tenant here, surrendered the whole of Stirchley up to Buildwas Abbey, the prayers of the monks being the consideration.

STIRCHLEY CHURCH.

Originally a chapel subject to Idsall, this ancient structure appears to have been founded by the lords of Stirchley, in the 12th century. The Priors of Wenlock had a title to it in 1238. Pope Nicholas' taxation in 1291 valued the church of Stucheley in the deanery of Newport at £2 13s. 4d. *per annum*. In 1341, the parish was rated 40s. to the *ninth*; there were no sheep here, etc. The *Valor* of 1534-5 gives the rector of Stirchley's income as £6 13s. 4d., less 6s. 8d. for procurations, and 1s. for synodals.

Early Incumbent.—Walter, chaplain of Stirchley, 1220-30.

Chetwynd is thus described in William the Conqueror's record:—"The same Turold holds Catewinde. The Countess Godeva held it [formerly]. Here iii hides geldable. The [arable] land is [sufficient] for viii ox-teams. In demesne are iii ox-teams; and vi neat-herds, ii villains, and iii boors, with i team. Here is a priest; and a mill, with ii fisheries renders 5s. and lxiv sticks of eels [annually]. There is a little wood. In the time of King Edward the manor was worth 25s. [per annum]. Now [it is worth] 50s. He [Turold] found it waste."[1]

---

[1] *Domesday*, fo. 257, b 2.

We have stated that Turold's manors passed to a family who, deriving their name of Chetwynd from this place, long continued to hold them under the Fitz-Alans. The wealthy Chetwynds, again, had their feoffees holding under them.

The *Nomina Villarum* of 1316 returns John de Chetewind as lord of Chetewind. Sir John fought on the rebel side at the battle of Boroughbridge, in 1322. His arms were *azure, a chevron between three mullets or.*

THE CHURCH.

Chetwynd Church appears to have been existent in 1086. The taxation of 1291 places it in the deanery of Newport, and represents it as worth £4 13s. 4d. *per annum*. In 1341, the assessors of the ninth of wheat, wool, and lamb taxed the parish £3 6s. 8d. The *Valor* of 1534-5 gives the rector of Chetwynd's preferment at £11 *per annum*, less 3s. 10d. for synodals and procurations.

Early Incumbent.—William, Parson of Chetwynd, 1272. The lords of the manor presented.

Pilson also once belonged to Turold de Verley, and, like his other manors afterwards became part of the fee of Chetwynd. "The same Turold," says *Domesday*, "holds Plivesdone. Earl Eduin held it [formerly]. Here is one hide geldable. The land is [enough] for iiii ox-teams. In the time of King Edward, the manor was worth 8s. [*per annum*]. Turold found it waste, and so it continues."[1]

When Roger de Pywelesdon, in 1293-4, attempted to levy in Wales the taxes necessary for the French war, the *insurrection of Madoc* ensued, when the infuriated Welsh hanged and beheaded the English king's collector.[2]

Sambrook, another member of Chetwynd is noticed in Domesday Book thus:—"The same Turold holds Semebre. Ulgar held it. Here a hide and a half. Here is land [sufficient] for vii ox-teams. A knight holds it under Turold, and has one ox-team; and there are v boors with ii teams; and a mill, paying a rent of 64d. In time of King Edward the manor was

---

[1] *Domesday*, fo. 257, b 2.   [2] POWELL'S *Chron.* p. 278.

worth 45s. [per annum]. Now it is worth 16s. Turold found it waste." [1]

Howle. "The same Turold," says *Domesday*, "holds Hugle, and Walter holds it of him. Batsuen held it [in Saxon times]. Here ii hides geldable. The land is [capable of employing] v ox-teams. In demesne are ii teams, and iiii neat-herds, and a mill of 64d. [annual value]. In the time of King Edward, the manor was worth 20s. [per annum]. Now it is worth 16s. He [Turold] found it waste." [1]

Kinnersley. Gerard de Tornai held five manors in Recordin Hundred under the Norman earl, namely Kinnersley, Uppington, Shawbury, Cherrington, and Chesthill. The first-named place is thus described in William the Conqueror's record:—"Gerard holds Chinardeseie of Earl Roger. Willegrip held it [in Saxon times.] Here i hide geldable. The land is [sufficient] for iiii ox-teams. In demesne is i ox-team; and [there are] iii serfs, iiii villains, and iii boors with ii teams. In time of King Edward, the manor was worth 21s. [per annum]. Now it is worth 18s." [2]

The Norman Gerard de Tornai's daughter Sibil married Hamo Peverel, who, in right of his wife, acquired Kinnersley, which he gave to Shrewsbury Abbey. The abbot retained the estate until the Reformation.

THE CHURCH.

There was a chapel at Kinnersley in 1174. In 1291, the church of Kinardeseye, in the deanery of Salop, was valued at £1 13s. 4d. per annum, besides a pension of 2s. therefrom to the abbot of Shrewsbury. The parish of Kinardesheye in the deanery of Newport, was assessed one merk (13s. 4d.) to the *ninth* in 1341. The *Valor* of 1534-5 represents the rector of Kynnasshey's income to be £6 13s. 4d., less 6s. 8d. for procurations, 1s. for synodals, and a pension of 4s. to Shrewsbury Abbey.

Early Incumbent.—Walkeline de Northampton, 1223; presented by the King because the abbaey of Shrewsbury was vacant.

---

[1] *Domesday*, fo. 257, b 2.　　[2] *Ibidem*, fo. 258, b 2.

Uppington, pleasantly situated under the Wrekin, also belonged to Gerard de Tornai in 1086. "The same Gerard," says *Domesday*, "holds Opetone. Goduin held it. Here ii hides geldable. There is land [sufficient] for v ox-teams. In demesne are iii teams; and [there are] vi neat-herds, v villains, and iiii boors, with ii teams. Here is a wood, i league in length, wherein is i Haye. In the time of King Edward, the manor was worth 25s. [per annum]. Now 31s. He [Gerard] found it waste."[1]

Eventually, like other Tornai escheats, Uppington lapsed to the crown, when Henry II. conferred the manor upon Roger Mushunte, his servitor in the matter of the purchase of Welsh horses for the king's use in Normandy. Roger held Uppington and Harrington on condition that he procured the king *a sore sparrow hawk* annually: an appropriate serjeantry to attach to the tenure of lands so close to the hawk eyries of Mount Gilbert (the Wrekin.)

Roger Mussun, "for the soul's health of his lord, King Henry the Second, and himself and his wife," gave land and "the chapel of Uppington," to Wombridge Priory; and by various grants from Roger's successive descendants, eventually that Priory was enabled to establish a clear title to the whole of the manor.

To Roger Mussun's charter to Wombridge was attached a round white waxen seal, charged with the figure of a bird, probably a hawk, stretching out its head and wings. On July 1, 1346, this charter was sent to Lichfield, and exhibited in the course of some legal proceedings affecting Wombridge Priory, when, by some accident, the seal happened to get so fractured that only the letters Rog' i Mussun of the legend remained. A Notary Public then present, upon this was employed to draw up a certificate of the disaster, and of what the seal had been, which curious certificate the canons of Wombridge carefully embodied in their chartulary, so essential was it then deemed to the validity of a document that its seal should be preserved.

Uppington parish originally formed part of the Saxon parish of Wroxeter.

Uppington chapel, as it has been stated, was given by the lord of the manor, about 1188, to Wombridge Priory; consequently, this ancient foundation is not specially mentioned, either in the

---

[1] *Domesday*, fo. 258, b 2.

taxation of 1291, the assessment of 1345, the *Valor* of 1535, or the Diocesan Registers.

Shawbury.

This name implies a camp or place of defence, by the side of a wood: in accordance with which we have Shawbury Park Wood, Withyford Wood, etc.

Shawbury is the subject of the following entry in Domesday Book:—"The same Gerard holds Sawesberie. Edric and Eliet held it [in Saxon times] for ii manors. Here a hide and a half geldable. The [arable] land is [sufficient] for viii ox-teams. In demesne is one team; and ii serfs. A church, a priest, iii boors, i freeman, and a mill of 5s. [annual value, are here.] In the time of King Edward the manor was worth 12s. [per annum]; now 16s."[1]

De Tornai's son-in-law, Hamo Peverel, succeeded him as lord of Shawbury; but Henry II., dissallowing such a mode of succession, resumed this Tornai escheat into his own hands, and the under-tenant accordingly became a tenant *in capite*. That tenant's name was Robert Fitz-Nigel, the same who, "for the soul's health of himself, his father, mother, and all his friends [gave] the advowson of the church of St. Mary of Schawgesbury" to Haughmond Abbey. Robert Fitz-Nigel's son, Wido Fitz-Robert, lord of Shawbury about the year 1200, was waylaid and murdered in the forest of Haughmond. Upon this, deceased's brothers Nigel and Richard successively became lords of the manor; but the latter, in 1206, having murdered Maurice de Shawbury, suffered outlawry and forfeiture.

King John then conferred the manor of Shawbury upon his favourite, Thomas de Erdinton, whose heirs retained it. Henry de Erdington II. is duly returned in the *Nomina Villarum* of 1316 as Lord of Shawbury.

The Church.

The Church of St. Mary of Shawbury, which is alluded to in the Domesday notice of the manor, was probably a Saxon foundation. It included in its parish the afterwards distinct chapelries of Acton Reynald, Moreton Corbet, Grinsill, and Great Withyford, in each of which vills the lords of the fee founded chapels and cemeteries during the reign of Stephen or Henry II.

---

[1] *Domesday*, fo. 258, b 2.

We have said that Robert Fitz-Nigel gave Shawbury Church to Haughmond Abbey. In the words of the chartulary, "*ex dono Roberti de Sagheberia ecclesiam ejusdem villæ cum Capellis de Mortone, Actone, et Wideford;*" and the bishop suffered the monks to appropriate Shawbury, with its chapels. In 1291, the church of Schawebur', in Salop deanery, was valued at £6 13s. 4d. per annum. In 1341, the parish was assessed £6 to the *ninth*. The *Valor* of 1534-5 represents the abbot as receiving £8 6s. 8d. for the ferm of Shawbury rectory. The vicar's income was £7 10s. per annum, less 2s. for synodals, and 6s. 8d. for procurations.

Early Incumbent.—Robert, priest of Shawbury in the latter half of 12th century, may have been either the last rector, or first vicar of Shawbury.

Cherrington.

"The same Gerard," says *Domesday*, "holds Cerlintone. Uliet held it. Here iii hides geldable. There is land [sufficient] for vi ox-teams. In demesne is one team and a half; and iii neat-herds, ii villains, and iii boors, with i team. In time of King Edward the manor was worth 23s. [annually]; now it is worth 22s. He [Gerard] found it waste."[1]

Sooner or later the canons of Wombridge obtained the best part of this manor, and they retained it until the Dissolution.

Chesthill.

"The same Gerard," says *Domesday*, "holds Cestulle. Leduui held it [in Saxon times]. Here i hide and iii virgates geldable. The land is [capable of employing] v ox-teams. In demesne is one ox-team; and [there are] ii serfs, ii boors, and one Radman with i team. In the time of King Edward it was worth 15s. [per annum]; now [it is worth] the same."[1]

From another part of Domesday Book, we ascertain that the Bishop of Chester held the other half of the manor. "The same Bishop holds Cesdille, and held it [in Saxon times]. Here i hide and one virgate of land. There is land enough for ii ox-teams. Its former value was 8s. [per annum]; now it is waste."[2] Chesthill, which name is now lost, occupied the angle formed by the confluence of the Bailey Brook and the Tern.

---

[1] *Domesday*, fo. 258, b 2.   [2] Ibidem, fo. 252, a 2.

Longner-upon-Severn, in 1086, also belonged to the Bishop of Chester, for *Domesday* says that:—" The same Bishop holds Languenare, and Wigot holds of him. Here i hide. There is land [enough] for ii ox-teams. In demesne is one team; and ii serfs, and ii villains have i team. The manor was and is worth 8s. [*per annum*]." [1]

"Even to this day," says Eyton, "does Longner retain a strongly-marked feature of its ancient *status*. It is an isolated portion of the Shrewsbury parish of St. Chad. Now St. Chad's church was founded, endowed, and for ages governed by the bishops of the Mercian diocese; and they threw their manors into the parish of St. Chad, wherever distance would permit such an arrangement." [2]

Stoke-upon-Tern. The Norman Earl of Shrewsbury gave to his vassal, Roger de Laci, three manors in Recordin Hundred; namely, Stoche, Uptone, and Wideford. The first of these is noticed in the Conqueror's record, thus:—" The same Roger holds Stoche. Edmund held it [in Saxon times]. Here vii hides. In demesne are iii ox-teams; and vi serfs and iii female serfs. Here is a church, a priest, xi villains, iii radmans, and i Frenchman with x teams between them all; and there might be v more teams besides. There is a mill of 12s. [annual value], and a third part of one league of wood. In time of King Edward the manor was worth £6; afterwards it was waste; now it is worth £7." [3]

The De Lacys had for tenants in their great manor of Stoke, the important family of de Say; but when, upon the decease of Walter de Lacy, lord of Ludlow, in 1241, John de Verdon became co-heir to his barony and seigneural lord of Stoke, he purchased the tenant-interest of Hugh de Say, by an equivalent of lands in Ireland.

A list is given of the members of Stoke-upon-Tern, in one instance called *Stoke Say*, in the other *Stoke Lacy*, in the Feodaries of 1284-5. These were Allerton (now Ollerton), Eton, Wystaneswyk, Stoke Aubry, Wodehus, Heselschawe (Helshaw), Pechesay (Petsey), Morton Say, Stuche (now Stych), Blecheley,

---

[1] *Domesday*, fo. 252, a 2. [2] *Antiquities of Shropshire*, vol. viii. p. 205.
[3] *Domesday*, fo. 256, b 1.

Aldeley, Oldefeld, Hull, Waranshall, and Parrok (now Park). Theobald de Verdon held the whole *in capite* of the king, as a member of his barony of Ludlow.

The notices relating to the various members of Stoke-upon-Tern are scanty and uninteresting. They were held by various feoffees under the seigneural lord of the central manor.

The Church.

The church of St. Peter, at Stoke-upon-Tern, is alluded to in the *Domesday* notice of the manor. In all likelihood it was one of the original Saxon churches of the district. In 1291, the church of Stokesay, as it was then called, in the deanery of Newport, was valued at £6 13s. 4d. In 1341, the parish of *Stoke-super-Teyrn* was rated £5 6s. 8d. to the *ninth*. The Valor of 1534-5 gives the rectory of Stoke-upon-Tyrn as £21 *per annum*, less 8s. 4d. for procurations, 6s. 8d. for synodals, and 5s. for procurations at visitations.

Early Rector.—Master Henry de Bray, on March 24th, 1304, was instituted to this church at presentation of Sir Theobald de Verdon, sen[r.]

Waters Upton, or Upton Parva, is noticed in *Domesday* thus :—" The same Roger holds Uptone [of the earl], and Seuuard [holds] of him. Gamel held it [in Saxon times]. Here iii hides. In demesne are ii ox-teams ; and iiii neat-herds, iiii villains, one boor and one radman with ii teams, and still there might be ii more teams. There is a mill of 12s. 1d. [annual value]. In time of King Edward the manor was worth 40s. 4d. [*per annum*], and afterwards it was waste ; now it is worth 30s. 2¼d." [1]

By some way or other becoming annexed to the barony of Wem, Pantulf's feoffee here, Walter Fitz John, gave to the place that distinctive title of Walters or Waters Upton, by which it is now known. The Hundred Roll of 1255 represents the tenants here as holding *Hopton* " by service of one knight at Wem, for forty days, at their own cost, in time of war."

Waters Upton Church.

From the circumstance that this church paid a pension to the priory of St. Guthlac, at Hereford, it may be inferred that it was

---

[1] *Domesday*, fo. 256, b 1.

founded by those Lacies who took so great an interest in St. Guthlac. About 1245, Nicholas de Upton gave the advowson of Waters Upton to Shrewsbury Abbey.

No mention is made of this chapel in 1291, except that St. Guthlac received a pension of 2s. therefrom. In 1341, the chapelry of Upton Parva was assessed 16s. to the *ninth*; there had been a murrain among the sheep, and the corn crops had failed. In 1534-5 the rector of Upton Parva's preferment was worth £4, less 2s. for procurations, and 10½d. for synodals.

Early Incumbent.—Peter, parson of Upton, found dead in bed; 1256.

Little Withiford.

In 1086, the Norman Roger de Lacy was seigneural lord also of half Withiford. The fact is thus recorded in Domesday Book :—" The same Roger holds Wideford, and Robert [holds it] of him. Leuenod held it [in Saxon times]. Here is half a hide and half an ox-team; and there might be another half-team. The former value was 2s. [*per annum*]; now its value is included in the ferm of Stoche." [1] Lacy's estate afterwards became annexed to Shawbury, to which it still remains attached.

Fulcuius held the other half of Withiford, under the Norman Earl of Shrewsbury, for in another part of King William the First's record, we read that :—" The same Fulcuius holds Wideford. Godric held it. Here half a hide. The land is [sufficient] for ii ox-teams. Here is one team; and it [the half manor] pays a ferm of 3s. [*per annum*]. In the time of King Edward it was worth 8s." [2]

Withington

also was held by Fulcuius when the Conqueror's Commissioners surveyed Shropshire. *Domesday* says that :—" Fulcuius holds Wientone of Earl Roger. Uluuin and Uluric held it [in Saxon times] for ii manors. Here ii hides and a half. The land is [capable of employing] iiii ox-teams. In demesne are ii ox-teams; and iiii serfs, and i female serf; and iii

---

[1] *Domesday*, fo. 256, b 1.   [2] Ibidem, fo. 259, a 2.

villains and i boor, with i team and a half. In time of King Edward the manor was worth 15s. [*per annum*]; now it is worth 21s. He [Fulcuius] found it waste."[1]

Fulcuius' descendants, if any he had, lost those manors which he had held in 1086, and Withington escheating to the Crown, half the manor was annexed to the fief of Fitz-Alan, whilst the other half was made a serjeantry. The duty of the tenant was to provide a knight who should conduct the Welshmen of Powis land, whenever they had to visit the English Court. In other words, Robert de Haughton, the lord of Withington's charge, was to provide safe conduct for Welsh embassies between Montfordbridge and Shrewsbury, whether going to or returning from the English Court: a service appropriate to the great feudal position which the Haughtons formerly occupied on the Shropshire border.

In process of time the Withington serjeantry became extinct, and the whole manor was held for half a knight's fee, under Fitz-Alan, the service due thereon being to provide one esquire, with a barbed horse, etc., at Oswestry, for 40 days.[2]

Concerning Withington church, although existent so early as 1159, those national records which treat of parish churches are silent; the reason is, that, originally a chapel of Upton Magna, it belonged to Shrewsbury Abbey.

Preston-on-Wealdmoors.

Upon arriving at his palatine earldom, Roger de Montgomery conferred upon his vassal, Ralph de Mortemer, three manors in Recordin Hundred; one of the three, Preston-on-Wealdmoors, is thus described in Domesday Book:—"Radulf holds Prestune of Earl Roger. Burrer held it [in Saxon times]. Here i hide geldable. The land is [sufficient] for iiii ox-teams. In demesne is one team; and ii neat-herds and iii villains with one team. Here half a league of wood. The old value of the manor was 40s. [*per annum*]; now 20s."[3] Rebelling against his king in 1088, Ralph Mortemer lost his Recordin manors. Ultimately, Preston was annexed by Henry I. to the fee of Hodnet, and so was held *in capite* of the Crown by the hereditary seneschals of Montgomery castle.

---

[1] *Domesday*, fo. 259 a 2.   [2] *Inquisitions*, 2 Edw. I., No. 30.
[3] *Domesday*, fo. 257, a 1.

The free chapel of *Preston-super-Wyldmore* is described in King Henry the Eighth's *Valor* as worth 60s. *per annum.*

Early Incumbent.—Roger, rector of this church, resigned September 6th, 1336.

Peplow is thus noticed in *Domesday*:—"Radulfus holds Papelau of Earl Roger. Orgrim and Uluric held it [in Saxon times] for ii manors. Here iii hides geldable. There is [arable] land enough for vii ox-teams. In demesne is i team; and [there are] ii serfs and v villains with iii teams. In the time of King Edward the manor was worth 46s. [*per annum*]; now [it is worth] 12s. 4d. [annually]. He [Radulf] found it waste."[1] Ultimately annexed to the fee of Hodnet, the early history of Peplow is associated with that of Preston-on-the Wealdmoors.

Isombridge, the remaining manor held of the Norman earl by the great Ralph de Mortemer, is thus alluded to in the Conqueror's record:—"Radulf holds Asnebruge of Earl Roger. Ulf held it [in Saxon times]. Here ii hides geldable. There is [arable] land [sufficient] for iiii ox-teams. In demesne is one team; and [there are] ii neat-herds, iiii villains, and iii boors with ii teams. Here is a mill paying [annually] iii measures of corn. A knight here has half a hide of this land. The manor was and is worth 20s. [*per annum*]."[1] Forfeited like his other lands in Recordin Hundred, Ralph Mortemer's manor of Isombridge appears to have been conferred by the Norman earl upon Ulger Venator, Chief Forester of Shropshire, whose descendants, the lords of Bolas, long continued to hold it.

The site of that free chapel at Esomebrigge described in the *Valor* of Henry VIII. as worth £1 6s. 8d. *per annum*, may still be identified.

Bolas Magna is not mentioned in Domesday Book, because in 1086 it was merely a member of Isombridge. Cotemporaneously, however, with the appointment by the Norman earl, of Ulger Venator to the chief forestership of Shropshire,

---

[1] *Domesday*, fo. 257, a 1.

Bolas became *caput* of the manor, and hence the hereditary foresters of Shropshire are often called foresters of Bolas. Ulger and his descendants long continued lords of Great Bolas. One of these, Roger Fitz John, on the great perambulation of the Shropshire forests being taken in 1300, is the first-named of the foresters then in office.

THE CHURCH.

In 1291, the church of Boulwas, in the deanery of Newport, is valued at £1 13s. 4d. *per annum*. In 1341, the parish was taxed 20s. to the *ninth*. In 1534-5, the rectory of Bollas was worth £8 *per annum*, less 6s. 8d. for procurations, and 4s. for synodals.

Early Incumbent.—Alan de Newton, in 1306, was presented to this church by King Edward I. as guardian of Roger Fitz John's heir.

Old Caynton, Meeson, Orleton, and Calvington, members of Bolas, were, in early times, held by various feoffees of the foresters of Bolas.

Sutton. Roger de Curcelle held two manors in Recordin Hundred, under Roger de Montgomery, the Earl of Shrewsbury. Sutton was one of them which, now a mere township in the parish of Market Drayton, in William the Conqueror's time was an important manor. We read in *Domesday* that:—"Roger de Curcelle holds Sudtone of Earl Roger. The Countess Godeva held it [formerly]. Here iiii hides geldable. In demesne is one ox-team; and ii neat-herds and ix boors, with i radman, have ii ox-teams; and there might be iiii more teams besides. Here is a mill, rendering [annually] 8 measures of corn. The value [of the manor] was and is 25s. [*per annum*]."[1] Roger de Curcelle's fief was ultimately annexed to Pantulf's barony of Wem.

Tibberton is thus noticed in Domesday Book:—"The same Roger holds Tetbristone. Ulgar held it. Here v hides geldable. In demesne is one ox-team; and two neat-herds, and four boors, with one team; and there might be vii more teams [employed].

---

[1] *Domesday*, fo. 256, a 2.

In King Edward's time the manor was worth 60s. [annually], and afterwards it was waste; now it is worth 10s."[1] The Bradford Hundred Roll of 1255 represents the tenants here as doing "ward at Wem Castle, in time of war, with a horse, a hauberk, a *chapel de fer*, and a lance, at their own cost."

Tibberton chapel, dependent on the church of Edgmond, although not mentioned in early records, nevertheless was an ancient foundation.

Woodcote.

The roads by means of which the Roman conquerors kept up an easy communication with their most distant possessions, present a fit subject both for our wonder and admiration. These roads extended from Spain and Barbary in the east to Assyria in the west, and from Great Britain in the north to Arabia and Egypt in the south. The difficulties that must have been encountered, and the perseverance required, in the completion of such stupendous works, are calculated to impress us with a very high estimate of Roman energy.

The Roman Watling Street enters Shropshire close to Weston-under-Lizard, south-east of Woodcote. From Weston-under-Lizard, a branch shoots out in a north-westerly direction, which, midway between Woodcote and Newport, bears the name of Pave Lane. This particular line is characterised by that great feature of a Roman road, namely, the direct course it takes from one point to another. The line once chosen, every natural impediment, were it mountain or morass, yielded to the inflexible determination of that great people.

Woodcote, situate on the eastern verge of Shropshire in 1086, was held under the Norman earl by Roger Fitz Tetbald. The circumstance is thus recorded in that venerable record the Domesday Book:—"The same Robert holds Udecote, and Tochi holds it of him. Aluric held it [in Saxon times]. Here iii hides. In demesne there is one ox-team; and ii neat-herds, one villain, iii boors and iii free men, with two teams between them; and there might be three more teams besides. The manor was worth [in King Edward's time] 20s. [annually]; now 10s."[2]

Robert Fitz Tetbald's seigneury at Woodcote passed, with his

---

[1] *Domesday*, fo. 256, a 2.   [2] Ibidem, fo. 256, b 2.

Sussex honour of Petworth, to Joseline de Lovain, and so to the world-renowned house of Percy. The Feodary of 1284 says, that "William Randulfe holds the vills of Wodecote and Eye of Henry de Percy, who holds of the king *in capite.*" This William Randulf, or Rondulf, was a thriving burgess of Newport. His eldest son, Geoffrey, even in his father's life-time, attained a high position as a burgess of Shrewsbury. He served the office of bailiff of Shrewsbury no less than six times between the years 1290 and 1323; and was returned as a burgess of Parliament for that town nine times between 1295 and 1318, his brother, Simon Rondulf, being one of his *manucaptors* on the last occasion.

Woodcote chapel is a very ancient structure. From the first it was, and it continues to remain, subject to the church of Sheriff Hales.

The Eye. "The same Robert holds a manor of one virgate of land, and Tochi holds it of him. It is in the same Hundred [namely, Recordin]. The land is [enough] for one ox-team. Here is one villain and ii serfs: they have nothing. The manor formerly was worth 5s [annually]."[1] Such is the *Domesday* account of a piece of land which, a little to the west of Leighton, enclosed by the winding of the Severn, is now known as Eye Farm.

Brockton, near Longford, is supposed to be twice alluded to in Domesday Book, thus :—" Richard holds of the earl [Roger de Montgomery], in Brochetone, half a hide. The land is sufficient for i ox-team. Aisil held it [in Saxon times] for one manor. Here is one free man. He pays xvi pence [annually]."

Again :—" Richard holds of the earl Brochetone. Aisil held it [in Saxon times]. There is half a hide geldable. The land is enough for i ox-team. Here one free man pays a rent of xvi pence."[2]

Haughton, in the modern Hundred of Bradford South, is the subject of the following entry in *Domesday* :—" Roger Venator

---

[1] *Domesday*, fo. 256, b 2.   [2] Ibidem, fos. 257, a 1, and 259, b 2.

holds Haustone [of the earl]. Edwi held it [in Saxon times]. Here i hide geldable. There is land [sufficient] for ii ox-teams. Here is one tenant [*homo*] rendering a ferm of 6s."[1]

About the year 1245, Roger Fitz Gilbert, of Halghton, gave to Haghmon Abbey two acres in the field of Halghton, which Gilbert, his father, had bequeathed, with his body, to sustain the lights before the high altar in the church of Haghmon. Witnesses, Henry de Sibbeton and others.

Uffington signifies the town of the children of Uffa. Intersected by the Severn, pleasantly situated, Uffington is noticed in *Domesday* thus:—"The same Helgot holds Ofitone [of Earl Roger]. Genut and Elveva held it [in Saxon times] for ii manors and were free. There are v hides geldable. Here is land enough for xii ox-teams. In demesne is a team and half, with iii male and iiii female serfs; and [there are] iii villains, ii boors, and ii Frenchmen, with ii teams. Here is half a league of wood. In King Edward's time the manor was worth 30s. [*per annum*]; now [it is worth] the same."[2]

Robert de la Mare, the crusader, as he lay on his death-bed at Benevento in 1192, bequeathed the whole of Uffington to Haughmond Abbey, and the monks held the estate until the Reformation.

Uffington chapel, whenever founded, continued for centuries an affiliation of St. Alkmund's, Shrewsbury.

Poynton, in the parish of High Ercall, is alluded to in the following extract from Domesday Book:—"Uluiet holds Peventone and Tuncstan of the earl. He also held it [in Saxon times] for ii manors. Here i hide and a half. The [arable] land is [enough] for iii ox-teams. In demesne is one team and ii serfs. [In time of King Edward] the manor was worth 11s.; now 12s."[3]

Remains of an ancient chapel here are still visible.

Lilleshall. When William the Conqueror's Commissioners surveyed Shropshire in 1086, it was found that six manors in Recordin Hundred belonged to the collegiate church of St.

---

[1] *Domesday*, fo. 259, a 2.   [2] Ibidem, fo. 258, b 1.   [3] Ibidem, fo. 259. b 2.

Alkmund, at Shrewsbury; three out of the five being held by Godebold, the priest, Earl Roger's friend and adviser.

Lilleshall, one of St. Alkmund's manors, is described in Domesday Book as follows:—"The same church held and holds Linleshelle. Here x hides. In demesne are ii ox-teams; and [there are] x villains, v boors, and iii serving Frenchmen, with viii teams between them; and yet there might be ix more teams. Here are iiii neat-herds, and a mill; but it pays nothing. Here is i league of wood. In the time of King Edward the manor was worth £6 [*per annum*]; now £4. Godebold, the priest, holds it."[1]

Godebold's prebendal estates passed from his son to Bishop Richard de Belmeis, Viceroy of Shropshire, whose younger nephew, Richard de Belmeis II., Archdeacon of Middlesex, acquiring "all the churches, lands, and things," which having in the first instance been held by Godebold and Robert, his son, had since been held under the king by the late bishop; he founded

Lilleshall Abbey.

This great monastic establishment was designed for those Arroasian canons of the order of St. Augustine, who, introduced into Shropshire, had been domiciled in his manor of Tong by the lord of Lilleshall's elder brother. For reasons best known to himself, Stephen the usurper consented to the prayer of Archdeacon Richard de Belmeis, and conceded to his shorn protégés "the prebend which the said Richard had in the church of St. Alchmund at Salopesbury, and all his demesnes and stock; and, moreover, all the other prebends of the aforesaid church, whenever they should fall vacant:" Pope Eugenius III., and the diocesan bishop, Roger de Clinton, consenting to this great transfer of church property; thus the prebendal estates of the once opulent college of St. Alkmund went, about 1145, to found Lilleshall Abbey. The confirmatory charter of Theobald, Archbishop of Canterbury, which details the circumstances, seal and all complete, is still preserved among the Duke of Sutherland's muniments at Trentham.[2]

Stephen's rival, "Matilda the empress, daughter of King Henry," also received "William, abbot of Lylleshull, and the canons there serving God, for the souls of Henry her father, Matilda her mother, etc., etc., and for the welfare of himself and hers, under her tutelage and protection."[3] Henry II.'s charter to the canons

---

[1] *Domesday*, fo. 253, a 1. [2] See *Monasticon* VI. 263 for copy.
[3] EMPRESS MATILDA'S *Charter*, *Lilleshall Chartulary*, fo. 44.

of Lilleshall followed. A contemporary royal precept granted the canons an exemption from *toll and passage* throughout the king's dominions, under a penalty of £10, recoverable from any one who should charge them with such dues; and thus, within four years of its founder's consecration as Bishop of London, the Augustine abbey of Lilleshall was firmly established. Papal privileges and archiepiscopal and regal confirmations, full and remarkable, were not wanting to the monks of Lilleshall. King John's charter, which cost the abbot 30 merks, gives to the canons these extraordinary franchises: namely, soc, sac, tol, them, infengenthef, and utfengenthef; also it acquits them of geld, Dangeld, suits of counties, and hundreds, waste, forest regard, army aids, aids to sheriffs, or their serjeants, of stretward, hidage, pleas, and plaints pertaining to county, and of all secular services, saving such as might be reserved in the charters of any of the canon's suzerains. They were also to be quit of toll, passage, tolls of bridges, ways, ferries, or sea voyages, and of all tolls at fairs throughout the kingdom, except in the city of London, and in respect of such goods as could be proved to belong to themselves, or to have been purchased for their uses.

Pope Nicholas's taxation, in 1291, took into account only a few of the sources from whence the abbot of Lilleshall's income was derived; this computation, therefore, gives no accurate idea of the wealth of the abbey. King Henry VIII.'s *Valor* in 1535-6, however, represents the abbot of Lilleshull as returning the gross income of his monastery in temporalities and spiritualities at £326 0s. 10d. The abbot was in receipt of rents from the counties of Shropshire, Staffordshire, Cheshire, Derbyshire, Northamptonshire, Leicestershire, Yorkshire, and Warwickshire. He was also impropriator of eight churches, three of which were in Shropshire, the others were in the counties of Warwickshire, Leicestershire, Norfolk, Gloucestershire, and Devonshire respectively.

On October 16, 1538, the abbot of Lilleshall surrendered up his charge to the king, when Henry VIII., on November 28, 1538, granted the site of the house, etc., in *fee farm*, to William Cavendish, Esq. In the following year, it was granted to James Leveson, Esq. William, apparently first abbot of Lilleshall, occurs about 1148. The election of an abbot of Lilleshall required the assent both of the crown and the diocesan bishop.

To return to the manor of Lilleshall, over which meanwhile the abbot had continued lord: the Bradford tenure roll of 1285 says

LILLESHALL ABBEY, FROM THE NAVE.

FONT, LILLESHALL CHURCH.

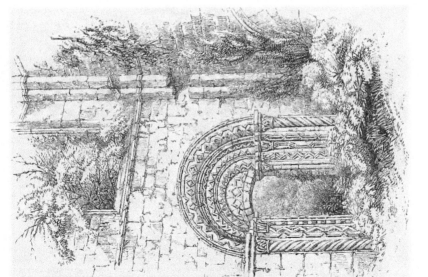

DOORWAY, LILLESHALL ABBEY.

that "the abbot of Lilleshill holds the manor of Lilleshill, with its members, viz., Donyngton and Mokeleston (Muxton); also the three vills of Attecham, Unkynton (Uckington), and Adbright-lee, of the king, *in capite sine medio*, as members of the church of St. Alchmund, Salop, by gift of the king, and by charter. The abbot has his free court, and holds pleas of bloodshed and *hue and cry*, and has gallows and free warren."

PARISH CHURCH OF LILLESHALL.

This, a very ancient foundation, was granted by Bishop Peche, about the year 1161, to the canons of Lilleshall. In 1291, the church of Lilleshall was valued at £4 13s. 4d. per annum. In 1341, the parish was taxed only £4 to the *ninth*, because there had been a general murrain among the sheep, etc. In 1534-5, the vicar of Lilleshall's income was £7 per annum, less 2s. 3d. for synodals. The rectory yielded the abbot £5 6s. 8d. per annum, less 6s. 8d. for procurations.

Early Vicar.—R, vicar of Lilleshall, about 1235.

Longdon-upon-Tern in 1086 also belonged to St. Alkmund's church. "The same church," says *Domesday*, "held [in Saxon times] and [still] holds Languedune. Here ii hides. In demesne there is one ox-team; and iiii boors with i team; and still there might be iii more teams here. There are vi . . . [1] among the male and female serfs; and a mill of 5s. annual value. In King Edward's time, the manor was worth 21s. [per annum]. Now it is worth 9s. 4d."[2] As one of the prebendal estates of St. Alkmund, this manor ultimately went to enrich Lilleshall abbey.

Uckington. "The same church [St. Alkmund's] held, and still holds Uchintune; and Godebold holds it of her [the church]. There are iiii hides geldable. In demesne are iii ox-teams; and ii radmans and iii boors, with i team, and there might be iii more teams besides. Here vi neat-herds. In time of King Edward, the manor was worth 24s. [per annum]. Now it is worth 30s."[2]

---

[1] In the original record a word is wanting here. [2] *Domesday*, fo. 253, a

From the middle of the 12th century to the middle of the 16th the abbot of Lilleshall exercised the seigneury over this manor.

𝔄𝔱𝔠𝔥𝔞𝔪. "The same church held [in Saxon times], and now holds Atingeham; and Godebold holds it of her. Here i hide. In demesne there is one ox-team and half; and ii villains and iii boors, with iii teams. [The manor formerly] was worth 10s. [per annum]. Now it pays a rent of 6s. 8d."[1] This manor, which, from time immemorial had belonged to the Saxon church of St. Alkmund, at Shrewsbury, passed, with the other estates of that church, to the abbot of Lilleshall, under whom it was held until the dissolution.

ATCHAM CHURCH.

Atcham church is not alluded to in the *Domesday* notice of the manor, yet it certainly was existent when William the Conqueror's commissioners made their report, for, on April 5, 1075, ten years before *Domesday* was compiled, Ordericus Vitalis, the celebrated monkish historian, was baptized in it. "I was born," says he, "on the 14th of the calends of March (Feb. 16), and was regenerated in the holy font of baptism by the ministry of Ordericus the priest, at Attingham, in the church of St. Eata the Confessor, which stands on the bank of the river Severn."[2]

In another place, this celebrated Anglo-Norman monk says, "I was baptized on the Saturday of Easter, at Attingham, a village in England, which stands on the bank of the great river Severn. There, by the ministry of Ordericus the priest, Thou [O God] didst regenerate me with water and the Holy Spirit, and gavest me the name borne by this priest, who was my godfather. When I was five years old, I was sent to school at Shrewsbury," etc.[3]

Atcham church then was dedicated to St. Eata, the friend of that St. Cuthbert of whom Bede tells us so much. St. Eata founded Ripon Minster. The name Attingham or Ettingham, by corruption Atcham, signifies *the Home of the Children of Eata*, and it is possible that here the descendants of the Saxon bishop, finding a dwelling-place, founded a church which they dedicated to their saintly ancestor.

---

[1] *Domesday*, fo. 253, a 1.　　[2] ORDERICUS VITALIS, B. V. ch. i.
[3] *Eccle. Hist. of Eng. & Nor.* B. XIII. ch. xlv.

ATCHAM CHURCH

Atcham church went with the manor to Lilleshall abbey, and Thomas à Becket suffered the canons to appropriate it. In 1291, the church of Ettingham, in Salop deanery, was valued at £6 13s. 4d. per annum. In 1341, the assessors taxed the parish only £5 to the *ninth*, because of the abbot's glebe, two virgates lay untilled, from tenant's want of means, etc. In 1534-5 the vicar of Attynham's preferment was valued at £11 10s. per annum, less 3s. 4d. for synodals and procurations.

Early Incumbent.—Ordericus the priest, who, in 1075, baptized and stood sponsor for the historian Ordericus, was probably incumbent of Atcham. If so, he is, as the author of "The Antiquities of Shropshire" has observed, "perhaps the earliest parish priest that can be named for any locality in Shropshire."

Albright-Lee.

"The same church," says *Domesday*, "held and holds Etbretolio. Here i hide. In domesne is i ox-team, and ii villains and one boor, with i team. Here is i league of wood, but Earl Roger has taken it from the church. [The manor] was and is worth 12s. [per annum.]"[1] The place thus described still continues in the parish of St. Alkmund.

Charlton near Shawbury.

"The same church held and holds Cerletone. Here i hide. There was and is one radman here. The manor [or the radman] used to pay 4s. rent. Now it [or he] pays 5s."[1] But Charlton seems to have been a divided manor in 1086, for in Domesday Book we find another entry to this effect:—"IN RECORDINE HUNDRED. Roger holds of the earl Cerlintone. Uluric held it [in Saxon times]. Here i hide. Here ii serfs have half an ox-team, and there might be an ox-team and a half besides. [In King Edward's time the manor] was waste. Now it pays 5s."[2] It is not quite certain that the above entry relates to Charlton near Shawbury.

---

[1] *Domesday*, fo. 253, a 1. [2] Ibidem, fo. 255, b.

DOMESDAY HUNDRED OF SCIROPESBERIE.

Modern Name.	Domesday Name.	Saxon Owner or Owners, T. R. E.	Domesday Tenant in capite.	Domesday Sub-Tenant.
Shrewsbury and its Suburbs	Civitas Sciropesberie	Rex Edwardus	Rogerius Comes	Abbatia Sti. Petri et Burgenses de Sciropesberie.
Monk Meole	Melam	Episcopus de Cestre	Episcopus de Cestre	
Meole Brace	Melam	Ecclesia Stæ. Mariæ	Rogerius Comes or Radulfus de Mortemer	Ecclesia Stæ. Mariæ.
Meole Brace	Melam	Eddid	Radulfus de Mortemer	
Shelton	Saltone	Episcopus de Cestre	Episcopus de Cestre	Ecclesia Sti. Ceddi.
Sutton	Sudtone	Ecclesia Stæ. Milburgæ	Rogerius Comes	Ecclesia Stæ. Milburgæ.
Hencot		Eccl. Sti. Almundi	Idem	Ecclesia Sti. Almundi.
		Eccl. Stæ. Julianæ	Idem	Ecclesia Stæ. Juliana.

SHREWSBURY in Saxon times consisted exactly of one hundred hides, the original condition probably of all Hundreds. That the hide was a measure of comparative value, rather than of extent, we have a proof in the Hundred of Shrewsbury, which, according to *Domesday*, paid geld upon a hundred hides. It would be ridiculous, however, to suppose that the city liberties contained an area equal to that of Recordin Hundred.

The present liberties of Shrewsbury involve all that was contained in the *Domesday* Hundred, and a great deal more beside.

Shrewsbury. Situated on an eminence that rises over the eastern bank of the Severn, and enclosed within a peninsula formed by the winding of that river, stands the capital of Shropshire, concerning the early history of which we have now to treat.

Shrewsbury appears to owe its origin to the Britons. Deserting the Roman Uriconium or Wroxeter, which the Saxons are said to have fired; the unhappy Britons retired before the fierce heathen invader, and sought a place of refuge higher up the Severn. Protected by the meanderings of that stream, they found a shelter at "the Hill or Head of Alders," *Pengwern* or *Amywddig*, both of which were ancient British titles for Shrewsbury. According to Leland, "the destruction of Roxcestr was by all likelyhood the caus of the erection of Shrewsbury."[1] Shrewsbury then, has no pretensions to the dignity of a Roman station, nor has a vestige

---

[1] LELAND, *Itin.* iv, pt. 2, p. 96.

of that extraordinary race ever been discovered within its circuit. Surrounded at that early period, as undoubtedly it was, by morasses, the site of Pengwern presented one of eminent natural strength to the fugitives, and if the supposition of the learned authors of the history of Shrewsbury be correct, this town was founded by the Britons about the year 570, one hundred and fifty years after the Romans abandoned Britain.

The blue-eyed heathen followed the Britons, however, to their new position. Attacking them, they fired their habitations; when the royal palace of Pengwern having become enveloped in flames, the unfortunate Britons in despair sought the western mountains.

The next authentic notice we have respecting Pengwern or Shrewsbury, is, as forming the capital of the British kingdom of Powis, of which kingdom the portion of Shropshire that was unoccupied by the Saxons constituted the fairest portion, the "*Paradise of the Cymry*," as it is enthusiastically called by the ancient British poet Llywarc.[1] Obscurity, however, prevails respecting those kings who wielded the sceptre of old Powis in the wattled halls of Pengwern.[2] Suffice it to observe, that they were patriotically engaged in perpetual hostilities against the Saxons, who nevertheless continued to encroach upon them, until, after a bloody and exterminating struggle of two centuries' duration, Offa the Terrible, of Mercia, permanently annexed Shropshire to the land of the Angles, or England. To secure his acquisition, the Mercian conqueror cast up the vast entrenchment known as Offa's Dyke, which, extending from the river Wye, six and a half miles northwest of Hereford, boldly traverses for upwards of a hundred miles mountain and plain, until it terminates in the parish of Mold, Flintshire, sixteen miles from the estuary of the Dee. In its course northwards, this stupendous work forms the boundary between Shropshire and Montgomeryshire, in the former of which counties it is still very complete for a distance of twenty miles.[3]

Pengwern, then, with its palace and houses of wattled twigs and clay, no longer the capital of British Powis, became the abode of the fair-haired Saxons, who gave it the title of Scrobbeŗ-byŗiʒ, or Shrewsbury, a name which it has ever since retained. *Scrobbes-*

---

[1] Llywarc Heñ, Prince of the Cumbrian Britons, whose poems, still extant, prove that he was well acquainted with the mountains, streams, and towns of Shropshire.

[2] The domestic architecture of our British ancestors was in the lowest state of rudeness, regal mansions even being constructed of peeled rods.

[3] HARTSHORNE'S *Salopia Antiqua*.

byrig signifies a *bury* or fenced eminence, overgrown with shrubs.

During the Anglo-Saxon era, if Shrewsbury was degraded from its position as the metropolis of a kingdom, on the other hand, it gained in substantial importance. Included now within the kingdom of Mercia, whose capital was London, nevertheless Shrewsbury may have been the seat of a subordinate governor. When Ethelfleda, Lady of the Mercians, succeeded in 912 to the government of her deceased husband's province, which had been shorn of London and much of its territory, the heroic daughter of King Alfred, in her frequent contests with the Welsh, must have visited Shrewsbury, for there she founded St. Alcmund's collegiate church. Indeed, the warlike Ethelfleda appears to have devoted much of her attention to Shropshire, in which county she built castles both at Chirbury and Brugge.

In the time of the great Anglo-Saxon King Athelstane, who reigned from the year 924 till 940, Shrewsbury was a borough, considered sufficiently important to have the privilege of a mint, and several pennies stamped Scrob, and bearing the name of that monarch have been found. Coins, also, were minted in Shrewsbury of the reigns of the Anglo-Saxon Kings Edgar and Ethelred; Canute, the Anglo-Danish king; Edward the Confessor; and Harold II. After the Norman Conquest, coins were struck at Shrewsbury of the reigns of William I., William II., Henry I., Henry II., and Henry III.; after whose time no coins appear to have been minted at Shrewsbury, until the reign of Charles I.

We learn from the Anglo-Saxon Chronicle,[1] that whilst the pagan host of Danes afflicted his kingdom with their dreadful visitations, Ethelred the Unready, in 1006 passed "over Thames into Shropshire, and there took his abode during the mid-winter's tide." "Meanwhile," adds Henry of Huntingdon, "King Ethelred lay in sorrow and perplexity at his manor in Shropshire, where he was often sharply wounded with rumours of these disasters."[2] Learned men have supposed, from the foregoing, that our Saxon kings had a settled residence in Shrewsbury.

Scrobbes-byrig, or Shrewsbury, was the occasional residence of King Ethelred's son-in-law and vicegerent, the infamous Edric Streonc, Earl of Mercia; for here it was that he caused Ælfhelm the Ealdorman, to be treacherously assassinated.[3]

---

[1] *Anglo-Saxon Chron* p. 398. Bohn's Ed.
[2] HENRY OF HUNTINGDON *Chron.* p. 186, Bohn's Ed.   [3] See page 91.

When, in 1015, Edric deserted his imbecile father-in-law and went over to the conquering Anglo-Danish King Knut, or Canute, the men of Shropshire followed the traitorous example of their earl, and made peace with the invader; for which, in the following year, they were severely punished by Edmund Ironsides.[1]

Under the Saxon rule, no less than five opulent ecclesiastical foundations sprang up in Shrewsbury. *Domesday* furnishes us with a very good description of the state of Shrewsbury in the reign of Edward the Confessor. From that venerable record we learn that:—

"In the town of Shrewsbury, there were 252 houses in the time of King Edward, with a burgess residing in each house; these altogether paid an annual rent of £7 16s. 8d. King Edward enjoyed the following branches of revenue in this town:—

"If any person wilfully infringed a protection given under the king's own hand, he was outlawed. He who violated the royal protection given by the sheriff, forfeited 100s.; and the same sum was exacted for an assault committed on the highway, and for a burglary. These three forfeitures were paid to King Edward in all his demesne lands throughout England, over and above the reserved rents.

"When the king resided in this town, twelve of the better sort of citizens kept watch over him; and when he went out a hunting, such of them as had horses guarded him. The sheriff used to send thirty-six footmen to the stand, when the king was present; and at Marsetelie park that officer was bound by custom to find the same number of men for eight days. When he made a progress into Wales, every person who did not obey his summons to accompany him forfeited 40s.

"A widow paid the king 20s. for a license to marry; a maiden 10s. for the same permission. If a house was burnt by accident without negligence, the burgess who inhabited it paid a fine of 40s. to the king, and 2s. each to his two next neighbours. The king had 10s. for a relief upon the death of every burgess dwelling within the royal demesne; and if it was not paid by the time which the sheriff appointed, a fine of 10s. more was exacted. If a man wounded another so as to draw blood, he paid 40s. for this offence. When the king departed from the town, if he went southwards, the sheriff sent twenty-four horses with him as far as

---

[1] SIMEON DUNELM, p. 172.

Leintwardine; and he furnished the sovereign with the same number also to the first stage in Staffordshire, when he travelled that way.

"The king had three moneyers in this town, who, after they had purchased their money dies in the same manner as the other moneyers of the country, were bound, within fifteen days after, to pay the king 20s. each, whilst the new coinage was in progress. Upon the whole, the town paid an annual rent of £30, two-thirds of which went to the king, and the remainder to the sheriff.

"In the reign of King Edward, this town was assessed to the Danegeld at the rate of an hundred hides; of which—

"The church of St. Alcmund held ii hides.

"St. Julian half a hide.

"St. Milburg i hide.

"St. Chad a hide and a half.

"St. Mary i virgate (or one-fourth of a hide).

"The Bishop of Chester i hide.

"Ediet iii hides.[1]

"The bishop of Chester possessed, in Shrewsbury, sixteen masures, each inhabited by a burgess; he also possessed other burgesses. He had also sixteen canons in the town, who were exempt from the payment of Danegeld."

Allowing a wife and three children for each of the 252 abovementioned burgesses, this would give a population of 1260 souls; and as, at that unsettled period, it would have been unsafe to have conducted the operations of husbandry at too great a distance from fenced towns, it is probable that, when the Conqueror's survey was taken, Shrewsbury was encircled by an earthen rampart, which included much arable land now covered with the streets, alleys, and gardens of modern Shrewsbury.

Excepting the latter clause of the above extract relating to the burgesses *possessed* by the bishop of Chester, the Shrewsbury burgesses do not appear in the same degraded aspect as those of many other towns mentioned in *Domesday*. We are perpetually reminded, in other parts of that record, of villains, slaves, labourers, and, in some towns, burgesses, confined to the soil, and transmitting hereditary and hopeless bondage to their children, but, with the exception alluded to, we read of nothing of the kind in connexion with Shrewsbury.

---

[1] *Domesday*, fo. 252, a 1.

The Norman Conquest, which subverted the English constitution and produced a total revolution in the ownership of landed property throughout the kingdom, of necessity brought changes to Shrewsbury. When England was invaded by the Normans, in 1066, Edwin and Morcar were joint earls of Mercia. Although opposed to the Norman duke, it nevertheless does not appear that either of them assisted their brother-in-law, King Harold, at the battle of Hastings; after which great event, one account represents these earls as concurring in placing the youthful Edgar Atheling on the vacant throne, another as aspiring themselves to the crown. At length, perceiving their inability to resist the victorious progress of William, Edwin and Morcar swore fealty to the Conqueror, who, in return, confirmed them in their possessions. The reader has already been made acquainted with the details of their revolt and subsequent hard fate.[1] Meanwhile the Welsh, who never ceased to scan with envious glance their former fertile province, acting in concert with Edric the forester, invaded Shropshire, and laid siege to the king's castle of Scrobesbury,[2] in which they were assisted by the Saxon townsmen. King William lost no time in despatching two earls, William and Brien, to the relief of the beleaguered stronghold; yet, ere they could arrive, the combined Saxon and Welsh host had decamped, after having burnt the town; at which the king was so enraged, that, early in the spring of 1069, he marched at the head of his forces to punish the rebels of Mercia. Then it was, that the Conqueror abolished the old Anglo-Saxon earldom of Mercia, and giving to his kinsman, Roger de Montgomery, nearly the whole of Shropshire, including a grant of the town of Shrewsbury, he conferred on him also the title of Earl of Shrewsbury.

In Shrewsbury, then, this Norman seigneur held high court. He pulled down the old castle which had previously existed here, and in its stead erected a Norman fortress on that narrow neck of land by which alone Shrewsbury could be approached.

From this stately castle Earl Roger could overawe the Saxon burgesses, or issue forth at the head of chosen counsellors and mail-clad warriors, to quiet and govern his province, and repress the Welsh.

The condition of Shrewsbury under its first Norman ruler, may be inferred from the following passages in *Domesday*:—" In

---

[1] See pp. 65 and 66.   [2] ORDERICUS, B. IV. ch. v

the year preceding this survey," says that record, "earl Roger received a rent of £40 from the town [which was £10 more than the burgesses had paid in Edward the Confessor's time, whilst their means of payment, as appears from what follows, were much diminished]. The Saxon burgesses complain that they pay the same Danegeld as they did in King Edward's days, although the castle erected by the earl occupies the site of fifty-one houses, while fifty houses lie waste, and forty-three, which paid to the taxes at that time, are now holden by Normans. Besides which, the earl himself has given thirty-nine burgesses to his abbey, who are, therefore, freed from the tax; and there are now two hundred houses, save seven, which pay nothing."

Over the burgesses the Norman earl set a *præpositus*, or provost: in plain English, a rent-collector, who doubtless extorted from the unhappy Saxons as much as he could, both for his proud master and himself. The sufferings which the English experienced at the hands of their Norman oppressors are, however, too generally known to require comment. It is not to be imagined, and indeed the extract from *Domesday* just given precludes the supposition that the English burgesses of Shrewsbury, with their families, were exempt from what was the common lot of their down-trodden countrymen. Our Anglo-Saxon forefathers experienced, in its dread reality, the fate of a conquered country. A retributive justice then inflicted on them a similar measure of misery to that which, five centuries before, they had so cruelly dealt out to the unfortunate Britons.

Far advanced in years, Roger de Montgomery, the first earl of Shrewsbury, died on July 17, 1094, and was honourably interred, says Ordericus, in the new church which he had founded at Shrewsbury.

Hugh de Montgomery succeeded his father Roger as Earl of Shrewsbury, who, much engaged in hostilities with his Welsh neighbours, eventually lost his life, in the year 1098, at the straits of Anglesey, whilst endeavouring to repel the invasion of Magnus Barefoot, King of Norway. Pierced by a Norwegian arrow, earl Hugh fell from his horse into the sea, when, his body having been with difficulty recovered, after the lapse of seventeen days, it was buried in the cloister of Shrewsbury abbey.

To the earldom of Shrewsbury then succeeded his brother, Robert de Belèsme, that monster of whom we have treated.[1] In

---

[1] See pp. 11—14.

concert with many other Anglo-Norman nobles, de Belèsme preferred the claim of the indolent Robert Curthose to the English throne to that of Henry I. Beauclerc, however, broke up the hostile confederacy, and, crushing as we have related, his turbulent vassal, banished him to Normandy.

Upon the fall of its third and last Norman earl, Shrewsbury, with the lands in Shropshire of those of Robert de Belèsme's vassals who had sided with their suzerain against Henry, reverted to the king; and henceforth, the earldom of Shrewsbury being vested in the Crown, the king governed the province by a succession of viceroys or stewards, who resided in Shrewsbury castle. The first of these was Richard de Belmeis, in whose time, doubtless, the condition of Shrewsbury was improved; for good sense, and his position as the occupant of a disputed throne, alike inclined de Belmeis' royal master to court the affections of his English subjects. Indeed, we learn that such was the case from the charter of King John, which expressly confirms to the burgesses of Shrewbury, *all liberties and free customs, and quittances as they held them in the time of King Henry, our great grandfather*: "Omnes libertates, et liberas consuetudines, et quietancias, sicut eas habuerunt tempore regis Henrici proavi nostri," are the identical words of John's charter.

Richard de Belmeis was succeeded in his viceregency by Pain Fitz-John, during whose period of office Henry I. visited Shropshire, and, it is supposed, Shrewsbury. That monarch, however, at London, amidst the solemn festival of Christmas in the year 1126, summoning around him his barons, spiritual and lay, in their presence "gave," says William of Malmesbury,[1] "the county of Salop to his wife, the daughter of the Earl of Louvain, whom he had married after the death of Matilda," when she appointed as her sheriff William Fitz Alan.

When the civil war, consequent on the usurpation of Stephen broke out, Fitz Alan loyally adhered to the cause of the Empress Maude. In July, 1138, the active usurper laid siege to Shrewsbury Castle, which, in the following month, he stormed and took. Ordericus[2] has furnished us with the following particulars of what occurred after the capture of Shrewsbury Castle. "Arnulf de Hesdin, the uncle of this young man (Fitz Alan), a bellicose and venturesome soldier, arrogantly refused the peace which the king

---

[1] *Modern History*, b. I.   [2] B. XIII. ch. xxxvii.

offered him on several occasions, and obstinately forced others who wished to surrender themselves, to persist in their rebellion. At last, when the fortress was reduced, he was taken amongst many others, and brought into the presence of the king, whom he had treated with contempt. The king, however, finding that his gentleness had lowered him in the eyes of the revolters, and that in consequence many of the nobles summoned to his court had disdained to appear, was so incensed that he ordered Arnulf and nearly ninety-three others of those who had resisted him, to be hung on the gallows, or immediately executed in other ways. Arnulf now repenting too late, and many others on his behalf, supplicated the king, offering a large sum of money for his ransom. But the king preferring vengeance on his enemies to any amount of money, they were put to death without delay. Their haughty accomplices were greatly terrified when they heard of the king's severity, and came in haste three days afterwards to the king, offering various excuses for having so long delayed their submission. Some of them brought the keys of their fortresses, and humbly offered their services to the king." Escaping from Shrewsbury Castle, Fitz Alan remained an exile until, in 1152, young Prince Henry having landed in England, among his brilliant successes, according to some,[1] was the re-capture of Shrewsbury Castle. At any rate, shortly afterwards the usurper died, when Henry II. mounting his grandfather's throne, restored to William Fitz Alan his vast possessions and the sheriffdom of Shropshire.

During the reign of Henry II. the burgesses of Shrewsbury probably enjoyed many of those privileges possessed by their forefathers in the days of Edward the Confessor. They were liable, however, to be taxed arbitrarily at the will of the Crown. Thus, in 1155, the year after Henry II. had ascended his throne, the burgesses of Salopesberie paid an aid of ten merks into the king's Exchequer—a sum equivalent to £350 of our present money. Again, in 1159, Shrewsbury paid through the sheriff of Shropshire into the king's Exchequer, a sum of five merks by way of a *donum*; but, in 1170, the burgesses of Shrewsbury, like those of Bridgenorth, made an effort to escape out of the clutches of the sheriff by fining with the Crown that, in lieu of the several payments and

---

[1] CARADOC OF LLANCARVAN, a cotemporary Welsh Chronicler quoted by Dr. Powell in his *History of Wales*, p. 172.

forfeitures for which they were continually liable, they might be permitted to pay a certain fixed rent. In 1185, they paid £20 and two coursers, *pro firma burgi,* that henceforth, they might pay their own ferm or chief rent direct into the Exchequer, without being subject to the extortions of the sheriff or any other intermediate officer.

King Henry II., it would appear, visited Shrewsbury more than once; and as that monarch engaged in frequent contests with the Welsh, although history has not recorded the circumstances, doubtless this town was the scene, during that unsettled period, of many a negociation and contest.

There can be no doubt that a written charter of liberties, granted to Shrewsbury by Henry II. once existed, as it is expressly referred to in King John's charter; yet the earliest charter now preserved in the archives of the corporation is that of Richard I. This, dated the 11th of November, in the first year of Richard's reign, grants the town of Salopesbiri to be holden by the burgesses thereof for forty merks of silver of annual rent—a sum equivalent to £1,104 of modern currency. Ten of these merks were a commutation for the two horses (*pro duobus fugatoribus*) due in the reign of Henry II.; from whence we ascertain the fact, that a hunter in that age cost as much as would purchase more than a score of oxen.

King John had not been a fortnight on the throne (1199) ere the Shrewsbury burgesses obtained from him two charters. "The first of these," say the historians of Shrewsbury,[1] "is a mere recital of the free customs of Henry I., and a confirmation of the charter of Henry II.; but the second, dated a week after the first, introduces several new privileges of very great importance to the welfare of the town.

"It sanctions the formation (if it does not suppose the existence) of a 'common council of the town,' in which it authorises the burgesses to elect two of the most loyal and discreet burgesses, and to present them to the sheriff of the county: one of these the sheriff is to present to the chief justiciary at Westminster, when he delivers in his accounts;[2] and these two burgesses, thus chosen, are well and faithfully to keep the præpositure (*i.e.,* the office of

---

[1] OWEN AND BLAKEWAY, *Hist. of Shrews.*, vol. 1, p. 83.
[2] Which was at Michaelmas, hence the chief magistrates of Shrewsbury have always been elected about that season.

provost or reeve), of the town, and shall not be removed as long as they behave themselves well in that bailiwick, except by the common council of the town. He also grants that, by the same common council, they may elect four of the more loyal and discreet burgesses to keep the pleas of the Crown,[1] and other things which belong to the Crown in the said burgh, and to take care that the provosts treat both rich and poor in a lawful manner."

Thus, King John's charter abolished for ever the odious and tyrranical office of the reeve, or provost, appointed first by the Norman earl, and afterwards by the king; henceforth the burgesses of Shrewsbury elected their own provosts in their own common council. Yet, because they were permitted to elect their chief magistrate, it must not be imagined that the burgesses of Shrewsbury at once stept into the enjoyment of that enlarged liberty which their descendants enjoy—the precious boon of constitutional freedom which Englishmen of the nineteenth century enjoy is the result of many centuries' struggle. As a borough belonging to the king, Shrewsbury for the present remained subject to arbitrary talliages.

On February 24th, 1204-5, John gave a third charter to Shrewsbury, the last clause of which granted to the burgesses liberty to hold a fair for three days on the 1st and two following days of June. In accordance with the practice of that age, John mulcted the honest burgesses of Shrewsbury of a very heavy sum for his various charters.

The reign of King John was one of stirring interest for Shrewsbury. Impelled by that noble and invincible love of freedom which has ever inspired them, the Welsh had always been restless and uneasy neighbours to the English. Llewellyn the Great now wielded the sceptre of North Wales—a prince whose enterprising spirit the Anglo-Norman monarch judged it expedient to conciliate, and John gave him in marriage his natural daughter Johanna, by Agatha, daughter of Robert Earl of Ferrars; for this base king did not scruple to pollute the noblest families of the realm by his licentious amours. With his daughter, John gave to Llewellyn the lordship of Ellesmere. The king also endeavoured

---

[1] The Pleas of the Crown here alluded to, were certain forfeitures due from the burgesses of Shrewsbury to the king, on the commission of offences; such as theft, arson, etc. These penalties had formerly been exacted by the provost or reeve of the town, who, having generally abused his office, the power he exercised was now taken from him, and vested in four of the most respectable burgesses.

to gain the prince to his side, by chiming in with his scheme of reviving the obsolete claims of his ancestors to a supremacy over all the Welsh princes; in accordance with which, John insidiously invited Gwenwynwyn, Prince of Powis, to Shrewsbury, where he threw him into prison. Yet Llewellyn, whose darling object was the independence of his principality, was not to be diverted from his project by the advances of the English king, and, taking advantage of the embroiled state of his father-in-law's affairs, he commenced hostilities. Upon this, John assembled an army at Whitchurch, on July 8th, 1211,[1] and marching into Wales, penetrated as far as Snowdon, and laid waste the surrounding country. Unable to resist, the Welsh submitted to the English king, who, taking with him twenty-eight hostages from among the most distinguished families of Wales, then withdrew. In the very next year, the Welsh broke their engagement, and advanced into England; when John, with savage ferocity, caused every one of his twenty-eight hostages to be hung, nor would the inhuman king take any refreshment until his horrid command had been obeyed. At this all Wales was flung into mourning.

Meanwhile, the Anglo-Norman lords fell out with their king, and civil war swept over the fair realm of England. Grateful, it may have been, for favours conferred upon them by King John, the Shrewsbury burgesses adhered to the king. On the other hand, the exasperated Welsh eagerly espoused the cause of the barons; and, headed by Llewellyn, in 1215, they marched to attack the town of Shrewsbury. Avoiding the Welsh bridge, where the burgesses awaited his approach, Llewellyn the Great suddenly appeared before the gates of the stone bridge; when, having set fire to the abbot's premises, he stormed the town, and took from the hated king of England, Pengwern, the seat of his ancestors.

Notwithstanding the extravagant strains of his bards, who now tuned their harps in notes of triumph to Llewellyn's well-pleased ear, Pengwern did not long continue in the hands of the victorious Welshman. In the year 1216, the last of his inglorious reign and life, John had recovered Shrewsbury, for he was here on August 14th of that year.

We have many notices of Shrewsbury in the time of Henry III. Planted as it was on the border, this important town figures con-

---

[1] ROGER DE WENDOVER. vol. 2, p. 255. Bohn's Ed.

spicuously amid that deadly feud which raged between the English and the Welsh during the greater part of Henry's long reign. In his second year, a royal mandate directed the good men of Salop to bestow all their diligence and care in strengthening and closing their town, lest the king's enemies should enter the same;[1] and to aid them in their loyal undertaking, a patent in the fourth year of his reign grants to the burgesses of Salop the privilege of taking once a week the following tolls :—

Of every cart bringing things for sale into the town, one half-penny.

If the cart belong to another county, one penny.

Of every horse-load of things brought for sale (wood excepted), one farthing.

Of every horse, mare, cow, or ox, exposed for sale, one half-penny.

Of ten sheep, goats, or pigs, one penny.

Of every vessel coming into the town by Severn, laden with goods for sale, fourpence.

The same tolls to endure for four years, from Midsomer, 1220.[2]

Aids for building the walls of this important frontier town were likewise granted in the 7th, 8th, 29th and 30th years of Henry's reign, in which last the grant appears in the form of murage.

Henry III. paid no less than six different visits to Shrewsbury; twice he was here in the year 1220, once in 1226, 1232, 1241, and 1267. These repeated visits appear to have been undertaken by the English king for the purpose either of making treaties with the Welsh, or chastising them for infractions of the truce. A complication of skirmishing and negotiating, as the reader may suppose, was not conducive to the prosperity of the fertile plains of Shropshire. At the beginning of 1234, Llewellyn, with his ally, the famous Richard Marshal,[3] entered this county with a powerful army, and they "spread fire," says Roger of Wendover, "wherever they went; so that, from the confines of Wales, as far as the town of Shrewsbury, there was not a place that escaped their ravages; they then burned the town of Shrewsbury, and then returned home with valuable booty."[4] Shrewsbury was destined also to share in the sufferings consequent on the civil war of the

---

[1] *Pat.* 2 Hen. iii. m. 1.
[2] *Pat.* 4 Hen. iii. m. 4.
[3] See page 28.
[4] Roger de Wendover, vol. ii. p. 581. Bohn's Ed.

latter end of Henry III.'s reign ; for its burgesses, like the generality of the great lords of Shropshire, being staunch royalists, this brought down on them the wrath of the pretended patriots. In fact, the "incurable loyalty" of this district well-nigh caused a severance of Shropshire and its county town from the crown of England; for Simon Montfort, in the name of the captive king of England, appears to have actually ceded them to his ally, the Welsh prince.[1] The royalist victory of Evesham, however, hindered the projected annexation. After recovering his freedom, King Henry III., "for the fidelity and constancy with which the said burgesses (of Shrewsbury) have heretofore adhered to us, and our son Edward, and also for the losses which they have sustained on the same account during the disturbance of late had in the realm," granted to the men of Shrewsbury sundry privileges.[2]

From such deplorable pictures of the state of our country in the *good* old times, it is pleasant to turn and witness the gradual approach of the burgesses of Shrewsbury towards a better era. They obtained from Henry III., in the eleventh year of his reign, a charter which manifests, say the historians of Shrewsbury, " a spirit unusually humane and enlightened, for the age in which it was issued, towards an unhappy race, of whom we know nothing but from books, and to the extinction of whose servitude in Shropshire this royal grant first opened the way."[3] The sixteenth clause of this charter stipulates, "That none of the king's sheriffs shall intermeddle with the burgesses in any plea, or quarrel, or claim, or in aught belonging to the said borough," etc. The eighteenth clause recognises and establishes the authority of the merchant gild at Shrewsbury, by providing that:—"The said burgesses and their heirs, may have a merchant gild, with a hanse,[4]

---

[1] T. WIKES, p. 69, quoted by OWEN and BLAKEWAY, *Hist. of Shrews.*, vol. i. p. 128.

[2] *Charter* of Hen. III., dated Sept. 22, 1265.

[3] *Hist of Shrews.*, vol. 1. p. 100.

[4] The terms Gild and Hanse are synonymous, and signify a society of men contributing to a joint-stock, or forming a joint company. Gilds are traceable to a remote antiquity, and were known in this country in Saxon times. From a set of nine parchment rolls, sewed together (the earliest preserved amongst the archives of the corporation), it is clear that the Gild of Shrewsbury existed antecedent to this charter of 1227. The first roll commences as follows :—

"May the Holy Spirit be present with us!

"The names of those who are in Gild Merchant in the burgh of Salop, and whose fathers were not before in the liberties of the Gild in the eleventh year of King John, and whose fine is 5s. 4d."

Then follow thirty names, etc., from whence it would appear, that there were persons in the merchant gild of this town in the eleventh year of King John (1209) *whose fathers were before in the liberties of the gild.* Henry III.'s charter, then,

and other customs and liberties belonging to such gild; and no one who does not belong to that gild shall exercise merchandize in the borough, without the consent of the burgesses."

The nineteenth clause of Henry's charter relates to the enfranchisement of serfs, a very numerous class in this country in the 13th century:—" If any native (born in villeinage or slavery) of any person shall remain in the said borough, and hold himself in the same gild and hanse, and in lot and scot with the said burgesses for one year and one day without challenge (i.e., without being claimed by his lord), he may not be again demanded by his lord, if he freely continue in the said borough." Finally, the twentieth clause grants, that " the burgesses of Shrewsbury, and their heirs, shall be free of toll, lestage, passage, pontage, stallage, lene, Danegelds, gaywite, and all other customs and exactions, both in England and all other the king's territories, saving the liberty of the city of London."

As if it had been overlooked when this passed the great seal, a second charter, consisting of a single clause, and dated the same day, also granted to the men of Shrewsbury, " that no person may purchase raw hides or undressed cloth within the borough, unless he be in lott and scott, and in assessments and talliages with the burgesses": that is, unless he contributed to the public burdens.

In accordance with the narrow-minded commercial notions of that period, this clause had for its object the securing to the burgesses the advantage of preparing those commodities for sale.

On the 10th of August, 1256, Henry III. granted two more charters to the loyal burgesses of Shrewsbury. One of the privileges conferred by these gave the burgesses the right "to answer by their own hand at the king's exchequer, for all their debts and summons issuing out of that court, and affecting their town." Again, "If any of their servants commit any offence which induces a forfeiture of goods, the goods of the burgesses, their masters, either found in the hands of the servants, or deposited by them anywhere, are saved from forfeiture, on proof that the goods are really the property of the burgesses."

These charters likewise conferred upon the burgesses of Shrewsbury the two following important privileges : 1st, that "if any of

---

compelled every one who would carry on business in Shrewsbury to become a member of this gild, which formerly was a voluntary association.

them died, with or without a will, their goods should not be confiscated by the crown, but that their heirs should enjoy the whole;" 2ndly, that "burgesses shall be convicted only by their peers, burgesses of the town; and shall be tried according to their liberties used and approved."

In the age of which we are writing, if a burgess of one town owed money in another, it was lawful for the creditor to detain any of the debtor's fellow-townsmen who might be travelling, in the ordinary course of business, that way with goods. King Henry III.'s charter, however, expressly confers upon the burgesses of Shrewsbury the privilege "that neither they nor their goods shall be arrested for any debt in which they are neither principal debtors nor sureties." Thus a better day gradually dawned upon the men of Shrewsbury.

Having returned from Palestine, Edward I. determined to carry out the ambitious project of annexing Wales to England. With this object in view, he summoned Llewellyn to meet him at Shrewsbury, and do him homage there. The brave Welsh prince, however, was in no hurry to comply with the English monarch's order, when Edward peremptorily summoned him to Westminster. As Llewellyn still continued refractory, he was condemned as a rebel, and military operations were commenced forthwith against him. Regardless of the inconvenience to which he put his subjects, and in violation of the terms of Magna Charta, which direct that the Court of Common Pleas was always to sit in the same place, in order to convince Llewellyn of his determination not to give up the contest until he had gained his end, Edward I. now transferred the seat of government to Shrewsbury. "A.D., 1277. In the fortnight after Easter," says the contemporary chronicler, "the king withdrew from Westminster, and hastened towards Wales with all the military force of the kingdom of England, taking with him his barons of the exchequer, and his justices of the king's bench, as far as Shrewsbury, who remained there some time, hearing suits according to the customs of the kingdom of England. Therefore the Welsh, fearing the arrival of the king and his army, fled to their accustomed refuge of Snowdon."[1] That Edward I. was in person at Shrewsbury in the autumn of that year, we know from certain writs which he expedited for the conveyance of stores to the army. He left it on the 16th of October, after which the

---

[1] *Matt. West.*, vol. ii. p. 471, Bohn's Ed.

powerful English king so vigorously pressed his Welsh antagonist, that before the end of the year Llewellyn was forced to yield to the conqueror's hard conditions, and do him homage twice. Having effected a reconciliation with his brother David, impelled by a sense of national ardour, the indignant Welsh prince, however, in 1282, again flew to arms, when Edward, upbraiding him with *ingratitude*, reassembled his army at Shrewsbury, and again removed his courts thither.[1] But death released Llewellyn from the grasp of Edward. The Welsh prince fell near Buelht by the hands of assassins, when, his head having been sent to London, it was derisively encircled by a wreath of ivy, and fixed upon the Tower.

Animated with the prospect of for ever crushing the British dynasty, King Edward now prosecuted the war with vigour, and having got Llewellyn's brother into his hands, he determined to make of him an example such as he judged might deter Welshmen in future from disputing his supremacy. For this purpose, Prince David was sent in chains to Shrewsbury, where a parliament was summoned to meet on September 30, 1283. "It was the first national convention in which the Commons had any share *by legal authority;* for that summoned by De Montfort cannot be called such. Besides one hundred and ten earls and barons, here were two knights from each county, and two deputies from certain of the principal cities and towns[2] of the kingdom, probably that they might witness the rigid justice of their monarch : so that Shrewsbury witnessed the earliest legitimate traces of that popular representation in the constitution to which, under God, Englishmen have been indebted for all their subsequent prosperity."[3] Tradition has it, that the lords sat in the castle, and the commons in a barn

---

[1] Journeying backwards and forwards so great a distance over bad roads, and by the awkward system of conveyance in vogue at that early period, could not be otherwise than productive of injury to our national records. We learn from Fabyan, that the rolls of the courts were greatly damaged by the rain on their journey back from Shrewsbury, and the tattered appearance of the original plea rolls of the year in question bears testimony to the hard service they have seen.

[2] In all twenty cities and towns, Shrewsbury being of the number.

[3] *Hist. of Shrews.*, vol. i. p. 147. The omission of writs to the bishops and abbots, commanding their attendance at this solemn convention is remarkable. The spiritual peers have no votes in cases of blood. Their not having been summoned on this occasion, therefore, looks very like as if the King of England anticipated the condemnation of the Welsh prince from the Parliament. Dr. Brady, in his treatise on boroughs, speaks of 23 Ed. I. (1295) as being the first time that citizens or burgesses were summoned to Parliament. From the above, however, it is certain that he is wrong.

belonging to the Abbot of Shrewsbury. From the circumstance, however, that Shrewsbury Castle was then probably being rebuilt (for Edward I. reconstructed this fortress) it is more likely that this Parliament sat either in the chapter house or the refectory of Shrewsbury Abbey. Prince David was tried by the Lords, his presumed peers; the Commons therefore, having no concern in his trial, meanwhile may have assembled for some unrecorded purpose in a barn within the precincts of the Abbey. That both Lords and Commons afterwards adjourned to Acton Burnell is however certain. Llewellyn's brother, after a short trial, was condemned, when Shrewsbury witnessed a horrible spectacle. The unfortunate prince, after having been dragged by horses through the streets and lanes of this town, was hung up for a short time, and then cut down alive. His heart and bowels were afterwards torn out and literally burned before his eyes; he was next beheaded, and his body having been cut into four parts, his head was sent to London, to be stuck up along with that of his brother, whilst the quarters meanwhile were fixed in four principal cities of the kingdom. Thus did the conqueror, according to the shocking practice of that age, seek to strike terror into the hearts of all opposed to his authority.

After the conquest of Wales, Shrewsbury lost that importance it had acquired in consequence of occupying a frontier position on a hostile territory, and henceforth it ranked as an ordinary provincial town.

The condition of the burgesses of Shrewsbury in the reign of Edward II. may be inferred from a taxation-roll of the liberty of the town of Salop, of a fifteenth part of all moveable goods granted to the king in 1313. At this date, the Shrewsbury burgesses, in addition to their ordinary trade or handicraft, appear to have been somewhat in the condition of little farmers, for most of them had some live stock: the produce of their little plot of land probably went to supply the necessities of their own household. We may judge how inquisitorial and oppressive this taxation must have been, from the circumstance that the assessors descended to the most minute particulars. Thus we learn from this roll, that:—

"Isabel, widow of Roger the Locksmith: [was possessed of] malt [to the value of] 6s.; a small heifer, 3s.; four pigs, 3s.; a pot, 4s.; . . . . . . 11s.; household utensils, 12d.;" [upon all which this widow had to pay to Edward II. the fifteenth part of their value].

"The Prior of St. John, three draught horses, 9s.; a cart and harness, 4s. 3d.; a quarter and a half of wheat, 6s.; a quarter of rye, 40d.; three quarters of oats, 6s.; three bushels of pease, 9d.; utensils, 8d.

"Nicholas de Bakelare: ten sheep, 10s.; an heifer, 3s.; a silver brooch, 20d.; wood, 10d.; flesh, 18d.

"Nicholas Ive: three draught horses, 10s.; flesh, 6s.; a mazer cup, [*i. e.* one of mixed metal], 4s.; two silver cups, 6s.; six silver spoons, 6s.

"Richard de Hultone: in money, 21s.; malt, 20s.; wheat 26s.; oats, ... ; rye, ... ; pledges, 6s.; a horse, 13s; flesh, 11s.; silk and sindon, 13s.; boots and gloves, 6s.

"Adam the Blacksmith, upon the Wyle: iron and coals, 15s." [out of this, which was the whole of his property, Adam had to pay 12d.].

"John Fisher: a boat, 3s.; nets, 2s.; wood, 12d.; two little pigs, 8d.; a calf, 6d.; utensils, 4d.

"Roger le Parmenter, opposite the Castle: washed skins, 13s. 4d.; lamb, fox, and rabbit skins, 13s. 4d.; furs, 20s.; malt, 6s.; wood, 4s.; household utensils, 3s."[1]

Edward II. was loyally received by the inhabitants of Shrewsbury when, assembling his forces, he marched through the west in pursuit of Lord Badlesmere. Clad in armour, the burgesses went out to meet the king, and conveying him into their fortified town, there he remained from the 15th to the 23rd of January, 1322, busily engaged in devising measures against his own antagonists, and those of his favourites, the Despencers. From Shrewsbury, the king issued a proclamation of general amnesty to all his subjects, Badlesmere excepted, of which when Roger de Mortimer of Wigmore and his uncle Mortimer of Chirk heard, they proceeded thither, and threw themselves at the king's feet. No sooner, however, did Edward II. find these barons in his power than, oblivious of his solemn assurance, he consigned them to the Tower of London. The disgraceful arrest of these two nobles within the walls of Shrewsbury, in the neighbourhood of which they had large possessions, appears to have disgusted the burgesses, and upon the subsequent revolution which terminated in the murder of Edward II., they actively assisted the king's enemies.

With the exception of a new charter which its burgesses obtained from the king, and a considerable relaxation of good order among the inhabitants of this town, owing to the great pestilence that twice during the reign of Edward III. swept with fearful

---

[1] From time immemorial there has been a skinner's yard under the castle.

violence over England, there is nothing of special interest connected with the history of Shrewsbury during that monarch's long and glorious reign.

Richard II. honoured this town with a visit in 1387. About six years afterwards, a fire broke out which destroyed St. Chad's church and a great part of the town of Shrewsbury, the private houses of which were then chiefly constructed of timber, and thatched.

Shrewsbury Abbey.

Occupying a low spot in the eastern suburb, at the confluence of Meole brook with the Severn, are the remains of Shrewsbury Abbey. We learn from Ordericus that Siward erected in Shrewsbury a chapel in honour of St. Peter. That it was a small wooden structure we glean from other good sources of information,[1] and in this condition it remained until Earl Roger de Montgomery gave it to his counsellor Ordelirius, the father of Ordericus, the monkish historian. In 1082, Ordelirius went on pilgrimage to Rome, where he vowed that if he should return in safety to Shrewsbury he would, in place of the wooden church, build a more imposing edifice of stone in honour of St. Peter and St. Paul. Returning to Shropshire, the Norman earl concurred in the design, and convening Warin the sheriff, Picot de Say, and others of his nobles, on Saturday, the 3rd of March, 1083, explained to them his intention, when Roger's vassals applauded the resolution. After the assembly had broken up, the earl repaired to St. Peter's, where, in the presence of many witnesses, he vowed that he would found an abbey, and, granting thereto the whole suburb lying without the eastern gate, he confirmed his donation by laying his gloves upon the altar. Rainald and Frode, two monks skilled in architecture, now came over from Normandy to superintend the erection of the proposed abbey, which gradually arose. At the time of *Domesday* the building was still going on; and we learn from that record that the earl had conferred upon the monastery "as many of his burgesses [39 was the number] and mills as brought in an annual rent to the monks of £12." At the period of the survey, the abbey also held four manors, and seven churches; the greater part of the produce of whose glebe the monks appropriated to themselves. Earl Hugh and Robert de Belèsme both

---

[1] *Monasticon* and *Malmesbury*.

were benefactors to their father's foundation, and what with grants from our various kings, from the great men of Shropshire, and gifts from their vassals, the monastery of St. Peter and St. Paul acquired a property, which, in less than one hundred and fifty years after its foundation, amounted to no fewer than seventy-one distinct grants of manors or lands, twenty-four churches, and the tithes of thirty-seven parishes or vills, besides very extensive and valuable privileges and immunities of various kinds. Rich although Shrewsbury Abbey once was, doubtless there were ample calls upon its income. The decoration and repair of their church and buildings, charity to the poor, hospitality to the stranger, besides the taking care of themselves, seldom left the monks much ready money.

As a *Baron and Peer of Parliament*, the Abbot of Shrewsbury sat in the House of Lords until the Dissolution.

In common with the shorn fraternity of other mediæval establishments, the monks of Shrewsbury studied to raise their house in public esteem by the acquisition of various relics. With this object in view, at no little trouble and cost, they acquired the bones of "the blessed virgin Wenefrede," the odour of whose sanctity was such, that, according to monkish authority, "a little dust out of the virgin's skull mixed with holy water" immediately cured a sick man.

By the end of Henry II.'s reign, the abbey treasury reckoned amongst a long list of miracle-performing stores, besides the body of St. Wenefrede, bones, hair, and vestments of various apostles and martyrs; some of the milk, the chemise, couch, and tomb of the Virgin; some cloth stained with the blood of Thomas (à Becket), the martyr, etc.

The site of the abbey comprises about ten acres. Surrounded by an embattled wall, which still encloses its north and eastern side, this stately abbey, with its refectory, kitchen, dormitory, infirmary, chapter-house, treasury, library, and abbot's lodging, above all of which towered its great church, must have once presented the appearance of a fortified town, and doubtless displayed a majestic group of architecture to the traveller as he approached the ancient capital of Shropshire. Alas! devastation has befallen every part of the conventual buildings.

The present parochial church of the Holy Cross embraces within its walls the nave, side aisles, porch, and western tower of the abbey church. Although barbarously mutilated and its fair proportions curtailed, a certain solemn dignity still clings to the venerable fabric. What, then, must have been the effect produced on the mind of the devotee in days of yore, when the setting sun shot his emblazoning rays through its stained windows upon the taper columns, and lofty fretted roof, richly dight mosaic pavement, and gorgeous high altar, and lit up the splendidly-attired sacerdotal procession, which was wont, on high festival days, with crosses and banners, to sweep chaunting along its solemn aisles!

The present remnant of the abbey church displays two distinct styles of ecclesiastical architecture. The whole basement of the fabric, the three plain semi-circular arches, and thick low round columns of the eastern portion of the nave, the west door as well as other parts distinguished for their massive solidity, were erected in the eleventh century. The western division of the nave, the magnificent west window, and whole superstructure of the tower, belong to the fourteenth century.

Fulchered was first abbot of Shrewsbury, appointed in 1087. We read that, indignant at King William the Second's irreligious appropriation of ecclesiastical benefices, "Fulchered, Abbot of Shrewsbury, a powerful preacher and eloquent expounder of God's law, ascended the pulpit" at Gloucester, and denounced the impending wrath of heaven. "Behold!" he exclaimed, "the bow of celestial anger is bent against the reprobate; and an arrow, swift to wound, is drawn out of the quiver;" on the very next day, Rufus was slain by Tyrrel's arrow, in the New Forest. Fulchered died in 1120, when, according to Ordericus, "Godefred succeeded, in the reign of Henry. Both were literate and religious pastors, and studied to educate the Lord's flock diligently for nearly forty years." After Godefred, Herbert " usurped the rudder of the infant establishment." The last abbot was Thomas Boteler, who, surrendering in 1539-40, had a liberal pension assigned him.

Notwithstanding the efforts of the Corporation of Shrewsbury, who petitioned the king "to erect the house of the late abbey into a college or free school," Henry VIII. granted the house and site of the dissolved abbey, with its appurtenances, "houses, barns, stables, dovecotes, gardens, orchards, pools, lands, etc., and all profits," woods, etc., in the premises to Edward Watson and Henry Herdson, two speculators in land, who, on the 23rd of July, 1546 (the very next day) conveyed their acquisition to William Langley of Salop, who transmitted the abbey estate to his descendants for five generations.

The MANOR OF THE FOREGATE over which, undoubtedly, the abbots once were lords, was granted by Queen Elizabeth to Robert Newdigate and Arthur Fountayne, who, the day following, conveyed it to Richard Prynce, Thomas Hatton, and Thomas Rock, gentlemen, and the heirs of the survivor. Hatton proved to be this survivor, in whose family the manor continued till the 10th of February, 1654, when it was conveyed to Sir Richard Prynce, knight, son of the original joint-grantee, whose descendant, the Earl of Tankerville, is now lord of this manor.

VICARAGE OF THE HOLY CROSS.—The endowment of this must have taken place at a very early period.

Early Incumbents.—William, Clerk of the Cross, supposed to have been vicar here, attested a deed in the chartulary of the abbey previously to 1228; Henry, vicar of the altar of the Holy Cross, about 1240.

The Abbot and Convent of Shrewsbury presented to this vicarage until the Dissolution.

In the abbey church of the Holy Cross is the mutilated effigy of a warrior, represented in the act of unsheathing his sword. This cumbent figure is said to represent Roger de Montgomery, founder of Shrewsbury Abbey; yet, if it is intended to commemorate the great Norman earl, judging from the costume, it must have been executed at least a hundred years after his decease. There is an interesting statue of Edward III. over the west window of the abbey church. On the fall of St. Chad's church, and demolition of old St. Alkmund's, several curious ancient monuments were removed to the abbey church, in the ample side aisles of which they are now to be seen.

CHURCH OF ST. GILES.

Those who were afflicted with that dreadful scourge of former times, the leprosy, used to consider St. Giles their patron saint; he was, in fact, the patron of cripples in general. Among the various hospitals erected in England for lepers, this at Shrewsbury appears to have been founded as early as most of them, for unquestionably it was existent in the reign of Henry II., who, among other indications of his bounty towards the infirm of Shrewsbury, granted the lepers of St. Giles "a handful of two hands of every sack of corn, and a handful of one hand of every sack of flour, exposed to sale in Salopesbiri market."

The church of St. Giles appears to have been originally intended for the service of the hospital, which formerly adjoined it on the west. It consists of a nave, chancel, north aisle, and small turret. The north aisle is divided from the nave by three pointed arches, resting on plain round pillars. A handsome pointed arch separates the nave from the chancel. The south door is as old as the time of Henry I.

St. Giles is a vicarage in the gift of the vicar of Holy Cross.

St. Chad's Church.

Offa, who reigned from 758 to 796, is said to have converted the palace of the Kings of Powis into a church, and founded St. Chad's. Ceadda or Chad, "that true and gentle servant of God," became Bishop of Lichfield, and died on the 2nd of March, 672. He was canonised in 779, and chosen by Offa for patron of the first Saxon church erected in Scrobbesbyrig. At that early period, churches were thinly scattered over the country, and, wherever they existed, a body of clergy lived together collegiate fashion. St. Chad's, then, was originally a Saxon collegiate church, and its secular priests or canons were presided over by a dean. The canons of St. Chad's were not useless members of society, for, diligently clearing and tilling the lands which had been assigned them, at the period of the Conqueror's Survey their estate comprised twenty-three carucates and a half, or 2,820 acres of arable land. After *Domesday*, St. Chad's estate became still greater; and King Edward III. claimed it as a royal free chapel, independent of all ecclesiastical jurisdiction, episcopal or even papal.

That St. Chad's was a stone church before the Conquest is proved by the fragments of Saxon sculpture discovered on the rebuilding of the present church. After the Conquest, a spacious Anglo-Norman structure, in which, however, the early English style was visible, crowned the summit of the southern eminence which Shrewsbury now covers. It was a heavy-looking conventual fabric of a cruciform shape. An unadorned low tower of two stories rose from its centre. The interior was majestic. Five boldly-moulded semi-circular arches springing from well proportioned round columns separated the nave and aisles. Above was the clerestory. Its choir presented a beautiful specimen of early English. The only portion of this fabric that remains is the Lady Chapel, most of which is of later work.

On the morning of July 9th, 1788, just as four o'clock had been chimed, the tower of St. Chad's fell with a tremendous crash upon the roof of the nave and transept, and hurled the greater portion of the venerable fabric to the ground. The first stone of the present Grecian-looking church of St. Chad's was laid, upon a new site, on the 2nd of March, 1790.

DEANS OF ST. CHAD'S.—The earliest which occur are—I. William de Colenham; II. William de Sewksworth; III. Robert Peet of Worcester, 1296.

The collegiate church of St. Chad fell by the Act of 1 Edward VI., 1547.

The parish of St. Chad's was and still is of great extent.

In Queen Elizabeth's time, and afterwards, the right of nominating to St. Chad's was considered to be vested in the Corporation, who repeatedly presented; but in 1637, the Crown claimed the presentation, with whom it now remains. In 1674, Nathaniel Tench, Esq., of London, largely augmented this living by restoring to St. Chad's the tithes of corn and hay of the grange of Crow Meole.

Early Incumbents.—Sir John Beget, vicar, 1334.: Sir Philip Lanley, vicar in St. Chad's, 1354; Sir John Sallowe occurs as vicar of the collegiate church of St. Chad, 1369.[1]

The College of St. Chad, of which scarcely a vestige remains, adjoined the south-western end of the old church.

ST. MARY'S CHURCH.

Comprising the greatest portion of the town after St. Chad's, and probably second in antiquity to it, was the foundation of St. Mary's Collegiate Church. "The collegiate or parish church of St. Mary was founded by King Edgar for the maintenance of a dean, seven prebendaries, and a parish priest," said Henry the Eighth's commissioners. As the learned historians of Shrewsbury, however, have observed, under the influence of St. Dunstan, as Edgar was, "nothing is more improbable than that he should have any concern in the foundation of a church which consisted of secular clergy."[2] All we know concerning this church in Saxon times is, that it held lands amounting in the aggregate to not quite 1,300 acres. When the Conqueror's survey was taken, it held the same property, which had then, however, become diminished in value. Yet, humble although its possessions were, in the latter half of the eleventh century, the fabric was considered the most important in Shrewsbury.

The dean, three of the prebendaries, and Horm or Orm, vicar

---

[1] *Lichfield Reg.*   [2] OWEN and BLAKEWAY's *Hist. of Shrews.*, Vol. 2, p.302.

of St. Mary's, occur as witnesses to a deed of the time of Henry II. The Hundred Rolls of 1255 say, that " the church of St. Mary is a free chapel of our lord the king, and there are there ten prebends," etc.; and Edward II., when master Rigaud de Asserio was sent to England by Pope John XXII, in 1317, for the purpose of enforcing the payment of Peter's Pence, stood up for the rights of his free chapel of St. Mary, and by *writ close* addressed to the papal agent, forbade him to "exact certain intolerable impositions" from its dean and prebendaries.[1]

In 1332, St. Mary's church was selected as the place where the Pope's legates held their court for the adjustment of the differences existing between the English king and Welsh prince.

St. Mary's church stands on an eminence on the north-eastern side of Shrewsbury. Of a cruciform shape, this venerable fabric consists of a nave, north and south aisles, transept, chancel, and two chantry chapels. A clerestory crowns the fabric, at the western end of which is a spire visible for miles around. Of the original Saxon foundation there exists no indication, unless it may be the low level of the floor. The church that now exists presents work of the mixed Anglo-Norman and early English styles, and is one of the finest in the county of Salop.

One of St. Mary's windows contains stained glass, formerly in the east window of old St. Chad's, of unrivalled antiquity, beauty, and curiosity. The inscription conjures the spectator to " Pray for Monsieur John de Charlton, who caused this glazing to be made, and for Dame Hawis his companion." Sir John de Charlton married Hawise Gadarn, the heiress of Powis, and died in 1353, before which date this glass must have been executed.

In this church, there is an interesting monumental effigy of a cross-legged knight. Tradition says it is the tomb of the celebrated Hotspur, who fell at the battle of Shrewsbury, fought 20th July, 1403. Yet Churchyard[2] informs us that it belonged to one of the Leybournes, formerly lords of Berwick, in the parish of St. Mary. This warrior-like effigy formerly reposed under an arch in the north wall of the south chapel, which chapel in 1447 was called *the Leybourne Chappell*.

EARLY DEANS OF ST. MARY.—Richard, time of Henry II.;

---

[1] Claus. 2 Edw. II., m. 10 dorso. *Monasticon.* [2] *Worthiness of Wales.*

William le Strange; Henry Marshall, before 1194, as in that year he was appointed Bishop of Exeter.

Early Incumbents of St. Mary.—Horm, apparently of Danish extraction, officiated as vicar here in the reign of Henry II.; Robert, the chaplain occurs in 1255; Ranulf de Wycumbe is called canon and chaplain of St. Mary, in the feodary of Shropshire, early in the reign of Edward I.; William de Preston was chaplain of the parish church of St. Mary, in 3 Richard II.

The FRATERNITY OF THE TRINITY, a species of charitable and pious institution, was existent in the parish of St. Mary in 1336. In 1461, this society was incorporated by King Edward IV, by the name of "*A Fraternity or Gild of the Holy Trinity of the men of the mystery of drapers of the town of Salop,*" and the poor of St. Mary's almshouses were to pray for the said fraternity.

ST. ALKMUND'S.

Alkmund, the last descendant of the Northumbrian line of Ida, appears to have perished in the bloody confusion attendant on the invasion of his country by the fierce heathen Northmen. In consequence of this his Saxon countrymen had him canonized.

St. Alkmund's church is supposed to have been founded by Ethelfleda, Lady of the Mercians before the year 915. Her great great-grandfather bore the name Alkmund; and this circumstance may have induced the daughter of King Alfred to select the martyred Saxon prince as the patron saint of her new church. Like St. Chad's, this was of a collegiate character. We learn from *Domesday*, that St. Alkmund's held eleven manors in Edward the Confessor's time, and when the survey was taken, this church held in Sciropesberie twenty-one burgesses, besides the twelve houses of its canons; and two of the one hundred hides, for which the city paid Danegeld. Two of its manors had, however, been wrested from St. Alkmund's after the Conquest. In short, its estate then consisted of 4,020 acres. Of these, the canons held 660 in demesne, that is, in their own hands, and farming the rest out, they received for it a rent of £8 11s. 8d., or nearly three farthings an acre. But early in the twelfth century, St. Alkmund's prebendal estates went to found Lilleshall Abbey; and this once opulent college sunk into a vicarage.

The old church of St. Alkmund was a large cruciform-shaped fabric, exhibiting a mixed style of architecture. Some parts of it were of Anglo-Norman work, whilst others belonged to the sixteenth century: it had also, a Grecian altar screen, which, handsome although it was, yet was quite out of character with the original structure.

With the exception of its tower, this venerable fabric was ruthlessly demolished, when the present church was erected upon its ruins. This was opened for divine service on November 8th, 1795.

Early Incumbents.—Sir Godefrid occurs in a deed without date ; Hugh Ive, 1287 ; 1313, 8 non. Jul., William Pope, chaplain. In 1318, he was admitted a burgess of the town; and, on the ides of August, 1325, had licence from his diocesan to make a journey to Rome. He resigned this vicarage in 1349.

ST. JULIAN'S INCLUDING ST. MICHAEL'S.

That a church dedicated to St. Julian existed at Shrewsbury in the Saxon era is certain, since *Domesday* informs us, that, previously to the Conquest it had held half a hide of land in the city : and this is about all we know respecting its early history. It was a royal free chapel, for the Hundred Rolls of 1255 represent it as of the donation of our lord the king; and there were two prebends, one of whom held the chapel of St. Michael in the castle. Respecting the latter, we have described the nature of the tenure by which Lower Poston was held of St. Michael's.[1] Besides Poston and Soulton, which it held at *Domesday*, St. Michael's very early acquired two districts immediately contiguous to Shrewsbury, one of which was called Derfald, a *deer-fold,* or *park* for *deer* : the hunting district attached to the Norman earl's castle. A detached part of St. Julian's parish, now called Darville, before it was stripped of its trees, must, with its shade, pasture, water, and diversified surface, have presented just the conditions necessary for a park of deer.

Like St. Julian's, St. Michael's was a royal free chapel. In 1410, Henry IV., in memory of his victory at Shrewsbury, founded the Abbey of Battlefield, and, amongst other things, gave it the royal chapel of St. Michael's in Shrewsbury Castle, with the chapel of St. Julian belonging thereto. St. Michael's stood on the east side of the castle, near the river. Not a vestige of it remains.

Old St. Julian's church was an Anglo-Norman structure. The first stone of the present St. Julian's was laid February, 1749.

Early Incumbents.—Peter the clerk appears to have been parish

---

[1] *See* Lower Poston : *Index.*

priest about 1220; William de Sancta Juliana; Sir Thomas Barker, chaplain of St. Julian's in 1456.

The DOMINICAN, PREACHING, or BLACK FRIARS, as they were called from their dress, very early in the reign of Henry III. built themselves a house in Shrewsbury, which, according to Leland, stood "a little without the wall, on Severn side, at the end of Marwell Street;" probably St. Mary's, Water Lane.

The FRANCISCAN or GREY FRIARS, also so called from the colour of their dress, must have had a house in Shrewsbury very early in the 13th century. Calling themselves Minorites, to denote their pretended humility, the supposed sanctity of the Friars Minors induced many in their last hours to select them for their confessors, thus affording the friars an opportunity of which they were not slow to avail themselves to wring from their dying penitents their worldly substance. A portion of this Friary, converted into houses, still remains. Lastly—

The AUSTIN FRIARS, or Friars Eremites of St. Austin, noted for their skill in disputation, were established in this town by 1254. Remains of their friary are still to be seen.

Yet besides the monastery, parish churches, and friaries we have alluded to, Shrewsbury, in former times, contained the CHAPEL OF ST. NICHOLAS, that Norman structure in Castle Street, built by Earl Roger de Montgomery, for the accommodation of such of his retainers as resided in the outer court of the castle, and ST. GEORGE'S HOSPITAL, situated in Frankwell, near the Welsh Bridge, not a vestige of which, however, remains. Near to it formerly stood ST. JOHN'S HOSPITAL, a "shelter for honest poverty and helpless old age." CADOGAN'S CROSS was a preaching station, near to which was a chapel that in 1605 was converted into a pest house. The CHAPEL OF ST. BLASE was situated somewhere in or near Murivance; ST. CATHERINE'S CHAPEL, at Coton Hill; ST. MARTIN'S CHAPEL, of which all we know is, that it was situated on the south side of High Street; ST. MARY MAGDALENE, and the CHAPELS OF ST. ROMALD and ST. WERBERG, respecting the situations of which all is conjecture.

Monk Meole.

Situated in the Hundred of Shrewsbury, in William the Conqueror's time, Melam belonged to the Bishop of Chester, for we read in *Domesday* that, "Isdem Episcopus habet unum Manerium : Melam. Non est neque fuit hospitatus. Reddebat xx solidos tempore Regis Edwardi. Modo [reddit] xvii solidos et iiii denarios." [1]

Bishop Clinton granted the manor in question, " with the burgesses, and with all things pertaining to the said land," to the monks of Buildwas, and hence Monk-Meole acquired its distinctive name.

Meole Brace.

We read in *Domesday* that, "The said Church [of St. Mary, Shrewsbury] held [in Saxon times], and now holds one virgate of land in Melam, the manor of Ralph de Mortemer. The [annual] value [thereof] was and is 4s." [2]

St. Mary's appears to have lost the estate alluded to, which cannot now be identified.

From another part of *Domesday*, we learn that, "The same Radulf [de Mortemer] holds Melam. Eddid held it [in Saxon times]. Here iii hides geldable. In demesne are iii ox-teams, and [there are] vi serfs, iiii female serfs, vi villains, and iii boors, with iii teams, and one radman with half a team. To this manor belong ix burgesses within the city [of Shrewsbury], and a mill of 20s. [annual value]. In King Edward's time, and afterwards, the manor was worth £7 [per annum]. Now it is worth £13 5s. 6d." [3]

This manor, then, had once belonged to the Saxon queen, Edith, and Ralph de Mortemer afterwards had obtained it from the Conqueror. Very early in the 13th century, a complicated litigation took place between Ralph's descendant, Roger de Mortemer, and Audulf de Braci, respecting this manor :—"Roger de Mortimer seeks against Audulf de Bracy the Manor of Moles, with its appurtenances, as his right, and as a manor whereof his ancestors, from the Conquest of England were seized." "Audulf appears, and denies the plaintiff's right to hold the manor in demesne, but he well acknowledges that the aforesaid Hugh [Roger de Mortemer's father] was once seized thereof in demesne, and that he [Hugh] gave the manor to a certain knight, William Martel to wit, for his homage and service, which William took *esplees* thereof, as in his own right, for many years; and he [William

---

[1] *Domesday*, fo. 252, a 2.   [2] Ibidem, fo. 252, b 2.   [3] Ibidem, fo. 261, b 1.

Martel] afterwards gave it to Audulf de Bracy, the defendant's father, for his homage and service; which Audulf took *esplees* thereof, and died seized thereof; and from him the manor descended to the defendant as his heir. And this [namely, that the land was so given] the defendant offers to try against the plaintiff, as he ought to try it;"[1] in other words, the defendant offered to decide the matter by a duel.

De Bracy named a free man of his own, of the name of Wigan, a low unprincipled bravo and professed duellist, as his champion; and Mortemer, accepting the challenge, named as his champion his free man, Robert de Brocton. Owing, however, to some treachery on the part of William de Cantilupe, De Bracy's attorney, there was no occasion for the wager of battle having been proposed. A fine ended a series of cross suits, and Cantilupe, giving to Roger de Mortemer, the man whom he had been employed to oppose, 300 merks of silver, he became mesne lord of this manor, Audulf de Braci holding a moiety of it under him.

The distinctive title, Meole Brace originated from this tenure of Audulf de Braci.

The Church.

The advowson of Meole Bracy church was given, before 1174, by Sir Hugh de Mortemer, to Wigmore Abbey. In 1291, the church of Molebracy, in the deanery of Pontesbury and the diocese of Hereford, or rather the rectory thereof, was worth £12 per annum; the vicar's portion was £5. In 1341, the parish of Moely-Bracy was taxed £5 6s. 8d. to the *ninth*. King Henry VIII.'s *Valor* gives the vicar of Milbrace's preferment as £4 13s. 4d. per annum, less 7s. 4d. for procurations and synodals. The Abbot of Wigmore's rectorial tithes appear to have been over £5.

Shelton, as well as Monk Meole, belonged to the Bishop of Chester; for *Domesday* says that, "The same bishop holds Saltone, and the church of St. Chad [holds it] of him. Here is a hide and half. In demesne there is half an ox-team, and there might be ii more teams. Here iiii villains have i ox-team and a half. The value of the manor was and is 12s. [per annum]. This land pays geld."[2]

---

[1] Eyton's *Antiq. of Shropshire*, vol. vi. p. 351—5.   [2] *Domesday*, fo. 252, a 2.

The muniments of St. Chad's College having been lost, all that is known respecting the history of this estate is, that, at the dissolution, neither the bishop nor St. Chad's retained the slightest interest in Shelton.

Sutton, so called from its being south of Shrewsbury, belonged to the monastery of St. Milburg:—"The said church held [in Saxon times] and [still] holds Sudtone. Here i hide. Including freemen and villains, there are eight men here, with iiii ox-teams. The old value of the manor was 12s. [annually]. Now it is worth 16s."[1]

The monks of Wenlock continued to exercise a seigneury over Sutton until Henry VIII.'s time.

SUTTON CHURCH.

Pope Nicholas' Taxation represents the chapel of Sutton in the deanery of Pontesbury and diocese of Hereford as of less than £4 annual value. The parish was rated only 6s. 8d. to the *ninth*, in 1341, because the prior of Wenlock had lands here, and there were no sheep in it, etc. The *Valor* of 1534-5 does not mention this chapel.

Early Incumbent.—John de Hodenet, 1276, presented by the proctors of the prior of Wenlock.

St. Alkmund's Manor. *Domesday* continues:—"The church of St. Almund holds, in Sciropesberie xxi burgesses, besides the xii houses of its canons. These burgesses pay rents of 8s. 8d The same church has ii of the hundred hides which are computed in the geld of the city. These two [hides] are held by ii canons, who have here i ox-team and a half, and iiii villains having ii teams and a half. The [annual] value is 15s."[2] The town property here alluded to lay in the castle ward and castle foregate. Hencot was the suburban estate of St. Alkmund, and it, with all the other possessions of St. Alkmund, eventually passed to Lilleshall Abbey.

St. Julian's Manor. It seems as if every religious

---

[1] *Domesday*, fo. 252, b 2.   [2] Ibidem, fo. 253, a 1.

house in Shropshire had made it a point to acquire some tenement in the county town, for *Domesday* adds:—" The church of St. Juliana holds half a hide, and here has i ox-team; and ii burgesses labouring on this land pay 3s. rent [to the church]. The manor was and is worth 8s. [annually]."[1] We gather from another part of the Conqueror's record, that the half hide alluded to formed part of the hundred hides which constituted the liberties of Shrewsbury; but St. Julian's lost all interest in the estate in question, which cannot now be identified.

---

[1] *Domesday*, fo. 253, a 1.

DOMESDAY HUNDRED OF CONDOVER.

Modern Name.	Domesday Name.	Saxon Owner or Owners, T. R. E.	Domesday Tenant in capite.	Domesday Mesne, or next Tenant.	Domesday Sub-Tenant.	Modern Hundred.
Condover	Conendovre	Rex Edwardus	Rogerius Comes			Condover.
Netley	Netelie	Elmar	Idem			Ibidem.
Broome	Brame	Turstin and Austin	Idem			Ibidem.
Berrington	Beritune	Thoret	Idem	Rainaldus Vicecomes	Azo	Ibidem.
Longnor	Lege	Eldred	Idem	Rainaldus Vicecomes	Azo	Ibidem.
Cound	Cuneet	Morcar Comes	Idem	Rainaldus Vicecomes		Ibidem.
Acton Pigot	Æctune	Gheri	Idem	Rainaldus Vicecomes	Odo	Ibidem.
Kenley	Chenelie	Edric	Idem	Rainaldus Vicecomes	Odo	Ibidem.
Golding	Goldene	Suen	Idem	Rainaldus Vicecomes		Ibidem.
Eaton Mascott	Etune	Toret	Idem	Rainaldus Vicecomes	Fulcher	Ibidem.
Woolstaston	Ulestanestune	Chetel and Aluric	Idem	Robertus fil. Corbet		Ibidem.
Ratlinghope	Rotelingehope	Seuuard	Idem	Robertus fil. Corbet		Purslow.
Womerton	Umbruntune	Auti, Einulf, Aregri, and Archetel	Idem	Robertus fil. Corbet		Munslow.
Oaks	Hach	Ernuit	Idem	Robertus fil. Corbet		Condover.
Brompton	Brantune	Seuuard, Ernut and Elmer	Idem	Robertus fil. Corbet	Picot	Condover.
Welbatch	Huelbec	Hunine	Idem	Rogerius fil. Corbet		Liberties of Shrewsbury.
Staploton	Hundeslit	Huning	Idem	Rogerius fil. Corbet	Ranulfus	Condover.
		Ælric	Idem	Alward		
Acton Burnell	Actune	Godric	Idem	Rogerius fil. Corbet	Rogerius	Ibidem.
Hawksley	Avochelie	Elric	Idem	Teodulfus		Ibidem.
			Idem	Teodulfus		Liberties of Shrewsbury.
Pulley	Polelie	Eddid	Radulfus de Mortemer			
Edgebold	Edbaldinesham	Eddid	Idem			Liberties of Shrewsbury.
Sheinton	Schentune	Azor, Ælgar, & Saulf	Rogerius Comes	Radulfus de Mortemer	Helgod	Condover.
Preen	Prene	Eduinus	Idem	Helgot	Ricardus Godeboldus	Ibidem.
Harley	Harlege	Edric, Ulmar, Elmund, and Edric	Idem	Helgot		Ibidem.
Belswardine	Bellenrdine	Elmund	Idem	Helgot		Ibidem.
Bayston	Begestan	Edric, de Episcopo de Hereford	Idem	Willelmus Pantulf		Ibidem.
Norton	Nortune	Uluric	Idem	Willelmus Pantulf		Ibidem.
Wigwig	Wigewic	Elmar	Idem	Turoldus		Wenlock.
Pitchford	Piceforde	Edric, Leuric, and Uluric	Idem	Turoldus		Condover.
Lydley Heys	Litlega	Anti	Idem	Auti		Munslow.
Lee-Botwood	Botewde	Auti	Idem	Auti		Condover.
Frodesley	Frodeslege	Siwardus	Idem	Siwardus		Ibidem.
Overs	Ovre	Sewardus	Idem	Sewardus		Purslow.
Pulverbatch	Polrebec	Hunnic and Uluiet	Idem	Rogerius Venator		Condover.
Wrentnall	Wereutenehale	Urnul and Chetel	Idem	Rogerius Venator		Ibidem.
Cressage	Cristesache	Edric	Idem	Ranulfus Peverel		Ibidem.
Cantlop	Cantelop	Edric	Idem	Normannus		Ibidem.
Langley	Languelege	Suain	Idem	Toret		Ibidem.
Cothercote	Cotardicote	Hunnic	Idem	Avenel		Ibidem.
Smethcott	Smerecote	Edmund	Idem	Edmund	Eldred	Ibidem.
Wilderley	Wildredelega	Chetel	Idem	Hugo filius Turgisi		Ibidem.
Emstrey	Eiminstre	Eduinus Comes and Aluric	Idem	Eccl. Sancti Petri		Ibidem.
Moreton	Burtune	Ecclesia Sancti Petri	Idem	Eccl. Sancti Petri		Ibidem.
Inghley		Episcopus de Cestre	Idem	Eccl. Sctæ Milburgæ	Filius Alurici	Wenlock.
Betton	Betune	Episcopus de Cestre	Episcopus de Cestre			Condover.
Snildwas	Beldewes	Episcopus de Cestre	Episcopus de Cestre			Bradford South.

WE have now come to the *Domesday* Hundred of Condover, and observe, by way of preface to a description of its manors, that when the Hundreds of Shropshire were re-arranged, in the time of Henry I., the Manor of Ratlinghope was annexed to Purslow Hundred. In the 12th and 13th centuries, Condover sustained a further diminution of its territory. To give the general result in few words: the modern Hundred of Condover contains nothing which was not in the *Domesday* Condover; yet, as will be seen by the Table, it has lost eleven manors.

In the Anglo-Saxon King Edward's time, two-thirds of the profits of the Hundred-court belonged to the king, as lord of the manor of Condover. At the period of the survey, the whole profits of the Hundred went to Roger de Montgomery, a circumstance illustrative of that Palatine dignity he possessed, which combined the prerogatives of both king and earl. Moreover, the Norman earl appears to have been seigneural lord over forty-six out of the fifty manors of which Condover then consisted.

Upon the forfeiture of Robert de Belèsme, the revenues of Condover Hundred went to make up that £265 15s. for which the sheriff of Shropshire was annually responsible at the Exchequer. The sheriff, anxious to make as much out of his office as possible, sublet this and other hundreds to various fermors or bailiffs at as high a rent as he could get; these subordinate officers, in turn, eagerly sought a profit, and the result of the system was much oppressive extortion.

In 1292, Roger de Frodesley was chief-bailiff of Condover, that is, he farmed it for the sheriff, who accounted six merks a year to the crown as the proceeds of this Hundred.

Condover. The Celtic word *Cond* signifies a mouth, as of a river, hence Cound, the extremely ancient village near the mouth of the stream which traverses the Hundred of Condover. The fair-haired Saxons came, and finding this village in existence, founded another further up the same stream, to which they gave, by way of distinction, the title of *Conedovre*, namely, *Over* or *Upper* Cound.

Domesday says:—"The earl himself holds Conendovre. King Edward held it. To this manor appertain ten berewicks. Here xiii hides are subject to geld. In demesne there are vii hides, and thereon are iiii ox-teams, and xii villains, and a priest with vii ox-teams; and yet there might be iii other teams here. There are viii neat-herds and a mill of 8s. 6d. [annual value].

"To this manor [formerly] belonged two [out of every three] pence [arising] from the hundred of Conendoure. In time of King Edward, the manor yielded £10 [annually]. Now, together with the hundred, it yields £10.

"Of the land of this manor, Roger Venator holds i hide, Osbern i hide, and Eluuard iiii hides. Thereon is one team; and iiii villains, ii boors, iii radmans, and ii neat-herds between them all have iii ox-teams; and there might be viii additional teams. The whole is worth 41s. [per annum]."[1]

From the above extract, we learn, then, that in Saxon times Condover was a royal manor, *caput* of the hundred to which it gave a name, and that at the period of the survey, Earl Roger de Montgomery retained more than half the manor in his own hands, and was lord of the hundred of Condover.

The barons of Pulverbatch, Roger Venator's descendants, retained an interest in the manor of Condover until the 13th century, but Osbern's and Eluuard's interest had ceased when Henry I. became seized *in demesne* of the whole manor, excepting the tenement of Roger Venator.

The great Beauclerc visited Condover more than once; and, as a manor of *ancient demesne*, Condover came into the hands of his grandson, Henry II.. Of the £265 15s. assessed upon Shropshire, £12 13s. was the ferm which the sheriff accounted for at the Exchequer as arising from the king's manor of Condover; and the fiscal value of this manor remained unaltered during the reigns of Richard and John. Like Claverley, Worfield, and other manors of royal demesne, the affairs of Condover were managed by the sheriff; it was his duty to keep the king's manor well stocked, and doubtless he participated in the profits. Condover was assessable to tallages; but Henry III., being at Shrewsbury on August 29, 1226, notified to the sheriff of Shropshire that, "he has committed to his beloved sister Joan, wife of his faithful and beloved Lewellyn, the royal manor of Cunedour, to be held by the said Joan so long as the king shall please:" hence, for a time, it passed from the sheriff's hands. Lewellyn, prince of North Wales, however, was soon again in arms against his brother-in-

---

[1] *Domesday*, fo. 253, a 2.

law; border warfare ensued, when, after a number of petty successes on either side, a pacification was concluded. Condover, therefore, was restored to the princess Joan, who had suffered a temporary forfeiture of her manor. By 1231, Condover and Lewellyn's manor of Ellesmere were again seized into the king's hands, as fresh hostilities had broken out between the Welsh prince and his liege lord. Lewellyn devastated the marches, from Brecknockshire to Montgomery. On the other side, the Anglo-Norman king prosecuted the campaign of Elvein with peculiar ferocity.

Condover now continued in the hands of Henry III. until the 11th of June, 1238, when the king gave it, with other manors, to Henry de Hastings and Ada his wife, in lieu of Ada's share in the inheritance of her brother, John Scot, the late earl of Chester. Hastings therefore became seigneural lord of the manor, and he transmitted it to his descendants, one of whom gave Condover to Bishop Burnell, in exchange for Woton, Northamptonshire. The inquisition taken in July, 1294, on the death of Philip Burnell, nephew and heir of the bishop, states him to have held the manor of Conedovere *in capite*, by service of finding twelve foot soldiers for the army of Wales." [1]

CONDOVER CHURCH.

The collegiate Saxon church of St. Andrew, Condover, indicated in *Domesday* merely by the mention of a priest, had for its parish originally a district of great extent. We learn, that shortly after the survey, Earl Roger de Montgomery gave to Shrewsbury Abbey the "*Church of Chonedoura*," with all things appertaining to it. Pope Nicholas' Taxation in 1291, valuing the church of Conedovere, in the deanery of Salop, at £23 6s. 8d., adds, that the abbot of Shrewsbury received £1 therefrom. In 1341, the parish was taxed only £16 13s. 4d. to the *ninth*, because the corn crop was deficient, etc. The *Valor* of 1534 gives the vicar of Condover's preferment as £5 13s. 4d., out of which 13s. 4d. went yearly for procurations and 6d. for synodals. The abbot's rectorial tithes, however, amounted to £27 6s. 8d. of which he paid a pension of £7 6s. 8d. to the Dean and Chapter of Lichfield, out of Condover church. Thus the cathedral and the abbey divided the spoil.

Early Incumbents.—Thomas de Charnes, subdeacon, deceased in 1324, was last rector of one portion in this church; Henry de

---

[1] *Inquisitions*, 22 Edw. I., No. 45, c.

CONDOVER CHURCH, NORTH-WEST.

Lichfield, last incumbent of the other portion was dead in July, 1324; when John Husee became first vicar of Condover, admitted July 17, 1324, on presentation of abbot and convent of Shrewsbury.

Netley, now a township in the parish of Stapleton, is mentioned in *Domesday* thus:—"The earl himself holds Netelie. Elmar held it [in Saxon times] and was a free man. Here i hide geldable. The [arable] land is sufficient for ii ox-teams. It is and has been waste. It was worth 12s. [annually in Saxon times]."[1] The waste land referred to here became annexed to the forest. We learn that Nethelegh was one of the places disforested by the great perambulation of 1300-1.

Broome, now a township in the parish of Cardington, is the subject of the following entry in Domesday Book:—"Earl Roger holds Brame. Turstin and Austin held it. Here half a hide geldable. The land is for ii ox-teams. Of this land, Rainald has half a virgate."[1]

Berrington. Rainald the sheriff held seven manors in Condover Hundred under the Norman Earl. One of these is thus described in *Domesday*:—"The same Rainald holds Beritune, and Azo holds it of him. Thoret held [in Saxon times of the church] of St. Andrew half a hide in this vill by [certain] services. Besides this half hide, he [Thoret] held ii hides geldable [here]. In demesne are ii ox-teams; and vii serfs and vi villains, with i team; and still there might be ii other teams here. St. Peter, in Shrewsbury, holds the church and priest of this vill. In King Edward's time [the manor] was worth 30s.; afterwards, 14s. Now [it is worth] 40s. [*per annum*]."[2]

Toret appears to have lost his manor of Beritune amidst the general transfer of property from Saxon to Norman hands after the Conquest, when Rainald the sheriff became mesne lord of this manor, and Azo its subtenant.

A feodary of Fitz Alan's estates, taken in 1397-8, inserts Robert

---

[1] *Domesday*, fo. 259, b 2. [2] Ibidem, fo. 254, b 1.

de Lee as tenant of Berrington, by service of half a knight's fee. The Lees long continued to be lords of Berrington.

The White Nuns of Brewood, as well as Haughmond Abbey, had an estate at Berrington.

BERRINGTON CHURCH.

From the notice in *Domesday*, that the "Church and Priest" of Berrington belonged to St. Peter's Abbey, Shrewsbury, we may infer that Berrington church was in existence at the period of the survey, if not in Saxon times. We learn also from Earl Roger's charter, that it had been granted to the abbey by Warin, the first Norman sheriff of Shropshire. In 1291, the church of Byryhton, in Salop deanery, was valued at £5 9s. 4d., besides a pension of 24s. to Shrewsbury Abbey, and one of no less a sum than £6 13s. 4d. to Lichfield Cathedral.

In 1341, the parish was assessed £8 13s. 4d. to the *ninth*. The *Valor* of 1534-5 gives the gross value of this rectory as £20 12s., but pensions payable to Shrewsbury abbey, Lichfield cathedral, and the abbot of Haughmond, with 6s. 8d. for procurations, and 6d. for synodals, reduced the £20 12s. to £10 12s. net value *per annum*.

Early Incumbent.—Andrew, priest of Biriton about 1170.

Berrington church contains the mutilated monumental effigy of a knight carved in wood. Neither armorial insignia or inscription, however, remain to inform us whom it commemorates.

Longnor, anciently called *Lege*, is the subject of the following remarkable entry in Domesday Book :—"The same Rainald holds Lege, and Azo [holds] it of him. Eldred held it [in Saxon times] and could go whither he would.[1] Here ii hides geldable. In demesne is one ox-team ; and one serf and v villains with ii teams ; and there might be vi more teams here.

"Roger Venator holds the caput of this manor under Earl Roger, and the two hides which Azo holds exonerate his land, which is *Inland*,[2] from geld. In Roger [Venator's] demesne are

---

[1] "*Potuit ire quo voluit*," remarks Eyton, "is a common phrase in *Domesday*, indicating a particular franchise of certain Saxon freeholders, viz., that they could subject themselves (*Se commendare*), with or without their lands, to any patron or suzerain they pleased."

[2] The Saxon term *Inland*, is supposed to have been equivalent to the Norman *demesne*, but uncertainty prevails respecting the meaning of the whole of the above sentence.

ii ox-teams; and iii serfs, ii neat-herds, and ix boors with i team; and there might be iii other teams besides.

"Here a wood that will fatten 600 swine; there are iii *Firm Hayes*,[1] and a mill. The whole in time of King Edward was worth £8 [annually]; afterwards 20s. Now it is worth 64s."[2]

That the *Domesday* Lege was identical with the beautifully-situated Longnor of the present day, we have the first indication in Azo Bigot's grant to Shrewsbury abbey of half a hide in *Langanara*. This Azo was the same as the *Domesday* lord of Lege. Another circumstance tending to show that Lege and Longnor are only two different names for the same manor, is the fact, that, like the rest of Azo's tenures under Rainald the sheriff, the manor in question afterwards came to be held by the elder house of le Strange under Fitz Alan.

The Sprenghoses, a family who attained to great eminence, held Longnor for more than a hundred and fifty years under the Le Stranges. We read of Alric de Longenalra, alias Alric Sprencheaux, attesting one of the prior of Wenlock's charters about 1170. To Alric succeeded Roger Sprencheaux I. who, in 1185, gave with his body (when deceased) the mill of Langenore to Haughmond Abbey. Having served the office of coroner for Shropshire, this Roger was succeeded by a son, alluded to in the Forest Perambulation of 1235, as having had timber from "the Bosc of Wimbrinton" (Womerton), wherewith to fortify his "House at Langenalre." After Roger II. came Roger Sprenghose III., in whose time the house of Sprenghose became connected with the Princes of Powis.

Roger lived in stirring times; yet, following his liege lord, John le Strange III., in the path of loyalty, he drew his sword on behalf of the king, and after the battle of Evesham, Roger was rewarded by a grant of the forfeited lands of Sir Hugh Wrottesley, until they were redeemed under the *Dictum de Kenilworth*, when Sprenghose got 60 merks for surrendering them.

As constable of Montgomery, we find this Roger writing to Walter de Merton, Chancellor of England, to say that he had duly directed certain of his people to attend the abbots of Haughmond and Dore, on January 20th, 1273, when those commissioners were appointed to go to the Ford, beyond Montgomery, and there

---

[1] The *Haia* was that enclosed part of a wood into which beasts were driven; and the expression Firm Hayes, perhaps, means that the fences were in good repair.

[2] *Domesday*, fo. 254, b 1.

receive the oath of fealty due from Lewellyn ap Gruffyth, Prince of Wales to King Edward I.; yet, added the constable, "The commissioners waited at that ford till long past noon, but Lewellyn neither came nor sent any message." [1]

Sir Roger Sprenghose was sheriff of Shropshire and Staffordshire, from 1279, till May, 1286; and he was one of the knights of the shire returned for Shropshire in November, 1295, to the Parliament then held at Westminster. Sir Roger's successor at Longnor was Griffin de la Pole, otherwise Gruffith Vachan, fifth son of Griffin ap Gwenhunin, Prince of Powis, who, in 1310, was lord of this manor. He sold it to Sir Fulk le Strange.

There appears to have been several under-tenants in Longnor.

LONGNOR CHAPEL, as an affiliation of Condover church, belonged to Shrewsbury Abbey; owing, therefore to this state of subjection, it is not noticed in early records.

Cound was another of Rainald the sheriff's Condover manors. *Domesday* says of it, that "The same Rainald holds Cuneet. Earl Morcar held it. Here are 4½ hides geldable. In demesne are ii ox-teams; and [there are] vi male and iiii female serfs, vi villains, and vi boors with iiii teams. Here ii mills of 20s. [annual value], and a wood capable of fattening 50 swine. In time of King Edward, the manor was worth £4 7s. [annually]. Now [it is worth] £10." [2]

For ages after the Conqueror's survey had been taken, Rainald's successors the Fitz Alans held 3½ hides of Cound *in demesne*. Harnage, the remaining hide, by 1291, had fallen into the hands of the monks of Buildwas, who retained it until the dissolution.

COUND CHURCH.

The ancient church of Cound appears to have been a Saxon foundation, although the first mention we find of it is in 1216. In 1291, the church of Conede, in the deanery of Salop, with its chapels, was valued at £20 *per annum*. In 1341, the parish was rated at £16 18s. 6d. to the *ninth* of wheat, wool, and lamb. In 1534-5, the rector of Cound's income was represented as £33 13s. 4d., less 13s. 4d. for procurations and synodals.

Early Incumbent.—Robert de Gaham, 1216.

As late as the year 1553, the Fitz Alans presented to Cound.

---

[1] *Fœdera*, I, 499. [2] *Domesday*, fo. 254, b 1.

FONT, ACTON BURNELL (*see* p. 217).

FONT, COUND.

Acton Pigot. "The same Rainald," says *Domesday*, "holds Æctune, and Odo [holds it] of him. Gheri held it, and was able to give or sell it. Here iii hides geldable. In demesne is i ox-team; and iii serfs and iiii villains, with i team. A wood here will fatten xx swine. In King Edward's time, the manor was worth 20s.; afterwards 12s. Now it is worth 13s. 4d. [per annum]."[1] The status of Acton Pigot, in the twelfth century, was precisely that of Kenley.

Kenley is thus noticed in King William's record:—"The same Rainald holds Chenelie, and Odo [holds it] of him. Edric held it [in Saxon times], and was a free man. Here i hide geldable. In demesne is one ox-team, and other iiii teams might be here. There is a wood capable of fattening 400 swine. In the time of King Edward, the manor was worth 30s.; afterwards it was waste. Now it is worth 4s. [annually]."[1] The seigneural interest of Rainald over Kenley descended, in the usual course, to the Fitz Alans, and the interest of Fitz Odo, the mesne lord, in like manner descending down the line of his elder representatives, went, first to the de Wilileys, and then, at the close of the thirteenth century, to the Harleys.

The chapel of Acton Pigot, now a ruin, as well as the church of Kenley, in ancient times were affiliations of Cound church. The parish of Acton Pygot was rated one merk to the *ninth* in 1341.

Golding, one of the two remaining Condover manors of Rainald the sheriff, is described in the Conqueror's record thus:—"The same Rainald holds Goldene, and Odo [holds it] of him. Suen, a free man, held it [in Saxon times]. Here half a hide geldable. In demesne is one ox-team, iii serfs, and one boor; and another team might be employed here. [The manor formerly] was worth 8s. [annually]; now 5s."[1] The early seigneural and also mesne lords of this small manor, now a mere member of Pitchford, were identical with those of Kenley.

Eaton Mascott was the seventh and last manor in Condover Hundred which Rainald the sheriff held under the Norman

---

[1] *Domesday*, fo. 254, b 1.

earl. Of it *Domesday* says:—"The same Rainald holds Etune, and Fulcher [holds] of him. Toret held it [in Saxon times], and was a free man. Here iii hides geldable. In demesne is one ox-team; and iiii serfs, iii villains, and iiii boors, with one team; and two other teams might be [employed] here. Here is a mill of 4s. [annual value]. In time of King Edward [the manor] was worth 20s. [annually]; afterwards 24s. Now [it is worth] 20s."[1] Fulcher's interest here appears to have reverted to Rainald's successor, Fitz Alan, who then granted it to one Marescot, by birth a Scot, as his name implies. Of knightly degree, this man was probably a friend of that Walter Fitz Alan (brother to the seigneural lord of this manor) who, during Stephen's usurpation, became seneschal of Scotland, and eventually ancestor of the royal house of Stuart. Descendants of the Scotch knight for generations afterwards continued to be lords over Eaton Mascott.

Woolstaston.

There are two artificial mounds at Woolstaston, one ten feet high by thirty-two across its centre; the other, which adjoins it, has a descent on three sides. Naturally elevated above the adjacent land, this has its height further increased by an artificial raising of six feet, forming a figure in the shape of a parallelogram one hundred paces wide from north to east, and a hundred and fifty-two from north to south. These works resemble rather the remains of a Norman Keep and Baly than a Tumulus.

After Rainald the sheriff, Robert Fitz Corbet was the next greatest holder under the earl in Condover Hundred. He held four manors, besides having an interest in Brompton. *Domesday* alludes to one of his manors thus:—"Robert, son of Corbet, holds Ulestanestune under Earl Roger. Chetel and Aluric held it [in Saxon times] for ii manors, and those men were free. Here ii hides. In demesne is i ox-team, and vii villains, with i team and a half; and iii teams more might be here. There is a wood which will fatten xii swine. In time of King Edward, the manor was worth 40s. [annually]; now 12s."[2] During the reign of Henry I. the barony of Robert Fitz Corbet is said to have been divided between his daughters, one of whom became ancestress of the

---

[1] *Domesday*, fo. 254, b 1.   [2] Ibidem, fo. 256, a 1.

baronial house of Fitz Herbert, and the other of the baronial house of Boterell, or Botreaux. When this partition was made, the manor in question went to Boterell, whose descendants for generations afterwards retained the seigneury over Woolstaston.

The Boterell's feoffee here, about 1160, was Roger Anglicus, one of whose descendants, towards 1280, parted with the manor to Burnel, Bishop of Bath and Wells.

The Church.

We learn from the Assize Roll, that, about 1272, this church afforded sanctuary to certain felons. Described in the Taxation of 1291 as the church of Wolstanestone, in Wenlock deanery and Hereford diocese, it is set down as of less than £4 annual value. The parish of Wolstanton was assessed only 13s. 4d. to the *ninth*, on account of a murrain amongst its cattle, etc.

Early Incumbent.—Edmund de Lodelowe, 1316.

Ratlinghope.

Roteling-hope signifies the *hope* or valley of the children of Rotel.

"The Castle Ring," says Hartshorne,[1] "is a British encampment immediately above *Ratlinghope*, and contains within its area about an acre and a half. The ascent from the west and south sides is precipitous, and, as being unnecessary here, the vallum and fosse have been slight: whereas, on the east side, where the ground falls but gently, the works have been more elevated. The camp is nearly oval. The gorge is at the east. The general height of the vallum seems to have been ten feet, and the work is encircled by one ditch only. There are indications of another camp due south of *Castle Ring*, between this place and *Bilbitch Gutter*; and a British trackway appears to run between these two places, for the purpose of communication between the two positions." *Domesday* briefly alludes to this manor in the following terms:—"The same Robert holds Rotelingehope. Seuuard held it [in Saxon times]. Here ii hides. Waste they are and were."[2]

Situated in a lonely country, the approach to which, from Church Stretton, across the Longmynd range of hills, is at times, in the winter season, impassable, Ratlinghope had become a priory or cell of Wigmore Abbey by 1209.

---

[1] *Salopia Antiqua*, p. 87. [2] *Domesday*, fo. 256, a 1.

Ratlinghope Church.

This was originally founded, perhaps, by Wigmore Abbey in connection with the priory. The parish of Rotlynghope was assessed only 20s. to the *ninth* in 1341, on account of the poverty of its tenants.

Early Incumbent:—Laurence Johnson, a canon of the dissolved abbey of Wigmore, is the first rector we hear of in connection with this church. He was instituted by the Bishop of Hereford on February 15th, 1555, on presentation of Philip and Mary.

Womerton. "The same Robert holds Umbruntune. Auti, Einulf, Aregri, and Archetel held it [in Saxon times] for iiii manors. Those Thanes were free. Here ii hides and a half geldable. Here are ii villains, with half an ox-team. Most part of this manor is waste. In King Edward's time, altogether it was worth 68s. [annually]; now 10s. The land is [sufficient] for 5 teams."[1] Annexed to the adjacent royal demesne of Church Stretton, the land thus described eventually sank into a forest district.

Oaks. "The same Robert holds Hach. Ernuit held it, and was a free man. Here ii hides geldable. In demesne is half an ox-team; and ii serfs, i radman, i villain, and i boor with a team; and yet there might be iiii more teams here besides. In King Edward's time [the manor] was worth 40s.; afterwards 10s. Now 8s. [annually]."[1] Beyond the presumed *Domesday* notice of it, there is nothing particularly interesting in the early history of Oaks.

Brompton. Besides holding the four preceding manors, under Earl Roger de Montgomery, Robert Fitz Corbet held of him also a portion of Brompton. The fact is thus alluded to in *Domesday*:— "Robert holds of the Earl, Brantune. Seuuard held it in [Saxon times]. Here is half a hide. It was and is waste."[1] From another part of the Conqueror's record, however, we learn that by far the larger portion of Brompton was held by Picot de Say. *Domesday* says:—"Picot holds of Earl Roger, Brantune. Ernui

---

[1] *Domesday*, fo. 256, a 1.

and Elmer held it [in Saxon times] for ii manors, and were free men. Here iii hides geldable. There is [arable] land enough for vi ox-teams. In demesne is one team and a half; and iii neat-herds, vii villains, and ii boors with ii teams and a half. In time of King Edward, the manor was worth 25s.; afterwards 20s. Now 40s. [annually]."¹ Very shortly after the above was written, the Norman, Picot de Say, gave the *vill* of Brompton, with all its tithes, to Shrewsbury Abbey, to assist the monks in building and repairing their conventual church.

Welbatch. By referring to the Table, the reader will see that Roger Corbet held three manors in Condover Hundred, under the Norman earl; one of which is thus described in *Domesday*: "Roger Fitz Corbet holds of Earl Roger, Huelbec; and Rannulf [holds it] of him. Hunine held it, and was free with this land. Here i hide geldable. In demesne is one ox-team, ii serfs, and ii boors. Here is a mill, which will grind in winter but not in summer. In the time of King Edward, the manor was worth 20s. [*per annum*]; now [it is worth] 5s."² There is nothing of special interest attached to the early history of this small manor.

Stapleton. *Staplus*, in low Latin, means a tomb: this points to something sepulchral. We are not surprised, therefore, at learning that some years ago a large Tumulus was opened at Stapleton, Salop. All that was discovered in it was a funeral urn, formed of clay baked in the sun, which it was supposed held the ashes of the person to whose memory the barrow was raised.

We read in Domesday Book that:—"The same Roger [Fitz Corbet holds] Hundeslit, a manor of one virgate and a half geldable; and Rannulf holds it of him. Huning held it [in Saxon times], and was free. The land is for i ox-team. Here is one villain. The [manor formerly] was worth 16d. [annually]; now 12d."² In another place we read:—"Alward holds of the earl, Hundeslit. Ælric held it. Here one hide and half a virgate. The land is [capable of employing] ii ox-teams and a half. In demesne there is half a team, and one radman, and one villain, with i team. Its old value was 3s. [annually]; now [it is worth]

---

¹ *Domesday*, fo. 258, a 1.   ² Ibidem, fo. 255, b 1.

4s."¹ Hundeslit must be Stapleton, otherwise the former has no representative in the modern hundred of Condover, nor the latter in *Domesday*.

This divided manor appears to have derived its name from some former Saxon lord, called Huni; *Huning*, the patronymic of him who held the manor in Edward the Confessor's time, signifying the son or descendant of *Huni*.

Roger Corbet and his tenant Ranulf, it seems, surrendered their interest here to King Henry I., who, having also acquired the Saxon Alward's share, annexed the whole to the Honour of Montgomery. Henceforth, therefore, the successive lords of Montgomery exercised a seigneury over this manor, under whom again it was held by a race of feoffees springing from that Norman Baldwin de Meisy, who, in the reign of Stephen, was lord of Stapleton and Wistanstow. Long after the troubled career of the Usurper had drawn to its close, the descendants of Baldwin maintained their position here.

THE CHURCH.

It was in King Stephen's time that Hundeslit acquired the name Stepel-tun, owing to a church having been added to the manor. In 1291, the church of Stepelton, in the deanery of Salop, was valued at £4 *per annum*. In 1341, the parish was rated only £1 16s. 8d. to the *ninth*, on account of the low state of its cultivation. In 1534-5, Stepulton rectory was valued at £7 *per ann.*, but a pension of 10s. was payable to the rector of Shrewsbury Abbey, and 2s. 8d. went for procurations and synodals.

Early Incumbent.—Richard de Adbaston, presented to the "rectory of the chapel of Stepelton" October 25th, 1307, by Sir Robert de Stepelton.

Acton Burnell.

"The same Roger," says *Domesday*, "holds Actune, and one Roger [holds it] of him. Godrie held it [in Saxon times], and was a free man. Here iii and a half hides geldable. In demesne is one ox-team; and ii serfs, one villain, iiii boors, and i radman, with a team and a half. In time of King Edward [the manor] was worth 30s. [annually]; afterwards 15s. Now [it is worth] 20s. One team more might be employed

---

¹ *Domesday*, fo. 259, b 1.

here." [1] The Conqueror took the Saxon Godric's manor from him, and gave it to the Norman earl of Shrewsbury, who in turn conferred it on Roger Fitz-Corbet; accordingly, the seigneury over Actune remained with Fitz-Corbet's descendants, the barons of Caus.

It is supposed, that Roger, the Domesday tenant of Actune, was ancestor of those Burnels from whom afterwards the manor took its distinctive title of Acton Burnel. The first Burnel we hear of is William Burnel, who, previously to 1176, attested one of the Prior of Wenlock's charters. The family then appears as consisting of two distinct branches, both of whom claimed to have an interest in Acton Burnel. Thomas Burnel was the representative of the supposed elder branch: the Burnels of Acton Burnel and of Langley. Gerin, or Warin Burnel was the representative of the younger branch. It is with the latter that we have more particularly to do.

To Gerin Burnel succeeded Hugh his son; after whom came Gerin Burnel II., who, with William Corbet and others, at the instigation of Thomas Corbet, robbed a monk of Buildwas. A list of Thomas Corbet's barony gives William and this Geryn Burnel as holding one knight's fee in Acton in 1240.

William Burnel, here alluded to, slew two men, for which sentence of outlawry was pronounced against him, after which the king must have had his share of Acton Burnel for a year and a day, when, in the ordinary course, it would revert to the suzerain, Thomas Corbet of Caus.

To Gerin succeeded Roger Burnel, after whom came Robert Burnel, who, purchasing the fee simple of the whole manor, eventually became sole lord of Acton Burnell.

This extraordinary man enjoyed, in a remarkable degree, the favour and confidence of Edward I., and was his chief adviser in all his measures. Early betaking himself to civil and ecclesiastical employments, then generally combined, Burnel soon distinguished himself. While yet a young man, he was introduced to Prince Edward, who, pleased at his address, learning, and ability, made him his chaplain and private secretary. There is proof, that during the baron's wars, Robert Burnel was employed by the prince. It is uncertain whether or not he actually attended Edward to the Holy Land; but, on June 18, 1272, Prince Edward,

---

[1] *Domesday*, fo. 255, b 1.

then at Acre, in Palestine, made a will, in which he appointed Robert Burnel one of his executors. On September 21, 1274, King Edward, now on his father's throne, bestowed the Great Seal on Robert Burnel himself. When appointed to the office of chancellor of England, Burnel had reached no higher ecclesiastical dignity than that of Archdeacon of York. Four months afterwards, however, he was raised to the see of Bath and Wells.

He presided at the Parliament which met in May 1275, and passed "the Statute of Westminster the First," the code rather than Act of Parliament which has obtained for Edward I. the title of "the English Justinian." "The chief merit of it," says Lord Campbell, "may safely be ascribed to Lord-Chancellor Burnel, who brought it forward in Parliament."

The advice which Burnel tendered his sovereign intimately connects him with the conquest of Wales. After the defeat of Lewellyn, the chancellor was employed to devise measures for the pacification and future government of the conquered principality. He held courts of justice at Bristol, for the southern counties, and, giving general directions for the introduction of English institutions among the Welsh, he prepared a code under which Wales was governed till the reign of Henry VIII.

In 1283, to gratify his faithful minister, King Edward summoned a Parliament, to meet at Acton Burnel, in the mansion of his favourite. Speaking of the gable ends shown at Acton Burnell as those of the barn in which, according to tradition, the commons met, whilst the lords sat in Burnel's mansion, the learned historians of Shrewsbury contend that these did not belong to a barn. They add, "we have little doubt that they belonged to a great hall erected by the munificent prelate for the entertainment of his sovereign; and it is in the highest degree probable that the three estates of the realm, the lords spiritual and temporal, and the commons, sat within its walls."[1] Here was passed the admirable statute, "De Mercatoribus," otherwise known as the "Statute of Acton Burnell," for the recovery of debts, "shewing," says Lord Campbell, "that this subject was as well understood in the time of Chancellor Burnel as in the time of Chancellor Eldon or Chancellor Lyndhurst."

A patent of January 28, 1284, allows that "Robert, Bishop of Bath and Wells, our chancellor, may, he or his heirs, strengthen

---

[1] *History of Shrewsbury*, vol. I. p. 150.

with a wall of stone and lime, and also embattle their mansion of Acton Burnell."

While Burnel continued in office, the improvement of the law rapidly advanced. Various acts were passed, some of which have since become celebrated; for instance, "the Statute of Mortmain," and the "Ordinatio pro Statu Hiberniæ" (17 Ed. I.), for effectually introducing the English law into Ireland, and for the protection of the natives from the rapacity and oppression of the king's officers, "a statute framed in the spirit of justice and wisdom," says Campbell, "which, if steadily enforced, would have saved Ireland from much suffering, and England from much disgrace." Nor was King Edward's favourite a statute-framer only. As head of the law, Burnel exercised a vigilant superintendence over the administration of justice, and in the Parliament held at Westminster in 1290, the chancellor brought forward very serious charges against the judges, for taking bribes and altering the records, when, with two honourable exceptions, they were all convicted.

Lord Chancellor Burnel conducted King Edward I.'s claim to the superiority over Scotland, and pronounced the sentence by which the crown of that country was disposed of to be held under an English liege lord. He accompanied the martial monarch of England and his powerful army to Norham, and there addressed the Norman derived nobility of Scotland in the French language. The prelates, barons, and knights of Scotland having mustered on the green sward to the left of the Tweed, opposite Norham castle, in pursuance of the leave given them to deliberate in their own country, Burnel went to them in his master's name, and asked them "whether they would say anything that could or ought to exclude the King of England from the right and exercise of the superiority and direct dominion over the kingdom of Scotland, which belonged to him," etc., to which the indignant but helpless Scots made no particular objection. Upon this, the chancellor recapitulated all that had been said at the last meeting relative to Edward's claim; and, a public notary being present, the right of deciding the controversy between the several competitors for the crown of Scotland was entered in form for the King of England. Then Burnel, beginning with Robert Bruce, lord of Annandale, asked him, in the presence of all the bishops, earls, barons, etc., "whether, in demanding his right, he would answer and receive justice from the King of England as superior and direct lord over the kingdom of Scotland?" Bruce answered, that "he did acknowledge the King of England superior and direct lord of the kingdom of Scotland," and that he would before him, as such, demand, answer, and receive justice. The same question being put to all the other competitors, each and all of them obsequiously replied as Bruce had done.

Not satisfied, however with having obtained their verbal assent to Edward's ambitious proposal, the crafty English chancellor required the competitors to sign and seal a solemn instrument to the same effect, which they accordingly did, "quickened by hints thrown out that the candidate who was the most complying would have the best chance of success."[1] One hundred and four Scottish and English commissioners were now appointed to take evidence and hear the arguments of all who were interested. They met at Berwick-upon-Tweed, and Burnel presided over them. King Edward having been obliged to return south to attend the funeral of his mother, left Burnel behind, to watch over the grand controversy. It was Robert Burnel who gave judgment in favour of Baliol.

Lord Chancellor Burnel never returned southward, as he died on October 25, 1292.

Summing up the character of this remarkable man, Lord Campbell says of him, "As a statesman and a legislator, he is worthy of the highest commendation. He ably seconded the ambitious project of reducing the whole of the British isles to subjection under the crown of England. With respect to Wales, he succeeded, and Scotland retained her independance only by the unrivalled gallantry of her poor and scattered population. His measures for the improvement of Ireland were frustrated by the incurable pride and prejudices of his countrymen. But England continued to enjoy the highest prosperity under the wise laws which he introduced."[2]

The inquisition taken after the decease of Robert Burnel shews that the deceased prelate had accumulated a vast possession in Shropshire; nor had the minutest gains of territory in this his native county been beneath his notice. His tenure of Acton Burnell, under Sir Peter Corbet was by service of half a knight's fee. Philip Burnel, the bishop's nephew, was his heir, who, a spendthrift, among other manors, gave that of Acton Burnell to

---

[1] *Parl. Hist.* 40. [2] *Lives of the Lord Chancellors*, vol. i. p. 172.

certain merchants of Lucca, in liquidation of his enormous debts.

ACTON BURNELL CHURCH.

This appears to have been originally a chapel subject to the mother church of Cound. In 1291, it was valued at only £2 per annum. The parish was assessed 24s. to the *ninth* in 1341, at which date, a great part of it lay uncultivated. In 1534-5, the rectory of Acton Burnell, in the deanery and archdeaconry of Salop, was valued at £7 per annum, less 10s. 1d. for procurations and synodals.

Early Incumbents. — Robert de Acton, clerk, 1227—1272; Thomas, parson of Acton Burnell, killed about 1287.

Hawksley. We learn from *Domesday* that when the survey was taken:—"Teodulf held of the earl, Avochelie. Elric held it, and was a free man. Here half a hide geldable. It was and is waste. Here a wood which will fatten 40 swine. This manor is at ferm for 6d. [per annum]."[1] Shrewsbury abbey very early acquired the small woodland estate alluded to. Under the monks, the Burnells held this manor, which in time became appurtenant to Acton Burnell.

Pulley, in Saxon times, belonged to Edith the Lady, Edward the Confessor's queen. In 1086, however, this was a divided manor; one part of it was held under the Norman Earl Roger by the same Teodulf, who held Hawksley; the other portion of it Ralph de Mortemer held immediately of the king. Concerning Teodulf's share, *Domesday* says:—"The same Teodulf holds Polelie. Eddid held it [in Saxon times]. Here iii virgates of land geldable. The land is enough for i ox-team. It [the ox-team] is here, together with i serf and ii boors. [The half-manor] was and is worth 6s. [annually]."[1]

With respect to Mortemer's share of Pulley, we learn from Domesday Book that, "The same Radulf holds Polelie. Eddid held it [in Saxon times]. Here i hide and one virgate, geldable.

---

[1] *Domesday*, fo. 259, a 2.

The land is for v ox-teams. Here are iii radmans, iiii villains, and v boors with vii ox-teams. In the time of King Edward, it was worth 30s. [per annum]. Afterwards and now it was and is worth 40s."[1] In close proximity to Mortemer's greater manor of Meole, in process of time the manorial distinction between the two became effaced. The Polelie of the above extract must, therefore, be sought for in the parish of Brace Meole.

Edgebold. "The same Radulf [de Mortemer] holds Edbaldinesham [of the king]. Eddid held it. Here i hide geldable. The land is [capable of employing] ii ox-teams. Here is one free man, who pays a ferm of 8s. [annually]. The wood here will fatten xx swine. In King Edward's time [the manor] was worth 40s. Afterwards it was waste."[1] Edgebold became annexed to Meole under similar circumstances to Mortimer's share of Pulley. Singularly enough, about 200 years after the Conqueror's survey had been taken, the lord of Edgebold was paying to Cantilupe, who then held the manor under Mortimer, exactly the same rent of 8s. which the *Domesday* tenant had paid.

Sheinton. We learn from King William's record, that:— "Radulf de Mortemer holds Scentune [of Earl Roger], and Helgod holds it of him. Azor, Ælgar, and Saulf held it [in Saxon times] for iii manors, and were free, with their lands. Here ii hides geldable. In demesne, there is i ox-team and a half; and ii serfs and one frenchman, with ix boors, have ii ox-teams; and there might be a third team here. Here is a mill of 10s. [annual value], and a wood that will fatten 100 swine. It was worth 17s.; now 20s. [*per annum*]." Supplementary, and apparently by way of correction to the above, in another part of *Domesday*, Sheinton is described as being held by Mortemer *in capite* of the king, thus:—"The same Radulf holds Scentune, and Helgot [holds it] of him. Azor, Elgar, and Saul held it for iii manors. Here ii hides geldable. There is a wood which will fatten 100 swine, and a mill of 10s. [annual value]. The whole is worth 20s"[2]

---

[1] *Domesday*, fo. 260, b 1.   [2] Ibidem, fos. 256, b 2 & 260, b 1.

Involved in that large section of Helgot's barony which passed to de Girros, this manor was held by a succession of knights who derived their name of de Sheinton from the place. The knight de Sheinton then held the manor of de Girros or his heirs; de Girros held it of the lords of Holgate; the lords of Holgate held it under Mortimer of Wigmore, who again held it of the Crown.

The Church.

The *Valor* of 1534-5 represents the rectory of Shaynton, in the deanery of Salop, and the diocese of Lichfield and Coventry, as worth £6 13s. 4d., less 3s. 4d. for procurations, and 11d. for synodals.

Early Incumbent.—Roger, parson of Sheynton, about 1272.

Preen. Besides Sheinton, Helgot held three other manors in Condover Hundred, Preen, Harley, and Belswardine. Concerning the first of these, *Domesday* says, that:—" The same Helgot holds Prene, and Richard holds it of him. Eduin held it [in Saxon times], and was a free man. Here iii hides geldable. The [arable] land is for iii ox-teams. In demesne is one ox-team and iiii serfs. Of this land, Godebold holds i hide, and there he has one ox-team, one serf, one villain, and one boor with i team. A wood here [will fatten] 100 swine. In time of King Edward, the manor was worth 20s. [annually]; now 10s. He [Helgot], found it waste."[1] The two hides which Richard held here came afterwards to be known as Great, or Church Preen, from the circumstance that Wenlock priory very early acquired them. Owing to the distance of this manor from Wenlock, the monks founded a cell here, in conjunction with which they built the church or chapel of Preen.

Godebold, *Domesday* tenant of the remaining hide of Preen, was a priest, and the land he once held now goes by the name of Holt Preen. Godebold's successors at Preen were the de Girros. The Templars acquired the principal tenant-interest here, which they held until the forfeiture of their order in 1308, when this with their other estates passed to the rival order of the Knight's Hospitallers.

Harley. *Domesday* says, that:—" The same Helgot holds

---

[1] *Domesday*, fo. 258. b 1.

Harlege. Edric, Ulmar, Elmund, and Edric held it [in Saxon times] for iiii manors, and were free men. Here iiii hides geldable. The land is [enough] for 4½ ox-teams. In demesne are 1½ teams; and iii serfs, one villain, and one boor. Here is a mill, and a wood capable of fattening 100 swine. In time of King Edward [the manor] was worth 21s. [annually]; now 40s. He [Helgot] found it waste."[1] The seigneury over Harley passed from Helgot's heirs, when the manor was annexed by King Henry I., to the honour of Montgomery. Early in the reign of Henry II., a family were seated here who, deriving a name from the place, afterwards became illustrious. The coronets of de Vere and Mortimer have been borne by the representatives of that house whose humble origin must be sought for in connection with this manor.

In the first half of the twelfth century two successive lords of Harley, Edward and Ernulf by name, were concerned in granting *easements* and pasture in Harley wood to the monks of Wenlock; one or other of these men was ancestor of the Harleys, and genealogists labour in vain to prove a higher antiquity for that noble house.

To Edward and Ernulf, succeeded Malcolm de Harley, who attested Bishop Novant's famous charter to Buildwas Abbey in 1192. After Malcolm, William became lord of Harley, to whom succeeded Richard de Harley, represented in 1240 as then holding a knight's fee in Harle, of the fief of Cantilupe, lord of Montgomery. This man became one of the coroners of Shropshire, in which office he died. To him succeeded Robert, his son and heir, and then Richard de Harley, who, marrying, first Burga de Wililey, and afterwards Margaret de Brompton, the vast estates these heiresses brought him conduced greatly to the importance of his family. Richard de Harley's public employments, towards the close of Edward the First's reign, were very numerous. In 1297, he was assessor and collector of taxes in Shropshire and Gloucestershire. In 1299, 1300, 1301, and 1306, he was a commissioner of array, a purveyor of provisions, or in other ways connected with the king's forces. He was a justice of *Oyer and Terminer* in 1300, in which year and also in 1305, 1306, and 1307, he sat in Parliament as a knight of the shire of Salop. He also held very numerous public offices in the time of Edward II.

---

[1] *Domesday*, fo. 258, b 1.

Harley Church.

This, originally a chapel, founded probably about the middle of the twelfth century, appears to have been subject to Cound. In 1291, the church of Harleye, in the archdeaconry and deanery of Salop, and diocese of Lichfield was worth £3 6s. 8d. *per ann.* In 1341, the parish was rated only 30s. to the *ninth*, because storms had destroyed the corn crops, a murrain had prevailed among the sheep, and the inhabitants were so poor as scarcely to be able to till the ground, etc. The *Valor* of 1534-5 represents the preferment of the rector of Harley as worth £6 *per ann.*, less 6s. 8d. for procurations, and 1s. 3d. for synodals.

Early Incumbent.—Richard de Kynsedcleye, 1301. Patron, Sir Richard de Harley.

Belswardine. "The same Helgot," continues *Domesday*, "holds Belleurdine. Edmund held it, and was a free man. Here half a hide geldable. The [arable] land is [sufficient] for ii oxteams. In demesne, is half a team, and [there is] one serf and ii boors with half a team. [Formerly] it was worth 10s. [per annum]; now [it is worth] 4s."[1] The seigneury over Belswardine continued for centuries with Helgot's successors, the lords of Castle Holgate.

Bayston is the subject of the following entry in Domesday Book, which, on account of the ambiguity attaching to its second sentence, is given to the reader in the original Latin:—"Isdem Willelmus tenet Begestan. Edric tenuit de Episcopo de Hereford, et non poterat ab eo divertere quia de victu suo erat et ei prestiterat tantum in vitâ suâ. Ibi est i hida geldabilis. Terra est iii carrucis. In dominio est una [carruca] et iiii servi et ii bordarii. Valebat x solidos. Modo xxv solidos."[2] The propriety of William Pantulf's tenure appears, then, to have been questioned by the *Domesday* commissioners upon the ground, that, as Edric Sylvaticus had formerly held the manor of the Bishop of Hereford, who, it seems, had derived from it certain produce in kind, the seigneury over Bayston could not be changed. The decision of

---

[1] *Domesday*, fo. 258, b 1. [2] Ibidem, fo. 257, a 2.

William's commissioners appears to have been acted upon; the church recovered its lost manor, and accordingly, the Feodary of 1284 represents Walter Sprenghose, lord of Bayston, as holding it of the Bishop of Hereford.

Norton.
"The same William," says *Domesday*, "holds Nortone [of the earl]. Uluric held it [in Saxon times], and was a free man. Here i hide geldable. The land is [sufficient] for ii ox-teams. Here iii villains with i boor have i team. In the time of King Edward it was worth 30s. [annually]; afterwards 9s. Now [it is worth] 25s."[1] William Pantulf's successors, the barons of Wem, long retained their seigneury over Norton, near Condover.

Wigwig.
"Turold," says *Domesday*, "holds Wigewic [of the earl]. Elmar held it, and was free. Here i hide geldable. There is land [enough] for ii ox-teams. Here it [one ox-team probably] is in demesne; and iiii serfs, ii villains, and i boor, with half a team. The wood will fatten 50 swine. In King Edward's time [the manor] was worth 15s. [*per annum*]; afterwards 3s. Now 10s."[2] Given by Turold's son Robert to Shrewsbury Abbey, Wigwig, before the reign of Richard I., had passed from the monks of Shrewsbury to the monks of Wenlock, who retained it until the time of Henry VIII.

Pitchford.
The bituminous well at Pitchford, still the subject of much curiosity, doubtless formerly attracted the notice of the Roman conquerors of Britain, for a branch of their great highway, Watling Street, passed very close to it. Hence the name Pitchford, which the Saxons, borrowing from the Latin *Pix*, termed Pic-ꝼonb, Picford.

This was another of Turold's manors, as we learn from *Domesday* that:—"The same Turold holds Piceforde [of the earl]. Edric, Leuric, and Uluric held it [in Saxon times] for iii manors, and were free. Here iii hides geldable. The [arable] land is [capable of employing] v ox-teams. In demesne are iii teams; and iii serfs,

---

[1] *Domesday*, fo. 257, a 2.   [2] Ibidem, fo. 258, a 1.

iii neat-herds, i villain, and iii boors, a smith, and one radman with ii teams. Here is a wood that will fatten 100 swine. In the time of King Edward, the manor was worth 8s. [annually]; afterwards 16s. Now 40s."[1] The Saxons alluded to above were dispossessed of their property, when Turold, having become mesne lord of Piceford, he enfeoffed as tenant here that Ralph who, styled de Pitchford, behaved so gallantly at the siege of Brug.[2] The descendants of this Ralph, retaining the name which their ancestor had derived from this place, continued to hold Pitchford under Turold's successors, the Chetwynds, until the year 1298, when Ralph de Pitchford sold the manor to Walter de Langton, Bishop of Lichfield and Coventry. The prelate transmitted it to his heir, Edmund Peverel, whose daughter Margaret, having married William de la Pole, he parted with the manor in 1358 to Sir Nicholas Burnel.

A gigantic lime tree grows at Pitchford, which, according to

LIME TREE, PITCHFORD.

tradition, has been known for centuries as *The Tree with a House in it*. The annexed wood-cut omits the house which, however, is

---

[1] *Domesday*, fo 258, a 1.   [2] See page 33.

still carefully maintained. A branch of the Pitchford lime, which fell in 1828, was ascertained to contain 149½ cubic feet of timber. Another, which fell in 1856 contained 93 cubic feet. Doubtless, this gnarled and twisted vegetation, had it a voice, could tell us something of Pitchford and its old lords.

The Church.

Pitchford church appears to have been founded by Ralph de Pitchford, during the reign of Henry I. or Stephen. Sundry bits of masonry in its walls tally with this supposition. In 1291, the church of Picheford, in the diocese of Lichfield and Coventry, and the deanery of Salop, was valued at £5 *per annum*. The parish of Pychford was taxed in 1341 only £2 to the *ninth*, because there were only 60 sheep in it, etc. In 1534-5, this rectory was worth £6 13s. 4d., less 6s. 8d. for procurations, and 1s. 4d. for synodals.

Early Incumbents.—Engelard de Pitchford, brother of Ralph de Pitchford I., lord of the manor.

In Pitchford church is a very fine monumental effigy which, full seven feet in length, is, together with the slab whereon it reposes, carved out of one solid trunk of dark oak. Armed *cap-a-pié*, the figure is habited in knightly costume of the latter end of the 13th century. An illustration of this interesting relic of a by-gone era is given; from whence it will be seen, that around the sides of the monument are various armorial bearings. Tradition says, that this figure represents *Sir Hugh de Pitchford*, yet heraldry points rather to Sir John de Pitchford, who died in 1285.

Lydley Heys.

"Auti," says *Domesday*, "holds of the earl, Litlega. He himself held it [in Saxon times], and was a free man. Here i hide geldable. There is land [enough] for ii ox-teams. Here [those teams] are, with ii radmans. A wood here will fatten 30 swine. Its old value was 10s.; now it is worth 8s. [*per annum*]."[1]

The Saxon Auti or Outi lost Lydley, when the manor appears to have been given by Henry I. to Herbert Fitz Helgot, whose son, Herbert de Castello, granted it to the Knights Templars. Lydley, thereupon, became head-quarters in Shropshire of the

---

[1] *Domesday*, 259, b 1.

MONUMENT IN PITCHFORD CHURCH.

monastic and military order of the Knights of the Temple of Solomon, and here they fixed their Preceptory. Upon the abolition of the order of Knights Templars, in the early part of the 14th century, Lydley, together with the other acquisitions of the brethren, passed to the Knights Hospitallers.

Lee Botwood.

A quarter of a mile west-north-west of Leebotwood church, is Castle Hill. The extreme length of this mound at the top is two hundred and sixty-five feet; its summit is about forty feet above the subinjacent plain. On the north side there is a considerable fall, but a very gradual one on the south. This eminence, partly natural, was originally either a barrow, a beacon, or, as its name implies, a defensive work.

At the period of the Conqueror's survey, Leebotwood also belonged to Auti the Saxon; for we read in *Domesday*, that:—" The same Auti holds Botewde. He himself held it [in Saxon times], and was free. Here is half a hide geldable. The land is for one ox-team. Here that team is with ii radmans. [The manor] was and is worth 5s. [annually]." [1]

The half hide in question was annexed to the palatine or royal manor of Condover, when, stript of every human being, Botewde gradually became a forest. In this condition, it reached King Henry the Second's hands, who bestowed it upon Haughmond Abbey, and the abbey retained the estate until the dissolution.

About the year 1170, a hermit, by name Bletherus, dwelt in the forest of Botwood, whose hermitage, transferred into an oratory or chapel by the Haughmond monks, was the origin of the present church of St. Mary's, Lee Botwood.

The ancient document [2] has it " *Legam in forestâ de Bottewde*," Lega, in the forest of Bottewde, in short, Lee in Botwood, or the modern Leebotwood.

Lee Botwood Chapel, being subject to Haughmond Abbey, is not mentioned in the *Taxation* of 1291. In 1341, however, the chapelry assessed to the *ninth* as a distinct parish, was rated at only £1 6s. 8d., because, under stress of poverty, many tenants had thrown up their holdings, etc.

---

[1] *Domesday*, fo. 259, b 1. [2] *Harleian* MS. 3868, fo. 11.

Frodesley. We read in Domesday Book, that :—" Siward holds Frodeslege of the earl. He himself held it [in Saxon times], and was free. Here i hide geldable. The land is [sufficient] for iiii ox-teams. Here iii villains and iii boors have i ox-team. Here is a wood which will fatten 100 swine, and there are iii hayes. [Formerly] it was worth 10s. [annually] ; now 8s."[1] Siward, the Anglo-Dane, then, was permitted by the Normans to retain his manor under the Earl of Shrewsbury. The cause for this apparent clemency on the part of the conquerors, can be traced to the circumstance that Siward le Gros, the party in question, was, as Ordericus tells us, a kinsman of Earl Roger, whose own great-grandmother was a Dane. Indeed, the Normans as a race, sprang from the sea-kings of the north, who, taking from Charles the Simple the northern province of France, at that time called Neustria, abandoned their heathen habits, and, settling down in the territory they had conquered, founded a mighty state, which was called Normandy, the land of the north-men.

Siward transmitted his interest in Frodesley to his son Aldred, after whom the succession cannot be traced. Eventually, this manor was annexed to the fief of Fitz Alan.

THE CHURCH.

Frodesley, included in the churches of Salop deanery and Lichfield diocese, in 1291 was valued at £2 *per annum*. In 1341, the parish was assessed 15s. to the *ninth*. King Henry the Eighth's *Valor* represents the preferment of the rector of Froddesley as worth £5, less 1s. for synodals, and 5s. for procurations.

Early Incumbent.—Hugh de Aldenham, 1306.

Overs. We learn that :—" In Ovre there is half a hide geldable. It is worth 3s. [per annum]. Seuuard held in time of King Edward." The statement implies, that this was a manor of Earl Roger's demesne. Such, however, was not the case, and, accordingly the *Domesday* commissioners corrected their former error by inserting in another part of the record the following entry :—" Seward holds Ovre of the earl. Himself held it [in Saxon times]. Here half a hide geldable. Here are ii villains with half an ox-team. It was and is worth 3s. [annually]."[2] The

---

[1] *Domesday*, fo. 259, b 1.   Ibidem, fos. 254, a 1, and 259, b 1.

place alluded to, which does not now exist either as a manor or township, is situated about a mile south-west of Ratlinghope, to which it belongs parochially.

Pulverbatch. The district in question being, in the summer season, literally "a bed of dust," accounts for the first portion of the name Pulverbatch; the Latin *Pulveris* and the old French *poldre* signifying dust. As for the terminative *batch*, it probably derives from the Mercio-Saxon word *bach*, signifying a *bottom* or *valley*.

Besides the interest which he had in Condover and Longnor, Roger Venator held two manors in the Hundred of Condover, under the Norman Earl of Shrewsbury. One of these is thus alluded to in *Domesday* :—"The same Roger holds Polrebec. Hunnic and Uluiet held it [in Saxon times] for iii manors. Here ii hides geldable. The land is [sufficient] for v ox-teams. In demesne are ii [teams], and iiii serfs and vii villains with iii teams. The wood here will fatten 100 swine. Here are ii radmans. In the time of King Edward, it was worth £6 ; now 30s. When he [Roger Venator] received it, it was worth 20s. [annually]."[1] The Conqueror's record shows how greatly diminished in value this manor had become since it had been torn from its Saxon owners.

Pulverbatch was once the head of Roger Venator's barony, and here he erected his castle. In 1135, Venator's representative also bore the name Roger ; and genealogists say that this baron was ancestor, through females, of several Shropshire families, the Constantines, of Eaton Constantine and Oldbury ; the Uptons, of Waters Upton ; the Stapletons, of Stapleton and Wistanstow, etc. Roger Venator's representative in the reign of Henry II. was Reginald de Pulverbatch, whose daughter and sole heir, Emma, carried the barony of Pulverbatch to her husband, Herbert de Castello. But Emma and her husband were dead without issue in 1193, when, as the Hereford Pipe Roll informs us, John de Kilpeck proferred £100 for the *Barony of Purbech*, and obtained it.

Of pure Norman descent, this John was great-grandson of that William Fitz Norman who figures in the Herefordshire *Domesday* as holding largely under the king. In the province of Arcenefelde he held the manor of Kilpec, hence his name. John's father was

---

[1] *Domesday*, fo. 259, a 2.

that Henry Fitz Hugh, the forester, who is represented in the Pipe Roll of 1189 as owing an arrear of thirteen hawks, which he ought to have furnished to the king from the Herefordshire forest of Trivel.[1]

He who now succeeded to the barony deceased in 1204, when Pulverbatch castle was entrusted to the keep of William de Cantilupe; the sheriff of Shropshire, being ordered to surrender it to him, with all its arms and chattels. Cantilupe, also, had the wardship of John de Kilpec's heir; whose marriage, however, the king reserved to himself.

Meanwhile, Juliana, widow of John de Kilpec, gave to the king 50 merks and a palfrey, that she might have her dower and be permitted to marry any one she chose, save to an enemy of the king, after giving the king due notice of her intention; but, in 1207, William Fitz Warin taking a fancy to the lady or else her estate, fined a *destrier* and a good palfrey, that he might have her to wife, when King John sent her a letter urging her, without excuse or delay, to accept Fitz Warin as her husband. She did so, for the king's acknowledgement of the receipt of the destrier is still in existence.

Upon obtaining his majority, Hugh de Kilpec II. succeeded to his hereditary office of custos of the royal forests of Herefordshire; and, in August, 1223, he had letters entitling him to collect the scutage of Montgomery from his tenants in the counties of Salop, Staffordshire, Herefordshire, Wilts, and Gloucestershire. Being about to accompany Henry III. into Brittany, Hugh obtained on April 20th, 1230, a patent of protection during his absence in foreign parts. At Michaelmas, 1235, and again at Easter, 1236, he paid for the honour of Pulverbatch two merks to the *aid* on marriage of the king's sister.

This baron left two daughters to share his inheritance; the eldest of whom, Isabella, became wife of William Waleraund; Johanna, the younger, married Philip Marmion; these doing homage to the king, obtained their respective shares of Kilpec's estates. Pulverbatch, with the advowson of Pulverbatch, now went to Philip and Johanna Marmion, upon whose decease the manor fell to their widowed daughter, Joan de Morteyn. She held the manor *in capite* as a knight's fee until her death in 1295, when Ralph le Botiler, her nephew, succeeded to Pulverbatch.

---

[1] *Rot. Pip.*, : Ric. I., p. 142.

In the *Nomina Villarum* of 1316, he figures as holding the manor, which continued with his descendants, in the male line, until the reign of Elizabeth.

There were undertenants here.

The Church.

Dedicated to St. Edith the Virgin in 1291, the church of Pulverbache, in the deanery of Pontesbury, was valued at £6 *per annum*. In 1341, the parish was taxed £4 to the *ninth*. In 1534-5, the preferment of the rector of Powdurbach was worth £10 0s. 8d., less 7s. 2d. *per annum* for synodals.

Early Incumbent.—Richard de Smethcote, rector, 1270.

Wrentnall is described in *Domesday* as follows:—" The same Roger [Venator] holds Werentenehale [of the earl]. Ernui and Chetel held it [in Saxon times] for ii manors. Here ii hides. The land is [capable of employing] v ox-teams. In demesne, are iii teams; and v serfs, iii villains and one radman with i team. Here a wood that will fatten 100 swine, and one haye. In King Edward's time [the manor] was worth 60s. [per annum]; now it is worth] 30s. When he [Roger Venator] received it, it was worth 5s.

" Of this land, the church of St. Chad lays claim to a hide and a half; and the county bears witness, that [the said hide and half] had been in the church before the time of King Edward, but [the county] is ignorant as to the mode in which [the said hide and half] left [the church]."[1] St. Chad's did not recover its lost manor; and eventually Wrentnall became annexed to Pulverbatch, of which, both parochially and manorially, it remains a member to this day.

Cressage derives its name from the Saxon Cpirtep-ác, literally Christ's Oak. About a quarter of a mile from the village of Cressage, on the road to Shrewsbury, is the shattered trunk of an old oak tree. Tradition has it, that under the once wide-spreading branches of this identical oak, Christian missionaries preached to our pagan Saxon forefathers the unsearchable riches of Christ.

---

[1] *Domesday*, fo. 259, a 2.

After Romish error had corrupted the purer faith of the early British church, the tree alluded to acquired the title of the Lady Oak, in honour of the Virgin Mary.

Domesday says, that:—"Rannulf Peurel holds Cristesache of Earl Roger. Edric held it, and was a free man. Here i hide and a half geldable. In demesne are iii ox-teams; and viii serfs, vii villains, xi boors, and iiii cottars,[1] have iiii teams; and still there might be ii more teams here. Here is a fishery of 8s. [annual value], and a wood capable of fattening 200 swine. In time of King Edward the manor was worth 110s. [annually]; now £10. When he [Rannulf] received it, it was worth £6."[2] The Norman scribe who penned the above appears to have been very particular in preserving the name Cristesache. The fishery spoken of here, doubtless, was a weir in the adjacent Severn; the wood, Cressage Park.

We have before alluded to the mystery respecting the Peverels.[3] A forfeited estate, Cressage reached the hands of Henry II., who annexed it to the barony of de Lacy, as a member of which the Lacys of Cressage long held the manor.

THE CHURCH.

Cressage church was for many centuries a chapel dependant on Cound.

Early Incumbent.—Robert, parson of Cristeshethe, 1232.

Cantlop. Normannus Venator held one manor in Condover Hundred, for we read in Domesday Book, that, "Normannus holds Cantelop of Earl Roger. Edric held it [in Saxon times], and was a free man. Here i hide geldable. There is land enough for iiii ox-teams. In demesne are ii teams; and vi serfs and iiii villains with one team. Here is a mill, of 10s. [annual value]. In time of King Edward, the manor was worth 20s.; afterwards £4 10s.; now 110s. [annually]."[4] As a general rule, Shropshire manors became much depreciated in value by the Conquest. The reader, however, will not fail to observe how remarkably the value of this manor had increased since it had come into Norman hands. Cantlop is now a township in Berrington parish.

---

[1] The *Cotarii* of Domesday were tenants of cottages, and appear to have been a degree above the *villains*.
[2] *Domesday*, fo. 256, b 2.
[3] See page 67.
[4] *Domesday*, fo. 259, a 1.

THE LADY OAK, CRESSAGE.

p. 230.

Langley. "Toret," says *Domesday*, "holds of the earl Languelege. Suain held it, and was free. Here half a hide geldable. The [arable] land is enough for i ox-team. Here that team is [together] with iiii serfs. [The manor] was and is worth 5s. [per annum.]"[1] Toret appears to have been one of the favoured few of Saxon origin suffered by the Conqueror to hold land, under any condition, in the country of their forefathers; and it was probably in lieu of compensation for his losses that the Saxon Suain's manor was wrenched from him and bestowed upon his more fortunate countryman. From some cause or other, however, Langley quickly reverted to the suzerain, when, being transformed into a tenure by serjeantry, either Henry I. or Henry II. bestowed it on one of the Burnels, upon condition, that, "every year the lord of Langley was to convey a goshawk from the gate of Shrewsbury castle to Stepney in Essex." It does not say who was to provide the bird, which was evidently to go to Stepney for the king's use whilst he sojourned at the royal palace of Havering.

Langley with Ruckley now form a township in the parish of Acton Burnell.

In 1341, the parish of Rokeley was taxed 16s to the *ninth*. The assessors did not rate it higher, owing to much of its land lying uncultivated.

Cothercote. This delightfully situated member of Church Pulverbatch is also mentioned in the Conqueror's record, for "Avenel," says *Domesday*, "holds of the Earl Cotardicote. Hunnic held it [in Saxon times]. Here half a hide. The land is [sufficient] for i ox-team. Here that team is, with ii serfs. [Formerly the manor] was waste. Now it is worth 3s. [annually]."[1]

Avenel's interest here lapsed to the crown when Henry I. annexed Cothercote to the Honour of Montgomery. In 1204, the lord of Montgomery granted this manor to Haughmond abbey; and the abbot retained it until the ruthless hand of Harry the Eighth spoiled him of his possession.

Smethcott. There is reason to suppose that at some time or other a sanguinary conflict took place in this neighbourhood:

[1] *Domesday*, fo. 259, b 1.

perhaps a battle between the Britons and the Roman invader. In the year 1838, as some labourers were engaged getting clay, a little below the north side of the churchyard they came upon a vast quantity of human bones, that had evidently been deposited here at a very early period. In a meadow not far from Smethcott church is a barrow.

We read in *Domesday* that, "Edmund holds of the earl Smerecote, and Eldred holds it of him. He [namely Edmund] himself held it [in Saxon times]. Here i hide geldable. The land is [enough] for iii ox-teams. Here ii radmans and i boor with i team. The wood will fatten 50 swine. The manor was and is worth 4s. [annually]."[1] Smerecote did not continue with the heirs of either Edmund the Saxon or his fellow countryman Eldred; for, probably forfeited, it is certain that Henry I. annexed the manor to the Honour of Montgomery. The lords of Montgomery then, enfeoffing a tenant here, for centuries exercised a seigneury over Smethcott.

Early in the 13th century, the monks of Haughmond abbey obtained a footing in Picklescott, which they continued to improve until the dissolution.

SMETHCOTT CHURCH.

A rude font within this church, and two circular-headed windows, indicate the Norman character of the building. Smethecot parish was taxed £1 13s. 4d. to the *ninth* in 1341. The reason of the assessment being thus low, was because many tenants had thrown up their lands on account of poverty, etc. In 1534-5, Smethcote rectory, in the deanery of Salop and diocese of Coventry and Lichfield, was worth £4 13s. 4d., less 3s. 4d. for procurations and 1s. for synodals.

Early Incumbent.—Sir Richard, rector of Smythecote, died in 1311.

Wilderley, now a township in the parish of Church Pulverbatch, is thus alluded to in *Domesday*:—"Hugh [Fitz-Turgis] holds Wildredelega of the earl. Chetel held it, and was free. Here ii hides geldable. The land is for iiii ox-teams. In demesne is one team, and iiii serfs and iii villains with one team. The

---

[1] *Domesday*, fo. 259, b 1.

wood here will fatten 100 swine. In time of King Edward the manor was worth 30s. Now 20s. When he [Hugh] received it, it was worth 10s." [1] This was another of those Shropshire manors which Henry I. annexed to the then newly-founded Honour of Montgomery, whose successive lords continued paramount at Wilderley.

Emstrey. Beautifully situated on the western bank of the Severn, this extensive manor, in Saxon times, belonged to the earls of Mercia. From Atcham, it stretched a distance of nearly three miles up to Shrewsbury Abbey Foregate, and, lying thus contiguous to his own foundation, the Norman earl gave this valuable estate to the monks of Shrewsbury. Accordingly, says *Domesday*, "The same church [of St. Peter] holds Eiminstre. Earl Eduin held it. Here ix hides geldable. In demesne are iv ox-teams, xxii villains, v boors, and one fronchman, with xii ox-teams between them all. Here xx serfs, and a wood that will fatten xl swine. In the city [of Shrewsbury] one masure of land of 2s. [annual value belonged to this manor]. In the time of King Edward, the manor was worth 100s. [per annum]; afterwards £4. Now [it is worth] £11." A supplementary entry adds that, "In this vill, Aluric held one hide, geldable, in King Edward's time, and he could go whither he would. This land was worth 5s. [per annum]. Now St. Peter holds it, and it is waste." [2] Shrewsbury abbey retained possession of this great manor until the Reformation.

Emstrey, with its members, Cronkill and Chilton, was in the Saxon parish of Ettingham, now Atcham.

Boreton also belonged to Shrewsbury abbey, for we read in *Domesday*, that, "the same church holds Burtune, and held it in the time of King Edward. Here i hide geldable. In demesne is one ox-team, and vi boors with i team, and [also] ii neat-herds here. [Formerly] it was worth 5s. [annually]. Now 8s." [2] To read his charter,[3] one would suppose that Roger de Montgomery

---

[1] *Domesday*, fo. 258, b 2.   [2] Ibidem, fo. 252, b 1.
[3] *Monasticon*, vol. iii., p. 519, No. 3.

had been the original donor of Bourton to the monks. *Domesday*, however, clearly shows that it had belonged to the Saxon church of St. Peter before the Conquest, after which the Norman earl merely restored it. The abbot of Shrewsbury continued lord of Boreton until the reign of Henry VIII.

Hughley. Under the heading, "*Quod tenet Æcclesia Sanctæ Milburgæ*," *Domesday* treats of the possessions of Wenlock priory. At the bottom of the section is the following notice of a manor, which although unnamed, is placed in Condover Hundred:—
"Sancta Witburga [Milburga it should be] holds half a hide, geldable, and the son of Aluric [holds it] of *him* [her]. Here is one villain with i ox-team, and there might be another [team] here. It is worth 3s. [annually]." [1]

The above must allude to Hughley, which is known to have belonged, from a very early period, to Wenlock Priory. From the 12th to the 16th century, Hughley was held under the prior by feoffees, who derived a surname from this place, which, subsequently to *Domesday*, was invariably written *Lega* or *Lee*. Its tenants, we say, took their surname of Lee from this place. On the contrary, the place, curiously enough, acquiring the Christian name of one of its early lords, Hugh, in process of time became known by its present name: Hughley.

The Church.

Hughley chapel, founded before 1176, was an affiliation of the church of Wenlock, until the lords of the manor obtained the advowson from the priory. In 1291, the church of Huley, in the deanery of Wenlock, and diocese of Hereford, was of less than £4 annual value. In 1341, Hughley does not appear to have been considered a distinct parish, for it was not assessed to the *ninth*. In 1534-5, the rector of Hughlye's preferment was worth £4 13s. 8d., less an ancient pension of 2s. to the prior of Wenlock, and 6d. for synodals.

Early Incumbent.—Osbern, the chaplain, mentioned about 1170.

Betton, now divided into Abbot's Betton and Betton Strange, belonged to the Bishop of Chester, for *Domesday* affirms, that:—

---

[1] *Domesday*, fo. 252, b 2.

"The same Bishop holds Betune, and held it in King Edward's time. Here ii hides geldable. In demesne, there is one ox-team and a half, and iiii villains with ii ox-teams and a half. Here iii serfs. [In Saxon times] the manor was worth 15s. [annually]; now [it is worth] 16s."[1] The monks of Shrewsbury very early acquired also this manor; and, from the circumstance, that Earl Roger mentions in his foundation charter, that he had had the counsel of Robert de Limesey, Bishop of Chester, when, appointing the first abbot of Shrewsbury, it is conjectured, that the manor in question was this prelate's contribution to Shrewsbury Abbey. Be this as it may, the abbots continued lords over Betton for some four hundred and fifty years, even until the dissolution.

Buildwas. The following entry occurs in Domesday Book:—
"TERRA EPISOPI DE CESTRE. *Isdem Episcopus tenet Beldewes, et tenuit tempore Regis Edwardi. Ibi i hida geldabilis. In dominio sunt ii carucæ, et iii villani cum præposito habent iii carucas. Ibi v servi, molinum, et Sylva cc porcis. T. R. E. valebat xlv solidos, post xl solidos: modo xlv solidos.*"[2]

We glean from the above, that the Bishop of Chester held Beldewes in Saxon times, and also when the survey was taken; that the manor consisted of one hide geldable, two carucates of which were held in demesne, whilst other three were cultivated by iii villains and v serfs, over whom was placed a resident provost or bailiff. It appears that the manor contained a mill, and some woodland; and finally, that its value at the period of the survey, was exactly what it had been in the time of King Edward.

Buildwas Abbey.

Buildwas Abbey, the extensive and interesting ruins of which adorn the lovely scenery amid which they lie—ruins " sacred to departed genius and taste; sacred to the ever-living beauty of grandeur and repose;" Buildwas Abbey is said to have been founded in 1135 by Roger de Clinton, Bishop of Chester. The usurper's charter[3] confirmed Bishop Roger's grant, and allowed to the monks many privileges, which were afterwards respected by his lawful succes-

---

[1] *Domesday*, fo. 252, a 2. [2] *Domesday*, fo. 252, a 2.
[3] *New Monasticon*, vol. v. p. 356.

sors on the throne. Far from grim war's bloody confusion, then, or the turmoil of cities, in this secluded spot, the Cistercian brethren reared a sacred fabric, and spent their days in prayer. Meanwhile, their founder, escaping from the internecine war that deluged England with blood, joined the crusade of 1147, and died at Antioch in the following year.

Originally, Buildwas was an affiliation of the Norman house of Savigni, which, in turn, acknowledged the rule of the Cistercian Abbot of Citeaux. After the king and bishop, Philip de Belmeis was the next benefactor to this abbey; he granted Ruckley to "Saint Mary and Saint Chad," of Buildwas. William Fitz Alan I. was another very early benefactor to Buildwas, for he gave Little Buildwas to the monks: and thus the territorial acquisitions of the abbey gradually extended.

Very early in the reign of Henry II. the abbot of Savigni committed to the abbot of Buildwas the *cure* and *disposition*, as it was expressed, of the Savigniac houses of St. Mary's, Dublin, and the Flintshire house of Basingwerk, which accordingly became subject to the abbot of Buildwas.

We learn from the Staffordshire Pipe Roll, that, in 1157, the monks of Buildwas were excused their quota of the Danegeld, and of the *Donum* then assessed on that county. In the following year, they were again excused their quota of the *donum* then collected in Staffordshire and Shropshire; and, in 1162, 2s. of the Danegeld of Staffordshire.

Among various royal charters of privileges to this abbey, that of Edward I. deserves notice. It allowed to St. Mary's of Buildwas all lands and tenements already granted thereto, that the monks should hold not only these but all lands which they might hereafter acquire, quit of geld, Danegeld, scutage, fines for murder and larceny; also, of hidage, suits to shire or hundred, military services, sheriffs and all other aids; also that this church was to be "free of any amercement set upon the county or hundred, of toll, of passage and of pontage belonging to the king, of all work at castles, bridges, vivaries, walls, or parks, of fencings, of pleas, plaints, and all other customs; of all secular service, exaction, and servile work."[1] This charter is dated September 14, 1290.

According to the Taxation of 1291, the income which Buildwas Abbey derived from its various lands and rents, that is its *tempo-*

---

[1] *Placita de quo Waranto*, p. 145.

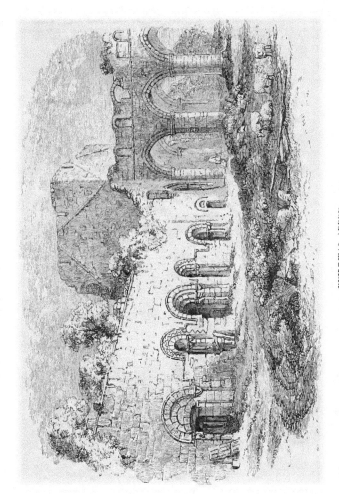

BUILDWAS ABBEY.

SEDILIA, BUILDWAS.

ralities, excluding churches, tithes, etc., amounted to £113 19s. 5d. *per annum*, of which sum the Abbey Grange yielded £4 10s. on six carucates of land, and £10 10s. on live stock. In 1535, the abbot of Buildwas declared the total temporalities and spiritualities of his house to be £129 6s. 10d., but the minister's accounts of the following year make it £30 more.

In 1538, Edward Grey, Lord Powis, obtained from Henry VIII. the site of Buildwas Abbey and all its possessions in Shropshire, Staffordshire, and Derbyshire.

Ingenulf was the name of the first abbot of Buildwas.

THE LONG FOREST involved within its regard nearly the whole of the *Domesday* Hundred of Condover, besides a number of manors belonging to other Hundreds. Embracing a vast district bounded on the south-east by the mountainous range known as Wenlock Edge, which extends fifteen miles in a direct line north-east; the Long Forest anciently included all the country between Wenlock Edge and the Long Mynd and Lyth Hills. The extensive tract alluded to contains much broken and sterile mountain land, unfitted for the purposes of agriculture. Hence the protracted existence of the Long Forest, which was very slowly disforested. In the Anglo-Norman period, the jurisdiction of the Long Forest was strictly maintained; and the Forest Roll of 1180, proves that, excepting in the case of a few favoured *vills*, no concessions in the way of *assart* or *imbladement* had been allowed to the inhabitants of the district; on the contrary, various amercements were inflicted for *waste*. In 1209, however, the *regard* of the Long Forest shows that indulgencies had been extended to the lords, or inhabitants, of a far greater number of *vills* within its jurisdiction, these having been suffered to increase the area of their cultivation, or permitted to compound for having so done. From the survey of Shropshire forests in 1235, we learn what were the woods or boscs subject to the jurisdiction of the Long Forest; these were the fragments, if it may be so expressed, of the once great primeval forest. Lythwood, Bushmoor, and Haycrust were the only three *hayes*, or royal preserves, kept intact within the Long Forest. In 1250, the jurisdiction of the Long Forest was further relaxed, a sign of advancing civilization; and this forest continued to be gradually encroached upon, until it was finally broken up in the reign of Edward I.

Domesday Hundred of Patinton.

Modern Name.	Domesday Name.	Saxon Owner or Owners, T. R. E.	Domesday Tenant in capite.	Domesday Mesne, or next Tenant.	Domesday Sub-Tenant.	Modern Hundred, or Franchise.
Much Wenlock	Wenloch	Ecclesia Sanctæ Milburgæ	Rogerius Comes	Ecclesia Sanctæ Milburgæ		Wenlock.
Ticklerton with Eaton-under-Heywood	Tichelevorde	Ecclesia Sanctæ Milburgæ	.... Idem	Ecclesia Sanctæ Milburgæ		..Ibidem.
Madeley	Madelie	Ecclesia Sanctæ Milburgæ	.... Idem	Ecclesia Sanctæ Milburgæ		..Ibidem.
Little Wenlock	Wenloch	Ecclesia Sanctæ Milburgæ	.... Idem	Ecclesia Sanctæ Milburgæ		..Ibidem.
Shipton	Scipetune	Ecclesia Sanctæ Milburgæ	.... Idem	Ecclesia Sanctæ Milburgæ		..Ibidem.
? ?	Petelie	Ecclesia Sanctæ Milburgæ	.... Idem	Ecclesia Sanctæ Milburgæ		? ?
Burton	Burtune	Ecclesia Sanctæ Milburgæ et Alnric	.... Idem	Ecclesia Sanctæ Milburgæ	Edric	Wenlock.
Stoke St. Milburg	Godestoch	Ecclesia Sanctæ Milburgæ	.... Idem	Capellani Comitis		..Ibidem.
Acton Round	Achetune	Uluiet	.... Idem	Rainaldus Vicecomes		Stottesden.
Abdon	Abetune	Uluuinus	.... Idem	Rainaldus Vicecomes	Azo	Munslow.
Tugford	Dodefort	Eluuinus	.... Idem	Ecclesia Sancti Petri Rainaldus Vicecomes	Raynerus	..Ibidem.
Stanway	Stanweie	Aluric	.... Idem	Rainaldus Vicecomes	Odo	..Ibidem.
Gretton	Grotintune	Airic Otro	.... Idem	Rainaldus Vicecomes Robertus	Odo	..Ibidem.
Easthope	Stope	Ernu Uluric	.... Idem	Rainaldus Vicecomes	Fulcher	..Ibidem.
Lutwyche	Loteis	Goduinus Semer	.... Idem	Rainaldus Vicecomes	Ricardus	..Ibidem.
Brockton	Broctune	Eliard Ednin	.... Idem	Rainaldus Vicecomes	Ricardus	..Ibidem.
Castle Holgate	Stantune	Genust, Æluuard Dunning, Elveva	.... Idem	Helgotus		..Ibidem.
Clee St. Margaret	Cleie	Aluric	.... Idem	Helgotus		..Ibidem.
Millichope	Melicope	Gamel	.... Idem	Helgotus		Wenlock and Munslow.
Oxenbold	Oxibola	Edric Sluuard	.... Idem	Helgotus		Wenlock.
Long Stanton	Stantune	Eluuinus	.... Idem	Rogerius de Laci	Herbertus	Munslow.
Patton	Patintune	Aluuinus	.... Idem	Rogerius de Laci	Herbertus	..Ibidem.
Rushbury	Riseberie	Æluuinus	.... Idem	Rogerius de Laci	Odo	..Ibidem.
? ?	Buchehale	Elmer	.... Idem	Willelmus (Pantulf)		? ?
Ruthall	Rohalle	Oschil	.... Idem	Gerardus	Gerelmus	Munslow.
Beckbury	Becheberie	Azor	.... Idem	Rogerius Venator		Brimstree.

Manor probably in Patinton, but whose Hundred is not stated in Domesday.

Ditton Priors	Dodintone	Eduinus Comes	Rogerius Comes			Wenlock.

PASSING now to the *Domesday* Hundred of Patinton, concerning which the subjoined is a tabular representation, we should premise, that it was swept away in the time of Henry I. when its manors were annexed to the then newly-created Hundreds of Munslow, Stottesden, and Brimstree. Afterwards, when Richard I. created the present *franchise* of Wenlock, a number of these manors were re-transferred to it; and, as a glance at the Table will show, in Wenlock Liberty they still remain.

Much Wenlock. Under a section, the heading of which is "QUOD TENET ECCLESIA SANCTÆ MILBURGÆ," *Domesday* treats of the possessions of the church of St. Milburg, thus:—"Earl Roger hath made the church of St. Milburg an abbey. The said church holdeth Wenloch, and held it in time of King Edward, Here are xx hides. Of these, iiii hides were free from geld [Danegeld] in time of King Chnut [Canute], and the rest were geldable. In demesne are nine and a half ox-teams; and ix villains, iii radmans, and xlvi boors have between them all xvii ox-teams; and other xvii [teams] might be here. Here are xv serfs and ii mills, providing for the monks. Here i fishery. The wood will fatten 300 swine; therein are ii hayes. In time of King Edward [the manor] was worth £15 [per annum]; now £12."[1] In speaking of this vast manor, a difficulty is experienced in determining what were its *Domesday* constituents. At no time, however, after the period of King William's survey, is it alluded to in its original entireness.

Wenlock Priory.

Wenlock priory, the oldest and wealthiest of the religious houses of Shropshire, according to Capgrave, was founded by St. Milburg. Milburg was daughter of Merewald, the Christian founder of Leominster priory, and granddaughter of Penda, the pagan King of the Mercians. It is added, that St. Milburg herself presided over Llan Meilien, which was an older name for this nunnery, and that dying, she was buried here. But the heathen Danes, in their unrelenting hostility to the faith, left nought of St. Milburg's church but a charred and blackened ruin, and in this melancholy condition it remained, until a hundred and fifty years afterwards Leofric, the Mercian earl, attracted to the spot by the veneration still clinging to the memory of St. Milburg, refounded Wenlock. The establishment which this munificent Saxon specially endowed here, partook of the usual character attached to the religious houses of the Saxons, and combined a college for secular clergy, with more or less of the monastic element. As appears from the *Domesday* notice of its lands, four hides of these, owing to an immunity granted to the church of St. Milburg by the Anglo-Danish King Knut, were not assessable to the Danegeld, for Knut the Great, although the son of an

---

[1] *Domesday*, fo. 252, b 1.

apostate to Christianity, displayed great zeal for the church. As we gather also from *Domesday*, the possessions of St. Milburg, in the time of Edward the Confessor, comprehended 74 hides and a quarter, equivalent to nearly 18,000 acres of that time.[1]

Upon the forfeiture of Earls Morcar and Edwin, the grandsons of its great restorer, this magnificent Saxon foundation came, almost entirely deserted, into the hands of Roger de Montgomery, when the Norman earl, again restoring it, completely remodelled the church of St. Milburg at Wenlock. "Earl Roger," says *Domesday*, "hath made the church of St. Milburg an abbey"; that is, he converted, according to Norman custom, the old Saxon college into a strictly monastic institution. This he did about the year 1080. Wenlock, therefore, was an older house than Shrewsbury, which was not founded until three years afterwards. Thus restored, the territories of St Milburg, at the period of the general survey, were nearly identical with those of Wenlock monastery in the time of Edward the Confessor; but its value was far otherwise; for whereas, formerly there was arable land sufficient for the employment of $141\frac{1}{2}$ teams of oxen, now, under the Norman, but $80\frac{1}{2}$ teams were employed; a difference, doubtless, attributable to the disturbances of the period.

Wenlock monastery was subject to the priory of La Charité in France, to which it paid an annual rent of 100s.—the priory of La Charité itself being one of the earliest affiliations of the great Benedictine abbey of Clugny, in Burgundy.

The 26th of May, 1101 was a day to be had in reverence by the shorn fraternity of Wenlock, for on it St. Milburg's remains, which had been discovered by the ingenious monks, were translated, or removed to their final resting-place, in front of the high altar of the new church. Miraculous were the cures reported; great the enthusiasm of the multitude. Wenlock had at length acquired the bones of its sainted Saxon foundress, a discovery fraught with pecuniary advantages to the foundation; accordingly, in gratitude, the brethren made their rents payable upon that day, and from thence dated their documents.

In Henry I.'s time a question arose, which led the priory to assert that St. Milburg's wide-spreading lands constituted but one parish: that is, were parochially subject to none but the mother church of Wenlock. This spiritual claim, so illustrative of the

---

[1] Our modern statute acre is much smaller than the acre of that period.

WENLOCK PRIORY. THE CHAPTER-HOUSE.
(AS IT STOOD A.D. 1793).

growing influence of Wenlock priory was keenly contested, until, at length, two great synods having deliberated on the question, the claim of the priory was established by Bishop Richard de Belmeis, Viceroy of Shropshire.

When the Shropshire Walter Fitz-Alan, steward of Scotland, conceived the idea, in 1163, of founding a Clugniac priory at Paisley, he bethought him of Wenlock Priory; so, coming to an agreement on the subject with its Prior, thirteen monks from Wenlock accompanied their chief across the border, and colonized the house at Paisley, which, for fifty years afterwards, continued an affiliation of the great Shropshire monastery. Dudley priory was another affiliation of Wenlock, whose prior could place any of his own monks at Dudley, and appoint its prior. The ancient renown of the great Shropshire house also was attested by the circumstance of its possessing a colony in the distant Isle of Wight, the Clugniac priory of St. Helen's.

Isabel de Say, baroness of Clun, largely augmented the patronage of Wenlock by granting to it the church of St. George at Clun with its seven subject chapels. But it was during the reign of Richard I. that the monks of Wenlock obtained the great aggrandizement to their house comprehended in that monarch's charter, creative of a new franchise in Shropshire, of which the seigneury was conferred upon the prior of Wenlock. The new liberty, composed of manors taken from the old Hundreds of Munslow, Condover, and Brimstree, was almost identical with the modern franchise of Wenlock. It is not known what induced the lion-hearted to grant to St. Milburg's freedom from "sac, soc, toll, team, and infangethef," with other franchises belonging to the crown, and a total exemption from all obligation to do *suit* at other Hundred Courts, or even at the greater court of the county; it is not known, we say, what was the Anglo-Norman king's motive for conferring on the new franchise such extensive privileges. Richard's charters relating to the subject are dated Roche Andeley, in Normandy, from the keep of Chateau-Galliard, that renowned fortress, then just erected, concerning which, when he had completed the whole system of its enormous works and defences, the delighted Richard with pride exclaimed, "Is she not fair, my daughter of a year?"[1] It is not improbable, therefore, that Richard granted these privileges in return for some large subsidy

---

[1] BROMPTON, *Hist. Angl. Scriptores Antiqui*, col. 1276.

the prior had granted to the warlike monarch, in furtherance of his engineering chef-d'œuvre on the banks of the Seine.

On the 29th of August, 1226, Henry III. halted at Wenlock, on his way from Shrewsbury to Brug. That king stayed at this priory several times afterwards: on one occasion, namely June 7, 1233, receiving in his *wardrobe* at Wenlock a sum of £106, being an instalment of the tax of the *fortieth* assessed in the previous year on Staffordshire, from which tax, however, the lands of the prior of Wenlock were exempt.

Yet heavy was the hand of Geoffrey de Langley, the justiciar, upon Imbert, the able prior of Wenlock, for, in his Iter of 1250, he mulcted Wenlock in extraordinary penalties. The prior, it would seem, had been assarting forest lands in all directions, without licence, for which the severe justiciar not only fined him in the large sum of £126 13s. 4d., but subjected him to future rent-charges.

In 1252, the good prior of Wenlock owed £6 for two purchases he had made of the king's wines. The liberty of Wenlock was the subject of a separate return in 1255, when its constituent manors, stated to be held under the prior, were said to owe suit to his court only.[1]

One of the commission appointed to treat with Llewellyn, Imbert, prior of Wenlock, was a party to the formal pacification agreed on between the Welsh prince and the English king, at Montgomery, on Sunday, August 22nd, 1260; but, shortly afterwards dying, the royal escheator, contrary to precedent, seized into the king's hand the estates of the priory. So extortionate was the rigour with which this functionary executed his office, that the granges, vivaries, woods, and parks of the priory were damaged to the extent of upwards of 10 merks; 20 merks also were wrenched from St. Milburg's tenants, and at length the sub-prior and convent were forced to hand over to the escheator 100 merks before they could participate in any of its profits during the vacancy. But this did not last long, for, on April 8, 1261, King Henry III. enjoined his escheator, Geoffrey de Northampton, custos of the priory, to give seizin thereof to Aymo de Montibus, formerly prior of Bermondsey, whom the king had admitted prior of Wenlock, on presentation of the prior of La Charité, when Wenlock recovered from the oppressions it had been subjected to by the king's justiciar

---

[1] *Rot. Hundred,* ii. pp. 84—86.

and escheator. Upon the death of prior Aymo, in 1272, Wenlock was again seized by the crown; yet not in the former harsh manner, a fine of 100 merks procuring for the convent custody of its house and lands during the vacancy, a vacancy filled up in the following year.

As we learn from the inquest of 1274, Wenlock priory had *gallows, and assize of bread and beer* within its liberty; and when, in 1283, a writ of King Edward I. exempted Cistercian houses from the tax of the *thirtieth* then collecting, Wenlock Priory was one of the very few Houses not of that order which had a similar reprieve.

In short, contributing very rarely to the King of England's exchequer, and but moderately assessed in respect to its subjection to the foreign house of La Charité, Wenlock long continued to flourish; its possessions gradually increased, and the prudence and sobriety of its Clugniac inmates steadily told upon their finances. Indeed, we may infer, from the extraordinary charter of privileges held by this priory, that every acre that belonged to it became doubly valuable, the tenants who held of this House being all privileged men.

According to Pope Nicholas' Taxation, the temporalities of Wenlock, in 1291, realised an income of over £144 per annum, of which £19 9s. 4d. arose from profits on farming stock. Its advowsons were worth £130 per annum, and it also had an income of £6 or £7 arising from various church pensions and portions.

When in 1333, the prior of Wenlock contributed 10 merks to the aid on marriage of the sister of King Edward III., only nine English monasteries contributed a greater amount. In less than four years afterwards, however, the English monarch, anticipating war with France, forbade Wenlock and other alien priories to transmit any revenue to the foreign houses of which they were affiliations; and when the war broke out Edward seized upon Wenlock, and appropriated to his own requirements the 100s. annually paid by the priory in Shropshire to the House of La Charité in France.

Wenlock was one of the twenty-one English priories threatened in 1343 with utter confiscation, if, upon any pretext, they sent money to a foreign superior."[1]

In consideration of 600 merks, which this convent paid to

---

[1] Claus. 17 Ed. III. p. 2 m. 19 dorso.

Richard II. in 1395, that king enfranchised Wenlock from the priory of La Charité, or the abbey of Clugny, upon which it used immediately and mediately to depend. Times had become altered: the English kings no longer had foreign interests to care for. Yet nearly a century elapsed ere this separation was recognized either by the parent monastery or the pope.

In 1534-5 the temporalities of Wenlock, valued at £333 16s. 10¾, and the spiritualities at £100 4s. 4d., gave a total of £434 1s. 2¾. Upon January 26, 1540, this religious house surrendered to Henry VIII., when the prior and convent were pensioned off upon £100 a year, divided between them. Of this sum the prior received £30, the sub-prior and eleven monks sharing the remainder.

Among *Early Priors of Wenlock*, Peter occurs first in 1120: to whom succeeded Rainald, prior of Wenlock, 1138—1150. Attending the council at Rheims, in 1148, in company with his friend, Robert de Bethun, bishop of Hereford, he waited on that prelate when he died there. To Rainald, accordingly, William of Wycumbe appropriately addressed his life of the bishop.[1] Humbald, 1155—1170: it was he who colonized the Scottish monastery of Paisley. To him succeeded Peter de Leia, who, in 1176, was promoted to the see of St. David's.

THE BOROUGH OF MUCH WENLOCK.—"The corporate towns of the 13th century," says Eyton, "were of three principal classes, viz., those which were held by royal charter, those which had arisen under sufferance of some feudal chief, and those which were of the patronage of the Church, that is, incorporated by the lords of a spiritual fief. Shropshire affords instances of each class. Shrewsbury and Bridgnorth were of the first; Oswestry and Ludlow of the second; Wenlock and the Abbey Foregate of Shrewsbury belonged to the third."

Where now stands the corporate, market, and parliamentary town of Much Wenlock, in the time of the Conqueror existed a purely agricultural district. The town, however, gradually sprang up, under the auspices of the priory, when, at length, owing to successive concessions of the priory, its burgesses acquired a corporate government. The first mention of a provost of Wenlock is in the year 1267, about which period it is probable, that the borough of Wenlock began to be governed by a corporate body.

---

[1] *Anglia Sacra*, vol. ii. pp. 296—318.

WENLOCK PRIORY, SOUTH SIDE OF CHAPTER-HOUSE.

WENLOCK PRIORY AND PARISH CHURCH.

p. 244.

CHURCH AND PARISH OF THE HOLY TRINITY AT WENLOCK.

The old Saxon parish of St. Milburg, of vast extent, involved, yet was immeasurably greater than, the Norman parish of the Holy Trinity that succeeded it. Again, the ancient parish of the Holy Trinity comprehended not only the modern parish of Much Wenlock, but eleven other places, in all of which there are now separate churches or chapels. Burton is the only one of these places within the modern parish of Much Wenlock.

The church of the Holy Trinity, Wenlock parish church, was founded shortly after *Domesday*. It was originally a rectory in the gift of the prior and convent, when William de Vere, Bishop of Hereford, in 1186-1199, granting it to the priory, the church of the Holy Trinity became a vicarage.

Pope Nicholas' Taxation values the church of Wenlock at £34 13s. 4d. *per annum*. It is not clear what was the precise extent of that parish of Wenlock assessed to the *ninth*. Yet, whatever its extent, it was assessed only £16, because, owing to tempests, the corn-lands had been unfruitful, there had been a murrain among the sheep, etc.

The *Valor* of 1534-5 gives a total of £35 4s. as the prior's rectorial income from the parish of the Holy Trinity. The vicarial income of Wenlock was £13 3s. 4d., of which 13s. 8d. went for procurations and synodals.

Early Incumbent.—Hervey occurs as vicar of Wenlock before 1238.

BRADLEY, formerly West Bradley near Burton, BENTHALL, BARROW, THE MARSH MANOR one of the prior's principal Granges, with ATTERLEY and WENLOCK WALTON, BRADLEY near Broseley formerly Bradley Grange, with its adjuncts Wyke, Farley, Posenthal, Calloughton, and the vill of Prestenden which cannot now be identified, were all included in the 20 hides alluded to in *Domesday* as attached to the church of St. Milburg. Held under the prior by tenants of various rank and importance, these constituted so many distinct estates, members of the vast fief of the church of Wenlock.

Contiguous to Wenlock, in former times, existed the *forest of Shirlot*. Compared with that of Morf, Shirlot Haye exercised not nearly so wide a regard or jurisdiction, yet this pervaded a district the length of which has been estimated at twelve miles, and its breadth at five. It is difficult to define the boundaries of

Shirlot forest and its adjuncts, which lay generally to the westward of the Severn. Suffice it to observe, that, the district in question was in close proximity to Morville and Chetton, manors where Saxon kings and Mercian earls once dispensed a rude, yet unbounded, hospitality: it was characteristic of the Norman earls who succeeded to their vacant seats, to reserve to themselves the right of hunting and fishing; finally, as after the forfeiture of de Belèsme, the Anglo-Norman kings themselves visited their own castle of Brug, and frequented, as guests, Wenlock priory; it evidently was the interest of each of these parties to maintain Shirlot forest intact. Quite a number of "vills and boscs pertaining to the Haye of Schirlet" were disforested in the time of King Edward I., whose policy in respect to royal forests, by the way, was much more liberal than that of his Anglo-Norman predecessors.

Tickleyton, in former days, belonged to Wenlock priory. *Domesday* says:—"The same church holds Tichelevorde, and held it in time of King Edward. Here vii hides geldable, and iii other hides quit of geld. In demesne is one ox-team, and vi villains, vi boors, and i radman, with v teams; and there might be vi more teams [employed] here. Here iii serfs, and a wood for lx swine. In time of King Edward, the manor was worth 100s. [annually]; now [it is worth] 50s."[1] The place alluded to, doubtless, derived its name from Tichel, some former Saxon proprietor. It was Tichel's *worthing*, or village, from whence the transition to the more modern termination of *ton* or town is natural.

Eaton-under-Heywood, originally merely one of its members, very early became the caput or centre of this manor, which was held chiefly in *demesne* by Wenlock priory. Hence, in 1255, the jurors of Wenlock liberty returned "Eton, with its appurtenances, as the manor of the lord prior." And a very pretty picking did the lord prior of Wenlock get out of Eaton and its appurtenances. These were Herton (now Harton), Tycleworthin, Longefewd, (Longville), Lussekote (Lushcote), Wolverton, and Hatton; the rents and ferms of the prior's manor of Eton being valued in 1541-2 at £30. 9s. 4d.; perquisites of court £1 3s. 6d. more; to say nothing of that large additional income which the prior received in the shape of eggs,

---

[1] *Domesday*, fo. 252, b 1.

poultry, fish, venison, for the kitchen of the priory, and labour-dues, concerning the latter of which we have a sample, under date 1237, when "Imbert, prior of Wenlock, demanded that Robert de Hatton should provide ten men for one day in autumn, to carry the prior's hay at the said men's own cost."

Church of Eaton-under-Heywood.

Eaton church, contemporaneously with Wenlock church, was granted as an appropriation to Wenlock priory by William de Vere, Bishop of Hereford; his reason for so doing being the excessive hospitality which he knew to be exercised by the monks. About 1225, however, the prior's right to Eaton was disputed, when Bishop Foliot, for reasons best known to himself, specially devoted Eaton church to the better provision of the monk's kitchen, saving the due maintenance of a vicar there. In 1290, Bishop Swinfield visited Etone, when the prior of Wenlock found forage for 36 horses of the prelate's train.

Pope Nicholas' Taxation valued the church of Etone at £10, and its vicarage at £4 6s. 8d. The parish of Eton Priors was assessed £6 8d. 4d. to the *ninth* in 1341. The *Valor* of 1534-5 returning the rectorial corn-tithes of Eton as among the *spiritualities* of Wenlock priory, gives them as worth £8 15s. 4d. *per annum*: the vicarage £5, upon which 7s. 8d. was charged for procurations and synodals.

Early Incumbent.—Sir Osbert, called Godman the priest, 1289.

Madeley was another of the church of Wenlock's possessions. *Domesday* notices the manor thus:—" The same church holds Madelie, and held it in time of King Edward. Here is i hide not geldable, and iii other hides geldable. In demesne are ii ox-teams, and vi villains and iiii boors with iiii teams. Here iiii serfs; and there might be vi other teams here besides. There is wood enough to fatten 400 swine. In time of King Edward, the manor was worth £4 [per annum]; now 50s."[1] The British *lle* signifies a place, the Saxon *leaʒ* a district, whilst the *Mad*-brook, which takes its rise in this place, contributed to form the name Madeley. The etymology of stream and district, perhaps, are found in Mæð, the Saxon for mead or meadow.

---

[1] *Domesday*, fo. 252, b 1.

Respecting Madeley and its member Coalbrookdale, we read that, in 1322, Walter de Caldebrook fined 6s. to the prior as lord of the manor, to be allowed to have a man, for a year, to dig sea-coal in Le Brocholes. The mineral treasures of this district were as yet, however, but slightly recognized.

MADELEY CHURCH.

This was taxed 12 merks in 1291. In 1341, the parish was assessed £2 16s. to the *ninth*; the causes of the low assessment being great storms, want of sheep stock, the surrender of six tenants, etc. In 1343, Madeley church was granted as an appropriation to Wenlock priory, when it became a vicarage. In 1534-5, under the head of portions receivable from certain *vills*, the rectorial tithes of Madeley appear as £2. The vicar's income was £5 5s., less 7s. 2d. for procurations and synodals.

Early Incumbent.—Richard de Castillion was rector of Madeley in 1267.

Little Wenlock is easily distinguishable from Much Wenlock in the Conqueror's survey, by the comparative smallness of its extent. *Domesday* says:—" The same church [St. Milburg's], holds Wenlock, and held it in time of King Edward. Here i hide not geldable, and other ii geldable. In demesne is one ox-team, and iiii villains, and ii boors with iii teams. Here ii neat-herds. The wood will fatten 300 swine, in which [wood] are two hayes [or enclosures], and a hawk's aerie.[1] In time of King Edward the manor was worth 70s. [annually]; now 40s."[2] According to the prior's rent-roll of 1510-11, there were four tenements in Huntyngton, and seventeen, of which one was a mill in Little Wenlock. These were held under Wenlock by three kinds of acknowledgments, ordinary rent; a rent called wood-silver, which varied from 9d. to 4d. per tenure; and rent of fowls in kind—generally one or two to each holding. The totals were, ordinary rents, £14 16s. 5½d.; wood-silver, 8s. 5d.; fowls, twenty-four. The receipts from Wenlock Parva and Huntington, including ferm of coal mines, in 1541-2, amounted to £23 15s. 5d.

LITTLE WENLOCK CHURCH AND PARISH.

From the circumstance, that the parishes of Badger, Beckbury,

---

[1] *Aira accipitris.*   [2] *Domesday*, fo. 252, b 1.

Madeley, and Little Wenlock are included in the diocese of Hereford, the boundary of which in this quarter is very irregular, it is supposed, that the boundary of St. Milburg's lands determined that of the diocese. This is very likely, since the see of Hereford was founded A.D. 676, an era coeval with that of the sainted Saxon foundress of Wenlock.

Little Wenlock is a rectory to this day, it not having been subjected to appropriation by the priors. In 1291, it was returned at £4 6s. 8d. In 1341, the parish was assessed only £1 12s. to the *ninth*; because the crops had been destroyed by the weather, there were no sheep, and much land lay uncultivated, and because the small tithes, etc., were not reckoned in estimating the *ninth*. In 1534-5, this preferment was valued at £11 10s., of which 2s. 2d. went for procurations and synodals, and a pension of £1 to the prior of Wenlock.

Early Rector.—Peter de Langon, a Burgundian; Peter de Aquablanca, Bishop of Hereford, also a Burgundian, being patron, although how he came to be so does not appear. This alien bishop dying, John le Breton, his successor, in 1269 ousted Langon from Little Wenlock, when Langon instituted proceedings in the papal court against his diocesan. The suit dragged its slow and tortuous existence through the expensive Roman chancery until, in 1290, more than twenty years afterwards, sentence was given in the Pope's Palace at Orvieto, for the restoration of Langon to all his preferments.

This brief notice of an alien rector of Little Wenlock, recalls to memory not only the period when English disputes were accustomed to be carried for decision to the foreign and corrupt papal court of Rome; but it reveals to us that unendurable condition of affairs which, when Henry the Third was king, led our ancestors in bitterness to exclaim, that " the natives of the country were as dirt in the sight of the foreigners." In the Parliament held in London in 1258, in reply to the urgent demand of Henry III. for pecuniary assistance, the Anglo-Norman nobles flatly told the king that they neither could nor would any longer submit to his misrule. Long enough England had groaned under it, said they. Resuscitating, therefore, the celebrated league of former years, the guardians of the Great Charter once more extended to each other their mailed hands, and swore upon the Holy Gospels, that they would reform the kingdom, and, upon pain of losing their lands, purge the country of its alien enemies and disturbers. Armed *cap-a-pié*, and attended by those who owed them knightly service, the great barons then rode to Oxford, and, acting in concert in the Parliament there held, they passed the celebrated "Ordinances."

Shipton. We read that, "The same church held [in Saxon times] and still holds Scipetune. Here half a hide, not geldable, and iii other hides, geldable. In demesne is one ox-team and v villains, and v boors with v teams, and ii serfs. [In time of King Edward, the manor] was worth 30s. [annually]. Now 4d. more."[1] The prior of Wenlock continued lord of Shipton until the dissolution.

SHIPTON CHURCH.

This church is first heard of about 1110. In 1291, the church or chapel of Shipton was returned as of £6 annual value. In 1341, the parish was assessed only £2 5s. to the *ninth*, because the corn was in great part destroyed; there were no sheep here; a third of the land lay untilled from inability of the tenants, on account of poverty, etc. In 1534-5, the prior of Wenlock received corn tithes to the value of £5 6s. 8d. per annum from Shipton, and a portion of £1 6s. 8d. from the vills of Larden and Brockton, whilst the unendowed chapel of Shipton is not even mentioned.

Petelie was another of the Priory's manors:—"The same church held and holds Petelie. Here is half a hide not geldable. In demesne is one ox-team, and iii boors with i team, and ii serfs. The wood [is capable of] fattening xl swine, and therein is i haye. [Formerly] it was worth 8s. Now 6s."[1] Its name being lost, the situation of this manor can only be surmised.

Burton. "The same church," continues *Domesday*, "held and holds Burtune, and Edric [holds it] of her. Aluric, Edric's father, held it [in Saxon times] and could not recede from the church.[2] Here ii hides and iii virgates of land geldable. In demesne is half an ox-team, and iiii villains, iiii radmans, and iii

---

[1] *Domesday*, fo. 252, b 1.   [2] "*Non poterat recedere ab ecclesiâ.*"

boors with iii teams and a half; and there is i serf and i mill serving the manor-house, and i haye. In King Edward's time [the manor] was worth 50s. [annually]. Now it is worth 40s. There might be ii more teams [employed] here." [1]

The circumstance of this manor being held by a Saxon under the Church, appears to have secured to Edric, its *Domesday* lord, a degree of protection. Nevertheless, in time, Burton passed wholly into the demesne of the foreignised monks of Wenlock, the locality being selected for holding the Hundred Courts of their franchise. These consisted of the greater and lesser Hundred Courts, the former of which were held twice a year, the latter every three weeks; and numerous are the instances in which manors belonging to Wenlock liberty are said to owe suit to the greater or lesser Hundred Courts of Burton.

Stoke St. Milburg.

The Saxon word Stóc signifies an inhabited place or village. Stoke St. Milburg was formerly called God-Stoke from its connection with St. Milburg, who it appears had lands here which she often visited. "Stokes," therefore, became the scene of many of those miracles which its saintly Saxon proprietress was said to be in the habit of performing; and for centuries afterwards St. Milburg's fields were believed to be supernaturally defended from the depredations of the wild fowl which infested the lands of her neighbours.

The beauty of Milburg attracted many suitors, but she made a vow of chastity, and rejected them all. Once upon a time, one of her suitors, who was the son of a king (a Welsh one, probably), determined to carry off Milburg by force, and he planned to surprise her while she was on a visit to Stoke. St. Milburg, however, was informed of her danger, and in haste fled towards Wenlock. Her royal lover closely pursued, until the Saxon saint, having reached the Corve, which at that particular spot was a mere streamlet, no sooner had the fair one leaped over the rivulet than suddenly it swelled into a torrent, and thus the designs of her enamoured pursuer were baffled.

This extensive manor is thus alluded to in William the Conqueror's survey:—"The same church held Godestoch [in Saxon

---

[1] *Domesday*, fo. 252, b 2.

times]. Earl Roger gave it to his chaplains, but the church ought to have it. Here are xx hides. Of these, iii are not geldable; the others are geldable. In demesne are ii ox-teams, and xxv villains and v boors with ix teams, and iiii neat-herds; and xix more teams might be here. In time of King Edward [the manor] was worth £13 [annually]. Now £9."[1] Stoke St. Milburg appears to have reverted to Wenlock priory as the earl's chaplains died off, when the early priors of Wenlock retained the bulk of the manor, partly in demesne, but chiefly leased out to life-tenants. According to Pope Nicholas' Taxation, in 1291, the prior of Wenlock's interest in this manor consisted of six carucates of land [held in demesne, £4]; four acres of meadow, 8s.; assized rents, £9 6s. 8d.; tallage, £6 13s. 4d.; pleas, perquisites [of Court], and labour dues, £1 6s. 8d.; total, £21 14s. 8d.

The Wenlock fine-roll of 1321-2 contains many entries relating to Stoke St. Milburg; we give the following:—" Stok, October 13th, 1321. The tenants of the manor fine 6s. 8d. with the lord [the prior], that he will commute a certain rent of geese, hitherto payable by them in kind, for a rent in money, viz., at the rate of 3d. per goose." On the same day, " two tenants give the lord twelve pullets for license to convey the one to the other some meadow land near St. Milburg's Cross." " Stok, April 19, 1322, a tenant fines for licence to marry." " Stok, July 6, 1322. A tenant surrendering a garden, another takes it for life. Both give a fine of 12d."

In 1541-2, after the Dissolution, the crown officers returned the large sum of £38 19s. 5d., as representing the prior of Wenlock's late interest in "Stoke Milbrudge."

PARISH AND CHURCH OF STOKE ST. MILBURG.

From time immemorial, a church has existed here. Its parish included the manor of Stoke, and also that of Clee Stanton. In 1291, the rectory was valued at £10 13s. 4d. per annum, besides a portion of £3 which the prior of Wenlock derived therefrom. In 1341, the parish was assessed only £4 10s. to the *ninth*, because the wheat had been destroyed by dreadful storms, there were no sheep, eleven tenants had quitted, etc. Soon afterwards, this church became subject to an appropriation by the prior of Wenlock. The *Valor* of 1534 represents the vicarage as worth £6 13s. 4d., less 14s. 4d. for synodals and procurations. A cotemporary return

---

[1] *Domesday*, fo. 252, b 2.

THE HEATH CHAPEL.

p. 252.

of the prior and convent of Wenlock mentions "a portion of £4 6s. 8d. from the vill of Stoke Milburg," by which is meant the rectorial income.

Early Incumbent.—Adam de Stretton, rector, 1272, presented by King Henry III., Wenlock priory being then vacant.

The *Domesday* manor of Godestoch included Stoke, the Moor, Clee-Downton, Newtown, Bockleton, Kinson, Norncott, and the Heath.

The architectural remains of the Heath chapel bespeak its antiquity. Founded probably by some pious layman, yet parochially subject to the church of Stoke St. Milburg, no record even mentions this chapel during the first four centuries of its existence. Hence we may infer, that its altar was unserved during the greater portion of this long period; for, jealous of the temporal interests of their church as they were, yet, little, we fear, in a general way, did the rich lord abbots and priors of old concern themselves about the souls of the people around them.

𝔇𝔦𝔱𝔱𝔬𝔫 𝔓𝔯𝔦𝔬𝔯𝔰, held in demesne by the Norman Earl of Shrewsbury, was probably exempt from external jurisdiction, at the period of the survey. Hence its Hundred is not specified in the Conqueror's record. Ruthall, in the same parish, however, is described in *Domesday* as a Patinton manor.

Ditton Priors, then called Dudinton from the Saxon Duƃƃinʒ-tun, namely, the town of Dudding, is thus described in *Domesday* :—" The Earl himself holds Dodintone. [Formerly] Earl Eduin held it, with iiii berewicks. Here xii hides geldable. In demesne are v ox-teams; and x serfs xx villains, and viii boors with vi teams; and there might be other xiii teams here. In Wich there is one salt-pit, returning 2s. In time of King Edward [the manor] paid £10 [annually]. Now £11."[1] In treating of Donington, we have explained what is meant by a salt-pit in *Domesday*. Upon the forfeiture of Robert de Belèsme, Ditton fell into the hands of Henry I., who granted Ashfield, one of its berewicks, along with other lands, to the ancestor of the Beysins, to be held *in capite* of the king, by service of keeping the king's hawks. Unshorn of any of its other members, Henry II. succeeded to

---

[1] *Domesday,* fo. 253, b 2.

Ditton, when that king granted it, with Corfham and Culmington, to Hugh de Periers. That this Norman had drawn his sword on behalf of legitimacy against the usurper Stephen appears evident, from his attesting a charter of the Duke of Normandy, which passed at Coventry in 1153, the very year in which the successful campaign of the young duke in the midland counties took place, when, "after a night of misery, peace dawned on the ruined realm of England." His service in the cause of royalty may also be inferred from the circumstance, that within the first year of his reign Henry II. gave De Periers these manors.

We are informed by the Pipe Roll, that Hugh's interest in Ditton Priors ceased at Christmas, 1175, shortly after which the monks of Wenlock acquired the whole of the manor. It would seem that De Periers, feeling his end drawing nigh, surrendered himself, according to the superstitious practice of that age, to the monks of Wenlock. He wished to die a member of their fraternity, and be buried within their walls. On this account, he gave them his manor of Ditton, subject to conditions which secured from the priory the same tenant-rights for his men as they had formerly enjoyed when holding under himself. Agreeably to which the "*verdict* of the Liberty of Wenlock," in 1255, states the prior to be lord of the manor of Dodinton, and that it was once a king's manor; that King Henry gave it to Hugh de Peres, and he gave it to the priory.[1]

Church of Ditton Priors.

The right to this advowson, about 1196, was contested between the Dean of Brug and the prior of Wenlock, when the pope's arbitrators decided that Ditton church should remain with the priory; but the dean and his successors were to receive an annual acknowledgment of two pieces of gold at Michaelmas from the priory.

The church of Dodyton, in Stottesden deanery, in 1291, was valued at £12, besides a portion for the vicar of £4 6s. 8d. In 1341, this parish was assessed only £5 4s. to the *ninth*, on account of storms, absence of sheep stock, and the surrender of nine impoverished tenants, etc. In the *Valor* of 1534-5, Ditton Priors vicarage is stated to be worth £6 13s. 4d., less 10s. to the prior, and 7s. 8d. for procurations and synodals.

Early Incumbent.—Master Nicholas de Hamtun, vicar, end of 12th century.

---

[1] *Rot. Hundred*, II, 85.

Acton Round. Ãc, in Saxon, signifies an oak tree, tun, a town, and hence derive all Actons. With respect to the terminal, Round, by which this place is distinguished, its etymology is not so certain. Sir Thomas Boteler, vicar of Much Wenlock, about the middle of the 16th century, says, that, "the chapell of Acton Round was sometyme round, like a temple." Now it is certain, that the Templars were introduced into Shropshire by the Fitz-Alans, lords of Acton Round; they are known to have built round churches; it is not improbable, that the form of the chapel in question was suggested by some contemporary building of the Templars at Lidley; and hence it may be the etymology of Acton Round.

Rainald, the Norman sheriff of Shropshire, held, under the Earl of Shrewsbury, no less than eight manors in Patinton Hundred. Acton, one of these, is thus noticed in Domesday Book:—"The same Rainald holds of the Earl, Achetune. Here iiii hides geldable. Uluiet held it, and was free, with this land. In demesne are ii ox-teams; and vii serfs, ix villains, and iiii boors with iiii teams; and there might be iii teams more besides. Here is a mill of 32d. [annual value]. In time of King Edward [the manor] was worth 60s. Now 40s."[1] Rainald and his successors, the Fitz-Alans, continued to hold this manor, principally in demesne, that is, as lords of the manor, they kept the greater portion of the land in their own hands; yet they enfeoffed vassals in a part of it.

Muckley, Upper Monk-Hall, and Lower Monk-Hall, were members of this manor. By 1496, Wenlock priory had acquired an interest in the former; and, if their titles do not mislead, the shaven crowned brethren had also something to do with both of the latter.

CHURCH OR CHAPEL OF ACTON ROUND.

The chapel of "Acton Rotunda" was granted as an affiliation to Wenlock priory, by Bishop Swinfield, in 1284, simply because it was constructed on St. Milburg's land. Hence its occupant was deprived, and the future chaplains had to pay a pension of 2s. per annum to the mother church.

As belonging to the prior of Wenlock, and in the deanery of Wenlock, Acton Round Chapel, in 1291, was valued at £6 13s. 4d. per annum. In 1341, the parish was rated at £2 16s. only to

---

[1] *Domesday*, fo. 254, a 2.

the *ninth*, because of destruction of wheat-crop, absence of sheep-stock, non-cultivation of holdings through poverty of tenants, etc. The *Valor* of 1534-5 gives £3 6s. 8d. as the "portion" which the prior of Wenlock received from the vill of Acton Round, out of which it appears an annual pension of 14s. went to the rector of Cownde for the chapel of Acton Round.

Early Incumbent.—Adam, parson of Acton in 1227.

Abdon. The Titterstone mountain, near Abdon, doubtless originally derived its name from the Icelandic *Titra*, which signifies to *tremble*; and Hartshorne, by a personal investigation, proved that there existed on this eminence *a rocking stone.*

Abdon Burf is 1805 feet above the level of the sea at low water. Upon its summit are indications of upwards of forty circles of stone, enclosed within a huge vallum of basalt or *dû* stone. The enclosed area is of an oval form, and measures 1317 feet from north to south, and 660 feet from east to west. Geologists fail to account satisfactorily for the appearances on Abdon Burf and the two other Clee Hills, namely, Clee Burf and the Titterstone; the summits of both of which, likewise, appear to have been surrounded with a vallum of stones, within which, again, are numbers of smaller circles. It has been conjectured, that these are artificial enclosures, which, at some period of remote antiquity, were devoted to idolatrous or Druidical purposes: purposes, probably, partly devotional, partly sepulchral. It may have been, that Abdon Burf was one of those condemned high places set apart, in ancient times, for the mysterious worship of Baal, or the sun. Leland says, "Cle Hills be holy in Shropshire;"[1] and if it be true, that Abdon Burf and its neighbour eminences are vast monuments of an extinct hill-worship, then the tradition acquires a remarkable significance.

Betwixt Abdon Burf and the village of Clee St. Margaret is the Roman station, Nordy Bank, one of the most perfect remains in the kingdom of the Roman period. In shape, it is a parallelogram, the angles rounded. A fosse, twelve feet wide, surrounds the whole. The vallum is twenty-six feet wide at its base, and six across its crest. The interior slope is twelve feet, the scarp eighteen, and the counterscarp, six. There are four gorges or

---

[1] *Itinerary*, vol. viii fo. 89 b.

openings due north, the original ones being at the east and west. This important station gave the Roman general not only the command of Corve Dale, but it commanded also the valley on the southern side of the Burf. As it has already been pointed out by the great authority on matters relating to the earthworks and ante-Norman fortresses of Shropshire and the Welsh border;[1] the existence of this very perfect Roman work immediately below Abdon Burf proves, that the enclosure on its summit was a *religious*, not a *defensive* one, since the Roman general would hardly have pitched his camp in a position which the Britons could have assaulted with so much advantage.

Abdon is described in William the Conqueror's record as follows:—"The same Rainald [the sheriff] holds Abetune [of the earl], and Azo [holds it] of him. Uluuin held it [in Saxon times], and was free with this land. Here iii hides geldable. Here i oxteam and iii serfs, one Frenchman, ii villains, one radman, and ii boors with i team; and still there might be iii more teams [employed]. [In time of King Edward] it was worth 20s. [annually]. Now 12s."[2]

Azo, the *Domesday* sub-tenant of this manor, held other lands in the fief of Rainald the sheriff. Under his Norman name, Azo Bigot, he granted lands in Abeton to Salop Abbey, before 1136, for until so long after the survey did Azo continue lord of this manor. Azo's wife also, for the soul of Rainald her son, granted land to the monks in the town of Shrewsbury, which yielded them 10d. annually. Robert, the knight, another son of Azo, was also a benefactor to the Church, concerning whose gift we read that the seigneural lord, "William Fitz-Alan, conceded the donation which Robert his knight made to the church of St. Peter at Salop, of the vill which is called Abbeton, which was of his (Fitz-Alan's) fee; and this was at the request of the same Robert. But for this concession, which with his own hand he (Fitz-Alan) placed upon the altar, the monks conceded to him, for the soul of his mother who was lately deceased, one annual service; and out of the slender means of their church, they gave him fifteen merks of silver and one palfrey. Witnesses: Roger, archdeacon; Richard and Heming, priests; and many others of the men of the same William.—But when the same Robert, his lord allowing it, offered the said vill upon the altar of St. Peter, Richard, his nephew,

---

[1] HARTSHORNE, *Salopia Antiqua*, p. 151. [2] *Domesday*, fo. 254, a 2.

willingly conceded the thing, and with him made the donation. Witnesses: Roger, archdeacon, and others."[1] Notwithstanding which, by some mischance, Abdon slipped between the fingers of the monks, and in 1165, it formed part of two knight's fees of new feoffment,[2] which John le Strange then held of Fitz-Alan's barony. The Le Stranges long continued seigneural lords over Abdon.

PARISH AND CHAPEL OF ABDON.

About 1138, Bishop Betun assigned Abdon Chapel to Shrewsbury Abbey. In 1291, this church was returned as worth under £4. The parish was rated only 11s. to the *ninth*, in 1341, non-cultivation of the land, owing to poverty of the tenants, being the reason alleged. In 1534-5, Abdon Rectory was valued at £3, less 6d. for synodals.

Early Incumbent.—Walter de Bermingham, priest, presented by the abbot and convent of Salop, 1307.

Tugford. William the Conqueror's record says:—"The same Rainald hath given Dodefort to the church of St. Peter, for the soul of Warin, his antecessor.[3] Eluuin held it and was free with the land. Here three and a half hides. In demesne are iii ox-teams and iii serfs, iii neat-herds, iii villains, and viii boors with v teams. Here is a mill of 4s. [annual value]. [In time of King Edward the manor] was worth 20s. Now 40s. Of this land, Rayner holds i hide of Rainald. Here he has i ox-team and i neat-herd; iii villains and i boor, with i team. Its value is 8s."[4]

The manor thus described, as the reader will see by referring to the Table, was one of those eight Patinton manors that belonged to the sheriff of Shropshire, the "greatest of Earl Roger's feoffees whose lands were hereditary, and whose office was quasi-hereditary, from the Norman conquest of Mercia to the reign of King John." The first Norman sheriff of Shropshire was Warin, and he it was, and not Rainald, his successor as *Domesday* has it, that gave to Shrewsbury Abbey by far the larger portion of this manor. Warin died before the year of the survey, when Rainald, marrying

---

[1] Recitatory charter, quoted by Eyton, from *Salop Chartulary*.
[2] New feoffment: that is, had arisen since the time of Henry I.
[3] *Antecessoris sui*. [4] *Domesday*, fo. 254, a 2.

his widow, succeeded him as sheriff: hence, in *Domesday*, Warin is called Rainald's antecessor: namely, predecessor in office and estate.

Including that of the first palatine earl, there are six imperial charters of general confirmation to Shrewsbury Abbey, in all of which the grant in Tugford is ascribed to "Warin, the sheriff." The abbot's collective receipts from the Tugford estate were returned, in 1534, at £13 17s. 2d.

The etymological changes have been great with respect to this place.

TUGFORD CHURCH.

The chapel of Tugaford is mentioned in 1138. The Taxation of Pope Nicholas in 1291, values the church of Tugford, in Wenlock deanery, at £5 6s. 8d., besides a portion of 2s. to the abbot of Shrewsbury. Formerly belonging to Shrewsbury abbey, by 1301 the Bishop of Hereford had acquired the patronage of this church. In 1341, the parish was assessed only 30s. for the *ninth* of its wheat, wool, and lamb, because the tenants, under stress of poverty were not tilling the land; six of them were mendicants, etc.

Early Incumbent.—John de Mosewell, clerk in 1291, resigned Tugford.

Stanway was another of the Patinton manors of "Rainaldus Vicecomes." It is noticed in *Domesday* thus:—" The same Rainald holds Stanweie of the earl, and Odo holds it of him. Aluric held it, and was a free man. Here ii hides geldable. In demesne are ii ox-teams, and iiii serfs, iii villains, and i boor, with ii teams; and there might be iii teams more besides. In time of King Edward [the manor] was worth 40s. [annually]; now [it is worth] 30s. It was waste when he [Rainald] received it." [1] How came this manor which, in Saxon times was worth 40s., to be "waste" when Rainald, the Norman, received it? The cut-throat scum of Europe, which William's victory at Hastings saddled upon England, robbed the Saxons and ravished their women. The English sought redress for these outrages, but in vain: their insolent oppressors laughed at them. With Earls Morcar and Edwin at their head, they then made a desperate attempt to throw off the

---

[1] *Domesday*, fo. 254, a 2.

Norman yoke; and in the fearful struggle which ensued doubtless it was, that, overrun in all directions, the manor in question was pillaged and burnt, and its Saxon inhabitants put to the sword. Something like this is but too often indicated, when the term " wasta fuit " is made use of in the Conqueror's survey.

Of Aluric, its Saxon proprietor, it follows, that nothing further is heard. Odo de Bernières, his Norman successor, was founder of the family of Fitz Odo. Holding other manors besides Stanway, Odo was a chief among the knights of Shropshire.

The *vills* Upper Stanway, Lower Stanway, and Stone Acton, the bulk of the *Domesday* manor of Stanweie, passed in time from Odo's descendants to Herbert de Rushbury, who gave " the whole of the land of the two Staneweys, with all their appurtenances," to Henry de Audley, about 1225. He again quitted all his right in Stanway to Madoc de Sutton. Madoc, therefore, became mesne-tenant at Stanway, holding it under Fitz Alan, a member of whose barony this manor continued to be.

Stanway and Stone Acton are now in the parish of Rushbury.

Gretton. *Domesday* thus describes this manor :—" The same Rainald, with one Robert, holds Grotintune of the earl. Odo holds it of them. Alric and Otro held it [in Saxon times] for ii manors. Here ii hides geldable. Those thanes [Alric and Otro] were free. Here are v villains with ii ox-teams, and there might be other two teams here. In time of King Edward, the manor was worth 32s.; now it is worth 10s. When they [namely Rainald and Robert] received it, it was waste." [1] Here we have another case of waste. The fields they loved to cultivate, and those well-stocked Saxon homesteads, around which their wives and blue-eyed little ones had fondly clung, were devastated and burnt by the ruthless oppressor; and the free thanes Alric and Otro, if they perished not in the vain attempt to shield all that was dearest to them, at least had been driven from the estate which had been their father's. Odo, the Norman tenant of two different mesne-lords, appears to have partially recovered this ruined manor, for, at the period of the survey it was worth 10s. : yet, how great the difference to its value in Saxon times. Odo's descendants, for two centuries after him,

---

[1] *Domesday*, fo. 254, a 2.

continued to hold one moiety of Gretton under Rainald and his successors the Fitz Alans. The other moiety, namely, that hide which Odo held under the Norman mesne-lord Robert, had a various history. Upon the forfeiture of the Norman earls, of course Robert's tenure became a tenure *in capite* of the Crown, yet, as nothing further is heard of Robert, it is presumed, that, participating in de Belèsme's rebellion, he also became involved in the ruin of his suzerain, when half the manor of Gretton became forfeit to the Crown. If such were the case, his tenant Odo, as was usual in similar circumstances, would become a tenant *in capite*, that is, he would hold the moiety of Gretton which Robert had held immediately of the Crown. Yet, whether it was so, or whether King Henry I. granted Robert's interest to his viceroy, Richard de Belmeis, is not known. Certain it is, however, that one moiety of Gretton did not leave the tenure in fee of Odo's eldest representative, until both moieties, being re-united late in the 13th century, the whole manor was enjoyed by his descendant.

𝕰𝖆𝖘𝖙𝖍𝖔𝖕𝖊 is described in Domesday Book as follows:—" The same Rainald holds Stope of the earl, and Fulcher [holds it] of him. Ernu and Uluric held it, and were free. Here ii hides geldable. In demesne is i ox-team, and iiii serfs, one villain, and v boors with i team; and still there might be ii teams more [employed] here. In time of King Edward [the manor] was worth 15s.; now 20s. When he [the sheriff] received it, he found it waste." [1]

Under the fostering care of Fulcher, its tenant, this waste manor had so recovered that it was actually worth more at the time of the survey than it had been in the time of Edward the Confessor. The Norman Fulcher held other manors besides this under Rainald the sheriff. It is doubtful, however, whether his descendants continued to enjoy Easthope; yet, the tenure of Roger, who, in 1165, held it, was of old feoffment, that is, it was existing before the death of King Henry I. Roger's successor, in 1255, was found to be John de Esthop, who, a man of repute, became coroner of Shropshire, an office ranking in importance only next to the sheriff. For more than fifty years, this man was in possession of Easthope.

---

[1] *Domesday*, fo. 254, a 2.

He held the manor by service of finding a man and horse at Oswestry, for 40 days in time of war. He held it of the seigneural lord Fitz Alan, doing suit to the hundred, and paying the king 2s. annually for *stretward* and *motfee*.

EASTHOPE CHURCH.

According to the Taxation of 1291, the church of Esthop, in the deanery of Wenlock, was under £4 annual value, out of which a pension of 3s. went to the rector of Cound. In 1341, the parish was taxed only 9s. to the *ninth,* because there were no sheep in it; and, what with murrain, diverse taxes, etc., the best part of the vill was annihilated. The *Valor* of 1534-5 gives the rectory of Estope as worth £3 6s. 8d. *per annum,* less a pension of 3s. 4d. payable to the church of Cound, and 4d. for synodals.

Early Incumbents.—Roger, parson of Easthope about 1240. On June 8th, 1383, William Garmston, priest, was deprived of this benefice, he having murdered the patron, John de Esthope, lord of the manor.

Lutwyche. "The same Rainald," continues *Domesday,* "holds Loteis, and Richard [holds it] of him. Goduin held it, and was a free man. Here is i hide geldable. In demesne is one ox-team, and ii neat-herds, one villain, and one boor with half a team. It was and is worth 8s."[1]

Brockton, in the parish of Long Stanton, is noticed in Domesday Book as follows:—"The same Rainald holds Broctune, and Richard [holds it] of him. Semær, Eliard, and Eduin held it [in Saxon times], and were free with this land. Here ii hides geldable. In demesne is half an ox-team; and ii serfs, iii villains, ii boors, and i Frenchman, with i team between them all; and still there might be iiii more teams here. In time of King Edward the manor was worth 28s. [per annum]; now 15s. When he [Rainald] received it, he found it waste."[1] The mesne-lords of Lutwyche and Brockton were identical, descending from that Norman Richard who held both under Rainald the sheriff.

---

[1] *Domesday,* fo. 254, b 1.

Castle Holgate, formerly Stanton. Under one notice, *Domesday* thus alludes to two different manors similarly named :—" The same Helgot holds Stantune [of the earl]. Chetel held it [in Saxon times], and was a free man. Here are ii hides geldable. The land is for iii ox-teams. Here is one radman with half a a team, and one serf and i boor. [In time of King Edward] it was worth 8s.; now 3s. [per annum]."[1] Again :—"The same Helgot holds Stantune. Genust and Æluuard, Dunning and Elveva held it for four manors, and were free with their lands. Here iii hides geldable. There is land [enough] for vi ox-teams. Here Helgot has a castle and ii ox-teams in demesne, and [he has] iv serfs, iii villains, iii boors, and one Frenchman, with three and a half teams. Here is a church and a priest. In time of King Edward [the manor] was worth 18s.; now 25s. [Helgot] found it waste."[1] The manors thus described, in time lost their *Domesday* appellation of Stantune, and, becoming one great manor, the name Holgate was given to it, after the baronial residence of its first Norman lord.

When Shropshire passed to the Norman Earl Roger, he conferred upon Helgot, his follower, nineteen manors in the county. This knight who, doubtless, had seen service at Hastings, fixing therefore his seat at Stantune, reared his stronghold in the upper valley of the Corfe, over the rich repose of which, in ancient times, it spread its gloomy shadow. Unlike, however, the generality of those fortresses with which its Norman Conquerors networked England, the site of Helgot's castle presented no feature of natural strength, and, as it was far from the Welsh border, it figures but little on the page of history.

The first Norman lord of Stantune granted Monkmoor to Shrewsbury abbey, and passed away. Herbert Fitz Helgot then succeeded to his barony, and, as appears from a charter of Beauclerk's, dated " *apud castrum Helgoti in Scalopecyra,*"[2] King Henry I. partook of Fitz Helgot's hospitality at Corfe. Like his father, Fitz Helgot gave lands to the church. He gave to Shrewsbury Abbey " the church of Stanton, with all the tithes of himself,' and of his knights, and with all things which pertained to the same church."[3]

Eutropius, his eldest son, does not appear to have lived to

---

[1] *Domesday,* fo. 258, b 1. [2] *Monasticon* I. 248, Num. xvii.
[3] *Salop Chartulary,* No. 35.

succeed his father, and, dying without issue, Herbert, his brother, styled De Castello, became third baron of Castle Holgate. Herbert left no child, and the heir to his barony, after a dispute between the de Girros family and the descendants of Richard de la Mere, which lasted ten years, was found to be in de la Mere's line.

Richard de la Mere was one of those Anglo-Normans, who fought under the banner of Cœur de Leon, in Palestine. Upon the abandonment by the Christian forces of the third crusade, in journeying homewards, de la Mere was seized with mortal sickness in Benevento, Italy, when his last act was to grant his *vill* of Uffington to Haughmond abbey, by a deed in which the particulars of his illness being recited, is attested by the preceptor and one of the brethren of a house of Knights Hospitallers at Benevento. It was Thomas Mauduit, grandson of the deceased crusading knight, who, on coming of age in 1203, became lord of Castle Holgate. Accordingly, in regard to this Shropshire barony, he stands acquitted on the fifth, sixth, and seventh scutages of John, levied respectively in the years 1204-5-6. Thomas Mauduit, lord of a great fief in Hampshire, as well as Castle Holgate, accompanied King John over to Ireland in 1210. He served also in that unlucky French campaign, which terminated in Philip Augustus' victory at Bovines.

In 1216, Mauduit joined the barons against John, when Castle Holgate was given to Hugh de Mortimer of Wigmore. Nor did Thomas, like many, return to his allegiance on the accession of young Henry III, as we learn that on March 16th, 1217, all his lands in Shropshire and Hampshire were given to Robert de Ferrars during the king's pleasure; but shortly afterwards the rebellious baron, doing homage, his lands were restored.

To Thomas Mauduit, William his son succeeded in 1244, whose homage receiving, the king ordered the sheriffs of Shropshire, Hampshire, and Wiltshire to give him seizin of his inheritance in those counties. Styling himself "Lord of Castle Holgate," this William gave to Haughmond abbey that mill out of which, when he bequeathed them his body, his father had given to the monks 20s. rent to celebrate his *anniversary*. In 1254, this barony was assessed at five fees to the *aid* for knighting prince Edward. It was William Mauduit who alienated this Shropshire barony to Richard Plantagenet, the rich but covetous king of the Romans. The brother of Henry III., therefore, became lord of Castle Hol-

DOOR-WAY, HOLGATE.

gate, when he forthwith conveyed it to the order of Knights Templars. After the suppression of that order, Robert Burnel, Bishop of Bath and Wells, acquired Castle Holgate, he holding it *in capite* by service of two knights, in time of war, at Montgomery, and the prelate transmitted this the greatest of his territorial acquisitions to his heirs.

Holgate Church.

This, the remains of a Saxon foundation, was given as stated, by Herbert Fitz Helgot, in Henry the First's time, to Shrewsbury abbey. But a deed which passed in 1210, exhibits Holgate church as held by three portionists or prebendaries, the advowson of two of which pertained to Salop Abbey; the lords of Holgate presenting to the other. Soon after 1280, the patronage of two of the Holgate prebends passed from Shrewsbury abbey to the see of Hereford; eventually all three prebends were consolidated in a single rectory.

Pope Nicholas' Taxation values the three portions in this church separately; the first at £6, the other two at £4 13s. 4d. each. In 1341, the assessors taxed the parish only £4 13s. 4d. to the *ninth*, because there were no sheep or lambs, four acres of land lay uncultivated, etc. The *Valor* of 1534 gives this preferment, including a pension of 4s. receivable from the rector of Aston Botterell, as worth £13 7s. 4d. *per annum*, less 7s. 8d. for procurations and synodals. The vicar of Leighton also paid a pension of 5s. to the rector of Holgate.

Prebendaries of Holgate.—Helias, a priest, was incumbent of the Presbytral prebend in 1210. At that time, the Diaconal prebend, to which the lord of Castle Holgate presented, was vacant; but Osbern, a priest, had the sub-diaconal prebend.

Clee St. Margaret, like Cleobury, derived its name from the great Clee Hill. St. Margaret, the name of the patron saint to whom its church was dedicated, being added to distinguish it from other Clees.

We read in Domesday Book that:—"The same Helgot holds Cleie. Aluric held it, and was a free man. Here i hide geldable. The [arable] land is [capable of employing] iiii ox-teams. In demesne, there is one team and iiii serfs and ii villains, with i team, and ii boors and a mill serving the court-house. [Formerly] it was worth 8s. [per annum]; now 10s."[1] Helgot, who reared his feudal stronghold in the valley of the Corfe, held also this manor under Roger de Montgomery, and the succeeding lords of Castle Holgate owning it after him, in their time, Clee St. Margaret became gradually dismembered, for the abbeys of Salop and Haughmond, Wenlock priory, and the Knights Hospitallers, by grant after grant, had acquired nearly the whole of the manor.

CHURCH OF CLEE ST. MARGARET.

The first notice relating to it is in the Taxation of 1291, when, entered as the church of "le Cleye St. Milburge," in the deanery of Ludlow, it is said to belong to the Hospitallers of Dinmore. Its value is not stated. This parish does not appear to have been assessed to the *ninth* in 1341, but in 1534-5, "the chapel of St. Margaret de Lee Clee" was valued at £3 *per annum*, out of which an annual pension of 14s. was payable "*to the Commander of the Commandery of St. John of Dynmore.*"

Early Incumbent.—The first we hear of in connection with this church, is Richard Rushton, parson, in 1546-7.

Millichope. Domesday says:—"The same Helgot holds [of Earl Roger] Melicope. Gamel held it [in Saxon times], and was free. Here i hide geldable. The land is [capable of employing] iii ox-teams. In demesne there is one [such team] and iiii serfs. It [formerly] was worth 50s.; now 15s."[1] We hear no more of Helgot's interest in this manor, although shortly after *Domesday* it was given by the Norman earl Roger de Montgomery to St. Milburg's church, in exchange for Eardington. Early in the 12th century, however, Stephen, rector of Munslow, claimed the two Milinsopes to belong to his parish; but Bishop Richard de Belmeis, viceroy of Shropshire, decided that all St. Milburg's lands were parochially subject to the mother church of Wenlock. "There is, nevertheless," added the viceroy, "conceded to Stephen, not in virtue of his claim, but for the sake of peace and for love of his lord (the lord of Munslow), the tithe and the sepulture of the rustics of Lower Milinsope, and the third garb of the tithe of the same lord";—the result of which concession is, that to this day Lower Millicope is in Munslow parish, while Upper Millicope

---

[1] *Domesday*, fo. 258, b 1.

and Hungerford are in St. Milburg's parish of Eaton. The foreign rent-roll of Wenlock priory of 1521-2 includes 20s. as still receivable from the "lord of Nether Millynchope."

The feoffees who held Upper Millichope under the priors of Wenlock, were also hereditary foresters of that vast jurisdiction, known in ancient times as the Long Forest. There still exists at Upper Millichope a house, the architectural details of which belong to the 13th century. It is presumed to have been the lodge of the hereditary foresters of the Long Forest. The precautions against attack are elaborate.

Oxenbold.

This name appears to have agricultural ideas associated with it. We learn from *Domesday*, that:—"The same Helgot holds Oxibola. Edric and Siuuard held it for two manors, and were free. Here i hide geldable. The land is [enough] for iv ox-teams. In demesne is half [a team], and one neat-herd, one villain, one boor, and one Frenchman, with a team and a half. [In time of King Edward] it was worth 11s.; now 8s."[1] In the days of Henry II. this manor was held by Robert de Girros, the same who also held Charlcott and Burwarton under the lords of Castle Holgate. About 1244, Robert, a descendant of this man, granted Oxenbold to Wenlock priory, for which "the prior received the said Robert into all benefits, prayers, etc., which should be offered up in his house for ever." Wenlock retained the manor until the harsh hand of bluff Harry the Eighth severed the accord. Yet the prior, foreseeing the impending storm, in order to subsist when he should be out of his house, raising the fines high, leased the manor out at a low rent, hence the minister's accounts of 1541-2 give only £17 13s. 4d. as the ferm of Oxenbold.

Monk-Hopton, Weston, and Far Monk-Hall or Priors Muchall, originally members of Oxenbold, also all belonged to Wenlock priory.

Long Stanton.

Stán in Saxon, signifies a stone, and it is probable that this place acquired its distinctive appellation from

[1] *Domesday*, fo. 258, b 1.

the length of its parish greatly exceeding its breadth. It is thus alluded to in *Domesday*:—"The same Roger [de Laci] holds [of the earl] Stantune, and Herbert [holds it] of him. Eluuin held it [in Saxon times], and was a free man. Here iii hides geldable. In demesne is one ox-team and a half, and [there are] ii serfs and one boor with half a team. [The manor formerly] was worth 6s. [annually]; now 12s."[1]

When Roger de Laci, in 1095, conspired with Robert de Moubray against the Red King, his fief, forfeit to the Crown, became dismembered, when Long Stanton was shared out amongst various tenants. One obtained from the king a portion of Long Stanton by sergeantry of acting as a "constable of 200 foot-soldiers whenever any king of England invaded Wales." One of these constables granted whatever he had in Long Stanton to a tenant in fee, yet his right to do so being afterwards questioned, his descendants had to compound for the act by an annual payment to the Crown. The tenant's name was Simon de Stanton, and he, during the thirty-six years he held this estate, granted many subinfeudations thereof. The abbot of Haughmond acquired an interest here, so also did the Knights Templars: nor had Wenlock priory been forgotten.

Church and Parish of Long Stanton.

In 1081, the church of this parish was probably at Patton, with which it has always been connected. A century afterwards, we hear of Walter, chaplain of Stanton. Before 1275, the prior of Wenlock gave this advowson to the dean and chapter of Hereford, when it became a vicarage in their gift. In 1291, the church of Long Stanton, in the deanery of Wenlock, was valued at £13 6s. 8d. per annum. Yet the parish, in 1341, was assessed only £3 10s. to the *ninth*, because of destruction of corn by storms, murrain among sheep, surrender of eleven tenants, whose lands lay uncultivated, etc. The *Valor* of 1534-5 gives the vicarage of Long Stanton as worth £7 0s. 8d, less 7s. 8d. for procurations and synodals.

Patton is thus noticed in *Domesday*:—"The same Roger holds of the Earl, Patintune. Aluuin held it, and was a free man. Here i hide geldable. Herbert holds it of Roger. In demesne he has

---

[1] *Domesday*, fo. 256, b 1.

i ox-team; and ii serfs, one villain, and one radman with i team; and yet there might be iii teams more [employed]. Here is a priest and one boor. In time of King Edward [the manor] was worth 10s. [annually], and afterwards it was waste. Now [it is worth] 24s."[1]

Patton and Long Stanton have always been in the same parish. Roger de Lacy was *Domesday* lord of both. Herbert held them of him. Doubtless, also, Aluuin, the Saxon lord of Patintune, was identical with Eluuin the Saxon proprietor of Stantune: finally, when De Lacy lost his barony, both manors underwent a similar disintegration. Then half of Patton passed to the seigneury of Wenlock Priory, when, according to the custom of the priory, it was leased out to life tenants. In 1363, the prior of Wenlock obtained the king's licence to purchase the other moiety of this manor; and so, at length, he reduced the whole, and his successors retained jurisdiction over Patton until the Dissolution.

This place formerly was *caput* of the Domesday Hundred to which it gave a name.

Rushbury was formerly a Roman station, the Devil's Causeway being the direct line of communication betwixt it and Nordy Bank. It is thus alluded to in that Anglo-Norman record, Domesday Book:—"The same Roger holds Riseberie, and Odo [holds] of him. Æluuin held it [in Saxon times] and was a free man. Here v hides geldable. In demesne are ii ox-teams, and iiii serfs, i villain, iii radmans, and ii boors with v teams. Here is a mill, a wood for fattening xl swine, and a hawk's aerie. In time of King Edward, the manor was worth 60s., and afterwards it was waste. Now [it is worth] 35s., and there might be ii more teams here."[1] After Roger Fitz-Odo, Herbert de Rushbury was lord of this manor in 1200, holding it under Walter de Lacy, in whose Irish interests he participated, since we read of Herbert de Rissebiry and Elias de Say, another of Lacy's Shropshire feoffees, being joint claimants of land in Meath against William Parvus. Herbert's interest in Rushbury eventually passed to his heirs, De Willey and De Bitterley, whose houses inheriting the manor, hence Rushbury came to be split up into no less than six manors, namely, Rush-

---

[1] *Domesday*, fo. 256, b 1.

bury proper, Eastwall, Westwall, Wall-sub-Heywood, Coates, and Wilderhope. It would serve, however, but to disgust and weary the reader to trace all the various sub-infeudations that sprung up in the manor of Rushbury. A single sample will suffice. In 1255, Eastwall, merely one of the six constituents of Rushbury, was held by Roger Sprenghose of Adam de Brinton, who held under the heir of Nicholas de Williley, the said heir under Margery de Lacy, the said Margery, in dower, under the heirs of Walter de Lacy, and the said heirs *in capite* of the crown.

RUSHBURY CHURCH.

This church, the architectural remains of which bespeak its antiquity, was probably founded by Roger de Laci, the *Domesday* baron, and by him given to that priory at Hereford in which both his father and himself took so much interest. In 1291, the church of Ryssebury, in the deanery of Wenlock was valued at £13 6s. 8d., besides a portion of 13s. 4d., which the prior of Hereford had therein. In 1341, the parish was assessed only £5 to the *ninth*; the reasons were, "destruction of wheat by tempest, murrain of sheep, poverty and desertion of tenants," etc. The *Valor* of 1534-5 gives the church of Rusburye as worth £19 15s. 4d. per annum, less 7s. 8d. for procurations and synodals.

Early Incumbent.—Richard, rector of Rushbury in 1250.

Buchehale, in Patinton Hundred, is thus briefly noticed in *Domesday* :—" William [Pantulf] holds Buchehale. Elmer held it. Here i virgate. The land is for half a team. It was and is waste." [1] Neither the name, or situation of the manor can now be identified.

Ruthall. Concerning this place, *Domesday* says :—" The same Gerard holds Rohalle [of the earl], and Gerelmus holds of him. Oschil held it, and was a free man. Here half a hide geldable, The land is [enough] for ii ox-teams. In demesne, there is half a team and ii neat-herds, and iii boors with half a team. In time of King Edward, it was worth 6s. Now 8s." [2]

---

[1] *Domesday*, fo. 257, b 1.   [2] Ibidem, fo. 259, a 1.

It appears, then that Gerelmus held Ruthall of Gerard de Tornai, Gerard of the Norman earl, and the earl of the king. When the Norman earl rebelled, his vassal Gerard shared both in the revolt and forfeiture of his lord; the mesne tenures between Gerelmus and the crown, therefore, were effaced, and henceforth the Sandfords, successors of Gerelmus, held Ruthall and another place, of the name of Sandford, from whence they derived their name immediately of the crown. The collective tenure, at first, was by service of half a knight's fee, but afterwards by serjeantry of finding one horseman at Montgomery for forty days, in time of war, at the tenant's own cost.

Ruthall, with Ashfield, now constitutes a township in the parish of Priors Ditton. Unlike the rest of the parish, however, this township is in Munslow Hundred; for the prior of Wenlock, although lord of Ditton, never succeeded in obtaining ingress into Ruthall or Ashfield.

Beckbury.

Domesday says:—"The same Roger [Venator] holds Becheberie [of Earl Roger]. Azor held it, and was a free man. Here i hide geldable. The [arable] land is [capable of employing] ii ox-teams. Here one knight pays [to Roger] 20d. rent. In time of King Edward [the manor] was worth 12s." [1]

Azor, who held this manor in Saxon times, was lord also of Burwarton and Neenton. Scarcely anything is known of either Norman, Roger, or Ulger Venator. Roger Venator's manors, as a general rule, went to form the fief of Pulverbatch, yet not the one in question, which appears to have passed, if not wholly, in greater part, to the prior of Wenlock.

In 1255, Philip de Beckbury was lord of the vill, holding it of the prior at a rent of 25s. Exactly the same amount was receivable by the prior, in the shape of chief rent, from Beckbury, upwards of 260 years afterwards.

At the forest assizes of March, 1209, the following charge was brought against the lord of this manor:—" Richard de Prestewode (a forester, apparently), going through his bailiwick of Morfe, followed two men till he came up with them, viz., Hugh de Bectebury and Thomas, his brother. They had with them three grey-

---

[1] *Domesday*, fo. 259, a 2.

hounds, out of leash, and five hares; but when Richard had arrested Hugh, Thomas drew his sword and released him. Both then took to flight; and Richard, raising the *hue and cry*, pursued till night took the fugitives from his sight." A very heavy fine, doubtless, was proffered for this flagrant violation of the forest laws by the lord of Beckbury, " that he and Thomas, his brother, might be quit as to this: that they had taken hares in the king's forest." [1]

BECKBURY CHURCH AND PARISH.

Beckbury, and Badger formerly described, evidently both belonged to the great Saxon parish of St. Milburg, a condition to this day evidenced by their forming detachments of the diocese of Hereford.

The church of Beckbury, in the deanery of Wenlock and diocese of Hereford, was, in 1291, of less than £4 annual value. There is no mention of an assessment to the *ninth* here. The *Valor* of 1534-5 gives the rectory of Beckburye, as worth £5 6s. 8d. per annum, out of which the prior of Wenlock had his pension of 3s., and 4d. went for synodals.

Early Incumbent.—Master Ralph de Bikebir', parson of the church of Bikebir', 1296.

Linley, near Broseley, is not mentioned in Domesday Book. It appears, however, from a very early period, as a manor, held in *socage*, under Wenlock priory. The architectural remains of Linley Chapel bear evidence of great antiquity.

---

[1] *Forest Rolls*, No. 11, m. 1, 3.

FONT, LINLEY.

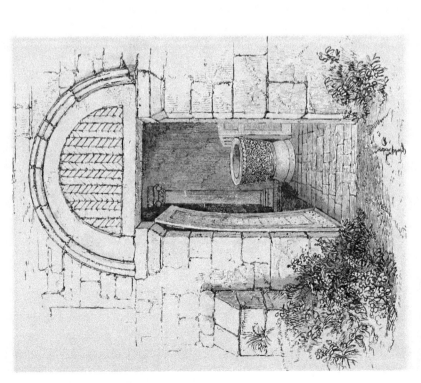

DOOR-WAY, SOUTH SIDE, LINLEY.

Domesday Hundred of Condetret.

Modern Name.	Domesday Name.	Saxon Owner or Owners, T. R. E.	Domesday Tenant in capite.	Domesday Mesne, or next Tenant.	Domesday Sub-Tenant.	Modern Hundred.
Cleobury Mortimer	Claiberie	Eddid	Radulfus de Mortemer			Stottesden.
Mawley	Melela, Lel, and Fech	Tres Teini	Idem			Ibidem.
The Low	Lau	Ecclesia Sancti Petri	Idem	Ricardus		Ibidem.
Cleobury Lodge	Nene	Uluric	Idem	Ricardus		Ibidem.
Neen Savage	Nene	Huni	Idem	Ingelrannus		Ibidem.
Stepple	Steple	Godric	Idem	Goisfridus		Ibidem.
Kinlet	Chinlete	Eddid	Idem	Ricardus		Ibidem.
Higley	Hugelei	Godeva Comitissa	Rogerius Comes	Radulfus de Mortemer		Ibidem.
Walton Savage	Waltone	Edric	Idem	Radulfus de Mortemer	Ingelrannus	Ibidem.
Baveney	Barbingi	Alsi and Fech	Idem	Radulfus de Mortemer	Fech	Ibidem.
Wall Town	Walle	Uluric	Idem	Radulfus de Mortemer	Ricardus	Ibidem.
Catsley	Catescheslei	Edric	Idem	Radulfus de Mortemer	Ulf	Ibidem.
Overton	Ovretone	Edric	Idem	Radulfus de Mortemer	Ingelrannus	Ibidem.
Hopton Wafre	Hoptone	Siuuard	Rogerius de Laci	Widard		Ibidem.
Wheathill	Walthā	Elmund	Rogerius Comes	Rogerius de Laci		Ibidem.
Neen Sollars	Nene	Siuuard	Osbernus filius Ricardi	Siunardus		Overs.
Ingwardine	Ingurdine	Eduin	Rogerius Comes	Willelmus Pantulf		Stottesden.
Farlow	Ferlau		Widard			Woolphy, Herefordshire.
Norton	Nortone	Toret	Rogerius Comes	Rainaldus Vicecomes	Toret	Stottesden.
Detton	Dodintone	Eluuard and Elric	Idem	Rainaldus Vicecomes	Robertus	Ibidem.
Harcott	Havretescote	Elnuard	Idem	Alcher		Ibidem.

Manor probably in Condetret, but whose Hundred is not stated in Domesday.

Stottesden	Stodesdone	Eduinus Comes	Rogerius Comes			Stottesden.

THE above manors that, in William the Conqueror's time, belonged to the Hundred of Condetret, were, during the reign of Henry I., transferred to the then newly-created Hundred of Stottesden. The existing Hundred of Stottesden, therefore, embraces manors which, at *Domesday*, were in Condetret, Patinton, Alnodestreu, and Bascherch Hundreds; none of which now exist. Also two manors anciently in Staffordshire, four in Warwickshire, and a portion of the *Domesday* Hundred of Overs. Farlow in the above list was, at the time of the survey, and still is, in Herefordshire; although surrounded by the Shropshire Hundred of Stottesden.

Stottesden. We must seek in the Saxon Scōð, Scōðer, signifying *a stud of brood horses*, and in ðen *a valley*, or ðún *a hill* or *down*, the etymology of Stottesden. *Domesday* thus describes the manor :—" The same earl [of Shrewsbury] holds Stodesdone. Earl Eduin held it, with vii berewicks. Here ix hides. In demesne are iiii ox-teams, and viii serfs, iii female serfs, xviii villains, v boors, and vi semi-serfs,[1] with xi teams. Here is a mill of 10s. [annual value], and two leagues of wood. In time of King Edward [the manor] was worth £20 [per annum]; now [it is worth] £10.

The church of St. Peter holds the church of this manor, together with ii hides and a half. Here are x villains with ii ox-teams; and there might be ii other teams [employed] here. It is worth 20s. [per annum]."[2] This was one of the unfortunate Earl Edwin's manors, which, shorn of half its value, passed to the demesne of the palatine earl, Roger de Montgomery. Upon the rebellion of Robert de Belèsme, son of the first Norman earl, Stottesden reverted to the Crown, when Henry I., retaining the central manor in demesne, granted away, on various conditions, its berewicks or adjuncts. Reputed as of *ancient demesne*, this central manor of Stottesden came into the hands of Henry II., who gave it to Godfrey de Gamages in 1159.

Godfrey was a scion of that Norman family whose castle and vill of Gamache, from whence they derived their name, situated in the Norman Vexin, gave name to a deanery in the archdiocese of Rouen. The name Gamages figures on the roll of Battle abbey[3] as that of one who contributed by his long sword to place the Conqueror upon the English throne; hence, he to whom Henry II. gave Stottesden, inherited two knight's fees of old feoffment in the Herefordshire barony of de Lacy, the estate in question being the meed of that knightly service his ancestor had rendered at Hastings. From the circumstance that Godfrey received from Henry II. other gifts besides that of Stottesden, it is inferred that he fought against the usurper Stephen; yet, be this as it may, by 1176, Mathew, his son, had succeeded to his estates both in Normandy and England.

As was the case generally with those who held lands on both sides of the channel, the situation of this Anglo-Norman noble now became critical.

---

[1] "*Coliberti.*" These appear to have been serfs partially enfranchised. Like the villains, they were *ascripti glebæ*, they belonged to the land, and required further manumission to make them free.
[2] *Domesday*, fo. 254, a 1.
[3] Duchesne's *List*.

Richard Cœur de Leon ceded to Philip Augustus of France, by the treaty of Issoudun in 1195, the Norman Vexin territory, including the castle of Gamache. It was a mistake on the part of the Anglo-Norman king, who, although a consummate warrior, was a bad politician. Upon the renewal of hostilities in the following year, the castle of Gamache was re-captured, when, as an outpost commanding a debateable frontier, it was immediately strongly fortified. Such was the position in which Mathew de Gamages stood, and such it continued to be, until, in 1203, notwithstanding all the bribes lavished on him by the fratricidal king of England, Matthew, like other Anglo-Norman nobles, preferred holding under the chivalrous French monarch to continuing a vassal of King John's. Stottesden accordingly became forfeit to the Crown: a temporary possession of it was then obtained by Ivo and Hugh Pantulf, but in 1222, this estate was restored to William de Gamages, brother of him who had forfeited it. He who now became lord of Stottesden doubtless fought for the king in that civil war which closed John's career, and distinguished the earlier years of young Henry the Third's reign; for we read that royalty conferred on William de Gamages various favours.

Upon his decease, Henry III., in violation of hereditary rights, recovered Stottesden from Godfrey, son and heir of William, and bestowed it upon his favourite, John de Plessitis, sometime Earl of Warwick. Accordingly, the jurors in 1255, said that the manor of Stottesden "was an escheat of the lord king of the *Land of the Normans*, which Sir John de Plessy holds *in capite* of the king, who is enfeoffed in the same vill by royal charter, and for service of *half a knight's fee*, etc." Upon the death of John de Plessitis, Hugh, his son, paid his relief of 100s. and had livery of this manor, which, in 1270, he gave in frank marriage with Christiana, his infant daughter, to John de Segrave, then 14 years of age; consistently with which the Feodary of March, 1316, gives John de Segrave as lord of Stottesden. It was this John, who, at the head of his London brigade, made the onset against the Royalists at the famous battle of Lewes.

The Church.

Stottesden church appears to have been one of those Saxon foundations which had for its parish a very extensive district. It was given to Shrewsbury abbey by Earl Roger de Montgomery, previously to 1085; hence, as *Domesday* observes, "the church of St. Peter holds the church of this manor, together with two hides and a half"; its glebe, in fact. About 1283, this church became a vicarage, Bishop Swinfield having granted an appropriation of it to the abbot of Shrewsbury; in return for which favour, when Swinfield afterwards visited this part of his diocese, the abbot found forage for 41 horses of his train.

The abbot's rectorial income from Stottesden was valued in 1291 at £26 13s. 4d.; the vicarial portion was £13 6s. 8d.; besides which, the abbot of Wigmore had a portion of 13s. 4d., the rector of Cornley £1, the precentor of Wenlock priory 13s. 4d., and the dean of Brug 6s. 8d. from Stottesden church. In 1341, the assessors of the *ninth* rated the parish at only £15 6s. 8d., because 500 acres lay untilled; there were no sheep or lambs, and the tenants had quitted on account of poverty, etc. The *Valor* of 1534 gives £8 13s. 4d. as the amount of the abbot of Shrewsbury's tithes from Stottesden and Duddlewick. Stottesden vicarage was worth £15 12s. 8d., less 10s. for procurations, and 2s. for synodals.

Early Incumbent.—John Fitz Walter, 1100-35.

Cleobury Mortimer is thus mentioned in Domesday Book:— "The same Radulf [de Mortemer] holds Claiberie [of the king]. Eddid held it [in Saxon times]. Here iiii hides geldable. The land is [enough] for xxiiii ox-teams. In demesne are iiii teams, and xiiii serfs, xx villains, a priest, ii radmans, and viii boors have between them all xx teams. Here is a mill rendering ii horseloads of corn.[1] A wood capable of fattening 500 swine renders 40s. In time of King Edward, the manor was worth £8 [per annum]; afterwards its value was the same. Now it is worth £12."[2]

Eddid, mentioned above, was none other than the noble, intelligent, and modest Saxon beauty, whom Edward the Confessor married. Edith, the lady or queen of England, was daughter of the great Earl Godwin. "As the thorn produces the rose, so Godwin produced Edith," was the saying of the time, even of those who disliked her family. Yet beautiful in mind and in person as Edith was, the Confessor King cared not for her: she dwelt in his palace a wife only in name. And the king spent his days in visions of superstition.

---

[1] *Sumas annonæ.*   [2] *Domesday*, fo. 260, a 1.

STOTTESDEN CHURCH.

FONT, STOTTESDEN.

p. 276.

Whether the circumstance that the unhonoured wife of King Edward is described as having singly held Claiberie during the life-time of her husband indicates the estrangement that existed between them, or whether this and other Shropshire and Herefordshire manors had been given Edith by her father is unknown; yet, *Domesday* proves that after the death of her brother Harold, the last Anglo-Saxon king, Queen Edith was deprived, at least of Claiberie, if not of all her other estates.

We infer from *Domesday* that the Conqueror had bestowed Claiberie and its adjuncts on William Fitz Osborn, Earl of Hereford; and that, in turn, he enfeoffed Turstin de Wigmore therein.[1] Now Fitz Osborn was slain in Flanders, on February 20th, 1071; and as Edith died at Winchester on December 14th, 1074, it is clear that she had been bereft of Claiberie. The Saxon ex-lady of England died a sad-hearted woman, when, with much funereal pomp, King William assigned her a resting-place by the side of Edward the Confessor in Westminster Abbey.

Upon the forfeiture, in 1074, of Earl Roger de Britolio, Fitz Osborn's successor, Mortemer, the conqueror of Edric the forester, obtained Cleobury, Wigmore, and other estates that had formerly been Fitz Osborn's, from the king, when Turstin the mesne-tenant having been removed, Mortemer made Cleobury his headquarters.

BARONY OF MORTIMER.

RALPH DE MORTEMER, to whom William I. gave the manor of Cleobury, was son of Roger de Mortemer, of Castle Mortemer, in the Pays de Caux, who was cousin in the second degree of affinity to Robert the Devil, father of William the Conqueror. Ralph's brother Hue, Wace tells us, rendered an important service at Hastings. "The English fell back upon a rising ground, and the Normans followed them across the valley, attacking them on foot and horseback. Then Hue de Mortemer, with the Sires d'Anviler, D'Onebac, and Saint-Cler, rode up and charged, overthrowing many."[2] The *Domesday* baron succeeded to his father's estates in Normandy, and, as stated, upon the forfeiture of Earl Roger de Britolio, and his nearly simultaneous reduction of Sylvaticus, Ralph de Mortemer acquired an extensive fief in Shropshire and Herefordshire, which he held *in capite* of the king. Ralph was related to Earl Roger de Montgomery, much in the same way as

---

[1] *See* MAWLEY, p. 282. [2] WACE'S "*Roman de Rou*," by Taylor, p. 239.

he was to the king: all three descended from Gunnora, wife of Richard I., count of the Normans, and her two sisters. Mortemer appears to have held the office of seneschal to the Norman earls, yet he shared neither in the rebellion nor subsequent forfeiture of Roger de Belèsme. To the *Domesday* baron succeeded—

HUGH DE MORTEMER, his son, who, upon the accession of Henry II., fortified against that king Bridgnorth Castle, which Stephen had permitted him to hold, probably on account of his traditional office of seneschal over the royal demesnes of Shropshire. As a general rule, the appointments of the usurper were reversed by Henry II., hence the quarrel between Mortemer and the king. We have seen how Henry II. destroyed Cleobury castle, and reduced his turbulent vassal.[1] Great consideration, however, appears to have been shown to De Mortemer, who in regard to his Shropshire barony, had special immunities from scutages and aids allowed; in this respect, Mortemer's standing alone among the Shropshire baronies. Hugh founded Wigmore abbey, and, dying in 1181, was succeeded by—

ROGER DE MORTIMER, his son, who having shortly before waylaid and murdered Cadwallan, a prince of South Wales, as, under the king's guarantee of safe-conduct, he was returning from court, he suffered a two years' forfeiture and imprisonment for the offence. About 1195, this baron was signally defeated by Rees, prince of South Wales, under the walls of Radnor castle. Besides acquisitions in Wales, Mortimer held estates in no less than thirteen English counties, and the vast hereditary fief in Normandy of St. Victor-en-Caux. Uniformly adhering to King John in his contest with the King of France, on the revolution that ensued, Roger lost his Norman barony. On the other side, his English estates were augmented; for, owing to the disqualification of the lord of Ferrières, her brother, consequent on his siding with Philip Augustus, Isabel, his wife, acquired the Gloucestershire manors of Lechlade and Longborough, and Oakham, Rutlandshire.

In May, 1213, Roger de Mortimer was one of the twelve barons who stood sponsors for the good faith of King John, when, succumbing to the pope, he solicited the return of Archbishop Langton to England. About the same time, Mortimer, with his wife, proffered for the custody and lands of William de Beauchamp of Elmley, a fine, the enormous amount of which may be inferred

---

[1] Page 15.

from the circumstance, that, in June 1214, £1011 of it still remained unpaid. To Roger succeeded—

HUGH DE MORTIMER II., who, at the time of his father's death, was serving in Poitou, his wife, a daughter of the ill-fated Braose, remaining, meanwhile, the victim of John Plantagenet's cruelty. The king returned from Poitou in October, 1214, when, in deference to the prayer of the legate, he ordered the lady to be liberated. Notwithstanding the treatment which his wife had experienced at the hands of John, Hugh de Mortimer steadfastly adhered to that king throughout his troubles; and Hugh's attestation to John's last charter, which passed at Lincoln on Sept. 28, 1216, but three short weeks before he was no more, proves his fidelity to the king, even in his extreme. In return for his adhering to the cause of his father, young Henry III., by a patent dated Jan. 27, 1217, gave Hugh de Mortimer the lands of all the king's enemies which were of Mortimer's fee; in other words, an authority to confiscate all the estates of his anti-royalist tenants.

The first scutage of King Henry III. was about to be collected in October, 1217, when the sheriffs of seventeen counties were ordered to assist Hugh de Mortimer in enforcing payment on his tenants, the sheriffs of nine counties at the same time receiving orders to assist his wife to collect of her tenants. Hugh served in person at the siege of Biham, and on May 31, 1223, the king gave him 20 merks towards strengthening Wigmore castle. In 1226, Henry III. granted Hugh the privilege of holding an annual fair in his manor of Cleybiry, to last for three days, viz., September 13, 14, and 15.

In the following year, Hugh died, leaving no issue, when Cleobury, and the numerous estates of the deceased baron, devolved upon his brother—

RALPH DE MORTIMER II. Heavy liabilities, however, attached to Mortimer's barony, the late noble, at the time of his decease, owing to the king a destrier, two hawks, and no less than £1015 2s. 4d., the larger half of which sum had been contracted fourteen years before, and of the balance of the debt, not a farthing had the deceased baron paid to the king during thirteen years. It was a characteristic of the haughty Mortimers to be indifferent to their pecuniary obligations with the crown. He who now became lord of Cleobury, married Gladuse Duy, daughter of Llewellyn the Great, by Joan, the illegitimate daughter of King John, and by her Ralph de Mortimer acquired lands; and on the failure, at a subsequent period, of all other legitimate descendants of Llewellyn the Great, the Principality of North Wales was said to be in the representatives of Gladuse Duy. To Ralph succeeded—

ROGER DE MORTIMER II., who, at the time of his father's decease, was only seventeen years of age. He married the eldest daughter and co-heir of William de Braose, and she, bringing him a third of the Honour of Braose of Brecknock, and also a share in the Honour of the Earls Marshal, Baron Mortimer thus acquired large estates in England, Wales, and Ireland. On June 11, 1259, Mortimer was appointed a commissioner to demand satisfaction from Llewellyn ap Griffyth for breaches of truce, with power to prolong the truce and treat of peace, and a fortnight afterwards the commissioners concluded a year's truce at Montgomery. At that time the Marches were in a fearfully disturbed state. On July 17, 1260, the Welsh took Builth castle, which Mortimer had custody of on behalf of Prince Edward, and complaining to the Anglo-Norman king, in June 1262, of Mortimer's infraction of the truce, the enraged Llewellyn besieged and took his enemies' castles of Knoklas and Keuenches, when ensued a regular Welsh war.

Upon the rupture between the Crown and the Barons, with other warlike lords-marchers, Roger Mortimer declared in favour of the royal cause, and, in December, 1263, with Prince Edward, he was on the king's side against the confederate lords, when both parties swore to defer to the arbitration of the king of France. Roger fought by the side of Henry III. when the barons were defeated at Northampton, and, according to some,[1] was present at Lewes when the royalists met with that disastrous reverse which ended in King Henry III. and Prince Edward both being captured. Escaping from the battle-field, Roger, with other western barons, then stirred up war in the Marches against Llewellyn and Simon Montfort; but the result is the subject of discordant accounts.

It was Roger de Mortimer who, acting in concert with Roger de Clifford, contrived to effect the escape of Prince Edward from Hereford castle. It was managed in this way: on May 30, 1265, the prince obtained permission from his guards to take exercise in a field outside the city, and to amuse himself with trying the speed of their horses. At length, after tiring out all the others,

---

[1] MATTHEW OF WESTMINSTER, vol. ii. p. 419, Bohn's Ed.

he mounted a fresh good steed, and giving him the spur, Prince Edward bade farewell to his guards. Accompanied by two knights and four esquires, his personal attendants, who had been made acquainted with his design, the prince, crossing the river Wear, directed his course to Mortimer's castle of Wigmore. Recovering from their surprise, his guards pursued; but, on seeing the banners of Mortimer and De Clifford, who, by preconcerted appointment, now appeared, they saw that they had been out-manœuvred, and returned to Hereford. Within ten weeks after, the battle of Evesham was fought, Simon Montfort, the leader of the rebels, was slain and the king restored to his prerogative. After that decisive victory, no reward was too great for Mortimer, whose steady loyalty and conspicuous valour had largely contributed to the grand result. Among other acknowledgments of his services, the baron obtained from the king a charter by which Cleobury and Chelmarsh henceforth were to constitute a single manor, it, with its members, to remain independent of all suits to county or hundred. Taking advantage of a vaguely worded charter, the baron then proceeded to annex some twenty manors to the new franchise, and, setting up his central court at Cleobury, the royal Hundred of Stottesden lost the suit of many manors. This Roger was one of the trustees appointed by Prince Edward to take charge of his estates whilst he fought in Palestine. To Roger succeeded—

EDMUND DE MORTIMER, his son, who, doing homage, had livery of his lands, on November 24, 1282. It was he who commanded the detachment when Llewellyn fell at Builth. The unfortunate Welsh prince's head was cut off and carried to London, where, in mockery crowned with ivy, and fixed to a stake, his brutal enemies erected it upon the Tower of London. Edmund de Mortimer was sued under writs of *quo warranto* for the various franchises arrogated by his father. The king's writ of *Diem clausit extremum*, upon the decease of this baron, is dated Stirling, July 25, 1304, whither, doubtless, Mortimer had followed his sovereign, King Edward I., in his ambitious scheme against the liberties of Scotland.

ROGER DE MORTIMER III., son and heir of the deceased, now became lord of Cleobury, whose great power on the border suggested his elevation to the earldom of March. His mad career ended on a scaffold. The lineal representatives of the haughty and powerful barons Mortimer in the seventh generation were Edward IV. and Richard III., two sceptred kings.

Owing to the exclusive nature of Mortimer's seigneury, little is known concerning the undertenants of Cleobury.

CLEOBURY MORTIMER CHURCH.

The church of Cleobury, perhaps originally founded by Queen Edith, was, in 1179, given by Hugh de Mortimer to that abbey of Wigmore he founded. Accordingly, Pope Nicholas' Taxation in 1291, represents the church of Clebury Mortymer, in the deanery of Burford, as belonging to the abbot of Wygmore, and of the annual value of £10: the vicar's portion being less than £4. In 1341, the parish was taxed £6 13s. 4d. to the *ninth*. In 1534-5, the vicar of Clyberye Mortymer's income was £12 18s. 6d., less 7s. 8d. for procurations and synodals. The abbot of Wigmore's cotemporary return gives £16 16s. as his rectorial income.

CHANCEL-ARCH, CLEOBURY MORTIMER.

Early Incumbent.—John Scheremon, priest, 1321.

The chantry of St. Nicholas in this church was founded by Roger de Mortimer previously to 1360.

𝔐𝔞𝔴𝔩𝔢𝔶. By way of supplement to its description of Cleobury, *Domesday* adds:—"The same Ralph [de Mortemer] holds Melela [a manor] of i hide, and Lel of i virgate, and Fech of i virgate of land. These iii manors were geldable; iii thanes held them [in Saxon times], and were free men. When Turstin de

Wigemore received them from Earl William, he joined them to the superior manor of Cleberie, and both then and now they were and are valued therein."[1] By Melela, is undoubtedly meant Mawley, south-east of Cleobury.

Earl's Ditton. After describing these small estates, *Domesday* proceeds:—"In Ovret Hundred is i hide, Dodentone, which itself also is valued in the same," namely in Cleobury. Unquestionably the *Domesday* Dodentone is represented by Earl's Ditton, and the *Doddington liberty* of Cleobury Mortimer. Ditton is simply a contraction for Dodentone, the prefix, "Earl's" attached, indicating the former seigneury of the Mortimers, Earls of March.

The Low. The Anglo-Saxon *hlaw, lowe,* signifies a tumulus, and generally speaking where the syllable *low* forms either singly or in combination the name of a place, we may expect to hear of a tumulus or place of burial. *Domesday* says:—"The same Ralph holds Lau, and Richard [holds it] of him. The church of St. Peter held it. Here i hide geldable. The land is for ii ox-teams. In demesne is one team, and ii villains and i boor with i team. [In Edward the Confessor's time] it was worth 5s.; now 10s. He [Richard] found it waste."[2] The church of St. Peter alluded to above, was that Saxon parish church, in the eastern suburb of Shrewsbury, which, under the auspices of the first Norman earl, expanded into the Benedictine abbey of St. Peter and St. Paul. As Mortemer took no interest in Shrewsbury Abbey, he transmitted his seigneury over the Low to his descendants, under whom, a family deriving their name from the place, held the estate for upwards of two centuries.

Neen is thus noticed in *Domesday*:—"The same Ralph holds Nene, and Richard [holds] of him. Uluric held it and was a free man. Here i hide and a half geldable. The land is [capable of employing] iii ox-teams and a half. Here i serf and i villain, with half a team. In King Edward's time, the manor was worth 15s. [per annum]; afterwards it was worth 3s.; now it is similarly

---

[1] *Domesday*, fo. 260, a 1. [2] Ibidem, fo. 260, a 2.

worth 3s."[1] The place thus described, in the opinion of one to whose judgment we defer,[2] is now represented by Cleobury Lodge, in the west foreign division of Cleobury Mortimer, it having been annexed by Mortimer to his capital manor of Cleobury.

Neen Savage. The Celtic *nene* signifies a river, and the word *nan* a brook, is said to be a remnant of a primitive language. Certain it is, that two of the Shropshire Neens are intersected by a stream.[3] Neen Savage is the subject of the following entry in Domesday Book :—" The same Ralph holds Nene, and Ingelrann [holds] of him. Huni held it [in Saxon times], and was free. Here iiii hides geldable. The [arable] land is [enough] for v ox-teams. In demesne is one team, and iiii serfs, iii villains, and iii boors, with one team. Here is a mill of 2s. [annual value]."[1] Neen and Neen Savage were held by two several feoffees of Ralph de Mortemer, who himself held of the king. The family of Le Savage descended from the *Domesday* Ingelrann, hence the latter place acquired the name Neen Savage, its present title.

NEEN SAVAGE CHURCH.

This was also bestowed upon Wigmore Abbey by Hugh de Mortemer, and the abbot's rectorial income from it in 1291 amounted to £6 13s. 4d.; the vicar's portion being under £4. In 1341, the parish was assessed only £4 10s. to the *ninth*, because there had been a murrain among the sheep, there were no lambs or wool in it; eight acres lay untilled, etc. The *Valor* of 1534-5 represents Nyende Savage vicarage as worth £5 17s. 6d., less 13s. 4d. to the abbot of Wigmore, and 7s. 8d. for procurations and synodals.

Early Incumbent.—John de Stepleton, 1317.

Stepple, formerly a manor in itself, is now a member of Neen Savage. It is noticed in the Conqueror's record, thus:—" The same Radulf holds Steple, and Goisfrid holds it of him. Godric held it, and was free. Here i hide and a half geldable. The land is for iiii ox-teams. In demesne is i team, and iii serfs and vi

---

[1] *Domesday*, fo. 260, a 2. [2] BLAKEWAY. [3] The river Rea.

boors with i team. In time of King Edward, the manor was worth 12s.; afterwards and now it was and is worth 7s." [1]

Kinlet. *Cyne* in Saxon signifies royal, and Læð a *lathe* or district; hence the etymology of Kinlet, which formerly belonged to Eddid, namely Edith, the Lady, Edward the Confessor's queen. "The same Radulf," says *Domesday*, "holds Chinlete and Richard [holds] of him. Eddid held it. Here iiii hides. There is land for viii ox-teams. In demesne are ii teams; and vi serfs, viii villains, ii radmans, vi boors, and one frenchman, with vi teams. In King Edward's time, the manor was worth 60s. [annually]; afterwards 30s.; now 40s." [2] Mortemer acquired this manor probably in the same way as he had done Cleobury.

The successors of Richard the *Domesday* tenant, were the Bromptons, descending from a male ancestor cotemporary with, yet quite distinct from, Richard. Brian de Brompton, the last of the elder male line of his house, was dead on December 28th, 1294, as on that day a writ of *Diem clausit extremum* was issued by Edward I., when the jurors who reported the Shropshire tenures of the deceased said, that Brian had held twenty acres of the king *in capite* in Kinlet park, by service of a twentieth-part of a knight's fee, and that he had done homage to the king for the said tenure, which was worth 6s. *per annum*.[3] Glancing at the wide-spreading domains of the Bromptons, it seems extraordinary that a single tenure *in capite* of twenty acres by knight's service, should have entitled the Crown to control the whole; yet, such was the fact; and, his having held this insignificant slip of land of the Crown, gave the king a right to dispose of the two daughters of Brian de Brompton in marriage. Accordingly, Edward I. gave Margaret de Brompton, then not three years of age, to "his beloved clerk," Malcolm de Harley, for his nephew Robert. Hence it came that, in the beginning of the present century, Brompton Bryan was in the hands of Edward Harley, Earl of Oxford and Mortimer, as the lineal descendant of Robert de Harley and Margaret de Brompton.

Kinlet Church.

From the French chronicle of Wigmore, we learn that Kinlet church was given by John de Brompton to that abbey (1179); the seigneural lord concurring. Bishop Swinfield visited Kinlet

---

[1] *Domesday*, fo. 260. a 2.   [2] Ibidem.   [3] *Inquisitions*, 23 Edw. I., No. 136.

in 1290, staying there from Sunday, April 16th, until the following Tuesday. His celebrated letter to Pope Nicholas IV., alleging the miracles performed at the tomb of his predecessor Cantilupe, and soliciting the canonization of that prelate, was dated at Kinlet. As rector of Kinlet, the abbot of Wigmore found corn and fuel for baking bread to Swinfield's suite, besides forage for the thirty-six horses of his train.

The *Taxation* of 1291 gives £10 as the value of the rectory of Kynleth; the vicar's portion being under £4. In 1341, the parish was assessed only £5 10s. for the *ninth* of its wheat, wool, and lamb, because the abbot had land here, etc. The *Valor* of 1534-5 gives the vicar of Kynlett's preferment as £8 10s., less 7s. 8d. for procurations and synodals.

Early Incumbent.—William Philippe, 1288.

Higley. Besides the seven manors just described, which he held *in capite* of the Crown, Ralph de Mortemer held six others in Condetret Hundred under Roger de Montgomery, the Norman Earl of Shrewsbury. We proceed now to notice these latter places, in the order in which they are entered in Domesday Book, premising, however, that there is little connected with their early history of a nature to interest the reader.

According to the Conqueror's record:—"The same Radulf holds Hugelci [or, as it is now called, Higley]. The Countess Godeva held it [in Saxon times]. Here iii hides geldable. In demesne there is one ox-team and a half; and vi villains, vi boors, and one radman have two teams and a half, and yet there might be ii more teams [employed here]. There is a wood which will fatten xxxvi swine. In time of King Edward, the manor was worth 15s. [per annum]; afterwards 3s. Now 18s."[1] In 1255, Robert de Lacy was lord of Hugele, holding it of Roger de Mortimer, by service of doing ward for one knight's fee at Wigmore castle in time of war for forty days.[2]

The Church.

Before 1148, Hugh de Mortimer's feoffee, the lord of Higley, at the request of Mortimer, then in one of his fits of piety, at a great assembly at Leominster, presided over by Bishop Robert de Betun, gave the church of Huggcley to certain Augustine canons

---

[1] *Domesday*, fo. 257 a 1.   [2] *Rot. Hundred*, ii. 81.

KINLET CHURCH.

settled at Shobdon, the germ of Wigmore Abbey. Hence, in 1291, the church of Hugleye, in the deanery of Stottesden, is described as the abbot of Wigmore's, and of £2 13s. 4d. annual value. In 1341, the parish was taxed only 22s. to the *ninth*, because the greater part of it was uncultivated. In 1534-5, the vicar of Higley's preferment was worth £7, less 1s. for synodals, and a pension of £1 to the abbot.

Early Incumbent.—Nicholas de Oxon, instituted to *Hugefeld* 15th March, 1279.

Walton Savage, in ancient times, was a manor distinct in itself. *Domesday* says:—"The same Radulf holds Waltone, and Ingelrann holds of him. Edric held it, and was a free man. Here half a hide geldable. In demesne is i ox-team, iiii serfs, and vi boors. [The manor formerly] was worth 10s. Now 8s. He [Radulf] found it waste."[1] In at least seven manors, one of which was the Hampshire manor of Anne, afterwards called Anne Savage, Mortemer's tenant, Ingelrann, was succeeded by Le Savage, which leads to the inference that Ingelrann was ancestor of the Le Savages. It is not a little singular, however, that although four of these manors, namely, Overton, Walton Savage, Eudon George, and Rudge, belonged, in Saxon times, to Edric the Savage; yet, between him and the family who afterwards held them, there was no blood relationship. By 1255, the Le Savages' interest in this manor had been transferred to Wigmore Abbey, hence the return of the Stottesden jurors, who said, that "the abbot of Wygemore is lord of Walton Savage." The minister's accounts of 1539-40 enter a total of £5 12s. 8d. as the interest of the late monastery in Walton.

Baveney is noticed in *Domesday* thus:—"The same Radulf holds Barbingi, and Fech [holds it] of him. Alsi and Fech held it [in Saxon times] for ii manors. Here half a hide. One virgate of these two [virgates comprised in half a hide] lay in Claiberie. Here now ii radmans and ii boors have i ox-team. [The manor formerly] was worth 10s. Now 6s."[1] Baveney was and still is in the parish of Neen Savage.

---

[1] *Domesday*, fo. 257, a 1.

Wall Town. The name of this place is suggestive of a Roman origin; and Blakeway, following up the idea, describes a Roman encampment at Wall Town. Indications of this encampment are still to be traced. It was an exact square, each side of which measured 400 feet. Entering at the Prætorian, and passing out at the Decuman gate, the old road from Bridgnorth to Cleobury passed right through the centre of it.

Wall Town is thus alluded to in King William's record:—"The same Radulf holds Walle, and Richard holds of him. Uluric held it. Here i hide geldable. The land is [sufficient] for ii oxteams. Here is one [team] with ii neat-herds. Its former value was 6s. [annually]. Now it is worth 8s."[1]

Catsley. "The same Radulf holds Catescheslei, and Ulf [holds] of him. Edric held it. Here half a hide. In demesne is i ox-team, and ii neat-herds, one villain, and ii boors with i team. [In time of King Edward] the manor was worth 6s. 6d. Now 8s."[1] Ulf, the Saxon, who held this manor of Mortemer previously to *Domesday*, had been lord of Isombridge, North Shropshire, from whence he had been ousted by the Norman seigneur, and placed at Catsley. In his new abode, however, the unfortunate Saxon was not suffered to remain long, he being compelled to make way for the Lingen's descendants of the Norman, Turstin de Wigmore. Although manorially independent, Catsley was and still is in Kinlet parish.

Overton. Of it, *Domesday* says, that:—"The same Radulf holds Ovretone, and Ingelrann [holds it] of him. Edric held it. Here ii hides. In demesne is one ox-team, and ii neat-herds, iii villains, and ii boors, with one team. It was and is worth 20s."[1] Overton is now a township in Stottesden parish.

Bewdley, formerly Wyre Forest, was another of those great primæval woody regions, which anciently covered mile upon mile of British soil. The Romans had a station in this forest that they called Wyre-ceastre, hence Worcestershire and Worcester. But civilization intersected and cut up this wilderness, until at length, in the Conqueror's time, the portion of it which occupied the south-

---

[1] *Domesday*, fo. 257, a 1.

eastern angle of Shropshire constituted its larger half. *Domesday* is silent respecting these forests. There is a strong probability, however, that, within easy distance as it was of Cleobury and Kinlet, manors once belonging to the Saxon crown, as appurtenant to them, the Shropshire portion of Wyre Forest passed, with these manors to William Fitz-Osborn, Earl of Hereford.

In process of time, vills sprang up in Wyre Forest, one of which, Earnwood, namely, Eagle-wood, bears in its very name a conviction that the spot was so called before it was known as a habitation of man. Originally a forest residence of the Mortimers, Earnwood is now a manor in the parish of Kinlet.

Hopton Wafre,

in 1086, belonged to the Norman Roger de Laci. He held it of the king. *Domesday* says:—"The same Roger holds Hoptone, and Widard [holds it] of him. Siuuard, a free man, held it [in Saxon times]. Here iii hides geldable. The land is [capable of employing] iiii ox-teams. In demesne there is one [team], and one serf, one radman, ii villains, and iii boors, with i team. In time of King Edward, the manor was worth 10s.; afterwards 12s. Now 9s. 2d."[1] Four out of the five Shropshire manors which Roger de Laci held immediately of the crown, had formerly belonged to Siuuard. Siward probably descended from a viking rover; the name, at least, is Anglo-Danish. Of Widard, the *Domesday* tenant here, nothing is known. Like Cleobury North, Hoptone passed from the fief of Lacy to that of Bernard de Newmarch, the conqueror of Brecknockshire, when the Le Wafres held both manors immediately under the lords of Brecknock. Hence this place acquired its name, Hopton Wafre.

Church of Hopton Wafre.

In 1236, the tithes of this belonged to Brecknock Priory; before 1278 the advowson belonged to the abbot of Wigmore.

In 1291, described as in the deanery of Burford, the annual value of this church was £4 2s. 6d., besides a portion of 6s. 8d. to the prior of Brecon, and a similar pension to the abbot of Wigmore. In 1341, the parish was assessed £1 6s. 8d. only to the *ninth*, the reasons being diminution of sheep stock, and non-cultivation of

---

[1] *Domesday*, fo. 260, b 1.

two carucates from poverty of tenants, etc. In 1534-5, this rectory was valued at £5 14s. 8d., less the pensions of the abbot and prior, and 6d. for synodals.

Early Incumbent.—William de Bray, 1279.

Wheathill. The following entry in Domesday Book is conjectured to refer to Wheathill:—"The same Roger [de Laci] holds of the earl, Waltha. Elmund held it. Here iii hides. In demesne are ii ox-teams, and x serfs, and iiii villains, with a provost, have ii teams. In time of King Edward, the manor was worth 40s. [per annum]. Now it is worth 60s., besides a rent of one sparrow-hawk."[1] Scribes were as prone to err in the 11th century as they are in the 19th, otherwise one might be inclined to doubt whether the *Domesday* Waltha really meant Wheathill, so great is the change. Yet the evidence is pretty clear on the point. It was the only manor in Condetret Hundred which Roger de Laci held of the Norman earl.

At the inquest on Stottesden Hundred, held in November, 1274, the Jurors reported how that John de la Watere, constable of Corfham, had extorted half a merk (a considerable sum) from Roger le Burger, of Wethul, for taking a bundle of thorns from the woods of the lord of Corfham; and a similar sum from Richard Fitz-Agnes, of Wethul, for taking one hazel rod from the same.

Wheathill Church.

This, a dependency of Stottesden Church, in 1291, was valued at £5 per annum. In 1341, the parish was assessed at the unusually low rate of 25s., because four virgates lay fallow, etc. The *Valor* of 1534-5 gives this rectory as worth £7 6s. 6d., less 1s. for synodals.

Early Incumbent.—Reginald, son of Reginald Fitz-Stephen, of Ludlow, 1284. A patent of King Edward III., on July 6th, 1342, appoints special Justices to inquire "what malefactors seized John Hakette, late parson of Whethull, by night, at Whethull, and took him to Lodelowe, and feloniously drowned him in the water called Temede (the Team)."

---

[1] *Domesday*, fo. 256, b 2.

SOUTH DOOR, WHEATHILL.

Neen Sollars is thus described in *Domesday*:—" The same Osbern holds Nene, and Siuuard [holds it] of him. The same Siuuard held it [in Saxon times] and was a free man. This manor was never hidaged, nor ever paid geld. The land is [capable of employing] v ox-teams. In demesne is one team and x serfs. There is a mill which renders a bushel of corn. In time of King Edward, the manor was worth 40s. [annually]. Now it is worth 18s."[1] This manor was the only one Osbern Fitz-Richard, lord of Richard's castle, held in Condetret Hundred, and he held it of the king. Afterwards Neen was annexed to Overs Hundred, in which Osbern exercised a paramount interest.

Siward, the Anglo-Dane alluded to above, in the time of Edward the Confessor, held largely in Shropshire, partly under the church of Worcester. He has been mentioned in connection with Hopton Wafre. Before 1185, Siward's interest in this manor had passed to Baldwin le Poer, upon whose decease the lord of Richard's Castle, " Hugh, son of Hugh de Say, grants to Roger de Solers, Neen, which Osbern Fitz-Hugh, his uncle, did give to the childe Baldwine." De Solariis, therefore, became mesne lord of this manor, holding it under the barons of Richard's castle: hence its title, Neen Sollars.

The Church.

Pope Nicholas' Taxation represents the church of Nene Solers, in the deanery of Burford, as worth £8 per annum, besides a portion of 3s. which the abbot of Wigmore had therein. The parish was taxed only £5 to the *ninth*, in 1341, because three carucates lay fallow, on account of poverty of tenants, etc. In 1534-5, Nyende Solas and Milson constituted one rectory, worth £13 10s. 5d., less 7s. 2d. for procurations and synodals.

Early Incumbent—Richard le Fort, 1314. Patron, Sir Roger de Mortimer, lord of Wigmore.

Milson, as connected with Nene, in Condetret Hundred, is thus described in *Domesday*:—" To this manor there is adjacent one berewick, Mulstone. In Ovret Hundred. Here three and a half hides geldable. The land is for vi ox-teams. Here iii radmans and iii villains have iii teams. In time of King Edward, it was

---

[1] *Domesday*, fo. 260, a 1.

worth 14s. Now 10s. He [Osbern Fitz-Richard] found it waste." When Neen became annexed to Overs Hundred, the anomaly of a manor being in one Hundred whilst its berewick remained in another, was done away with, and to this day Neen Sollars and Milson continue in Overs Hundred. Their former manorial connection has, however, vanished.

MILSON CHURCH.

From certain architectural features of this small church, we judge it to be ancient. Subject to Neen Sollars, it is still annexed to that rectory.

Ingwardine. It is said, in the Conqueror's record, that:— "The same W [Willm. Pantulf] holds Ingurdine. Eduin held it [in Saxon times] and was a free man. Here i virgate of land geldable. There is land for half an ox-team. It [namely, the half-team] is in demesne, with one serf. [The manor] was and is worth 5s."¹ Inʒ, in Saxon, signifies meadow.

Farlow. "In Condetret Hundred," says King William's record, "Widard has one manor, Ferlau, of i hide and iii virgates of land. It lies in Leominstre, the king's manor in Herefordshire, and there it is valued. He [Widard] holds it of the king;"² a statement, the accuracy of which is proved by referring to that portion of *Domesday* which treats of the great manor of Leofminstre. *Fernelau* is there spoken of, and one *Vitard* is mentioned as paying 3s. per annum to the central manor.

Norton, in Condetret Hundred, belonged to Rainald, the sheriff. We read in *Domesday*, that:— "The same Rainald holds Nortone [of the earl] and Toret [holds it] of him. He [Toret] held it freely in time of King Edward. Here ii hides geldable. In demesne is one ox-team; and vi serfs and v villains with ii teams, and other two teams might be here besides. In King Edward's time, the manor was worth 20s. [per annum]. Now

---

¹ *Domesday*, fo. 257, b 1.   ² Ibidem, fo. 259, b 2.

15s."¹ The Saxon Toret, who held this manor both before and after the Conquest, did not transmit it to his descendants, which is nothing wonderful, since it was Norman policy to remove even the most favoured Saxons from their ancient possessions, transferring them elsewhere. It is supposed that Rainald removed Toret from Norton, and annexed the *vill* to Aston Botterel. Hence, to this day Norton remains parochially and manorially a member of Aston Botterell.

Detton. Of it, *Domesday* says:—" The same Rainald holds Dodintone, and Robert holds it of him. Eluuard and Elric held it for two manors, and were free. Here ii hides geldable. In demesne are ii ox-teams and vii serfs, one villain, iiii boors, and one radman, with i team only. In time of King Edward, the manor was worth 24s. Now 15s. He [Rainald] found it waste."¹ Concerning the early history of this manor, now represented by Detton Hall, in the parish of Neen Savage, little is known.

Harcott. Of it, *Domesday* says:—"Alcher holds of the Earl, Havretescote. Eluuard held it [in Saxon times] and was a free man. Here i hide geldable. The land is for v ox-teams. In demesne there is i team, and iii serfs and vi boors with iiii teams. [In King Edward's time] it was worth 7s. [per annum], and afterwards 5s. Now 12s."² Upon the forfeiture of the Norman earls, this tenure under them it was that made the Fitz-Aer's descendants from Alcher tenants *in capite* of the crown, the service attached being to find " one serving foot-soldier, with a bow and arrows, to attend the king's army in Wales." Parochially Harcot is a member of Stottesden.

---

¹ *Domesday*, fo.255, b 1.   ² Ibidem, fo.259, b 2.

Domesday Hundred of Ovre.

Modern Name.	Domesday Name.	Saxon Owner or Owners, T. R. E.	Domesday Tenant in capite.	Domesday Mesne, or next Tenant.	Domesday Sub-Tenant	Modern Hundred.
Burford	Bureford	Ricardus pater Osberni	Osbernus filius Ricardi.			Overs.
Milson*	Mulstone	Siuuardus	...... Idem			Ibidem.
? ?	Tedenesolle	Sauuardus	...... Idem			Ibidem.
Corley	Cornelle	Siuuardus	Radulfus de Mortemer			Stottesden.
Earls Ditton†	Dodentone		...... Idem			Ibidem.
Cainham	Caiham	Morcar Comes	Rogerius Comes	Radulfus de Mortemer	Veci, Walterius	Ibidem.
Bitterley	Buterlie	Goduinus	...... Idem	Rogerius de Laci		Overs.
Henley	Haneleu	Elmundus	...... Idem	Rainaldus Vicecomes.	Rogerius	Ibidem.
Lower Ledwich		Ecclesia Sanctæ Mariæ	Ecclesia Sanctæ Mariæ			Munslow.
Silvington		Ecclesia Sancti Remigii	Ecclesia Sancti Remigii			Overs.

OVERS and Condover are the only two Shropshire Hundreds which retain their *Domesday* appellations, the boundaries of the former remaining to this day much the same as they were in the time of the Conqueror. This was owing to the circumstance that the lords of Richard's Castle had the chief manorial interest here, as well as the soke or hundredal jurisdiction.

In 1066, Richard Fitz Scrobi, one of those Normans whom the weakly Confessor King had suffered to batten on the vitals of England, and who repaid the generosity of the English by secretly intriguing for their destruction, was lord of Ovre Hundred; his eventual successors in the seigneury being the Mortimers, barons of Burford and Richard's Castle.

Burford, deriving from the Saxon Buph *a town*, and Foŋb *a ford*, is thus described in *Domesday* :—" Osbern Fitz Richard holds Bureford of the king. Richard, his father, held it [in Saxon times]. Here vi hides and a half geldable. The [arable] land is [capable of employing] xxix ox-teams. Here Osbern has ii mills, rendering xii quarters of corn; and here are vi serfs, xii villains, iii radmans, xxiv boors, vii coliberti, and a church with two priests. Among them all, they have xxiii ox-teams. Here is a wood that will fatten 100 swine, and therein is a haye. In time of King

---

* Described, page 291. † Described, page 283.

Edward the [annual] value [of the manor] was 106s.; now [it is] £4."[1] Burford was the *caput* of Osbern Fitz-Richard's Shropshire.

BARONY OF BURFORD AND RICHARD'S CASTLE.—The father of Osbern Fitz Richard who, according to *Domesday*, held Burford of the king, was the Richard Scrob, alias Richard Fitz Scrobi, just alluded to. Upon the rupture between the Normandised Court of Edward the Confessor and Earl Godwin in 1052, when the potent Saxon, triumphing over his enemies, a decree of banishment was pronounced against the foreigners, Fitz Scrobi was one of the few Norman favourites of the king suffered to remain in England. Another foreigner permitted to remain was Robert the Deacon, whose daughter Fitz Scrobi had married. The meek Anglo-Saxon monarch had been extremely kind to these aliens, Fitz Scrobi, according to *Domesday*, having held in Saxon times four manors in Worcestershire and Burford in Shropshire; besides an interest he had in Herefordshire, in which county, at the time of the survey, Osbern Fitz Richard, Scrobi's son, was seized of no less than sixteen manors, the gift to him probably of his father. Upon the invasion of England by the Normans in 1066, Scrobi, or Scrupe as he is called in one part of *Domesday*, ungenerously lent his influence to crush the liberties of that people upon whose bounty he had for so long a time existed; he, with the Norman garrison of Hereford, making frequent inroads upon the lands of Edric the forester, who still bravely held out in the west. Fitz Scrobi's efforts were not successful; and we learn that, summoning to his aid Blethyn and Rhywallon, the princes of North Wales and Powis, in retaliation Edric then laid waste the county of Hereford, as far as the bridge of Lugg, and carried off much booty.[2] It is affirmed by some, that Richard Scrupe built Richard's Castle, Herefordshire, and that from him the stronghold derived its name. He died before the survey, at which period—

OSBERN FITZ RICHARD, his son, held largely in Herefordshire, Shropshire, Worcestershire, Warwickshire, and Bedfordshire, under the king or the Norman Earl of Shrewsbury. To Osbern succeeded Hugh, son of Osbern, or—

HUGH FITZ OSBERN, who lived in the reign of Henry I. He married Eustachia de Say, who left her surname with their

---

[1] *Domesday*, fo. 260, a 1.   [2] FLORENCE OF WORCESTER, *Sub. ann.* 1067.

descendants. She and her son founded the nunnery of Westwood, in Worcestershire. That son's name was—

OSBERN FITZ HUGH, who succeeded to the barony of Burford before 1140. He married Amicia, daughter of Walter de Clifford, and sister to Fair Rosamond. Fair Rosamond died in 1175 or 1176, when, for her soul's health and that of her mother, Osbern, at the request of her father, Sir Walter de Clifford, gave to the nunnery of Godstow, where Rosamond was buried, his salt-pit in Wich; King Henry II. assenting to the grant. Osbern Fitz Hugh was also a benefactor to Haughmond Abbey, to which he gave a very valuable gold cup. In 1185, Osbern was deceased without issue, when his brother,

HUGH DE SAY fined 200 merks for livery of his lands. To him succeeded—

HUGH DE SAY II., his son, who was employed in the wars of Wales. We learn that at Michaelmas, 1191, the sheriff of Shropshire had paid Hugh 25 merks for ward of Norton castle, Radnorshire, and £6 8s. for 40 swine to victual it; and, in 1195, the sheriff of Herefordshire paid him 100s. to fortify the castle of Blidewach, by order of Archbishop Hubert. De Say was killed in the Welsh wars. His daughter and sole heir marrying—

HUGH DE FERRARS, who had obtained her marriage by fining 300 merks with the Crown; he next became baron of Richard's Castle: yet he did not long enjoy it, for he died in 1204. Among others who then aspired to the hand of the rich Margaret de Say, who remained a child although a widow, was Thomas de Galwey, afterwards Earl of Athol, who, in 1205, furnished certain ships manned with mercenaries for King John's service, the king agreeing to go halves with the bravadoes in whatever they should pillage from his enemies.[1] Galwey proffered to the king a fine of 1,000 merks "that he might have the land of Hugh de Say," yet he never actually married Margaret; as, falling under the king's displeasure, about 1211—

ROBERT DE MORTIMER fined for, and obtained the marriage of Margery de Say, and became baron of Richard's Castle. Although bearing the name, it does not appear that this baron was related to Mortimer of Wigmore, the paternal inheritance of Mortimer of Richard's Castle lying in Essex. Faithfully adhering to King John, that sovereign, at Oswestry, on August 9th, 1216, gave him

---

[1] *Patent*, p. 51.

all such lands in his Worcestershire fief as were held by tenants adverse to the king; and, three days afterwards, at Shrewsbury, King John granted him a right to hold a weekly market on Thursdays, at Richard's Castle, and a yearly fair at the feast of St. Owen (August 26th), to last for six days. Robert died in 1219, and on July 5th of that year, young Henry III. received the homage of Margaret de Say at Gloucester, and ordered the sheriffs of Northamptonshire, Oxfordshire, Berkshire, Herefordshire, Worcestershire, Gloucestershire, Warwickshire, and Shropshire, to give her seizin of Richard's Castle, and all other lands of her inheritance. Only four months after the decease of Mortimer, Margaret married a third husband—

WILLIAM DE STUTEVILL, who thereupon became lord of Richard's Castle. Assessed to various scutages and aids during the reign of Henry III., in 1255 this William was returned as holding Bureford *in capite*. He held his barony, however, merely by *courtesy of England*, as it was termed, in right of his wife who had long before died. The king's writ of *Diem clausit extremum*, issued on the decease of William de Stutevill in 1259, when the inquests that followed found that Margaret de Say's son was heir to the barony, and accordingly—

HUGH DE MORTIMER, that son, did homage to the king, his relief being fixed at £100. This baron took an active part in the civil war that raged towards the close of the reign of Henry III., and suffered for his loyalty at the hands of Simon Montfort.[1] He fought on behalf of the king at Evesham; after which victory, among other rewards the king bestowed on his faithful adherent, was a privilege to hunt the hare, fox, weasel, and wild cat in any of the king's forests in Shropshire. A charter, dated Kenilworth, November 16th, 1266, likewise granted Hugh a weekly market on Saturdays, and an annual fair of three days (March 24, 25, and 26) at Burford. At the inquest held at Burford, on December 15th, 1274, upon the decease of Hugh de Mortimer, the jurors found that he had held two carucates in demesne in Burford manor, that two out of the three portions of Burford church belonged to him as patron; that the barony of Burford commanded no less than $32\frac{1}{2}$ knights' fees in different counties; and that Robert de Mortimer, son and heir of the deceased was $22\frac{1}{2}$ years old, etc. At an inquisition made at the same time by the justices at

---

[1] See DUGDALE'S *Baronage*, i. p. 152-153.

Shrewsbury as to the state of Overs Hundred, the jurors reported, that, after the battle of Evesham, the late Hugh de Mortimer had procured Burford to be made a *free borough* by Henry III.,[1] from which we may presume that about this period it became a corporate town.

ROBERT DE MORTIMER, who now became baron of Burford, had summons to muster with horse and arms at Worcester, on July 1, 1277, to march against Lewellyn. Ten years afterwards he was dead, when succeeded—

HUGH DE MORTIMER II., last baron of his line, whose summonses, both military and parliamentary, are numerous between 1297 and 1301, the dates inclusive of his public career. He left two daughters, Joan and Margaret. Upon the decease of her first husband, Joan de Mortimer became wife of Richard Talbot. Margaret, before she had attained the age of twelve years, was married to Geoffrey de Cornwall. Between these co-heiresses, the manor of Burford, therefore, was divided, and among their descendants the barony is still in abeyance.

WINDOW, BURFORD.

BURFORD CHURCH.

Alluded to in *Domesday*, this church probably existed in Saxon times. Pope Nicholas' Taxation in 1291, represents Burford church, in the deanery of Burford, as consisting of three portions, valued respectively at £16 13s. 4d., £9, and £5 6s. 8d. The assessors of the *ninth* of wheat, wool, and lamb, in 1341 rated the parish at only £12 0s. 3d., because eleven virgates lay

---

[1] *Rot. Hundred*, ii. 103.

fallow, being held by incapable tenants, etc. In 1534-5 the three portionists of Burford certified their collective preferment to be worth £23 13s. 4d. *per annum*, less 15s. 4d. for procurations and synodals, and an average charge of 17s. 9d. for the bishop's triennial procurations.

Early Incumbents.—In 1278, Stephen de St. George was incumbent of the first portion; Master William de Mortimer had the second portion; Geoffrey de Bureford was incumbent of the third portion.

Nash and Boraston chapels were affiliations of Burford church, but, as if independent, the church of Grete, in Burford deanery, in 1291 was valued as under £4. The inquisition of 1341 takes no notice of it; but the *Valor* of 1535 represents Grete as a rectory worth £5 *per annum*. Greet chapel appears to have been transferred to Whitton.

Tedenesolle is noticed in *Domesday* as follows:—"The same Osbern [Fitz Richard] holds Tedenesolle. Sauuard held it [in Saxon times] and was a free man. Here i hide geldable. The land is for iii and a half ox-teams. In demesne is one team, and iii serfs and iii boors with half a team. A wood here will fatten xl swine. In time of King Edward, the manor was worth 6s.; now 10s."[1] The manor thus alluded to, in later documents, is sometimes called Mærebroc. Whether it was situated in the south-eastern or in the north-eastern extremity of Overs Hundred is, however, a question.

Corley. Of this manor, William the Conqueror's record says:—"Radulf de Mortemer holds of the king Cornelie. Siuuard held it for ii manors, and was a free man. Here ii hides geldable. The land is [sufficient] for iiii ox-teams. In demesne is one team, and iiii serfs, one villain, ii boors, and one radman with half a team. In King Edward's time [the manor] was worth 48s. [per annum]; now 10s. When he [Mortemer] received it, it was worth 3s."[1] In 1255, Geoffrey de Overton, le Savage's successor

---

[1] *Domesday*, fo. 260, a 1.

at Corley, held the two hides alluded to in *Domesday*, under Mortimer for half a knight's fee. Corley was one of those manors which, after the battle of Evesham, Mortimer, to the king's injury, annexed to his honour of Cleobury.

CORLEY CHURCH.

In 1261 a robber took sanctuary here. The Taxation of 1291 values the church of Cornleye, in the deanery of Burford at £6; the rector had also a portion of £1 from the church of Stottesden. The parish was assessed only £2 to the *ninth* in 1341, because there were no sheep in it; four virgates lay uncultivated, etc. The *Valor* of 1534-5 represents this preferment as worth £6. The pension from Stottesden was no longer receivable at this date, but instead thereof Corley paid one of 6s. 8d. annually to Wigmore Abbey, and 7s. 8d. for procurations and synodals.

Early Incumbent.—William, parson of the church of Cornleye, 1278.

Cainham. The highly interesting British fortification known as Cainham Camp, is situated on a gentle eminence about two miles and a half south-east of Ludlow. "It is a double camp, fortified by a high vallum, and a fosse; the latter is only at that end where the two camps join. The entrance is at the east, and is about six paces wide. Here a good section of the vallum is obtained. Its base is as much as thirty-four yards wide, and the relief of the wall rises nearly twenty feet above it. On three sides the land falls somewhat precipitously. The mound is highest on the eastern side, where the slope is easiest. At the western end of the easterly camp, there are two openings into the other. The top of the vallum of both is planted."[1]

Concerning Cainham *Domesday* says:—"The same Radulf holds Caiham. Earl Morcar held it. Here viii hides geldable. In demesne are iiii hides, thereon are ii ox-teams; and there are ii serfs, x villains, and v boors, with iiii teams. Here is a mill; and two horse-loads of salt from Wich [belong to the manor]. The wood will fatten 200 swine; therein are iii hayes. In the whole manor the [arable] land is [capable of employing] xix ox-teams. Of the said land of this manor, Robert Veci holds iii hides, and Walter i hide, of Radulf. In demesne they have ii teams, and

---

[1] *Salopia Antiqua*, p. 214.

vii serfs; and there are iiii villains, and iiii boors, with i team only. The whole manor, in King Edward's time, was worth £8; and afterwards it was worth 60s. Now, that which Radulf [de Mortemer] holds is worth 40s. That which his knights hold is worth 38s."[1] Cainham was the only manor in Overs Hundred Ralph de Mortemer held of Roger de Montgomery.

Respecting the moiety of Cainham, including its member Snitton, which, in the time of the Conqueror, Ralph de Mortemer held in demesne, we learn from the French Chronicle that "Hugh de Mortimer gave Caynham to the said abbey [of Wigmore which he founded] with his body," in anticipation, doubtless, of his burial at Wigmore.[2] But Roger, his successor, challenged the title of the monks to Caynham and took from them Snitton, it being a convenient halting-place between Wigmore and Cleobury. Upon a certain occasion, however, it happened that whilst journeying between these places, Mortimer's wife, Isabel, was suddenly seized with the pangs of child-birth at Snitton. The infant died. The mother's own danger was great. Superstitious dread mingled with solemn reflection.

The circumstances presented exactly that opportunity which the churchman of the middle ages was so skilled in turning to profit. . In short, Isabel was led to believe that she was suffering on account of the sacrilege of her husband, when, at his wife's earnest entreaty, the baron restored Snitton to the abbey, to hold with Caynham for ever. Then the abbot of Wigmore assumed the privileges of having a gallows, and of assizing bread and beer in the manor, and retained it until the dissolution.

CAINHAM CHURCH.

In 1291, the church of Kayham, in the deanery of Ludlow, described as the abbot of Wigmore's (it probably having been involved in Mortimer's gift to the abbey), yielded the abbot, as rector, £3 6s. 8d.; the vicar's portion being under £4. The church of Bitterley also had a pension from Kayham. The parish was assessed only £3 0s. 8d. to the *ninth* in 1341, because two virgates lay untilled, etc. The *Valor* of 1534-5 represents this vicarage as worth £4 9s. *per annum*, less 1s. for synodals.

Early Incumbent.—Achelard, parson of Caynham, died about 1179; soon after which, the canons of Wigmore having obtained possession of this church, it became a vicarage.

---

[1] *Domesday*, fo. 256, b 2.   [2] WRIGHT'S *Ludlow*, pp. 121, 126, 127.

Hope Baggot was the portion of Cainham held either by Robert Veci or Walter at the time of the Conqueror's survey. It never passed to Wigmore Abbey, but was held under Mortemer as

CHANCEL, CAINHAM.

a distinct manor, by feoffees, whose name, Bagard, accounts for the distinctive title by which the place is now known.

The Chapel.

Hopbagard chapel, in 1291, is described as of less than £4 annual value. In 1341, the parish was taxed only 20s. The *Valor* of 1534-5 styles this chapel a rectory, worth £3 *per annum*, less 6d. for synodals.

Early Incumbent.—Roger Bagart, 1288, whose brother was patron.

Bitterley. "The same Roger [de Lacy] holds Buterlie. Goduin held it, and was a free man. Here iii hides geldable. In demesne is one ox-team, and there are iiii [teams] among the serfs, male and female. There is a church, a priest, vi villains, and one boor, with iii teams; and there might be iii other teams here. Here ii hayes. In time of King Edward, the manor was worth 60s. annually; and afterwards it was waste. Now [it

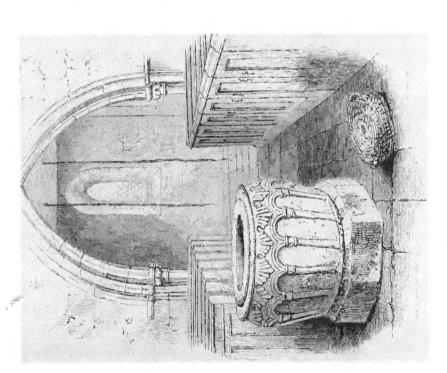

FONT, BITTERLEY.

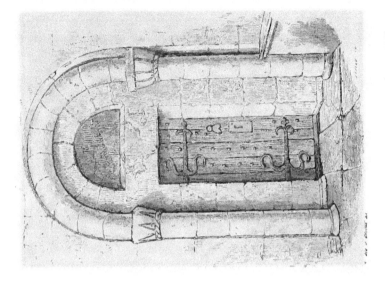

DOORWAY, SOUTH SIDE, SILVINGTON, (see p 305).

p. 302.

is worth] 40." ¹ *Domesday* describes "iiii teams among the serfs, male and female." Are we to understand from this that female serfs worked at the plough?

In 1165, the national record, called the Liber Niger, represents Roger de Esketot, a cadet of the family of Esketot, or Scotot, as holding a knight's fee, by *new feoffment*, under De Lacy.² That fee was Bitterley, for we learn, from the Chartulary, that shortly afterwards, Roger de Scotot gave 4s. rent out of his mill of Butterleg to Haughmond Abbey, Hugh de Lacy, seignoral lord, confirming the grant. The Scotots afterwards appear to have dropped their original surname, and to have taken a new one from the place over which they were mesne lords. Thus, in 1255, Sir Stephen de Buterleg "held iii hides, in Bitterley, of Dame Margery de Lacy, by service of one knight, and did suit to Overs Hundred."

Sir Stephen's descendants long continued to be lords of the *vill*, whilst under them held under-tenants.

BITTERLEY CHURCH AND PARISH.

Doubtless this church was one of those Saxon foundations whose vast parishes comprehended more than can now be determined. Like other churches of Lacy's Shropshire fief, Bitterley was charged with a pension to St. Guthlac's Priory at Hereford. Pope Nicholas' Taxation, in 1291, returns the church of Buterleye, in the deanery of Ludlowe, as worth £21 6s. 8d. per annum, which sum included pensions from Cainham and Hope Bagard. The prior of Hereford also had a portion of £1 10s. in Bitterley church. In 1341, the parish was taxed only £9 7s. 8d. to the *ninth*, because four virgates lay fallow, etc. In 1534-5, this rectory was worth £22 11s. 8d., upon which the charges were 30s. to the prior of St. Guthlac, £1 3s. 4d. to the prior of Wenlock; 14s. 4d. for procurations and synodals, and an average of 17s. 9d. yearly for the bishops' triennial visitation.

Early Incumbent.—Roger, parson of Butterley, about 1205.

Henley is noticed in *Domesday*, for we read in that record that:—"The same Rainald [the sheriff] holds Haneleu [of the earl], and Roger holds it of him [viz., Rainald]. Elmund held it

---

¹ *Domesday*, fo. 256, b 1.   ² *Liber Niger*, i. 153, 154.

[in Saxon times], and was free with this land. Here i hide geldable. In demesne is half an ox-team, and [there are] iiii [teams] among the serfs, male and female; and ii villains and one boor with i team. Here is a mill of 4s. [annual value]. The manor was and is worth 12s. [per annum]."[1]

Lower Ledwich, now in Ludford parish, was anciently called Priest Ledwich, from the circumstance that it belonged to the great Saxon church of St. Mary's of Bromfield. Accordingly, under the heading "*Quod tenet Ecclesia Sanctæ Mariæ,*" Domesday says, that:—" The same church held [in Saxon times] and still holds half a hide in Ovret Hundred. It was waste, and so remains."[2] This wasted half hide afterwards came to be called Ledwich. In the time of Henry III, the Prior of Bromfield withdrew the suit of Ledwich from Overs Hundred, and hence it came to be annexed to that of Munslow.

In the Conqueror's record, the church of St. Mary's Bromfield is confused with that of St. Mary's Shrewsbury. "*Domesday,*" say the historians of Shrewsbury,[3] " was put together in London from loose notes collected in the country; and it is highly probable that the officers of the exchequer, finding two sets of entries of a church of St. Mary in Shropshire, erroneously classed them together." To which the author of " Antiquities of Shropshire" adds, " I would here remark how *Domesday*, that unrivalled record of facts, is instructive even in its omissions. The officers of the exchequer unhesitatingly adopted a classification which took it for granted that more than one great church dedicated to St. Mary was not to be reckoned on in a single county. We have in this an illustration of the fact that the *Domesday* churches in Shropshire were very few in number."[4]

Silvington, with the marginal affix, "*In Ovret Hundred,*" and under the title of, "*Terra Sancti Remigii,*" Domesday says, that:—"The church of St. Remigius held [in Saxon times] and

---

[1] *Domesday*, fo. 255, a 1.
[2] Ibidem, fo. 252, b 2.
[3] *Hist of Shrewsbury*, ii. 303, *note*.
[4] Eyton's *Antiq. of Shrop.* vol. iv. p. 377.

holds of the king one manor of i hide ; and here there were and are ii ox-teams. Its former and present value was and is 10s. 8d."[1] It was a strange thing for Algar, the Anglo-Saxon earl of Mercia, to give land to a French monastery. Yet this was why he gave it : Aldred, the Saxon archbishop of York, going on a mission to Rome, early in 1061, was accompanied by many noble Englishmen, Burchard, the son of Earl Algar, being among the number. The object of their journey accomplished, as they passed through Rheims, on their way back to England, Burchard was seized with mortal sickness. Before he died, he asked to be buried in the abbey of St. Remigius, promising, in return, that certain lands that belonged to him should be given to that house. The monks buried the illustrious youth according to his desire, when the sorrowing father, with consent of Edward the Confessor, fulfilled his son's dying promise. Hence it came, that, at the period of the survey, besides the manor above described, the great Benedictine abbey of St. Remigius at Rheims owned four other estates in England, all of them being of Earl Algar's gift.

SILVINGTON CHURCH.

Dedicated to St. Nicholas, this was probably originally subject to Bitterley. The Taxation of 1291 represents the church of Silvyntone, in the deanery of Ludlow, as worth less than £4 per annum. In 1534-5, it was a rectory of the annual value of £3 6s. 8d., less 6d. for synodals.

Early Incumbent.—William, rector of Silvinton : 1307.

---

[1] *Domesday*, fo. 252, a 2.

DOMESDAY HUNDRED OF CULVESTAN OR COLMESTANE.

Modern Name.	Domesday. Name.	Saxon Owner or Owners, T. R. E.	Domesday Tenant in capite.	Domesday Mesne, or next Tenant.	Domesday Sub-Tenant.	Modern Hundred, or Franchise.
Stanton Lacy	Stantone	Siuuard	Rogerius de Laci			Munslow.
Stokesay	Stoches	Ældred	Idem			Ibidem.
Aldon	Alledone	Siuuard	Idem			Ibidem.
Corfton	Cortune	Alsi	Rogerius Comes	Rogerius de Laci	Herbertus	Ibidem.
Middlehope	Mildehope	Aelsi	Idem	Rogerius de Laci	Herbertus	Ibidem.
Onibury	Aneberie	Episcopus de Hereford	Episcopus de Hereford	Rogerius de Laci		Ibidem.
Upper Ledwich	Ledewic	Uluric	Rogerius Comes	Willelmus Pantulf	Bernerus	Ibidem.
Middleton Higford	Middeltone	Uluric and Eduin	Idem	Willelmus Pantulf	Bernerus	Ibidem.
Little Sutton	Sudtone	Aluric	Idem	Willelmus Pantulf		Ibidem.
Merston	Merstun	Gamel and Uluric	Idem	Willelmus Pantulf		Ibidem.
Great Sutton	Sudtone	Alnric	Idem	Helgot	Herbertus	Ibidem.
Steventon	Scevintone	Renensuard	Idem	Helgot		Ibidem.
Poston	Possetorne	Aluric	Idem	Helgot		Ibidem.
Bouldon	Bolledone	Seunard and Elmund	Idem	Helgot		Ibidem.
The Sheet	Sethâ	Leuenot	Radulfus de Mortemer	Ingelraunus		Ibidem.
Huntington	Hantenetune	Ludi	Rogerius Comes	Radulfus de Mortemer	Turstinus	Ibidem.
Upper Ashford		Azor	Idem	Radulfus de Mortemer	Ricardus	Ibidem.
Ashford Carbonel	Esseford	Ledi	Osbernus fil. Ricardi			Ibidem.
Aston and Munslow	Estune	Elmund	Rogerius Comes	Rainaldus Vicecomes		Ibidem.
Cardington	Cardintune	Austin	Idem	Rainaldus Vicecomes		Ibidem.
Hope Bowdler	Fordritishope	Edric Salvage	Idem	Hugo filius Turgisii		Ibidem.
Clee Stanton	Clee	Ecclesia Sanctæ Milburgæ	Rogerius Comes	Ecclesia Sanctæ Milburgæ		Wenlock.

MANORS SITUATED IN CULVESTAN, BUT WHOSE HUNDRED IS NOT STATED IN DOMESDAY.

Modern Name.	Domesday. Name.	Saxon Owner or Owners, T. R. E.	Domesday Tenant in capite.	Domesday Mesne, or next Tenant.	Domesday Sub-Tenant.	Modern Hundred, or Franchise.
Corfham Diddlebury	Corfan	Rex Edwardus	Rogerius Comes			Munslow.
Sicfton	Sireton	Edricus	Idem			Ibidem.
Culmington	Comintone	Edricus	Idem			Ibidem.
Lower Poston	Possetorn	Chetel	Idem	Ecclesia Sancti Michaelis	Unus homo reddens fascem busci	Ibidem.
Bromfield	Brunfelde	Ecclesia Sanctæ Mariæ	Idem	Robertus		

IN the change that took place in the divisional system of Shropshire, in Henry I.'s time, the old Culvestan Hundred was done away with, and its manors were transferred to the then newly-created Hundred of Munslow, in which, with one exception, they still continue. St. Milburg's manor of Clee Stanton is the exception, it having been annexed to the franchise of Wenlock in the reign of Richard I.

Corfham is thus described in *Domesday*:—"The Earl himself

holds Corfan. King Edward held it, with iiii berewicks. Here iiii hides geldable. In demesne are v ox-teams, and a sixth might be [employed]. Here iii villains and iii boors have iii teams, and still there might be ii more teams. Here are x neat-herds.

"Of this land, one of the earl's knights holds half a hide, and has thereon i ox-team, ii serfs, and ii villains, with i team. It is worth 5s. [annually].

"The church of St. Peter holds the church of this manor, with i hide. The land is [sufficient] for iii ox-teams. It yields to the monks 18s. [per annum].

"To this manor pertains the whole of Comestane Hundred and Patinton Hundred. In King Edward's time [the manor] with two pennies from the Hundreds, yielded £10 of ferm.[1] Now, with the Hundreds, it yields to the earl £6."[2] United, like many of King Edward's manors, with an *Hundredal* jurisdiction, Corfham, in Saxon times, and at *Domesday*, was *caput* of the Hundreds of Culvestan and Patinton. Upon the forfeiture of Earl Robert de Belèsme, his seigneuries reverted to King Henry I., when he, re-arranging the Hundreds of Shropshire, Corfham, combined with Siefton and Culmington, two adjacent manors, came into the hands of Henry II. In 1155, this estate was given by Henry II. to Hugh de Periers, who, dying in 1175, it reverted to the king, when the sheriff accounted at the rate of £31 per annum for Corfham, Siefton, and Culmington, as if they again constituted an estate of royal demesne, rated at so much in the county ferm. At Michaelmas, 1178, however, the sheriff described the estate as *the land* of Corfham, and claimed quittance for himself of the £31, saying that he had delivered it up according to the king's precept; and for twelve years, namely until 1190, a similar entry was repeated on every Pipe-Roll. What could be the reason, then, for excluding from the Pipe-Roll the name of him to whom Henry II. had made the grant? Shame dictated the concealment of a gift, which, in truth, was but the wages of dishonour—Walter de Clifford, father of fair Rosamond, King Henry's paramour, being the grantee in question, to whom

---

[1] That is, 2d. out of every 3d yielded by the pleas and perquisites of the Hundred Courts, the third penny belonging, as usual, to the earl of the county: which office, during the last years of the Saxon rule, belonged to the great Mercian earl Leofric, Alger, his son, and Edwin, his grandson, successively.

[2] *Domesday*, fo. 253, b 1.

the king had given this demesne "for love of Rosamond, his daughter."

BARONY OF CLIFFORD.

The second son of Richard Fitz-Ponce, Walter de Clifford, probably became heir to his uncles, Walter and Drogo Fitz-Ponce, who, at the time of the *Domesday* survey, held manors in the various counties of Oxfordshire, Berkshire, Wiltshire, Gloucestershire, Worcestershire, and Herefordshire; and, by 1138, he had succeeded his father. Upon the accession of Henry II, Walter de Clifford received various grants from the king. He seems, however, to have made no return of his tenures *in capite*. With respect to his daughter, Fair Rosamond, she appears to have been very young when Duke Henry seduced her. But lately married to the worthless Eleanor, divorced by Louis VII. of France, it is a historical fact that the births of William and Geoffrey, the sons of Henry and Rosamond, took place between the births of William and Henry, the two eldest children of Henry and Eleanor. King Henry's marriage took place on May 18, 1152: Prince Henry, his second legitimate son, was born February 18, 1155.

In March, 1173, began that grand domestic rebellion which embittered the later years of Henry II. Shortly afterwards, his jealous queen, who had planned the whole affair, being captured by her husband, Henry kept her a close prisoner for the remaining sixteen years of his life, when Rosamond Clifford, who previously had been domiciled at Woodstock, openly became the king's paramour. But Rosamond died 1175-6, and obtaining sepulture at Godstow, Walter de Clifford, for his soul's health, and for the souls of his wife Margaret and their daughter Rosamond, with consent of the king and his own heirs, gave to the nuns of Godstow his mill of Framton, with a meadow near by, and also his salt-pit in Wich.

Dying about 1190, it is a remarkable circumstance, that Richard de Clifford's second son succeeded to Corfham and his father's Shropshire estates, by paying a fine of 300 merks to King Richard. Why did the king permit the rights of the elder brother to be ignored by such an anomalous succession? Eyton attributes it to the anger and disgust with which King Richard associated De Clifford's name with his mother's wrongs, so that when called on to confirm his father's grant of one of the finest crown estates in Shropshire to the heir of the first grantee, regarding it as connected with his father's infamous passion, he refused, although he gave it to a younger brother. In support of this, Eyton refers to the circumstance, that about two years after King Richard's accession, the body of Rosamond Clifford was, by order of a bishop of Lincoln, ignominiously expelled from Godstow church, and re-buried without its walls; yet the view which this learned writer takes of the subject hardly agrees, we think, with that extraordinary contrition for his undutiful conduct, known to have been manifested by Richard on the death of his father; neither does it tally with the subsequent riches and honours the king lavished upon William Longespee, son of Fair Rosamond, who obtained from Richard, in preference to all her other suitors, the rich and beautiful Ela in marriage, and the earldom of Salisbury.

To return: Walter, eldest son of De Clifford, was seized, during King Richard's reign, of other estates, although not of Corfham. He was one of the lords marchers of Herefordshire, having, in 1191, custody of Knighton castle. In 1196, and in 1199, he paid scutage for lands he held in Wiltshire and Berkshire respectively. This brings us to the reign of John, by whose charter, dated Chambrais, August 3rd, 1199, the manor of Corfham " as King Richard, our brother, granted and confirmed the same to Richard de Clifford, the grantee's brother, whose heir the said Walter is," secured by a fine of 300 merks, was confirmed to Walter de Clifford, the elder brother, and his heirs. Litigation ensued, upon the ground that King Richard's previous grant had made Corfham the appanage of a younger brother; the result was a fine, and Richard de Clifford, for a valuable consideration, renounced all claims in favour of Walter.

Secure in the possession of these Shropshire estates, one of Walter's first acts was a grant to Haughmond Abbey. For the sustenance of their kitchen and their refections in fresh fish, the successful litigant gave to the canons his mills of Culmington and Siefton, half a virgate in Siefton, etc. A courtier and a favourite of John's, Walter's name frequently appears on the rolls of that king's reign, sometimes as *custos* of royal castles, at another time as sheriff of Herefordshire; one while he figures as the recipient of presents of deer from the king's forest, at another hostages and escheated lands are entrusted to his keeping; he meanwhile, knowing well how to take care of himself, and secure a continuance of his worthless master's favour, by fines; paying upon one occasion as much as 1,000 merks to King John to stifle enquiry. Walter died January 1221, when his son, Walter de Clifford, junior, succeeded to his estates.

Agnes de Cundy, lady of Cavenby and Glentham, the wife of Walter de Clifford the elder, by bringing him vast estates in Lincolnshire and Nottinghamshire, Essex and Kent, materially increased the importance of his house.

A steadfast adherent of John's throughout his troubled reign, at length, by writ of Henry III., Walter succeeded to his paternal inheritance, his relief being fixed at £100. Annoyed at the king's infatuated partiality to foreigners, he confederated with the gallant but unfortunate Richard Marshal, when, without judgment of his court or sentence of his peers, Henry III. ordered his arrest, and gave his lands to the Poictevins. Unlike Marshal's rebellion, however, de Clifford's was of short duration, as, in 1234, having previously made peace with the king, H. de Trubleville received orders to give up Clifford castle to its lord, to whom the king had restored it. Both in 1235, and in 1236, this baron was assessed in Shropshire for the aid due on marriage of the king's sister.[1] Advanced in years, and father of an only daughter then twelve years of age, a patent of April 30th, 1244, informed de Clifford of the king's desire to match the young heiress with Longespee, great-grandson of Fair Rosamond. By this marriage, William Longespee became husband of his father's second cousin, Matilda de Clifford. Longespee was killed in a tournament at Blithe in 1256.

Under date 1250, M. Paris observes: "Walter de Clifford, who was one, not of the least importance amongst the barons of the Welsh borders, either in power, wealth, or liberties, was accused before the king of having, in contempt of the said king, violently and improperly treated his messenger, who bore his royal letters, and having forced him to *eat the same, with the seal.* Walter being proved guilty of this before the king, did not dare to stand trial, but threw himself on the king's mercy, whereby he, although with difficulty, escaped death or disinheritance, but lost his liberty, and all the money he possessed or could procure, amounting to about a 1,000 merks, and was then allowed to return home without being imprisoned, on the bail of some especial securities."

Estimated to contain 7½ hides, the manor of Corfham, in 1255, including Culmington, Siefton, and Diddlebury, was held of the

---

[1] *Testa de Nevill,* pp. 60, 61.

king by Sir Walter de Clifford, by service of one knight. He had a franchise here, gallows, assize of bread and beer, and held *pleas of bloodshed, hue and cry*, with other lesser pleas. It was Roger, the nephew of this Walter, who, in concert with Mortimer, assisted Prince Edward to escape from Hereford castle.

After the decease of Walter de Clifford and his second wife, Margaret, daughter of Llewellyn, Prince of Wales, Longespee's young widow, Matilda, succeeded to the whole barony of her father, when John Giffard, of Brimsfield, took her by force from her manor-house to his castle.[1]

A patent of 1271 legalizing the marriage, accordingly in the *Feodary* of 1284, it is said, that, "John Giffard holds the manor of Corfham by right of Matilda de Longespeye, formerly daughter and heir of Walter de Clifford, for one knight's fee."

Giffard died in 1299, when the heirs of his first wife, Matilda de Clifford, were found to be Margery, wife of the Earl of Lincoln (to whom she had been affianced by Longespee, her father, when she was five years old), and Matilda's three daughters by John Giffard. Between these four co-heiresses, therefore, the De Clifford estates were divided, when Corfham falling to Eleanor, Giffard's second daughter, and she afterwards marrying Fulk le Strange, hence the return of March, 1316, styles him lord of Corfham. But the *old barony* of Clifford had fallen into an abeyance.

DIDDLEBURY CHURCH.

By the *Domesday* entry, "the church of St. Peter holds the church of this [Corfham] manor, with one hide," it is meant that Diddlebury church, with its hide of land, yielded 18s. annually to Shrewsbury Abbey, to which Earl Roger de Montgomery had granted it. In the words of his charter, "I gave," says the Earl, "the church of Dudclebury, with all things which pertain thereto."

The dispute between the Norman abbey of Seez and Shrewsbury abbey, being soldered up about 1147, among the various transfers and concessions then agreed on, the abbot of Shrewsbury gave to the abbot of Seez the church of "Dudenebury." About 1236, however, the abbot and convent of Seez having felt "great danger," as it is expressed, "inasmuch as living in foreign parts they could not, as was right and decent, provide a fitting pastor for this church," they besought the Bishop of Hereford to devise

---

[1] DUGDALE'S *Baronage*, p. 500.

some remedial plan; accordingly, the bishop gave Diddlebury church to his own chapter.

The church of Duddelebury, in the deanery of Ludlow, was valued in 1291 at the high rate of £38 13s. 4d., a portion in the church of Alberbury amounting to £1 6s. 8d. also belonging to its rectory. The vicarage was then worth £7 6s. 8d. *per annum*. In 1341, the parish was assessed at only £9 to the *ninth*, because six carucates lay untilled on account of various taxes which oppressed the tenants, etc. In 1534-5, the rectories of Diddlebury and Long Staunton were returned as jointly worth £40 *per annum*; the vicarage of Diddlebury £13 6s. 8d. Out of this latter sum, 7s. 8d. went for procurations and synodals, and 17s. 9d. the annual proportion of the bishop's triennial visitation charge.

Early Incumbents.—Aluric and Osbern, rector and vicar, 1115.

Siefton. Like Corfham, this was a manor of Earl Roger's demesne, as we read in Domesday Book, that:—" The same earl holds Sireton. Edric held it. Here v hides. In demesne are iii ox-teams, and ii female serfs, iii villains, and iii boors, with i team; and still there might be vii teams more here. In King Edward's time it was worth £6; now 100s." [1] The Saxon owner alluded to above was probably Edric the Savage, of whose manors some were bestowed by the Conqueror on Roger de Montgomery. Escheated to Henry I., Siefton was held as royal demesne, until Henry II. giving it first to Hugh de Periers, and then to Walter de Clifford, at length it became a dependency to Corfham.

Culmington. "The same earl holds Comintone. Edric held it. Here v hides geldable, with iii berewicks. In demesne are ii ox-teams; and iiii serfs and xii villains with iii teams; and there might be vii more teams here besides. In King Edward's time the manor was worth £4; now £6." [1] In its Saxon ownership, as well as in its subsequent history, Culmington is associated with Siefton.

---

[1] *Domesday*, fo. 254, a 1.

THE CHURCH.

The church of Culmynton in the deanery of Ludlow, in 1291 was taxed at £10. In 1341, the parish was assessed only £3 1s. to the *ninth,* because much land lay untilled, owing to various burdens on the tenantry. The *Valor* of 1534-5 represents the net value of this rectory as £18 9s.

DOUBLE PISCINA, CULMINGTON.

Early Incumbent. — John de Wrocestre (Wroxeter), about 1223.

Adjoining the last named manors, in ancient times flourished the great Clee Forest, a well-wooded expanse, which, in the Saxon era, was appurtenant either to the Mercian earl's manor of Ditton, or to the Anglo-Saxon king's manor of Corfham. At the Conquest, this wood became a palatine, and afterwards one of the royal forests of Shropshire, when Henry II. giving Corfham, Culmington, and Siefton to Walter de Clifford, along with them he gave to him the Clee Forest. Here, therefore, the Anglo-Norman seigneur exercised those rights which ordinarily belonged to royal forests, and here the lordly de Cliffords, for generations afterwards, jealously maintained their forest rights.

The Forestership of Clee was claimed as their hereditary right by the Wyards, a family descending from "Wiard the Forester," who trod the green glade previously to 1199.

Clee Forest flourished where Loughton, in the parish of

Chetton, now stands. This manor consisted of reclaimed forest land. We read that Walter de Clifford, son of Walter de Clifford and Agnes de Cundy, "grants to Salop Abbey, in *pure almoign*, 120 acres of the Bosc of the said monks of Luhtone, of which the Bosc and site were already theirs, to assart, fence, and dispose of as they liked; provided the beasts of his forest should be able to pass in and out according to the custom of the Forest;" upon which, doubtless, the monks industriously set to work and reduced the land thereabouts to pretty nearly its present condition.

Stanton Lacy is thus minutely described in *Domesday Book*:—"The same Roger [de Lacy] holds Stantone. Siuuard held it [in Saxon times], and was a free man. Here are xx½ hides geldable. The land is sufficient for L ox-teams. In demesne are x teams, and xxviii [teams] amongst the male and female serfs; and lxvii villains, ii smiths, v boors and four cozets[1] have between them all xxiii teams. Here is a church having i hide and a half [of land], and ii priests with ii villains have iii teams. Here ii mills of 26s. [annual value]. St. Peter of Hereford has here i villain. Of this land, in the above manor, Richard holds i hide and a half, Azeline i hide and a half, Roger i hide and a half. These [three] have in demesne vi teams, vi serfs, ii semi-villains,[2] v boors, and ii cozets with i team, and a mill of 10s. [annual value]. Out of the same manor iiii serving-men have land [enough] for iii teams, and [have] a ferling, and they have iiii teams and x acres of land. Here are iii radchenistres[3] having land [capable of employing] ii teams and a half, and here they have that number of teams. And one man, Auti, holds one member of this manor wherein are iii hides; and thereon he has one team with a semi-villain. The whole manor in King Edward's time was worth £24 [*per annum*]: now it is worth £25."[4]

The circumstance that Roger de Lacy held this great and well-stocked manor immediately of the crown in 1086, leads us to the consideration of—

---

[1] The *Cozets* like the *Cotarii* of Domesday were tenants of cottages, and appear to have been a degree above the mere villains.

[2] The *Dimidii villani* appear to have been villains partially enfranchised.

[3] The Radchenistres and Radmans of *Domesday* appear to have been identical. *See* Note, p. 50.

[4] *Domesday*, fo. 260, b 1.

THE BARONY OF DE LACY.

WALTER DE LACY, father of Roger de Lacy, who held Stantone at the time of the survey, was that *Sire de Lacie* who, with others brave as himself, "forming one troop, fell on the English offhand, fearing neither fence nor fosse;"[1] in other words, he was, as Master Wace informs us, one of the heroes of Hastings; and for the hazard he encountered on that eventful occasion, Walter afterwards received ample remuneration. An approved warrior, lands were assigned him in the west, so that he might help to restrain the Welsh; yet what was the extent of that territory he held under William Fitz-Osbern, the first Norman Earl of Hereford, is unknown. Upon the rebellion of Fitz-Osbern's successor Earl Roger de Britolio, a vast fief was placed at the Conqueror's disposal, who conferred it upon Walter de Lacy. Walter died on March 27, 1085, in consequence of a fall received whilst superintending the building of the "Church of St. Peter," at Hereford. A monastic record informs us that Walter gave to that monastery ten villains in ten distinct *vills* of his fief, that is, he gave as much land in each instance as was held in villainage by one tenant, which accounts for the statement *Domesday* makes in connection with Stantone, that "St. Peter of Hereford has here one villain." To Walter succeeded his son and heir—

ROGER DE LACY, the *Domesday* Baron, who at the period of the survey held no less than a hundred different manors in Shropshire, Herefordshire, Worcestershire, Gloucestershire, and Berkshire, besides the Norman fief of Lassy, which descended to him from his father, and whence his family derived its name. But Roger rebelled against Rufus and was banished in 1095. The king gave Roger's forfeited estates to his brother—

HUGH DE LACY, who thereupon became seignoral lord of Stanton. Of him little is known, excepting that he greatly enriched the famous monastery of Lanthony, in that Ewias-land which Hugh had acquired by conquest. Hugh de Lacy died without issue previously to 1122, and at his decease, his estates escheated to the crown. Pagan Fitz-John, the same who, as Viceroy of Shropshire, we described as holding court at Brug castle, then occupied a portion of De Lacy's fief, by gift of Henry I. Pagan fell in a Welsh foray, pierced through the head by a spear. After him, Joceas de Dynan, by gift of Stephen,

---

[1] ROMAN DE ROU (Taylor) p. 220.

held a large portion of the Honour of De Lacy; but, about 1143, the title of—

GILBERT DE LACY, nephew of the deceased baron, was recognised by Stephen, and accordingly he became lord of Ewias. Living in a time when all law and kingly authority were in abeyance, "a prudent man, and one of great foresight and activity in any military undertaking," as Gilbert is described to have been, could readily turn his sword to good account. We hear of him first at the court of the Empress, whose charters he attested; when she being either unwilling or unable to fulfil his expectations, Lacy changed his political faith, and went over to the Usurper. Upon this, the Empress deprived him of his Norman fief, which she granted to the Bishop of Bayeux: but Stephen amply compensated Gilbert for the loss he had sustained in changing sides, by conferring on him his uncle's estates in England. After winning a reputation for valour, before his death Gilbert de Lacy took upon himself the habit of a Templar and retired from the world. Dying about 1163, his son—

HUGH DE LACY II., upon his succession, obtained from King Henry II. a charter confirming Stanton Lacy, Ludlow, Ewias and other estates to him. When the order was given, in 1165-6, for every tenant *in capite* of the crown to return a list of all who held under him by knight's service, Hugh de Laci complied, and accordingly we find in the record called the *Liber Niger*, or Black Book of the Exchequer, a statement of this Shropshire Barony. As the great chief probably compiled the document himself, it merits attention. Sir Hugh considered himself entitled to the services of 58¾ knights' fees, whereof 53¼ were of *old feoffment* that is, had existed from the days of Henry I., and 5½ of *new feoffment*. He had besides nine tenants who held from 6 *librates* down to a *virgate* of land, yet without any specific knights' service assessed on their tenements. Some of these lived in Sir Hugh's household, some were in his Welsh mansions; and he provided the necessaries of life to both the latter classes. The return does not allude to the long forfeiture which Sir Hugh's father had suffered.

This baron figures in early Irish history, as one of its Anglo-Norman conquerors. In October, 1172, Hugh de Lacy accompanied Henry II. in his expedition to Ireland. "The King," says the contemporary historian,[1] "crossed over with four hundred

---

[1] HOVEDEN, Vol. i. p. 350. Bohn's Ed.

large ships, laden with warriors, horses, arms, and provisions." He crossed from Milford Haven, and landed near Waterford. Having received the homage of a number of its petty kings, circumstances arose which compelled Henry II. to return to England; "but before he left Ireland, he gave, and by his charter confirmed, to Hugh de Lacy the whole of the lands of Meath, with all their appurtenances; to hold in fee and hereditarily of himself and his heirs, by a hundred knights' service, and gave in his charge the city of Dublin, and appointed him Justiciary (Viceroy) of Ireland." [1]

Meanwhile, backed by the French monarch, Prince Henry had raised the standard of revolt in Normandy, against his father, when the king recalled Hugh de Lacy from Ireland, to aid him at this critical juncture. The important frontier town of Verneuil, entrusted to his charge, was invested on July 6, 1173, by King Louis VII. of France; yet, under the governorship of De Lacy and Beauchamp, it gallantly held out until the English monarch relieved it in person. Throughout that crisis of the king's affairs, Hugh de Lacy chivalrously adhered to him. Revisiting Ireland, however, in 1177, Hugh married a daughter of the king of Connaught, without the royal license, when Henry II. suspecting Lacy of an intention to found an independent kingdom for himself in Ireland, viewed the matter as nothing less than high treason. A temporary escheat therefore befell the house of Lacy. On the 25th of July, 1185, Hugh de Lacy was assassinated at Durrow, in Ireland.

WALTER DE LACY, the eldest of the deceased baron's four sons, in 1189 had his father's lands restored to him. He paid scutage in 1194 for King Richard's redemption from his Austrian prison, being assessed at the rate of £1 per fee on $51\frac{1}{4}$ fees. "During this year," says Stapelton, "the ravages committed by Walter de Lacy in conjunction with John de Courcy, lord of Ulster, upon the territory of the king in Ireland, caused a seizure of his lands into the king's hands;" and we learn, from the Pipe Roll of 1198, that "Walter de Lacy renders account of 3,100 merks [£2,066 13s. 4d.] for having the king's good-will and seizin of his lands." Potent, indeed, was the Anglo-Norman Lacy. His Norman fief being as great as his English, and, perhaps, as his Irish possessions. Some notion of its magnitude may be gathered

---

[1] HOVEDEN, Vol. i. p. 354. Bohn's Ed.

from the fact, that the king's escheator actually received therefrom in the year before it was restored to the heir, £750 in money, besides produce in kind—grain, wine, and fish.[1] When Normandy was severed from England, however, Lacy lost his Norman fief.

Unsteady in his allegiance to King John, Lacy confederated with Braose, his father-in-law, and arrayed Meath, Ulster, and Munster against the English king. At length, in the summer of 1210, John made a campaign against the rebels in Ireland, which, being successful, closed with the outlawry and banishment of Walter and Hugh de Lacy, and of the elder Braose. They retired to France. The wife and the eldest of Braose's sons fell into the king's hands; and tradition has it that they were starved to death in the dungeons of Windsor. It is said that Walter de Lacy and his brother took refuge in the monastery of St. Taurin, at Evreux, where for some time they maintained themselves by servile employments; but at length, the abbot, discovering who they were, interceded with King John on their behalf. Gratitude for the kindness they had received at the hands of the abbot then, may have been the reason why Walter and Hugh de Lacy afterwards founded and endowed the monastery of Foure, in Ireland, a cell to the Norman abbey of St. Taurin.

By payment of an enormous fine, Walter de Lacy obtained the restoration of his estates; and, in 1215, we have many instances of the good-will and trust with which King John at last regarded this influential but often disloyal baron. One while Walter de Lacy is charged with commissions of great import in Shropshire; at other times he is found at court with the king. King John presents him with a *Destrier*, allows him to hunt in Dean forest, gives him custody of escheated lands, and prevents him being unduly taxed; releases his brother William from a four years' prison, Walter being one of the *manucaptors* for his future fidelity. Even after the kingdom had practically departed from him, like other barons of the west, unmindful of former grievances, de Lacy was found loyal to King John. Addressing Walter himself, on October 10th, 1216, the king gave a tract of land in Acornbury forest to Margaret de Lacy, Walter's wife, that she might found thereon a house of religion for the souls of William de Braose her father, Matilda her mother, and William her brother, the victims of

---

[1] *Rot. Scacc. Normanniæ*, A.D. 1198, m. 5 dorso.

John's former cruelty. Lacy was on his way to the king at the time, for he transacted business for him at Lincoln on the 17th of October. On the 19th King John died.

An uninterrupted good understanding appears to have existed between the lord of Stanton Lacy and Henry III., who looked upon him with confidence and favour. In 1218, Lacy's Shropshire fees were assessed to the first scutage of Henry III. In 1221, this noble had quittance of the scutage of Biham. In the following year, and again in 1224, de Lacy was in Ireland. His brother Hugh, lord of Ulster, in concert with the men of Meath, it seems had risen in rebellion against the Anglo-Norman king, and Henry III. sent Walter de Lacy to subdue his own brother, and his own vassals. Hence the writ of March 30th, 1224, enjoining the viceroy of Ireland to provide accommodation in Trim Castle for Walter de Lacy and his followers, so long as he should be in that quarter levying war on the enemies of the king and of himself.

Acquitted of the scutage of Brittany, a patent of April 20th, 1230, dated at Portsmouth, names Walter de Lacy among those whose property was to be protected while they were with the king in foreign parts. The arrangement thus indicated must have been reversed, however, as Roger de Wendover informs us that, in the following July, Walter de Lacy commanded one of the divisions of that army which inflicted such signal chastisement upon the King of Connaught, when, taking advantage of the Anglo-Norman king's absence on the continent, he sought to extirpate the English from Ireland.

Pre-eminent among the nobles of Ireland, blind from old age, however, and otherwise bodily afflicted, Walter de Lacy died in 1241. Walter's granddaughters, Matilda and Margaret, were his heirs, the former of whom had been given in marriage to Peter de Geneva, a Provençal favourite of Henry III.; the latter married John de Verdon. Between these co-heiresses the manor of Stanton Lacy, and the other lands of the deceased baron, therefore, were divided, when Ludlow castle, de Lacy's chief residence, fell to Peter de Geneva. The Provençal did not long enjoy the honour; for, dying, Matilda de Lacy re-married to Geoffrey de Genevill or Joinville, who accordingly, in right of his wife, became lord of Ludlow and the Irish castle of Trim. John de Verdon, also, had military summonses as a baron marcher of Shropshire, who, loyally adhering to Henry III., when the confederate lords leagued against their king, his Warwickshire castle of Brandon was demolished by the barons. Upon the return of peace, John de Verdon accompanied Prince Edward, as a crusader to the Holy Land. He died in 1274.

The Feodary of 1316 describes Roger de Mortimer, Earl of March, who married Johanna, granddaughter of Geoffrey de Genevill and Matilda de Lacy, as lord of Stanton *juxta* Ludlow.[1]

Stanton Lacy appears formerly to have been free from all hundredal subjection, hence the public records supply but scant information respecting this manor. Its seigneural lords claimed to have a gallows, to hold pleas of bloodshed and hue and cry, and to assize beer; also to try, under *writ of right*, all civil causes within their jurisdiction.

Stanton Lacy Church.

Previously to 1084, Walter de Lacy gave two-thirds of the tithes of Stanton to his monastery of St. Peter, at Hereford, the remaining third was probably retained for the parochial church. Early in the 12th century, however, the advowson must have been given by Hugh de Lacy I. to Lanthony, in Monmouthshire, as in the Taxation of 1291, the prior of Lanthony is described as being rector of Stantone Lacy, in the deanery of Ludlow, his interest here amounting to no less a sum than £36 13s. 4d. *per annum*; the vicar's portion was £11 extra. In 1341, the parish was taxed only £10 to the *ninth*. The *Valor* of 1534-5 gives the vicar of Stanton Lacy's preferment as worth £14 13s. 4d., less 7s. 8d. for procurations and synodals, and an annual average of 17s. 9d. for the bishop's triennial visitation.

PISCINA, STANTON LACY.

Early Incumbent.—Adam de Bromhal, instituted October 7th, 1300, on presentation of prior and convent of Lanthony.

---

[1] *Parliamentary Writs*, IV. 397.

STANTON-LACY CHURCH.

p. 320.

DOORWAY, STANTON LACY.

p. 320.

Stokesay was one of those ten distinct *vills* of his fief, in which Walter de Lacy, endowing St. Peter's at Hereford, granted a villain; in other words, Walter gave as much land in this manor to his newly-founded church as was held in villainage by one tenant. He also gave to St. Peter's two-thirds of the tithes of this *vill*. Walter de Lacy, the donor in question, lost his life in the year before the survey. Accordingly, *Domesday* describes Stoches as held by the deceased baron's son, Roger, *in capite* of the Conqueror, thus:—" The same Roger holds Stoches. Ældred held it and was a free man. Here vii hides geldable. The land is [capable of employing] xiiii ox-teams. In demesne are v teams, and [there are] xvi teams among the male and female serfs, and xx villains, with viii teams, and ix female cottars. Here a mill rendering ix quarters of corn [annually], and here is a miller and a keeper of bees. In the time of King Edward the manor was worth £10."[1] Ældred, the dispossessed Saxon alluded to above, probably was the same as he who was permitted to hold, under its Norman lord, "one member of land" of the neighbouring manor of Aldon.

Before 1115, the seigneural Lord Lacy enfeoffed the Says in this manor, whose descent was in this wise. Theodoric de Say, living in the reign of Henry I., appears to have been a cadet of that baronial house, whose ancestor, Picot de Say, was lord of Clun at *Domesday*. To Theodoric succeeded Helias de Say, who attested Philip de Belmeis' grant to Buildwas Abbey in 1138-9. Helias is presumed to have been father of Hugh de Say, who, becoming Lacy's vassal in this manor, gave Stokesay Church to Haughmond Abbey, his seigneural lord confirming the grant. To him succeeded Helias de Say II., who, previously to 1224, for the souls of Amicia his wife, Hugh de Say his father, and Olympias his mother, gave the mill of Stoke and Wetlington to Haughmond Abbey. Helias or Elias de Say, by his will, also "commends his soul to God, his body to the church of Haghmon, and, together with his body, gives (besides the mill) also six oxen and one horse from Southstoke, and ten quarters of rye growing on the ground at Northstoke, and ten quarters of oats in the barn of Southstoke,"[2] and dying before 1224, his brother Robert, a clerk in holy orders, became lord of this manor. To him succeeded a third brother,

---

[1] *Domesday*, fo. 260, b 2.
[2] Coeval extract from original will in possession of Richard Corbet, Esq., of Adderley.

Walter de Say, who is represented as holding, in 1240, Stokesay and its members, two knight's fees under the Baron de Lacy. Upon his decease, Hugh de Say, his nephew, became lord of Stokesay, who gave the manor in exchange for property in Ireland to his suzerain, John de Verdon. In short, alienating all or nearly all his property, de Say settled in Ireland, and hence it arose that his descendants are not afterwards heard of in connection with this place.

John de Verdon, then, was lord of the fee-simple of Stokesay, being duly registered in the Inquisition of 1255 as lord of Stoke Say, Wetliton, and Neuton. This co-heir of Lacy held the manor of the general estate of Lacy. He held Stokesay by service of two knights, due at Ludlow Castle. The manor also owed the service of one knight in ward of Montgomery castle, in time of war, for forty days. Sir John de Verdon had for tenant here Reginald de Grey, whose son again, about 1281, conveyed the whole manor to Laurence de Ludlow, who thereupon came into full possession of Stokesay. In the feodary of 1284, Laurence de Ludlow is said to hold the vill of Stokesay, for one knight's fee, under John de Grey, which John held it under Theobald de Verdon, who, in turn, held of the king. It was Laurence de Ludlow who obtained licence from King Edward I., in 1290-1, to strengthen his mansion with a wall of stone and lime, and to crenellate or embattle the same. The remains of this fortified manor-house are now known as Stokesay Castle, an extremely interesting relic.

STOKESAY CHURCH.

We have said that Hugh de Say gave this church "of St. John of Suthestokes" to Haughmond Abbey. A bishop of Hereford granted to that abbey an appropriation of it before 1248. The Taxation of 1291, describing the church of Stokesay, in the deanery of Ludlow, as the abbot of Haughmond's, values the rectory thereof at £8 per annum; besides, the prior of Wenlock had a portion therein of £1 4s.; the prior of Bromfield one of 8s. 4d.; and the prior of Lanthony, 6s. 8d. The vicar's portion was £4 6s. 8d. In 1341, the parish was assessed only £3 to the *ninth*, because six virgates lay untilled, etc. In 1534-5, the preferment of the vicar of Stokesay was valued at £4 8s. 4d., less 7s. 8d. for procurations and synodals, and an annual average of 17s. 9d. for the bishop's triennial visitation.

Early Incumbent.—Master Adam, rector of Stoke, 1200—1234.

STOKESAY CASTLE.

Aldon, also held immediately of the crown by Roger de Lacy, is thus particularly noticed in *Domesday*:—"The same Roger holds Alledone. Siuuard held it, and was a free man. Here 2½ hides geldable. The land is for xv ox-teams. In demesne are ii teams, and there are viii teams among the male and female serfs; and xxiiii villains, ii boors, and one cottager, with viii teams among them all. Here is a mill of 5s. [annual value]. Of the land of this manor, Richard holds i hide, and Ældred one member of land. Thereon is one team, and xii villains, vii boors, and iii serfs, with iii teams. The church has half a hide [of land], and the priest one team, with one cottar. The whole manor in the time of King Edward, was worth 105s. Now, that portion which Roger [de Laci] holds is worth £8. That which his men [Richard and Ældred have is worth] 16s.; that which the priest has is worth 5s."[1] The church mentioned in *Domesday*, in connection with this manor, in process of time was transferred to Stokesay, it having become the most important place in the parish.

Corfton. Besides these manors just described, which he held of the king, Roger de Lacy held two other Culvestan manors of Earl Roger de Montgomery, and one under the Bishop of Hereford. *Domesday* says:—"The same Roger holds Cortune [of the earl], and Herbert holds it of him. Alsi held it. Here iii hides geldable. In demesne are ii ox-teams, and iiii neat-herds, iiii villains, and one boor with ii teams, and other ii teams there might be. Here is a *haye* for taking kids. [The manor in Saxon times] was worth 16s. Now 12s. [per annum]."[2] In Cortune, the dispossessed Saxon Alsi gave place to the Norman Herbert, who, accordingly, held this manor of the baron, Roger de Lacy. Corfton eventually passed to Burnel, bishop of Bath and Wells, who died in 1292 seized of it.

Middlehope. "Roger de Laci holds Mildehope, and Herbert holds it of him. Ælsi held it. Here i hide geldable. In demesne are ii ox-teams, and iiii serfs, ii villains, iiii boors, and i

---

[1] *Domesday*, fo. 260, b 2.   [2] Ibidem, fo. 256, b 1.

radman, with ii teams. In time of King Edward, the manor was worth 7s.; afterwards 2s. Now 20s."[1] Under Corfton we have spoken of Alsi or Ælsi the Saxon and his Norman successor Herbert. Herbert's descendant, De Furcis, early in the 13th century, enfeoffed in a portion of this manor a William de Middlehope, who, in 1203, was one of the coroners of Shropshire. Long after, this man's descendants continued to hold in Middlehope, under its seignoral lord. Like Corfton, Middlehope is now a township in the parish of Diddlebury.

Onibury was held by Roger de Lacy of the bishop of Hereford, in 1086, for *Domesday* records, that:—"The same bishop held, in King Edward's time, and now [holds] Aneberie. Roger de Laci holds it of him [the bishop]. Here iii hides geldable. In demesne is one ox-team, and iiii villains in gross, vi semi-villains, a priest, and one cottar with iii teams. Here is i serf. Here i knight holds i hide, and has i ox-team and v villains. In time of King Edward, there were in this manor ix ox-teams, and it was worth 40s. [annually]. Now it is worth 20s."[2] Roger de Lacy showed the respect which he entertained for the memory of Earl Roger de Montgomery by giving the tithes of Aniberie to Shrewsbury Abbey, on the day of the burial of his suzerain and political ally. The great Norman earl was buried in July, 1093-4; in 1095, the donor was banished. Roger de Lacy's brother Hugh then became mesne lord of Onibury, whose baronial successors continued to hold the manor by service due on a single knight's fee.

In 1175, William de Wootton was Lacy's under-tenant at Onibury, and he held both it and Walton, for half or three-quarters of a knight's fee, according as his lord required a military or a pecuniary *aid*. Eventually, Philip Burnel, nephew of the bishop, acquired Onibury.

THE CHURCH.

From the mention of a priest in the *Domesday* notice of Aniberie, it may be concluded that a church was then existent here. Nor does the circumstance that Roger de Lacy gave the tithes of Aniberie to the abbey of Shrewsbury render this less likely, for the Normans thought a great deal more of the institutions of

---

[1] *Domesday*, fo. 256. b 1.   [2] Ibidem, fo. 252, a 2.

monachism than they did of parochial necessities. In 1291, the church of Onebury, in Ludlow deanery, was valued at £10. The parish was assessed 50s. only to the *ninth* in 1341, because so heavy were the local burdens on the tenantry, that thirty virgates lay untilled, etc. 1534-5 the rector of Onybury's preferment was valued at £3 13s. 10d. per annum, less 11s. for procurations and synodals.

Early Incumbent.—Roger de Lodelowe, rector of Onebury, about 1276.

Upper Ledwich.

At the time of the survey, the Norman William Pantulf held four manors in Culvestan Hundred, all of which he held of Roger de Montgomery. One of them is thus described in Domesday Book:—" The same William holds Ledewic, and Berner [holds] of him. Uluric held it [in Saxon times]. Here ii hides geldable. The land is [capable of employing] iiii ox-teams. In demesne is one team, and [there are] ii neat-herds, ii villains, and iiii boors with i team. In the time of King Edward, the manor was worth 13s. 4d. Now 10s. He [Pantulf] found it waste."[1] The early history of this manor is involved with that of the neighbouring manor of Middleton.

Middleton Hugford.

According to *Domesday* :—" The same William holds Middeltone, and Berner [holds it] of him. Uluric and Eduin held it for ii manors. Here ii hides geldable. The land is for viii ox-teams. In demesne are ii teams and iiii neat-herds, one villain, and viii boors with i team, and a mill of 2s. [annual value]. [The manor] used to be worth 20s. Now 14s."[1] The Saxon Uluric or Aluric made way in no less than seven distinct manors for the Norman Pantulf. Berner, the Norman sub-tenant of Middleton, is presumed to have been ancestor of those Hugfords, who, long after Pantulf's seigneury over it had ceased, continued to hold Middleton, first under Lacy, and then under Fitz-Alan.

The chapel of Middleton, subject at first to Bitterley church, afterwards belonged to Wenlock priory.

---

[1] *Domesday*, fo. 257, b 1.

Little Sutton. "The same William," continues *Domesday*, "holds Sudtone. Aluric held it. Here half a hide geldable. The land is for ii ox-teams. In demesne is one team with ii neat-herds and one boor. The manor was worth 3s. [annually]. Now it is worth 9s. He [Pantulf] found it waste."[1]

The seigneury of William Pantulf over this small manor vanished from some cause or other, when the king making it a serjeantry, a family who derived their name from the place held Sutton under the crown by service of accompanying the sheriff, twice in each year, when the latter conveyed the ferm of the county to the Exchequer; the king paying all expenses.

Lawton. Not mentioned in *Domesday*, this place now forms one township with Little Sutton, with which from ancient times it has been associated. Like Little Sutton, Lawton, in the twelfth century had become a serjeantry, held *in capite* by the Baskervilles, who held estates not only in Shropshire, but in Herefordshire and Northamptonshire. The serjeantry by which Lawton was held varied. In 1211, the duty of its tenant was to provide one serving-man, with a lance, for the king's army of Wales.[2] According to the Munslow Jurors, Lawton was held in 1255 by serjeantry of the king; the service due being to find one archer, with bow and arrows, for fifteen days, in time of any Welsh war, at the tenant's cost.

Merston. "The same William holds Merstun. Gamel and Aluric held it. Here i hide and a half geldable. The land is for iii ox-teams. In demesne is one team, ii serfs, and iii boors. It was worth 15s.: now 10s."[3] Merston is conjectured to have been in Diddlebury parish.

Great Sutton. Helgot held of the Norman Earl, in the *Domesday* Hundred of Culvestan, four manors; namely, Great Sutton, Steventon, Poston, and Bouldon. Describing the first of these, *Domesday* says, that—"The same Helgot holds Sudtone, and Herbert holds of him. Aluric held it [in Saxon times] and was free. Here ii hides geldable. The [arable] land is for v ox-teams. In demesne are ii [teams] and iiii neat-herds, iiii villains and one boor, with iii teams. Here is a mill of 3s. [annual value.]

---

[1] *Domesday*, fo. 257, b 1.   [2] Testa de Nevill, p. 55.   [3] *Domesday*, fo. 257, b 1.

In the time of King Edward, the manor was worth 20s. [annually]: now 25s. [Helgot] found it waste."[1] Changes took place. The lords of Castle Holgate, Herbert's successors, had lost the seigneury over this manor by 1165; as in that year, Herbert de Castellis, the then lord of Castle Holgate, is returned by Hugh de Lacy as holding two fees of *new feoffment* in his barony. Great Sutton, including Wichcott, constituted one of these fees which Herbert held by service at Ludlow castle. The lords of Castle Holgate continued to hold under the heirs of Lacy, until, about 1257, the Earl of Cornwall having purchased the Shropshire estates of the former, he alienated the whole to the Knights Templars, who accordingly became lords of Sutton and Wichcott. Soon afterwards, the Templars' interest here passed to Robert Burnel, Bishop of Bath and Wells.

Steventon, although now only a member of the parish of Ludford, at *Domesday* was a manor complete in itself. We read that,—"The same Helgot holds Scevinton. Reuensuard held it and was a free man. Here i hide geldable. The land is for iiii ox-teams. In demesne are ii [teams]; and iiii male and ii female serfs, and iii villains with ii teams. In King Edward's time, it was worth 12s. Now 15s."[1]

Poston. "The same Helgot holds Possetorne. Aluric held it. Here i virgate of land geldable. There is land for half an ox-team. The manor was and is waste."[1]

Bouldon. "The same Helgot holds Bolledone. Seuuard and Elmund held it for ii manors, and were free. Here ii hides geldable. The land is for iii ox-teams. In demesne are ii teams and iiii neat-herds. [The manor formerly] was worth 8s. [annually]: now 15s. Helgot found it waste.[1] Before the end of the reign of Henry I. either Helgot or his successor had enfeoffed in this manor one who, deriving a surname from the place, figures in the *Liber Niger* as William de Bullardon; the knight's fee which he held under Herbert de Castellis being of *old feoffment*. More than a hundred and fifty years afterwards, this William's descendants still held Bouldon, under the lord of Castle Holgate.

---

[1] *Domesday*, fo. 258, b 2.

𝕿𝖍𝖊 𝕾𝖍𝖊𝖊𝖙, now merely a township in Ludford parish, was a *Domesday* manor held by Ralph de Mortemer immediately of the king. "The same Radulf holds Sethâ, and Ingelrann holds it of him. Leuenot held it with i berewick. Here ii hides geldable. There is land enough for iiii ox-teams. In demesne are ii teams, and iiii neat-herds, and ii villains with half a team. In the time of King Edward, the manor was worth 5s.; afterwards 2s.; now, 10s.[1]

𝕳𝖚𝖓𝖙𝖎𝖓𝖌𝖙𝖔𝖓, now a member of Ashford Carbonel, in 1086 was a manor held by Ralph de Mortemer of the Norman Earl. "The same Radulf holds Hantenetune, and Turstin holds it of him. Ludi held it. Here i hide and a half geldable. In demesne are ii ox-teams and iiii *serfs*,[2] ii villains, ii boors, and i radman with i team; and there might be another team here. Here is a mill of [i.e. paying a rent of] 400 eels. [The manor formerly] was worth 10s.; afterwards 5s.; now 10s."[3] It was a singular rent to pay, 400 eels for a mill.

Turstin, mentioned above, perhaps, was that Turstin de Wigmore, whom Ralph de Mortemer removed from Cleobury, giving him, it is not unlikely, Huntington and other manors in exchange. If so, Turstin, as appears from *Domesday*, was a man of great connections and wealth. He took his distinctive appellation of de Wigmore probably from something which he held in the *Chatellany* of Wigmore. His wife's great uncle, Osbern, was one of those Norman favourites whom the weak Edward the Confessor enriched at the expense of his own English subjects. Alured de Merleberge, his father-in-law, figures in the Conqueror's survey as holding manors in Surrey, Hants, Somersetshire, Herefordshire, and Wiltshire; and Turstin himself at the time of the survey, besides Huntington, had considerable tenures elsewhere; one of them, Merchelai, being held by him under Turstin Fitz-Rolf, or Rollo, the same who bore Duke William's gonfalon at the battle of Hastings.

Genealogists affirm that Turstin de Wigmore was ancestor of the great Herefordshire family of Lingen; and it is certain that

---

[1] *Domesday*, fo. 260, a 2.
[2] This word is underlined in the original record and *Bovarii* [neat-herds] written over it in correction.
[3] *Domesday*, fo. 256, b 2.

the Lingens held in the thirteenth century, under the Mortimers, the identical manors, Huntington among the number, which Turstin had held in the eleventh.

The following apparently well-attested tale of female devotion is recorded of a member of the house of Lingen:—In the year 1253 a marriage took place between Grimbald, son and heir of Richard Pauncefort, and Constantia, daughter of John Lingayn, which was celebrated amid such circumstances as could only be expected between families of the first rank and opulence. Impelled by the general enthusiasm of the age, Grimbald joined in the expedition against the Mahommedans of Tunis, but being taken prisoner, a joint of his wife was demanded by the Moorish captor as the only price of his liberty. Possibly the fame of the lady's beauty may have suggested to the swarthy heathen this cruel ransom; yet, urged by affection for her husband, and perhaps by zeal in what was deemed a sacred cause, Constantia did not hesitate to comply with the proposed terms, and cutting off her left hand above the wrist, she sent it to her husband in Africa. Grimbald accordingly was released, and returned home to that wife whose heroic love had saved him. When they died, Grimbald and his lady were buried at the east end of the south aisle of Cowarne church, and an altar with their effigies erected over them.

The crusader's monumental figure habited like that of an Anglo-Norman knight reposed cross-legged, whilst his lady's exhibited her left arm couped above the wrist. Only some dispersed fragments of this sculptured record of woman's love now remain; but the following is Mr. Silas Taylor's account of it, who examined it in the 16th century:—"To gainsay the report about it, I diligently viewed the accord which might have been between the two figures; the female laid next the wall of the south aisle, on her right side, by which means his left side might be contiguous to her right, the better to answer the figure; also, the stump of the woman's arm is somewhat elevated, as if to attract notice; and the hand and wrist, cut off, are carved close to his left side, with the right hand on his armour, as if for note."[1]

Upper Ashford. Following its notice of Huntington, comes this entry in *Domesday*:—"The same Radulf holds here-

---

[1] MS. *Harl. Bibl.*, quoted in Duncumb's *Herefordshire*, vol. 2, p. 99.

abouts one manor, and Richard holds it of him. Azor held it. Here i hide and a half geldable. In demesne, there is i ox-team and a half, and iiii serfs, ii villains, and ii boors, with one team. [Formerly] it was worth 5s.; now 10s."[1] Although the name is not specified, the above description refers to Upper Ashford or Ashford Jones. For two centuries, this small manor was held of the Mortimers, by the Burleys, under whom again held undertenants.

Ashford Carbonel was the only manor which the barons of Richard's Castle held in Culvestan Hundred:—" The same Osbern [Fitz Richard] holds Esseford. Ledi held it [in Saxon times]. Here are ii hides geldable. The land is for iiii ox-teams. Here one frenchman and iiii villains have ii teams. Here a mill [which renders annually] iii quarters of corn. In King Edward's time [the manor] was worth 16s.; now 8s. He [Osbern] found it waste."[2] It is doubtful whether or not the Frenchman alluded to above was ancestor of the Carbonels, who, as appears from the following charter of feoffment, had held this manor from a very early period :—" Osbern Fitz Hugh [baron of Richard's Castle, 1140—1185] grants, with consent of Hugh his brother, to William Carbunel and his heirs, to hold of the grantor and his heirs, all his land, viz., Hesford [Ashford] and Huvertone [Overton, in Burford manor], for service of half a knight's fee. Witnesses, Hugh de Say, Hugh his son," and twenty-one others. The original of this charter was with Sir Simon Archer in 1637. It had two seals, one representing a knight on horseback, charging sword in hand; it was the seal of Osbern Fitz Hugh. The other had the figure of a lion passant on it, and the words HUGONIS DE SAI of the legend still remaining.[3]

Hugh Carbonel figures in the *Nomina Villarum* of March, 1316, as lord of the *vill* of Ashford.

St. Mary's, Ashford Carbonel, now a perpetual curacy annexed to the vicarage of Little Hereford, appears originally to have been a chapel subject to that mother church.

Estune. Rainald, the Norman sheriff of Shropshire in 1086, held this large manor under the Earl of Shrewsbury; the fact is

---

[1] *Domesday*, fo. 256, b 2. [2] Ibidem, fo. 260, a 1.
[3] DUGDALE'S transcript of this ancient charter is in the Asmol. Lib., v. K.

thus recorded in Domesday Book:—"The same Rainald holds Estune. Elmund held it in King Edward's time. Here viii hides and a half geldable. In demesne are ii ox-teams, and vi serfs, v villains, viii boors, a priest, one frenchman, and one radman, with v ox-teams among them all; and yet there might be ix more teams [employed] here. There is a mill of [or yielding] iii measures of corn [annually]. In the time of King Edward, the manor was worth 65s.; now 40s. He [Rainald] found it waste."[1] It is conjectured that the ancient Estune is represented in the modern *vill* or township of Aston near Munslow.

MUNSLOW and ASTON MUNSLOW. To speak of Estune as represented by these manors; Henry I. probably granted the manorial estate to Richard Banastre, a man who, standing high in provincial importance, as lord of Munslow and Aston Munslow, appears to have held them *in capite* of the king. To him succeeded Thurstan Banaster, his son, in whom or else his successor of the same name ended the elder male line of this house (1154—1189). Thurstan left as his co-heirs two daughters, Margery wife of Richard Fitz Roger, and Matilda wife of William de Hastings.

BARONY OF HASTINGS.

William de Hastings' uncle Ralph, steward (*dapifer* or dispensator) in Queen Eleanor's household, appears to have enjoyed, in a high degree, the favour of Henry II., and to Ralph's estate, and also the great domains in Leicestershire, Warwickshire, Bucks, and Middlesex, of Erneburga de Flamville his own mother, William became heir. Considered in respect to the lands he also acquired with his wife, the daughter of Banaster, de Hastings therefore was a great holder, and his descendants heirs to a large inheritance. Yet, notwithstanding his riches, William was cut off in his prime. Matilda, his wife, survived him forty years. Of this noble's eldest son Henry, it is told by Brakelond, how, on the 1st of April, 1182, the youth, led by his uncle,[2] who had him under his protection, and surrounded by a brilliant retinue of knights, proudly appeared before the abbot and monks of St. Edmundsbury, to claim that hereditary office of *seneschalcy* held by his ancestors; but the good abbot objecting to the incompetency of the youth, a

---

[1] *Domesday*, fo. 255, a 1.
[2] Thomas de Hastings, who, according to genealogists, became ancestor of the Earls of Huntingdon of the Hastings' name.

deputy was for a time appointed. In 1190, the young baron followed King Richard to Palestine; a scutage on the fees he held under St. Edmundsbury in 1191 excusing him on that account. De Hastings fell a victim to crusading zeal; at any rate, he was dead without issue in 1194, as in that year his brother William offered 100 merks for his *relief* of the lands and serjeantry of said Henry. It was this William de Hastings III. who married Margery, daughter of Roger Bigod, the great Earl of Norfolk. De Hastings attended the parliament at Lincoln in November, 1200, when William, King of Scots, did homage to King John for the territory he held in England of the English king. A Feodary of St. Edmundsbury of the same year gives William de Hastings as holding five knight's fees under the abbey, but as he sided with the barons against King John, a writ, of April 10th, 1216, ordered the constable of Norwich to destroy William's castles and lay waste his lands, whilst another writ gave up to the abbot of St. Edmund's all lands the rebel held in his fee. Dying on January 28th, 1226, the deceased baron's son and heir, Henry, had livery for a fine of 50 merks of his lands.

Under 1240, we find Henry de Hastings enrolled as *tenant in capite* of one-fourth of a knight's fee in Eston and Mosselawe, and cotemporary notices of his tenures under the Crown, the Earls Ferrars, the Lords Marmion, and others in different counties; some of which lands descended to him from his father, whilst others accrued to him by his marriage with Ada, youngest sister and co-heir of John Scot, the great Earl of Huntingdon.

To treat more particularly of Munslow and Aston :—In 1167, being then held under Matilda Banaster and her husband by Robert Fitz Walkeline, these *vills* were amerced half a merk and one merk respectively by Alan de Nevill, justice of the forest.

In 1255, William de Venables was mesne-lord of Munslow, holding it of Henry de Hastings. In 1316, Robert de Beek, enrolled as lord of Munslow and Aston, appears to have been Hastings, immediate tenant in Munslow. The Hertwalls were Hastings' tenants at Aston; whilst John de Aston, Thomas de Munslow, and others of a lower degree, held under one or other of the greater tenants of Munslow and Aston.

CHURCH AND PARISH OF MUNSLOW.

The church indicated by the *Domesday* mention of a priest at Aston, is conjectured to have been subsequently transferred to

MUNSLOW CHURCH.

Munslow, as the more important place. Known as the church of Munslow before 1115, it claimed jurisdiction over an extensive Saxon parish of Shropshire. In 1291, the rectory of the church of Munslow, in Wenlock deanery, was valued at £11 6s. 8d. *per annum*; the vicar's portion was under £4. In 1341, the assessors of the *ninth* rated the parish at £3 only, as storms had destroyed the corn, there had been a murrain among the sheep, five carucates of land lay untilled, etc. In 1534-5, Monslowe rectory was valued at £21 15s. 2d. *per annum*.

WINDOW, MUNSLOW.

Early Incumbent.—Stephen, rector of Munslow, 1115.

Cardington. According to *Domesday*:—"The same Rainald holds Cardintune [of the Earl]. Austin and another Austin held it in King Edward's time for ii manors. Here v hides. In demesne is one ox-team, and v serfs, xv villains, and i radman with vii teams between them all, and there might be viii more teams here. There are ii leagues of wood here. In time of King Edward, the manor was worth 40s. [annually]; now it is worth the same."[1] Cardington, described above, comprised Enchmarsh, Chatwall, and Willstone. Alan Fitz Flaald and his descendants the Fitz Alans, succeeded to the *Domesday* estates of Rainald the sheriff, when William Fitz Alan I. evinced zeal on behalf of oppressed pilgrims to Jerusalem, by giving to the Knights Templars, soon after the establishment of that order, Cardington, Enchmarsh, and half the *vill* of Chatwall; also 3 merks annually from the church at Cardington, and 5s. from Cardington mill.

---

[1] *Domesday*, 255, a 1.

Having opposed Stephen throughout his usurpation, William died in 1160.

In 1167, named "Templars' Cardington," this vill was amerced 2 merks by Alan de Nevill, justice of the forest.[1] From a survey of the Templars' Shropshire estates in 1185, we learn that they had in Carditon 18 tenants holding half a virgate[2] or more, and 16 tenants holding less, rents varying from 3s. 4d. to 2s. per half-virgate; 2d. per acre being paid for a less quantity. Among the tenants were Inard the priest and his *wife*, who, curiously enough, are both entered as participating in the privileges of this monastic and military order, being charged 6d. and 4d. respectively. In 1187, and again in 1200, the *vill* of Cardington was amerced for waste by the justices of the forest, but, acting on their charter in the following year, the Templars obtained a king's writ ordering their acquittance. Immunities which, for 150 years, the Templars enjoyed in the manor of Cardington, however, came to an end on the suppression of that corrupted order by the Council of Vienna in 1311, when the farms and manors it possessed throughout Europe, by an edict of Pope Clement V., passed to the Hospitallers, excepting those estates which reverted to the heirs of the donors. Of such, many were in England, and among them Cardington, as we read that "the knights [Hospitallers] granted it to Edmund Fitz Alan, Earl of Arundel," the heir in question, who accordingly figures in the territorial survey of 1316 as "lord of the *vill* of Cardington."

CARDINGTON CHURCH AND PARISH.

Cardington, even in the time of the Conqueror, was an extensive parish. Its church, very ancient, was held by the Templars, who had the rectory, as well as the advowson of its vicarage, to whom as belonging, in 1291, the church of Cardynton, in the deanery of Wenlock, was valued at £13 6s. 8d., the vicar's portion being £4 per annum additional; and it was exempt from the *tenths* paid by English parochial churches, at that period, to the Roman see. In 1341, the parish was taxed only £5 to the *ninth*, owing to non-cultivation of lands, murrain among sheep, etc. The rectorial value of this church is not mentioned in the *Valor* of 1534-5, but the vicarage was then worth £6 10s., less 7s. 8d. for procurations and synodals.

Early Incumbent.—Arnolf, rector, in 1185.

---

[1] *Rot. Pip.* 13 and 16 Hen. II., Salop.   [2] A virgate consisted of 40 acres.

Hope Bowdler. The Celtic *Hope*, in composition, denotes a small valley between two mountains. Camden understood it to signify a "hill-side." In early Saxon times, this place was known as the hope or valley of Forthred, hence its name of Fordritishope in *Domesday*. "The same Hugh [Fitz-Turgis] holds [of the earl] Fordritishope. Edric Salvage held it. Here iii hides geldable. The land is for vi ox-teams. In demesne are ii teams and iii serfs, ii female serfs, and ii villains with i team. There are two leagues of wood. In the time of King Edward, it was worth 25s. Now 15s."[1] Hugh Fitz-Turgis, mentioned above, held also Wilderley and Chelmick under Earl Roger; but ere long, through some cause or other, these were annexed to the fief which Henry I. bestowed on Baldwin de Bollers. It was while this manor was held by the De Bollers, that it acquired the distinctive appellation of Hope Bollers or Buthlers, of which Bowdler is the modern representative.

THE CHURCH.

In 1291, the church of Hope Boulers, in the deanery of Wenlock, was valued at £4 13s. 4d. per annum. The rector of Rushbury had also a portion of 2s. therein. In 1341, owing to its general poverty, the assessors of the *ninth* taxed the parish only £1 6s. 8d. In 1534-5, this preferment was valued at £6 13s. 4d., less 6d. per annum for synodals.

Early Incumbent.—Nicholas, "parson of Hope Bulers," in 1248, was amerced one merk for a false claim before the justices then in *eyre* at Salop.

Clee Stanton is described in *Domesday* as follows:—"The same church [St. Milburg's] held [in Saxon times] and now holds Clee. Here ii hides. Here is one tenant and one ox-team, and six other teams might be here. Its old value was 18s. Now [it is worth] 6s. per annum."[2] Wenlock priory retained possession of the manor till Henry VIII.'s time.

Lower Poston is described in *Domesday*, under the title, *Quod tenet (ecclesia) Sancti Michaelis*, thus:—"The church of St. Michael holds Possetorn of the earl. Chetel held it. Here is one

---

[1] *Domesday*, fo. 258, b 2.   [2] Ibidem, fo. 252, b 2.

virgate of land. The [arable] land [is enough] for half an ox-team. One tenant renders for the same a bundle of box on Palm Sunday." [1] Reft from Chetel, its former Saxon proprietor, the small manor in question was then bestowed by the Norman Earl Roger upon that chapel in Shrewsbury Castle which, appropriately dedicated to Michael, the warrior-angel, is known in *Domesday* as the" Church of St. Michael." The church then sublet its acquisition to a tenant who held the manor, upon condition that he should annually furnish a bundle of box, to deck St. Michael's on Palm Sunday. As the palm did not grow in England, branches of box-tree were invariably used as a substitute.

Bromfield. Under the heading, " *Quod tenet Ecclesia Sanctæ Mariæ,*" we read in the Conqueror's record, that :—"The same church holds Brunfelde, and there it is built. Here are now x hides, and in demesne vi ox-teams, and [there are] xii neat-herds, xv villains, and xii boors, with viii teams. It is worth 50s. [annually] to the canons; and Nigel the physician, has 16s. [annually] from this manor. In this manor there were, in King Edward's time, xx hides, and xii canons of the said church had the whole. One of them, Spirtes by name, had alone x hides. But when he was banished from England, King Edward gave these x hides to Robert Fitz-Wimarch, as to a canon. But Robert gave the same land to a certain son-in-law of his, which thing, when the [other] canons had shown to the king, forthwith [the king] ordered that the land should revert to the church, only delaying till, at the court of the then approaching Christmas, he should be able to order Robert to provide other land for his son-in-law. But the king himself died during those very festal days, and, from that time till now, the church hath lost the land. This land Robert now holds under Earl Roger, and it is waste and was found waste. One part with another, the arable land is sufficient to employ liiii ox-teams." Nigel or Nihel, the clerk alluded to in this interesting extract, was physician to Earl Roger de Montgomery. Spirtes lived in the reigns of two Anglo-Danish kings, namely, Harold and Hardacanute, and also in the time of the Anglo-Saxon king, Edward the Confessor. Whether the circumstance that Spirtes had been a favourite with the sons of Canute

---

[1] *Domesday*, fo. 252, b 2.

indicates a Danish descent in him or not, we cannot tell; but, for some cause or other, Edward the Confessor banished him.

Robert Fitz-Wimarch, to whom, upon the banishment of Spirtes, King Edward gave the ten hides of Bromfield, is presumed to have been identical with Robert the deacon, that Norman ecclesiastic whose daughter Richard Scrob married; and doubtless the un-named son-in-law of the *Domesday* entry just quoted was Scrob. When, in 1052, the English, at the instigation of Earl Godwin, insisted upon the banishment of the Norman favourites of Edward the Confessor, exceptions were made in favour both of Robert, the deacon and his son-in-law, who were indulgently suffered to remain in the land that had enriched them.

The canons of St. Mary objecting, as it seems, to the alienation by Robert Fitz-Wimarch of half this, their manor, laid the matter before Edward the Confessor, when the Basileus "ordered that the land should revert to the Church, only delaying till, at the court of the then approaching Christmas, he should be able to order Robert to provide other land for his son-in-law. "But the king himself," continues *Domesday*, "died during those very festal days." At reading these words, the circumstances attending the demise of the king alluded to are recalled to memory. Edward the Confessor wore, as was his wont, his crown, on the solemn festival of Christmas, at London, in the year 1065, when, attacked by more than ordinary ailment, the king ordered that church which, some years previously, in performance of a vow he had commenced to build in the "Isle of Thorns," at once to be dedicated to St. Peter, for he felt that he was dying. Three days afterwards, on the 28th of December, 1065, accordingly, Westminster Abbey was consecrated.

As he drew near his end, weakly in mind as in body, strange visions appeared to the sick Edward. Singular premonitions of hostile invasions scared the distraught intellect of the Confessor. "The Lord has bent His bow; the Lord has prepared His sword; He brandishes it like unto a warrior; He manifests His anger in steel and flame," exclaimed involuntarily the king, and Edward's pale face, upon which now fast settled the death-dew, flushed with unwonted excitement, as, with sightless eyes and relaxed grasp, he sank back on his pillow exhausted. The archbishop Stigand smiled at what he considered merely the ravings of dotage; yet many who stood around were apprehensive of the truth of the dying monarch's predictions: fears and alarms being then unaccountably rife throughout England. Who may tell what anxious what remorseful thoughts pressed upon the brain of the expiring Edward, in that hour of Nature's weakness ? Conscious of having aroused the hyena passions of the warlike Norman, who indeed shall unravel the entangled skein of his reflections, as, perturbed for the future of his unfortunate kingdom, the childless Confessor king fast hastened to his account. After having reigned twenty-three years, six months, and twenty days, he died on Twelfth-Day Eve, January 5th, 1066, and on Twelfth-Day, in the Minster which so recently he had caused to be hallowed, amid "bitter grief," they buried the last legitimate Anglo-Saxon king. So much for what passed in "those very festal days" spoken of in the *Domesday* entry relating to Bromfield.

Bromfield Priory.

The Saxon and collegiate church of St. Mary of Bromfield after the conquest became a regular monastic institution; and the fact that Osbert, *Prior* of Bromfield, attested about 1115 an ordinance of the Viceroy de Belmeis, proves that a change had taken place in the Saxon constitution of this church by that date. Owing to the non-existence of any Bromfield Chartulary, little is known concerning the history of this religious establishment; yet certain it is, that very early in the reign of Henry II. Bromfield had become a Benedictine Priory, subject to Gloucester Abbey, and so it continued until the dissolution.

The manor of Bromfield and its members, BURWAY, CLAY FELTON, RYE FELTON, WHITBATCH, HALFORD, and DINECHOPE, appear to have been held in demesne by the monks. Pope Nicholas' Taxation, in 1291, gives the following estimate of the Prior of Bromfield's income, as lord of this manor:—Eight carucates of land yielded £4 *per ann*. The hay (ten loads at 1s.6d.) was worth 15s. The *assized rents* and *tallage* of *natives* amounted to £22 13s. 4d. Pleas and perquisites of court, the labour-dues and fines (on copyhold land) were £3. The *pannage* of swine yielded 2s., three mills £3, and £7 2s. which arose from profits on stock (8 cows and 260-ewe sheep) made a total of £40 12s. 4d. *per ann*. £78 19s. 4d. was about the income which the Priory derived from the manor of Bromfield and its adjuncts in 1534-5.

BROMFIELD CHURCH AND PARISH.

The original Saxon parish of Bromfield was of vast extent.

BROMFIELD CHURCH.

HALFORD CHAPEL.

In 1291, the church of Brompfield, in the deanery of Ludlow, represented as the prior's own, was valued at £23 6s. 8d.; the vicar's portion being less than £4: moreover, a portion of £1 went to the prior of Wenlock. In 1341, the parish was rated only £9 to the *ninth* of its wheat, wool, and lamb, because four carucates lay uncultivated, etc. In 1534-5, the tithes which the prior of Bromfield received as rector of this church amounted to over £21 6s. The vicar's net income at the same time being £5 5s. 7d.

Early Incumbent.—Sir Thomas de Bromfend, 1285; patrons, the abbot and convent of Gloucester.

LITTLE BROMFIELD, LITTLE HALTON, HILL HALTON, and OAKLEY, appear to have been members of Bromfield, alienated however by very early feoffment. The interesting chapel of Halford bespeaks great antiquity, yet the first recorded notice of it is in the *Valor* of 1534-5, where its chaplain is described as receiving £2 from the prior of Bromfield for his services.

Shropshire, at the time of the Conqueror's survey, contained several members which are now in Herefordshire: on the contrary, the *Domesday* Herefordshire included some places which are now in Shropshire. The latter applies to the greater part of the territory once attached to Richard's Castle, that stronghold which Richard Scrupe founded in Herefordshire, where the *vill* of Richard's Castle to this day remains. The Shropshire constituent of the honour of Richard's Castle in 1255 contained five hides, which, collectively called the *Franchalimot of Wollerton*, was divisible into the following distinct estates:—Wollerton, Overton, Ashford Bowdler, Batchcott, Mora now Moor Park, Turford, and Whitebroc, all of which were held by different tenants of the ancient lords of Richard's Castle.

Ludlow.

As being situated also in Cutestorn Hundred, Herefordshire, a manor is described in *Domesday* as follows:—
"The same Osbern [Fitz Richard] holds [of the king] Lude, and Roger de Laci [holds it] of him. Saisi held it [in Saxon times]. Here ii hides, geldable. In demesne are ii ox-teams, and one villain, a bailiff [*prepositus*], and a smith with ii teams. [The manor] was worth 25s. [annually in Saxon times]; now 30s." [1]

---

[1] *Domesday*, fo. 186, b 2.

The mention of a provost and a smith, coupled with the improved value of the manor, although they might not suggest, yet they tally with the notion of an existent borough, or intended residence of a great feudal chief. At any rate, the above is the only entry in *Domesday* likely to refer to the now parliamentary borough of Ludlow.

Authorities of note [1] interpret the name *Ludlow* as Léobe-hlæþ, Leode-hlæw, the *tumulus*, grave or hill of the people. Eyton [2] supposes rather that the original *vill* was called Lude from some adjacent ford of the river Teme, and that after *Domesday* Ludlow got its distinctive name from the *low* or *tumulus* which was a prominent feature of the town.

Osbern Fitz Richard's seigneury over Lude was soon transferred to his potent tenant Roger de Lacy, who built Ludlow Castle. The foundation of Ludlow has been ascribed to Earl Roger de Montgomery;[3] yet it can be shown from *Domesday* that the territory upon which that fortress was erected, did not belong to him. Considering, therefore, that close to Ludlow, on the northwest, lay Lacy's enormous manor of Stanton, in whose hundred of Culvestan this baron also had other great interests; add, that Roger de Lacy had no castle in Shropshire, and that Ludlow became the seat of his successors, and it will appear extremely probable that this baron reared Ludlow castle. This first-class Anglo-Norman fortress would appear to have sprung into existence between the years 1086, when *Domesday* does not mention it, and the year 1095, when Roger de Lacy was banished.

Ludlow castle then had for its lord, Hugh de Lacy, brother of the exiled baron, and afterwards it appears to have been entrusted by Henry I. to the keeping of Pagan Fitz-John, in whose time it is probable that its bulwarks had more than once to withstand the attack of the exasperated Welsh. The Welsh managed to kill the "Lord of Ewias" at last, when King Stephen, seizing Ludlow, appointed Joceas de Dynan to be its castellan. But Joceas rebelled against his benefactor; and Stephen, after his visit to Worcester in state on April 30th, 1139, diverged to Ludlow, when, rearing two counter-forts against the castle, he laid siege to it.[4] The generally accurate Norman chronicler tells how the Scottish Prince Henry, then with the usurper, riding under the walls of

---

[1] WRIGHT's *Ludlow*, p.13.   [2] *Antiq. of Shropshire*, vol.5, p.238.
[3] *Hist. of Fulk Fitz Warine* (Warton Club, 1855), p.3.
[4] FLORENCE OF WORCESTER, p. 267. Bohn's Ed.

Ludlow was seized by an iron grapple, which the besieged flung out, and being dragged from his horse, would have been hauled into the castle had not Stephen daringly rescued him. It does not appear that the brave usurper succeeded in reducing Ludlow.

The early history of Ludlow, meagre and unsatisfactory, is somewhat relieved by the following :—" War arose between Sir Hugh de Mortimer and Sir Joce de Dinan, then lord of Ludlow, insomuch that this same Joce could not freely or at pleasure enter or quit his castle of Ludlow for fear of Sir Hugh, so pertinaciously the latter pursued the war. And because Joce could prevail nothing against Sir Hugh by force; he set spies along the roads where he heard that Sir Hugh was to pass unattended, and took him and held him in his castle in prison, until he had paid his ransom of three thousand merks of silver, besides all his plate and his horses and birds (hawks)."[1] The Fitz Warine chronicle confirms the truth of this story when it speaks of Sir Joce de Dynan, lord of Ludlow, "mounting the highest tower in the third bail of the castle, which is now called by many Mortimer. And it has the name of Mortimer for this reason, that one of the Mortimers was in it a good while imprisoned."[2] The circumstance alluded to took place before the accession of Henry II. in 1154, more than seven hundred years ago; yet still, Mortimer's tower is pointed out among the ruins of Ludlow castle.

Tradition dwells also upon a sanguinary feud between the lord of Ludlow and the lord of Ewias, " for which discord many a good knight and many a brave man lost his life; for each invaded the other, burnt their lands, plundered and robbed their people, and did much other damage . . . . . One summer's day, sir Joce rose early in the morning, and ascended a tower in the middle of his castle, to survey the country ; and he looked towards the hill which is called Whitcliff, and saw the fields covered with knights, squires, sergeants, and valets, some armed on their steeds, some on foot ; and he heard the horses neigh, and saw the helms glittering. Among whom he saw the banner of Sir Walter de Lacy, blazing new with gold, with a fess of gules across. Then he called his knights, and ordered them to arm and mount their steeds, and take their arblasters and their archers, and go to the bridge below the town of Dynan, and defend the bridge and the ford that none passed it. Sir Walter and his people thought to pass safely; but

---

[1] WRIGHT'S *History of Ludlow*, p.113.   [2] *History of Fulk Fitz Warine*, p.34.

the people of Sir Joce drove them back, and many on both sides were wounded and killed. At length came Sir Joce 'and his banner, all white with silver, with three lions passant, of azure, crowned with gold; with five hundred with him, knights and servants on horse and foot, besides the burgesses and their servants who were good. Then, with great force, Joce passed the bridge, and the hosts encountered body to body. Joce struck Godebrand, who carried the banner of Lacy, through the body with a spear. Then the Lacy lost his banner. Then the people exchanged blows, and many on both sides were slain. But the Lacy had the worst; for he went off flying and discomfited, and took his way beside the river of Teme. The lady, with her daughters and her other damsels, had ascended a tower, whence they saw all the battle, and prayed God devoutly, to save their lord and his people from hurt and defeat." Distinguishing De Lacy by his coat-of-arms, flying all alone, Joce struck spurs into his steed and overtook him, when Lacy, seeing nobody but Joce, turned, and fought him. Partizans of both soon joined in the fray. At length, after a desperate encounter, in which the Lacy bravely defended himself, he was taken, and led over the river to Ludlow. The knight's wounds were seen to, and Lacy being carried " into a tower which is called Pendover," there he was guarded with great honour.

De Lacy, however, escaped from his prison, and captured by stratagem the stronghold in which he had been imprisoned; when a savage struggle ensuing, *Dynan* or Ludlow was burnt, half-destroyed, and so forth.[1]

Upon the suspected treason of Hugh de Lacy in 1181, Henry II. laid hands on Ludlow Castle, and it continued to remain in *manu regis* until after 1190, as in that year the sheriff of Shropshire charged £10 9s. 8d. for storing it with corn, oats, bacon, and wine, and had paid, under authority of the Chancellor Longchamp, to Gilbert de Essartis 100s. for custody of the castle. Walter, son of Hugh de Lacy, had not long recovered possession of Ludlow when King Richard, and afterwards King John, held in their hands both Ludlow town and castle, apparently as a security for the fealty of their potent lord. In 1212, " the castle and *vill* of Luddellawe, with their appurtenances," were still in the hands of King John, but upon November 2nd, 1214, John sent to the sheriff of Herefordshire the following characteristic writ :—" The King to

---

[1] *History of Fulk Fitz Warine*, p. 24 and following.

LUDLOW CASTLE.

Engelard de Cygon, greeting. What thou reportest thyself to have done in the matter of the swine is well done; and; although it may be better worth while to restore the castle of Ludelawe [to Lacy] than to pay 40 merks *per annum* for its custody, yet keep you the said castle in our hand, and let Walter de Lacy have the *vill* according to the agreement between him and us, because we don't wish to flinch from the said agreement."[1] At length, on April 12th, 1215, King John ordered Engelard to deliver up to "our faithful and beloved Walter de Lacy his castle of Ludlow," and the leal-hearted western lord-marcher stood by the ill-fated king to the last.

A patent of Henry III., dated at Worcester 5th of July, 1223, offers safe conduct to Lewellyn, Prince of Wales, if he will meet the king at Ludlow, but the Cymrian prince rejected the offer.

Eyton draws attention to a charter[2] of Walter de Lacy, dated at Trim, Ireland, 1st August, 1234, in which that great Irish lord concedes to William de Lucy, for his homage and service, the seneschalship of his English possessions, and in consideration of certain land which the baron gave him, " William and his heirs were to be constables of Lodelawe castle, which they should keep, or cause to be kept, at their own cost for ever. They were further to maintain a chaplain, a porter, and two sentinels there, as they had been maintained aforetime. This was to be the rule when the grantor or his heirs proposed to make any *short* stay at Ludlow castle; but in time of hostility, the grantor and his heirs should garrison the castle, and the grantee and his heirs should remain in the *outer bailey*, so long as such garrison should be there. The grantee and his heirs were further to take, in the grantor's absence, such rates, taxed upon bread and beer, in the *vill* of Ludelawe, as the grantor had been accustomed to take, or could lawfully take, when present. The repairs which William de Lucy and his heirs were to do at the walls and dwellings of the castle were to be at the grantor's cost, under *view* (*i.e.* valuation) of two lawful men of the *vill*. The grantee and his heirs should have fuel from the same *bosc*, as former constables. If William or his heirs, by command of the grantor or his heirs, should go any whither on the grantor's territory to hold a court, to audit accounts, or expedite other of the grantor's affairs, they should be provided in all necessaries of food and drink for themselves and five horses. Further,

---

[1] Claus. I., 173. [2] DUGDALE'S MSS., K. fo. 19.

the grantor would provide, for the grantee and his heirs male, all garments and accoutrements as for a knight of his own household," etc. Among the witnesses to this charter were Sir Richard, Bishop of Meath, Sir Geoffrey de Marisco (late viceroy of Ireland), Symon and Almeric de Lascy, Hugh de Stanton then chancellor to Walter de Lacy, and William de Ponte, clerk, the notary who drew up the deed. It was attested by the grantor's seal, charged with a simple *fesse*, the well-known cognizance of his house.

As in the case of Bridgnorth and other fortresses, services of castle-guard were due at Ludlow from neighbouring manors; for instance, two virgates in Wigley were held by Robert Duvile by service of fifteen days' ward in the tower of Ludlow castle in wartime.

About 1264-5, Simon de Montfort, backed by Lewellyn, is said to have reduced Ludlow castle; but ere Evesham was fought the royalists had recaptured it.

The donjon or keep of Ludlow, the oldest part of the castle, was built, says Wright, probably soon after the year 1090. "This massive tower, which rises to the height of 110 feet, is a very fine example of the style which was introduced by Bishop Gundulf, as it is seen at Rochester."[1] The keep of Ludlow has, however, sustained several alterations since it was first erected. The original entrance was on the first floor at the east turret, and as a precautionary measure it was probably approached by a flight of steep steps running down by the side of the tower. The old entrance still exists, but its inconvenience being felt in the 15th century, the steps were taken away and a new entrance worked in the mass of the wall, with a doorway of the time of Henry VIII., leading by a flight of steps to the first floor, and opening into the chief room of the keep, at the foot of the newel staircase, which runs up the northern turret, and formed the communication between the different floors and the top of the tower. Underneath was the great dungeon or vault, which appears originally to have been approached by a passage descending in the mass of the wall from the old entrance. In later times, a door was made in the north-east side, on a level with the ground.

Most of the windows and doorways of the keep of Ludlow, display the round Norman arch. The castle appears to have been completed by Joce de Dynan, in the reign of Henry I., when it

---

[1] WRIGHT'S *History of Ludlow*, p.86.

LUDLOW CASTLE, INTERIOR.

probably covered the same ground as at present. It consisted of three wards : first, the keep, or last stronghold in case of extremity ; secondly, the castle properly so-called, or the mass of buildings within the inner moat round what is now popularly termed the inner court; thirdly, the large court without, also surrounded by strong walls and towers, and a moat. Into this court it was that the townsmen, with their property, the cattle, and the neighbouring peasantry were wont to hurry for shelter whenever a hostile invasion took place. The place of one of the fosses or moats is now occupied by walks on the side of the town. The opposite side of the castle being reared upon the verge of a precipitous rock, was not so liable to attack, consequently it did not require the protection of a moat.

The chapel of St. Mary Magdalene, Ludlow Castle, seems to have been built in the reign of Henry I. All that now remains of it is the nave, a circular building, similar to the round church at Cambridge, and the Temple church, London. Ludlow chapel is entered from the west by a richly-decorated Norman doorway. Opposite is a large and beautifully-ornamented Norman arch, which once formed the entrance into the choir, now, alas! entirely destroyed. The circular structure still existing has three semicircularly headed Norman windows : the arcade within is formed by round arches, having alternate plain and zigzag mouldings resting on small pillars with indented capitals. This chapel is a very noble monument of the period at which it was erected.

The BOROUGH or town of Ludlow, existent long before the Conquest, in point of antiquity ranks second only to Shrewsbury. This can be proved by a very satisfactory species of historical evidence, namely, the evidence of coins. Coins stamped Lud, Luda, or Lude, were struck by authorised Ludlow moneyers in the reigns of Edgar (A.D. 959), Edward II., Ethelred II., Canute, Harold I., and Edward the Confessor. Shrewsbury had its moneyers as early as the reign of the Anglo-Saxon King Athelstane (A.D. 925).

Excepting the notice in *Domesday* of the *prepositus reeve* or bailiff resident at Lude, no further allusion is made to the borough of Ludlow until the reign of Henry III., when there is more than one notice of it. The insignificance of Ludlow during the 12th century is evident from the circumstance, that it possessed no religious house before the reign of King John.

In 1187, Robert Marmion and his associates visiting Shropshire amerced Herbert, provost of Ludelaw, £5, because he had not produced before the justices a certain money-forger who had lodged in his borough. Licensed minting in Ludlow ceased about the reign of William I. : to judge, however, from the number of cases of money-forging connected with the early history of Ludlow, some of its former inhabitants appear to have been loth to part with their ancient craft.

At the assize of 1203, the *vill of Ludelawe* appeared as an independent liberty. In the reign of John, there was a bridge at Ludford, which is mentioned in charters of Henry III. : it was known by the name (*pontem de Temede*) Teme bridge.

A patent, issued on December 17th, 1232, conferring facilities for a plan of enclosing the town of Ludlow with a wall, and in 1260, Geoffrey de Genevill was empowered to levy customs or *murage* for five years towards walling Ludlow. Patents for *murage* at Ludlow also occur in 1267, 1272, 1280, 1285, 1290, 1294, 1301, and 1304.

Ludlow appears to have enjoyed the usual privileges of free boroughs. Its corporate body of themselves discharged certain responsibilities which, in unchartered towns, presented an excuse for the interference of the sheriff, escheator, or other officers of the crown. The men of Ludlow had the privilege of buying and selling at Montgomery without paying any toll. We search in vain, however, for any detailed account of the customs and privileges formerly exercised by the municipality of Ludlow.

One of the first things that engaged the attention of Edward I. after his return from Palestine, was to put a check upon that spirit of lawlessness which had been fostered by the weak rule of his father Henry III. For this purpose, King Edward caused inquisitions to be made throughout the hundreds in every county ; and the results which have been preserved in the Hundred Rolls present us with numerous instances of the insecurity of person as well as property at that period. The jealousies between the feudal lords and the towns, and even between one town and another, gave rise to frequent scenes of violence. The townsmen of Ludlow appear to have been frequently ill-treated by the retainers of the lords of Wigmore and Corfham. One day, the foresters of Wigmore seized on Elias Millar of Ludlow on the highway between Ludlow and the Sheet, and took from him his sword and bow, and having tied his hands behind him, led him thus to Steventon, where they further extorted two shillings from him and then let him go.[1] On another occasion, as the bailiffs of Castle Holgate were bringing six quarters of oats towards Ludlow, as they passed by Corfham, they were attacked on the high road by the bailiffs of John Giffard of Corfham, who, leading the horses into the demesne of their lord, sowed the oats and harrowed the ground with the horses that had carried them. We read also that at another time, as a cart of John Giffard, lord of Corfham, was passing through Ludlow, it smashed a chaldron belonging to Richard de Olreton, one of the burgesses, when the carter, not having wherewith to pay for the damage, left one of his horses in pledge. No sooner did the constable of Corfham hear of this, however, than he ordered the cattle of dame Sibil de Olreton to be seized, and he detained them eight days till Richard de Olreton (who was probably her husband), not only gave up the horse but consented to pay a fine of 60s., 45s. 7d. of which he was obliged to pay down, apparently all the ready money he could procure. Again, we are told by those rolls, that the constable of Wigmore seized forty head of cattle belonging to burgesses of Ludlow, as they were passing through the barony of Clun from Montgomery fair; and, driving them to Wigmore castle, he detained for a piece of cloth of a woman of Wigmore, which he pretended had been cut and sold in the town of Ludlow. Such was the state of justice at the period alluded to on the border.

Foremost among the wealthy burgesses of Ludlow, stood Laurence de Ludlow, founder of the prosperous family of Ludlow. He flourished towards the close of the 13th century. Acquiring enormous wealth, as a Ludlow clothier, Laurence then exchanged his mercantile for a territorial importance, and became lord of the castle and manor of Stokesay.

The following names occur as burgesses of Ludlow in Edward the First's time. Robertus Clericus (the clerk); Rogerius Monetarius (the coiner or money-dealer); Reginaldus le Fulur (the fowler); Elyas Molendarius (the miller); Stephanus le Grindar (the grinder); Thomas Cyrothecarius (the glover); Galfridus Aurifaber (the goldsmith); Willelmus Pistor (the baker); Reginaldus Tinctor (the dyer); Hugo le Mercer (the mercer). These names belonged to the persons exercising the trades and callings alluded to, and at the present would be represented by the titles—Robert Clark, Roger Coiner, Reginald Fowler, Elias Miller, Stephen

---

[1] *Rot. Hundred*, II, 99.

Grinder, Thomas Glover, Geoffrey Goldsmith, William Baker, Reginald Dyer, and Hugh Mercer. We glean from these names the number and character of the trades exercised at Ludlow in the reign of Edward I.

Numerous are the notices of shops and messuages in ancient Ludlow. At the period of which we write, premises were *let* after this fashion:—" October, 1277. Hugh Brayn and Alice, his wife, enfeoff Philip Fitz-Stephen in a messuage, for 40s. paid, and a ½ rent." Or, as in this case:—" November, 1285. Peter Furbet, and Oldeburgh, his wife, enfeoff Laurence de Ludlow in a messuage and shop in Ludlow, to hold of the grantors and the heirs of Oldeburgh, at a rent of *one rose*. One *sore sparrow-hawk* is said to be paid for this grant."

CHURCH OF ST. LAURENCE.

Existent, perhaps, in the time of King Athelstane, the church or chapel at Lude, at that remote period, was probably a dependence of the Saxon church of St. Mary's, Bromfield. Generally speaking, our parochial and ecclesiastical boundaries have been preserved far more intact than our civil and manorial boundaries; as therefore Ludlow is represented as giving name to a deanery in even the earliest written records, the great ecclesiastical antiquity of Ludlow may be hence inferred.

In 1199, the people of *Ludelau*, finding their church too small for the growing necessities of their town, determined on enlarging it by lengthening it towards the east. The *lowe* or *tumulus*, from whence originated the name of the town, presented, however, an obstacle to their undertaking. It was levelled, when, as a matter of course, it was found to contain human remains. This was a notable discovery for the slenderly-paid clerks officiating at Ludlow, who, forthwith transforming stinking bones into relics of saints, collected them carefully, placed them in a coffer, and, on the 11th of April, with great reverence, deposited them in Ludlow church. A scroll, well preserved, inwardly by wax and outwardly by lead, which the Ludlow clerks said they had also found, conveniently explained all about the disentombed skeletons: they were no other than the remains of three Irish saints, namely, St. Fercher, father of St. Brendan; St. Corona, St. Brendan's mother, and St. — Cochel, brother of St. Corona. By way of explanation as to how three Irish saints came to be found in that out-of-the-way place, the scroll added that these worthies had " lived on the spot for fifteen years, what time they adopted the protection of

LUDLOW CHURCH.

p. 348.

the saints of Britain, distrustful [of their own country], after the death of Luda." Clerks, living under the shadow of the castle of a great Irish lord, would find small difficulty in learning somewhat concerning Irish saintship. The easy-minded, superstitious, good folk of Ludlow failed to detect the pious fraud that was being palmed off on them; and, for many a long year afterwards, these precious bones yielded a goodly income to the formerly poor clerks of Ludlow.

Among the Harleian MSS. in the 'British Museum [1] is a book which, at the end of the 13th century, or beginning of the 14th, belonged to St Laurence's, Ludlow. The greater portion of the volume is written in the Anglo-Norman language. Its contents are of a mixed theological and literary kind, and illustrate the class of reading then fashionable with a man of taste of the clerical order. At the commencement of the book is a calendar, which informs us that the church of St. Laurence was dedicated on the 13th of February, but the year is not stated. Next follows a copy of the early Anglo-Norman prose version of the Psalms. Thirdly, a metrical Anglo-Norman version of some parts of the Psalms; fourthly, the Bestiaire d'Amours, a poetical description of animals, etc., with curious moralisations; fifthly, the rules given by Robert Grosteste for regulating the household and lands of a nobleman; sixthly, the French version of Turpin's History of Charlemagne; seventhly, a French treatise on confession; eighthly, various fragments, among which are many charms, and a treatise on chiromancy; ninth, the "Manuel des Pechés," a well-known religious poem, attributed to Robert Grosteste; tenth, an account of St. Patrick's purgatory, in French verse; eleventh, a French poem, entitled La Pleinte d'Amour; twelfth, various religious matters, in Latin.

In its present shape, St. Laurence's, Ludlow, was built either in the reign of Edward II., or early in that of Edward III.

Pope Nicholas' Taxation values the church of Lodelawe, in the deanery of Lodelawe, at £13 6s. 8d. per annum.

In 1341, a special jury taxed Ludlow, as a mercantile town, to the current assessment, when the great sum of £72 12s. 11d. was returned as the *ninth* of the moveable goods of its burgesses. In 1534-5, the rectory of Ludlow was worth £20 per annum, less 7s. 8d. for procurations and synodals.

---

[1] *Harl. MS.*, No. 273.

Early Incumbent.—Sir John de Mendone, instituted Feb. 18, 1278, the lords of Ludlow castle presenting.

Formerly there was a chantry in this church, for we read of "the altar of St. Mary and St. Gabriel, the archangel, in the nave of Ludlow Church."

LUDLOW HOSPITAL. Situated on the north side of the Teme, near the bridge, formerly stood the Hospital of St. John the Baptist, which Peter Undergod, a rich burgess of Ludlow, founded about 1225. The establishment in question ceased to exist about 1535.

THE ST. AUGUSTINE FRIARS once had an establishment at Ludlow. We are assured by the annals of Worcester, that, in 1282, the prior of the Augustine Friars of Ludlow, along with a number of knights and others, saw three suns at Kinlet, one in the east, one in the west, and one (the real one probably) in the south.[1]

THE CARMELITE, or WHITE FRIARS' HOUSE, stood in Corvegate Street. But little is known respecting either of these religious foundations.

The *Abbeys* of Wenlock and Wigmore, together with Cresswell Priory, had interests in Ludlow. So also had the Hospitallers.

---

[1] *Anglia Sacra*, i. 506

Domesday Hundred of Ruesset.

Modern Name.	Domesday Name.	Saxon Owner or Owners, T. R. E.	Domesday Tenant, in capite.	Domesday Mesne, or next Tenant.	Domesday Sub-Tenant.	Modern Hundred.
Alberbury	Alberberie	Rex Edwardus	Rogerius Comes	Rogerius filius Corbet	....	Ford.
Winsley	Wineslei	Seuuard	.... Idem	Rogerius filius Corbet	....	..Ibidem.
Rea	Un-named	Morcar Comes	.... Idem	Rogerius filius Corbet	....	..Ibidem.
Woolaston	Willavestune	Uluiet	.... Idem	Rogerius filius Corbet	....	..Ibidem.
Bausley	Beleslie	Siward	.... Idem	Rogerius filius Corbet	....	Deythur, Montgomeryshire.
Eyton	{ Etuoe / Etune }	{ Elmar / Siuuard and Uluric }	.... Idem / .... Idem	Rogerius filius Corbet / Elric	....	Ford.
Loton Park	Lncbetune	Edric	.... Idem	Rogerius filius Corbet	....	..Ibidem.
Yockleton	Loclehuile	Edric	.... Idem	Rogerius filius Corbet	....	..Ibidem.
Pontesbury	Pantesberie	Ernui	.... Idem	Rogerius filius Corbet	Ernui	..Ibidem.
Fairley	Fernelege	Ernuin	.... Idem	Rogerius filius Corbet	Ernuin	..Ibidem.
Hanwood	Hanewde	Edic	.... Idem	Rogerius filius Corbet	....	Liberties of Shrewsbury.
Westbury	Wesberie	Ernui	.... Idem	Rogerius filius Corbet	....	Ford.
Wattlesborough	Wctesburg	Edric	.... Idem	Rogerius filius Corbet	....	..Ibidem.
Cardeston	Cartistune	Leuenot	.... Idem	Rogerius filius Corbet	Gislebertus	..Ibidem.
Whitton	Wibetnne	{ Lenenot, Leimer and Ulchetel }	.... Idem	Rogerius filius Corbet	....	..Ibidem.
Marsh	{ Messe / Mersse }	{ Leniet, Dainz, and Weniet / Aluric }	.... Idem / .... Idem	Rogerius filius Corbet / Robertus filius Corbet	.... / Ernui	..Ibidem.
Onslow	Andreslaue	Ernui	.... Idem	Robertus filius Corbet	Ernui	Liberties of Shrewsbury.
Woodcote	Udecote	Uluric	.... Idem	Robertus filius Corbet	Unus Burgensis	..Ibidem.
Longden	Langedune	Leuric	.... Idem	Robertus filius Corbet	....	Ford.
Wigmore	Wigemore	Aluric	.... Idem	Robertus filius Corbet	....	..Ibidem.
Amaston	Enbaldestune	Elmundus	.... Idem	Elmund et Alward filius ejus	....	..Ibidem.
Rowton	Rutune	Quatuor Teini	.... Idem	Alward filius Elmundi	....	..Ibidem.
Polemere ?	Pole	Lemer, Elmer	.... Idem	Alward filius Elmundi	Ordmer	....
Bentball	Benehale	Elmar	.... Idem	Alward filius Elmundi	....	Ford.
Preston Montford	Prestune	Eccl. Sti. Almundi	.... Idem	Ecclesia Sti. Almundi	Eluuardus	Liberties of Shrewsbury.
Dinthill	Duntune	Eccl. Sti. Almundi	.... Idem	Ecclesia Sti. Almundi	....	..Ibidem.

Manors situated in Ruesset, but whose Hundred is not stated in Domesday.

Modern Name.	Domesday Name.	Saxon Owner or Owners, T. R. E.	Domesday Tenant, in capite.	Domesday Mesne, or next Tenant.	Domesday Sub-Tenant.	Modern Hundred.
Caus	Alretone	Rex Edwardus	Rogerius Comes	Rogerius filius Corbet	Quinque Milites	Ford.
Minsterley	Menistrelie	Rex Edwardus	.... Idem	Rogerius filius Corbet	....	..Ibidem.
Ford	Forde	Eduinus Comes	.... Idem	....	....	..Ibidem.

IN the reign of Henry I., the *Domesday* Hundred of Ruesset was swept away, and the Hundred of Ford substituted for it. With the exception of some changes, the most important of which was, that Alberbury ceased to be, and Ford became the *caput* of the Hundred, the modern Hundred embraces all that the ancient one did.

Caus, formerly Alretone, is thus noticed in *Domesday*:—
"The earl himself holds Alretone. Roger [holds it] of him. King Edward held it [in Saxon times]. Here xx hides geldable.

The [arable] land is [capable of employing] xl ox-teams. Excepting ii hides, it was waste. In demesne is one ox-team; and v villains, with i free man have iii teams; and certain Welshmen here tilling[1] the ground pay 16s. [rent]. The woods are ii leagues [in extent]. Waste land is here for xxxi ox-teams.

"In this manor, five of Roger's knights have vi teams and a half in demesne; and ii villains, vi boors, ii Welshmen, and one radman with iii boors and vi neat-herds, have between them all iii teams. In time of King Edward, the manor paid 8s. [annually]. Now [it pays] altogether £4."[2]

ROGER FITZ CORBET, for he it was who with his knights held Alretone of the earl, was son of the Norman Corbet who came to Shropshire from the Pays de Caux, in Normandy. "The ancestry of the Corbets," says Blakeway, "ascends to a very remote antiquity. The name denotes in Norman-French a raven; whether in allusion to the famous Danish standard (the Reafan), of which their ancestor might have been the bearer from Scandinavia under Rollo, the movement of which portended to that people the event of their expeditions; or whether, from a less noble source" cannot be determined. It is certain that Corbet came, with his second and fourth sons, Roger and Robert, to the invasion of England by Duke William of Normandy. Besides the two sons, who settled in Shropshire, the eldest and third sons, Hugh and Renaud, stayed behind. Hugh Corbet, like his father, a knight, is mentioned in some charters of the abbey of Bec, in Normandy. Renaud Corbet, the third son, was in Palestine in 1096, with his two sons, Robert and Guy. From the last of these descended five generations, all of them men of eminent rank in France, distinguished crusaders in the Holy Land, and castellans or viscounts of St. Pol, which the Corbets continued to hold until Hugh Corbet, knight, fourth descendant of Guy, sold his viscounty to the Count de St. Pol, in order to raise money that he might follow St. Louis on his crusading expedition against the Moors of Africa with greater splendour. Robert, son of Hugh, accompanied his father to Tunis, and was drowned there in 1270. Hugh, his son, settled near Cambray; and his descendants for four generations lived at various places in the Netherlands, till James Corbet, sixth in descent from the last-named Robert, removed to Antwerp; and Robert, grandson of James, migrated to Spain, where he left a fair posterity.

---

[1] Laborantes.   [2] *Domesday*, fo. 253, b 1.

These Corbets of France and Flanders bore three ravens for their arms, in token of their descent from the third brother. A branch also of the Corbet family settled in Scotland, and were even allied to the royal family there; for, in 1255, the Archbishop of St. Andrew's writes a letter to the English chancellor, Walter de Merton, on behalf of his "beloved and especial friend, Nicholas Corbet, cousin of my lord the king,"[1] who had then certain affairs pending at the court of Henry III.

To return to the Shropshire Corbets. Soon after *Domesday*, building himself a castle at Alreton, Roger named it Caus in honour of his birth-place. The castle of Caux was one of those border fortresses which, throughout the Anglo-Norman period, was called on alternately to serve the purposes of aggression and defence. Planted in a position of inherent strength, it commanded a wide extent of country; and from its battlements the warder might descry from afar every danger that approached by way of the valley of the Rea. But a fragment of it now remains; yet the site of its massy keep, and the situation of its enormous well, can be traced, and these enable the imagination to picture the frequently-enacted scene of old, when, to escape the fierce irruption of the Welsh, men, women, and children hurried to seek refuge within its walls. Exposed to the turmoil of a hostile frontier, this oft-assailed fortress served as a home for the barons of Caus.

We learn from Ordericus that Earl Roger de Montgomery, who probably organised the frontier defences of Shropshire, was ably seconded in the government of his province by Corbet and his sons Roger and Rodbert. Roger Corbet is mentioned as the first of the three commanders to whom the Norman Earl Robert de Belèsme entrusted the castle of Bridgenorth, when it was besieged by King Henry I. in 1102. Roger Fitz-Corbet, the *Domesday* baron, gave the *Vill* of Wineslega (Winsley) to Shrewsbury Abbey, and, dying about 1121, was succeeded by—

WILLIAM CORBET, his eldest son, in whose time Caus Castle was taken and burnt by the Welsh. It is probable that William died childless, and was succeeded in the barony of Caus by his brother—

EBRARD CORBET. To Ebrard succeeded—

ROGER CORBET II., who was in attendance on Henry II. at the

---

[1] *Rymer, sub ann.*, quoted by BLAKEWAY in *Sheriffs of Shropshire*, p. 38.

siege of Brug in the summer of 1155. The period during which he held Caus Castle, was by no means a peaceful one on the border; and we learn from the sheriff of Worcestershire's account, that in 1165, he had paid £14 11s. 8d. to the soldiers or garrison of Chaus. To Roger succeeded his nephew—

ROBERT CORBET, who, in 1176, was amerced 20 merks for trespassing on the royal forests. It has been stated, that this baron fought by the side of King Richard at the siege of Acre; such, however, is not the fact, and it may be accepted as a general truth, that a lord-marcher usually had his hands full enough at home, without requiring to go so far as Palestine to find scope for his valour. When the scutage for King Richard's redemption was levied in Shropshire, Robert Corbet was charged and paid £4, his quota in that county. He was also assessed to various other scutages in the reigns of Richard and John: his barony being reputed, as far as scutages and military service were concerned, to consist of five knights' fees: *Robertus Corbet, Baro, tenet in capite, et debet servicium v militum,* says a Feodary of the year 1211. Among various notices relative to this baron, we find that in 1196 the sheriff of Shropshire paid Robert Corbet 10 merks: it was a present from King Richard "to support Corbet in the king's service in the parts of Wales." Wenunwin de Kevelloc, Prince of Powis, married Robert Corbet's daughter. Robert loyally adhered to King John throughout his troubled reign; but his eldest son, Thomas, took a different course, and young Henry III. for a time seized the castle of the loyal father, as a precaution against the malpractices of the son. "For the love of God, for the health of of the grantor's soul, and of all his progeny," Robert Corbet gave liberally to the monks of Shrewsbury and Buildwas Abbey; and, dying in 1222—

THOMAS CORBET, his son, fined £100 for his relief, and doing homage to the king, the sheriff of Shropshire was certified accordingly. That this baron was fond of the chase, appears from the king's *writ close*, dated at Montgomery, October 4th, 1224, ordering the sheriff to allow Corbet to pursue any three boars through the forests of Shropshire, which he might unkennel in his own forest. In 1236, Henry III. confirmed by charter to his faithful and beloved Thomas Corbet the whole forest of Teynfrestanes (Stiperstones), quit of all foresterage and exaction, with such right of hunting and venison, as Roger, his uncle, had had in the time of Henry II. In 1248, this baron marcher was appointed sheriff of Shropshire and Staffordshire.

We gain an insight into the immunities claimed by the barons of Caus by the statement which Thomas Corbet made in 1250-1, before the barons of Exchequer. Corbet said, that, *"He had had five antecessors since the Conquest of England, and that none of them had rendered any relief to the king or to his antecessors for those five knight's fees which he (Corbet) now held of the king in capite."* It is certain that he was the first recorded lord of Caus who had paid the baronial fine of £100.

Thomas Corbet was one of those vassals of the crown who, when the news reached the King of England that the Welsh had stormed Builth castle, and put its garrison to the sword, received summons to muster, with horses and arms, at Shrewsbury, on September 8, 1260. The details of border history at this period would furnish a stormy chapter for the page of history. Throughout this troubled time, Corbet adhered to Henry III., yet his loyalty does not appear to have partaken of an active character; old age, perhaps, or a peculiarity of temper, which involved him in quarrels with his vassals, his kinsmen, his compatriots of the Marches, and even in a lawsuit against his own son, were the reasons why he did not co-operate more actively with the members of his party. Having completed his foundation of the chapel of St. Margaret at Caus (the castle chapel), this baron died in 1274. The Inquest which was held on the 23rd of October following found that his barony consisted of $8\frac{3}{4}$ knight's fees, and that he owed thereon the service of 5 knight's fees in time of war. His whole income had amounted to £101 11s. 9d. per annum. In Caus itself he had had four carucates in demesne. Twenty-eight burgages, there paid a rent of 1s. each. The garden was worth 6s. 8d., and the dove-cote 5s. per annum. Peter, his son and heir, would hold his estates of the king, etc. Upon the 2nd of November, 1274, King Edward I. accepted the homage of—

PETER CORBET, who, accordingly, now became Baron of Caus. Peter, whose summonses, military and parliamentary, are numerous, served in the campaign which closed the career of Lewellyn. He also fought in King Edward's Scottish wars. Like his father, being a "mighty hunter," a patent, dated May 4th, 1281, commissioned Peter Corbet to destroy all wolves, wherever they could be found, in the counties of Salop, Stafford, Gloucester, Worcester, and Hereford, using men, dogs, and other devices for the purpose: from which it appears that the Anglo-Saxon King, Edgar, had not so completely extirpated this ferocious animal from England as is generally supposed.

The baron of Caus arrogated rights of *haut justice,* or the power of inflicting capital punishment, and imprisoning and releasing at his pleasure, and pleading immemorial usage of his ancestors. Corbet claimed that no sheriff, coroner, or other officer of the crown could enter his *vills.* But the king's attorney replied, that Caus, etc. were in Shropshire; that the king was King of England, Shropshire included; and that these very franchises constituted the essence of sovereignty. It does not appear, however, that Edward I. recovered all those rights, which, as he alleged, his vassal had usurped. Peter Corbet died in 1300, leaving his second son—

PETER CORBET II., to succeed him. As *Dominus de Cauz,* he joined in the famous letter of the barons to Pope Boniface VIII., asserting King Edward's right to the crown of Scotland. Lord of numerous estates in Shropshire and Devonshire, the heir of Peter Corbet II. was his brother, John Corbet, who spent his life in ineffectually prosecuting a claim on the Valletort estates, of which he was the co-heir in right of his grandmother, Isabel, sister of Reginald de Valletort, of Trematon, Cornwall. Reduced in circumstances by the joint artifices of his own kindred and the king's injustice, John Corbet, the last baron of Caus, if such he can be called, died without issue in 1347, whilst Beatrix, his sister-in-law, was yet seized of his barony.

With respect to Beatrix, wife of Peter Corbet II., she was sister of John, Baron Beauchamp of Hache. After Peter Corbet's decease, she remarried with Sir John de Leybourne, who accordingly presented to Caus chapel, in 1346. Beatrix died in 1347, seized in tail of the whole Shropshire manor of the Corbets, which then passed to the great-grandchildren of her first husband's aunts, Alice and Emma, daughters of Thomas Corbet. Alice, the eldest, had married Robert, Baron Stafford; accordingly, one moiety of the barony of Caus was annexed to the barony of Stafford. The other moiety was subdivided, and the share of Emma, youngest daughter of Thomas Corbet, and wife of Brian de Brompton, is now in the heirs of Harley, and in the heirs of Cornwall of Kinlet.

The Corbets of Leigh and Sundorne, according to Blakeway,[1]

---

[1] BLAKEWAY'S *Sheriffs of Shropshire,* pp. 42, 65.

are descended from John, the last male Corbet of the elder line. The said John, however, died without lawful issue. Eyton says that the *Roger Corbet of Legh juxta Caus, knight,* who, by writ of May 9th, 1324, was summoned to attend the great council of Westminster, "was assuredly ancestor of the Corbets of Leigh." "Of Corbets which have branched off from the house of Caus," says the same authority, "none of them can be descended from any later baron than he who died in 1222."

Minsterley. "The camp on Callow Hill, near Minsterley, is rectangular, and surrounded by a fosse, four yards wide. This form favours the supposition of its having been thrown up by the Romans. It is eighty-six paces from east to west, and fifty-eight from north-west to south-east. The corners are gently rounded; that at the east-north-east more so than the rest."[1] This camp commands the beautiful valley of Minsterley, the neighbourhood of which is rich in lead mines.

The name Minsterley seems to indicate that this place was formerly the site of one of those Saxon collegiate churches whose parishes were so extensive. Of the manor, *Domesday* says:— "The earl himself holds Menistrelie, and Roger [Fitz Corbet holds it] of him. King Edward held it. Here vi hides geldable. In demesne are ii ox-teams, and other ii might be here. Here viii villains and iiii boors, with viii teams. Here iiii neat-herds. There are two leagues of wood. In time of King Edward, it was worth 60s. [annually]. Now 5s. more."[2] From the above, it appears that the Saxon king had been lord of Minsterley, which probably included Habberley. We have seen how it is recorded as one of the ancient customs of Shrewsbury, that when the king resided there the sheriff used to send thirty-six footmen to his [hunting] stand, but "at Marsetelie Park, that officer was bound by custom to find the same number of men for eight days."[3]

MINSTERLEY CHAPEL. Instead of being, as in Saxon times, the mother-church of Westbury, Minsterley is now dependant on Westbury. The first notice we have of this chapel is in 1694.[4]

HABBERLEY CHURCH. Like Minsterley, Habberley Chapel was anciently subject to the church of Westbury. The *Valor* of

---

[1] *Salopia Antiqua,* p. 155.
[2] *Domesday,* fo. 253, b 1.
[3] See p. 169.
[4] *Diocesan Reg.*

Henry VIII., however, representing it as then independent, gives the preferment of the rector of Haburley, in the deanery of Pontesbury, as £4 0s. 2d. per annum, less 6s. for synodals. The barons of Caus presented. *Early Incumbent.*—Sir Roger, parson of Habberleye, close of 13th century.

Alberbury.

We learn, from the Conqueror's record, that:— "The earl himself holds Alberberie, and Roger [Fitz-Corbet holds it] of him. King Edward held it. Here i hide. In demesne is i ox-team, and viii boors with ii teams; and [there are] ii neat-herds here. To this manor appertains Reweset Hundred. In time of King Edward [the manor] was worth 5s. Now 20s. [annually]."[1] Corbet's first feoffee in Alberbury was Ralph the Fat, who, in the reign of Stephen, gave the church of Alberberie to Shrewsbury abbey. Whether he was heir to Ralph or not, is unknown, yet Fulk Fitz-Warin, lord of the castle of Whittington, was Corbet's vassal in Alberbury, in Henry II.'s time, and the lordly Fitz-Warins for many generations afterwards continued to do homage to the barons of Caus for this manor. A feodary of Thomas Corbet's barony, of the year 1240, gives Fulk Fitz-Warin as holding one knight's fee in Aldeburi. He it was who was deputed by the assembly of angry nobles which met at Dunstable on June 30, 1245, to proceed to London, and give the pope's nuncio formal notice to quit the kingdom. The nuncio obeyed the peremptory order.

On November 22, 1248, a fine was levied between Thomas Corbet and Fulk Fitz-Warin, concerning the customs and service required by Corbet on a knight's fee held by Fitz-Warin in Alberbury. Corbet required that Fitz-Warin should do him homage and service of one knight, and do suit every three weeks at the court of Caus, and find one knight or two servientes for ward of Caus castle, at his [Fitz-Warin's] cost, for forty days, whenever there was war between the English king and the Welsh. Fitz-Warin now acknowledged all these obligations. It was this Fulk Fitz-Warin III. who founded Alberbury priory.

The following entry, so illustrative of the feudal system, is on the Salop Assize Roll, of January, 1256:—"An Assize comes on, to make recognition whether Thomas Corbet hath disseized Fulk

---

[1] *Domesday*, fo. 253, b 1.

Fitz-Warin, junior, of his free tenement in Albebyr, viz., of about 120 acres.

"Thomas says that the land is of his fief, and that the plaintiff, before many magnates and lieges of the king, rendered back his homage and the said land to the defendant, and positively declared that he never would hold either that or any other land of the defendant. For this reason, the defendant put himself in seizin of the said land, as it was lawful for him to do, the moment that Fulk abandoned it to him."

"Fulk says [in reply] that he never rendered back land nor homage, and asks judgment on this special point: whether, even if it were true that under anger and excitement he had verbally rendered back his homage, yet had not subsequently changed his state, but had continuously remained in seizin; whether it was competent to the defendant to dis-seize him on the ground of a mere word. As to his never having spontaneously and of good will surrendered the land, he puts himself on an assize" (i.e., appeals to a jury).

"The jury declares that a certain day of reconciliation was fixed upon between Thomas Corbet and Griffin ap Wennonwyn, touching several matters of contention; that many magnates met together on the occasion, and that Fulk, the present plaintiff, was of the number; that Fulk and Thomas Corbet quarrelled together; that Corbet called Fulk [Fulk's father] a traitor; that Fulk announced to Corbet, that, seeing he charged his father with such a crime, he [Fulk junior] would render back his homage to Corbet, and would never hold land of him again."

"The jurors, being asked [by the Court] whether Fulk, in his own person, made the said surrender, say that he did not; indeed, that he made the surrender through Hamo le Strange."

"The jurors, being further asked whether Fulk, after he had sent that message, returned to his seizin, say 'Yes;' and that Fulk is still in seizin of the castle of Alberbyr, which is the *capital manor* pertaining to the said land; and that Fulk caused eight days' ploughing to be done on the land, in the interval before Corbet ejected him."

Judgment was given in favour of Fitz-Warin. "The court decides that Fulk do recover his seizin."[1] About eight years afterwards the Fulk Fitz-Warin of the above entry fought for

---

[1] *Assizes*, 40 Hen. III. m. 15, quoted by EYTON, *Hist of Shrop.*, vol. vii. p. 80.

Henry III. at Lewes, where he lost his life, not in the thickest of the fight, but drowned in the neighbouring stream." [1]

ALBERBURY CHURCH.

This was originally a Saxon collegiate church. When Fulk Fitz-Warin III. founded Alberbury Priory, he doubtless gave up the patronage of Alberbury church and its prebends to the Priory; the Barons of Caus concurred, when, the friars having procured an appropriation of the church, its prebends were suppressed, and a vicarage only remained, of which the friars were patrons.

In 1291, the rectorial income of the church of Alberbury, in Pontesbury Deanery, was valued at £25 *per ann.*; the vicar's portion was £6 13s. 4d. We learn from the Assize Roll of 1292, that a Welsh murderer, some time previously, had taken Sanctuary in Alberbury church, where he remained five weeks, till he was rescued by his countrymen. Here we have a remarkable illustration of the superstitious awe for the precincts of a shrine, which prevailed during those lawless ages in which our Anglo-Norman ancestors lived.

In 1341, Alberbury Parish was assessed only £10 4s. to the *ninth,* because the greater portion of it was in the *parts of Wales;* three virgates of land lay uncultivated on account of poverty of tenants, etc. In 1534-5, the Vicar of Alberbury's preferment was valued at £5, less 1s. for archdeacon's synodals, and 13s. 4d. for bishop's procurations.

Early Incumbent.—Gregory de Clon, 1284.

Alberbury Priory.

Although its foundation charter is lost, there is reason to believe that Alberbury Priory was founded by Fulk Fitz-Warin III., between the years 1220 and 1230.

"Fulk," says the Fitz-Warin Chronicle, "in remission of his sins, founded a priory, in the honour of our Lady, St. Mary, of the Order of Grandmont, near Alberbury, in a wood, on the river Severn." [2] The French House of Grandmont, in Limousin, of which, strictly speaking, Alberbury was a mere cell, adopted the Benedictine rule. We learn that, "Fulk Fitz-Warin gave his

---

[1] MATTHEW PARIS, vol. iii. p. 348, Bohn's Ed.
[2] *Hist. of Fulk Fitz-Warine.* T. Wright, p.176.

ALBERBURY CHURCH AND CASTLE.

body to the Priory [of Alberbury] to be buried there; and that therewith he gave [besides his former donations] a certain messuage in Wytmere, in pure and perpetual alms." The possessions of this priory were soon increased by various other benefactors. "There was formerly," says an MS. authority,[1] "a chapel dedicated to St. Stephen, within the site of the Monastery, in which was buried Fulk Warin, its founder, with many other benefactors of the priory;" and therein a priest performed services for the souls of the said founder and benefactors.

Pope Nicholas' Taxation represents the Prior of Alberbury's annual income to be, in temporalities, £2 7s.; in moveables, £1 9s. The former item was derived from lands and assized rents: 9s. of the latter arose from 6 cows, and £1 from 60 sheep. Upon the breaking out of the great war with France, Edward III. seized into his hands the alien Priory of Alberbury, which continued an escheat of the crown until Henry VI.'s time. This king, at the request of Chicheley, Archbishop of Canterbury, on May 11, 1441, granted this suppressed priory, with all its tithes, advowsons of churches and chapels, etc., in free and perpetual alms to All Souls' College, Oxford, then recently founded by Chicheley.

Peter de Corcellis, apparently a foreigner, was Prior of Alberbury, 1289-90. He is the only one whose name has been preserved.

Winsley. Roger Fitz-Corbet held this manor of the Norman earl in the year 1086; for *Domesday* says that,—"The same Roger holds Wineslei. Seuuard, a free man, held it [in Saxon times]. Here ii hides geldable. In demesne are ii ox-teams; and one villain and one radman with i team and a half. [The manor] was and is worth 15s. [annually]."[2] We have mentioned that the *Domesday* Baron of Caus gave Winsley to Shrewsbury abbey. The *Valor* of 1534 reckons among the temporalities of Shrewsbury abbey, 35s. of assized rents in Wynnesley.

The Rea. "The same Roger holds half a hide in this Hundred [Ruesset], which Earl Morcar held. Here is one villain with half an ox-team. It was and now is worth 32d."[2] The

---

[1] MS. at Loton Park.   [2] *Domesday*, fo. 255, b 1.

above un-named manor afterwards came to be called "the Rea," because it was situated on the river Rea. For a time a family, who derived their name of Rea from the place, held it under Corbet of Caus; but eventually this manor becoming absorbed into the baron's surrounding demesnes the situation of it cannot now be ascertained.

Woolaston. "The same Roger," continues *Domesday*, "holds Willavestune. Uluiet held it and was a free man. Here half a hide geldable. Waste it was and is, and yet it yields a rent of 12d."[1] Woolaston chapel was from the first and still continues to be a dependency of Alberbury.

Bauseley. On the summit of Bauseley Hill is a British entrenchment, which still continues in a very perfect state. The eastern side being precipitous did not require artificial means to strengthen it. The western has two concentric ditches, each with counterscarp of ten feet.

We learn from *Domesday*, that "The same Roger holds Beleslei. Siuuard held it. Here i hide not geldable. Here are two Welsh with i ox-team. [The manor] was and is worth 2s. and yet it is at *ferm* for 6s. 8d."[1] The *Domesday* Commissioners appear to have received conflicting evidence respecting the value of Bauseley, and they have left on record the paradox they were unable to account for. In process of time the Corbets of Caus withdrew this manor into their jurisdiction of *Walcheria*, where it remained until after the conquest of Wales. Bauseley is now in the Montgomeryshire hundred of Deythur. With the Leightons, as co-heirs of Robert and Matilda Corbet, Bauseley remained till 1711, when it passed to a younger branch of the Leightons, who now possess it.

Eyton, near Alberbury, is the subject of two entries in Domesday Book. First we are informed that:—"The same Roger [Fitz Corbet] holds Etune. Elmar held it. Here i hide and iii virgates. Here ii boors with v oxen are ploughing. The value is 3s. The

---

[1] *Domesday*, fo. 255, b 1.

land is for ii ox-teams."¹ Secondly we are told that:—" Elric holds of the earl Etune. Siuuard and Uluric held it for ii manors. Here iii virgates of waste land."²

𝕷𝖔𝖙𝖔𝖓 and the Hayes, now appurtenances of Watlesborough, formerly constituted a distinct manor, as we read in *Domesday* that:—" The same Roger [Fitz Corbet] holds Luchetune. Edric held it. Here i hide geldable. In demesne is i ox-team and one serf, and one haye. [The manor] is worth 5s.; and ii more teams besides might be here."¹

𝖄𝖔𝖈𝖍𝖑𝖊𝖙𝖔𝖓. "The same Roger," continues *Domesday*, "holds Loclehuile. Edric held it and was a free man. Here vi hides geldable. In demesne are iii ox-teams; and viii serfs, xix villains, and vi boors with viii teams. Here a mill renders one measure of barley.³ The wood will fatten 100 swine. In King Edward's time, it was worth £8 [annually]; now £6."¹ Loclehuile, Yocklehull, or as it is now written Yockleton, like Minsterley, was almost uniformly held in demesne by the barons of Caus.

STONEY STRETTON appears to have been formerly a Roman station. Both Yockleton and Stretton parochially belonged to Westbury.

𝕻𝖔𝖓𝖙𝖊𝖘𝖇𝖚𝖗𝖞. The lead mines of the Ponsert [Pontesford] hill were worked, and perhaps originally discovered, by the Romans. Some lead, partially fused, was found a few years since, nearly on the summit of Ponsert hill, in which were embedded pieces of charcoal. The fragment alluded to evidently belonged to the Roman period. Indeed, the names Pontesbury (the former part of which is derived from the Latin *Pontes*), Stoney Stretton, and Watlesborough, sufficiently indicate that this locality was known to the Romans.

Under date A.D. 661, the Anglo-Saxon chronicle informs us that:—" This year, during Easter, Kenwalk fought at Pontesbury, and Wulfhere, the son of Penda, laid the country waste as far as Ashdown."

The camp upon the summit of Pontesford hill is British, and,

---

¹ *Domesday*, fo. 255, b 1.   ² Ibidem, fo. 259, b 1.   ³ "*Summam brasii.*"

according to Hartshorne, may be assigned to the year 661. "It is a double camp, having its ditches and walls in conformity to the nature of the ground. The hill is very steep on all sides, especially towards the east, where the declivity is nearly perpendicular. The lower camp, which is the southerly one, is three hundred and seventeen yards long, and varies from twenty-five to thirty-five in width. The upper and northerly division is the same width, and two hundred and sixty-five yards in length. There is an entrance due north into the upper one, and one due south into the lower." [1]

Pontesbury is thus described in *Domesday* :—"The same Roger [Fitz Corbet] holds Pantesberie [of the earl]. Ernui held it [in Saxon times], and still holds it under Roger [Fitz Corbet]. Here $4\frac{1}{2}$ hides geldable, and $1\frac{1}{2}$ hides not geldable. In demesne are iiii ox-teams, and vii serfs, x villains, v boors, and i radman, with v teams; and iii teams more might be here. A mill here renders an annual corn-rent. The wood will fatten xl swine. In time of King Edward [the manor] was worth £8 [annually] ; now £6." [2] Eventually dispossessed of all his manors, for Ernui, the Saxon lord of Pantesberie, had been a man of good property in Edward the Confessor's time ; after *Domesday*, the baronial Fitz Herbert's held Pontesbury under the barons of Caus. They held it until, in 1305, Rese ap Howel purchased the manor. Very shortly afterwards he gave Pontesbury to the king in exchange for other lands. Upon this, Edward II. gave the manor to his *beloved valet* John de Cherlton, who thereupon became lord of Pontesbury, and as such he is duly entered in the *Nomina Villarum* of 1316.

PONTESBURY CHURCH.

This was originally a Saxon collegiate church, and gave name to the deanery in which it is situated. At all recorded periods, down to the present day, St. George's, Pontesbury, has consisted of three portions, rectories or prebends. In 1291, two of these portions were valued at £10 13s. 4d. *per annum* each. The remaining one at £5 6s 8d. In 1341, the parish was assessed £17 15s. 8d. to the *ninth*. The *Valor* of 1534-5 represents the three prebends as collectively worth £42 17s. *per annum*, less 17s. 9d. for procurations and synodals.

Early Incumbents.—Of the first, Decanal or David portion, David Fitz Reginald, 1272 ; second, Nicholas or Child's Hall

---

[1] *Salopia Antiqua*, p. 179. [2] *Domesday*, fo. 255, b 1.

PONTESBURY CHURCH, NORTH-WEST.

portion, Walter Fitz Reginald Fitz Peter, 1277; third, Cold-Hall, or Ratford portion, Master Thomas de Wynton, 1278.

Fairley is noticed in *Domesday* thus:—"The same Roger holds Fernelege, and Ernuin [holds] of him. [Ernuin] himself held it in King Edward's time, and was free with his land. Here i hide geldable. In demesne is one ox-team, iii serfs, and iii boors; and there might be ii teams more here. It was worth 4s.; now 3s."[1]

Hanwood. "The same Roger," continues *Domesday*, "holds Hanewde. Edic [Edric probably] held it and was free. Here ii hides geldable. In demesne there is half an ox-team, and v serfs, iii villains, and ii boors with 2½ teams; and one team more might be employed here. The former and present value was and is 10s. [annually]."[1]

HANWOOD CHAPEL.

In 1291, the chapel of Hanewode, in Pontesbury deanery, was valued at £4 6s. 8d. *per annum*. In 1341, the parish was taxed only 6s. to the *ninth,* because there were no sheep or lambs in it, and four virgates of land lay untilled, etc. The *Valor* of 1534-5 represents the rector of Han-

FONT, HANWOOD.

[1] *Domesday*, fo. 255, b 2.

wode's preferment as worth £2 6s. 8d. *per annum*, less 6d. for synodals.

Early Incumbent.—R., rector of Hanwood in 1277.

Westbury is mentioned in Domesday Book thus:—"The same Roger holds Wesberie. Ernui held it, and was free. Here ii hides geldable. In demesne is one ox-team, and one serf, two priests, and v villains, with iii teams. [In Saxon times] it was worth 20s.; now 25s."[1] At the period of the survey the baron of Caus held Westbury in demesne; but before the close of the 12th century, Sir Odo de Hodnet, otherwise Odo de Westbury, ancestor of the hereditary seneschals of Montgomery Castle, became Corbet's feoffee here, whose descendants continued vassals of Corbet of Caus.

Westbury Church.

The mention of two priests in the *Domesday* entry relating to Westbury, indicates the existence of a collegiate church in this place. Minsterley collegiate church then appears to have been transferred to Westbury by the year 1086. The two priests of *Domesday* were types of the two prebendaries or rectors, who, in all later records, appear as sharing the emoluments of this church. In 1291, the church of Westbury, in the deanery of Pontesbury, was valued at £20 *per annum*. In 1341, the parish was taxed £13 6s. 8d. to the *ninth*; a great part of it then lay untilled, the tenants being poor. In 1534-5, the preferment of the rector of *Westbury-in-Dextra-parte* was worth £14 7s., less 17s. 9d. for procurations and synodals. The rector in *Sinistra-parte* had an annual income of £12 7s., less 14s. 4d. for procurations and synodals.

Early Prebendary in *Dextra-parte.*—Sir Henry Corbett died April 24th, 1288. *Early Prebendary* in *Sinistra-parte.*—Master Robert de Stoles, portioner in 1277.

Wattlesborough appears to have been originally a Roman station, and there is reason to believe that a Roman road, a branch of the great Watling Street, formerly traversed the district.

Domesday mentions Wattlesborough thus:—"The same Roger

---

[1] *Domesday*, fo. 255, b 2.

WATTLESBOROUGH CASTLE FROM THE NORTH-WEST.

[Fitz Corbet] holds Wetesburg [of the earl]. Edric held it [in Saxon times]. Here ii hides geldable. In demesne are iii ox-teams, and iii neat-herds, ii villains, one boor, and one radman, with v oxen; and ii teams more might be here. In King Edward's time it was waste. Now it is worth 20s. [annually]."[1] From the 12th century, Wattlesborough was held by a race of knights, who, descended from Roger Fitz Corbet, the *Domesday* baron. Already divergent, in Henry the Second's time the connecting link between the baronial and the knightly Corbets has been lost; and all we are certain of is, that Richard Corbet entered on the Shropshire Pipe Roll of 1179-80 as a vassal of the barony, is the first of his line who can be named as holding Wattlesborough under the barons of Caus. A century later, and we have this Richard's grandson, Sir Robert Corbet, prepared to do full military service under his suzerain Peter Corbet of Caus against Lewellyn.

The flat Norman buttress of the tower of Wattlesborough castle, the lower part of which still exists, bespeak a high antiquity for this monument of the past. The moat can still be partially traced. Descending from the Corbets to the Mouthès; from them to the Burghs; and from them to the Leightons; Wattlesborough castle was successively maintained as a residence by each of these families till the year 1712.

Cardeston.

"The same Roger holds Cartistune, and Giselbert [holds it] of him. Leuenot held it, and was a free man. Here i hide geldable. In demesne is one ox-team, and iiii serfs, one villain, and one boor; and here iii additional teams might be employed. In King Edward's time, the manor was worth 30s. Now 20s."[1] Cardeston was annexed to the fee of Corbet of Wattlesborough, before 1255.

CARDESTON CHAPEL.

The chapel of Cardiston, in Pontesbury deanery, was represented, in 1291, as of less than £4 annual value. In 1341, Cardeston parish was taxed 16s. to the *ninth*. King Henry VIII.'s *Valor* gives the preferment of the rector of Karston as worth £3 6s. 8d. per annum, less 6d. for synodals, and a pension of 8s. to the abbot and convent of Wigmore.

Early Incumbent.—William de Cardiston, 1276.

---

[1] *Domesday*, fo. 255, b 2.

Whitton, formerly a member of Corbet's barony, is mentioned in *Domesday,* thus:—"The same Roger holds Wibetune, Leuenot, Leimer, and Ulehetel held it and were free. Here i hide and half geldable. In demesne is one ox-team; and ii neat-herds, one villain, v boors, and one radman, with i team only; and other ii teams might be here. In King Edward's time, it was worth 9s. Now 15s."[1]

Marsh. "The same Roger [Fitz-Corbet] holds Messe. Leuiet, Dainz, and Weniet, held it [in Saxon times] for iii manors, and were free. Here iii virgates, geldable. In demesne is one ox-team and ii neat-herds. It was worth 9s. Now 5s."[1] In another part of *Domesday,* we find it entered, that:—"The same Robert [Roger Fitz-Corbet's brother] holds Mersse. Alurie held it, and was a free man. Here ii hides, geldable. In demesne are ii ox-teams, vi serfs, i boor, and i radman. There might be iiii ox-teams here. In time of King Edward, it was worth 15s. Now 12s."[2] Uncertainty prevails respecting the position of the manor first alluded to. Robert Fitz-Corbet's share of Marsh descended to his co-heirs, the Boterells, lords of Longden, whose chief tenants here were the Marshes.

Onslow, in Pontesbury parish, is mentioned in Domesday Book:—"Robert [Fitz-Corbet] holds Andreslaue of the Earl, and Ernui [holds it] of him. The same [Ernui] held it [in Saxon times] and was a free man. Here i hide, geldable. In demesne is one ox-team, and iii villains with i team. [The manor former-ly] was worth 10s. [annually]. Now 12s."[2] Part of Onslow descended to Boterell, as co-heir of Robert Corbet.

Woodcote, with Horton, now constitutes an outlying township of the Shrewsbury parish of St. Chad. In William the Conqueror's time, however, Woodcote was a distinct manor, one of that series which Robert Corbet held of the Norman earl. "The same Robert," says *Domesday,* holds Udecote. Uluric held it, and was a free man. Here one hide and a half, geldable. In demesne

---

[1] *Domesday,* fo. 255, b 2.   [2] Ibidem, fo. 256, a 1.

is i ox-team; and i villain and i boor, with i team, and still there might be i more [team] here; and there is one burgess paying 8s. [rent]. The manor was worth 8s. Now it is worth 15s."[1] Robert Fitz-Corbet, the *Domesday* lord of Woodcote, was brother to Roger Fitz-Corbet, baron of Caus. The fief which Robert held was less than that of his elder brother. In 1121, the brothers appear together, attesting Henry I.'s charter to Shrewsbury abbey. Yet Robert's relationship with that king was not reputable; for Sibil, or, as she is otherwise called, Adela Corbet, his eldest daughter, was one of the numerous mistresses of Henry I., by whom she had at least two sons, and probably a daughter. Roger, the elder of these illegitimate offshoots of royalty, was surnamed De Dunstanville. Sibil Corbet afterwards became the lawful wife of Herbert, son of Herbert, the king's chamberlain, and her descendants by him eventually acquiring a share in Robert Fitz-Corbet's barony, they exercised the seigneury over Woodcote. The Hortons and the De Woodcotes held Woodcote under the baronial Fitz-Herberts.

Longden. Robert Fitz-Corbet held also Longden of the Norman earl, for *Domesday* says:—"The same Robert holds Languedune. Leuric held it, and was a free man. Here iii hides geldable. In demesne are ii ox-teams, and iiii serfs, one villain, ix boors, iii radmans, and vi cottars between them all have ii ox-teams, and there might be iii additional teams here. The wood will fatten 60 swine. In time of King Edward, the manor was worth £4, and afterwards 30s. Now it is worth 40s."[1] Robert Fitz-Corbet, the *Domesday* baron, had two daughters, viz., Sibil and Alice, who eventually became his heirs. Of Sibil Corbet, the elder sister, we have just spoken. Alice, youngest daughter and co-heir of Robert Fitz-Corbet, marrying William Boterell of Cornwall, upon the death of Reginald, earl of Cornwall, the Boterells obtained, like the Fitz-Herberts, their moiety of Robert Corbet's barony, and thenceforth Longden was reputed to be caput of the Shropshire barony of Boterell or Botreaux. Sir William de Boterell IV. alienated Longden to Robert Burnel, bishop of Bath and Wells, in exchange for lands in Somersetshire. Accordingly, the feodary of 1284 states, that "the bishop holds Langedon of the

---

[1] *Domesday*, fo. 256, a 1.

king, *in capite*, for half a knight's fee, doing the service of two foot soldiers in time of war, for 40 days, at his own cost."

Parochially, Longden is a member of Pontesbury.

𝕎igmore, now a township in the parish of Westbury, is noticed in *Domesday* thus:—"The same Robert holds Wigemore. Aluric held it, and was a free man. Here i hide, geldable. There are iiii villains, with i ox-team, and there might be another team besides. It was and is worth 5s."[1] Wigmore also descended to Boterell as coheir of Robert Corbet.

𝔸maston and Rowton, joint townships in the lower quarter of the parish of Alberbury, are both noticed in King William's record. Concerning Amaston, *Domesday* says:—"Elmund and his son Alward hold of the Earl Enbaldestune. He himself [namely Elmund] held it [in Saxon times] and was free. Here ii hides, geldable. The land is for iii ox-teams and a half. Here iiii villains and iii boors have i team and a half. It used to be worth 10s. Now 7s."[2]

𝕉owton. "The same son of Elmund holds Rutune. Four thanes held it before him for iiii manors, and they were free. Here ii hides, geldable. The [arable] land is [capable of employing] iiii ox-teams. Here are ii radmans. In time of King Edward, it was worth 9s. Now 3s. They [the two manors of Enbaldestune and Rutune probably is meant] were waste, and still are generally so."[2] Elmund and his son Alward having been displaced, Amaston and Rowton were annexed by Henry I. to the Honour of Montgomery, which Honour descended through the families of Bollers, Courtenay, and Cantilupe, to Zouch of Haryngworth.

𝕡ole. Besides Rowton, Alward the Saxon held also the manors of Pole and Benthall at the period of the survey. *Domesday* records the fact thus:—"The same [Alward, son of Elmund] holds Pole, and Ordmer [holds it] of him. Lemer and Elmer held it for ii manors, and were free men, and paid geld. Here

---

[1] *Domesday*, fo. 256, a 1.   [2] Ibidem, fo. 259, b 1.

half a hide. There is land for i team and a half. In demesne is half a team, with i serf and one boor. It was worth 4s. Now 2s."¹ The situation of Pole cannot be identified.

Benthall. "The same [son of Elmund] holds Benehale. Elmaer held it, and was a free man. Here i hide, geldable. The land is for iii ox-teams. Here i radman, ii villains, and ii boors, with i team. The former value was 13s. 8d. Now 5s.¹ Parochially Benthall is a member of Alberbury.

Preston Montford, at the period of the Conqueror's survey, belonged to the church of St. Alkmund, Shrewsbury:—"The same church held [in Saxon times], and still holds Prestune. Here i hide geldable. In demesne is one ox-team, and two villains with i team. Formerly it was worth 8s.; now 5s. Eluuard holds it [of the church]."²

Dinthill. "The same church held and still holds Duntune. Here i hide geldable. In demesne is one ox-team, and there are one villain and i boor with half a team. It was and is worth 8s."² St. Alkmund's manors descended to Lilleshall Abbey; and accordingly, the abbot figures as Lord of Preston and Dunthull in the *Nomina Villarum* of 1316.

Ford was situated in Reusset, although its Hundred is not stated in *Domesday*. "The earl himself holds Forde. Earl Eduin held it, with xiiii berewicks. Here xv hides. In demesne are x ox-teams; and xx serfs, vi female serfs, L villains, and xiiii boors, with xxix teams. Here a mill renders 3 *ores* [*i.e.* 60 pence] and a half. A fishery [yields] 2s. In time of King Edward [the manor] paid £9 [annually]; now [it pays] £34."³ From the above, we learn that the Saxon Earl of Mercia had held this important manor previously to its coming into the hands of the Norman earl. Upon the forfeiture of Earl Robert de Belèsme, Ford devolved to King Henry I., whose grandson, Henry II., in 1155-6 granted it to his uncle Reginald, Earl of Cornwall.

---

¹ *Domesday*, fo. 259, b 1. ² Ibidem, fo. 253, a 1. ³ Ibidem, fo. 253, b 2.

Reginald de Dunstanvill, son of Henry I., by Sibil, daughter of Robert Corbet of Longden, was born before 1115. Styled "Reginald, son of King Henry," this illegitimate magnate figured in the court of the usurper Stephen in March, 1136, but quickly changing sides, he afterwards materially aided the cause of his half-sister, the Empress.

That Reginald Fitz Roy should take an interest in Shropshire, the county of his mother's family, was natural. In 1141 he attested the Empress' charter to Shrewsbury Abbey, and in 1155 he accompanied his nephew, Henry II., to the siege of Bridgenorth. Under such circumstances, it is not to be wondered at, that Reginald should seek to obtain from the young king Ford, which occupied a central position with respect to the bulk of his grandfather Corbet's manors—lands over which Earl Reginald held the seigneury during his life. At the time Henry II. granted Ford to his uncle, it was reputed to pay an annual ferm of £5 13s. 4d. to the king's exchequer; and, from 1156 to 1175, the sheriff of Shropshire deducted that amount from his own liabilities, and assigns it under the head of *Terræ datæ* to Earl Reginald. Yet, besides his Shropshire estates, Earl Reginald held lands in Wiltshire, Northamptonshire, Devonshire, Herefordshire, Somersetshire, and Dorsetshire, to say nothing of that vast Cornish fief which yielded to the son of King Henry a princely revenue.

Ford having returned into the king's hand at the death of Earl Reginald in 1175, it continued in the crown during the reigns of Richard, John, and the earlier part of the reign of Henry III. in which period the manor was subject to a wholesale destruction of fire and sword at the hands of the Welsh. On August 5, 1230, however, the king, then at Bordeaux, grants to Henry de Audley the manor of Ford, "to hold in fee-farm of the king and his heirs, to the grantee and his heirs, for an annual rent of £12, payable at the Exchequer, in lieu of all services. The grantee is to be quit of suits to county or hundred, and his men are to be quit of all talliage for the king's use; but the grantee may *talliate* the manor for his own use, as often as the king *talliated* the royal demesnes."[1]

HENRY DE AUDLEY, who now became lord of Ford, was of a Staffordshire family of knightly degree. Sheriff of Shropshire and Staffordshire in 1229, skilful and loyal, Henry amassed a barony. His commissions as a lord-marcher are numerous.

---

[1] *Cartæ Antiquæ*, F.F. 7, quoted by Eyton.

JAMES DE AUDLEY, his son, succeeded him in 1246, whose homage the king having accepted, the sheriff of Salop and Staffordshire had orders to take security for his relief, and give him seizin of his father's lands and castles. As loyalist sheriff of Shropshire, Audley did good service to the cause of Henry III. during that eventful period which preceded the battle of Evesham, when, in 1272, having broken his neck—[1]

JAMES DE AUDLEY II., his son, did homage to the king, and forthwith had livery of his inheritance. He held the barony but a short while; for dying—

HENRY DE AUDLEY II. succeeded his brother as lord of Ford in November, 1273. On April 22, 1276, the king's writ of *Diem clausit* announced the decease of this baron, when—

WILLIAM DE AUDLEY, his brother, succeeding, he soon after fell in the wars of Wales.

NICHOLAS DE AUDLEY, brother and heir to William, succeeded to Ford in 1282, who, dying in 1299—

THOMAS DE AUDLEY, his son, a youth ten years old, became his heir. This young noble died in 1308, whilst in ward to the king.

NICHOLAS DE AUDLEY II., who then succeeded his brother, is returned in the *Nomina Villarum* of March, 1316, as lord of the *vill* of Forde. In December following, he also died, making, singularly enough, seven successive lords of this barony, all of whom had been cut off within the short space of forty years. To Nicholas succeeded—

JAMES DE AUDLEY III., who, present at the famous battle of Poictiers, according to Walsingham, "broke through the French army and caused much slaughter that day to the enemy." "The lord James Audley," says Froissart, "with the assistance of his four squires, was always engaged in the heat of the battle. He was severely wounded in the body, head, and face; and, as long as his strength and breath permitted him, he maintained the fight, and advanced forward: he continued to do so until he was covered with blood; then, towards the close of the engagement, his four squires, who were as his body-guard, took him, and led him out of the engagement, very weak and wounded, towards a hedge, that he might cool and take breath. They disarmed him as gently as they could, in order to examine his wounds, dress them, and sew up the most dangerous." After the battle was won, the

---

[1] *Baronage*, p. 748.

Black Prince enquired from those knights who were about him, of Lord James Audley, and asked if any one knew what was become of him. "Yes, sir," replied some of the company; "he is very badly wounded, and is lying in a litter hard by." "By my troth," replied the Prince, "I am sore vexed that he is so wounded. See, I beg of you, if he be able to bear being carried hither; otherwise I will come and visit him." Two knights directly left the prince, and coming to Lord James, told him how desirous the prince was of seeing him. "A thousand thanks to the prince," answered Lord James, "for condescending to remember so poor a knight as myself."

He then called eight of his servants, and had himself borne in his litter to where the prince was. When he was come into his presence, the prince bent down over him and embraced him, saying: "My Lord James, I am bound to honour you very much; for by your valour this day, you have acquired glory and renown above us all, and your prowess has proved you the bravest knight." Lord James replied, "My lord, you have a right to say whatever you please, but I wish it were as you have said. If I have this day been forward to serve you, it has been to accomplish a vow that I had made, and it ought not to be thought so much of." "Sir James," answered the prince, "I and all the rest of us deem you the bravest knight on our side in this battle; and, to increase your renown, and furnish you withal to pursue your career of glory in war, I retain you henceforward, for ever, as my knight, with five hundred marcs of yearly revenue, which I will secure to you from my estates in England." "Sir," said Lord James; "God make me deserving of the good fortune you bestow upon me."

Being very weak, he then took leave of the prince, and his servants carried him back to his tent. Arrived at his tent, Lord James then sent for his brother, Sir Peter Audley, the Lord Bartholomew Burghersh, Sir Stephen Cossington, Lord Willoughby of Eresby, and Lord William Ferrers of Groby; they were all his relatives. He then sent for his four squires that had attended upon him that day, and, addressing himself to the knights, said: "Gentlemen, it has pleased my lord the prince to give me five hundred marcs as a yearly inheritance; for which gift I have done him very trifling bodily service. You see here these four squires, who have always served me most loyally, and especially in this day's engagement. What glory I may have gained has been through their means, and by their valour; on which account I wish to reward them. I therefore give and resign into their hands the gift of five hundred marcs which my lord the prince has been pleased to bestow upon me, in the same form and manner that it has been presented to me. I disinherit myself of it, and I give it to them simply, and without a possibility of revoking it."

The knights present looked at each other, and said, "It is becoming the noble mind of Lord James to make such a gift."

When the Black Prince was informed how Lord James had made a present of his pension of five hundred marcs to his four squires, he sent for him, and the noble being carried into his presence in his litter, the prince received him graciously and said, "Sir James, I have been informed that after you had taken leave of me, and were returned to your tent, you made a present to your four squires of the gift I presented to you. I should like to know if this be true, why you did so, and if the gift were not agreeable to you." "Yes, my lord," answered Lord James, "it was most agreeable to me, and I will tell you the reasons which induced me to bestow it on my squires. These four squires, who are here, have long and loyally served me, in many great and dangerous occasions, and until the day that I made them this present, I had not any way rewarded them for all their services; and never, in this life, were they of such help to me as on that day. I hold myself much bound to them for what they did at the battle of Poictiers; for, dear sir, I am but a single man, and can do no more than my powers admit, but, through their aid and assistance, I have accomplished my vow, which for a long time I had made, and by their means was the first combatant, and should have paid for it with my life, if they had not been near to me. When, therefore, I consider their courage, and the love they bear to me, I should not have been courteous nor grateful, if I had not rewarded them. Thank God, my lord, I have a sufficiency for my life to maintain my state; and wealth has never yet failed me, nor do I believe it ever will. If, therefore, I have in this acted contrary to your wishes, I beseech you, dear sir, to pardon me; for you will be ever as loyally served by me and my squires, to whom I gave your present, as heretofore." The prince answered, "Sir James, I do not in the least blame you for what you have done, but, on the contrary, acknowledge your bounty to your squires whom you praise so much. I readily confirm your gift to them; but I shall insist upon your accepting of six hundred marcs, upon the same terms and conditions as the former gift." [1] Surviving his wounds, the chivalrous James de Audley, lord of Ford, died at the age of 71.

Now a mere township partly in Alberbury parish, Ford gives name to the hundred and division.

Ford Chapel.

Almost the whole of the *Domesday* manor of Ford was in the parish of Pontesbury, leaving as the parish attached to Ford chapel merely the vill of Ford. Ford Chapel was subject to St. Michael's church, Shrewsbury, along with which the advowson of Ford went to that college at Battlefield which Henry IV founded. Accordingly, in the *Valor* of Henry the Eighth, the master of Battlefield returns among his annual receipts £3 16s. 8d., the ferm of the tithes of the chapel of Foorde, in the diocese of Hereford.

---

[1] *Froissart Chron.* By Johnes, vol. I., pp. 441—449.

Domesday Hundred of Odenet.

Modern Name.	Domesday Name.	Saxon Owner or Owners, T. R. E.	Domesday Tenant in capite.	Domesday Mesne, or next Tenant.	Domesday Sub-Tenant.	Modern Hundred.
[od]net	Odenet	Rex Edwardus	Rogerius Comes			Bradford North.
[W]em	Weme	Wighe, Leuuinus, Alveva, Ælveva	.... Idem	Willelmus Pantulf		..Ibidem.
[W]olverley	Ulwardelege	Wigba and Elmer..	.... Idem	Willelmus Pantulf		..Ibidem.
[G]reat Withyford	Wicford	Carle	.... Idem	Willelmus Pantulf		..Ibidem.
[H]orton	Hortune	Elveva	.... Idem	Willelmus Pantulf		..Ibidem.
[T]irley Castle	Tirelire	Uluric, Rauesuard	.... Idem	Willelmus Pantulf		Pirehill, Staffordshire.
[E]dstaston	Stanestune	Ordui and Alveva..	.... Idem	Willelmus Pantulf		Bradford North.
[C]otton	Cote	Wigbe & Grichetel	.... Idem	Willelmus Pantulf		..Ibidem.
[A]lkington	Alchetune	Elmer	.... Idem	Willelmus Pantulf		..Ibidem.
[M]arket Drayton	Draitune	Godnin	.... Idem	Willelmus Pantulf		..Ibidem.
[H]arcourt	Harpecote	Turtin	.... Idem	Willelmus Pantulf		..Ibidem.
[E]ston	Estune	Uluiet and Elmer..	.... Idem	Willelmus Pantulf	Walter	..Ibidem.
[S]andford	Sanford	Uluiet	.... Idem	Gerardus		..Ibidem.
[E]llardine	Elleurdine	Dodo	.... Idem	Gerardus		Bradford South.
[C]old Hatton	Hatune	Godric	.... Idem	Gerardus		..Ibidem.
[B]etton in Hales	Baitune	Ulchete	.... Idem	Gerardus		Bradford North.
[L]ongslow	Walenceslau	Ulniet	.... Idem	Gerardus		..Ibidem.
[E]ghtfield	Istefelt	Uluiet	.... Idem	Gerardus		..Ibidem.
[W]oolerton	Ulvreton	Oschetel	.... Idem	Gerardus		..Ibidem.
[M]archamley	Marcemeslei	Seuuar and Aluric	.... Idem	Rainaldus Vicecomes	Walter	..Ibidem.
[H]igh Hatton	Hetune	Ælric, Ulfac, Uluiet, Leuric	.... Idem	Rainaldus Vicecomes	Ricardus	..Ibidem.
[S]tanton upon Hineheath	Stantune	Sanuard	.... Idem	Rainaldus Vicecomes		..Ibidem.
[G]reat Withyford	Wicford	Sten and Wilegrip	.... Idem	Rainaldus Vicecomes	Alcher	..Ibidem.
[G]ravenhunger	Gravehungre	Æluric and Ulgar..	.... Idem	Willelmus Malbedeng		..Ibidem.
[M]oore	Waure	Lenuin and Edric..	.... Idem	Willelmus Malbedeng		..Ibidem.
[D]orrington	Derintune	Leuuin and Edric..	.... Idem	Willelmus Malbedeng		..Ibidem.
[O]nneley	Anelege	Edric	.... Idem	Willelmus Malbedeng		..Ibidem.
[M]oreton Say	Mortune	Elmund	.... Idem	Rogerius de Laci	Willelmus	..Ibidem.
? ?	Lai	Eluni	.... Idem	Rogerius de Laci		..Ibidem.
[H]opton	Hotune	Edric	.... Idem	Rogerius de Laci		..Ibidem.
[L]acon	Lach	Elnod	.... Idem	Ranulf Peverel		..Ibidem.
[W]eston under Red Castle	Westune	Edric Salvage	.... Idem	Ranulf Peverel		..Ibidem.
[W]hixall	Witehala	Ældid	.... Idem	Ranulf Peverel		..Ibidem.
[E]dgeley	Edeslai	Aluric	.... Idem	Rogerius de Curcellé		..Ibidem.
[D]odington	Dodetune	Eduinus Comes	.... Idem	Rogerius de Curcelle		..Ibidem.
[S]teele	Stile	Algar, Colline, Brictric, Turgar	.... Idem	Rogerius de Curcelle		..Ibidem.
[B]earstone	Bardestune	Ulgar	.... Idem	Turoldus		..Ibidem.
[L]ittle Drayton	Draitune	Godeva Comitissa	.... Idem	Turoldus		..Ibidem.
[N]orton in Hales	Nortune	Azor	.... Idem	Helgot		..Ibidem.
[L]ec Brockhurst	Lege	Uluiet, Wictric, Eltac	.... Idem	Normannus		..Ibidem.
[M]oston	Mostune	Dodo and Ulgar	.... Idem	Rogerius Venator		..Ibidem.
[R]owton	Routune	Morcar and Dot	.... Idem	Eddiet		Bradford South.
[P]rees	Pres	Episcopus de Cestre	Episcopus de Cestre	Anschitil, Fulcber		Bradford North.
[A]dderley	Eldredelei	Edric	Rogerius Comes	Nigellus		..Ibidem.
[B]avington	Savintune	Dodo	.... Idem	Nigellus		..Ibidem.
[S]poonley	Sponelege	Dunning	.... Idem	Nigellus		..Ibidem.
[C]alverhall	Cavrahalle	Edmær & Eluui	.... Idem	Nigellus		..Ibidem.
[M]oulton	Suletune	Brictric	.... Idem	Ecclesia Sancti Michaelis		..Ibidem.
[W]hitchurch	Westune	Heraldus Comes	.... Idem	Willelmus de Warene		..Ibidem.

Part of Domesday Hundred of Pireholle, Staffordshire.

[C]heswardine & Chipnall	Ciseworde and Ceppecanole	Godeva	Robertus de Stafford	Gislebert		Bradford North.

THE annexed Table shows that the *Domesday* Hundred of Odenet is mainly represented by the modern Hundred of Bradford North.

𝔥𝔬𝔡𝔫𝔢𝔱 was formerly caput, and gave a name to the old Hundred of Odenet. After the conquest of Mercia, when Earl Roger de Montgomery, the Norman earl of Shrewsbury, distributed amongst his followers the various manors of Odenet, he retained this important locality himself, for we read in Domesday Book, that:—" The earl himself holds Odenet. King Edward held it.

Here i hide and a half. In demesne are iii ox-teams; and xii villains, ii boors, a priest, and a provost, with vii teams; and still there might be ix more teams here. There is a small wood, producing nothing. The church of St. Peter holds the church of this manor. In the time of King Edward, this manor yielded [an income of] £3 6s. 8d. [per annum]. Now with the Hundred which pertains thereto, it yields £8."[1] Hodnet, then, once

---

[1] *Domesday*, fo. 253, a 2.

HODNET CHURCH, FROM THE NORTH-EAST; A.D. 1816.

WEM CHURCH;—TAKEN DOWN IN 1811.

belonged to the Saxon king, Edward the Confessor, from whom it passed to the Norman earls, and, upon their forfeiture, to Henry I., who, when he founded the seneschalcy of Montgomery, endowed that hereditary office with Hodnet and other manors. The hereditary seneschals of Montgomery taking their name of De Hodnet from this place, continued for centuries to exercise the seigneury over Hodnet.

HODNET CHURCH.

This, a Saxon foundation, is mentioned in *Domesday.* We glean from King William II.'s confirmation-charter to Shrewsbury abbey, that the Norman earl Roger gave Hodnet church to that abbey.[1] In 1291, the church of Hodnet, with its chapels, was valued at £40 per annum, besides a pension of £1 6s. 8d. to the abbot of Shrewsbury. In 1341, the assessors taxed the parish 40 merks to the *ninth.*

The *Valor* of 1534-5 represents the rectory of Hodnet as worth £30 per annum, less 13s. 4d. for synodals, 6s. for procurations, a pension of £3 to Marchamley chapel, and £1 6s. 8d. to the abbot.

Early Rector.—Master G. DeWeston was "Parson of Hodeneth" in 1241.

Wem. The Norman William Pantulf held no less than eleven manors in the old Hundred of Odenet. Of these, Wem, the reputed caput of Pantulf's barony, is thus described in *Domesday* :—" The same William holds Weme. Wighe, Leuuinus, Alveva, and Ælveva, held it [in Saxon times] for iiii manors, and were free. Here iiii hides, geldable. The land is [sufficient] for viii ox-teams. In demesne is i team; and ii serfs, iiii villains, and viii boors with i team. Here a hawk's œrie, a wood which will fatten 100 swine, and a haye. In the time of King Edward, [the manor] was worth 27s. [per annum]. Now 40s. He [Pantulf] found it waste."[2]

William Pantulf, first baron of Wem, concerning whom Ordericus Vitalis has told us so much, was lord of Noron, near Falaise. Following the potent Roger de Montgomery into England, from him he obtained no less than twenty-nine manors in Shropshire, besides several in Staffordshire and Warwickshire, and he became one of the chief officers to whom Roger de Montgomery

---

[1] *Salop Chartulary*, No. 34.   [2] *Domesday,* fo. 257, a 2.

entrusted the administration of affairs in his earldom of Shrewsbury. After mentioning the name of Warin the Bald, "Roger de Montgomery," continues the Anglo-Norman ecclesiastical historian, " also gave commands in his earldom to William, surnamed Pantoul, Picot de Say, and Corbet, with his sons, Roger and Robert, as well as other brave and faithful knights, supported by whose wisdom and courage he ranked high among the greatest nobles." [1]

In 1073, " the knight named William Pantulf, at the instance of his friend, the venerable Abbot Mainier, and, with the permission of his lord, the earl Roger, gave to St. Evroult the churches at Noron, one of which was built in honour of St. Peter, and the other of St. Cyr the martyr, with his own enclosed park, and part of the wood of Pont-Ogeret, and his share in a farm called Molinx, and of another situated over the brook, commonly called Ruptices. He also gave the whole fee of William de Maloi, comprising about thirty acres of land. Thereupon he received, from the charity of the monks, sixteen pounds of Rouen money, to enable him to undertake a pilgrimage to St. Giles'. He also gave," etc. :—" all this, William Pantulf, and Lesceline, his wife, freely gave to God, for the repose of their souls, and of those of their friends, and they ratified the gift in the chapter of the monks of St. Evroult, convened generally, before many witnesses." " Afterwards, Abbot Mainier and Fulk the Prior, with William Pantulf, went to Earl Roger, who was then residing at Belèsme, and humbly petitioned him to confirm the said knight's grants by his own charter. He, being pious and liberal, received favourably their lawful petition, and ratified all their demands, in the presence of those who, on various affairs, were then attending his court. The feast of St. Leonard was then being celebrated at Belèsme ; to pay due honour to which, the count, with his usual munificence, had assembled a great number of guests," " bishops and abbots," " clerks and laymen, who were witnesses to the above-mentioned charter."

In the year 1077, " the illustrious Robert [de Grantmesnil, ex-abbot of St. Evroult, but then abbot of St. Euphemia, in Apulia], having assisted at the consecration of the churches of Caen, Bayeux, and Bec, which took place that year, and having had friendly intercourse with King William [the Conqueror], and others his friends and relations, whom he had not seen for many

---

[1] ORDERICUS VITALIS, Bk. IV. ch. vii.

years, went back to Apulia, taking with him William Pantoul, and Robert de Cordai, his nephew, with many other gallant knights. At that time Robert Guiscard (the celebrated Norman), commanded in Apulia, and had acquired the dukedom of Gisulf, Duke of Salerno. He was the son of Tancred de Hauteville, a person of moderate station, who, by his bravery and good fortune, had succeeded in acquiring great power in Italy. With the aid of his brothers and others of his countrymen who joined him, he imposed his yoke on the people of Apulia; and having most unexpectedly risen to great eminence, he was exalted above all his neighbours, amassed great wealth, and was continually enlarging his territories. He received William Pantoul with distinguished honours, and making him great promises, tried to retain him in his service on account of his merit. He made him sit by his side at dinner on the feast of Easter, and offered him three towns if he would remain in Italy.

"Meanwhile (that is, on the 5th December, 1082), the Countess Mabel (Earl Roger Montgomery's tyrannical wife) had perished by the sword of Hugh D'Igé, the revengeful knight; and this murder was the cause of great troubles after William Pantoul's return from Apulia. For he was accused of treason, and the charge was prosecuted with great animosity by some of his rivals. The deceased lady had (unjustly) taken possession of the castle of Perai, which had been given to William; on which account there had long existed a violent hostility between them. It was hence suspected that William had contrived her death, particularly as he was on terms of intimacy and frequent communication with Hugh. Earl Roger, therefore, and his sons seized his whole estate, and sought an opportunity of putting him to death. In consequence, William and his wife took refuge at St. Evroult, where they remained for a long time under the protection of the monks, but in the greatest alarm. The knight boldly denied the crime of which he was accused; and no one was able to convict him of it by certain proof; but while he asserted his innocence, no opportunity was allowed him of lawfully clearing himself of the charge, as he offered to do. At length, however, by the interference of many of the nobles, it was determined by the king's court that the accused should purge himself from the stain attached to him, by undergoing the ordeal of hot-iron at Rouen, in the presence of the clergy, which was done; for having carried the flaming iron in his naked hand, by God's judgment, there was no appearance of its being burnt, so that the clergy and all the people gave praise to God. His malicious enemies attended the trial in arms, intending, if he was declared guilty by the ordeal of fire, to have immediately beheaded him. During the troubles to which William Pantoul and his family were exposed, he was much comforted by abbot Mainier and the monks of St. Evroult, who rendered him all the help they could both with God and man. This increased their mutual regard, and William offered to St. Evroult four of the richest palls he had brought from Apulia (the produce doubtless of the silk looms of Southern Italy), out of which were made four copes for the chanters in the church, which are preserved there to this day, and used in the solemn services of divine worship." [1]

To judge from the *Domesday* record of 1085-6, William Pantulf, at that date, had been reinstated by the Norman earl in all his possessions.

"William Pantoul betook himself [again] to Apulia, and having a great respect for St. Nicholas, made diligent enquiries after his relics. By God's blessing on his endeavour (continues the monk) he obtained from those who had translated the body, one tooth, and two fragments of the marble urn. William Pantoul was a gallant soldier, endowed with great talents, and well-known among the nobles of England and Italy, as one of the wisest and richest among his neighbours. Having obtained the tooth of so great a man, he returned to Normandy, and, on an appointed day, called together a number of persons at his own domain called Noron, to receive the relics in a worthy manner. Accordingly, in the year of our Lord 1092, the tooth of the blessed confessor Nicholas, with other relics of the saints brought by William Pantulf from Apulia, was deposited with great reverence in the church of Noron, erected in ancient times in honour of St. Peter. He invited Roger, abbot of St. Evroult, and Ralph, who was at that time abbot of Seez, but who afterwards became Archbishop of Canterbury, to be present at the ceremony; and, in the month of June, they received the holy relics amid great devotion of the monks and rejoicings of the laity, carefully placing them in a silver coffer, liberally provided by the before-mentioned knight. The deposit so often spoken of became in frequent request by persons suffering from fevers and other maladies, whose devout

---

[1] ORDERICUS. B. V. ch. xvi.

prayers, aided by the merits of the good bishop Nicholas, obtained what they desired in the recovery of their health." [1]

There is no evidence to show how Pantulf was treated by Earl Hugh after the decease of Roger de Montgomery; but Robert de Belèsme, the third earl of Shrewsbury, and Pantulf, could not agree at all. "He," (namely, Robert de Belèsme), "had disinherited William Pantoul, a brave and experienced knight," says Ordericus, [2] "and had even given him a sharp repulse when he proffered his valuable services at the time they were urgently needed. Being thus rejected with disdain, William Pantulf went over to the king [Henry I., at that time engaged in the siege of the turbulent De Belèsme's stronghold of Bridgnorth], who, having already proved his vigour of mind, received him graciously. He gave him [Pantulf] the command of two hundred men, and entrusted to him the custody of Stafford Castle, in the same neighbourhood. This knight proved Robert de Belèsme's worst enemy, never ceasing from persecuting him both by his counsels and his arms, till his ruin was completed." It was by Pantulf's negotiation with his neighbours, the defenders of Bridgenorth, that that fortress was surrendered, and King Henry I. succeeded in crushing the terrible earl.

On account of the important services he had rendered to his king, Henry I. restored Pantulf to his lost possessions, and further rewarded him.

"In the year of our Lord 1112, that is to say, the twelfth year of the reign of Henry, King of England, and the fourth of that of Lewes King of France, William Pantoul came to St. Evroult, it being the fortieth year after he founded the cell for monks at Noron, [3] and mindful of his former friendship and the grants which, as we have already related, he before made, he recapitulated them, and, with his wife Lesceline, confirmed them all in a general chapter of the monks. At the same time, Philip, Ivo, and Arnulph, his sons, confirmed all the grants of their father to the monks of St. Evroult; and they all, that is to say, William and Lesceline, and their three sons, Philip, Ivo, and Arnulph, laid the grant on the altar together."

"William Pantoul, so often mentioned, lived long, respecting

---

[1] ORDERICUS. B.VII. ch. xiii.
[2] *Eccles. Hist. of Eng. and Nor.* B. XI. ch. iii.
[3] Among other gifts with which William Pantulf enriched the monks of that place, he gave them the manor of Traditon (Market Drayton, in Shropshire) with the church and mill of that village.

the clergy and being kind to the poor, to whom he was liberal in alms; he was firm in prosperity and adversity, put down all his enemies, and exercised great power through his wealth and possessions. He gave sixty marks of silver towards building the new church at St. Evroult, undertaking a work of great beauty to the honour of God, which death prevented him from completing. His sons succeeded to his estates—Philip in Normandy, Robert in England—but they have failed of prosecuting their father's enterprises with equal spirit."[1]

'So much for the account which Ordericus has given us of William Pantulf. We have preferred allowing the honest monk of St. Evroult to tell his own tale, for two reasons; first, on account of the insight which the reader thereby gains into the history of that period in which the writer lived and moved; secondly, because Ordericus Vitalis, born, as we have seen, in Shropshire, was personally acquainted both with the Norman earl and William Pantulf, one of the greatest of his feudatories. Such was William Pantulf, from whom the barons of Wem descended; such the first Norman lord of the dispossessed Saxon's manor of Wem. It was this man's descendants who, in after times, acquired by charter of King Henry III. the right to have a market and fair at Wem. There also they held their free court twice in the year; and had pleas of bloodshed, hue and cry, and the grim privilege of a gallows.

Wem Castle was reported to be in a ruinous condition on April 7th, 1290.

WEM CHURCH.

The manorial lords were probably the founders, as they continued the patrons, of Wem church. In 1291, the church of Wemme, in the deanery of Salop, was valued at £13 6s. 8d. per annum. In 1341, the parish was rated £11 to the *ninth*. The *Valor* of 1534-5 represents the income of the rector of Wemme to be £26 13s. 4d., less 9d. for synodals and procurations.

Early Incumbent.—Ivo Pantulf was rector of Wem very early in the 13th century.

Wolverley, west-north-west of Wem, is thus described in *Domesday* :—" William Pantulf holds Ulwardelege of Earl Roger.

---

[1] ORDERICUS VITALIS, B.V. ch. xvi.

Wigha and Elmer held it for ii manors, and were free men. Here iii hides geldable. The land is for iiii ox-teams. There are iii villains with i team, and a radman. In time of King Edward, it was worth 17s.; now 8s. He [Pantulf] found it waste." [1]

Great Withyford. In 1086, William Pantulf held of the Norman Earl Roger part of Withyford, for *Domesday* says, that:— " The same William holds Wicford. Carle held it. Here half a hide geldable. The land is [capable of employing] ii ox-teams. Here i villain and one boor have i team. In King Edward's time, [the manor] was worth 10s.; afterwards 8s.; now 10s." [1] According to the Hundred Roll of 1255, " a virgate and a half in Wythyford was held by John Fitz Aer, of the barony of Weme; and that for the said land, he rendered the service of two foot-soldiers, with bows and arrows, for fifteen days, in time of war at Weme."

Horton. That this township of Wem was a distinct manor in 1086, is proved by the following entry in Domesday Book:— " The same William [Pantulf] holds Hortune. Elveva held it, and was a free woman. Here ii hides geldable. The land is [enough] for iiii ox-teams. In demesne is half a team; and ii serfs and iii boors, with half a team. Here a wood which will fatten lx swine. It was and is worth 10s." [1]

Tirley, now in Staffordshire, in 1086 was considered to belong to Shropshire. It was attached to Pantulf's Barony of Wem. " The same William Pantulf holds Tirelire. Uluric and Rauesuard held it for ii manors and were free. Here i hide geldable. The land is for ii ox-teams. Here iiii villains and one serf with i team. It was worth 17s.: now 20s." [1] Tirley castle was founded by Pantulf's descendant, the Baron of Wem, about the year 1280.

Edstaston, north north-east of Wem, is noticed in Domesday book thus:—" The same William holds Stanestune. Ordui and Alveva held it and were free. Here ii hides geldable. The land is for ii ox-teams. Here iii villains have i team. The wood will

[1] *Domesday,* fo. 257, a 2.

fatten 60 swine. In time of King Edward it was worth 7s.: now 20s. He [Pantulf] found it waste."[1] Concerning the interesting ancient chapel here early records are silent.

Cotton, another member of Wem, in the time of King William I. also formed a distinct manor. "The same William holds Cote. Wighe and Grichetel held it for two manors and were free men. Here ii hides geldable. The land is for iii ox teams. Here ii radmans with i villain have i team. In time of King Edward it was worth 20s.: now 12s. The wood here will fatten lx swine, and there is one haye."[1]

Alkington, in the parish of Whitchurch, also formerly was subject to the Barons of Wem. "The same William holds Alchetune. Elmer held it and was a free man. Here i hide and one virgate geldable. The land is for v ox-teams. In demesne is half a team; and one serf ii villains and one boor with half a team. The wood will fatten 100 swine. In time of King Edward [the manor] was worth £4 3s. [annually]; and afterwards the same: now 10s. only."[1]

Market Drayton is the subject of the following entry in Domesday Book: "The same William holds one berewick, Draitune. Goduin held it [in Saxon times] and was a free man. Here ii hides geldable. The land is [capable of employing] viii ox-teams. In demesne is one team; and ii neat-herds, a priest, and ii boors with i team. [This berewick formerly] was worth 20s. Now [it is worth] 10s."[1]

We learn from the historian, Ordericus, that the knight, William Pantulf, after he had returned home from his second visit to Southern Italy gave to the monks of Noron, "*Traditon*[2] [Drayton] with the church and mill of that village, and the tithes of six hamlets, which belonged to that church." St. Peter's at Noron, founded by the first Baron of Wem himself, being a cell

---

[1] *Domesday*, fo. 257, a 2.
[2] M. LE PREVOST, in his valuable edition of Ordericus, has erroneously identified Traditon with Trotton, in Sussex; and, following him, the editor of Bohn's Translation has perpetuated the error. Eyton has clearly shown, however, that Market Drayton, in Shropshire, is the place alluded to by Ordericus.

EDSTASTON CHAPEL.

of the great Norman abbey of St. Evroult, consequently Pantulf gave in effect his Shropshire manor, with its appurtenances, to the parent abbey. The English interests of St. Evroult were attended to by the Prior of Ware, a cell of St. Evroult, in Hertfordshire. About 1133, however, the Abbey of Combermere was founded, when it having become the interest of the Combermere monks to have Drayton; accordingly, the Prior of Ware, with consent of his principal, the Abbot of St. Evroult, granted them a perpetual lease of the Manor. The monks of Combermere therefore became lords of Drayton; who, obtaining from Henry III. the privilege of holding a weekly market here, hence the place acquired that distinctive title by which it is now known. The following are the authorities upon which the foregoing statement is based:—

"On November 8, 1245, King Henry III., being at Worcester, grants to Simon, Abbot of Combermere, the privilege of holding a weekly market, on Tuesdays, at his manor of Draiton;—also, of holding an annual fair on the eve, the day, and the morrow of the Nativity of the Virgin (Sept. 7, 8, 9); also *Blodwite* and *Infangthef*;—also quittance of suits to county and hundred, of Wapentak, and of toll throughout the kingdom;—and such other franchises as were usually sought for a projected borough." Henry and James Audley, successive lords of the neighbouring town of Newport, attested the foregoing charter.[1]

The Bradford Hundred Roll of 1255, says, that—"The Abbot of Cumbermere holds Draiton of the Prior of Ware, with the church of Draiton, of the fee of Hugh Pounton [Pantulf]. And the abbot renders 20 merks *per annum* to the Prior of Ware, and has here a market by Royal Charter."

Again King Henry III., on April 4th, 1266, confirmed to the monks of Combermere the "Manor of Magna Drayton-in-Hales, by concession of the Abbot and Convent of St. Ebrulf, with all its franchises and appurtenances."

Under the fostering care of the Abbot of Combermere, Drayton steadily increased in trading importance; until the dissolution severed the connection between the abbot and the town of his creation.

One of many bloody contests between the Houses of York and

---

[1] *Rot. Chart.*, 4 Ed. III., m 3. Inspeximus, quoted by EYTON. *Antiq. Shropshire*, vol. ix. p. 185.

Lancaster took place on Bloor-Heath, near Market Drayton, and Lord Audley was slain in the skirmish: a cross marks the spot where he fell.

MARKET DRAYTON CHURCH.

This church, alluded to in the *Domesday* notice of Drayton, was probably the Saxon mother church of a district. It was given by William Pantulf, first Baron of Wem, to that church of St. Peter which he founded at Noron, in Normandy. In 1291, the church of "Drayton-in-Hales," in the deanery of Newport, was valued at £12 *per ann.*: besides a pension of £1 10s. to the Abbot of Shrewsbury; this was the rectory. The vicarage was worth £6 13s. 4d. In 1341, the parish of *Drayton-in-le-Halys* was rated £10 to the *ninth*. The *Valor* of 1534-5, gives this vicarage as worth £13 6s. 8d. *per ann.*, less 4s. for synodals, 8s. for procurations, 2s. 4d. for an annual pension to Tyrley chapel, and a pension of 1s. 9d. to the diocesan bishop. At the dissolution, it was found that the advowson of Market Drayton belonged to the Carthusians of Sheen, Surrey, to whom, as the asset of an alien monastery, it had been granted by Henry V.

Early Incumbent.—Robert, priest of Dreiton, and his son, Ivo, occur in 1136-7.

Harcourt. "The same William holds Harpecote. Turtin held it and was a free man. Here half a hide geldable. The land is for an ox-team and half. Here i radman has half a team. [Formerly] it was worth 8s.; now it is worth 2s."[1] Harcourt, a township of Stanton-upon-Hine-Heath, is the place alluded to, which formerly acknowledged the sway of the Barons of Wem.

Aston, which derived its name probably from its lying to the east of Wem, is also noticed in the Conqueror's record. "The same William holds Estune and Walter [holds] of him. Uluiet and Elmer held it for ii manors, and were free. Here i hide geldable. The land is for iii ox-teams. In demesne is one team, one serf, i neat-herd, and ii boors. The wood will fatten xl swine. It was worth 20s.: now 10s."[1]

Sandford. Next to William Pantulf, the Norman Gerard

---

[1] *Domesday*, fo. 257, a 2.

de Tornai, had the largest interest in Odenet Hundred. In this hundred he held seven manors under the earl. One of these, Sandford, a mile and a half north north-east of Prees, is thus described in Domesday book: "The same Gerard holds Sanford. Uluiet held it [in Saxon times] and was free. Here iii hides geldable. The land is [sufficient] for iii ox-teams. In demesne is a team and half a team; and ii serfs, and iiii villains with i team. There is a wood which will fatten 30 swine; and a haye. In the time of King Edward [the manor] was worth 15s. [annually]: now 10s. He [Gerard] found it waste."[1] From Gerard de Tornai the seigneury over Sandford passed to Hamo Peverel and Sibil his wife; and afterwards, in default of a lineal descendant, it escheated to the crown. Like other Tornai escheats, Sandford then became a *tenure in capite*, and the tenant, whether enfeoffed here by Gerard de Tornai himself, or his son-in-law Hamo Peverel, or by Henry I., at all events derived his surname of Sandford from the place. From Richard de Sandford, known to have been lord of this manor in 1167, it can be proved that its present owner is lineally descended in the male line. Very few Shropshire land-owners can lay claim to such a genealogy.

Ellardine.

"The same Gerard holds Elleurdine. Dodo held it and was a free man. Here i hide, and a third part of another hide, geldable."[2] King Henry II. conferred Ellardine, with Rowton and Sutton, on Gervase Goch, his *Latimarius*.[3]

Cold Hatton.

"The same Gerard holds Hatune. Godric held it and was free. There is half a hide and two-parts of a virgate geldable. The land in these two manors [Ellardine and Hatton] is sufficient for iii ox-teams. In demesne are ii teams; and [there are] iii serfs, ii neat-herds, and vi boors with one team. In time of King Edward, the two manors were worth 38s. annually. Now they are worth 20s. He [Gerard de Tornai] found them waste."[4] Before 1265, William Wischard, lord of the *vill*, gave it to Lilleshall Abbey, and King Henry III. confirming the grant, the Lord Abbot retained Cold Hatton until the Reformation.

---

[1] *Domesday*, fo. 258, b 2.
[2] Ibidem. The valuation and stock are given under Cold Hatton.
[3] See Sutton Maddock, p. 67.
[4] *Domesday*, fo. 258, b 2.

Betton-in-Hales. "The same Gerard holds Baitune. Ulchetc held it and was a free man. Here iii hides geldable. The land is for vi ox-teams. In demesne are ii teams and ii serfs, ii neat-herds, and iii boors with i team. There is a mill and a wood which will fatten lx swine; and here are ii *hayes*. In the time of King Edward it was worth 40s. Now 30s."[1] During the lifetime of Roger de Montgomery, Gerard gave the *vill* of Betton to that Abbey which his great suzerain had founded at Shrewsbury, and the monks retained his gift for more than 250 years.

Longslow. "The same Gerard," continues *Domesday*, "holds Walanceslau. Uluiet held it and was a free man. Here iii hides geldable. There is land for v ox-teams. In demesne is one team, and ii serfs; and there is one tenant[2] here, paying a rent of 40d. In time of King Edward it was worth 10s.: now 12s."[1] Longslow, north-west of Market Drayton, is alluded to in the above extract from *Domesday*. Like many of Gerard's manors, Longslow afterwards became a serjeantry; and the Bradford Hundred Roll of 1255, says that:—"Hugh de Wlonkislow, lord of the vill, held it *in capite*, by service of 40 days in time of war, at the castle of Shrawardine, or of Shrewsbury, at his own cost. He was to be provided with a horse, a breast-plate, a chapel-de-fer, and a lance. The *vill* paid 12d. yearly for *motfee* and 12d. for *stretward*, and did suit every three weeks to the Hundred-Court."

Ightfield. "The same Gerard holds Istefelt. Uluiet held it and was a free man. Here ii hides geldable. The land is for iiii ox-teams. Here a priest and ii boors with i team; a wood which will fatten 60 swine; and ii hayes. [Formerly the manor] was worth 15s. [per annum]: now 10s."[1] In the course of time, Ightfield became a serjeantry; the service of its tenant being to provide one foot-soldier for ward of the royal castle of Shrawardine. The *Nomina Villarum* of 1316, represents John de Garenne [Warrenne] as lord of the vill of Ythefeld.

The Church.

From the mention of a priest in the *Domesday* notice of the manor, it may be inferred that there was a church at Ightfield

---

[1] *Domesday*, fo. 259, a 1.   [2] "Homo."

in 1086, which probably was the mother church of the district. In 1291, the church of Ithefeld, in the deanery of Newport, and archdeaconry of Salop, was valued at £2 13s. 4d. *per annum*; besides a pension which the abbot of Combermere received therefrom. In 1341, the parish was rated £2 6s. to the *ninth*. In 1534-5, the rectory of Ightfelde, in the deanery of Salop, was worth £8 *per annum*, less 3s. 4d. for procurations, and 2s. for synodals. A chantry here was further endowed with £5 *per annum*.

Early Incumbent.—John, parson of Ightfield in 1272.

Woolerton, on the Tern, also belonged to Gerard de Tornai in 1086, for *Domesday* says:—"The same Gerard holds Ulvretone. Oschetel held it, and was a free man. Here i hide geldable. The land is [capable of employing] iiii ox-teams. In demesne are ii teams; and vii serfs, iii villains, ii boors, and one radman, with i team. Here a mill of 10s. [annual value], and a wood which will fatten four-score swine. In King Edward's time [the manor] was worth 15s.; now 25s. He [Gerard] found it waste."[1] Hamo Peverel, who, by marrying the daughter of Gerard de Tornai, became his successor, gave the vill of Woolerton to Shrewsbury Abbey, and the abbot continued lord over it until the dissolution.

Marchamley. Rainald, the sheriff, held five manors in the *Domesday* Hundred of Odenet. One of these, namely, Marchamley, is thus described in the record of King William I. "Raynald, the sheriff, holds Marcemeslei of the earl. Seuuar and Aluric held it in King Edward's time for ii manors, and were free. Here 5½ hides geldable. In demesne are ii ox-teams; and iiii serfs, vi villains, vii boors, and ii radmans having iii teams between them all; and there might be x more teams [employed] besides. Here a mill of 5s. [annual value]; a wood which will fatten 100 swine; and one haye.

"Of this land, Walter holds [under Rainald] 1½ hides, and thereon he has i ox-team and i serf; and [there are] a villain and a boor with half a team. The whole, in the time of King Edward, was worth 100s.; afterwards it was waste; now it is worth 46s. 4d."[2] Beyond the *Domesday* notice, there is nothing

---

[1] *Domesday*, fo. 259, a 1.   [2] Ibidem, fo. 254, a 2.

particularly interesting attached to the early history of Marchamley.

High Hatton, in 1086, also belonged to Rainald *Vicecomes*, for we read in *Domesday*, that:—"The same Rainald holds Hetune of the earl, and Richard [holds it] of Rainald. Ælric, Ulfac, Uluiet, and Leuric, held it for iiii manors in the time of King Edward. Here ii hides geldable. In demesne are one ox-team and iiii serfs; and ii villains and ii cottars with ii teams; and there might be v more teams besides. Those who [formerly] held these lands were free. In the time of King Edward [the manor] was worth 60s. [annually]; afterwards it was waste; now [it is worth] 10s."[1] The Corbets of Hadley and Tasley ultimately acquiring this manor, accordingly the Hundred Roll of 1255 gives Roger Corbet as lord of the *vill*. He held it of the fief of John Fitz Alan, and provided a horseman with horse, hauberk, lance, and *chapel de fer*, to serve at Fitz Alan's castle of Oswestry for forty days, and at Corbet's cost. The present lord of the manor is Roger Corbet's descendant.

Stanton-upon-Hineheath. "The same Rainald," continues *Domesday*, "holds Stantune of the earl, and Ricardus [holds it] of Rainald. Sauuard held it [in Saxon times], and was free with this land. Here i hide geldable. In demesne there is one ox-team and iiii serfs. The church, a priest, vi boors, and a smith, have among them all ii teams; and there might be a third team. Here is a mill of 10s. 8d. [annual value]. In time of King Edward [the manor] was worth 35s.; afterwards it was waste; now it is worth 22s."[1] Richard, the *Domesday* tenant of Stanton, it is supposed was ancestor of that powerful family who, deriving their name of De Stanton from the place, long exercised the seigneury over Stanton-upon-Hineheath, whilst under the De Stantons held under-tenants.

The Church.

Stanton church, a Saxon foundation, is noticed in Domesday Book. It is dedicated to St. Andrew. About 1230, William de Stanton, the lord of the manor, gave this advowson to Haughmond Abbey. In 1291, the church of Staunton, in the deanery of Salop,

---

[1] *Domesday*, fo. 254, a 2.

was valued at £12 *per annum*, besides a pension of 4s. to the abbot of Haghmon. The canons of Haughmond having obtained an appropriation of this rectory, on November 3rd, 1331, Bishop Northburgh instituted John Fayrchild, first vicar of Stanton, at presentation of the "abbot and convent of Haghmon, impropriators of the said church by papal authority, and patrons thereof." In 1341, the parish of Staunton was assessed £8 to the *ninth*. In 1534-5, the vicar of Staunton's preferment was worth £6, less 9s. 2d. for procurations and synodals.

Great Withyford.

We have already described Pantulf's share of Withyford. Other two parts of the manor belonged to Rainald, the sheriff. *Domesday* says:—"The same Rainald holds Wicford, and Alcher [holds it] of Rainald. Sten and Wilegrip held it, and were free with this land. Here 2½ hides geldable. In demesne are ii ox-teams and viii serfs, v villains, one radman, and one frenchman, with 3½ teams. Here a mill of 8s. [annual value]. In time of King Edward [the manor] was worth 28s.; afterwards it was waste; now [it is worth] 40s.

"The same Rainald holds in the same vill i hide geldable, and Albert [holds it] of him. Uluric and Carlo held it [in Saxon times] for a manor. Here is one ox-team, ii serfs, ii boors; and there might be another team. [In King Edward's time] this was worth 7s.; afterwards it was waste; now [it is worth] 7s."[1] Among the knightly families of Shropshire, none are traceable with a greater certainty to the time of William the Conqueror, than that family of Fitz Aer who descended from Alcher or Aher, Rainald the sheriff's tenant at Withyford. Besides Withyford, the Fitz Aers, for many generations held Aston Eyre of the barony of Fitz Alan.[2]

At an inquest held in 1356, the jurors stated that "John Fitz Aer died seized, etc. Hugh, his son and heir, enfeoffed William Canne, who settled Harcott on the said Hugh, his wife Alina, and their heirs. The heir of Hugh and Alina was their son Thomas, whose daughter and heir, Margery, married Alan, son of Alan de Cherlton. The latter died seized of 20 librates of rent, payable by his father for the Fitz Aer estates, at Aston and Withford, and John, son of Alan, now a minor, was son and heir of Alan de

---

[1] *Domesday*, fo. 254, a 2.   [2] *See* Aston Eyre, p. 52.

Cherlton, junior," The Charltons of Apley, therefore, descend from Fitz Aer.

Gravenhunger. William Malbedeng, the great Norman feoffee of Hugh Lupus, Earl of Chester, had little to do with Shropshire; nevertheless, when William the Conqueror's commissioners surveyed the county, they found that he held four manors in Odenet Hundred, under the Earl of Shrewsbury. Beyond the notices relating to them in Domesday Book, the early history of Malbedeng's Shropshire manors is uninteresting. Gravenhunger is thus described in the record of King William the First:— "William Malbedeng holds Gravehungre of Earl Roger. Æluric and Ulgar held it for ii manors, and were free. Here i hide geldable. There is land for iiii ox-teams. Here ii radmans have i team. Here i haye. In the time of King Edward [the manor] was worth 13s.; now 12s. He [William] found it waste."[1]

Woore. "The same William," continues *Domesday*, "holds Waure. Leuuin and Edric held it for ii manors, and were free. Here i hide geldable. The land is for iii ox-teams. Here ii radmans have i team with iii boors. The wood will fatten 60 swine. In time of King Edward, it was worth 23s.; now 10s. He [William] found it waste."[1] Parochially, Woore is in Staffordshire.

Dorrington. "The same William holds Derintune. Leuuin and Edric held it for ii manors, and were free. Here i hide geldable. The land is [capable of employing] iii ox-teams. Here is one radman, with i team and with one boor. The wood will fatten 100 swine. In the time of King Edward [the manor] was worth 14s.; now it is worth 8s. He found it waste."[1] The lordly Malbedengs or Malbancs, befriended the church, for it was Hugh, son of William Malbedeng, the *Domesday* baron, who founded the Cistercian abbey of Combermere. Again, one of his descendants gave Dorrington to the monks of Wenlock.

Onneley. "The same William holds Anelege. Edric held it.

---

[1] *Domesday*, fo. 257, b 1.

Here i virgate of land geldable. In the time of King Edward it was worth 5s.; now it is waste."¹ The virgate of land here alluded to early became annexed to Gravenhunger.

Moreton Say is the subject of the following entry in Domesday Book:—"Roger de Laci holds Mortune under Earl Roger, and William [holds it] of him. Elmund held it [in Saxon times], and was a free man. Here iii hides geldable. In demesne is one ox-team, and viii serfs, iiii villains, and iiii boors, with ii teams; and there might be vi more teams besides. The wood here will fatten 100 swine. In the time of King Edward [the manor] was worth 40s. [annually]; afterwards it was waste; now it is worth 30s."² It was from that great family of Say, who, for so long a period held Stokesay and Moreton under Lacy and his heirs, that Moreton Say acquired its distinctive title.

The church of Moreton Say was originally a chapel of Hodnet.

Lai. "The same Roger," continues *Domesday*, "holds Lai, and William holds it of him. Here i hide geldable. Eluui held it [in Saxon times], and was a free man. Here one free man has half an ox-team; and there might be one more team [employed]. [Formerly] it was worth 6s.; now 2s. He [Roger de Laci] found it waste."² This small manor cannot now be identified.

Hopton, near Hodnet. *Domesday* says:—"*In hôc Hundredo [scilicet Odenet] tenuit Edric unam berewicham, Hotune, de dimidiâ hidâ geldabilem; et non poterat hæc terra separari a manerio Stoches quem tenet Rogerius Laci. Hæc terra est appreciata in ipso manerio, in Recordin Hundredo.*"³ It was Roger de Lacy's manor of Stoke-upon-Tern that is alluded to in the above obscure *Domesday* notice of Hopton. Lacy's tenants, both at Stoke and at Hopton, were the De Says, one of whom named Elyas de Say gave Hopton, before 1172, to the monks of Haughmond Abbey.

Lacon. Ranulf Peverel held three manors in Odenet Hundred, under the earl, viz., Lacon, Weston, and Whixall. The first

---

¹ *Domesday*, fo. 257, b 1.   ² Ibidem, fo. 256, a 2.   ³ Ibidem, fo. 256, b 1.

of these is thus described in the Conqueror's record:—"The same Rannulf holds Laeh. Elnod held it and was a free man. Here 2½ virgates geldable. In demesne is half an ox-team with i boor, and still there might be another half team besides. The old value of the manor was 5s. [annually]; now it is worth 3s."[1] Lacon is two and a half miles north-east of Wem.

Weston-under-Red Castle.

"The same Ranulf," continues *Domesday*, "holds Westune. Edric Salvage held it. Here iii hides geldable. In demesne are ii ox-teams, and viii serfs, iii villains, one radman, and ix boors, with i team; and still there might be v more teams [employed]. In time of King Edward, the manor was worth 60s.; afterwards 5s.; now [it is worth] 40s."[1] Peverel's Shropshire manors did not continue with his house, and King Henry the Third's favourite, Henry de Audley, having purchased that portion of the manor on which was situated the rock called Red-Cliff, a patent of August 17th, 1227, empowered him to build the castle of Radeclif, which thenceforth became the Shropshire stronghold of the Audleys.

Weston chapel, an ancient foundation, was, from the first, a dependency of Hodnet.

Whixall.

"The same Rannulf holds Witehala. Ældid held it, and was a free man. Here i hide geldable. In demesne is i ox-team, ii neat-herds, ii boors; and there might be one more team. In time of King Edward, the manor was worth 8s.; now 5s."[1] The superior lords of Weston and of Whixall, were identical. William le Botiler, of Wem, died in 1369, seized of Quixhall, which he held under James de Audley by service of a pair of spurs.

Edgeley.

Earl Roger enfeoffed his vassal, Roger de Curcelle, also in three Odenet manors. One of them was Edgeley, which is thus noticed in Domesday Book:—"The same Roger holds Edeslai. Aluric held it, and was a free man. Here i hide geldable. Here is one radman, one villain, and v boors, with i ox-team; and v more teams might be here. Here one serf. In time

---

[1] *Domesday*, fo. 256, b 2.

of King Edward, it was worth 40s. [annually]; now 12s. He [De Curcelle] found it waste."¹ The place alluded to is a mile and a half south-east from Whitchurch. The Norman Roger de Curcelle's manors eventually were annexed to Pantulf's barony of Wem.

Dodington, "The same Roger holds Dodetune. Earl Eduin held it. Here i hide geldable. Here iiii villains and one radman with ii ox-teams; and other ii teams might be here. The wood will fatten lx swine. [Formerly the manor] was worth 16s.; now 9s."¹ Dodington now forms the southern portion of the town of Whitchurch.

Steele, in the parish of Prees, is thus described in *Domesday*:—"The same Roger holds Stile. Algar, Colline, Brictric, and Turgar held it for iiii manors, and were free men. Here i hide. Here are iiii villains and one boor, with i team; and two more teams might be here. A wood here will fatten xxx swine. In time of King Edward, the manor was worth 13s.; now 6s."¹

Bearstone, south-west of Woore, in 1086 belonged to Turold de Verley, for *Domesday* says, that:—"The same Turold holds Bardestune [of the earl]. Ulgar held it [in Saxon times], and was a free man. Here i hide geldable. The land is for v ox-teams. In demesne is one team; and [there are] ii neat-herds and iii boors with i team. Here a mill of 3s. [annual value]; and a wood which will fatten 60 swine. In time of King Edward it was worth 20s.; now it is worth 10s. He found it waste."² This, like Turold's other manors, eventually passed to the Chetwynds, who held it for a couple of hundred years at least. Although in Shropshire, Bearstone belongs to the Staffordshire parish of Mucklestone.

Little Drayton, bounded by the river Tern, is thus spoken of in Domesday Book: —"The same Turold holds Draitune. The Countess Godeva held it. Here i hide geldable. The [arable] land is [sufficient] for v ox-teams. In demesne is one team, with ii neat-herds, and one villain. In time of King Edward [the

---

¹ *Domesday*, fo. 256, a 2.   ² Ibidem, fo. 258, a 1.

manor] was worth 8s. [annually]; now 6s. 8d. He [Turold] found it waste."[1] We have already spoken of William Pantulf's *berewick* Draitone, now Market Drayton. The Draitune described in the above extract, is Little Drayton, which, in ancient days, belonged to the illustrious Mercian Countess Godeva. The Norman Turold de Verley, who succeeded the Saxon Lady here, gave Drayton Minor to Shrewsbury Abbey, and the lord abbot continued to rule supreme over Little Drayton until Henry the Eighth's time.

Norton-in-Hales.

We read in Domesday Book that:— "Helgot holds Nortune of Earl Roger. Azor held it, and was a free man. Here iii hides geldable. The land is for vi ox-teams. There is one radman with i team, and iiii villains with ii teams. A wood here will fatten 200 swine. In the time of King Edward it was worth 30s.; now 20s."[2] In Henry the First's time, Helgot's son Herbert gave this manor to Shrewsbury Abbey, and the monks retained it until the dissolution.

NORTON CHURCH.

Eyton says, " perhaps Herbert Fitz Helgot was the founder of Norton church, for his successors at Norton, the monks of Shrewsbury, were not addicted to such works." Pope Nicholas' Taxation in 1291, describes the church of Norton-in-Hales, as being in the deanery of Newport, but merely states that the abbot of Shrewsbury received a pension of 2s. therefrom. In 1341, the parish of *Norton-in-le-Halys* was taxed £1 6s. 8d. to the *ninth* of wheat, wool, and lamb. King Henry the Eighth's *Valor* in 1534-5 represents the preferment of the rector of Norton-in-Hales as worth £6 *per annum*, less 6s. 8d. for procurations, 2s. for synodals, and the abbot's pension of 2s.

Early Incumbent.—Richard was parson of Norton-in-Hales in 1294. Presented by the abbot and convent of Shrewsbury.

Lee Brockhurst.

The following entry in Domesday Book is supposed to relate to Lee Brockhurst:—" The same Normannus [Venator] holds Lege [of the earl]. Uluiet and Wictric and Elfac held it for iii manors and were free. Here i hide geldable. There is land for ii ox-teams. Those [two] teams are in demesne,

---

[1] *Domesday*, fo. 258, a 1.   [2] Ibidem, fo. 258, b 1.

with iiii neat-herds, and i boor. Here a mill of 6s. [annual value]. In time of King Edward [the manor] was worth 13s.; now £3. He [Normannus] found it waste."¹ Lege acquired that particular title by which it is now distinguished from Brockhurst, an adjoining tract of woodland.

Moston, a mile and a half north-north-west of Stanton Hineheath, is noticed in *Domesday* thus:—"The same Roger [Venator] holds Mostune [of Earl Roger]. Dodo and Ulgar held it for ii manors, and were free men. Here ii hides geldable. The land is for iiii ox-teams. Here one radman has i team, with ii villains. In time of King Edward, it was worth 40s.; now 15s. He found it waste."²

Rowton, in the parish of High Ercall, is also noticed in *Domesday*:—"Eddict," says that record, "holds Routone of the earl. Morcar and Dot held it for ii manors, and were free men. Here ii hides geldable. The land is for iiii ox-teams. In demesne is one team; and iii serfs, a priest, and iiii boors, with i team. The manor was worth 25s.; now 15s."³ It is supposed that Eddiet, who held this manor under the Norman earl, was a woman. After *Domesday*, Rowton is always spoken of in connection with Ellardine.⁴ Of that church or chapel which is indicated by the mention of a priest in the *Domesday* notice of Rowton, scarce a vestige remains.

Prees, in Anglo-Saxon as in Anglo-Norman times, belonged to the Bishop of Chester, for *Domesday* says:—"The same bishop holds Pres, and held it in King Edward's time. Here viii hides geldable. In demesne are iii ox-teams, x villains, a priest, and iii boors, with v teams. Here vi neat-herds, and a wood for 60 swine. Of this manor, Anschitil holds half a hide, and Fulcher ii hides under the bishop. In demesne they have ii ox-teams, and ii villains, with i team; and iii other men who till plough-land here pay 10s. rent; and [there are] ii neat-herds here. The whole manor, in King Edward's time, was worth 50s. [annually]; afterwards it was waste. Now, that which the bishop has is worth 40s;

---

¹ *Domesday*, fo. 259, a 1.
² Ibidem, fo. 259, a 2.
³ *Domesday*, fo. 259, b 1.
⁴ *See* page 389.

that which his men [Anschitil and Fulcher], have [is worth] 28s. Six more teams might be here."[1] Throughout the middle ages ecclesiastical property of every description was invested with great and exclusive privileges, hence we have but scanty notices of the early history of Prees. According to the Tenure Roll of 1285 :—
"The Bishop of Chester holds the manor of Prece, with its members, viz., Darlaston, Leeton, Wotenhull [now lost], Mitteley [Mickley], Willaston [Wooliston], and Milheyth [Millenheath], of the king *in capite sine medio*, freely, as a member of his barony of Eccleshall; and here the bishop has, from ancient time, his free court and gallows. Also he has here a market and fair, by charter of King Henry III."

In accordance with that Act of Parliament, of October 9th, 1646, which abolished all archbishopricks and bishopricks, and vested their estates in trustees, Prees was sold, on December 18th, 1647, to lay purchasers.

CHURCH OF ST. CHAD, AT PREES.

This, originally a Saxon Collegiate foundation, is indicated by the mention of a priest in the *Domesday* notice of the manor. It appears to have preserved its collegiate character until about 1280, when the greater portion of its revenues went to found a prebendal stall in Lichfield Cathedral.

Pope Nicholas' Taxation, in 1291, makes mention of an episcopal estate at Prees, and a prebend of Prees worth £26 13s. 4d. per annum, but says nothing about a vicarage. In 1341, the parish was taxed 20 merks to the *ninth* of its wheat, wool and lamb. King Henry VIII.'s *Valor* of 1534-5 represents the vicarage of Prees, in the deanery of Salop, as worth £10 annually; but the prebendary of Pipa Minor, alias Prees, was worth £19.

Early Incumbents.—T. and N., probably Thomas and Nicholas, were co-rectors of Prees in 1214. Thomas, parson of Prees, occurs in 1224. Robert de Radcwcy is the first recorded vicar of Prees, 1280-90.

Addenley, Shavington, Spoonley, and Calverhall, at the period of the Conqueror's survey, formed one compact estate, held of the Norman earl by Nigel, a clerk, who was also physician to Earl Roger de Montgomery. "Nigellus," says *Domesday*, "holds

---

[1] *Domesday*, fo. 252, a 2.

Eldredelei of Earl Roger. Edric held it [in Saxon times] and was a free man. Here iii hides geldable. There is [arable] land for 6½ ox-teams. In demesne is one team, and ii neàt-herds and iiii villains with i team. Here ii hayes. [The manor] was and is worth 15s. [annually]."[1] Upon the decease of Nigel, his Shropshire estates escheated to earl Hugh, when Adderley, Shavington, Spoonley, and Calverhall, were consolidated into one manor, of which, for two centuries, Adderley continued the centre. Upon the forfeiture of the Norman earls, this manor came into the hands of King Henry I., who gave it, along with Idsall, to Alan de Dunstanvill.[2]

The *Nomina Villarum* of 1316 represents Bartholomew de Badlesmere, as lord of Aderdeleye. Implicated in the rebellion of the earl of Lancaster, Lord Badlesmere was taken prisoner at the battle of Burroughbridge, when, being convicted of high treason, the lord of Adderley was drawn, hanged, and afterwards beheaded.[3]

THE CHURCH.

Adderley Church must have been founded before 1291, as, in that year, according to Pope Nicholas' Taxation, it was worth £5 per annum. In 1341, the parish of Adderdeleye was taxed £5 as the *ninth* of its wheat, wool, and lambs. In 1534-5, the preferment of the rector of Adderley was valued at £12 per annum, less 14s. for synodals and procurations. There is a curious ancient font in this church.

Early Rector.—Master Richard de Northampton, 1305.

Shavington.

"The same Nigellus holds Savintune. Dodo held it, and was free. Here half a hide, geldable. The land is for iiii ox-teams. In demesne is half a team, and ii serfs and iii boors with half a team. [Formerly] it was worth 12s. Now 15s. Nigellus found it waste."[1]

Spoonley.

"The same Nigellus holds Sponelege. Dunning held it and was free. Here i hide geldable. The land is for ii

---

[1] *Domesday*, fo. 259, a 1. [2] See page 81.
[3] DUGDALE's *Baronage*, ii. 58.

ox-teams. Waste it was and is. In time of King Edward it was worth 20s." [1]

Calverhall. "The same Nigellus," continues *Domesday*, "holds Calvrahalle. Edmær and Eluui held it for ii manors, and were free with these lands. Here i hide and iii virgates, geldable. The land [might employ] vi ox-teams. In demesne is one team; and ii neat-herds and iiii villains with one team. The wood will fatten 20 swine. In time of King Edward, the manor was worth 18s. [per annum]. Now 20s. And it furnishes one hawk." [1] After Adderley, Shavington, Spoonley, and Calverhall, or Cloverley, had been consolidated into one manor, the tenants of the three last-named places did suit at the court of the lords of Adderley. Adderley, with Shavington and Spoonley, constitute the present parish of Adderley, whilst Calverhall is in the parish of Prees.

Soulton, in the days of King William I., belonged to St. Michael's chapel, in the castle of Shrewsbury, to which it had been given by Earl Roger de Montgomery. "The same church holds Suletune [of the earl]. Brictric held it [in Saxon times] freely. Here i hide geldable. The land is for i ox-team. Here is half a team. [Formerly] it was worth 5s. [per annum]. Now it yields 4d. more." [2] St. Michael's long continued to exercise a seigneury over the chief tenant here, under whom again held under-tenants.

Whitchurch, at the time of the Conquest, was called Weston. It acquired this name, probably, from the circumstance of its lying on the extreme western edge of the part of Shropshire in which it is situate. Its position was that of a town bordering on the marches of North Wales: hence its early importance.

"Willelm de Warene," says *Domesday*, "holds Westune of Earl Roger. The Earl Herald held it [in Saxon times]. Here 7½ hides geldable. In demesne are iiii ox-teams, and ii serfs, and vi neat-herds, xxiii villains, ix boors, and one radman, with viii teams; and still there might be xiiii more teams here. Here a wood, which will fatten 400 swine; therein are iii hayes. In time of King Edward [the manor] was worth £8 [annually]. Now [it is

---

[1] *Domesday*, fo. 259. a 1.   [2] Ibidem, fo. 252, b 2.

worth] £10."[1] Shortly after the survey had been taken, a large church constructed of whitish-looking stone, was built at Weston. This was an extraordinary work in the eyes of the natives, who, abandoning that old title of Weston, by which the town had heretofore been known, henceforth distinguished it by the new name of Album Monasterium, Blancminster, or, in plain English, Whitechurch.

As appears, then, from the above extract, Whitchurch, in Anglo-Saxon times, belonged to the great Earl Harold, second son of Godwin, earl of Wessex. After the sudden demise of his father, Harold became the right hand, as it were, of his indolent and superstitious brother-in-law, Edward the Confessor. He fought his battles, and drove back to Nature's misty strongholds, Gruffith, dread chief of the Cymri: and hence, no doubt, it came to pass, that the reputed conqueror of Wales acquired Whitchurch.

King Edward loved Harold very much. He was "the king's darling," and dearest to him in all service. Not only to his infirm brother-in-law, the Confessor, was the name of Earl Harold dear; it was dear to all, save to the out-land men, the Normans. Upon Edward the Confessor's decease, Harold was chosen by a majority of the Witan, or English national council, to mount the vacant throne. "Harold, the earl, succeeded to the kingdom of England, even as the king had granted it to him, and men also had chosen him thereto," says the cotemporary writer in the Anglo-Saxon Chronicle. Crowned King of England, Harold II.'s brief reign of forty weeks and one day was characterised by vigor and a complete return to those old Saxon usages which had been despised by the late king and his Norman courtly favourites. Yet King Harold "with little quiet abode therein, the while that he wielded the realm ;" for the bastard count of the Normans, deeming that he had a better title to the throne of England than he who now sat upon it: hence the Norman invasion. The bold English king, after a forced march from York, whither he had gone to crush the hostile attempt of his unnatural brother Tosti, and his ally, the Norwegian giant, Hardraade; after an exhausting march of 250 miles, King Harold confronted, with a very inadequate force, that incongruous but magnificent mail-clad host which Duke William had mustered upon the field of Hastings. A great battle ensued, in the midst of which, pierced with an arrow in the eye

---

[1] *Domesday*, fo. 257, a 2.

the regal lord of Whitchurch paid the penalty of his ambition with his life, and William the Conqueror extended his iron sway over our country.

William de Warren, who succeeded Harold in this, his only Shropshire estate, was distantly related both to the Norman earl of Shrewsbury and to the Conqueror. By accepting an isolated feoffment in Shropshire, De Warren chivalrously entailed upon himself the warlike cares of a lord-marcher, and Weston castle became one of a series of strongholds that guarded the marches.

Under the earls, Warren and Surrey, Whitchurch was held by vassals, descending from William de Warren, alias Fitz-Ranulf, who was related to the elder line. He was the earliest known lord of Whitchurch, under the earls. His first appearance is on the Shropshire Pipe Roll of 1176, when he was security for his neighbour, the lord of Ightfield.

The service by which the manor was formerly held, was this: the lord of Whitchurch was to do duty as Earl Warren's huntsman, at the will and at the charges of the said earl.

The Church.

William de Warren, to whom the Conqueror assigned Weston or Whitchurch, a lover of the church, having founded Lewes and Castle Acre Priories, it is most likely also caused St. Alkmond's church to be built here. This church contains the monumental effigy of John Talbot, Earl of Shrewsbury, who, surnamed the English Achilles, fell at the battle of Bordeaux in 1453. His bones were removed from France, and interred in the old church at Whitchurch. When the present edifice was being erected, an urn was discovered in which the old warrior's heart was found, embalmed and covered up with a crimson velvet cloth.

In 1291, the church of Album Monasterium, in the deanery and archdeaconry of Salop, was valued at £13 6s. 8d. per annum. In 1341, the parish was taxed only £12 to the *ninth*, because a third of it was in Cheshire and a part in Flintshire, counties not included in the current assessment. The *Valor* of Henry VIII. gives £50 as the gross income of the rector of Whytechurche, out of which he had to pay 4s. 4d. *per annum* for synodals, 6s. 8d. for procurations, 4s. for procurations at the bishop's triennial visitation, and a salary of £4 13s. 4d. to the chaplain of the church of Merbury.

The old church of St. Alkmond fell down in the reign of Queen Anne. The present Grecian structure was erected in 1722.

THE OLD CHURCH OF ST. ALKMOND, WHITCHURCH.
(WHICH FELL DOWN, JULY 31, 1711).

Early Rector.—Jacob Taunceys, or Fraunccys, parson of Whitchurch, 1296.

Cheswardine and Chipnall are entered in Domesday Book as constituting a single manor in the Staffordshire Hundred of *Pireholle.* "The said Robert [de Stafford] holds [of the king] in Ciseworde and in Ceppecanole ii hides; and Gislebert holds of him. The land is for vi ox-teams. In demesne are ii teams, and xii villains and viii boors, with $3\frac{1}{2}$ teams. Here i acre of meadow. The wood is ii leagues long and half a league wide. [The manor] is worth 40s. [annually]. Godeva [the Countess] held it [formerly], but from Ceppecanole she used to pay 2s. to the church of St. Chad." [1] Severed from the county and barony of Stafford, as a manor of royal demesne, Cheswardine came into the hands of Henry II., who, granting it previously to Michaelmas, 1155, to Hamo le Strange, for ages the Le Stranges exercised the seigneury over Cheswardine. The tenure *in capite* of Le Strange of Ness and Cheswardine was by service of $1\frac{1}{2}$ knight's fees, of which Cheswardine constituted the half fee. The lord of the manor had his free court, in which he held pleas of bloodshed and hue and cry. He did suit to the county, but not to the hundred. He exercised free warren, and had a castle and park at Cheswardine.

The Sprenghoses held Cheswardine under the Le Stranges, whilst various other tenants held Chipnall, Hull, and Magna and Parva Sudeley of the lord of the manor.

CHESWARDINE CHURCH.

This must have been founded before the year 1178, about which time John le Strange granted the advowson thereof to Haughmond Abbey. It is dedicated to St. Swithin. Fairs and wakes were usually sought to be held on the anniversary of the patron saint of the parish church; and accordingly, Roger le Strange, in 1304, obtained the king's charter for holding a yearly fair at Cheswardine, of three days' duration, namely, the eve, the day, and the morrow of the translation of St. Swithin.

In 1291, the church of Chesewurthyn, in the archdeaconry of Stafford, was valued at £6 13s. 4d. In 1341, the parish, then reputed to be in the Shropshire deanery of Newport, was taxed £5 6s. 8d. to the *ninth.* No mention is made of Cheswardine in the *Valor* of 1534-5.

Early Incumbent.—John Fitz Geoffrey, said to have been appointed by King Henry III.

---

[1] *Domesday,* fo. 248, b 2.

Domesday Hundred of Bascherch.

Modern Name.	Domesday Name.	Saxon Owner or Owners, T. R. E.	Domesday Tenant in capite.	Domesday Mesne, or next Tenant.	Domesday Sub-Tenant.	Modern Hundred.
Baschurch	Bascherche	Rex Edwardus	Rogerius Comes			Pimhill.
Fennymere	Finemer	Seuuardus	Idem			Ibidem.
English Frankton	Franchetone	Aldi	Idem	Rainaldus Vicecomes	Robertus	Ibidem.
Shrawardine	Saleurdine	Æli	Idem	Rainaldus Vicecomes		Ibidem.
Albright Hussey	Abretone	Seuuard	Idem	Rainaldus Vicecomes	Herbert	Liberties of Shrewsbury.
Little Ness	Nesse	Seuuardus	Idem	Rainaldus Vicecomes		Pimhill.
Middle	Mulleht	Seuuardus	Idem	Rainaldus Vicecomes	Albertus	Ibidem.
Welch Hampton	Hantone	Ældit	Idem	Rainaldus Vicecomes	Albertus	Ibidem.
Rosshall	Rosela	Hunni	Idem	Rainaldus Vicecomes	Albertus	Liberties of Shrewsbury.
	Aitone	Leuric	Idem	Rainaldus Vicecomes	Albertus	
Hadnall	Hadehelle	Goduin	Idem	Rainaldus Vicecomes	Osmundus	Ibidem.
Acton Reynald	Achetone	Seuuard	Idem	Rainaldus Vicecomes	Ricardus	Ibidem.
Albrighton	Etbritone	Gheri	Idem	Warinus Vicecomes (Nuper)	Alcher Nuper	Pimhill.
Walford	Waleford	Seuuard	Idem	Robertus Pincerna	Sturmid	Ibidem.
Stanwardine in the Field	Staurdine	Eldrid	Idem	Robertus Pincerna		Ibidem.
Petton	Pectone	Leuenot	Idem	Robertus Pincerna	Rudulfus	Ibidem.
Eyton near Baschurch	Hetone	Leuui	Idem	Robertus Pincerna	Robertus	Ibidem.
? ?	Crugetone	Eduinus Comes	Idem	Robertus Pincerna		Ibidem.
Colemere	Colesmere	Aldiet	Idem	Normannus		Ibidem.
? ?	Estone	Elnod	Idem	Normannus	Fulcher	?
? ?	Cheneltone		Idem	Normannus ?		?
? ?	Slacheberie	Aluiet	Idem	Roger Venator		
Broom Farm	Bruma		Idem	Luigatur		Pimhill.
Hordeley	Hordelei	Algar Dunniht	Idem	Odo		Ibidem.
Ruyton of the Eleven Towns	Uleford Ruitone	Leuenot	Idem	Odo		Oswestry.
Montford	Maneford	Elmer	Idem	Rogerius		Pimhill.
Preston Montford	Prestone	Godric	Idem	Rogerius		Liberties of Shrewsbury.
Forton	Fordune	Edmer	Idem	Rogerius de Laci	Osbernus	Pimhill.
Fitz	Witesot	Hunnith	Idem	Picot		Ibidem.
Merrington	Gellidone	Hunnith	Idem	Picot		Liberties of Shrewsbury.
Moreton Corbet	Moretone	Hunnit and Uluiet	Idem	Turoldus	Hunnit and Uluiet	Bradford North.
Preston Brockhurst	Preston	Hunnit and Uluiet	Idem	Turoldus	Hunnit	Pimhill.
Besford	Betford	Oschetel and Dodo	Idem	Gerardus	Robertus	Ibidem.
Grinshill	Grivelesul	Leulet, Godlic, Seuuard, Algar	Idem	Walcholinus		Liberties of Shrewsbury.
Felton Butler	Feltone	Aluric, Æluard Alchen	Idem	Helgot	Bernardus	Pimhill.
Leaton	Letone	Hunni	Idem	Anschitil		Liberties of Shrewsbury.
? ?	Iagedone	Elduinus	Idem	Elduinus		?
Sleap Magna	Eslepe	Uluric	Idem	Willelmus Pantulf		Bradford North.
? ?	Sudtelch	Asci	Idem	Willelmus Pantulf		? ?
Astley	Hesleie	Ecclesia Stæ. Mariæ	Idem	Ecclesia Stæ. Mariæ		Liberties of Shrewsbury.
Mytton	Mutone	Ecclesia Stæ. Mariæ	Idem	Ecclesia Stæ. Mariæ	Picot	Pimhill.
Broughton	Burtune	Ecclesia Stæ. Mariæ	Idem	Ecclesia Stæ. Mariæ		Liberties of Shrewsbury.
Broughton	Burtone	Ecclesia Sti. Cedde	Idem	Ecclesia Sti. Cedde		Ibidem.
Yorton	Lartune	Ecclesia Sti. Cedde	Idem	Ecclesia Sti. Cedde		Ibidem.
Bicton	Bichetone	Ecclesia Sti. Cedde	Idem	Ecclesia Sti. Cedde		Ibidem
Little Rosshall	Rosela	Ecclesia Sti. Cedde	Idem	Ecclesia Sti. Cedde		Ibidem.
Onslow	Andrelau	Ecclesia Sti. Cedde	Idem	Ecclesia Sti. Cedde		Ibidem.
Preston Gobalds	Prestone	Ecclesia Sti. Almundi	Idem	Ecclesia Sti. Almundi	Godeboldus	Ibidem.

MANORS SITUATED IN BASCHERCH, BUT WHOSE HUNDRED IS NOT STATED IN DOMESDAY.

Modern Name.	Domesday Name.	Saxon Owner or Owners, T. R. E.	Domesday Tenant in capite.	Domesday Mesne, or next Tenant.	Domesday Sub-Tenant.	Modern Hundred.
Great Ness	Nessham	Morcar Comes..	Rogerius Comes	Robertus, Ecclesia Sti. Petri........	....	Pimhill.
Loppington	Lopitone......	Edric Salvage..	.... Idem	....	....	Ibidem.
Ellesmere	Ellesmeles......	Eduinus Comes	.... Idem	Mundret, Rainaldus..	....	Ibidem.
Great Berwick	Berewic	Edric Salvage..	.... Idem	....	....	Liberties of Shrewsbury.

THE Bascherch Hundred of William the Conqueror's time was, in the 13th century, generally represented by the Hundred of Pimhill. Although still mainly represented by Pimhill, yet 18 manors, which at *Domesday* were included in the Hundred of Bascherch, are now involved in the Liberties of Shrewsbury. Other minor changes have taken place, as the reader can see by glancing at the annexed Table.

Respecting its jurisdiction :—In Edward the Confessor's time, the Hundred Court was held at Baschurch, and two-thirds of its revenues went to the king; the remaining third to the Earl of Mercia. After the conquest, the palatine Earls of Shrewsbury took the whole profits of the Hundred. When, however, upon the forfeiture of the third earl, Henry I. became lord of the Hundred, inasmuch as Shrewsbury Abbey had acquired the manor of Baschurch, the Hundred Court was henceforth held at Pimhill.

The Hundred of *Pemhull* is entered as attending by its jury at the Shropshire assizes, held in the autumn of 1203, the earliest of which detailed records remain.

Baschurch. The British poet Llywarc Hên, who lived in the 6th century, bore a distinguished part in defending his unfortunate country against the Saxon invader, and consequently, was an eye-witness of the actions he records. After being driven from his principality of Cumbria, Llywarc sought shelter in the court of Cynddylan, the British Prince of Powis, at Pengwern (Shrewsbury). But the fierce Saxons compelled the Britons to retire still further, before their superior force ; when it is supposed by some,[1]

---

[1] BLAKEWAY.

that Cynddylan made his last stand in the marshy neighbourhood of Baschurch.

"Pierced through the head by Twre [or the Hog]," the brave British prince died defending the patrimony of his sire; and then his sorrowing friend sang—

> "The churches of Bassa afford space to-night
> To the progeny of Cyndrwyn—
> The grave-house of fair Cynddylan!"[1]

About a mile and a half north-east of Baschurch stands the British fortress known as *the Berth*. The British term *berth*, signifies *a violent thrust*, which tallies with the event for which this spot is venerable. "The works at the Berth," says Hartshorne, "consist of two distinct fortresses, lying in a morass, but which are connected with each other by an artificially-raised causeway, one hundred and fifty yards long and twelve feet wide, formed with vast labour, of small stones." Another causeway, the communication between the camps and the main land, takes a sinuous line across the bog towards the higher ground at Marton. Both these causeways are built of stones brought from a gravel-pit a quarter of a mile distant.

"The upper work occupies a circular eminence of three acres, and rises about forty-five feet above the level of the land at its base. It is strengthened on three sides by a morass; upon the south, or fourth side, by a deep pool of water, covering eight acres. A concentric trench and vallum encircle the whole work; in some parts this is still tolerably perfect, chiefly so on the north side, but having been formed of stones according to the British method of construction, the greater portion of it is destroyed, and what remains is daily growing less conspicuous, in consequence of the materials being used for draining the surrounding wet land. The fosse was at first as much as ten feet wide. The crest of the vallum is at present about twenty feet above the level of the marsh. On the north-north-east side are remains of the original entrance. The gorge or gangway is seven feet wide. It had a tower on either side, or some erection which answered the same purpose, for there are two great heaps of stones still on the surface, notwithstanding the thousands of loads that" have been carried away. "A stream runs round this side of the work, that cuts off the causeway from reaching to the very entrance. There is no doubt that this

---

[1] *Heroic Elegies of Llywarc Hên*, translated by W. Owen. Lon. 1792, p. 85.

was intentional, and served the purpose of preventing all approach to the superior fortress, unless its inhabitants let down a plank or drawbridge to allow their friends to come over." Proceeding along the causeway which connects the two, the inferior work is entered "between two slightly elevated mounds, which formed the original gate of admission. The inferior fortress is of an elliptical form. It was defended by a morass on all sides, and even intersected by a ditch that was supplied with water to render all access to it still more difficult. The works on the side next the superior fortress are considerably higher than those in the other quarters." "In whatever way we look at these two fortifications," concludes the intelligent writer just quoted, "they cannot fail to strike us as most remarkable examples of castrametation for the age when they were constructed. They evince a degree of military knowledge that is highly curious and surprising; whilst they furnish us with a connecting link in the history of martial tactics, that is well deserving the attention of the antiquary and the soldier."[1]

The *Domesday* notice of Baschurch is as follows:—"The Earl himself holds Bascberche. King Edward held it. Here are iii hides and a half. Of this one [hide] is in demesne, and there are iiii ox-teams, vi villains, and ii boors, with ii teams. Here are viii neat-herds and iii Fisheries worth xxii pence [*per annum*].

"To this manor belong ii pence of the same hundred. The whole [in King Edward's time] was worth £7; now it is worth £6 to the lordship of the Earl.

"Of this manor, the church of St. Peter holds of the Earl ii hides and a half, and the church of the vill. The [arable] land is capable of employing v ox-teams, and here are [v teams] with xiii boors. [The manor] is worth xxvi shillings and viii pence."[2]

We learn from the above, that Edward the Confessor had held in demesne at Baschurch a hide of land, and two-thirds of the Hundred Pence, or profits of the Hundred Court. From these two sources the king received £7 *per annum*. In 1086, the hide, with the whole profits of the Hundred Court, yielded to the Norman Earl Roger £6. The remaining 2½ hides belonged to Shrewsbury Abbey; and like good farmers, as they were, the monks it appears had taken care to keep their land well stocked with team-power.

Upon his accession to the earldom of Shrewsbury, the son of

---

[1] *Salopia Antiqua*, p. 174—176.   [2] *Domesday*, fo. 253, a 2.

Earl Roger gave that hide which his father had held in demesne also to Shrewsbury Abbey. "It constituted the sole eleemosynary offering which the annals of Shropshire can record for the memory of Earl Robert de Belèsme." Baschurch therefore, both church-fee and manor, became the property of the monks.

A charter of December 28, 1339, informs us, that—"With the unanimous consent of his convent, Adam, Abbot of Salop, gives and concedes to his tenants and burgesses of the *New Vill*[1] of Baschirche (natives excepted) that they may hold their Burgages, recently built, or thereafter to be built, for 100 years, each such Burgage paying to the abbey an annual rent of 2s. in lieu of all services, except suit of the Manor-Court, and a heriot of 2s. at the decease of any burgess. The abbot further imparts to his burgesses his own franchise of selling free of toll throughout England. He gives them rights of common throughout the manor, and liberty *to assize bread and beer*, and to elect their own bailiff." So the Baschurch people acquired from the Abbot of Shrewsbury a corporate government, and a position superior in some respects to the inhabitants of a royal borough. The Minister's Accounts of 1541-2 give a total of £26 19s. as the Abbot's late income from Baschurch and its members, Newton, Prescott, Acton, (now Boreaton), Byrche, Nonyley, and Bageley.

THE CHURCH.

The Church of All Saints at Baschurch, originally a Saxon collegiate church, was given by Earl Roger de Montgomery to Shrewsbury Abbey. Bishop Novant, about 1190, allowed the monks to appropriate this Rectory.

In 1291, the church of Bascherch, *i.e.* the rectory, was valued at £16 *per annum*, and the vicarage at £5. In 1341, the parish was assessed only £12 to the *ninth*, "because the usual stock of sheep was not kept up in the parish, and because all the lambs produced in the current year had been sold for two quarters of oats. Moreover, the wheat crop had failed in a great measure, and the community were pauperised by different taxes of constant occurrence."

In 1534, the abbot represented his tithes of Baschurch, including Bagley and Noneley, to be £16 15s. 4d., but the Minister's Accounts of 1541-2 give them as £39 4s. 4d. The vicarage of Baschurch was valued at £11 10s. *per annum*, less 10s. for procurations and 4s. for synodals.

---

[1] A part of Baschurch is still called Newtown.

THE CHURCH OF ALL SAINTS, BASCHURCH.
(FROM A SKETCH TAKEN IN 1808).

Early Incumbents.—{ William Brun and Herbert Fitz-Alard, } last co-rectors of Baschurch were both living in 1190. William occurs as first vicar about 1265.

Fennymere. "The earl himself," says *Domesday*, "holds Finemer. Seuuard held it and was a free man. Here half a hide geldable. The land is for i ox-team. It was and is waste."[1]

Great Ness. According to *Domesday*—"The earl himself holds Nessham. Earl Morcar held it with iiii berewicks. Here v hides. In demesne are v ox-teams; and [there are] x neat-herds, xv villains and v boors with vi teams; and there might be [employed here] iii teams besides. Here vi Welshmen pay 20s. There is i league of wood. The church of St. Peter holds the church of this manor, with one virgate of land. One Robert has iiii villains who pay 5s. In time of King Edward [the manor] was worth £3 [per annum]; now [it yields] £13 10s."[2] The Norman earl's policy in the marches appears to have been successful; and here we have an instance of the Welsh holding under the Normans.

After the forfeiture of Robert de Belèsme, Ness came into the hands of Henry II., as a manor of royal demesne, when it acquired the title of King's Ness. King Henry made a temporary grant of the manor to Cadwallader, one of those renegade Welsh princes, whom the English sovereigns used as tools to disintegrate the unity of North Wales; but by 1157-8, as we learn from the Shropshire *Pipe Roll*, the English king had taken Ness from the Welsh prince and given it to John le Strange. Henceforth, therefore, the baronial and powerful Le Stranges, distinguished as a race for their abilities in the field and at the council, and yet more so for their steady loyalty, exercised the seignoury over Ness; and from them it was that the manor acquired the distinctive appellation of Ness-Strange.

CHURCH OF ST. ANDREW OF NESS.

This, originally a Saxon collegiate church, was given by the Norman earl, before *Domesday*, to Shrewsbury Abbey. In 1291, the church of Nesse Extranea, in the deanery and archdeaconry

---

[1] *Domesday*, fo. 259, b 2.   [2] Ibidem, fo. 253, b 2.

of Salop, was valued at £10 *per annum*, besides the abbot's pension of 10s. therefrom. In 1341, the parish of Nesse-Strange was taxed £4 only to the *ninth*, because much of the parish was in Wales; there had been a general murrain among the sheep, etc. About the middle of the 15th century, Shrewsbury Abbey obtained an appropriation of this church. King Henry VIII.'s *Valor* gives the vicar of Nesse-Strange's income as £9. The rectorial tithes, which went to Shrewsbury, were represented at the same time as worth £12 6s. 8d.; but this sum was chargeable with sundry pensions and payments.

Early Rectors of Ness:—Orneus, 1180. John, Rector of Ness, about 1265.

Early Vicar of Ness:—Sir William Bickley was instituted first Vicar of Ness, on April 3, 1452. Patrons, the Abbot and Convent of Salop.

Loppington.

"The Earl himself," says *Domesday*, "holds Lopitone. Edric Salvage held it. Here v hides geldable. In demesne are ii ox-teams and iiii serfs, and xv villains with vi teams; and there might be ii [other] teams besides. In the time of King Edward [the manor] was worth £3; now £6 10s."[1] In process of time, Loppington escheated to the crown, when it became a tenure *in capite*, by service of one knight's fee. The first recorded lord of the manor is Alexander de Loppington; who, about the year 1190, "gave the church of Lopinton to Wombridge Priory, for the souls of himself, his father, mother, and ancestors, and by consent and request of Richard his heir."[2]

On January 10, 1278, "the king accepted the homage of William le Botiler, son and heir of Ralph le Botiler, of Wemme, for the manor of Lopinton, which the said William had by concession of the Abbot of Lilleshull and of Richard de Lopinton;" and, continuing part of the barony of Wem for several generations, Loppington descended to the Lord Ferrers, of Wem, and to the Barons Greystock.

The Church.

Loppington was originally subject to Baschurch. We have noticed how, in 1190, it was given to Wombridge priory. The prior and canons of Wombridge were allowed to appropriate this church, in 1232. In 1291, the church of Lopington, in the

---

[1] *Domesday*, fo. 253, b 2.   [2] Wombridge Chartulary.

deanery and archdeaconry of Salop, was valued at £5 per annum, besides a pension of 2s., which the vicar of Bassechurch received therefrom. In 1341, the parish was taxed only £3 to the *ninth*, because a great part of the land lay untilled, on account of the poverty of the tenants; there had been a murrain among the sheep, etc. The *Valor* of 1534-5 gives £6 13s. 4d., less 1s. 3d. for synodals, as the annual income of the vicar of Lopynton; whilst the canons of Wombridge received as farm of tithes of Loppington the sum of £3 16s. 8d.

Early Incumbent.—Brother John Dynmowe, a canon of Wombridge, was instituted on September 5th, 1374, to the newly constituted vicarage of Loppington. The prior and convent of Wombridge presented.

Ellesmere. Delightfully situate amid scenery diversified with hill and dale, on the north-western extremity of Shropshire, lies Ellesmere. Of English origin, the town derives its name from the extensive *mere* or lake on its eastern side. This fine sheet of water covers some 116 acres, and is well stocked with fish. The meres, six in number, form a peculiar and attractive feature in the neighbourhood. They present, also a good field for the botanist, as fifteen or sixteen species of fern are to be found; and, in one of the meres, namely, Colemere, moss-balls, *confervæ*, are also found.

Ellesmere is noticed in Domesday Book as follows:—" The earl himself holds Ellesmeles. Earl Eduin held it [formerly]. Here iiii hides and a half. In demesne are v ox-teams, and x neatherds, xxxvi villains, and xiiii boors, with ii priests, have xiiii teams [among them]. Here a mill. In King Edward's time [the manor] yielded a fee farm [rent of] £10. Now [it yields] £20. [Of the land] of this manor, Mundret holds i hide, and Rainald i hide. Here they have ii ox-teams and iiii serfs, iiii villains, and vii boors, with iii teams and a half. [The manor] is worth 23s."[1] The Rainald mentioned above, was no other than Rainald the sheriff; the hide he held, Lea, which, as we learn from Earl Roger's charter, Rainald gave to Shrewsbury abbey.

From the record of William I., we learn that the important manor of Ellesmere, in Saxon times, had belonged to the earls of

---

[1] *Domesday*, fo. 253, b 2.

Mercia, and that, after the conquest, the Norman earl of Shrewsbury retained it in demesne. Upon the forfeiture of Robert de Belèsme, third and last Norman earl of Shrewsbury, Ellesmere came into the hands of King Henry I., who granted it, along with several border manors of less importance, to William Peverel of Dover, one of that family concerning whose origin there is so much mystery.

After the death of his royal benefactor, Peverel, in concert with Fitz-Alan and other Shropshire adherents of the empress, in 1138, raised the standard of revolt against Stephen the usurper. "The young William, surnamed Peverel," says Ordericus, "had four castles, namely, Bryn, Ellesmere, Overton, and Geddington, and, elated at this, he augmented the force of the rebels." [1] But Stephen resisted the rebel lords, and, marching to Shrewsbury, stormed and took by assault its castle ; yet, whether or not Ellesmere castle then yielded to the usurper is a point upon which we have no information. Suffice it to observe, that, sickened with the internecine strife that caused his unhappy country to mourn, William Peverel dedicated himself to the service of the cross, and eventually found his grave in Palestine.

Upon the restoration of Henry II., the coheirs of Peverel were excluded from Ellesmere, which, as a manor of ancient demesne, came into the hands of that king. David-ap-Owen, prince of North Wales, married Emma, sister of Henry II.: accordingly, the English king, in 1177, conferred "the land of Ellesmare on David Fitz-Owain, who had married his sister." [2]

But David now suffered a lengthened imprisonment at the hands of his nephew, Lewellyn, of which King John, taking advantage, seized Ellesmere, and retained it. At Michaelmas, 1203, the sheriff of Shropshire charged that king 100s., which he had expended in repairs at Ellesmere castle ; again, the Michaelmas Pipe Roll of 1204 shows that Ellesmere castle had been repaired at the king's expense.

The policy of the English monarch evidently was to conciliate the prince who wielded the sceptre of North Wales. John therefore gave in marriage to Lewellyn the Great, Joan, his natural daughter, and ordered the sheriff of Shropshire to assign 20 librates of lands as her marriage portion, which assignment took place

---

[1] ORDERICUS VITALIS, B. XIII. ch xxxvii.
[2] Hales was afterwards called Hales-Owen, from Owen, son of this princess.

partly in Ellesmere. A patent of March 23rd, 1205, also instructed Thomas de Erdinton, then custos of Ellesmere castle, to give the same up to Lewellyn. Yet, notwithstanding that title of endearment, "our beloved son," by which the English king styled the Welsh prince, amity did not long endure between them, and Lewellyn, rebelling against his father-in-law, forfeited Ellesmere.

In 1212, the justices of the forest amerced the town of Ellesmere 20s. for some fault.

Young Henry III. had not been long upon the throne, when, entering into negotiations with the Welsh prince, he restored Ellesmere to Lewellyn, who retained it until in 1231, hostilities having again broken out between the Welsh and English, Lewellyn for ever lost his grant. The castle and manor of Ellesmere now remained in the custody of successive sheriffs of Shropshire until 1253, when a patent of July 20th announced that the king had demised the manor and Hundred of Ellesmere to John de Grey, for a term of fifteen years, at an annual rent of £20. Guilty of abridging the king's prerogatives at Ellesmere, however, long before his lease had expired, De Grey had forfeited Ellesmere by judgment of the barons of exchequer, and, in 1256, Henry III. granted the manor to Prince Edward for a term of ten years, at a rent of £30 per annum.

Meanwhile, in anticipation of its becoming the residence of the king's son, and doubtless also in anticipation of the stormy period at hand, the sheriff had expended a large sum in the repair of Ellesmere castle, and the king's house in it. As difficulties, provoked by his own weak misrule, multiplied around the throne of the third Henry, the barons grew bolder; and it appears that the Parliament of Oxford, known as the *mad Parliament*, thrust upon the king Peter de Montfort as custos of the castle and manor of Ellesmere. Something of the sort certainly happened, and a patent of June 30th, 1258, empowers Peter de Montfort to levy customs for five years, to enable him to wall the town of Ellesmere.

A patent of December 16th, 1263, gives Hamo le Strange, the royalist sheriff of Shropshire, seizin of the manor, castle, and Hundred of Ellesmere, with all appurtenances; and these, it is probable Le Strange held for the king throughout the civil war which immediately succeeded. The barons, as is well known, defeated the king, and took him prisoner at Lewes, on the 14th of

May, 1264, when, among other pseudo-patents which Simon Montfort issued, there is one of June 18th, 1265, which reveals the fact that Montfort offered to Lewellyn, for the sum of 30,000 merks, among other things, the Hundred of Ellesmere. Thus he who ranks as one of the great founders of the English constitution, did not scruple at dismembering from England this important possession. The event of the battle of Evesham, however, liberated the king, when Henry III., in recognition of his loyal services, conceded the manor, castle, and Hundred of Ellesmere to Hamo le Strange, until he could be otherwise provided for. It is supposed that, soon afterwards, this great royalist accompanied Prince Edward to the Holy Land, and, like a previous lord of Ellesmere had done, perished fighting against the Mahommedans.

In 1276, Ellesmere was settled by Edward I. on Hamo's brother, Sir Roger le Strange, for life, with remainder to the crown. Sir Roger died in 1311, when Ellesmere reverted to the crown. King Edward III., in 1330, gave the manor and castle of Ellesmere to his valued servant, Eubolo le Strange, and his wife Alice. In 1335, Eubolo died without issue, when Ellesmere went to his nephew, Roger le Strange, Baron of Knokin, who accordingly became Baron Knokin and of Ellesmere. He held the fortalice and Hundred of Ellesmere *in capite* of the king, by service of one twentieth of a knight's fee, and, dying in 1349, was succeeded by Roger le Strange II., his son. Ellesmere continued with the barons Strange of Knokyn until their heir general carried it to the Stanleys. "Now, the baronies of Knokyn and of Ellesmere, as well as that of Stanley," says Eyton, "are in abeyance between the descendants and representatives of the three daughters and co-heirs of Ferdinando Stanley, fifth earl of Derby of his line."

There is little of interest connected with the early history of the numerous members of Ellesmere.

The Church.

That Ellesmere was originally a Saxon collegiate church is evident from the mention of two priests in the *Domesday* description of the manor. When Lewellyn was lord of Ellesmere, in the earlier half of the thirteenth century, he granted this advowson to the Knights Hospitallers located at Dongelwal, North Wales, who having, at some unknown period, obtained an appropriation of this rich benefice, the collegiate status of the church vanished..

In 1291, the vicarage of Ellesmere, in the deanery and arch-

ELLESMERE CHURCH.
(FROM A SKETCH TAKEN IN 1840).

deaconry of Salop, was worth £5 per annum. In 1341, Ellesmere, with its members, excepting English Frankton, Colemere, Lea, and Welch Hampton, were reputed to be in Wales, and consequently were exempt from the inquisition of the *ninth*. The four hamlets alluded to, however, were taxed £4 6s. 8d. to the current assessment, not more, as a general murrain had devastated the sheep-folds.

In 1534-5, the vicar of Ellesmere's income was £19, less 12s. for procurations, and 10s. for synodals. The Hospitallers continued, at that date, to hold the rectory, the then value of which, however, is not known.

Early Co-Rectors of Ellesmere.—
    Reyner, parson of Ellesmere } 1205.
    Geoffrey (resigned)

Early Vicar.—John de Woubourne, instituted June 4th, 1313, at presentation of Brother William de Tothale, prior of the Hospitallers of Jerusalem, in England.

Great Berwick, in the parish of St. Mary's, Shrewsbury, is thus noticed in *Domesday* :—"The earl himself holds Berewic. Edric Salvage held it. Here i hide and a half. In demesne are ii ox-teams; and iiii serfs, one female serf, and xi villains, with v teams. In the time of King Edward, it was worth 30s; now £9."[1] From Edric, the brave Saxon forester, this manor passed to the Norman Earls of Shrewsbury, who retained it in demesne. Upon their forfeiture, Berwick came into the hands of Henry I., who, adopting a policy calculated to qualify the ascendancy of the Norman aristocracy, enfeoffed here William de Gorram, an emigrant from Maine. De Turnham and the Leybournes, descendants of this William, continued for 250 years afterwards to hold *in capite* of the Crown the manor of Berwick. They held it by the following curious service. In war-time, whenever the king passed into Wales, the lord of Berwick was to provide one horseman, one man, and one greyhound, carrying with them one gammon of bacon; these were to follow the king till the gammon of bacon was consumed, after which, if they remained, it was to be at the king's charges. According to the description given of this serjeantry in the Tenure Roll of 1284, the consumption of the

---

[1] *Domesday*, fo. 253, b 2.

gammon of bacon was to be regulated by the king's marshal—a very necessary precaution against too limited a service.

Berwick chapel belonged to Lilleshall Abbey.

English Frankton.

In his elegy on Cynddylan, Llywarc Hèn says—

Ni çafai Franc tanc o'i ben."

which means—

"From his mouth the *Frank* would not get the word of peace." Commenting on this passage, Owen Pughe asks, " Did the *Franks* emigrate with the *Saxons* in such numbers as to cause the introduction of their name into this island, as a separate body of people ? "

Rainald, the Norman sheriff of Shropshire, was lord over no less than eleven manors in Bascherch Hundred. He held them of the Earl of Shrewsbury. One of these is thus described in Domesday Book:—"The same Rainald holds Franchetone, and Robert [holds] of him. Aldi held it in the time of King Edward. Here ii neatherds and iii villains, with i ox-team. In King Edward's time it was worth 10s.; now 15s." [1]

Shrawardine,

also belonged to Rainald in 1086, for we read in *Domesday* that :—"The same Rainald holds Saleurdine. Æli held it in King Edward's time. Here ii hides. In demesne are ii ox-teams, and iiii neat-herds, iii villains, and iiii boors with ii teams and a half. It was and is worth 40s. [per annum]." [1]

Shrawardine castle must have been built before 1165, in which year Philip Helgot, acknowledging his service of castle-guard as returnable at Shrawardine, says, that it was "the same as his antecessors had been used to render." Lying in the rear of Oswestry, Knokyn, Carrechova, and Whittington, those advanced posts of border warfare, Shrawardine with Ellesmere and Ruyton castles, in ancient times, constituted an interior line of defence against Welsh aggression. Although founded in Fitz Alan's fief, it would appear that Shrawardine was originally built and garrisoned by the Crown. The Pipe Roll informs us, that, in 1171 the sheriff, in obedience to a king's writ, had expended £10 18s. 4d. on the works of the castle of Schrawurdi. In 1187, the same

---

[1] *Domesday*, fo. 255, a 1.

officer charges 19s. 1d. for repairing the king's house in Srwardin castle. The Welsh probably razed this royal castle in their march to Shrewsbury in 1215, when the Crown, abandoning Shrawardine to its hereditary lords, the Fitz Alans rebuilt the castle. Tradition tells of a young Fitz Alan who, either through his own infantine temerity or the carelessness of his nurse, fell from the battlements of this stronghold, and so perished. Shrawardine castle, the ruins of which are still visible, was destroyed during the civil wars of the 17th century.

The Church.

It is certain that in the reign of King John there was a church at Shrawardine, for he presented a rector thereto. In 1291, the church of Shrewardyn, in the diocese of Hereford, the archdeaconry of Salop, and the deanery of Pontesbury, was valued at £5 per annum. In 1341, the parish of Shrawarthin was assessed only £2 to the *ninth,* because 3 carucates lay waste, owing to the poverty of the tenants; moreover, a vast quantity of growing wheat had been destroyed by a flood

FONT, SHRAWARDINE.

of the Severn, etc. In 1535, the income of the rector of Scrawardyn was £10, less 6s. 8d. for procurations, and 1s. for synodals.

Early Incumbent.—Robert de Cerne, presented November 10th, 1213, by King John, who then held the estates of the late William Fitz Alan.

𝔄𝔩𝔟𝔯𝔦𝔤𝔥𝔱 𝔥𝔲𝔰𝔰𝔢𝔶. The manor, afterwards known by this name, is alluded to in one if not both of the following extracts from *Domesday* :—" The same Rainald holds Abretone. Seuuard held it. Here are ii hides not geldable. There are iii villains, i radman and one frenchman with iiii boors; and they have ii ox-teams and a half. [The manor] was and is worth 15s." Again :— " The same Rainald holds Etbretone, and Herbert [holds it] of him. Seuuard, a free man, held it. Here ii hides. In demesne is one ox-team, and viii villains and iiii boors with ii teams. [Formerly] it was worth 14s.; now 25s."[1] After *Domesday*, the Husseys became lords of Albrighton, and from them the manor acquired its distinctive appellation of Albright Hussey.

ALBRIGHT HUSSEY CHAPEL.—Annexed to Battlefield Abbey, this gradually fell into decay, and in the present century its eastern end formed the division between two barns.

Little Ness. "The same Rainald," continues *Domesday*, "holds Nesse. Seuuard held it in the time of King Edward. Here iii hides. In demesne are ii ox-teams; and iiii villains and iii boors, with ii teams; and other ii [teams] might be [employed] besides. There is a mill [which pays an annual rent of] xx shillings and 600 eels. In King Edward's time [the manor] was worth £3, and afterwards £4; now 10s. more."[2] Rainald's successors, the Fitz Alans, long continued to hold Little Ness in demesne.

MILFORD.—This member of Little Ness derives its name, perhaps, from that mill mentioned in *Domesday* as so valuable an adjunct of the manor being situated here. ADDCOTT was given in *frank almoign* about 1260 to Haughmond Abbey, by Thomas de Rosshall, when Fitz Alan, the lord of the fee, concurring, the grantor's tenants, families, as well as chattels, passed with the vill to the abbot. The ancient chapel of Little Ness has ever been a dependency of Baschurch.

Middle is thus described in the Conqueror's survey :—" The same Rainald holds Mulleht. Seuuard held it in the time of King Edward. Here viii hides. In demesne is one ox-team; and viii boors, a priest, and ii frenchmen. Here is a wood which will fatten xl swine. The land is for xx ox-teams. In time of King Edward [the manor] was worth £6, and afterwards £4; now it is

---

[1] *Domesday*, fo. 255, a 1 and 2.   [2] Ibidem, fo. 255, a 1.

worth £3 10s."¹ Before 1165, John le Strange had acquired the greater portion of the *Domesday* manor of Middle; and his descendants for centuries continued to hold it under the Fitz Alans, Rainald's successors. A patent of April 1st, 1308, permits John le Strange to fortify and crenellate his *mansion of Medle* with a wall of stone and lime; remains of which castle are still to be seen.

MIDDLE CHURCH.

The church of St. Peter, at Middle, originally a Saxon foundation, had been given before the Conqueror's survey was taken by Warin, the Sheriff, to Shrewsbury Abbey. The pre-existence of this church is implied by the mention of a priest in the *Domesday* entry relating to the manor. Middle church was never appropriated by the monks. In 1291, it was valued at the large sum of £20 10s. *per annum:* out of this a pension of 10s. went to the abbey. In 1341, the parish was taxed only £8 to the *ninth*, because five carucates of land lay untilled, and there had been a murrain among the sheep, etc. In 1535, the income of the rector of Middle was £16; less £2 to the chaplain of Hadnall, 13s. 4d. to Shrewsbury Abbey, and 19s. 6d. for procurations and synodals.

Early Incumbent.—Howel-ap-Maddoc-ap-Griffin de Bromfeld, a younger son of the contemporary Prince of Lower Powis, is the first rector of Middle of whom we hear—1232.

Welch Hampton. In composition with some preceding word, Hampton signifies the house, village, or town of the hamlet, *Ham-Tun.* This place is thus mentioned in the Conqueror's survey:—" The same Rainald holds Hantone. Ældit held it in the time of King Edward. Here iii hides. Albert holds it of Rainald. In demesne is i ox-team, and iii serfs, vi villains and iiii boors with ii teams; and other ii teams might be here. In the time of King Edward [the manor] was worth 15s.; now 30s."²
WELCH HAMPTON CHAPEL was originally a mere affiliation of Ellesmere church, but in 1391, John de Kynaston, with the consent of the vicar of Ellesmere, erected a more independent foundation, of which he and his heirs had the patronage.

Rosshall and the Isle, as well as Welsh Hampton, in the reign of William I., were held by Albert, under Rainald the

---

¹ *Domesday*, fo. 255, a 1.   ² Ibidem, fo. 255 a 2.

sheriff, who in turn held them of the Norman earl. There is not much connected with their early history of a nature to interest the reader. *Domesday* records the following relative to the first of these manors:—"The same Rainald holds Rosela, and Albert [holds it] of him. Hunni held it in the time of King Edward. Here i hide. In demesne is i ox-team; and iiii serfs, ii villains, and iiii boors, with i team; and there might be other [teams employed] besides. [Formerly] it was worth 20s.; now 12s."[1]

The Isle. Concerning it *Domesday* says, that—"The same Rainald holds Aitone, and Albert [holds] of him. Leuric held it in time of King Edward. Here ii hides. In demesne is i ox-team; and iiii serfs, ii villains, and iii boors with i team. There is a mill of 10s. [annual value]. [In Saxon times the manor] was worth 15s.: now 25s"[1] Contiguous, and both held by the same knightly family, the two manors of Rosshall and Eyton became united, and eventually were known only by the former name. The church or chapel of Rosshall is valued in the Taxation of 1291 at £1 13s. 4d. *per annum*. Up-Rossall and the Isle are in the Shrewsbury parish of St. Chad.

Hadnall is thus noticed in *Domesday*:—"The same Rainald holds Hadehelle, and Osmund [holds the manor] of him. Godwin held it. Here iiii hides geldable. In demesne is one ox-team; and ii neat-herds, vi villains, one boor, and ii frenchmen with iii teams, and there might be iiii [more] teams employed besides. Here is a wood which will fatten xl swine. In the time of King Edward the manor was worth 60s.; and afterwards 10s.; now 20s."[1] In the 12th, 13th, and 14th centuries, the Banastres, lords of this manor, by various grants, conferred upon Haughmond Abbey a large part of Hadnall. Hadnall, with its members, Hardwick, Shotton, Haston, and Smethcott, being in the parish of Middle, Hadnall Chapel, whenever founded, was and still continues subject to the church of Middle. The earliest recorded notice of this chapel, namely in Henry VIII.'s *Valor*, represents it as supported by a pension of 40s., payable by the rector of Middle.

---

[1] *Domesday*, fo. 255, a 2.

Acton-Reynald. "The same Rainald holds Achetone and Richard [holds] of him. Seuuard held it in King Edward's time and was a free man. Here iii hides geldable. There is [arable] land [enough] for v ox-teams. Here ii knights have i team. Here is a wood which will fatten xxx swine. [In time of King Edward the manor] was worth £4; and now 10s."[1] The Stantons, presumed to have descended from Richard, the *Domesday* lord of Acton, continued to exercise the seigneury here until the extinction of their male line in the reign of Edward I. Under the De Stantons, a family long held the manor who derived their name of De Acton from the place. Acton Reynald chapel, founded in King Stephen's time, was from the first a dependency of Shawbury church. Shawbury belonged to the canons of Haughmond, who are represented in the *Valor* of 1535-6, as paying a salary of 20s. to the officiating chaplain of Acton Reyner.

Albrighton, or Monks' Albrighton. "Alcher," says *Domesday*, "held of Warine who was Rainald's antecessor, Etbritone. Gheri held it and was a free man. Here are iii hides geldable. There is land for vi ox-teams. In demesne are ii teams and iiii serfs, one Frenchman, vi villains and one boor with iii teams. In time of King Edward the manor was worth 20s. and afterwards 15s.: now [it is worth] 30s."[2] We glean from Earl Roger's charter, that the Alcher, or "Aher," mentioned in *Domesday*, "dedicated Etburtone with its appendages," to Shrewsbury Abbey; and hence it came to pass, that this place acquired the distinctive title of Monks' Albrighton. The monks retained the manor until the Dissolution.

ALBRIGHTON CHAPEL. The ancient font in the present church is a relic of the former chapel.

Walford. After Rainald the Sheriff, Robert Pincerna was the greatest lay holder in Bascherch Hundred, under the Norman earl, at the period of the survey. He held five distinct manors, the first of which, namely Walford, is the subject of the following entry in Domesday Book. "Robert Pincerna holds of Roger the Earl, Waleford, and Sturmid [holds it] of him. Seuuard held it in the time of King Edward. Here ii hides. In demesne is half

---

[1] *Domesday*, fo. 255, a 2.   [2] Ibidem, fo. 255, b 1.

an ox-team; and [there is] one neat-herd, ii villains, and ii boors with i team and a half. In time of King Edward [the manor] was worth 15s.; afterwards it was waste. Now it is worth 20s."[1] Robert Pincerna appears to have held the office of chief butler to the Norman Earls of Shrewsbury, and probably shared in the forfeiture of his suzerain, Robert de Belèsme, in 1102; for King Henry I., when he founded the Honour of Montgomery, annexed thereto the escheated estate of Robert Pincerna. Hence it happened that those lands, over which this magnate once had exercised the seigneury, afterwards were held under the successive lords of Montgomery.

In 1240, Philip de Hugford was holding Walford under the lords of Montgomery; and he again had a tenant here who held a virgate of land under him upon these conditions:—He was, when ordered, to ride in the company of his suzerain at any time of the year, and to any part of Shropshire, at his own charges; but if he went out of the county, his expenses were to be paid. It was this singular service probably which obtained for the tenant that soubriquet of *Le Knight* by which he was known.

Stanwardine-in-the-Field.

"The same Robert holds Staurdine. Eldred held it. Here ii hides. There is one villain, one boor, and a smith with half an ox-team; and there might be ii teams [employed] besides. It was and is worth 10s."[1] The *Nomina Villarum* of 1316 represents William de la Zouche, lord of Montgomery, as seigneural lord of 'Stanworthin-y'-the-feld.'

Petton.

"The same Robert," continues *Domesday*, "holds Pectone and Radulf [holds it] of him. Leuenot held it [in Saxon times]. Here i hide and a half. In demesne [there] is one ox-team and ii villains, and ii boors with i team. [Formerly] it was worth 5s.: now 10s."[1] Like Pincerna's other manors, Petton was subsequently held under the lords of Montgomery; the service of the tenant here being to attend for fifteen days in war time upon his suzerain, with a bow and two unfeathered arrows, at the suzerain's cost.

Petton Chapel.

This was founded before 1159, and at first was subject to Baschurch, as the chartulary of Shrewsbury Abbey proves. Pope

---

[1] *Domesday,* fo. 256, a 2.

Nicholas' Taxation, in 1291, makes no mention of this chapel; yet in 1341, the parish was assessed only 10s. to the *ninth*, because there had been a general murrain of sheep, etc. In 1534-5, the rector of Petton's income was £3 6s. 8d. *per annum*, less 11d. for synodals and 1s. 8d. for procurations.

Early Incumbent.—John de Pecton, 1306.

Eyton. "The same Robert holds Hetone, and another Robert [holds the manor] of him. Leuui held it. Here i hide. Here is one villain and iii boors with i ox-team and a half. It was waste. Now it is worth 5s."[1] Eyton-juxta-Baschurch lost its standing as a distinct manor soon after the above had been recorded.

Crugetone. "The same Robert," continues *Domesday*, "holds Crugetone. Earl Eduin held it. Here a hide and a half. In demesne is one ox-team; and ii serfs, one female serf, ix villains, ii boors and one free-man with iii teams. Here are iiii fisheries worth 13s. 4d. [per annum]. In the time of King Edward [the whole] yielded a rent of £3 13s. 4d. Now [it pays] £4 and a thousand eels."[2] Absorbed probably into other manors, the position of the valuable *Domesday* manor of Crugetone cannot now be determined.

Colmere. When William the Conqueror's Commissioners surveyed Shropshire, it was found that Norman Venator held under Earl Roger de Montgomery two manors in Bascherch Hundred, namely, Colemere and Estone. Excepting the notices relating to them in Domesday Book, their early history is however uninteresting. Respecting the former, we are told that:—" The same Norman holds Colesmere. Aldiet held it. Here ii hides geldable. The land is for iiii ox-teams and a half. In demesne is one [such team]; and ii villains and ii boors with half a team: and iiii strangers here pay [a rent of] xl pence. In King Edward's time it was worth 10s.: now 30s. It was waste [when] he [Norman] got it."[3]

Estone. "The same Norman holds Estone and Fulcher of him. Elnod held it. Here are ii hides and a half geldable.

---

[1] *Domesday*, 256, a 2.   [2] "*Mille Anguillarum.*"—*Domesday*, fo. 256, a 2.
[3] *Domesday*, fo. 259, a 2.

The land is for vii ox-teams. It was waste. Now it is at fee farm for 36s."¹ Neither the locality of Estone, nor that of—

Cheneltone, of which the following is the brief *Domesday* notice, can now be determined:—"In Cheneltone is one hide, which was waste in the time of King Edward and is [so still]."¹ The entries relating to Estone and Cheneltone immediately succeed the *Domesday* notice of Colemere, and both fall under the marginal affix of Bascherch Hundred.

Slacheberie is another of those manors which have been expunged from the map of Shropshire; yet in the Conqueror's time, Roger Venator held it of the Norman earl. *Domesday* says:—"Roger Venator holds of Earl Roger Slacheberie. Aluiet held it. Here i hide geldable. [The manor] was worth 5s. in the time of King Edward. Now it is waste."¹ Slacheberie doubtless was absorbed into Ellesmere.

Brome. By way of supplement to the notice of Slacheberie, *Domesday* has the following entry:—"In this hundred lies Bruma of i hide, and it belongs to Hantone [Welch Hampton], Albert's manor. From thence a lawsuit is pending between the earl's vassals."² Bruma is now represented by Broom Farm, in the township of Tetchill, about two miles south-west of Ellesmere.

Hordeley. "Odo," says *Domesday*, "holds of Earl Roger Hordelei. Algar and Dunniht held it [in Saxon times] for ii manors and were free. Here ii hides geldable. There is land for iii ox-teams. Here v villains and v boors with ii teams. The wood will fatten lx swine. In time of King Edward, [the manor] was waste. Now it yields 15s. [per annum]."³ Very soon after the Norman scribe had penned the above, Odo gave Hordeley to the monks of Shrewsbury, who doubtless retained it until Henry the Eighth's time.

---

¹ *Domesday*, fo. 259. a 2.   ² *Inde litigant Homines Comitis—Domesday*, fo. 257 b 2.
³ *Domesday*, fo. 257, b 2.

The Church.

St. Mary's, Hordeley, was originally a dependency of Baschurch. In 1291, the church of Ordeleye, in Salop deanery and archdeaconry, was valued at £2 13s. 4d., besides a pension of 2s. therefrom to Shrewsbury Abbey. In 1341, the assessors to the *ninth* treated "*Hordel*" as a chapelry, and taxed the parish only 20s., because there were no sheep in it, etc. In 1535, the income of the rector of Hordeley was £4 2s., less 2s. for procurations, and 11s. for synodals.

Early Incumbent.—Richard de Derynton was rector of Hordyleg chapel in 1310.

Ruyton juxta Baschurch, or Ruyton-of-the-eleven-towns, a name acquired from the eleven towns which at some period, perhaps, constituted the manor, is thus described in the Conqueror's record:—"The same Odo holds Udeford and Ruitone. Leuenot held them for ii manors. There i hide and a half geldable. The land is for iiii ox-teams. Here iiii villains and ii boors have ii teams. In demesne is one team and ii neat-herds. There is a wood which will fatten xl swine, and v fisheries in the estate of [or underlet to] the villains.[1] In the time of King Edward [the land] was waste, and afterwards it was worth 13s.; now 20s." The Saxon Leuenot having been displaced, his manors were given by the Norman earl to his vassal, Odo. The fisheries spoken of as being here, were doubtless on the river Perry.

Early annexed to Fitz Alan's barony, through the influence of this great chieftain doubtless it was, that Ruyton came to be annexed to the Hundred of Oswestry, over which Fitz Alan's interest was paramount. Appropriated thus to his exclusive jurisdiction in the marches; a district where the baron suffered neither sheriff or king to interfere in matters appertaining to its civil jurisdiction: Ruyton became almost lost to English records.

Ruyton was part of that fief which the le Stranges held under the Fitz Alans; but about the year 1300, John Le Strange (V.) sold Ruyton, with all its homages and fees, to his suzerain, Edmund, Earl of Arundel.

In ancient times, there were three mills connected with the manor of Ruyton. One of these was very early acquired by Haughmond Abbey; "the Platt Mill" was given to Shrewsbury

---

[1] "Et v piscariæ in censu villanorum." *Domesday*, fo. 257, b 2.

Abbey. Concerning the third mill, we read that *Johannes extraneus quartus* [John le Strange IV.] gave and confirmed, for the souls of himself and his wife Johanna, his mill of Heath, with its fishery and appurtenances, and with timber to repair the same out of his wood of Rednall, and with a place near the mill convenient for winnowing. One moiety of the profits of this mill was to go to the canons themselves; with the other moiety, the monks were to provide two candles, to burn at the head and foot of the tomb of the aforesaid Johanna, the grantor's wife. [1]

RUYTON CHURCH.

Originally this was an affiliation of Baschurch, and as such was in the advowson of the abbot of Shrewsbury. In 1291, the church of Ruyton, in the archdeaconry and deanery of Salop, was valued at £8 *per annum*. Under the fostering care of the lords of the fee, Ruyton had grown into an independent rectory, when, having been consigned to monastic patronage, the result as usual was, appropriation; and the spoils of Ruyton rectory went to the kitchen of the convent. The Pope's Bull, giving his holiness' consent to the transaction, was recited by Roger Northburgh, Bishop of Lichfield, on February 27th, 1331, and on January 4th, 1332, William de Tykelwardyn was admitted the first vicar of Ruyton, at presentation of Haughmond Abbey.

Ruyton was not assessed as a distinct parish to the *ninth* in 1341, it being in Oswestry Hundred. In 1535, the vicar of Ryton's income was £6 *per annum*, less 2s. for synodals: the abbot's rectorial tithes were £7 2s.

Early Incumbent—Walter, parson of Ruton about 1235.

Montford, pleasantly situated some five miles from Shrewsbury, on the northern bank of the Severn, is thus noticed in Domesday Book:—"Roger holds of the earl Maneford. Elmer held it [in Saxon times]. Here are iii hides. In demesne is one ox-team and a half, and xiii villains with vi teams; and there might be iii teams and a half besides. Here is half a fishery, and a wood which will fatten xxiiii swine. In the time of King Edward [the manor] was worth £4 [annually], and afterwards 20s.; now it is worth £4 10s. 'Hoc manerium calumniatur Episcopus, R.'" [2] There appears to have been some uncertainty as

---

[1] *Haughmond Chartulary*, fo. 106.   [2] *Domesday*, fo. 255, b 2.

CHURCH OF RUYTON OF THE ELEVEN-TOWNS.

to whom this manor really did belong when the survey was made, hence the scribe who penned the clause just quoted, omitted to state whether Roger who held Maneford, was Roger Fitz Corbet or Roger de Lacy. From the circumstance, that two centuries afterwards, descendants of the latter are found holding the manor, we should infer it was Roger de Lacy's tenure. Montford bridge is famous in history as the scene of many a parley between the ambassadors of England and North Wales.

The Church.

The advowson of Montford was granted to the White Nuns of Brewood, in the 13th century. In 1291, the church of Moneford, in the deanery and archdeaconry of Salop, was valued at £5 6s. 8d. *per annum*. In 1341, the parish was taxed only £4 to the *ninth*, because 6 carucates of land in it lay waste, there had been a murrain among the sheep, and a Severn flood had destroyed most of the growing corn, etc. The *Valor* of 1535 represents the vicar of Monsforde's income as £5 6s. 8d., less 6s. 8d. for procurations, and 1s. 6d. for synodals. The rectory produced the White Nuns £8, less a pension of 10s. to the prior of St. Guthlac, at Hereford.

Early Vicar.—Sir Richard de Aula, presented in 1331 by the priory and convent of White Nuns of Brewood.

Preston Montford.

Following the entry relating to Montford, and apparently as if it was held by the same Roger, *Domesday* notices a small piece of land in these terms:—"Roger holds of the earl Prestone. Godric held it and was a free man. Here is one virgate of land. In demesne is half an ox-team. It was and is worth 3s. The wood will fatten x swine."[1] The small part of Preston here alluded to as in Baschurch Hundred, afterwards involved with the larger part in Ford Hundred, went with it to Lilleshall Abbey, and is now in the Liberties of Shrewsbury.

Forton,

now a hamlet in Montford parish, was, at *Domesday*, held of the Norman earl by Roger de Lacy. "The same Roger holds Fordune, and Osbern [holds it] of him. Edmer held it [in Saxon times]. Here iii hides. In demesne is one ox-team and ii neat-herds, one villain, and xiii boors, with ii teams and a half;

---

[1] *Domesday*, fo. 255, b 2.

and other ii [teams] might be here. The wood here will fatten c swine. In time of King Edward [the manor] was worth 20s., and afterwards the same; now [it is worth] 25s."[1]

Fitz is described in Domesday Book as follows:—" The same Picot [de Say] holds Witesot. Hunnith held it, and was a free man. Here iii hides geldable. The land is for v ox-teams. In demesne are ii teams, and [there are] ix serfs, iiii villains, one radman, and a smith, with ii teams between them all. In the time of King Edward it was worth 40s., and afterwards 60s.; now [the manor is worth] £6."[2] We learn that the Norman Picot de Say gave two-thirds of the tithes of his demesnes of *Philtesho* and of *Gulidone* for the building and maintenance of Shrewsbury Abbey. Associated sometimes under the common name of Fitz, Fitz and Gulidone came, in due course, to Isabel de Say, baroness of Clun, and passed from her to her descendants by the first William Fitz Alan.

Fitz Alan's feoffee here was Robert de Girros, who, partial to Haughmond, between the years 1239—42, gave to that abbey his lands in Fittesho and Gulidon, including "appurtenances, easements, *natives* [that is, men], and their chattels." The prayers and good offices of the abbey were the consideration.

Fitz Chapel.

Originally a dependence of St. Mary's, Shrewsbury, Fitz chapel was the subject of litigation between that church and Haughmond Abbey in the year 1200. Robert de Girros, claiming the advowson, had alienated it to Haughmond Abbey, hence the angry dispute. At length, the protracted suit between the abbot of Haughmond and the Dean and Chapter of St. Mary was actually settled by *wager of battle*, and the abbot's champion came off victorious. A writ of King Henry III., dated at Westminster, October 18th, 1256, addressed to the Bishop of Coventry and Lichfield, then informed that prelate of the recent suit, and how a duel had been *armed* and *foughten* between the parties; since which the Dean and Chapter (the defendants) had come into court and renounced their right; the bishop was, therefore, to admit the abbot's presentee to the said parsonage. In 1341, the parish of Fittos was taxed 20s. to the *ninth*. King Henry the Eighth's

---

[1] *Domesday*, fo. 256, b 1.   [2] Ibidem, fo. 258, a 2.

Valor represents the preferment of the rector of Fettys as worth £5 10s. *per annum*, less 1s. for synodals, and 3s. 4d. for procurations.

Early Incumbents.—Richard de Lynton, presented by the dean and chapter of St. Mary's, Shrewsbury, was forcibly ejected in 1253, and Robert de Acton, the nominee of Haughmond abbey, intruded in his place. He resigned in 1254.

Merrington

formerly Gellidone, or Gullidone, the early history of which has just been alluded to, is noticed in *Domesday*, thus:—"The same Picot holds Gellidone. Hunnith held it. Here ii hides geldable. The land is for v ox-teams. In demesne is one [team], and iiii serfs, iii villains, iiii boors, and one radman, with ii teams between them. The wood here will fatten xxiv swine. In time of King Edward [the manor] was worth 15s., and afterwards the same. Now 40s."[1]

Moreton Corbet.

"The same Turold," says *Domesday*, "holds Mortone, and Hunnit, with his brother [hold the manor] of him. The same [Hunnit and his brother, in Saxon times] held it, and were free men. Here i hide geldable. The [arable] land is for ii ox-teams. Here are [ii teams], with v serfs and one boor. [Formerly] it was worth 10s. Now 16s."[2] Amid the social revolution attendant on the Norman Conquest of England, the Saxon Hunnit and his brother lost their estates, some of which were given to their more fortunate countryman, Toret. "Whatever," says an authority,[3] "were the misfortunes of Hunnit and his brother Uluiet, it is certain that the descendants of their contemporary and compatriot, Toret, succeeded to some of their estates, and it is also certain that a lineal descendant of the said Toret is at this day lord of Moreton Corbet. These are terms in which very few Shropshire estates can be spoken of." The lineal descendant alluded to is the present Sir Vincent R. Corbet, Bart.

There is a tradition that, once upon a time, the heir of Moreton Corbet went to the Holy Land, and was detained in captivity so long, that he was supposed to be dead, and his younger brother engaged to marry that he might continue the line. On the

---

[1] *Domesday*, fo. 258, a 2. [2] Ibidem, fo. 258, a 1.
[3] EYTON, *Antiq. of Shropshire*, vol. x. p. 181.

morning of the marriage, however, a pilgrim came to the house to partake of the hospitalities of that festal occasion, and, after the dinner, he revealed himself to the assembled company as the long-lost elder brother. The bridegroom would have surrendered the estate, but he declined the offer, desiring only a small portion of the land, which he accordingly received. This pilgrim was ancestor of the Corbets of Moreton, whose primogeniture is established by their armorial bearings, the single raven. The real progenitor of all the Shropshire Corbets was Roger Fitz-Corbet, the *Domesday* baron, mentioned under Caus.

Moreton Corbet Castle, the ruins of which still remain, was erected, in the 16th century, on the foundations of the ancient castle.

Moreton Corbet Church.

Originally styled a chapel, this, in 1148, was subject to Shawbury church. The abbot and convent of Haughmond, therefore, had the advowson of Moreton Corbet. Before Henry VIII.'s time, however, the change from a vicarage to a rectory having taken place, the *Valor* of that king's reign represents the rector of Moreton Corbet's income as £5 6s. 8d., less 1s. 8d. for synodals, and 1s. 6d. for procurations. St. Bartholomew's consists of a nave and chancel, south aisle, transept, and tower. In the south aisle are two interesting monuments, with recumbent effigies of knights and ladies.

Early Vicar.—Hugh de Peppelowe, 1300.

Preston Brockhurst was also held of the earl by the Norman Turold de Verley at *Domesday*. The fact is thus recorded in King William I.'s record :—"The same Turold holds Preston, and Hunnit [holds] of him. Hunni and Uluiet themselves held it for ii manors and paid geld, and were free men. The land is for ii ox-teams. In demesne is one [team], and ii serfs and iii villains. It was and now is worth 13s."[1] The Saxon Hunnit's manor of Preston, like Moreton, fell into the hands of Toret, his favoured countryman, from whom they both descended to the Corbets of Moreton and Wattlesborough.

But Preston Brockhurst, in the Conqueror's time, was a divided manor, and whilst the portion referred to in the foregoing extract

---

[1] *Domesday*, fo. 258, a 1.

MORETON-CORBET CHURCH.

remains in Pimhill Hundred, *Domesday* thus alludes to the smaller portion, which is now in the parish of Shawbury, and in the Hundred of Bradford North ;—" The same Gerard [de Tornai] holds Prestone, and Robert [holds it] of him. Bertunt held it, and was a free man. Here i virgate of land. The land is for half a team. It was and is waste." [1]

Besford. "The same Gerard holds Betford, and Robert [holds the manor] of him. Oschetel and Dodo held it for ii manors, and were free men. Here iii hides geldable. The land is for iii ox-teams. In demesne is one [team], and [there are] iii serfs, iii villains, and ii single women,[2] with i ox-team. In time of King Edward, it was worth 7s., and afterwards 5s. Now 20s." [3] A tenure roll of 1284-5 states, that:—Roger Pryde, a burgess of Salop, holds Besford, a member of Schawbere, in Pymhull Hundred." Very shortly after, Robert Corbet purchased the whole manor from Roger. Parochially, Besford is in the parish of Shawbury.

Grinshill is noticed in *Domesday*, thus :—" Walchelinus holds of earl Roger, Grivelesul. Leuiet, Godric, Seuuard, and Algar held it for iiii manors, and were free. Here ii hides, geldable. There is land for ii ox-teams. Here are iii free men, and they pay 7s. per annum. This land was worth 32s. in King Edward's time." [4] Much that is merely conjectural is mixed up with the early history of Grinshill, yet it is certain that, previously to the Reformation, the monks of Haughmond had a very pretty picking out of the manor. Grinshill chapel, an ancient foundation, was originally a dependency of Shawbury.

Felton Butler was the only manor which Helgot held in Bascherch Hundred. *Domesday* says :—" The same Helgot holds Feltone. Aluric, Æluuard, and Alchen held it for iii manors, and were free men. Here iii virgates of land, geldable. The land is for v ox-teams. In demesne is one team, and iii serfs and iii villains, with i team. Bernard held [the manor] of Helgot. In

---

[1] *Domesday*, fo. 259, a 1.
[2] Viduæ Feminæ.
[3] *Domesday*, fo. 259, a 1.
[4] Ibidem, fo. 257, b 1.

the time of King Edward it was worth 14s. Now 15s."¹ Feltone derived its distinctive appellation of Felton Butler from that family of Butlers who, from an early period, held the manor under Helgot's successors.

Leaton is described in William the Conqueror's record, thus:—"Anschitil holds Letone of the earl. Hunni held it, and was a free man. Here i hide, geldable. There is land [sufficient] for ii ox-teams. In demesne is one [such team], and there are ii strangers paying 4s. 8d. [Formerly] it was worth 8s. Now 10s."² In 1211, Adam de Leton, the tenant here, held his land by service of doing ward at Shrewsbury castle with his *balista*. Eight days he was to serve at his own charges; if, however, he stayed there longer, it was to be at the expense of the king.³ About the year 1300, a descendant of this Adam held Leaton by a different serjeantry. "His tenure was by 40 days' ward at Shrewsbury castle, during which period he was to provide one man with a bow and three shafts unfeathered, in event of war; and after the 40 days ended, the man was to shoot his shafts into three quarters of the said castle, and to depart, unless the king wished to detain him."

Jagdon. "Elduin holds of the earl Iagedone. He himself held it [in Saxon times] and was a free man. Here half a hide geldable. The land is for i ox-team. Here is [one team] with ii boors. It was and is worth 5s."⁴ The situation of the half hide alluded to cannot be identified.

Sleap-Magna. "The same William [Pantulf] holds Eslepe. Uluric held it [and] was a free man. Here is half a hide geldable. The land is for i ox-team. Here is one free man with i team. There is a wood which will fatten vi swine. [The manor] was and is worth 5s."⁵

Sudtelch. "The same William," continues *Domesday*, "holds Sudtelch. Asci held it and was a free man. There is half a hide

---

¹ *Domesday*, fo. 258, b 1. ³ Testa de Nevill, p. 55.
² Ibidem, fo. 259, b 2. ⁴ *Domesday*, fo. 259, b 2.
⁵ *Domesday*, fo. 257, b 1.

geldable. The land is for ii ox-teams. It was worth 5s.: now it renders 2s."[1] Nothing further is known respecting this manor.

$Astley$, in 1086, belonged to the church of St. Mary, at Shrewsbury, for *Domesday* says:—" The same church held and holds Hesleie. Here are iii hides geldable. Here a priest with ix villains and ii boors have iii ox-teams; and there might be ii other teams besides. The wood will fatten L swine. [The manor] used to be worth 20s.: now 25s."[2] According to the Pimhill tenure-roll, of 1279, Astley was held "by the men of Astley, in free socage, under the canons of St. Mary, which canons held in frank-almoign of the crown." The priest resident at Astley in 1086, a canon perhaps of St. Mary's, indicates the existence of a church here at that date. Little is known, however, respecting the early history of this benefice.

DOORWAY, ASTLEY.

$Mytton$, in the parish of Fitz, also belonged to St. Mary's in William the Conqueror's time. "The same church," continues *Domesday*, "held [in Saxon times] and [still] holds Mutone, and Picot [de Say holds it] of her. Here ii hides geldable. Here iiii

---

[1] *Domesday*, fo. 257, b 1. [2] Ibidem, fo. 252, b 2.

villains with ii ox-teams. It was worth 12s.: now it is at fee-farm for 11s." [1]

Broughton, in Saxon and throughout the Anglo-Norman period, was divided between the Shrewsbury churches of St. Mary and St. Chad. Respecting St. Mary's share, which is now represented by Clive and Sansaw, two townships in the parish of St. Mary's, Shrewsbury, *Domesday* observes, that:—"The Church of St. Mary held and holds Burtune. Here v hides geldable. One priest has here half an ox-team, and [there are] vii villains with ii teams and a half; and there might be iii more teams here. A wood here will fatten xxiiii swine. In the time of King Edward it was worth 10s.: now 15s." [1] The chapel of All-Saints at Clive is evidently a very ancient foundation.

Concerning the part of Broughton which belonged to St. Chad's, we read, that:—"The same church held and holds Burtone. Here ii hides geldable. There is land for v ox-teams. Here iii villains have ii teams. It used to be worth 10s.; now 11s. 2d." [2] This manor is represented by the modern Broughton. Broughton chapel was a dependency of St. Chad's.

Yorton, which with Broughton now constitutes the parish of Broughton in the Liberties of Shrewsbury, in ancient times also belonged to St. Chad's church, for Domesday Book, that great basis of all local investigation, says:—"The same church held and holds Lartune. Here ii hides geldable. There is land for iiii ox-teams. Here is a priest and one villain with i team. [The manor formerly] was worth 8s.; now 5s." [2]

Bicton was also held from the Saxon era up till the time of Harry the Eighth by the church of St. Chad:—"The same church," says *Domesday*, "held Bichetone. Wiger held it of her. Here ii hides geldable. In demesne is i ox-team, and iiii villains and one free man with ii teams; and there might be ii other [teams]. [In King Edward's time] it was worth 10s.; now 15s." [2]

---

[1] *Domesday*, fo. 252, b 2.   [2] Ibidem, fo. 253, a 1.

CLIVE CHAPEL.

BROUGHTON;—RUINED CHANCEL OF THE OLD CHURCH.

Little Rosshall also belonged to St. Chad's.—"The same church held and holds Rosela. Here i hide geldable. Two radmans with vii boors have iii ox-teams and a half. [Formerly] it was worth 8s.; now 15s." [1]

Onslow also belonged in part to St. Chad's, as according to *Domesday*:—"The same church held and holds Andrelau. Here i hide geldable. It was waste [formerly]. Here iii villains have i ox-team. [The manor] was worth 4s." [1] The distinction which endured for centuries between Robert Corbet's and St. Chad's shares of Onslow is destroyed, and both are now in the Liberties of Shrewsbury.

Preston Gobalds, which derives its name from Godebold the priest, in Saxon times, as at the period of the Norman conquest, belonged to the church of St. Alkmund in Shrewsbury. We read in *Domesday*, that:—"The same church held and holds Prestone, and Godebold holds it of her. Here are iiii hides. In demesne is one ox-team, and ii villains, iii boors, and ii frenchmen with ii teams; and there might be ii other teams [employed here]. [The manor formerly] was waste. Now it is worth 10s." [1] Preston Gobalds, like St. Alkmund's other estates, passed to Lilleshall Abbey, the monks of which retained it until the Reformation.

The ancient church of Preston Gobalds continued a mere dependence of St. Alkmund's until after the Dissolution. Nothing, therefore, is known respecting either its early history or emoluments.

---

[1] *Domesday*, fo. 253, a 1.

Domesday Hundred of Mersete.

Modern Name.	Domesday Name.	Saxon Owner or Owners, T. R. E.	Domesday Tenant, in capite.	Domesday Mesne, or next Tenant.	Domesday Sub-Tenant.	Modern Hundred.
Maesbury and Oswestry	Meresberie	Rex Edwardus	Rogerius Comes	Rainaldus Vicecomes	x Walenses, etc.	Oswestry.
Whittington	Wititone	Rex Edwardus	....Idem	....	Walenses, etc.	..Ibidem.
? ?	Wiferesforde	Rex Edwardus	....Idem	....		..Ibidem.
Halston	Halstune	Edric	....Idem	Rainaldus Vicecomes	{ ii Walenses i Francigena }	..Ibidem.
Weston Rhyn	Westone	Senuard	....Idem	Rainaldus Vicecomes	Walenses, etc.	..Ibidem.
Morton and	Mortune and Aitone	Seuuard	....Idem	Rainaldus Vicecomes	v homines	..Ibidem.
Maesbrook	Meresbroc	Leuenot	....Idem	Rainaldus Vicecomes	i Walensis	..Ibidem.
? ?	Tibetune	Uluiet	....Idem	Rainaldus Vicecomes	ii Walenses	..?
Melverley	Meleurlie	Edric	....Idem	Rainaldus Vicecomes	ii Walenses	..Ibidem.
Weston Cotton	Westune	Seuuard	....Idem	Rainaldus Vicecomes	Walenses, etc.	..Ibidem.
Wooton	Udetone	Edric	....Idem	Rainaldus Vicecomes	Robertus	..Ibidem.
Woolston	Osulvestune	Uluric	....Idem	Rainaldus Vicecomes	i Miles	..Ibidem.
West Felton	Feltone	Seuuard	....Idem	Rainaldus Vicecomes	i Miles	..Ibidem.
Cynlacth and Edeyrneou	Chenlei and Derniou	....	....Idem	Rainaldus Vicecomes	Walenses	{ Montgomeryshire. Merionethshire. }
Osbaston and Kynaston	Sbernestnne and Chimerestun	Seuuard and Aluni	....Idem	Rainaldus Vicecomes	....	Oswestry.
Aston	Estone	Uluric	....Idem	Robertus Pincerna	xii Walenses	..Ibidem.
Wykey	Wiche	Eduinus Comes	....Idem	Odo	....	..Ibidem.
Kinnerley	Chenardelei	Dunning and Algar	....Idem	Ernucion	i Walensis	..Ibidem.
? ?	Newetone	Turgot	....Idem	Iward	....	? ?
.... and Porkington	Hanstune and Burtone	Seuuard	....Idem	Madoc	....	..Ibidem.

Welsh Districts also included in the Shropshire Domesday.

| Maelor Saesneg | Una Finis terræ Walensis | .... | Rogerius Comes | Tuder Walensis | .... | Flintshire.. |
| Yale | Terra de Gal | .... | ....Idem | Hugo Comes | { 2 Presbyteri 32 homines } | Denbighshire. |

AS the annexed Table shows, excepting the Welsh districts of Chenlei and Derniou, every manor of the *Domesday* Hundred of Mersete is contained in the modern Hundred of Oswestry.

Maesbury and Oswestry. There are two hoar stones in the neighbourhood of Oswestry; one, six feet ten inches above the surface, and three feet six inches across the western face, lies near Offa's Dyke. It goes by the name of CAREG-Y-BIG or THE POINTED STONE. The other hoar stone, which is called GARREG LWYD or THE GREY HOARY STONE, measures nine feet by three, and lies a few yards to the right of the Holyhead road, a mile on the Shrewsbury side of Oswestry. This, a sand-stone, unlike what is found in the neighbourhood, must have been brought from a distance here.

FONT, PRESTON GUBBALDS.

OSWESTRY CHURCH.

(FROM A SKETCH TAKEN IN 1807).

A hoar stone is an ancient, single, upright and unhewn stone of memorial, erected to define the limits of territory. The actual hoar stones that now exist are few.

The lovely scenery amid which Oswestry stands, doubtless witnessed in ancient times many a bloody conflict—dark episodes in border history; yet there is no proof that the Romans ever occupied the district. Llanymynech hill, six miles to the south, appears to have been the nearest point to which the Latin invader carried his arms; the unconquered Cymri, therefore, still defiantly manned the crest of their vast earthwork Hên Dinas. Fortifications of British origin generally have but a couple of ditches drawn round the quarter most liable to attack; in the extraordinary fortress of Hên Dinas, at Old Oswestry, however, there are four or five concentric ditches.

Maes, Maesdir, signifies the *open field* or *champaign*; the name probably by which the Cymrian occupants of Hên Dinas denominated the surrounding country.

In the vicinity of Maesbury was fought the great battle in which King Oswald was killed. Oswald, the Christian king of the North-Humbrians—Bretwalda, of Britain, who ruled supreme over all the kings of the Angles, the Picts, the Cymri, and the Scots—that powerful yet lowly-minded Saxon, upon whom even the jealous Britons bestowed the epithet of "Bounteous-hand"— Oswald was slain in battle at "Maserfeld," in the year 642, by Penda "the Strong." A terrible fellow was this restless pagan head of the South-Humbrians. He savagely caused his fallen Christian opponent's body to be cut into pieces, and the spot where Oswald's mangled remains had been suspended, the Saxons called *Oswald's treow*, Oswald's tree, afterwards Oswestry. The Welsh named it *Croes Oswalt*, Oswald's Cross. The place where the pious Christian king parted with life, continued for many years to receive an extraordinary amount of superstitious reverence at the hands of his Saxon countrymen. Venerable Bede, speaking of Oswald and Maserfeld, observes :—"How great his faith was towards God, and how remarkable his devotion, has been made evident by miracles since his death; for, in the place where he was killed by the pagans, fighting for his country, infirm men and cattle are healed to this day. Whereupon many took up the very dust of the place where his body fell, and, putting it into water, did much good with it to their friends who were sick. This custom came so much into use, that the earth being carried away by degrees, there remained a hole as deep as the height of a man."[1] The writer of the foregoing died in 735, nearly a hundred years after Oswald had been slain.

To restrain the incessant inroads of his Welsh neighbours, apparently about the year 765, Offa, King of Mercia, caused Watts dyke to be erected. It runs hard by to the east of Maesbury. But when, after twenty years' fighting, the "Terrible" Mercian had succeeded in driving his Cymrian foes further back towards their mountain fastnesses, he cast up in a parallel line some two miles westward of Watts dyke, that vast entrenchment which still bears his name. Maesbury lay between those two remarkable earthwork barriers, Offa's dyke and Watts dyke, and thus, essentially a border settlement, its position must have entailed on its ancient inhabitants all the stirring vicissitudes of border life. Unfortunately, however, we are in possession of but few of the facts relating to its early history.

Domesday says that:—"The earl himself holds Meresberie with v berewicks, and Rainald [holds the manor] of him. King Edward held it [formerly]. Here vii hides geldable; and here Rainald has built Luure castle. In demesne [Rainald] has ii ox-teams, and x Welsh with a priest have viii teams; and there might be vi more teams [employed]. Here a church. Here iiii neat-herds. There is a wood worth little or nothing. Of the same land Robert holds half a hide, and Hengebaldus ii hides; and they have ii teams. To this manor belongs Mersete Hundred. In the time of King Edward it was waste. Now it is worth 40s. [annually]."[2]

From the Conqueror's record, then, we learn that in King Edward's time the important manor of Maesbury was waste; in other words, it yielded no revenue to its royal owner: a condition doubtless to be attributed to that alliance between Algar, the rebel Earl of Mercia, and Gryffyth ap Llewellyn, Prince of North Wales, which caused his enemies to harry the Confessor's manor. But the Saxon king's vicegerent, Harold, marched against the Welsh and subdued them.

Upon the forfeiture of the earls Edwin and Morcar in 1071, William the Conqueror conferred the palatinate of Shropshire on his kinsman, Roger de Montgomery. The Norman Earl of Shrewsbury, politic as strong, with the assistance of Warin his sheriff and other wise warriors, succeeded in gaining the ascendancy over

---

[1] BEDE, *Eccles. Hist.* B. III., ch. 9.   [2] *Domesday*, fo. 253, b 1.

the Welsh border, when, giving Maesbury to Warin, it descended to his successor Rainald, who held the manor when the *Domesday* Commissioners made their report. Instead, however, of its being good for nothing as it had been in King Edward's time, the manor, with the jurisdiction of the hundred attached, yielded 40s. annually to its Norman lord; moreover, it was peacefully occupied in part by the Welsh. The church spoken of in *Domesday* as connected with this manor, doubtless had been erected over that sacred spot where stood Oswald's tree. As we learn from Earl Roger's charter to Shrewsbury Abbey, this church was called "*ecclesiam Sancti Oswaldi*," the church of St. Oswald: around the sacred edifice a *vill* gradually sprang up. To it Rainald the sheriff, for strategic reasons, added a castle, that great military work emphatically styled Luure or L'Œuvre in *Domesday*; and the town which thus arose under Norman influences in the manor of Maesbury, named Oswestry, soon became *caput* of the manor.

Oswestry was either recovered by, or ceded to, the Welsh in the reign of Stephen, as we learn from good authority [1] that "at the close of the year 1148, Madoc, the son of Meredith ap Blethyn, did build the castle of Oswestrie, and gave his nephewes, Owen and Meyric, the sonnes of Gruffyth ap Meredyth, his part of Cyvelioc." Amid the hostilities of Stephen's reign, it is not unlikely that the Welsh, having succeeded in gaining a temporary ascendancy over the border, may have rebuilt the castle of Oswestry, which had been destroyed. It is certain, however, that the Anglo-Norman William Fitz-Alan died in 1160, lord of Oswestry. Called *Blancminster*, the sheriff, Guy le Strange, had custody of the castle here from 1161 till 1175. It was an unsettled period, and from his accounts we glean that one knight, two watchmen, two porters, and twenty men-at-arms—the ordinary garrison of Oswestry castle—cost £48 13s. 4d., or something like £2,000 per annum modern currency. This was independent of the outlay caused by sinking a new well, war stores, castle-palisades, and in frequently providing a large body of *Servientes*, as a temporary addition to the garrison; all of which expenses the sheriff, by direction of the Crown, had incurred in order that he might hand over Oswestry castle in a state of efficiency to its young lord. Upon the death of William Fitz-Alan II. in 1210, Oswestry, by reason of the minority of his heir, again was placed at the disposal

---

[1] POWEL, p. 147. (Ed. 1811).

of the Crown, and King John made it a rendezvous for his invasion of Wales. John Fitz-Alan sided with the barons in rebellion against his liege lord, when the king, concentrating his fury against the west, appeared before Oswestry on the 6th of August, 1216, and by the 10th the town was reduced to ashes. It does not appear, however, that the infuriated John succeeded in capturing Fitz Alan's stronghold.

Oswestry, in 1226, was appointed by King Henry III. and Prince Lewellyn as the place of conference between the latter and certain lords-marchers to whom he owed restitution. A *writ-close* of September 19th, 1233, enjoins the bailiffs of Shrewsbury to allow merchants to carry their merchandize as far as Album Monasterium (Oswestry).

John Fitz-Alan III. died in 1272, when an Extent, or general valuation, of his Shropshire estates being made, it was found that the net annual income which the deceased baron had received from Arundel, Clun, Shrawardine, Blancminster, and the Walcheria of Blancminster, amounted to £506 8s. 1d., a sum equal to £25,000 of our modern money. Out of this total, Oswestry, with its demesnes, manor-court, mills, tolls, rents of burgages and other tenements, yielded £88 17s. 3d., whilst the tenants of the *Walcheria* of Oswestry, paid further rents or services amounting to £42 2s. 9½d., and were subject besides to an assessment, the object of which was to supply the drink (*poturam*) of certain serjeants of the peace appointed for the district. The burgages within and without the bailey of the castle are distinguished. One of the obligations of the lord of Oswestry's tenants related to the keep and conveyance of his hounds.

We may be sure that the Welsh border was subject to disturbances of no ordinary character during the reign of Edward I. Accordingly, we find that on December 6th, 1283, the king being then at Acton Burnell, expedited a patent whereby the bailiffs and burgesses of Oswaldestre were permitted to take a 1d. for every measure of corn exposed for sale, and to levy, for a period of twenty years, similar duties in aid of the repair and completion of their town wall. King Edward I. was in person at Oswestry on the 16th of January, 1284. That warlike and ambitious monarch again visited Oswestry on June 24th, 1295: within two months after "Madoc, son of Llewellyn" was captured on the long mountain near Caus, when the Welsh, despairing of attaining their aim, abandoned war and quietly settled down to more profitable speculations. We need scarcely add, that the pacification of Wales and the border was fraught with prosperity to Oswestry.

CHURCH OF ST. MARY, OSWESTRY.

This, a Saxon foundation, first of all dedicated to St. Oswald, before 1085 had been given by Warin, the sheriff, to Shrewsbury Abbey. It is alluded to in the *Domesday* notice relating to the manor of Maesbury. Originally of a collegiate character, it was the mother church of an extensive district. The abbot and convent of Salop obtained the appropriation of Oswestry church about the year 1222, when it became a vicarage. In 1291, the rectory of the church of Oswalstra, in the deanery of Marchia, and diocese of St. Asaph, was valued at £26 13s. 4d., and its vicarage at £8 13s. 4d. The *Valor* of 1534 represents the vicarage of Oswestre, in the deanery of Marchia, as worth £26 13s. 4d., less 40s. for *lactualia*,[1] 15s. for procurations, and 2s. 10d. for the annual average payable at a bishop's visitation. The abbot of Shrewsbury's rectorial tithes, at the same time, amounted to £66 13s. 4d. per annum. Nothing is known respecting the early incumbents of Oswestry, or any other church in the diocese of St. Asaph.

In former times an hospital existed at Oswestry, which, founded about the year 1205, was endowed with great liberality.

Largely populated by the Welsh, it is difficult to define the extent of, or to say what were the various members of that vast jurisdiction that owned Fitz-Alan's sway in the Marches. The baron rendered no acknowledgment, except homage and fealty for the exercise of his prerogative, which was of a most exclusive character. Hence the materials for the history of this district are but scanty. Yet, if the greatest of the lords-marchers of Shropshire enjoyed unbounded privileges, his feudal obligation also was great—he had to maintain Oswestry castle in efficiency, and to guard the Welsh border.

Whittington is thus noticed in *Domesday*:—" The earl himself holds Wititone, with viii berewicks and a half. King Edward held it. Here xviii hides geldable. The land is [enough]

---

[1] Lactualia were the tithes of dairy produce, receivable by incumbents from their parishioners. The incumbents of the diocese of St. Asaph were bound to hand over a portion of these dues to their bishop.

for xxv ox-teams. In demesne are vi teams, and xv villains and vi boors, with xii teams. Here xii boors and certain Welshmen pay 20s.; and there is a mill here of 5s. [annual value]. Here is one league of wood. In King Edward's time [the manor] was waste. Now it yields £15 15s. [annually]. In the time of King Ethelred, King Edward's father, these three manors [doubtless Maesbury, Whittington, and Chirbury], yielded half the cost of a night."[1] It is clear, from the above description, that the Norman earl's policy, conciliatory or otherwise, was successful in at least this part of the border; for that which in King Edward's time was valueless, under Earl Roger's management returned £15 15s. per annum.

What a corrective to loose historical assertion such an invaluable record as Domesday Book is. We have seen it gravely stated, that in the year 843, Whittington castle was built by a British chieftain, whose descendants possessed it till the Conquest, when it was given to Peverel, the founder of the family of Peverels of the Peak. From *Domesday*, however, we learn that Wititone belonged to the Anglo-Saxon kings before the Conquest, and that when the Conqueror's commissioners made their report, the Norman earl himself was holding the manor. The real history of Whittington has indeed been surrounded with so much that is romantic, yet utterly false, that to present the sober truth to the reader may, perchance, turn out rather an unthankful office. The matter may be summed up in a few lines.

From Roger, the first Norman Earl of Shrewsbury, Whittington descended to his son, Robert de Belèsme, upon whose forfeiture it probably came into the hands of Henry I. It is certain that William Peverel was lord of Whittington in Henry the First's time, and it is most likely that he received it from that king. Nobody has ever yet found out who was father of the brothers, William, Hamo, and Pagan Peverel; but William Peverel of Dover, to whom Henry I. gave Whittington, being childless, his nephew, William Peverel, succeeded to Whittington, and fortified it against the usurper Stephen, in 1138.

Upon the decease of the younger William Peverel, it does not appear that his sisters and co-heirs were permitted by Henry II. to establish their claim upon Whittington, but as is proved by a series of payments made by the sheriffs of Shropshire, in the

---

[1] "Dimidium firmam noctis." *Domesday*, fo. 253, b 1.

WHITTINGTON CASTLE.

p. 444.

years 1160-1-2-3-4, resuming it in demesne, that king in 1165 gave Whittington to the Welshman, Roger de Powis.

From various entries on the Pipe Rolls, it is certain that Roger continued to hold Whittington, and to remain in the pay of the English king, until his death, when Mereduch, his son, and afterwards Mereduch Fitz Roger's brother, Meurich, successively became lords of Whittington.

The following from the Shropshire Pipe Roll, shows that the lord of Whittington, with a contingent, accompanied Richard the Lion-hearted, into Normandy in 1194:—" Et Meurich, filio Rogeri et vi servientibus, cum duobus equis et lx servientibus peditibus, 108 solidos, pro liberacionibus suis de octo diebus ad eundum in servitio Regis in Normanniam, per breve Regis." Again, we have it from the most unquestionable authority, that towards April, of the year 1200, " Meuric de Powis, of Wittinton, fined 50 merks with King John, to have the king's confirmation of Wittinton and Overton, which Henry II. did confirm to Roger, his father"; and that the king accepted the fine.[1] Succeeding his father, in the following May, Wrennoc, son of Meuric de Powis, "proffered a fine of 80 merks and two coursers to King John, for possession of the vills and castles of *Hitinton* [Whittington] and Overton," which John, accepting, confirmed him in the possession of; but, in 1204, Fulk Fitz-Warin III. established his right to the manor and castle of Whittington. It is uncertain what constituted Fitz-Warin's right to Whittington, whether relationship to the Peverels, the old lords of Whittington, or from one of Fitz Warin's ancestors having been enfeoffed by one of the Peverels in the greater part of the manor. There is, and probably ever will be, obscurity surrounding the question. The first Fulk Fitz Warin is known to have been connected by ties of vassalage to the second William Peverel in Cambridgeshire. There is no reason why he might not have been his vassal also at Whittington. Be it as it may, Fulk Fitz Warin III. got a judicial decision in his favour, and on October 17th, 1204, obtained from King John Whittington castle and estate, *as his right and inheritance.* The lordship of Whittington continued with the baronial Fitz-Warins until the extinction of the elder male line in 1420.

---

[1] *Rot. Chartarum*, 1 John, p.2, m.16.

Whittington Church.

In 1291, the church of Chwytunton, in the deanery of Marchia, and diocese of St. Asaph, was valued at £12 *per annum*. In 1534-5, the rectory of Whityngton was worth £25 4s. *per annum* net value.

Early Incumbent.—David Vewan, parson of Witinton, about 1218 attested two deeds of Reyner, Bishop of St. Asaph.

Wlferesforde. "Roger the earl," says *Domesday*, "holds Wlferesforde. King Edward held it. Here ii hides. The land is for vi ox-teams. It was and is waste. Here a little wood." [1] Nothing further is known respecting the above.

The following places are successively spoken of in Domesday Book as belonging to Mersete (now Oswestry) Hundred. When the Conqueror's record was compiled, Rainald the sheriff held all these different manors of the Norman earl. From Rainald, the seigneury over them descended to the Fitz-Alans; as members of whose exclusive jurisdiction they continued to remain for centuries. Excepting, therefore, the *Domesday* notice of them, there is scarcely anything known respecting their early history.

Halston. "The same Rainald holds Halstune. Edric held it with iii berewicks. Here vii hides geldable. The land is for viii ox-teams and a half. Here ii Welsh and one Frenchman, with ii men, have one team and a half. [The manor] is worth 4s. It was waste [in King Edward's time], and waste when [Rainald] got it." [2] Before 1221, the military order of Knights Hospitallers acquired Halston, and they, founding a preceptory here, for centuries realized a large annual income from their *bajulia* or bailiwick of Halston.

Halston Church was originally a private chapel attached to the preceptory. "Halston manor," says Eyton, "is extra-parochial to this day, and the church is donative—two things which are vestiges of that status which existed under the rule of the Knights Hospitallers."

Weston Rhyn. "The same Rainald holds Westone. Scuuard held it [in Saxon times]. Here are v hides geldable

---

[1] *Domesday*, fo. 259, b 2. [2] Ibidem, fo. 254, b 2.

with v berewicks. The land is [enough] for xv ox-teams. Here are ii Welshmen with ii teams. Of this land Robert holds i hide, and here he has i team with iii villains. [In King Edward's time the manor] was waste, and it was waste when [Rainald] obtained it. Now it is worth 10s. [annually]."[1]

Morton. "The same Rainald holds Mortune and Aitone. Seuuard held them for ii manors. Here. v hides. The land is for viii ox-teams. Here v men have ii teams. Here is a small wood worth nothing. [The land formerly] was waste; now it yields lxiiii pence."[1] The place named Aitone, in the above extract, cannot now be found.

Maesbrook. "The same Rainald holds Meresbroc. Leuenot held it in the time of King Edward. Here ii hides. The land is for iiii ox-teams. Here is one Welshman with i team, and he pays 5s."[1]

Tibetune. "*Isdem Rainaldus tenet Tibetune. Uluiet tenuit T. R. E. Ibi i hida. Terra est ii carucis. Ibi ii Walenses habent i carucam et reddunt iiii solidos. Hæc duo Maneria [Mɛresbroc et Tibetune] wasta fuerunt, ut multa alia.*"[1] The manor thus described, cannot now be identified.

Melverley. "The same Rainald," continues *Domesday* "holds Melevrlei. Edric held it in King Edward's time. Here i hide. The land is for ii ox-teams. Here ii Welshmen have one team, and they pay xxxii pence."[2] Melverley church is not mentioned in any very early document.

Weston Cotton. "The same Rainald holds Westune. Seuuard held it in King Edward's time. Here one hide geldable. The land is for iii ox-teams. In demesne are ii teams and iiii neat-herds, and iiii Welshmen with i team, and they pay 4s. The whole is worth 10s., and these [viz., the manors of Melverley and Weston] were waste."[2] Weston is now a small township about a mile and three-quarters south-east of Oswestry.

---

[1] *Domesday*, fo. 254, b 2. [2] Ibidem, fo. 255, a 1.

Wooton. "The same Rainald holds of the Earl Udetone, and Robert [holds] of him. Edric held it with ii berewicks. Here ii hides. The land is for iiii ox-teams. In demesne is one team and ii neat-herds, and viii Welsh with i team. It was worth 15s. Here ii leagues of wood."[1] Wooton is now a township, 3½ miles south-east from Oswestry, to which it belongs.

Woolston. "The same Rainald holds Osulvestune and a knight [holds the manor] of him. Uluric held it in King Edward's time with one berewick. Here i hide and a half. The land is for iii ox-teams. Here iiii Welsh have i team. It is worth 6s."[1] The berewiek here alluded to was Sandford. Sandford and Woolston are in the parish of West Felton.

West Felton. "The same Rainald holds Feltone and a knight [holds] of him. Seuuard held it. Here is half a hide. The land is for i ox-team. It was and is waste."[1] West Felton, with its member, Tedsmere, in the 13th century appears to have been held by Strange of Berrington, under Strange of Ness, who again held the Manor under Fitz-Alan.

WEST FELTON CHURCH.

This, the only church in Mersete Hundred which belonged to the diocese of Chester, in 1291, was valued at £10 *per annum*. Situated in Oswestry Hundred, the parish was exempt from payment of the *ninth* in 1341. In 1534-5, the rector of Felton's income was £21 *per ann.*, less 6s. 8d. for procurations and 1s. for synodals.

Early Incumbent.—John de Biriton, acolyte, instituted February, 27, 1305.

Cynlaeth & Edeyrneou. "The same Rainald holds in Wales two districts,[2] Chenlei and Derniou. From one he has 60s. rent: from the other, eight Welsh cows."[1] Chenlei or Cynlaeth lay to the west of the present boundary of Shropshire. As to the district called Derniou, it was at least twelve miles distant from the most western point of the Walcheria of Oswestry. Yet in

---

[1] *Domesday*, fo 255, a 1.   [2] "Duos Fines."

1086, its Welsh tenants were paying a rent in kind to the Norman Sheriff of Shropshire.

Osbaston & Kynaston are thus described in *Domesday*: "The same Rainald holds Sbernestune and Chimerestun. Seuuard and Aluui held them for ii manors. Here ii hides. The land is [capable of employing] vi ox-teams. Here are ii leagues of wood. [The manors] were and are waste."[1] The changes in the nomenclature of this district have been great. The site of the frontier fortress of Knockyn Castle was originally in the manor of Osbaston, around which the Stranges of Ness and Knockyn gradually amassed an extent of territory that made them formidable to their suzerains, the Fitz-Alans.

KNOCKYN CHURCH.

A Norman door in the chancel of this church proves that it was founded at least as early as the reign of Richard I. This architectural feature agrees with the circumstance that, about 1190-95, Ralph le Strange gave the chapel of Knokyn to Haughmond Abbey. Formerly included in Kinnerley, after the erection of this chapel, Knokyn became an independent parish. Reyner, Bishop of St. Asaph, before 1210, "for the support of the brethren and of the poor, and for the entertainment of guests," allowed Haughmond Abbey to appropriate Knockyn chapel.

In 1291, the church of Knwkyn, in the deanery of Marchia and diocese of St. Asaph, was valued at £3 6s. 8d. *per ann.* The *Valor* of 1534-5 represents this rectory as worth 100s. *per annum*.

The ancient family of Kynaston is said to be descended from Griffin-ap-Gervase Gohc, who, styled *Griffin de Kinerton*, was lord of Kynaston about the year 1200.

Aston, near Oswestry, in 1086 was held of Earl Roger by Robert Pincerna. "The same Robert holds Estone. Uluric held it. Here ii hides. The [arable] land is for iiii ox-teams. Here xii Welshmen have ii teams. It was worth 3s.: now 10s."[2]

Wykey, now a township of Ruyton-of-the-Eleven-towns, in Saxon times was an important manor, and belonged to the Mercian

---

[1] *Domesday*, fo. 255, a 1.   [2] Ibidem, fo. 256, a 2.

G G

earls. At the period of the Conqueror's survey, however, Odo the Norman held it of the Earl of Shrewsbury. "The same Odo," says *Domesday*, "holds Wiche. Earl Eduin held it. Here vii hides with iii berewicks. The land is for x ox-teams and geldable. In demesne are iii teams; and vi neat-herds, and iv boors with i team. Here is a fishery rendering nothing, and a wood in which is one haye. [Formerly the manor] was waste: now it is worth 15s."[1]

Kinnerley is mentioned in Domesday Book thus:—Ernueion holds of the earl Chenardelei. Dunning and Algar held it [in Saxon times] for ii manors. Here i hide geldable. There is land enough for ii ox-teams. Here one Welshman pays a rent of one hawk, and here is half a league of wood."[2] Kinnerley was granted by Henry II. to his *Latimerius*, or interpreter, Gervase Goch, but eventually the Fitz-Alans engrossed the manor.

THE CHURCH.

Kinnerley Church, originally the mother church of a district, was granted by Griffin Goch, or his son Madoc, before 1248, to the Knights Hospitallers of Jerusalem, who became the impropriators of the rectory. The value of the church of Kynardyllef, in the deanery of Marchia and diocese of St. Asaph, is not stated in the Taxation of 1291; because the property of the privileged order of Hospitallers was exempt from the ordinary Papal decimation. According to the *Valor* of 1534-5, the vicarage of Kenerley was worth £7 6s. 8d. *per ann.* The rectory, appropriated by the Commandery of Halston, was worth £20.

Newton. "Iward," says *Domesday*, "holds of the earl Newetone. Turgot held it. Here half a hide geldable. The land might employ ii ox-teams. Here ii villains and ii boors have a team. It was worth 7s.; now 5s."[3] This manor cannot now be identified.

Porkington & Selattyn. "Madoe holds of the earl Haustune and Burtone. Seuuard held them. Here ii hides geldable. There is land for iiii ox-teams. It is waste."[3] Burtone in the 12th century was called Broginton, and Porking-

---

[1] *Domesday*, fo. 257, b 2.   [2] Ibidem, fo. 259, a 2.   [3] Ibidem, fo. 259, b 2.

ton in the 19th. Madoc, *Domesday* lord of Porkington, is said to have been a younger son of Blethyn-ap-Convyn, Prince of North Wales.

SELATTYN originally was merely a member of Porkington, the church, however, happening to be at Selattyn, this gave that place the parochial pre-eminence. In 1291, the church of Sulatwn, in the deanery of Marchia and diocese of St. Asaph, was valued at £6 13s. 4d. *per annum*. In 1534, the net value of Salatin rectory was £12 9s. 6d.

𝕸𝖆𝖊𝖑𝖔𝖗 𝕾𝖆𝖊𝖘𝖓𝖊𝖌 was another district in Wales held by a Welsh noble, in 1086, under the Norman earl. *Domesday* says:—"Tuder, a certain Welshman, holds of Earl [Roger] i district of Welsh land, and from thence pays £4 5s."[1] The territory alluded to now forms part of Flintshire.

𝕷𝖆𝖑𝖊 was another Welsh *commot* assigned by the crafty Conqueror to the palatinate of Shropshire. It was held by Hugh Lupus, Earl of Chester, under Earl Roger de Montgomery. "Hugh the Earl," says *Domesday*, "holds of Roger the Earl, in Wales, the land of Gal. This land extends v leagues in length and one league and a half in breadth. In the time of King Edward it was waste, and similarly [waste] when Hugh received it. In-demesne are iii ox-teams, and ii priests and xxxiii men have among themselves viii teams; and there might be another team besides. There is a mill yielding nothing. The value of the whole now is 40s."[2]

---

[1] *Domesday*, fo. 253, b 1. [2] Ibidem, fo 254, a 2.

DOMESDAY HUNDRED OF WITENTREU.

Modern Name.	Domesday Name.	Saxon Owner or Owners, T. R. E.	Domesday Tenant in capite.	Domesday Mesne, or next Tenant.	Domesday Sub-Tenant.	Modern Hundred.
Chirbury	Cireberie	Rex Edwardus	Rogerius Comes			Chirbury.
Middleton	Mildetune	Ertein	Idem	Ertein		Ibidem.
		Edric Salvage	Idem	Robertus filius Corbet		Ibidem.
Marrington	Meritune	Eluuard and Aluric	Idem	Robertus filius Corbet		Ibidem.
Priest-Weston	Westune	Sex teini	Idem	Robertus filius Corbet		Ibidem.
Rorrington	Roritune	Aluric	Idem	Robertus filius Corbet	Leuric	Ibidem.
		Eluuard	Idem	Rogerius filius Corbet	Osulf	Ibidem.
Worthin	Wrdine	Morcar Comes	Idem	Rogerius filius Corbet	Picot, Reinfrid, Goisfrid, and Grento	Chirbury. Ford.
Leighton	Lestune	Seunard	Idem	Rogerius filius Corbet		Montgomery.
Montgomery	Muntgumeri	Seunar, Oslac, and Azor	Idem	Rogerius filius Corbet Elluuard		Chirbury. Montgomery.
Rhiston	Ristune	Seunard	Idem	Elward		Chirbury.
Church Stoke	Cirestoc	Seunard	Idem	Elward	1 Walcis	Cawrse.
Wotherton	Udevertune	Elmund	Idem	Alward filius Elmundi		Chirbury.
	Muletune	Godric	Idem	Elward		Ibidem.
Lack	Lach	Leuric	Idem	Godebold		Ibidem.
Marton	Mertune	Ecclesia Sti. Ceddæ	Idem	Ecclesia Sti. Ceddæ	Eluuard	Ibidem.

Chirbury. Scattered through the extensive parish of Chirbury, are several barrows and traces of ancient encampments. Betwixt Church Stoke and Chirbury is the British work *Caer Bre*.

Chirbury is thus described in *Domesday* :—"The earl himself holds Cireberie. King Edward held it. In demesne are iiii ox-teams, and xiii villains with a priest have v teams. Here are viii neat-herds. Here ii churches with a priest, who has i team. To this manor belongs Witetreu Hundred. In King Edward's time it was waste; now it is worth 40s." [1]

In William the Conqueror's time, it appears then that Chirbury was caput of the hundred of Witentreu, as it still remains caput of the hundred to which it gives a name. The *Domesday* notice of this manor furnishes us with another proof that the Norman earl's policy in the Marches had been successful. Probably it was upon the forfeiture of the earls of Shrewsbury, that Chirbury reverted to the king; at any rate, when Henry I. re-arranged the hundreds of Shropshire, the seigneury of Chirbury Hundred, and every manor in it that was at the king's disposal, went to form the honour of Montgomery, which honour the king bestowed upon Baldwin de Bollers, when he married Sibil de Faleise, the king's niece. The manor of Chirbury continued with the descendants of Baldwin, until the honour of Montgomery was dismembered by Henry III.

---

[1] *Domesday*, fo. 253, b 1.

Reassumed by the Crown, Chirbury then became a royal borough.

Chirbury Priory,

Of which some vestiges still remain, was apparently founded and endowed by Robert de Bollers, lord of Montgomery, towards the close of the 12th century. In 1291, the prior of Chirbury's possessions and income yielded a total of £5 18s. 4d. This included an annual profit of 13s. 6d. on nine brood mares. The *Valor* of 1534-5 represents the net income of the priory to be £66 8s. 7½d. per annum. This included a sum of £5 12s. 10d. oblations at the several shrines of saints in the parish churches of the prior's advowson.

CHURCH OF ST. MICHAEL.

Originally the collegiate church of a vast Saxon parish, this was one of the two churches spoken of in the *Domesday* notice relating to Chirbury: Church Stoke probably was the other foundation. The advowson of St. Michael was part of that endowment which Robert de Bollers, lord of Montgomery, conferred upon his newly-founded priory of Chirbury. In 1291, the church of Chirbury, (that is the rectory), in the deanery of Pontesbury, the archdeaconry of Salop, and the diocese of Hereford, was valued at £30; besides a pension of 10s. to the precentor of Wenlock. In 1341, the parish was assessed only £9 13s. 4d. to the *ninth* of wheat, wool, and lamb, because part of it was in Wales, many tenants were going about begging, and their poverty had thrown 200 acres of land out of cultivation, etc. King Henry the Eighth's *Valor* gives a total of £29 5s. as the annual value of Chirbury rectory; the vicarage was worth £9 6s. 8d., less £1 7s. 10d. for procurations.

Early Incumbents.—Richard, last of the co-rectors or portioners of Chirbury, occurs about 1225; John, vicar of Chirbury, 1289; Richard de Chirbury, priest, was presented to this vicarage, March 6th, 1308, by the prior and convent of Chirbury.

Middleton,

in 1086, was a divided manor. In one part of Domesday Book, we read that:—"Ertein holds of the earl Mildetune. He himself held it [in Saxon times], and was a free man. Here iii virgates of land geldable. There is land for i ox-team. In demesne is [one team] with ii serfs. [In King Edward's time the manor] was worth 9s.; now 12s." ¹ In 1255 the tenants here were to perform the following services:—"To provide a man with bow or lance in ward of Montgomery castle for 15 days in wartime; to do suit thrice yearly to the court of Montgomery, and throughout the year to Chirbury Hundred Court; also to go hunting thrice yearly with the lords of Montgomery, and to victual the guards of Montgomery." ²

We are told in another part of King William's record that Robert Fitz Corbet held the other half of the manor under Roger de Montgomery:—"The same Robert holds Mildetune. Edric Salvage held it. Here iii virgates geldable. Here i radman, i villain, and ii boors, with half an ox-team; and there might be i team besides. It was worth 4s.; now 5s." ³

Marrington, situated on the river Camlad, which here flows through a lovely glen, is thus noticed in *Domesday*:—"The same Robert [Fitz Corbet] holds Meritune. Eluuard and Aluric held it for ii manors, and were free men. Here half a hide geldable. Here are ii radmans, and iii boors, with ii ox-teams; and [there is] a wood which will fatten xv swine. The old value was 7s.; afterwards 5s.; now iv pence more." ³

Priest-Weston, also a township of Chirbury, is thus mentioned in *Domesday*:—"The same Robert holds Westune. Six thanes held it for vi manors, and were free. Each had i virgate of land and paid geld. Now there are here vii radmans, with iii ox-teams, and they pay 20s. The land of two of the thanes was worth 10s. [that of] the others truly was waste." ³

Rorrington, in 1086, was a divided manor; one half of which was held of the Norman earl by Robert Fitz Corbet, and the other by Roger Fitz Corbet. "The same Robert holds Roritune. Aluric held it. Here i virgate not geldable. In demesne is i ox-team, and vii serfs and ii boors. Here is a wood which will fatten xv swine; and [there is] half a haye here. [The manor formerly] was worth 3s.; [annually] now, 6s. Leuric held it of Robert." ³

---

¹ *Domesday*, fo. 259, b 1.   ² *Rot. Hundred*, II. 60.   ³ *Domesday*, fo. 256, a 1.

Again:—"The same Roger holds Roritune, and Osulf [holds] of him. Eluuard held it and was a free man. Here i virgate, not geldable. In demesne is half an ox-team, and vi boors with half a team. The wood here will fatten xv swine, and [there is] half a haye. It used to be worth 7s.; afterwards 16d.; now 6s."[1]

Worthin.

Upon the summit of Cefn Digol, at the end of the Long Mountain, is the circular British entrenchment Caer Digol, otherwise called the *Beacon Ring*. Mentioned by Lomarchus, in the 7th century, and by Cynddellw in the twelfth, it may be inferred that Cefn Digol was a post generally occupied by the Britons in warfare. Several barrows are scattered about the parish of Worthin.

In 1086, Roger Fitz Corbet held, under the Norman earl, this great estate, which is thus minutely described in the Conqueror's record:—"The same Roger holds Wrdine. Earl Morcar held it [formerly]. Here are xiiii hides and a half geldable, with xiii berewicks. In demesne are ii ox-teams; and ii serfs, xiii villains, vi boors, and iii radmans, with x teams and a half. Here ii mills yield iii horse-loads of corn; and [there is] a wood ii leagues long in which are iiii hayes; and it is capable of fattening cc swine.

"Of the land of this manor, Picot holds of Roger iii hides, Reinfridus iii hides and a half, Goisfridus i hide and a half, and Grento half a hide. In demesne they have iiii ox-teams and a half; and [there are] iiii serfs, vii villains, and viii boors, with iiii teams, and iii neat-herds.

"In this manor there is [arable] land [sufficient] for xli oxteams. In Roger's demesne there might be iiii teams [more]. The whole, in the time of King Edward, was worth £10; and afterwards 10s. Now that which [Roger] holds [is worth] £5; that which [his] knights [hold] £4 10s."[1] About the year 1236, Thomas Corbet withdrew his great manor of Worthin from all connection with Chirbury Hundred, and exalted it into an independent jurisdiction; which accounts for so little being known respecting the early history of this district. But, after Wales had been conquered, the barons marchers were at a discount with the King of England; and Edward I. setting his lawyers at work to question Corbet's right to hold pleas of the crown, and to have

---

[1] *Domesday*, fo. 255, b 2.

market, fair, and wayf in his manor of Worthin; the result was a considerable diminution of the haughty noble's franchise.

WORTHIN CHURCH.

Although not indicated in *Domesday*, yet this undoubtedly was a very ancient Saxon foundation; the centre of a vast parish. In 1291, the church of Worthin, in the archdeaconry of Salop, and deanery of Pontesbury, was valued at £20 per annum. In 1341, the parish was taxed only £10 14s. 7d. to the *ninth*, because the greater portion of it was "in the parts of Wales," etc. In 1534-5, the rector of Worthyn's income was £30 per annum, less 6s. 8d. payable to the commissary, 1s. for synodals, and 17s. 9d. annual proportion of bishop's triennial visitation-fee.

Early Incumbent.—Hugh Corbet, rector of Worthin, 1245.

The *Domesday* berewicks of Worthin are, perhaps, included in the following places, all of which were anciently members of Worthin: Aston Pigot, Aston Rogers, Beachfield, Binweston, Brockton, Walton and Leigh, Hope, Bromlow, Grimmer, Hampton, Meadow-Town, Gatten, Habberley Office, Heath, and Shelve, famous in the 12th and 13th centuries for its lead mines. The rectory of Shelve, in the deanery of Pontesbury, according to the *Valor* of 1534-5, was worth £2 13s. 4d., less 6d. per annum for procurations.

Leighton,

between Offa's Dyke and the Severn, is thus noticed in *Domesday*:—"The same Roger holds Lestune. Seuuard held it, and was free. Here one hide, not geldable. In demesne is i ox-team, and one radman, and ii neat-herds. There is a wood here ii leagues long, and capable of fattening cc swine. It was and is worth 5s."[1]

Montgomery.

The retreat of Caractacus and his brave British force, before the advancing Roman general Ostorius, is indicated by numerous defensive vestiges scattered over neighbouring eminences, and by the Roman work at Caer Flôs. Situated above the eastern bank of the Severn, at the confluence of four valleys, a mile and a half north of Montgomery, the camp of the skilful Roman tactician served as a key to the whole district, as far as Bishop's Castle to the south-east, and the vale of the Severn to Newtown on the south-west.

---

[1] *Domesday*, fo. 255, b 2.

More than a thousand years had passed since Caractacus made his heroic stand against the Latin invader, when, a little to the west of the great Saxon work, Offa's Dyke, which, by the way, also had for its object the restraining of the Cymrians, the Norman Earl of Shrewsbury, to enforce his policy on the border, built a castle, which after his own name, he called Montgomery. This stronghold, with the chatellany attached, is the subject of the following entries in *Domesday*:—" Near to the castle of Montgomeri the earl himself has iiii ox-teams; and [he has] £6 of pence from one district of Wales pertaining to this chatellany. Roger Corbet has here ii ox-teams, and, with his brother, has from Wales 40s."[1] Again:—" The earl himself built the castle called Muntgumeri, adjacent to which [lie] lii hides and a half, which Seuuar, Oslac, and Azor [formerly] held of King Edward, quit of all geld. By that they had hunting.

"In Etenehop is i hide; in Estune ii hides; in Stantune vii hides; in Cestelop ii hides; in Mulitune iii hides; in Goseford iii hides; in Hoptune ii hides; in Benehale vii hides; in Dudestune i hide; in Wadelestun iii hides; in Elehitun half a hide; in Walecote i hide; in Ulestanesmude iii hides. These lands were held [in Saxon times by the] aforesaid iii thanes. Now Earl Roger holds [them]. They are and were waste. Of over L hides there are iii hides [only] in his demesne.

" The same iii thanes held Westune of iii hides; Staurecote of i hide; Horseford of half a hide; Torneberie of i hide; Heme of iii hides; Edritune of i hide; Furtune of half a hide; Urbetune of i hide; and Achelai of i hide. These lands Roger Corbet holds of the earl, except Achelai, which Eiluuard holds. In these, are in demesne ix ox-teams and a half; and xv villains, xiiii boors, with iii radmans, and viii serfs, have xii ox-teams and a half. [In King Edward's time these lands] were waste; now [they are] worth c shillings. In Heme are iii fisheries, and a wood with a haye. In Edritune there is a wood which will fatten lx swine. In Achelai one haye."[2]

Concerning the above, it may be observed, that the names of more than half the villages given, indicate a Saxon occupation anterior to the reign of Edward the Confessor. These extracts from Domesday Book also clearly prove how successful had been the policy, on the border, of the Conqueror's lieutenant, since a

---

[1] *Domesday*, fo. 253, b 1.   [2] Ibidem, fo. 254, a 1.

territory which was wasted through war in King Edward's time, in 1086 yielded Roger de Montgomery £6 of Welsh rent, and £5 to Roger Corbet; independently of 35½ hides of desert land, which the earl probably devoted to purposes of the chase.

About 1095, or some two years after the decease of its great founder, "the Welsh," says Florence of Worcester, "demolished the castle of Montgomery, and killed in it some of the retainers of Hugh, Earl of Shrewsbury; at which the king [William II.] was so incensed that he issued orders for an expedition, and, after the feast of St. Michael, led his army into Wales, where he lost many men and horses."[1] Re-built by the English, upon the fall of Robert de Belèsme in 1102 the castle and chatellany of Montgomery escheated to Henry I., who, augmenting the latter largely with distant estates, "granted it to Baldwin de Bollers, in marriage with Sibil de Faleise, his niece."

Upon the extinction of the male descendants of Baldwin and Sibil in 1207, William de Courtenay gained the barony, as heir of Baldwin and Sibil's daughter, Matilda, wife of Richard Fitz Urse. De Courtenay died without issue in 1214, when the succession to the honour of Montgomery became the subject of much contention.

The claimants were Vitalis Engaine, Thomas de Erdinton, Stephen de Stanton, Giles de Erdinton, Robert Wafre, and lastly, William de Cantilupe, who ultimately obtained everything belonging to the honour in Shropshire or the Marches.

Meanwhile, King John, and afterwards Henry III., affecting to treat the castle and honour of Montgomery as an escheat since the death of William de Courtenay, had retained the castle of Montgomery in their own hands. A writ-close of May 6th, 1215, orders the barons of the Exchequer to reimburse Erdinton for his outlay at Shrewsbury, Oswestry, Shrawardine, Morton, Clun, Montgomery, Mortoin, and other castles which were in his custody. A writ-close of August 8th, 1223, ordered the chief forester of Shropshire to admit the king's carpenters into Shirlot forest, there to prepare timber for the fortifications of the said castle, when need should arise. On October 7th of the same year, King Henry III. himself visited Montgomery to receive Lewellyn's submission. Nevertheless, the King of England continued his precautions, and sent, two days afterwards, to his Forest of Dean

---

[1] FLORENCE OF WORCESTER, p. 201. Bohn's Ed.

for 20 able miners to do certain works at the castle which he had built at Montgomery. Returned to Westminster, a writ of October 22nd speaks of the knights who were employed by Henry III. in the fortifications of the above castle. On November 8th, the king sent £200 to Montgomery, for liveries and castle-works. On the 22nd, from Gloucester he ordered 6,000 *quarrels*, manufactured at St. Briavells, to be conveyed here. A writ of the same day relates to a chapel "in the new castle." The king sent £300 more for works and liveries of knights and servientes at Montgomery, on December 9th, 1223, and another £300 on February 23rd, 1224. Again, the king dispatched £200 on August 22nd, 1224, to pay the liveries of the knights and servientes at his castle of Montgomery, and to continue the works there. On the 1st of October following, Henry III. revisited Montgomery, in company with his justiciary. On November 6th, 1224, £300 more was sent for the works and garrison of Montgomery castle, and many other cheques which Henry III. drew tend to show that this king had seizin of and actually rebuilt the castle of Montgomery; yet, whether he reconstructed it on the site of the old fortress, or in another situation, does not appear.

In the year 1227, the men of Montgomery, for a fine of £20, purchased their franchise as a free borough from King Henry III. " By his charter, dated at London on February 13th in that year, the king wills and concedes that his town of Montgomery be a free borough. The burgesses may enclose the town with a wall and foss. They may have a merchant-guild, with a *hanse*, and other customs. None, except those of the guild, may do merchandise there, without consent of the burgesses. If any *native* be received into the guild, and pay scott and lott for a year and a day, he may not be recovered by his lord without judicial process. The burgesses are to have *soc, sac, tol, theam,* and *infangenthef,* and to be quit of *tolls, lastaye, passage, pontage, stallage, lene,* and *danegeld*. They are to have all such franchises as the citizens of Hereford enjoyed. They are also to have two annual fairs; one of four days, at the feast of St. Bartholomew [August 24th]; the other of eight days, on the eve, day of, and six days after, the feast of St. Michael [September 28th—October 5th]. All merchants visiting the town are to be under royal protection; but the liberties of the city of London are to be reserved in all things." [1]

---

[1] *Rot. Chart.*, 2 Hen. III., p. 1, m. 27, quoted by EYTON.

But it is to Hubert de Burgh, the erewhile potent minister of the fickle Henry III., that Montgomery owes its more extended liberties as a free borough. In one of his moments of extravagant bounty, the king had given him Montgomery, when "Hubert de Burgh, Earl of Kent, and Justiciar of England," amongst other things, conceded to his burgesses of Montgomery, that "they may hold their town in fee-farm [at a rent of 60 merks], viz., all their lands and tenements, both in *new* and *old Montgomery*; also that they may have fairs and markets, with a merchant-guild, and all franchises and liberties appurtenant to the said fairs." "The burgesses were to elect two provosts of their own, to take custody of the town, which provosts were to swear before the earl, or [if absent] before his constable, to keep the town securely, for his advantage and the advantage of his heirs, and to administer justice to all, and to cause *right assizes* to be observed. The burgesses were also to have two coroners, who should faithfully attach all pleas of the Crown, and should keep such pleas till it were the earl's pleasure that they should be heard. All merchants might bring their goods with security to the town, and, paying the right dues, should be under the earl's protection. No constable or bailiff of the earl should take or buy anything from a stranger, save by that stranger's consent. The said constables and bailiffs might buy victuals from the men of the town, but must by no means defer payment for the same beyond 20 days."

MONTGOMERY CHURCH.

This originally was an affiliation of St. Michael at Chirbury, but about 1227, Montgomery became a rectory in the patronage of the crown. Pope Nicholas' Taxation, in 1291, values the church of Montgomery, in the deanery of Pontesbury and diocese of Hereford, at £25 *per ann.*, besides a pension of £2 10s. payable to the castle of Montgomery (the castle-chaplain's salary), and a pension of £1 10s. to the conventual Church of Chirbury. The *Valor* of 1534-5, represents the rector of Mountegomery's income to be £17 15s. 4d. *per ann.*, less 11s. for procurations and synodals, payable to the Archdeacon of Salop.

Early Incumbent.—William de Boulers, parson of Montgomery in 1227, was probably presented by the Prior of Chirbury.

William le Brun, presented Jan. 21, 1243, by King Henry III.

The twenty-two estates which *Domesday* names as members of Montgomery, were Etenehop, now Lower and Upper Edenhope; Estune, now Upper and Lower Aston; Stantune cannot now be identified; Castelop, now perhaps Castlewright; Mulitune, now Mellington; Goseford, now lost; Hoptune, now lost; Benehale, now lost; Dudestune, now Dudson; Wadelestun, now lost; Elchitun, now Hokelton; Walecote, now Walcot; and Ulestanesmude, now Wolston Mynd. The foregoing composed the 35½ hides of desert land which Earl Roger de Montgomery retained as a hunting adjunct to his castle.

Those which Roger Fitz-Corbet held were—Westune, now Great Weston, or Weston-Madoc; Staurecote, now lost; Horseford, also lost; Torneberie, now Thornbury; Heme, now Great and Little Hem; Edritune, now Edderton; Furtune, now Forden; Urbetune, now Wrobbeton, or Wropton; and Achelai, now Ackley.

Looking through the vista of eight hundred years, it is singular how slight have been the changes which have occurred in the names of the places that composed the Domesday Chatellany of Montgomery.

Rhiston is described in *Domesday* thus:—"Elward holds Ristune. Seuuard held it and was a free man. Here iii hides geldable. The land is (capable of employing) iiii ox-teams. Here i radman has i team with iii serfs, and [there are] ii villains with i team.[1] There is wood enough here to fatten xxx swine. [The manor] was worth 10s.; now 12s."[2] The Ristune of *Domesday* must be understood to include Brompton.

Church Stoke. "Elward holds Cirestoc. Seuuard held it and was free. Here v hides geldable. There is land for vii ox-teams. Here one Welshman has i team. The wood here will fatten 100 swine. It used to be worth 10s.; now 5s. 4d."[2] The chapel here, an affiliation of Chirbury, is described in King Henry the Eighth's *Valor* as worth £20 *per ann.*

Wotherton. The same [Alward son of Elmund] holds Udevertune. Elmund held it and was a free man. Here iii hides geldable. The land is for xiv ox-teams. In demesne is half a team, and vi villains, one boor, a priest, and iiii radmans with xii

---

[1] It is not often that *Domesday* describes villains as possessing a team.
[2] *Domesday*, fo. 259, b 1.

teams. Here is a mill which yields [a rental of] xxiv small vessels of corn.¹ In the time of King Edward [the manor] was worth £4 [per annum]; now a similar amount."² In 1255, "Henry de Wodenertun held it for half a knight's fee, doing three weeks' ward at Montgomery castle in war-time, and doing suit throughout the year to Chirbury Hundred, and going to hunt thrice yearly with the lords of Montgomery."

Muletune. "Elward holds Muletune. Godric held it and was a free man. There is i virgate of land geldable. The land is for i ox-team. There is [one team] in demesne with ii serfs. It was and is worth 5s." ² There is a doubt respecting the situation of the land thus described in *Domesday*.

Lack. "Godebold holds of the Earl Lach. Leuric held it. Here one virgate and a half of land geldable. It was waste. Now it pays xvi pence."² With Rhiston and Brompton, Lack now constitutes the English part of the parish of Church Stoke.

Marton, in Chirbury Hundred, belonged, in William the Conqueror's time, to the church of St. Chad, at Shrewsbury. "The same church," says *Domesday*, "holds Mertune, and held it [in Saxon times]. Eluuard holds it of the church. Here ii hides geldable. In demesne is half an ox-team, and iii villains, iii radmans, and one boor with iii teams and a half; and there might be ii more teams besides. The wood here will fatten L swine. In the time of King Edward [the manor] yielded 8s.; now it is worth 10s., but it pays only 6s. 2d."³

---

¹ "*Vascula Frumenti.*"   ² *Domesday*, fo. 259, b 1.   ³ Ibidem, fo. 253, a 1.

Domesday Hundred of Rinlau.

Modern Name.	Domesday Name.	Saxon Owner or Owners, T. R. E.	Domesday Tenant in capite.	Domesday Mesne, or next Tenant.	Domesday Sub-Tenant.	Modern Hundred.
Clun	Clnne	Edric	Rogerius Comes	Picot	Walterus, Picot Miles, Gisloldus, Duo Wales	Clun.
Myndtown	Munete	Lenric	Idem	Picot	Leuric	Purslow.
Clunton	Clutune	Elmund, Uluric, Æhnund	Idem	Picot		Ibidem.
Clunbury	Cluneberie	Suen	Idem	Picot		Ibidem.
Kempton	Chenpitune	Suen	Idem	Picot	Duo Waleis	Ibidem.
Hopesay	Hope	Edric	Idem	Picot		Ibidem.
Sibdon Carwood	Sibetnne	Suen	Idem	Picot		Ibidem.
Purslow	Posselau	Uuric	Idem	Picot		Ibidem.
Barlow	Berlie	Uluric	Idem	Picot		Ibidem.
Obley	Obelie	Ælmund	Idem	Picot		Clun.
Hopton Castle	Opetnne	Edric	Idem	Picot	Duo Waleis	Purslow.
Corston	Cozetune	Suein	Idem	Picot		Ibidem.
Edgton	Egednne	Suein	Idem	Picot		Ibidem.
Wentnor	Wantenovre	Edric	Idem	Rogerius filius Corbet		Ibidem.
Choulton	Cautnne	Gunnert	Idem	Robertus filius Corbet		Ibidem.
Lydbury, North	Lideberie	Episcopus de Hereford	Episcopus de Hereford	Quidam Franco, Willelmus Clericus		Ibidem.

Manor situate in Rinlau, but whose Domesday state was Independent.

Lydham	Lidum	Edric Salvage	Rogerius Comes			Purslow.

TO judge from the above table, the modern Hundred of Purslow represents the *Domesday* Hundred of Rinlau: yet Purslow contains seven manors that were not in the ancient hundred. *Domesday* does not state where the caput of Rinlau Hundred was situated. The Barons of Caus, for ages after *Domesday* had been compiled, claimed to be prescriptive lords of Purslow Hundred.

Clun. Situated on a very fine and commanding position betwixt Knighton and Clun, is the strongly entrenched British fortress, Caer-Caradoc. Pent-in among mountains, Caer-Caradoc, however reared its fortified crest far above the neighbouring summits, and stood a centre of communication for all those border fortresses which Caractacus manned to stay the victorious progress of the Roman legions. "The eastern side of the camp," says Hartshorne,[1] "is that most difficult of approach; and accordingly on this side less labour has been employed to make it defensible. From the north and north-western sides three different fosses and

---

[1] *Salopia Antiqua*, p. 52.

valla die away to the others. The entrances were at the north-eastern and western sides.

"We see in it," he continues, "an undisputed example of British castrametation. Unquestionably it bears the name of the British chief (Caradoc or Caractacus), and is associated traditionally with his exploits." There are no less than five different ancient British military works in the Forest of Clun.

About two miles to the west of Clun the celebrated Saxon earthwork, Offa's Dyke, is to be seen, in an excellent state of preservation.

Clun is the subject of the following entry in Domesday Book:—
"The same Picot holds Clune. Edric held it [in Saxon times] and was[1] a free man. Here xv hides geldable. There is [arable] land [sufficient] for lx ox-teams. In demesne are ii [teams] and v serfs, x villains, and iiii boors with v teams, and a mill which supplies the manorial hall: and iiii Welsh pay 2s. 4d.

"Of this land Walter holds ii hides of Picot, and Picot the knight iii hides, and Gislold ii hides. Here they have iii ox-teams, and [there are] ii serfs, ii neat-herds, viii villains, iiii boors, and ii Welsh with ii teams amongst them all. Here ii radmans pay a tax of ii animals.[2] The whole manor in King Edward's time was worth £25, and afterwards £3:[3] now what Picot has is worth £6 5s.; that which the knight has [is worth] £4, less 5s."[4]

Ficot, Pigod, or Picot's real name was Robert. The *vill* of Saium or Sai, from whence he derived his distinctive appellation of De Say was situated about nine miles west of Exmes the caput of Roger de Montgomery's Norman Viscomté. With his wife, Adeloya, and his two sons, Robert and Henry, Picot occurs in 1060 as a benefactor to the house of St. Martin, at Seez. Six years later and he fought under the banner of the Duke of Normandy at Hastings, for his name figures on the Battle Abbey Roll.[5] The historian Ordericus mentions, that besides entrusting the command of Shrewsbury to Warin the Bald (the sheriff), "Roger de Montgomery also gave commands in his earldom to William, surnamed Pantoul, *Picot de Say*, and Corbet, with his sons, Roger and Robert, as well as other brave and faithful knights, supported by whose

---

[1] A scribal error in *Domesday* has substituted the word *tenuit* for *fuit*, which is evidently meant.
[2] "*Reddunt* ii *animalia de censu.*"
[3] An enormous depreciation.
[4] *Domesday*, fo 258, a 2.
[5] The name Pigot appears in the list published by Duchesne; Pygot in that published by Leland.

CLUN CHURCH.

FONT, CLUN.

wisdom and courage, he ranked high among the greatest nobles." [1] Thus figuring as one of Earl Roger's chief vassals, Clun was the largest of the twenty-nine manors which the Norman Picot de Say held under the Earl of Shrewsbury.

After Picot, Henry his son, became lord of Clun, to whom succeeded Helias de Say, whose era was nearly co-equal with Stephen's usurpation. It was probably during this period of civil convulsion, that the baron of Clun converted Clun into an independent jurisdiction.

Isabel de Say, daughter and sole heir of Helias, married William Fitz-Alan I.; and thus the two privileged franchises of Oswestry and Clun became united in the house of Fitz-Alan.

Clun castle, after a long siege and many a fierce assault, was stormed by the Welsh Prince, Rees, about 1196 and committed to the flames.

Upon the decease of John Fitz-Alan III. in 1272, an extent of his barony was taken, when the jurors found that—" Clun castle was small but pretty well built. The roof of the tower wanted covering with lead, and the bridge wanted repairing. Outside the castle was a bailey, enclosed with a foss, and a certain gate in the castle-wall thereabouts, had been begun [but not finished]. The buildings in the said bailey, viz., a grange, a stable, and a bakehouse, were in a weak state. In the town of Clun there were 183 burgages, and 22 burgages had tenements in the assarts of the manor. Clun market, held on Saturdays, produced £10 *per annum*. Two fairs of three days each were held at Martinmas (November 11th), and at the feast of Pancrace, Nereus, and Achilles (May 12th). They realized £6 *per annum*. A tallage assessable by the lord of Clun, whenever the king had a tallage, produced £5. The pleas of the free-court realized £2; the pleas and perquisites of the portmote 2 merks *per annum*. Robert le Clerk paid a rent of 24 horse-shoes, or 12d., for his smithy. Certain of the burgesses were bound to provide 20 men, each to accompany the lord of Clun four days yearly on his hunting excursions." [2]

Church of St. George, at Clun.

Although unnoticed in *Domesday*, this probably was a Saxon foundation—the mother-church of a vast parish. In the time of Richard I., the lord and lady of Clun granted the advowson of

---

[1] Ordericus Vitalis, Bk. IV. ch. vii.   [2] *Inquis.*, 56 Hen. III., No 36.

Clun and all its chapels, to Wenlock priory, and the bishop shortly afterwards permitted the monks to appropriate them. The Taxation of 1291, says, that:—"The church of Clone, with its chapels, is the prior of Wenlock's, and worth £36 13s. 4d. per annum:" this was the rectory. "The vicar's portion in the same was worth £5 per annum." King Henry the Eighth's *Valor* gives the prior of Wenlock's rectory of Clun as worth £34 13s. 4d. per annum. The value of the vicarage is not stated.

DOORWAY, CLUN.

Early Incumbent.—Walter was probably the last rector of Clun, 1221; and Radulf de Clumbiry first vicar of Clun, November, 1221.

Myndtown, in 1086, also was held under the Norman earl by Picot de Say, for we read in *Domesday* that :—"The same Picot holds Munete, and Leuric [holds] of him. The same [Leurie] held it [in Saxon times], and was a free man. Here i hide and a half geldable. The land is for iii ox-teams and a half. In demesne is one team and a half; and [there are] ii serfs, iiii villains, and iiii boors, with ii teams. Here is i haye. In the time of King Edward [the manor] was worth 60s.; now 30s."[1]

---

[1] *Domesday*, fo. 258, a 1.

Myndtown Church.

The Taxation of 1291 represents this church as being of less than £4 annual value. In 1341, the parish of Munede was taxed only 30s. to the *ninth*, " because the lands lay fallow and untilled, the tenants being poor." King Henry the Eighth's *Valor* gives the rector of Mynton's preferment as £4 13s. 4d. per annum.

Early Incumbent.—Walter le Clerk, rector of *Munad*, 1210.

Clunton. "The same Picot holds Clutune. Elmund, Uluric, and Ælmund held it for iii manors, and were free. Here iiii hides geldable. The land is for xii ox-teams. In demesne are ii teams, and vi serfs, iiii villains, viii boors, and one radman, with ii teams. Here were v hayes. In time of King Edward it was worth £7 14s.; afterwards 5s.; now 40s." [1]

Clunbury. Nearly upon the summit of Clunbury hill, is a large upright stone. That it was carried thither is evident from its geological character, which differs from that of the hill on which it stands. In short, it is a memorial or hoar stone, marking the point where the parishes of Clunbury and Clungunford separate.

"The same Picot," continues *Domesday*, "holds Cluneberie, Suen held it. This manor never paid geld, nor was hidaged. In the time of King Edward it was worth £4. Here were vi ox-teams." [1]

Clunbury church, an affiliation of St. George, at Clun, is not mentioned in the Taxation of 1291; but, as an independent parish, Clunbury was assessed 45s. to the *ninth* in 1341. The *curate* of Clunbury's preferment in 1534-5 was worth £7 *per annum*, less a pension of 13s. 4d. to the prior of Wenlock, and 7s. 8d. for synodals.

Kempton. "The same Picot holds Chenpitune. The same Suen held it [in Saxon times]. Here iiii hides geldable. The [arable] land in these ii manors [viz, Clunbury and Kempton] was [sufficient to employ] xiiii ox-teams. In demesne are iiii [teams], xiii serfs, viii villains, and ii boors, with v teams; and ii Welsh

---

[1] *Domesday*, fo. 258, a 1.

pay xiiii pence. There is a wood here which will fatten c swine, and in it are iii hayes. These two manors, in King Edward's time, were worth £8; afterwards £3; now £6."[1]

𝔥𝔬𝔭𝔢𝔰𝔞𝔶 is thus alluded to in Domesday Book:—"The same Picot holds Hope. Edric held it, and was a free man. Here vii hides geldable. The land is for xiiii ox-teams. In demesne are ii teams, and vi serfs, xiiii villains, a smith, and a bailiff, with vi teams. Here ii hayes. In time of King Edward [the manor] was worth £10; afterwards £3; now £7."[1] Hope acquired that distinctive title, by which it is now recognized, from its first Norman lord, whose descendants for ten generations continued to hold his cherished demesne.

THE CHURCH.

In 1291, the church of Hopesay, in Clun deanery, and Salop archdeaconry, was valued at £6 per annum. The parish was taxed only 30s. to the *ninth* in 1341, as a fourth of the land lay uncultivated on account of the poverty of the tenants. In 1534-5 the rectory of Hope-Say was worth £17 per annum, less 7s. 8d. for synodals and procurations.

DOORWAY, HOPESAY.

---

[1] *Domesday*, fo. 258, a 1.

HOPESAY CHURCH.

FONT, LYDBURY NORTH, (see p. 472).

Early Incumbent.—Sir Roger Fitz-Alan, parson of Hopesay, 1278.

Sibdon Carwood.

"The same Picot holds Sibetune. Suen held it and was a free man. Here ii hides geldable. The land is for iii ox-teams. In demesne is one [team]; and iiii serfs and ii radmans with i team. Here a wood which will fatten c swine. In time of King Edward it was worth 20s.; now 30s."

The chapel of St. Michael, of Sibdon, as an appurtenance of Clun church, passed to Wenlock priory towards the end of the 12th century, and consequently is not mentioned in any early records. The first curate of Sibdon, named in the diocesan register, is under date 1587.

Purslow.

"The same Picot holds Posselau. Uluric held it and was a free man. Here i hide geldable. The land is for ii ox-teams. In time of King Edward it was worth 15s. It is [now] waste."[1] Parochially, Purslow is in the parish of Clunbury.

Barlow.

"The same Picot holds Berlie. Uluric held it. Here half a hide."[1] This short entry in *Domesday* is succeeded by one relating to—

Obley.

"The same Picot holds Obelie. Ælmund held it. Here ii hides. These lands [viz., Berlie and Obelie] were and are waste."[1]

Hopton Castle

is thus described in the Conqueror's record:—"The same Picot holds Opetune. Edric held it and was a free man. Here ii hides geldable. There is land for iiii ox-teams. In the time of King Edward [the manor] was worth 40s. Now it is waste."[1] In time this place became caput of that fief which the Hoptons held under the descendants of Picot de Say. Vestiges of Hopton Castle are still to be seen.

The Church.

St. Mary of Oppetune, was originally an affiliation of the church of Clun. In 1291, the church of Hopton, in Clun deanery, was of less than £4 annual value. In 1341, the parish was assessed only

---

[1] *Domesday*, fo. 258, a 2.

13s. 4d. to the *ninth*, because there had been a murrain among the sheep, etc. In 1534-5 the preferment of the rector of Hopton was worth £4 11s. per annum, less 6d. for synodals.

Early Incumbent.—Sir John Gyrois, 1290.

Corston. "The same Picot," continues *Domesday*, "holds Cozetune. Suein held it, and was a. free man. Here i hide geldable. The land is for iii ox-teams. In demesne is one [team], and ii villains and one boor with i team. In King Edward's time it was worth 20s. Now a similar [amount]."[1] Although far apart, singularly enough, Corston now forms one township with Shelderton; the former being in Purslow Hundred, whilst the latter is in that of Munslow.

Edgton. "The same Picot holds Egedune. Suein held it, and was a free man. Here ii hides geldable. There is land for ix ox-teams. In demesne are ii [teams], and vi serfs, v villains, and i boor, with ii teams. In time of King Edward it was worth 60s.; afterwards 15s.; now 30s."[1] The chapel of St. Michael, of Edgton, an appendage of Clun church, is not alluded to either in the Taxation of 1291, the assessment of 1341, or the *Valor* of 1534-5.

Early Incumbent.—William Kepeton, chaplain of Egeton, 1418.

Wentnor is described in Domesday Book as being, in 1086, held of the Norman earl by Roger Fitz-Corbet. "The same Roger holds Wantenovre. Edric held it, and was a free man. Here ii hides and a half geldable. In demesne are iii ox-teams; and xv serfs, v villains, and xi boors, with viii teams. Here iiii hayes. In the time of King Edward it was worth £6; afterwards 40s.; now £4."[2] In process of time, the abbeys of Shrewsbury, Haughmond, and Buildwas, acquired by successive grants from the Corbets, barons of Caus, by far the larger portion of the manor of Wentnor.

THE CHURCH.

Roger Fitz-Corbet, about the year 1095, gave the advowson of

---

[1] *Domesday*, fo. 258, a 2. [2] Ibidem, fo. 255, b 1.

Wentnor to Shrewsbury Abbey. In 1291, the church of Wentenore, in the deanery of Clun, the archdeaconry of Salop, and the diocese of Hereford, was worth £5 6s. 8d. per annum; besides a pension of 5s. to the abbot of Shrewsbury. In 1341, the parish was taxed only 30s. to the *ninth*, because a third of it lay untilled, etc. The *Valor* of 1534-5 represents the preferment of the rector of Wentnore as being worth £7 per annum, less 1s. for synodals.

Early Incumbent.—Galfrid, parson of Wentnor, 1292.

Choulton, now a township of Lydbury North, is mentioned in *Domesday*:—" Robert [Fitz-Corbet] holds of the Earl Cautune. Gunuert held it, and was a free man. Here ii hides geldable. In demesne are ii ox-teams, and one serf, and vii villains, with ii teams; and there might be other ii [teams employed] besides. It was and is worth 20s." [1]

Lydbury North. We read in the Saxon Chronicle, under date " A. 792. This year, Offa, King of the Mercians, commanded the head of King Ethelbert to be struck off." The guest of the "Terrible" Mercian, when thus suddenly and cruelly deprived of life, his countrymen accounted the blameless King of East Anglia a martyr; and, removing his remains to Fernley, numerous miracles performed at Ethelbert's shrine attested, it was said, his virtues.

Among others who imagined that they had been cured of their maladies by a visit to the shrine of St. Ethelbert, was *Egwin Shakehead*, the wealthy but paralytic owner of Lydbury, who, in return, offered to the Saxon saint his vast manor. Offa hearing of the cure, repented, it is said, of his evil deeds, and largely increasing the endowment of St. Ethelbert, over the spot where a thousand years ago the murdered Saxon King of East Anglia's bones reposed in the little vill of Fernley, now stands the stately cathedral of Hereford. The reader will, therefore, understand how it came to pass that in 1086, William the Conqueror's commissioners reported that Lydbury belonged to the bishop of Hereford.

"The bishop of Hereford," says *Domesday*, "holds of the king Lideberie, and he held it in the time of King Edward. Here are

---

[1] *Domesday*, fo.255, b 1.

liii hides geldable. In demesne are iiii ox-teams; and xxxviii villains, iiii boors, and viii radmans, with xxviii boors, have among them xxiii teams. Here ii serfs, and a mill supplying the manorial hall.¹ The wood will fatten clx swine.

Of this manor, one portion is held of the bishop by a certain frenchman and William the clerk, and the church of the same manor, with priests and land appertaining thereto; and here is one ox-team. In this manor there might be 92 teams more than there are. In the time of King Edward, it was worth £35; and afterwards £10; now [it is worth] £12. Of this land there are xxxii hides and a half waste."

The control and possession of over 18,000 acres of border territory, for such in ancient times was the extent of Lydbury North, of necessity compelled the Anglo-Norman bishop of Hereford to become a lord-marcher—hence the foundation of Bishop's Castle.

A *writ close* of August 17th, 1223, allows Hugh [Foliot], Bishop of Hereford, to summon all the knights and tenants of his fee to the parts of Lidebiry North, to defend the Bishop's Castle and lands there, against his and the king's enemies.²

It was Queen Elizabeth who confiscated the ancient demesnes of the see of Hereford.

LYDBURY CHURCH.

The advowson of Lydbury North was given by Robert de Betun, Bishop of Hereford (1131—1148), to those canons of Shobdon who were afterwards known as the abbot and convent of Wigmore. Accordingly, Pope Nicholas' Taxation in 1291, says that "the church of Lydebury [in the deanery of Clun], is the abbot of Wigmore's"; the rectory was worth £13 6s. 8d. per annum; the vicar's portion was £4 13s. 4d. In 1341, the parish was assessed only £6 10s. to the *ninth*, because the greater part of the arable land of it lay untilled on account of the tenants being poor, etc. In 1534-5, the abbot, as rector, received £27 per annum, corn and hay tithes of Byshopp Castell, Lydbery, and Bishoppes-launde; besides £6 0s. 10d. per annum for rents and ferms of Lydbury. The vicar of Lydbury's preferment was worth £13 4s. per annum, less 7s. 8d. for synodals and procurations.

Early Incumbent.—William, clerk, rector in 1086.

BISHOP'S CASTLE, originally called Lydbury Castle, was founded by the Bishop of Hereford, probably before 1127. Around

---

¹ "Molinum Serviens Aulæ." ² *Rot. Claus.*, vol. i., p. 559.

BISHOPS CASTLE CHURCH.

MORE CHURCH.

the prelate's stronghold, in ancient times, the inhabitants of this distracted border territory clustered for security : thus the borough gradually arose.

BISHOP'S CASTLE CHURCH.

This, as an affiliation of Lydbury, belonged to the abbot of Wigmore. In 1291, the abbot's rectorial tithes amounted to £8 per annum; the vicar's portion was £4 13s. 4d. In 1341, the parish was taxed £2 only to the *ninth*, because a part of it was in Wales; "a third of the land lay untilled for want of means," etc. In 1534-5, the annual income of the vicar of Bishop's castle was £10, less 7s. 2d. for procurations and synodals.

Early Incumbent.—Sir Walter de Bokenhull, 1332; presented by the abbot and convent of Wigmore.

Linley, Norbury and Hardwicke, Whitcott, Asterton, Plowden (where stands the hall of "a family (the Plowdens) who have enjoyed the estate from which they derive their name as far back as our records extend ") ;[1] Eyton, Walcot (from the lord of which, in the 13th century, the Shropshire family of Walcot can trace their descent in the male line) ; Oakley (to this day in the possession of the same family who held it in 1283); Totterton, Brockton, Lea, Colebatch, Woodbatch, and Upper and Lower Broughton ; all these, in ancient times, were members of the Bishop of Hereford's manor of Lydbury North.

Lydham, is the subject of the following notice in Domesday Book :—"The earl himself holds Lidum. Edric the forester held it in the time of King Edward. Here xv hides geldable. In demesne are iiii ox-teams ; and xiiii villains, with a bailiff, a priest, and vi boors have x teams ; and there might be xvi teams here besides. Here vi radmans and a mill pay [by way of rent] i hog.[2] ii leagues of wood [are here]. In time of King Edward [the manor] was worth £10 ; now £14." [3] Upon the forfeiture of the Norman earls, Lydham came into the hands of King Henry I., who annexed it to the honour of Montgomery.

THE CHURCH.

The *Domesday* mention of a priest in connection with Lydham, indicates that a church existed here in 1086. In 1291, the church of Lydom, in the deanery of Clun, was valued at £4 6s. 8d. per

---

[1] *History of Shrewsbury*, ii. p.335, *note* 1.   [2] "Porcum."
[3] *Domesday*, fo. 253, b 1.

annum. In 1341, the parish was assessed only 24s. to the *ninth* of wheat, wool, and lambs, because a third part thereof was in Wales; another third was untilled, etc. In 1534-5, the rectory of *Ledon* was worth £10 per annum, less 6d. for synodals.

Early Incumbent.—Adam, parson of Lydham; presented before 1243.

MORE, originally a member of Lydham, afterwards became a tenure by *grand serjeantry* :—" The lord of More was, as a constable of the king's host, to assume the command of two hundred foot-soldiers, whenever any king of England crossed the Welsh border in hostile array. The said constable was to march in the vanguard of the army, and with his own hands to carry the king's standard." To be the standard-bearer of an English host, struggling against Welsh strategy in one of their defiles, although an honourable, nevertheless was a very responsible, office.

MORE CHURCH.

The Taxation of 1291, represents the church of More, in the deanery of Clun, as worth £4 6s. 8d. *per annum.* In 1341, the parish was taxed only 30s. to the *ninth,* because the lands were untilled, on account of the poverty of the tenants, etc. King Henry the Eighth's *Valor* represents the rectory of More to be worth £8 13s. 4d. *per annum,* less 6d. for synodals, and a pension of 6s. 8d. to the abbot of Wigmore.

Early Incumbent.—Roger, parson of More, 1220—30.

DOMESDAY HUNDRED OF LENTEURDE.

Modern Name.	Domesday Name.	Saxon Owner, or Owners, T. R. E.	Domesday Tenant, in capite.	Domesday Mesne, or next Tenant.	Domesday Sub-Tenant.	Modern Hundred and County.
Leintwardine	Lenteurde	Rex Edwardus	Radulfus de Mortemer	Unus Miles		Wigmore, Herefordshire.
Stanway	Stanwel	Ælmær	Radulfus de Mortemer			Wigmore, Herefordshire.
Adferton	Alfertintune	Edric	Radulfus de Mortemer			Wigmore, Herefordshire.
Lingen	Lingham	Gunuer, Edric	Radulfus de Mortemer	Turstin		Wigmore, Herefordshire.
Shirley	Sirelei	Ælmar	Radulfus de Mortemer	Turstin		Wigmore, Herefordshire.
? ?	Lege	Ælmar	Radulfus de Mortemer	Unus Miles		? ?
? ?	Tumbelawe	Eldred	Radulfus de Mortemer			? ?
Letton	Lectune	Seunard	Radulfus de Mortemer	Ingelrannus	Unus Miles	Wigmore, Herefordshire.
Walford	Wallforde	Ulnuard, Blachemer, Duning	Radulfus de Mortemer	Ingelrannus		Wigmore, Herefordshire.
Buckton	Buctone	Saxi	Radulfus de Mortemer	Oldelardus		Wigmore, Herefordshire.
LlanvairWaterdine	Watredene	Eduni	Radulfus de Mortemer			Clun, Salop.
Brampton Brian	Brantune	Gunnar	Radulfus de Mortemer	Ricardus		Wigmore, Herefordshire.
Pedwardine	Pedewrde	Elric, etc.	Radulfus de Mortemer	Ricardus		Wigmore, Herefordshire.
Westhope	Weshope	Elmund	Rogerius Comes	Picot		Munslow, Salop.
Woolston	Wistanestune	Spirtes, Presbyter	Rogerius Comes	Picot	Duo Milites	Purslow, Salop.
? ?	Caurtune	Eccl. Sti. Almuudi	Rogerius Comes	Picot		? ?
? ?	Chinbaldescote	Eccl. Stæ Mariæ de Brunfelde	Rogerius Comce	Picot		? ?
? ?	Edretehope	Edric	Rogerius Comes	Picot		? ?
Lungunford	Clone	Gunwardus	Rogerius Comes	Picot & Rainaldus Vicecomes	Fulco	Purslow, Salop. Munslow, Salop.
Bedston	Betletetune	Uluric	Rogerius Comes	Picot	Fulco	Purslow, Salop.
? ?	Edelactune		Rogerius Comes	Picot	Bernard	? ?
			Radulfus de Mortemer	Helgot		
? ?	Hibrihteselle	Ulchetel	Rogerius Comes	Picot	Fulco	? ?
Bucknell	Buchehale	Elmer	Rogerius Comes	Pantulf		Purslow, Salop.
		Aluni	Radulfus de Mortemer	Helgot		
? ?	Humet	Osbernus filius Ricardi	Osbernus filius Ricardi	Duo Milites		? ?
Stanage	Stanege	Osbernus filius Ricardi	Osbernus filius Ricardi			Knighton, Radnorshire.
Cascob	Coscop	Edric	Osbernus filius Ricardi			Wigmore, Herefordshire. Radnor, Radnorshire.
ck Hill	Achel	Edric	Osbernus filius Ricardi			Radnor, Radnorshire.
Knighton	Chenistetune	Leflet	Hugo Lasne †			Knighton, Radnorshire.
Norton	Nortune	Leflet	Hugo Lasne			Radnor, Radnorshire.
Wistanstow	Wistaneston	Spirtes (de St. Almuudi)	Nigellus Medicus			Munslow, Salop. Purslow, Salop.
? ?	Clev.	Spirtes	Nigellus Medicus			? ?
Acton Scott	Actune	Euric	Rogerius Comes	Eldred		Munslow, Salop.
Helmick	Elmundewic	Edric	Rogerius Comes	Hugo fil. Turgisii		Munslow, Salop.
Laish	Plesham	Goduinus	Rogerius Comes	Rogerius de Laci	Bernerus	Munslow, Salop.
Strefford	Straford	Elmund	Rogerius Comes	Rainaldus Vicecomes	Azo	Munslow, Salop.
Cheney Longville	Languefelle	Siward	Rogerius Comes	Siwardus		Purslow, Salop.

† Hugh, the Ass.

ABOLISHED in name, there is no modern Hundred that can be said to particularly represent the *Domesday* Hundred of Lenteurde, which, singularly eccentric in its organization, spread over a large tract of modern Radnorshire, and part of Herefordshire, as well as Shropshire. The Table contains a list of those manors which composed the old Hundred of Lenteurde. By scanning it over, the reader may learn how great have been the territorial changes which have taken place in the boundaries of Shropshire since William the Conqueror's days. As, however, there is nothing particularly worth noting in the early history of those places marked with an asterisk, excepting the one relating to Leintwardine, the *Domesday* notices of places only are given which are included in the modern county of Shropshire.

Leintwardine.

The Saxon king, Edward the Confessor's manor of Leintwardine probably was the original caput of the hundred which derived a name from it. We read in *Domesday* that:—"The same Ralph [de Mortemer] holds [of the king] Lenteurde. King Edward held it [formerly]. Here iiii hides and one virgate. The [arable] land is [capable of employing] xxiv ox-teams. In demesne are iii teams; and vi neat-herds, x villains, viii boors, a bailiff, and ii radmans, with a priest, among them have viii teams. Here is a church, and a mill [which pays] 6s. 8d. and [a rent in kind of] vi sticks of eels.[1] Of this land, a knight holds i hide and a half, and here he has i ox-team, and [there are] v serfs, v villains, and iii boors, with two teams. Here ii men pay 4s. for [certain] allotments of land.[2] Here i league of wood. In the time of King Edward [the manor] was worth 40s.; afterwards 30s.; now £4."[3] Another part of the Conqueror's record assigns a small part of this important manor to Picot de Say:—"The same Picot holds of the earl three virgates of land in Lenteurde, and Fulco [holds] of him. The land is for two ox-teams. It pays 5s."

LEINTWARDINE CHURCH.

This was originally the Saxon mother-church of a parish of very great extent. Approaching his end, Hugh de Mortimer, about 1184, gave the church of Lyntwardyn to Wigmore Abbey. In 1291, the church of Leynthwardyn, in the deanery of Clun, with the chapels of Boriton and Dunton, was worth £20 *per annum*; this was the rectory: the vicar of Leynthwardyn's portion was £4 13s. 4d. "In the 14th century, nine chaplains chanted daily mass at the altars of Leintwardine church for the souls of Edward III., of Isabella his mother, and Philippa his queen, of Henry, Bishop of Lincoln, the Earl of Lincoln, his Countess Joan, and others, with all the faithful departed. The lands assigned for these comprehensive services were granted by Roger, Earl of *Mortimer*, and were exempted by royal favour from the Statute of Mortmain. The church contained a regularly appointed choir,

---

[1] "VI stiches anguillarum."   [2] "De locatione terræ."   [3] *Domesday*, fo. 260, a 2.

with stalls yet remaining ; thither the *monks* of Wigmore repaired in procession; and the abbot delivered an annual sermon, on the festival of the Virgin, the patron saint."

In 1341, ten of the eleven vills of the parish of Leyntworth were out of Shropshire. Jay, the eleventh, was taxed only 10s. to the *ninth*, because three virgates lay untilled for want of means, etc. In 1534-5, the vicar of Leyntwarden's income was £8 3s. 4d. *per annum*, less 7s. 8d. for synodals and procurations. The abbot of Wigmore's rectorial receipts amounted to about £20.

Severed by Mortimer of Wigmore from Shropshire, Leintwardine, with the whole of that potent baron's other Lenteurde manors, except one, namely Llanvair Waterdine, are now in the Hundred of Wigmore, Herefordshire.

Llanvair Waterdine, situated on the extreme south-western border of Shropshire, is the subject of the following entry in Domesday Book:—"The same Ralph holds Watredene. Eduui held it. Here v hides. There is land for xii ox-teams. It was and is waste."[1]

The chapel of St. Mary, of Waterdine, as an affiliation of St. George's, of Clun, passed with the mother church to Wenlock Priory, in the reign of Richard I.: accordingly, early records are silent respecting it.

Westhope, in Diddlebury parish, in 1086 belonged to the Norman Picot de Say, for:—"The same Picot," says *Domesday*, "holds Weshope. Elmund held it. Here ii hides geldable. There is land for iiii ox-teams. In demesne are ii [teams], and vi serfs, and iiii villains, with i team. In time of King Edward it was worth 15s.; afterwards 6s.; now 25s."[2]

Woolston. The following entry in *Domesday* is supposed to relate to Woolston, in the parish of Wistanstow:—"The same Picot holds Wistanestune, and ii knights [hold the manor] of him. Spirtes, the priest, held it [in Saxon times]. Here ii hides geldable. There is land for viii ox-teams. Here are vi villains, a priest, iii boors, and one radman, with iiii teams. It is worth 20s."[2]

---

[1] *Domesday*, fo. 260, b 1.   [2] Ibidem, fo 258, a 2.

Clungunford. A few yards to the north-east of Clungunford church, is a large circular mound, which, 15 feet high, measures 103 feet across its base, and 49 across its summit. This tumulus was carefully opened some years ago,[1] and, from discoveries then made, it is clear that this mound furnishes us with an instance of interment by cremation. There can be no doubt that, when this barrow was constructed, the ancient custom of burning the dead prevailed in this country. An interesting account of the opening of this tumulus is given in Hartshorne's Salopia Antiqua.[2]

The following notices in Domesday Book relate to Clungunford:— "The same Picot [de Say] holds Clone. Gunuard held it. Here vi hides geldable. There is [arable] land [sufficient] for xv ox-teams. In demesne are iii [teams], and viii serfs, viii villains, and iiii boors, with iiii teams. Here a mill of liiii pence [annual value]. Of this land, Fulco holds of Picot i hide and a half, and [he] has ii ox-teams in demesne; and [there are] iiii neat-herds,

PISCINA, CLUNGUNFORD.

iii villains, and iii boors, with iii teams, and a mill of xxxii pence [annual value]. The whole in King Edward's time was worth £12; afterwards 30s.; now [it is worth] altogether £4."[3] Again:—

---

[1] By the Rev. JOHN ROCK, of Clungunford.   [2] P. 102, et supra.
[3] *Domesday*, fo. 258, a 2.

"The same Rainald [the sheriff] holds Clone, and Fulco [holds] of him. Gunward held it in King Edward's time. Here ii hides geldable. There are v villains, and one boor, with ii ox-teams; and here there might be vi teams besides. Here are iii hayes. The whole is worth 12s."[1]

THE CHURCH.

Clungunford church is a very ancient foundation. Pope Nicholas' Taxation, in 1291, valued the church of Clungonford, in the deanery of Clun, at £6 *per ann.* In 1341, the parish was taxed only 40s. to the *ninth* of its wheat, wool, and lamb, because much land in it lay fallow, the tenants being poor and the king's taxes frequent. King Henry VIII.'s *Valor* estimates the rectory of Clongonwar at £16 *per ann.*, less 7s. 8d. for synodals and procurations.

Early Incumbent.—Stephen de Clon, 1277.

Bedston. "The same Picot holds Betietetune and Fulco [holds] of him. Uluric held it. Here ii hides geldable. The land is for iiii ox-teams. It was and is waste."[2]

THE CHURCH.

In 1291, the church of Bedeston, in the deanery of Clun, was valued at £2 *per ann.*, but the rector being beneficed elsewhere, was liable to pay tithes. In 1341, the parish was assessed only 13s. 4d. to the *ninth.* In 1534-5, the rector of Bedston's preferment was worth £4, less 6s. for synodals.

Early Incumbent.—Walter de Bedeston, 1283.

Stow, near Knighton, although not mentioned in *Domesday,* nevertheless appears to have been a Saxon settlement.

STOW CHURCH.

In 1291, the church of Stowe, in Clun deanery, together with the chapel of Knyttheton was valued at £6 *per ann.*, and it belonged to the Prior of Great Malvern. The Vicar's portion therein was less than £4. In 1341, the townships of Stow and Weston were assessed only 18s. to the *ninth,* because, owing to poverty and the pressure of taxes the lands were untilled; nine vills of the parish were in Wales, etc. The *Valor* of 1534-5, gives

---

[1] *Domesday,* fo. 255, a 1.   [2] Ibidem, fo. 258, b 1.

the vicarage of Stowe as worth £4 15s. *per ann.*, less 7s. 8d. for synodals and procurations. The rectory of Stow, with the annexed chapelry of Knighton, was then valued at £8 13s. 4d. *per ann.*

Bucknell is the subject of two distinct notices in *Domesday*; for in 1086, William Pantulf held a share of it under Roger de Montgomery, the Norman earl; whilst Ralph de Mortemer held the larger portion of it under the king. "William [Pantulf] holds Buchehale. Elmer held it. Here i virgate. The land is for half an ox-team. It was and is waste."[1] Again:—"The same Ralph [de Mortemer] holds Buchehalle and Helgot [holds] of him. Here ii hides. The land is for vi ox-teams. It was and is waste. Here i league of wood. Aluui held [the manor in Saxon times]."[2]

BUCKNELL CHURCH.

Before 1176, the Lord of Bucknell had given this advowson to Wigmore Abbey. In 1291, the church of Bokenhull, in the deanery of Clun, was valued at £5 6s. 8d. *per ann.* The vicar's portion therein was under £4. In 1341, the parish was taxed only 19s. to the current levy, because more than two-thirds of it were in Wales, and in the Liberties of Wigmore. In 1534-5, Bucknell vicarage was worth £5 5s. *per ann.*, less 7s. 8d. for procurations and synodals.

Early Incumbent.—Nicholas Commpyun, deacon, instituted 13th January, 1285, on presentation of the abbot and convent of Wigmore.

Wistanstow. About a mile north-west of Wistanstow stands the British defensive work, Castle Ring. The Roman Watling-street runs due north through Wistanstow. This place is the subject of the following notice in Domesday Book:—"Nigel the physician holds of the king Wistanestou. Spirtes the priest held it of [the church of] St. Alkmund, and it was in King Edward's time the support of the canons.[3] Here iiii hides. The land is for xv ox-teams. Here are vii villains with vii teams; and one frenchman having a mill, which renders v horse-loads of corn [annually]. In time of King Edward [the manor] was worth 30s.; now 20s. It was waste when [Nigel] got it."[4] After Nigel the

---

[1] *Domesday*, fo. 257, b 1.
[2] Ibidem, fo. 260, b 1.
[3] "Victus canonicorum."
[4] *Domesday*, fo. 260, b 2.

WISTANSTOW CHURCH.

STRETTON CHURCH, (*see* p. 483).

FONT, WISTANSTOW.

FONT, BUCKNELL.

physician's death, it appears that Gilbert de Cunedore, a layman, in defiance of the dean and canons of St. Alkmund, forcibly occupied Wistanstow; but at length, excommunicated, he repented and restored the prebend to the church. It is said, that Gilbert and his knights submitted to stripes and discipline administered in the sight of all the people, and that then "Gilbert was led along naked into St. Alkmund's church and there he offered up the prebend upon the altar."[1] When the possessions of St. Alkmund's church went to found Lilleshall Abbey, in King Stephen's time, Wistanstow passed also to the abbey, under which it long continued to be held.

THE CHURCH.

Wistanstow church, it is most likely, is a Saxon foundation; and the priest mentioned in *Domesday*, in connection with Woolston, was probably attached to Wistanstow church. In 1291, the church of Wynstanestowe, in the deanery of Ludlow, was worth £13 6s. 8d. *per ann.* The vicar's portion was £5. In 1341, the parish was taxed only £6 to the *ninth*, "because the pressure of taxes on the tenantry had caused twenty virgates of land to be thrown out of cultivation," etc. In 1535-6, the rectory of Wystanstowe was worth £17 17s. *per ann.*, less a pension of 40s. to the abbot of Lilleshall, 11s. for synodals and procurations, and 17s. 9d., being annual average of the bishop's triennial visitation.

Early Incumbent.—Philip de Lega, Rector of Wistanstow, 1260.

Acton Scott.

We read in *Domesday*, that:—"Eldred holds of the earl Actune. Edric held it. Here iii hides geldable. The land is for iiii ox-teams. Here ii villains and ii radmans have iii teams. Here one haye. [Formerly the manor] was worth 10s.; now 15s."[2]

THE CHURCH.

In 1291, the church of Acton, in Longfeld, in the deanery of Wenlock, was valued at £5 *per ann.* In 1341, the parish was assessed only £1 6s. 8d. to the *ninth*, because "the lands were untilled for want of means. There were no sheep," etc. In 1534-5, the preferment of the rector of Acton Scott was valued

---

[1] Monasticon, vii. 750, Num. xvi.   [2] *Domesday*, fo. 259, b 2.

at £5 16s. 8d. *per ann.*, less 6s. 8d. for procurations and 6d. for synodals.

Early Incumbents.—Robert, Parson of Akton, in Longefelddesdale, in 1259; Hugh, Rector of Acton-le-Scott, 1284.

Chelmick, in the Shropshire parish of Hope Bowdler, is noticed in *Domesday* :—" Hugh Fitz-Turgis holds of Roger the earl, Elmundewic. Edric held it with i berewick. Here iiii hides geldable. The land is for vi ox-teams. Here ix villains have iii teams. In time of King Edward it was worth 12s.; now 8s. It was waste [when Hugh obtained it]." [1]

The following places in Shropshire are also noticed in Domesday Book :

Plaish, north-east of Cardington, thus :—" The same Roger [de Laci] holds [of the earl] Plesham, and Bernard [holds] of him. Goduin held it. Here i hide geldable. In demesne is i ox-team; and one villain and one serf with half a team. It used to be worth 3s.; now 5s." [2]

Strefford, in the parish of Wistanstow, thus :—" The same Rainald [the sheriff] holds Straford, and Azo [holds] of him. Elmund held it. Here ii hides geldable. The land is for iiii ox-teams. There are no men here; notwithstanding [Rainald] has from thence 20s. In time of King Edward [the manor] was worth 30s.; and afterwards it was waste." [3]

Cheney Longville, thus :—" Siward holds of the earl Languefelle. [Siward] himself held it [in Saxon times]. Here i hide and a half geldable. The land is for vii ox-teams. Here one villain and iii boors have ii teams. The old value was 20s.; afterwards it was waste. Now it is worth 5s." [4]

Alcaston, in the parish of Acton Scott, thus :—" The same Helgot holds Ælmundestune. Edric held it. Here i hide geldable. The land is for iiii ox-teams. In demesne is one [team], and ii serfs and v villains with i team. The value used to be 20s.; now 8s." [5]

---

[1] *Domesday*, fo. 258, b 2.
[2] Ibidem, fo. 256, b 1.
[3] Ibidem, fo 255, a 1.
[4] *Domesday*, fo. 259, b 2.
[5] Ibidem, fo. 258, b 2.

𝕸𝖎𝖓𝖙𝖔𝖓 & 𝖂𝖎𝖙𝖙𝖎𝖓𝖌𝖘𝖑𝖔𝖜 are the subject of this brief notice in *Domesday*:—"In Lenteurde Hundred habuit Leuric Comes II. maneria, Munetune et Witecheslawe. Ibi iiii hidæ geldabiles. Hi [sic] duo maneria jacent in firma Rogerii Comitis ad Stratune."[1]

𝕮𝖍𝖚𝖗𝖈𝖍 𝕾𝖙𝖗𝖊𝖙𝖙𝖔𝖓, situated in a romantic vale, derives its name of Stretton, or Street-town, from its proximity to the Roman Watling Street. Westward of Church Stretton stretches the magnificent Longmynd range of mountains; whilst in a north-easterly direction towers Caer Caradoc, one of, if not the last of, the strongholds which Caractacus defended ere he was basely betrayed to the Romans.

Domesday says:—"The Earl himself holds Stratun. Earl Eduin held it with iiii berewicks. Here viii hides. In demesne, are iii ox-teams, vi serfs, and ii female serfs; and xviii villains and viii boors with a priest have xii teams. Here a mill and a church, and in the wood [aro] five hayes: there might be vi more teams [employed]. In the time of King Edward [the manor] was worth £13; now £5."[2]

Upon the forfeiture of Robert de Belèsme, the last Norman earl of Shrewsbury, Stretton came into the hands of the king, and he retained it. Among others who obtained a temporary grant of the royal manor of Stretton, was the great Hubert de Burgh, to whom Henry III. granted it in the year 1226.

At Stretton, there was formerly a royal castle. It appears to have occupied the site now known as Brockhurst Castle, the foundations and ditch of which are still traceable: although the castle itself has been dismantled for more than six centuries.

In 1336, King Edward III. gave the manor of Stretton to Richard, earl of Arundel, and his heirs for ever; in whose family it remained until the time of Queen Elizabeth.

STRETTON CHURCH.

The church of St. Lawrence, at Stretton, originally the Saxon mother church of a district, is alluded to in the *Domesday* notice of the manor. In 1291, the church of Strattonisdale, in Wenlock deanery, was valued at £15 *per ann.* In 1341, the parish was assessed £4 13s. 4d. to the *ninth.* In 1534-5, the rectory of

---

[1] *Domesday*, fo. 259, b 2.   [2] *Domesday*, fo. 254, a 1.

Stretton was worth £16, less 17s. 9d., the annual proportion of bishop's triennial procurations, and 7s. 8d. for archdeacon's procurations and synodals.

Early Incumbent.—Ralph de Nevill, 1214. This rector of Stretton was for a time Lord Keeper, under Henry III. He became Bishop of Chichester, November 1, 1222, when he vacated Stretton; and was appointed Chancellor in 1227.

INDEX OF PLACES.

	PAGE		PAGE		PAGE
Abbot's Betton	234	Bauseley	362	Broughton	436
Abdon	256	Baveney	287	Buchehale	270
Ackley	461	Bayston	221	Bucknell	480
Acton Burnell	212	Beachfield	456	Buildwas	235
Acton Pigot	207	Beamish Hall	45	Bulwardine	102
Acton Reynald	150, 423	Bearstone	397	Burford	294
Acton Round	255	Beekbury	271	Burton	250
Acton Scott	481	Bedston	479	Buttery	143
Adcott	420	Benthall	245, 371	Burwarton	96
Adderley	400	Beobridge	101	Burway	338
Adeney	121	Belswardine	221	Byrche	410
Alberbury	358	Besford	433	Cainham	300
Albrighton	71	Beslow	143	Calloughton	245
Albright-Lee	165	Berrington	203	Calverhall	402
Albright-Hussey	419	Berwick Maviston	131	Calvington	157
Aleaston	482	Betton	234	Cantlop	230
Aldenham	6	Betton-in-Hales	390	Cantreyn	6
Aldeley	153	Betton Strange	234	Cardeston	367
Aldon	323	Bieton	436	Cardington	333
Alkington	386	Billingsley	6	Castle-Farm	86
Alveley	104	Binnall	6	Castle Holgate	263
Amaston	370	Binweston	456	Castlewright	461
Apley	90	Bishton	74	Catsley	288
Apley Castle	120	Bitterley	302	Caus	351
Arleston	120	Blecheley	152	Charlton	165
Ashfield	253, 271	Bobbington	108	Charlcott	64
Ashford Bowdler	339	Boekleton	253	Chelmarsh	93
Ashford Carbonel	330	Bolas Magna	156	Chelmick	335, 482
Astall	90	Bold	64	Cheneltone	426
Asterton	473	Boraston	299	Cheney Longville	482
Astley	108	Boreaton	410	Cherrington	151
Astley	435	Boreton	233	Chesthill	151
Astley Abbots	6	Bouldon	327	Cheswardine	405
Astley Parva	6	Bradley	245	Chetton	35
Aston	101	Bratton	144	Chetwynd	146
Aston	388	Bridgenorth	11	Childs Ercall	130
Aston	449	Brockton	63	Chilton	233
Aston, Upper and Lower	460	Brockton	159	Chipnall	405
Aston Botterell	56	Brockton	262	Chirbury	452
Aston Eyre	52	Brockton	250	Choulton	471
Aston Munslow	331	Brockton	456	Church Stoke	461
Aston Pigot	456	Brockton	473	Church Stretton	210, 483
Aston Rogers	456	Bromlow	456	Claverley	99
Aston-under-the-Wrekin	120	Brompton	210	Clay Felton	338
Atcham	164	Brompton	461	Clee-Downton	253
Atterley	245	Bromfield	336	Clee St. Margaret	256, 265
Badger	57	Broom Farm	426	Clee Stanton	335
Bageley	410	Broome	203	Cleobury Mortimer	276
Barlow	469	Broseley	64	Cleobury North	96
Barrow	245	Broughton	101	Cleobury Lodge	284
Baschurch	407	Broughton, Upper and Lower	473	Clive	436
Batchcott	339			Clun	463

INDEX OF PLACES.

Place	Page
Rorrington	454
Rosshall	421
Rowton	370
Rowton	399
Ruckley	45
Ruckley	231
Rucroft	6
Rudge	111
Rushbury	269
Ruthall	270
Ruyton juxta Baschurch	427
Ryton	60
Sambrook	147
Sandford	388
Sansaw	436
Selattyn	451
Severn Hall	6
Shakerley	37
Shavington	401
Shawbury	150
Sheet, The	328
Sheinton	218
Shelderton	470
Shelton	196
Shelve	456
Shiffnall	80
Shipley	112
Shipton	250
Shotton	422
Shrawardine	418
Shrewsbury	166
Shurlow	118
Sibdon Carwood	469
Sidbury	94
Siefton	312
Silvington	304
Slachberie	426
Sleap	118
Sleap Magna	434
Smethcott	231
Smethcott	422
Snitton	301
Soulton	402
Spoonley	401
Stanley	6
Stanton	87
Stanton Lacy	314
Stanton-upon-Hineheath	392
Stanwardine-in-the-Field	424
Stanway	259
Stapleton	211
Steele	397
Stepple	284
Steventon	327
Stirchley	146
Stockton	69
Stoke	253
Stoke Aubry	152
Stoke St. Milburg	251
Stoke-upon-Tern	152
Stokesay	321
Stone Acton	260
Stoney Stretton	363
Stottesden	273
Stow	479
Strefford	482
Stych	152
Sudeley, Magna and Parva	405
Sudtelch	434
Sundorn	128
Sutton	101
Sutton	157
Sutton	197
Sutton Maddock	65
Tasley	6
Tedenesolle	299
Tern	118
Thornbury	461
Tibberton	157
Tibetuno	447
Ticklerton	246
Tirley	385
Tong	39
Totterton	473
Tugford	258
Turford	339
Uckington	163
Uffington	160
Underton	6
Upper Ashford	329
Upper Ledwich	325
Upper Monk-Hall	255
Upper Stanway	260
Uppington	149
Upton	87
Upton Cressett	50
Upton Magna	124
Walcot	120
Walcot	461
Walcot	473
Walford	423
Wall Town	288
Walton Savage	287
Walton and Leigh	456
Waranshall	153
Waters Upton	153
Wattlesborough	366
Welbatch	211
Welch Hampton	417, 421
Wellington	119
Wem	379
Wenlock Walton	245
Wentnor	470
West Felton	448
Westhope	477
Westbury	366
Weston	267
Weston Cotton	447
Weston Madoc	461
Weston Rhyn	446
Weston-under-Redcastle	396
Wettleton	322
Wheathill	290
Whitbatch	338
Whitchurch	402
Whitebroc	339
Whitcott	473
Whittimere	108
Whittington	443
Whitton	299
Whitton	368
Whixall	396
Wichcott	327
Wigmore	370
Wigwig	222
Wilderley	232
Wilderley	335
Willey	74
Wilsithland	118
Winsley	353, 361
Wistanstow	480
Withington	154
Wittingslow	483
Wlferesforde	446
Wollerton	339
Wolstou Mynd	461
Wolverley	384
Wolverton	246
Womerton	210
Woodbatch	473
Woodcote	158
Woodcote	368
Woodhouse	86
Woodhouse	152
Woolaston	362
Woolerton	391
Wooliston	400
Woolstaston	208
Woolston	448
Woolston	477
Woore	394
Wooton	109
Wooton	448
Worfield	102
Worthin	455
Wotherton	461
Woundale	102
Wrentnall	229
Wrockwardine	115
Wropton	461
Wroxeter	132
Wyke	86
Wyke	245
Wykey	449
Wystanesmero	102
Wystaneswyk	152
Yale	451
Yockleton	363
Yorton	436

GENERAL INDEX.

	PAGE
TABLES OF DOMESDAY HUNDREDS—	
Alnodestreu	1
Isolated Manors, intermixed with Manors of Alnodestreu, etc.	79
Recordin	114
Sciropesberie, or Shrewsbury	166
Condover	199
Patinton	238
Condetret	273
Ovre	294
Culvestan, or Colmestane	306
Rnesset	351
Odenet	377
Bascherch	406
Merscte	438
Witentreu	452
Rinlau	463
Lenteurde	475
FORESTS—	
Brewood	48
Coed, Morf, Kinver, Wyre	112, 113
Wrekin, or Forest of Mount Gilbert	120
Botwood	225
The Long Forest	237
Shirlot	245
Wyre, or Bewdley	288
Clee	313
BARONIES—	
De Dunstanvill (see Idsall)	80 et supra
Fitz-Alan	125 ,,
Pulverbatch	227 ,,
Castle Holgate	263 ,,
Mortimer	277 ,,
Burford and Richard's Castle	295 ,,
Clifford	308 ,,
De Lacy	315 ,,
Hastings	331 ,,
Corbet	352 ,,
Audley	372 ,,
Wem	379 ,,
ABBEYS, etc.—	
Morville Priory	4
Church of St. Mary Magdalene, Bridgnorth	24
Convent of White Ladies	49

	PAGE
ABBEYS (continued).	
Haughmond Abbey	128
Wombridge Priory	139
Lilleshall Abbey	161
Shrewsbury Abbey	185
St. Chad's Church	189
St. Mary's Church	190
St. Alkmund's Church	192
St. Julian's Church	193
Buildwas Abbey	235
Wenlock Priory	239
Bromfield Priory	338
Alberbury Priory	360
Chirbury Priory	453

EMINENT PERSONAGES MENTIONED—
Caractacus, iii, 456-7, 463-4, 483.
Cynddylan, 407-8, 418.
Llywarç Hên, 116, 167, 407-8.
Crida, 51, 137.
Penda the Strong, 239, 363, 439.
Wulfhere, 363.
Kenwalk, 363.
St. Chad, 189.
Offa the Terrible, iii, 167, 189, 440, 471.
King Oswald, 439.
Ethelbert, King of East Anglia, 471.
Alkmund, 192.
King Edgar, 190.
St. Eata, 164.
King Alfred, 7.
King Alfred's daughter, Ethelfleda, iv, 11, 12, 49, 168, 192.
Knut the Great, 91-2, 168-9, 239-40, 336.
St. Milburg, 239-40, 251.
King Ethelred "the Unready," 91-2, 168, 444.
Edmund Ironsides, 91, 169.
Edric Streone, 91-2, 168-9.
Wulfric Spott, 112.
Earl Leofric, 35, 103, 111, 239, 307.
Godeva the Countess (see Tables of Domesday Hundreds, 3rd columns), 35-6, 398, 405.
Earl Algar (see Tables, 3rd columns), 6, 71, 99, 111, 305, 307, 440.
Edwin and Morcar, iv, 65-6, 111, 171, 440 (see also Tables, 3rd column).

K K

490 GENERAL INDEX.

EMINENT PERSONAGES (*continued*).
Earl Sweyn, iv, 97-8.
Earl Harold, who afterwards became King Harold II., a Shropshire landowner, iv, *see* also Whitchurch, 402-4; coins of his reign minted at Shrewsbury, 168; brother to *Edith the Lady*, Edward the Confessor's Queen, 277; mentioned, 440.
Edith the Lady, iv, 195, 217, 276-7.
King Edward the Confessor, iv, *see* also 3rd column Tables; his vicegerent, 6, 403; resident at Shrewsbury and Marsetelie Park, 169-70, 357; coins of his reign minted at Shrewsbury and Ludlow, 168, 345; treatment of his Queen, and superstitious character, 276-7; a favourer of the Normans, 295, 328, 336-7; death and burial, 337-8.
Edric Salvage, or the Forester, iv, 91—93; 287.
Earl Roger de Montgomery, related to William the Conqueror, 277-8, 440; his great grandmother a Dane, 226; palatine Earl of Shrewsbury, iv; power and estate in Shropshire, vi, *see* also 4th and 5th cols. Tables of Domesday Hundreds and accompanying notices; acquires nearly the whole of Shropshire and becomes Earl of Shrewsbury, in which town he builds a castle and rules supreme, 171-2; first Countess, 8, 381; second Countess, 8, 9; his kinsman Siward le Gros, 226; prime minister, 124; physician, 336, 400; his friend Godebold the priest, 161; his counsellor Robert de Limesey, 235; Rainald, the Sheriff, the greatest of his feoffees, 258; confers on Helgot, his follower, nineteen manors, 263; and eleven manors in Odenet Hundred upon William Pantulf, 379; to whom De Montgomery also gives a command in his earldom, 380; organises frontier defences of Shropshire, 353, 440; policy in the marches successful, 452, 457-8; Welsh districts that acknowledged the Norman Earl's sway, 451, 457; proprietor of Quatford Castle, 8; foundation of Ludlow Castle erroneously ascribed to him, 340; hunting ground, 193; reserves to himself right of hunting and fishing, 246; founds Shrewsbury Abbey, 185; to which foundation he gives Morville Church, 4; and the churches of Donington, 38; Tong, 45; Wrockwardine, 116; High Ercall, 118; Wellington, 119; Edgmond, 121; Stottesden, 275; Diddlebury, 311; and the valuable manor of Emstrey, 233; builds Quatford Church, 9, 10, and the chapel of St. Nicholas, 194; converts the church of St. Milburg, at Wenlock, into an abbey, 239-40; to which he gives Millichope, 266; gives Lower Poston, 336, and Soulton, 402, to St. Michael's,

EMINENT PERSONAGES (*continued*).
Shrewsbury; unjustly gives Godestoch to his chaplains, 252; deprives the church of a league of wood, 165; buried, 324; supposed monument, 188.
Hugh de Montgomery, second Norman Earl of Shrewsbury, 11; Lord of Worfield, 102; his Castle of Montgomery demolished by the Welsh, 458; himself killed, 172.
Robert de Belèsme, transfers castle and borough of Quatford to Bridgnorth, 8, 9, 20; becomes third Norman Earl of Shrewsbury, and exercises great cruelties over the English and Welsh, 11; rears Bridgnorth Castle, and, conspiring against Henry I., that king captures his stronghold and banishes him, 12—14, 172-3; disagrees with Pantulf, 383; gives a hide of land to Shrewsbury Abbey, 410.
Warin the Bald, iv, 124, 185, 204, 258-9, 380, 440-1, 443.
Rainald the Sheriff, iv, *see* also Tables, 124-5, 258-9, 440-1.
Picot de Say, iv, 185, 464-5.
Gerard de Tornai, iv, 67.
William Pantulf, iv, 12, 13, 379, 384.
Robert Fitz Corbet, 369.
The *Peverels*, 67, 414.
Robert Pincerna, 423-4.
Turold, 75, 145.
Robert Fitz Tetbald, 80, 87, 88.
Godfrey de Gamaches, 274-5.
Alan Fitz Flaald, the progenitor of the royal line of Stuart, 125-6.
The *Le Stranges*, 104—106, 411.
William de Warren, 404.
Ordericus Vitalis, the historian, 164-5.
Richard de Belmeis, 39, 40, 173.
Ranulf de Broc, 35-6.
Peter de Rupibus, and his son Peter de Rivallis, 27—31.
John Mansel, 31.
Sir *William de Hugford*, 90.
The *Mortimers* of Chelmarsh, 93, 94.
The *La Zouches*, 41—44.
The *Black Prince* and *James de Audley* III., 373—376.
Lord Chancellor Burnel, 213—216.
The *Harleys*, 220.

A tale of female devotion, 329.

Illustrations—feudal period, 86-7, 358-9.

"Wager of Battle," 195-6, 430.

CURIOUS TENURES AND SERJEANTRIES, 11, 34, 36, 42, 47-8, 86, 108, 110, 121, 122-3, 132, 139, 141, 145, 149, 155, 202, 231, 248, 252-3, 268, 317, 326, 334, 336, 348, 358, 390, 392, 404, 417-8, 424, 434, 454, 462, 465, 474.

REMAINS, MILITARY OR OTHERWISE, OF CELTIC, BRITISH, ROMAN, AND SAXON PERIODS—
Burwarton, 96; Mound near High Ercall, 117; Wroxeter, 132; Watling Street, 158, 480, 483; Woolstaston, 208; the Castle Ring, 209; Tumulus, 211; Pitchford, 222; Castle Hill, 225; the "Lady Oak" Cressage, 229; Barrow, *see* Smethcott, 231; Abdon Burf, Clee Burf, and the Titterstone, 256-7; Nordy Bank, 256-7; Rushbury, 269; the "Devil's Causeway," 269; Wall Town, 288; Cainham Camp, 300; Camp on Callow Hill, 357; Entrenchment, Bauseley Hill, 362; Stoney Stretton, 363; Pontesbury—Camp Pontesford Hill, 363-4; Wattlesborough,

REMAINS, MILITARY, etc. (*continued*).
366; "The Berth," 408-9; Watt's Dyke, 440; Offa's Dyke, 167, 440, 464; Hoarstones, 438-9; 467; Old Oswestry, 439; Barrows, etc., Chirbury, 452; Caer Bre, 452; "The Beacon Ring," 455; Barrows, Worthin, 455; Caer Flos, etc., 456; Caer Caradoc, 463-4, 483; mound, Clungunford, 478.

DOMESDAY BOOK, v; how it was compiled, 3, *note* 99, 111-2, 304; what the Saxon scribe thought of it, 3.
Explanation of terms—*salt-pits*, 38; *radman*, 50; *haia*, 205; *cottarii*, or cottars, 230; *coliberti*, 274; *cozets*, 314; *dimidii villani*, semi-villains, 314; *radchenistres*, 314.

THE END.

CPSIA information can be obtained
at www.ICGtesting.com
Printed in the USA
LVHW101053280322
714493LV00009B/352